MICHIGAN

Pleasant Peninsulas for Romance
Abound in Four Complete Novels

GAIL GAYMER
MARTIN

BARBOUR
PUBLISHING

Out on a Limb © 2004 by Gail Gaymer Martin
Over Her Head © 2002 by Gail Gaymer Martin
Seasons © 1998 by Gail Gaymer Martin
Secrets Within © 2001 by Gail Gaymer Martin

ISBN 978-1-59310-434-4

Cover art by Workbook Stock.

All Scripture quotations, unless otherwise indicated, are taken from the HOLY BIBLE, NEW INTERNATIONAL VERSION®. NIV®. Copyright© 1973, 1978, 1984 by International Bible Society. Used by permission of Zondervan Publishing House. All rights reserved.

Scripture quotations on pages 119, 240, 339, and 362 are taken from the King James Version of the Bible.

Published by Barbour Publishing, Inc., P.O. Box 719, Uhrichsville, Ohio 44683, www.barbourbooks.com

Our mission is to publish and distribute inspirational products offering exceptional value and biblical encouragement to the masses.

ecpa Member of the Evangelical Christian Publishers Association

Printed in the United States of America.

Dear Readers,

I'm thrilled to have four of my novels set in Michigan placed together in this anthology. I've lived in Michigan all my life, presently in Lathrup Village. Often people ask, "Where's Lathrup Village," and I do what most people who live in Michigan do. I lift my left hand, then point to the spot where Lathrup Village is located on the Michigan mitten.

Michigan is called the Water Wonderland, but we are a state with many geographical features from the deep woods of the rural area to the national pine forests, from farmland to the pure white sand dunes of Lake Michigan's shore and the rocky beaches of the eastern shore. In Michigan, a person will be no farther from a significant body of water than six miles. We are truly a state of inland lakes, rivers, and streams, and we boast a shoreline surrounded by the famous Great Lakes. These four stories are set in many of these lovely places in Michigan.

My city, Lathrup Village, is a northwest suburb of Detroit. It's a small city within a metropolis and our streets, some dirt roads, are lined with older homes and stately trees. I share our home with my husband, Bob, who is truly a gift from God. He supports me in every way and even serves as the Webmaster for my Web site at www.gail-martin.com. Our two children have homes of their own, and we have one grandchild.

Besides hours behind the computer, I sing with a well-known Christian group in the Detroit area, serve my church, speak and teach at conferences all over the country, and somewhere in there, enjoy my family and friends.

I pray these stories make you laugh and cry, that they touch your heart with God's love, mercy, and saving grace. Thank you for allowing me into your homes in the form of Christian fiction. I hope you find my visit a blessing.

Gail Gaymer Martin

OUT ON A LIMB

Chapter 1

The sun spilled a dappled pattern along the wood's leaf-strewn path. Balanced high up on an oak branch, Karen Chapman drew in a deep calming breath. Trees and meadows burdened with Michigan wildflowers soothed her city nerves. In another month she would return to the city and her difficult job of working with the courts as a child advocate. Still, no matter what tense moments lay ahead, today was heaven.

Though not yet September, autumn hung in the air. Karen leaned her back against the rough bark and breathed in the scent of ripe apples that drifted on the breeze from her grandfather's orchard. Overhead the green leafy canopy splattered with gold and red hinted of cooler days.

God's handiwork glowed in the afternoon sun, and a song lifted in her heart. "For the beauty of the earth, for the glory of the skies." She began to hum, thinking about her newly widowed grandpa back at the house and praising God that He'd guided her to come to the farm for a visit.

The words of another hymn spilled from her thoughts to her lips. "Earth and all stars," she sang then chuckled when she lilted the verse about "engines and steel" and "loud building workers." Too much reality there, she thought, recalling the Detroit suburb's constant construction and traffic noise. Her song echoed through the trees, arousing the birds and exhilarating her spirit.

"Very nice, lady in the tree."

The voice from below unsettled her. Karen jammed her lips together, cutting off the last syllable and gazed down at the man standing beneath her. "Sorry. I thought I was alone."

"No need to apologize. I heard you singing out here yesterday."

Heat rose to her cheeks, and she eyed the branches below her, wondering how to make a quick escape rather than face the embarrassing situation. She bit her lip, seeing no human way to vanish from the limb. "I guess I'd better keep my singing for church."

He rested his weight on one booted foot and leaned his fist against his trim, jeans-covered hip. A smile curved his full lips, and his chuckle rose to meet her. "Why? I like free concerts." He leaned against the tree. "Mind if I stick around and listen?"

"You can do what you like, I suppose, but the concert's over. Anyway, these aren't my woods." The woods belonged to her grandfather, however, and she almost told him so.

"I know."

She eyed him. "What do you mean?"

"I mean it's not your woods."

An uneasy feeling shuffled through her. She peered at him through the tree limbs. "It's not your woods either, I don't imagine." She cringed, calculating that she'd passed her grandpa's property line and was now sitting in the Kendalls' tree.

"This is my grandfather's land." He lifted an eyebrow, his broad hands on his hips.

She winced.

"Lionel Kendall. Do you know him?" he asked.

"Not really." But she remembered him, all right. He scared her when she was young. His grandfather and hers had been battling for years. Knowing who the stranger was, she wanted nothing to do with him or his grandfather. "Well, if that's the case, let me get out of your tree."

With what decorum Karen could muster, she edged her straddled leg over the limb and slid the other one down to the next branch. So far so good. Somehow, it seemed easier climbing up than down. When she attempted to guide her leg down to the next branch, she couldn't release her other foot. Her shoe had lodged in a deep, angular crook of the tree limb.

Her hot cheeks heated to boiling. As Karen struggled to move her bound leg, he stood below her, a teasing smirk twinkling on his face. His laughter traveled up the trunk faster than she was climbing down.

"Stuck?" he asked.

His voice reeked with humor. So much so, she refused to answer. What did he think? She wasn't hanging in the tree for fun.

He stepped forward and grasped a lower branch. "I guess you are. Let me help." He clutched a limb, raised himself, and swung his lean, nimble leg over the branch.

She wanted to refuse his assistance, but it was one of those "cut off your nose to spite your face" situations. She grasped the limb with one hand and, with the other, reached above and tugged wildly at her jammed shoe.

The branch she clutched dipped then lurched, and she clung like gum to a sole, praying she wouldn't fall to the ground. But falling would at least free her from the situation. The image made her smile.

The man loomed beside her, the muscles of his arms swelling as he raised himself to the branch above.

"Okay," he said, "let's slip your foot out of your shoe. Then I'll get it loose."

His large hand gripped her ankle while the other unlaced her sneaker. Finally, her foot escaped its prison. Wearing one shoe, she clambered down the branches to the ground, feeling like a child rescued by a cocky policeman.

At the same time, her liberator dropped to the ground beside her, his grin like the Cheshire cat. He lifted his arm and held out her scuffed sneaker. "Cinderella? I believe I have your glass slipper."

She snatched the shoe from his hand, too embarrassed to look him in the eye, and muttered, "Thank you." Spinning on her shoed foot, she hobbled down the sun-speckled path toward the orchard, her shoe clasped in her hand.

"You're very welcome," he called out after her. "And you don't have to run away, Cinderella. It's not anywhere near midnight."

His footsteps padded behind her, and the closer he got, the quicker she walked. Suddenly her stockinged foot landed on a jagged stone, and she released a loud "Ouch." But without a break in her step, she hobbled away.

"If you slowed down. . .or put on your shoe, you might save a doctor bill."

She'd reached the orchard and glanced over her shoulder. Now he was on her grandfather's property. A bough heavy with apples stood within arm's reach, and she snatched one off the limb and, with a glance, tossed it over her shoulder toward him.

"An apple a day keeps the doctor away," she called. For good measure, she plucked one for herself and, with a snap, sank her teeth into the sweet tangy pulp. She didn't stop until she reached the meadow, and when she did, he was gone. Like finishing a lovely novel, she felt disappointed it had ended.

❧

Eric Kendall stood between two apple trees and watched her stumble through the meadow like the nursery rhyme: "One shoe off and one shoe on. Diddle-Diddle Dumpling. . ." Except she wasn't his son John. He didn't know who she was, exactly, but he knew she was from the Chapman house.

What he did know was she had spunk. And a lovely face like sunshine with freckles. He'd been enchanted hearing her sing one of his favorite hymns the day before when he took a walk through the woods to stretch his legs when he first arrived. But she'd vanished before he found her.

He chuckled, thinking of her comical descent from the tree. She sure had her dander in an uproar. From the woman's attitude, he'd guess she was related to Walter Chapman. For years, his grandfather and Walter Chapman had some kind of ongoing feud, but he could never fathom the reason.

He snatched a stem of timothy and put it between his teeth and gazed ahead at his grandparents' familiar old farmhouse. Coming here was like a step back in time. He'd spent wonderful summers at the farm as a child, and right now he needed something to cling to. Something warm and soothing like his gramma's peanut butter cookies.

In the past three months, he'd ended a dead-end relationship and faced a new career right here in Gaylord, but one with financial risk. Change seemed to come in twos and threes. Never one change alone that he could handle. The failed relationship, he could deal with. It had been coming for a long time, and he felt confident the Lord had guided his direction.

Admitting his weakness, he had to confess that sometimes a gorgeous figure and beguiling smile got in the way of common sense. But before it was too late, he realized Janine's values were far from his own Christian beliefs. Like Grandmother always said, "Eric, listen to God's Word. Don't get yourself yoked up with an unbeliever." Those words had banged around in his head until he finally listened.

Nearing the house, he saw his grandmother bent over in the small garden filled with straight rows of green peppers, tomatoes, and cucumbers. His grandfather wouldn't be outdone with his neighbor's gardening attempts.

When his grandmother spotted him, she pushed a wisp of white hair from her cheek and grinned. "Where've you been?"

"Listening to a concert in the woods."

She nodded. "You mean the birds. They do sing a lovely tune."

Eric chuckled and bent down to pluck a handful of green beans and dropped them in her plastic bucket. "Not birds, Gramma. But she could've been, perched in the tree like that." He pictured the woman nestled on the branch, mottled with sun and shade, her voice floating to heaven.

His grandmother lifted her freed hand and rested her palm on his forehead. "Too much sun, Eric. You're having a heatstroke."

He laughed and yanked her apron string. The ties loosened, and the calico print slipped down her skirt.

She grabbed the apron before it hit the ground. "I should take you over my lap." Grinning, she swung the bucket toward him. "What are you talking about, anyway? Who was perched in a tree?"

"That's what I was going to ask you," Eric said, retrieving the apron from her hand. He wrapped it around her ample waist and retied the strings.

"How should I know?" she asked. "Did you see me hidin' in the bushes?"

"She must be a relative of Mr. Chapman. When she left, she headed back through the orchard with one shoe on and one shoe off." He chuckled.

"Now I know you've had too much sun," she said, wrapping her arm around his, as they headed back to the house. "I made up some lemonade. A cold drink might help those delusions you're havin'."

"Dark blond like ripe wheat. Freckles on her nose. And spunky like you, Gramma. Even meaner, maybe. "

She squeezed his arm with a little shake. "You better watch out how you talk to me, young man. I can still wash your mouth out with soap."

"And she's almost as pretty as you, too."

"Go on," she said. "You're talkin' blarney now. You must've got those sweet talkin' Irish ways from my father." She patted his arm. " 'Cuz you sure didn't get them from your grandpa."

He pulled open the back door, and Bea walked into the kitchen. Eric followed and slid into the chair. "So who is she?"

Bea turned to face him. "You don't remember her? I'm guessin' she's Karen. Walter said she was comin' for a visit. . .one day when he was sociable." She shook her head, followed by a patient grin. "I'm glad, too. He's not doin' well since his wife died nearly a year ago. Loneliness. Gets to everyone eventually."

Eric eyed her, wondering if she was talking about herself. "And Karen is. . . ?"

"His granddaughter. Remember the cute little thing who would come over with her grandmother sometimes when you came to visit? She'd sing a song at the drop of a hat. She always steered clear of your grandfather."

"Karen?" He sent his mind marching back in time. A faint vision drifted across his memory. He remembered once chasing a saucy little blond girl through the cornrows and when he caught her, he kissed her. His first kiss. He was six or seven, maybe. A grin slid onto his face.

Bea glanced at him over her shoulder then turned back to the sink, snapping and washing the beans. "What's that smile for?"

"Just thinking, Gramma. Granddad didn't plant corn this year, did he?"

"Corn? No, why?"

"No reason."

He remembered her clearly now. Karen. She was as cute and spunky twenty-some years ago as she was today, and picturing her darting through the meadow a short time ago, he knew she'd definitely outrun him in the cornrows now.

Chapter 2

An apple a day keeps the doctor away. Karen wished she'd listened to her own advice and eaten the apple earlier. She sat in her bedroom, rubbing the bottom of her foot where she'd stepped on the rock. The foot had been bruised, she guessed.

She took a couple of practice steps, trying not to limp. Her grandfather would question her, and she didn't want to talk about her meeting with the Kendall man. Even mentioning the last name would rile her grandpa. She knew it.

Concentrating on not wincing, Karen headed into the kitchen to fix lunch, but before she got one foot through the doorway, her grandfather stood at the other end of the hall watching her.

"What's wrong with your foot?"

"Stepped on a stone," she said, continuing her journey through the doorway. She headed for the refrigerator and swung it open. She sensed her grandfather had followed behind her.

"Where were your shoes?"

She turned to face him, knowing an attempt to keep anything from the sharp eyes of her grandfather was pointless. "One was on my foot."

He ambled into the room and grasped the chair back, looking puzzled. "And the other?"

"In my hand."

A grin spread across his face, and he pulled out the chair and sat. "Sounds like an interesting story."

She pushed her head back into the refrigerator and mumbled a few words of explanation about a stranger upsetting her in the woods. When she pulled out a package of luncheon meats and the mayo jar, one bushy eyebrow had raised as he waited. Karen set the items on the table and returned for the lettuce. Then she faced him. "Wheat or sourdough?"

"Sourdough. . .with tomatoes, too."

Karen nodded and went back to the refrigerator for a tomato, hoping he'd forgotten the whole issue now that the conversation had changed to their lunch. She set about making the sandwiches without a word, feeling relieved as each second ticked away. She placed the sandwich in front of him on a paper plate. "Milk or lemonade?"

"Milk, and you have some, too," he said.

"I hate milk."

"It's good for you."

Karen gave up and poured him a tall glass and a few ounces for herself. She'd learned years ago that arguing with her grandfather seemed pointless. He could be stubborn as a tea stain on a white silk blouse.

She slid the glasses onto the table then sat. Her grandfather gave a blessing, and before she could echo his amen, he'd grabbed his sandwich.

A secret smile fought for recognition, but she kept it hidden, pleased she'd duped her grandfather into forgetting the conversation.

"Good sandwich," he said, wiping his mouth with a paper napkin he'd pulled from a holder.

"Thanks, Grandpa." Seeing him look content and less lonely made her day.

He laid the partially eaten sandwich back on the plate. "So tell me about the stranger in the woods."

She pulled her head upward, totally discouraged at his persistence. "Fine. Ruin your lunch."

"How's that?"

She knew what was coming. "He said his grandfather is Lionel Kendall. Now are you happy?"

His expression looked like he'd eaten a lemon coated with sawdust. His mouth puckered then twisted as if he had words to say, but he couldn't spit them out.

"See, Grandpa. I ruined your lunch."

"Speaking of that old codger, he's stinkin' up my backyard. He's got to stop, or I'm callin' the police."

Karen set her sandwich down, her appetite already ruined. "Why is he stinking up your yard?"

"He puts his garbage along the fence close to my house. I can't even sit on the back porch."

The smell had never bothered Karen, but she knew her grandfather would make his own stink until they were removed. She hid her grin, amazed at his penchant for finding fault with Mr. Kendall. "I'll see what I can do, Grandpa. Now eat your lunch."

He dug into the last of his sandwich while she watched, wondering why she'd even tried to hide her stone bruise from him. If she'd told him when she'd first returned, the whole conversation would have been over, and they might have enjoyed their meal together. "Are you opening the vegetable stand this afternoon?"

"I might. I was out there for a couple of hours this morning. Not much traffic, but I figure the people passing from work might stop by this afternoon." He finished the last crust then swilled down the milk. "Thanks for lunch." He eyed her half-eaten meal, and his expression shifted. "Not hungry?"

She shrugged. "I don't like hearing you get so angry, Grandpa. If Grandma were here, she'd quote you Proverbs. 'A gentle answer turns away wrath, but a harsh word stirs up anger.' You'd dislike Mr. Kendall if he sat outside and read his Bible."

13

"The man doesn't own a Bible."

Karen shook her head as she rose and cleared the table. Her sandwich became garbage. She'd see what she could do about the trash barrels, but she didn't think the problem was as serious as her grandfather made it out to be. It was part of his unending quarrel with the neighbor.

❦

Eric drew a circle on the condensation covering his iced tea glass. His thoughts were going nowhere, just like the big O he'd etched on the tumbler. Sometimes his life seemed like a zero, but now he had plans to make a change, to make a difference.

When he lifted his eyes, he saw his grandmother's curious stare. He pulled away his gaze and saw the same look on his grandfather's face.

"What's troubling you?" Lionel asked.

Eric took a long drink of tea to give himself time to think. He had a wonderful plan, but he wasn't ready to tell his grandparents about it—not until he knew the deal was settled. He did have other news that had rocked his world until he felt God's hand on his heart and knew he had done the right thing.

"Nothing really. I'm just looking at some changes in my life."

"What kind of changes?" his grandmother asked, her plump face settling into a frown.

"Don't worry, Gramma. Some changes happened months ago."

"Then spit 'em out," his grandfather said, leaning a thick arm against the table. "Don't make us lollygag with wonderin'."

"I don't want you to be disappointed. That's all." He saw his granddad's pursed lips and decided to just tell them. "I broke up with Janine a few months ago."

"B–but I thought you were almost ready to give her a ring." The frown deepened on his grandmother's brow.

"I thought that was the way to go, but something about our relationship bothered me. Something kept niggling me until I put it in the Lord's hands. The answer came as clear as a spring morning."

Bea shifted her plate and rested her arms on the dining room table. "But what happened?" She paused a moment, then added, "If I'm not meddling."

Eric reached across the linen cloth and patted his gramma Bea's hand. "You're not meddling." He delved into the depth of his mind to answer the question. The reason had been more like a feeling than an actual revelation from God. He tried to recall all the deductions he'd made to come up with the decision. "We had different purposes in life, I think."

"She was a Christian."

Her sentence sounded like a question rather than a statement. "Yes. Janine went to church, but she looked at life with more of an earthly purpose than I did. I don't seem to care that much about money or owning fancy cars and houses. She does."

His gaze traveled across the room. The mahogany buffet lined with family photos, the worn carpet beneath the table, and the loving nicks hidden by the linen tablecloth—all these homey things meant more to him than most luxuries. "I love this farmhouse, Gramma, but Janine wouldn't want this. She'd want a modern house in the suburbs and a new car every year."

"Nothing wrong with new things," his grandfather muttered.

"You didn't need them, Granddad. You love the farm. . .and so do I."

His grandmother studied his face for a lengthy time then gave a decisive pat to the table. "Then you did the Lord's bidding. If you feel in your heart God guided your decision, you followed His will. That's all that matters."

"Thanks," Eric said, pleased to hear his grandmother's validation on his once uneasy decision.

His grandfather made a few grumbling sounds before he spoke. "Not sure a farm would do you any good nowadays. Most have gone fallow, but I trust your conviction, Eric. You've made your decision about Janine, and your grandmother and I hope you find another nice girl one day."

"Your grandfather and I were just talking about you being married and giving us some great-grandchildren." His grandmother gave him a gentle smile.

"I'm not opposed to marriage, Gramma. I just need to find the right girl."

"I know one—the best one," his grandfather said. He reached across the empty space and grasped Bea's arm with a shake. "You missed out on her, though." He gave a chuckle. "She's a little old for you, anyway."

Eric grinned at his grandfather's lighthearted banter and enjoyed it much more than his usual growl. He wished he could tell them his other news. In time he could. When the building deal came through, he'd delight in telling his grandparents he'd be moving to Gaylord—closer to them. Since his parents had moved to Arizona, Eric knew his grandparents were lonely for family.

His grandmother loosened herself from Lionel with a teasing slap. She rose and began scraping the dinner dishes. Eric followed her example and gathered a load then carried them to the kitchen. As he helped with the scraps, Eric bundled the trash and tied the bag. "I'll take this outside."

"Thanks," she said as she rinsed the dishes beneath the tap.

Eric lifted the bag and stepped through the back door. The sun clung to the rooftops, spreading a fiery glow as it sank below the horizon. The air had cooled, and Eric drew in a deep breath, feeling whole and happy on the farm. He'd spent many summer days on the farm as a boy. So had Karen Chapman. The memories touched him again. They'd been summer playmates back then, despite the family feud raging strong.

The family feud. He wished he understood it.

He hoisted the white plastic bag and carried it across the lawn to the trash cans set along the fence. Eric eyed the containers, wondering why his grandfather put them so far from the house. Most people tucked them behind a shed or in a corner niche outside the house, but Granddad Lionel had lined them along the Chapman fence.

The answer struck him. Another "get even" for Granddad's silly bickering with Walter Chapman.

Eric lifted the lid and sank the bag into the metal can. As he lowered the lid, making sure it closed tightly, he heard a door slam and lifted his gaze. Karen strutted across the lawn like a warrior armed for battle. He considered grasping the trash can lid for a shield, but he noticed she had no visible weapon, no pitchfork or butcher knife, so he waited, unprotected from her wrath.

"Good evening," he said, watching her flared nostrils give a quick flutter.

"It might be good if you could do something with your grandfather."

He rested his hand on the white picket, admiring the flush of her cheeks. "What do you have in mind?"

Karen drew back then scowled. "I—you. . .how do I know? You should think of something. My grandfather is tired of these trash cans lining the fence. Why not put them around the corner of the house?" She swung her hand, indicating the location.

He glanced over his shoulder and saw the same place he'd been thinking about. "Good spot," he said and waited.

"Then?"

"They're not my trash barrels. I'll check with my granddad, but I'm sure this is the exact place he wants them. They wouldn't upset your grandfather if they were over there and out of the way."

Her proud shoulders slumped with resignation. "The feud. It's foolish."

"Look, I'll talk with him, but it's like talking to a mule. I doubt if he'll listen."

"I'd appreciate it."

"By the way, I'm Eric Kendall. I don't think we introduced ourselves." He grinned at her. "You're Karen. I. . .sort of remember you."

"Me, too." She stayed in place and looked at the grass. Her feet shifted from one side to the other, as if she had more to say. Finally she tilted her chin upward. "You really don't know what that whole feud thing is about?"

"Sorry. I don't have a clue. In fact, I'd wondered if you knew anything."

"Not a thing. Have you ever asked?"

He nodded. "Many times. Even my grandmother brushes it off and says they're just grumpy old men. I'm beginning to think it's like the legendary feuding families, the Hatfields and the McCoys. No one really remembers whether it was an argument over a pig or something else."

Karen's face broke into a smile. "I'm beginning to think the same thing."

He loved seeing her smile and wished she'd do it more often. "I'll see what I can do about the trash barrels, but don't count on it changing."

Kate stepped back and gave a nod. "I'd appreciate it."

Eric watched her saunter across the grass toward the back porch. Her stride was much slower and less determined as she walked away. He liked her looks.

Her looks? He liked Karen.

Karen looked out the back porch window toward the Kendalls' fence. The trash cans were still sitting where they'd been yesterday. She shook her head. The battle wasn't worth the effort. She didn't smell a thing, and she guessed her grandfather didn't either. It was the principle.

Her grandfather's footsteps alerted her, and Karen headed back into the kitchen to greet him. "Coffee, Grandpa?"

He nodded and eyed the stove top.

"I made pancakes. They're keeping warm in the oven."

He gave a grin and settled at the table. In moments, she'd piled the golden-brown cakes on his plate and handed him a bottle of syrup she'd kept warm. He bowed his head and said a blessing over the food, then dug in.

"Are we setting up the produce stand this morning?" she asked.

He nodded then swallowed before speaking. "Friday's usually a good day, but I'm worried. The sky looks cloudy. They're rain clouds for sure."

"Gray skies can't hold us back, Grandpa. Are the vegetables in the shed?"

"Yep, and some pecks of apples."

"Let me get started while you finish up." Before he could direct her action, she hurried onto the porch and outside.

Grandpa was correct. The clouds had heavy gray bottoms and hid any blue that might be above them. An occasional shift by the wind let a fraction of sunlight through and gave Karen a sliver of hope. She loaded the hand truck with baskets of the produce her grandfather grew in his fields and headed down the driveway.

Minutes passed as she lifted the front cover of the stand to form a wooden awning, then unloaded the baskets with corn, tomatoes, carrots, peppers, and slender cucumbers just right for pickles. As she lifted a peck of apples to the counter, her grandfather arrived and set out the prices. Karen unfolded two canvas chairs, and they sat.

A car rolled past then stopped on the shoulder and backed up. Karen jumped up, and soon other vehicles parked to check out the produce. With purchases bagged, her grandfather harvested the money. When business slowed, they settled into the chairs again.

The conversation moved from the weather to her grandfather's health concerns and lingered over stories about Karen's grandmother Hazel.

"Your grandma is everywhere in the house," her grandfather said.

Karen's stomach knotted. "I know, Grandpa. I picture Grandma in the kitchen, baking or canning. Sometimes both. The house always smelled of apples. Apple pies, apple jelly, apple kuchen. Even the memory makes my mouth water."

"She was a good cook, your grandma. . .and pretty as a lacy pillow."

Karen never thought of her grandmother as pretty. She recalled her as cuddly and loving. But when she thought back, Karen remembered seeing old photos of her grandma in her youth. She had been a pretty woman in her 1940s long straight dresses and wearing flowered hats and white gloves. Her grandmother had a lovely smile and eyes that glinted. Flirtatious eyes, they might be called today, but eyes with a pinch of mischief that welcomed everyone.

"She was pretty," Karen said, rethinking her earlier notion. "But she was so much more to me."

Her grandfather reached over and patted her hand. "She loved you so much. I remember her saying you'd make a beautiful bride one day." He tilted his head and gave her a questioning look. "No beaus in the picture, sweetheart?"

Karen felt a grin flicker on her mouth. "No. Not a one. You're the special man in my life now, Grandpa." She said the words, but her mind shifted to an image of Eric Kendall. Despite her efforts to push him out of her thoughts, they had a will of their own. Eric seemed to settle there daily, and she couldn't budge him. The feud didn't make her feel any easier.

The conversation soon quieted, but Karen's thoughts didn't. The silly business between her grandfather and Eric's still lingered in her mind. How could one argument last so long for a Christian man?

"Grandpa, I wish you'd explain your feud with Mr. Kendall. I keep protecting your rights, but I'd like to know what I'm defending. . .and why."

He brushed his hand across the air as if to erase her question. "The man's ignorant and a rotten neighbor. Always was. Always will be."

As the words left his mouth, a raindrop struck Karen on the arm. She looked upward toward a black hovering cloud and rose as another larger drop struck her followed by another.

She leaped from the chair. "We'd better get this cleared away. Looks like that rain you were worried about decided to pay us a visit." As she spoke, Karen had already begun loading the vegetables into the baskets.

Her grandfather leaned on the counter and looked upward. "It's Lionel again. He's over there sticking pins in a carrot, just asking for rain. The man jinxed me again."

Karen looked heavenward. *Lord, help Grandpa understand that you are in charge of weather and of all things, not Mr. Kendall. And please, Father, if I can work a tiny miracle in Your name, let me be the catalyst that changes things here. I only have a few weeks, so make it fast, Lord.* Her amen hit her thought at the same time as a crack of lightning.

She jerked in surprise and wondered if the thunder was God saying "yes."

Or was the Lord threatening a "no"?

Chapter 3

Karen wandered through the house, feeling trapped by the summer showers. She glanced out the window, watching the rain beat a steady stream against the lawn and roll in rivulets from the porch roof. Stopped-up eaves troughs, she thought. One day she'd check that out. She didn't want her grandfather climbing a ladder to clean the gutters.

Bored, she wandered into the kitchen and stared into the refrigerator. She'd bake something if she had the ingredients and a recipe. Cookies sounded good or maybe a cake. With pies, she was hopeless.

"I'm going to the grocery store," Karen called to her grandfather from the kitchen doorway. "Need anything?"

She heard him mumbling and finally a response. "Check the bread and milk. Oh, and peanut butter. I've been hungry for a peanut butter and jelly sandwich."

"Okay," she called. She grabbed her handbag and an umbrella. Even getting wet was better than getting nowhere. That's what she'd been doing since the rain started.

❦

Eric leaped from his SUV and ran into Glen's Market. He'd wanted an excuse to come into town and ended up with his grandmother's grocery list. His trip was motivated by curiosity. He hadn't heard from the Realtor and was anxious to learn if he'd had a counteroffer on the property. The man had no added news but promised to make a telephone call and get back to Eric.

Though he wanted nothing more than to tell his grandparents, even tell Karen, about his plans, he cautioned himself in doing so. As soon as he opened his mouth, he was sure he'd get complaints and people's advice. He didn't want that now. Eric had thought long and hard. He'd done his homework; he'd looked for a bargain and a good location. He'd done everything to make this endeavor a success. Besides all that, he feared competition. A good idea could be stolen as easily as a bicycle left on the sidewalk.

When he reached the entrance, he stomped his wet feet on the mat inside the door, grabbed a cart, and hauled out his list. As he passed the produce, he couldn't help but think of his plan. He'd dreamed for the past few years of opening a natural food and health product market in town. He wanted to include homegrown produce, too. So many of the farmers had given up farming, but those who still did had no efficient outlet for their products except at the roadside stands. Rain, cold, and busy highways made their job difficult, but in Eric's market, he could offer customers a pleasant atmosphere to purchase homemade jams and canned pickles, as well as fresh in-season crops. Everyone loved homegrown food.

He paused a moment at the meat counter then pushed away and headed down the next aisle. As he looked ahead, he noticed a familiar face at the far end. Karen. Even her name made his pulse skip a beat. He shook his head at his lack of control. She had no interest in a man who'd just broken up with a woman and was about to give his last shirt for a new business. Anyway, she hated him, he feared.

That fact settled uneasily in his chest. He liked Karen, and if he had a chance, he'd like to pursue getting to know her better. While his reasoning told him to back off, his heartbeat shifted to high gear, and he found himself moving past the food displays to catch up with her. He swung around the corner and headed two aisles over. He figured they'd meet in the middle of the aisle.

He was right. As soon as he took a few steps, Karen came around the far corner. With her eyes focused on the food display, she didn't see him until they were cart nose to cart nose. When she looked up, her face filled with surprise.

"Hi," he said, unable to think of anything more original.

"What are you doing here?" she asked, a questioning look in her eye.

He suspected she thought he'd followed her. "I'm not having my tires rotated," he said. As soon as the words left his mouth he'd wished they hadn't.

Karen's frown deepened, and to cover his dumb comment, he waved his grandmother's grocery list in the air. "I'm picking up a few items for the family."

"Me, too," she said, not waving anything. She turned her eyes toward the shelving and grasped a large jar of chunky peanut butter.

Eric peered at his empty cart and did the same. He set down the jar and stared at his list for a moment to gather his thoughts. "We needed the rain," he said, wondering why he'd mentioned it.

"Grandpa thinks your grandfather put a jinx on the weather. We had to close down the stand today because of the storm."

Eric felt his eye's widen. "And he blamed my grandfather?"

"Naturally." She propped her hand against her hip and shook her head. "Nonsense, but that's what he does."

Thinking about his market concept, Eric couldn't resist the moment. "It's too bad when summer's so short and the small farmer has to deal with weather problems."

"It is," she said, shifting past him and stopping at the canned goods.

Eric checked his list and followed. He saw no canned goods on the list, but he grabbed a tin of pinto beans. His grandmother would use them somehow, and he had to appear as if he were actually shopping.

"People look forward to buying fresh produce. I always consider homegrown fruits and vegetables the best," he said, studying her face.

"Right, but it's a short season."

"Short, and then add the rainy days. Farmers have problems."

She nodded and rolled the basket ahead of him.

She paused. "Aren't you going the wrong way? I thought you just came from this direction."

The truth hit him between the eyes. "When I saw you, I stopped shopping." The words flew past his lips.

"I'll take that as a compliment."

"Good," he said, feeling tongue-tied.

"I thought maybe you were following me," she said.

"Me? Follow you?" A sound left his throat between a laugh and a choke. "I'm shopping just like you are." He dropped another couple of items into his basket.

She looked into his basket and chuckled. "Baby shampoo?"

He cringed. He'd grabbed without looking. Eric had no answer that made sense, so he peered at his list and shrugged. He followed along, making an occasional comment, and when she made another reference to the rain, he eased in his last question. "Wouldn't it be nice to have a store that specialized in homegrown products? A place where people could buy them and not have to worry about the weather?" He felt a smile grow, anxious for her response.

She only shrugged. "I've never given it any thought."

He felt his face contort from a smile to a frown. "No, but it's a good idea. Don't you think?"

"I don't think it would impress people. . .especially not the farmers."

He thought it would please the local farmers, but how could he explain without telling her his plan? Karen's comment twisted his stomach in knots. Nevertheless, he tucked her words into the back of his mind. Rather than rebut her comment, he changed the subject. "Sorry about the trash cans."

"I noticed they weren't moved."

"Granddad had a million reasons why that's exactly where they should be. I'll try to talk with him some other time. He was in a mood yesterday."

"Like always, from what I heard." She manipulated her basket to get past his.

Eric blocked her. "Granddad is more bark than bite. You don't really know him."

"And not sure I want to."

When the words left her mouth, Eric noticed a look of repentance on her face. He waited.

"Sorry. I'm reiterating what Grandpa says. I don't really know your grandfather at all since I've become an adult. When I was a child, he just scared me a little."

He smiled. "One day you should stop by. I know you like my grandmother. At least you did when we were kids."

Karen's face brightened. "I do. She was always kind and sweet to us. She slipped us treats. Remember?"

He recalled. Despite his parents' warning, Gramma did a lot to develop Eric's sweet tooth.

Karen eyed her cart. "I need to be on my way. Grandpa will wonder where I am."

Eric shifted his cart. "See you over the back fence. . .or out on a limb."

A knowing grin spread across her face.

Eric watched her go, admiring her fair hair that rolled under at the ends and her trim form that bounced when she walked. He liked Karen—too much for his own good. But he knew himself too well. No family feud or discouragement would stop him. When he felt the Lord's hand on his arm, Eric accepted that God was moving him forward, and Eric was eager to move.

Maybe more quickly than God had planned, but Eric couldn't stop himself.

Karen pulled the batch of cut-and-bake cookies out of the oven. They were less work than making her own from scratch, and she could still say she baked them. That part was the truth. She grinned at her silly thought. Who cared?

When she'd gotten home, Granddad had decided to take a nap, but the smell roused him. He passed her in the kitchen doorway as she headed for the living room with a napkin full of warm goodies. Before she sat, Karen paused in front of an old bookcase, studying the book titles. As she scanned the covers, she noticed a stack of photo albums and scrapbooks on the bottom shelf. She set the cookies on a lamp table and pulled out one of the photograph books.

After settling onto the sofa, she nibbled the sweets and flipped the pages. Old pictures of her grandmother and grandfather intrigued her. This album held pictures of when they were young, probably high school or even earlier. Occasionally they stood with a group of friends, and Karen let her mind travel, imagining what their lives might have been like all those years ago. Her grandmother had died too young. She'd been a vital young woman, according to the photographs. She gazed at pictures of them on horseback and tobogganing. Each one made her more curious.

"Good cookies," her grandfather said, coming through the doorway.

"Thanks. I baked them myself." She chuckled at her comment.

He didn't question her on the issue.

After he was seated, Karen rose and carried the album to his side. She slid onto the arm of his chair and set the album in his lap. "Tell me about these photographs. Who was this guy?" She pointed to a photo where her grandmother stood beside a young man who Karen knew wasn't her grandfather.

To her surprise, he flipped the album cover closed. "I don't remember all that fiddle-faddle. You should pitch those books in the trash. They're just sentimental things your grandmother hung on to. They don't mean anything to me."

Karen rose, stunned by his words. She lifted the album and cradled it in her arms. Maybe he didn't want to see the pictures, but she did. She loved wandering back in time and learning more about her grandparents.

Sensing her grandfather's moodiness, Karen slipped the photos back onto the shelf with the others and stood in front of the window. While she had spent away the time, the rain had stopped, and the sun had returned. The rainwater had already baked away, leaving a heavy weight of humidity suspended on the air. An occasional breeze rustled the leaves. Karen returned to the kitchen and slipped two more cookies onto her grease-stained napkin. She'd pay for the calories later, but now she was soothing her depression. She couldn't believe her grandfather's abrupt reaction to the album.

Karen looked through the back window and eyed the bench beneath the large oak in the backyard. The setting drew her forward, and she headed outside, trying to make sense out of what had happened.

No sooner had she sunk onto the bench, when she caught sight of Eric crossing his grandfather's lawn. He reached the fence, grasped the picket cross-bars, and did a springing leap. He landed on both feet on her side of the fence. Neither her mind nor the fence served as a barrier to Eric's presence in her life. Her chest tightened as he neared her.

"Mind if I sit?" he asked, plopping beside her on the bench.

"No. Please. Have a seat." She gestured toward the spot he'd already sat on.

He laughed then eyed the napkin in her lap. "Did you bake those?"

She looked down at the one lone cookie. "Yes, I baked them."

"I love chocolate chip," he said.

"Be my guest." She handed him the napkin, and he took it without an argument. Before she could lower her hand, he'd consumed the whole cookie. A dusting of crumbs lay on his lip, and she longed to brush them away but controlled the urge.

Eric must have felt them. He used the paper napkin to wipe his mouth, then wadded it, and put it in his pocket. "Thanks. It was good."

She liked his smile and his easy way. So often life left her uptight and edgy, particularly her job, but Eric always had a genial manner and a quick wit. She liked that in a person. She liked it especially in Eric.

"Am I disturbing you?" he asked.

"No, I'm just sitting here."

"Doing nothing?"

"Right." In truth she was escaping her grandfather's mood. With the album coming to mind, she found herself wanting to talk about what happened. "I'm avoiding my grandfather right now."

"Really?" His eyebrows flew upward like two startled birds.

She told him about the photograph album incident.

Eric's face registered a kaleidoscope of emotions as he gazed across the yard while she spoke as if he were miles away.

She wondered if he were listening. "I guess it was nostalgia, but I loved seeing my grandparents young again."

When she'd finished the story, he turned to her. "Why would he tell you to pitch the albums?"

"I don't know. He reacted almost as he does when your grandfather's name comes into the conversation. Just too strange."

"I don't understand either one of them," he said, rubbing the back of his neck.

Karen's heart felt heavy. "I wish I could do something about it. Arguments shouldn't last a lifetime."

"Maybe not, but I think this one will. I doubt if they'll ever change."

Karen shook her head. "Not true. Things can change. God can do anything. The problem needs our prayer."

A look of interest spread across Eric's face. "You think so?"

She didn't know how to answer his curious question. "Yes," she said. "Don't you?"

She waited, but he didn't answer.

Chapter 4

Karen woke with Eric on her mind. As they had sat in the backyard talking the day before, she felt comfortable and surprisingly amiable. Even though he was a member of her grandfather's "dreaded enemy's" family, she saw only his kindness and understanding, and she loved his wit. Even when she wanted to be angry at him and stick by her grandfather's side in his dispute with Lionel Kendall, Eric made her laugh.

Looking at the photographs yesterday, Karen had thought about her grandmother. She missed her these past months since she died. Her grandfather tried to cover his sadness, but once in a while his face confirmed the loneliness and grief he felt for his loss. The look made Karen's heart ache.

For some reason today, Karen recalled her grandmother's comments about the feud and the words sent a pinprick down her back. "Lionel Kendall's a poor loser," she'd said. Poor loser? Karen couldn't imagine the eternal feud being over winning or losing a football scrimmage or a game of checkers. Now that she recalled the comment, she wished her grandmother were there to explain.

In the quiet of the morning, Karen knelt by her bedside and asked God what she could do to end the foolish bickering between the two elderly men. One word entered her mind—patience. If the Lord had sent that word into her thoughts, she needed to explain. *Father, I'm not a patient woman. Please, Lord, give me some other way.* She felt her eyes well with tears as she said "amen." The task seemed so hopeless.

In the quiet of her room, Karen felt God's presence, and she sensed His guidance, but the exact action He wanted her to take seemed lost. She rose from the carpeted floor and sat on the edge of her bed. Her Bible lay on the bedside table where she'd left it the night before. She grasped it and turned the pages to the Gospel of Luke. Fingering the tissue-thin sheets, she scanned the verses while her eyes sought the message God wanted to share with her.

Karen stopped, letting the words sink into her mind. *But love your enemies, do good to them, and lend to them without expecting to get anything back. Then your reward will be great.* So simple. Love was the answer. Somehow she had to help her grandfather see that nothing was solved with anger and spite, but love was the answer. Yet how? Would her stubborn grandfather ever listen?

Lord, she reflected, closing her Bible, *thank You for the clear and simple message that can change the world. Please give me the patience I need. In Jesus' precious name, amen.* She rose, straightened her knit top, and brushed off her jeans.

Drawing her shoulders back, she headed through the bedroom doorway toward the kitchen. She needed resolve.

Before she stepped through the doorway, she smelled her grandfather's cooking—burnt toast and strong coffee. "What's for breakfast, Grandpa?" she asked, knowing full well she'd settle for milk and cereal.

"Made some fried eggs," he said.

His voice sounded thick in his throat, and she noticed a strained look on his face. Concern settled over her.

"You helpin' me this morning?" he asked, dropping his fork onto the empty plate.

"At the stand?"

He nodded. "Saturday's busy. I could use the help."

"You know I will." She gave his cheek a pat then kissed him over the spot, feeling an unnatural warmth on his face. "You're not feeling well, are you?"

He shrugged.

"You can't fool me, so stop trying. I think I inherited a keen eye from Grandma. She always knew when anyone was sick."

"It's just a summer cold. My chest feels tight, and my throat's scratchy."

"Then don't open the stand today," Karen said as she sprinkled some cereal into a bowl. "You should rest."

"An old man needs a purpose or else he gets sicker. I like talkin' to the customers, and I'm not sick. I'm just a little slow today."

Karen knew she'd get farther talking to the wall. She ate her breakfast with speed and drank her milk. She would have preferred a good cup of coffee, but the stuff her grandfather had brewed could disintegrate a spoon.

After she rinsed off the bowl, Karen hurried to the shed for the handcart. Yesterday they'd left the vegetables loaded on the dolly. Later in the day her grandfather had added some new produce, making the job easy this morning. She pushed the cart outside and headed toward the front yard, but before she reached the driveway, a bellow echoed from the house. Karen dropped the cart handle and dashed toward the noise.

"What's wrong?" she called, as she raced through the back doorway onto the porch.

"It's that scoundrel," he yelled from the front of the house. "He's parked his car in front of my stand."

Karen followed her grandfather's voice to the front door, and sure enough, Lionel Kendall's automobile was stationed on the gravel shoulder, blocking her grandfather's roadside stand.

"I'll sue the buzzard. He's a low down, dirty—"

"Grandpa, please. You're a Christian, and you know better. What does God say you should do when you're upset with a neighbor?"

"Park my car in front of his roadside stand—that is, if he had one."

She faltered at his comment. "That's not what God says." Her voice softened.

"Sure does. 'An eye for an eye. A tooth for a tooth.' So why not a parked car for a parked car?"

Karen shook her head. "Grandpa, you know why." She rested her hand on his shoulder. "Should I get my Bible?"

He lowered his gaze, and her heart softened. She sensed God's urging. Instead of huffing and puffing, she calmed herself and sat in the chair beside him. "An eye for an eye is in the Old Testament. When Jesus came to earth, He gave us some new commands to follow. I know you've read them. Jesus said, 'I know you've heard "an eye for an eye and a tooth for a tooth," but I tell you, Do not resist an evil person. If someone strikes you on the right cheek, turn to him the other also.' " Her grandfather shifted his gaze from the floor as if he wanted to counter her comment, but he couldn't debate with the Lord.

Karen stared at him until he looked at her. "And you know what else the Bible says?"

He shrugged.

"Love your enemy and pray for him."

She watched him bristle. "I can pray for him," he sputtered, "but I can't love him."

"Just try, Grandpa. Not for me, but for yourself." She gave him a hug and rose. "Just think about it. Don't do it for me. Do it for yourself."

Before he could come back with a comment, she turned and made her way through the front doorway. She'd kept control of her frustration in front of her grandfather, but as she marched across the Kendalls' front lawn, her irritation sparked. When she reached the neighbors' door, her hand folded into a fist, and she pounded on the frame until something pinged in her mind. Instead, she unfolded her hand and gave a final tap. Patience and love, she reminded herself.

The door opened, and Lionel Kendall stood facing her with a scowl on his face.

"Hi, Mr. Kendall," Karen said, forcing a pleasant grin. "I'm Walter Chapman's granddaughter, Karen. Remember me?"

He pursed his lips but otherwise didn't move.

"I noticed that you accidentally left your car in front of my grandfather's produce stand. I wonder if you'd mind moving it so we can open up this morning."

He still didn't say a word, but his eyes narrowed, and she could almost hear the thoughts grinding through his head.

"What's up?" Eric said, sliding in beside his grandfather.

Karen gave a wave toward the roadside stand. "We have a little problem."

Eric pushed open the screen door and leaned out. He looked toward heaven then gave Karen a knowing look. "Sorry, Karen. I'm sure my granddad wasn't thinking when he—"

"I was too think—"

Eric cut off Lionel's words as smooth as a warm knife to butter. "He was thinking he should move the car. Right, Granddad?" He held out his hand, palm up. "If you give me the car keys, I'll save you the trouble of putting on your shoes."

Karen hid her smile and backed away. Eric had handled the situation like a pro, and she realized for the first time he really felt as frustrated as she had been, but his laid-back style didn't always reflect his feelings.

She breathed a relieved sigh. If she would only ask herself what Jesus would do before she acted, she might respond more like a Christian should, but sometimes the very human side of her won out. She strutted across the lawn, knowing her grandfather would be happy with the car moved, and the day could proceed without any more problems.

At least, she prayed that was the case.

🌿

Eric watched her bounce across the lawn and felt his pulse give a twitch. She stirred his emotions. Why was he having feelings for this woman? He barely knew her. The thought hung in his head. That wasn't exactly correct. He had known her well when they were kids, and she still seemed very much the same—full of spunk and very caring. He saw it in the way she handled her grandfather. Firmly, but with love and concern. Not only was she beautiful, but Karen seemed intelligent, too. Her conversations were enjoyable, and she wasn't afraid to offer an opinion. He hated to admit it, but she had made a good point about the farmers' possible attitudes toward his market idea. He needed to give that some thought.

The hard part was she confused him. Eric sensed that she liked him. When she let down her guard, he could see it in her face and hear it in her voice, but she seemed to withdraw when he got too close. He wondered why. Was it him or the family feud? Could it be something else? Perhaps she was involved with someone.

Eric stepped outside with the car keys and treaded across the lawn. Karen had vanished around the side of the house. Even thinking of her made his chest tighten. He needed to monitor his feelings. He'd tried and it didn't seem to be working.

By the time he moved the car, Karen had arrived at the stand with a handcart loaded with produce. Eric took a step toward his grandparents' house then changed his mind. "Need some help?" he asked.

She shrugged and seemed distracted.

"Something wrong?"

"My grandfather's not feeling well. He insisted on coming out here, so the only way I got him to stay inside was to promise I'd do this myself. I'm just praying I can handle it."

"No need to pray for that," Eric said, pleased that he could finally do something helpful for her. She'd only asked for one thing, and he'd batted zero in dealing with his grandfather. "I'll stick around as long as I can."

She paused, studying him as a bunch of carrots hung suspended in the air. "Why?"

"Because I'm a nice guy?" He answered it as a question and followed the words with a toying grin.

"You really are. Thanks for the offer."

They worked side by side, and before the first car stopped, the vegetables and apples were in place, and the price cards had been taped to the table. Eric was surprised how many drivers pulled off the road and climbed out to check the produce. He became the cashier and helped bag, since Karen seemed to have a good grasp of the questions customers asked about the vegetables and apples. She knew the variety of tomatoes and could tell the buyer the hour they'd been picked.

When a lull came, Karen joined him in one of the canvas chairs. She leaned her head back and drew in a lengthy breath. "I don't know how Grandpa does this. It's a lot of work."

"He's been at it for years, I suppose."

Karen nodded. "I'm very worried about him. He really doesn't look well, but he won't let me call a doctor. When my mom and dad lived nearby, they'd occasionally come over and help during the busy season, but now that they've moved out of state and since Grandma died, Grandpa's alone too much."

"I'm sure he is since your grandmother's gone. How long has it been?"

"Nearly a year. She died too young. It's been difficult for him."

He agreed. Death was so final for the living and something humans couldn't control.

She'd paused a moment. "Keeping busy, at least, helps me not think about things."

Hearing her comment niggled his curiosity. "What kind of things?"

She gave him a look as if she wished she hadn't said anything. "I've been at a sort of. . .well. . .crisis in my life, I guess."

Immediately he wondered if it was the same kind of crisis he'd faced. "You broke up with someone?"

Her eyes widened. "No. I'm having a job dilemma. I have a good job at a social service agency, but it's stressful and depressing. I'm an advocate for children, and we try to keep families together. We deal with health issues and domestic problems. You can guess that the odds are poor, and the troubles are continuous. I work with a family, and when things look good, another family arrives on my intake list who's in worse condition. It's never ending."

He couldn't imagine dealing with that day in and day out. "What do you want to do?"

Her gaze captured his. "That's the problem. I don't know. I love the work, in a way. I just wonder if it's the location. A big city has so many sad problems. I'd love to be where a little help can get someone on his feet and my efforts seem to accomplish something. Now I feel like a paper shuffler. Sometimes good ideas never get anywhere because of all the red tape."

"I know about red tape," he said. "The business world has more than its share."

"It does." She glanced at her watch then looked down the road in both directions. "I suppose I could close for a while. Grandpa always likes to have the stand open around the time work lets out so he can catch the stragglers. I have lots to do today, but I can't concentrate. I'm too worried about Grandpa." She gave him a smile. "But God will see me through."

As she began to gather up the produce, Eric joined her, pleased about her positive attitude and her strong faith. He wished his faith were as steadfast. He tended to be wishy-washy at times with his beliefs. He believed in God and salvation through Jesus, but he didn't demonstrate it the way he should, and he definitely wasn't comfortable talking to others about his faith, as Karen seemed able to do.

When they'd loaded the handcart, Eric stepped toward the handle. "Let me do that."

"I'll be fine," she said. "Thanks for your help this morning."

"Don't forget to let me know if you need me later."

"I will." She gave the cart a yank and dragged it up the gravel driveway.

Eric was happy to help her, but he sensed her drawing away again, and he didn't want to push his luck. If he tried too hard, he could envision her shying away like a young colt being saddled. She wanted no restraints, no reins.

Finally he turned away and headed home, wondering what he could do to change the way things were going. Karen's words struck him. Maybe he couldn't do this alone. Prayer. The possibility settled over him. The Bible said "ask and you shall receive." He remembered that much. Perhaps it was time to ask the Lord for direction.

While he was at it, he should probably tell the Lord what he really wanted to see happen.

Chapter 5

Karen stood in the kitchen trying to select something for dinner. Her back ached, and she felt sunburned. A sound caught her attention. Tap. Tap. Karen heard it again and headed for the front door. When she answered, she felt her mouth gape open like a baby bird waiting for a worm.

"Eric. What—" She paused. Asking him what he was doing there would have been rude. "Hi. This is unexpected." She pointed to the kettle he held between two colorful potholders. "What's that?"

"Gramma Bea sent this over for your grandfather and you. I hope you haven't made dinner."

Karen laughed. "No, not by a long shot. What's in the kettle?" She pushed open the door.

"Gramma's homemade chicken soup. It's more like stew, it's so thick. She believes chicken soup is medicine," he said, stepping inside.

"It is. I've seen it work." She flagged him toward the kitchen. "Tell her thanks so much. I'm aching all over. This gardening business is for someone else, not me."

He chuckled and set the pot on the stove. When he lifted the lid, the rich scent of chicken and noodles filled the air, and Karen's stomach churned with hunger. "Care to join us?"

"I already ate, but I might stay and visit."

"Okay," she said. "Let me get my grandfather." He surprised her by his willingness to stay. She had assumed he'd get out of the house as fast as possible, but he'd decided to take his chances on her grandfather.

She left the kitchen, motioning him to have a seat. When she reached the living room, she stood in front of her grandfather's recliner and watched him sleep. Before she walked away, he opened one eye and peered at her. "Who's here?"

"Eric's grandmother sent over some homemade soup. Chicken. It smells wonderful. Do you feel like eating?"

"Not anything from that house. Lionel probably dropped arsenic in the broth."

"Grandpa. Please stop that. Mrs. Kendall sent the soup to you out of the goodness of her heart. Grandma always said chicken noodle soup put a person back on the road to health." She bent down and stared at him nose to nose. "And you need to get on that road." She leaned closer and kissed his cheek.

Her grandfather kissed hers back and then straightened. "Is he gone?"

"Who? Eric?"

He nodded.

"No. He's in the kitchen, waiting. Do you know he spent all morning with me working at the stand? He did it to help you."

"He did?" He lowered his gaze, and his mouth worked around the thought that was waiting to be spoken. "If that's the case, I guess he can stay."

She lifted her shoulders in frustration and gave her grandfather her hand to help him rise. She felt helpless and wondered what the Lord had in mind to heal the rift.

Walter tottered into the kitchen, using the wall and doorframes as support. Karen could see he really wasn't feeling well. Tomorrow morning she wasn't going to listen to his "no" response any longer. He was going to see a doctor unless he bounded out of bed wearing a pair of tap shoes.

Karen stepped into the kitchen behind her grandfather, and Eric rose, giving them a nod. "I hope you're feeling better, sir."

Her grandfather sniffed the air then let his gaze linger on the pot of soup. "Thank you. . .and for the soup, too. Tell your grandmother I appreciate it."

As they ate, Karen talked about the vegetables she picked earlier and the number of customers she had. Eric mainly listened, but occasionally, he added a comment about the problems farmers have selling their produce while fighting bad weather. Her grandfather warmed up, and soon he was acting more like himself with Eric. The picture filled Karen's heart as much as the soup and crackers filled her stomach.

After dinner, Walter decided to rest, and when the kitchen was cleaned and the rest of the soup refrigerated, Karen prepared a plate of cookies and poured glasses of iced tea before inviting Eric into the living room.

He followed and needed no invitation to take one of the cookies before he found a seat. "These are tasty."

Honesty nudged her. "They're the cut-and-bake kind. You can buy them in the dairy case."

"Really?" He picked up another and took a bite. "I thought you said you baked them yourself."

"I did. I just didn't prepare the dough."

He gave her a wink as if he already knew that and was only teasing her.

She relaxed and tucked her legs beneath her on the sofa. "I told you about myself earlier today. Tell me about you. What do you do for a living?"

He hesitated, and his reaction threw Karen a curve.

"I—I'm sort of between jobs," he said. He looked uncomfortable with his answer.

"Between jobs? Then you're unemployed." She didn't like that at all.

❧

Unemployed?

Eric swallowed and wanted to kick himself. He should have seen this coming.

She told him all about herself earlier in the day, and he'd said nothing. He figured it was only natural for her to ask some question, but he didn't want to answer or explain. Not now.

"Not exactly," he said finally, "I'm looking into an investment."

"Investment? What kind?"

"Property," he said.

Her nose wrinkled. "I never thought of owning property as a business."

"It is when a person does something with it." He felt himself getting defensive. He just wished he could tell her the truth and get it over with, but she was way too opinionated for him to be that open. "I have plans for the property." He saw her question coming. "I'm still working on the project."

"Oh."

That was it. An empty response, but at least one that wasn't a challenge. He'd accept it for that. "I was working for an electronics firm. We made products that go into automotive electrical systems. I was a company representative. It was okay, but very unfulfilling. I prefer talking with customers who are buying the car, not a part to put in one. Much more rewarding. That's what I'm aiming for now."

Her face had softened, and her expression had grown tender. "I like hearing about you. You're excited about your new prospects."

He winced. "I don't like talking about myself. Maybe that's a man thing."

"Probably. Men don't want to show their emotions. It's nice to see you excited and protective about your new investment." Karen paused a moment, then straightened her legs and lowered them to the floor. She rested her elbow on her knees and propped her chin in her hands. "What about you? Do you have a special woman in your life?"

Her question caught him unaware, and he sucked in a breath in surprise. He'd been evasive about his work, but he couldn't do it now. Total honesty was important.

"I was seeing someone for a couple of years, but we broke it off recently."

A look of concern settled on her face. "I'm sorry, Eric."

"Don't be. I ended it." When the words came out, he knew it might have been the wrong thing to say. Her concern shifted to a frown. "It was better for us both."

"Really."

That was all she said. Eric wondered what it meant. Really, she didn't believe him or really, it was the best for them both. He didn't want to challenge her one-word comment, but he felt what he'd said needed an explanation. He tried to reveal why he'd decided to end the relationship. The more he talked, the feebler he sounded, almost as if he were looking for excuses. He hadn't been. Eric knew in his heart it was the right thing to do.

Karen looked at her watch, and Eric realized he was digging himself in deeper with every minute. "It's getting late," he said. "I'd better go."

She didn't stop him but rose and headed for the kitchen. "I'll get your grandmother's soup kettle."

When she returned, she handed it to him with a distant look in her eyes. "Tell your grandma thanks for the soup. It was delicious."

"I will," he said, stepping toward the door. "I hope I didn't bore you with all my talk. I shouldn't have said anything."

She placed her hand on his arm. "No. I'm glad you did."

She pushed open the screen, and he stepped out into the summer evening.

As Eric walked away his stomach tightened, wondering if he'd lost all chances now of getting to know Karen better. He'd hoped something special might develop between them. Tonight he doubted if she'd even consider being his friend.

🌿

Sunday morning Karen was relieved to see Grandpa Walter's surprising recovery. They laughed over whether or not it really was the chicken soup that brought him back to health. The next day her grandfather decided to leave the stand closed in the morning. Karen used the free time to look at the eaves troughs. She dragged a long extension ladder to the porch roof, and as she feared, they were clogged with debris. When she climbed down and stepped back, reality caught her by the throat. The house was two stories. She'd been okay on the ladder one story up, but two? She shook her head. Hiring someone made more sense. Still she wasn't sure her grandfather had that kind of money to waste.

After she brought out a large trash bag, Karen climbed the ladder again. She tied the bag to a top rung and began dragging out the mucky compost that had congested in the trough. Her mind drifted, as it always did, to Eric. He'd disappointed her Saturday with his two bits of news—unemployed and fresh from a romantic breakup. Karen didn't see him as a saint, but she'd sensed he had two feet placed tightly to the ground. She'd apparently been very mistaken, and that changed everything.

She paused a moment, looking at the rotting mess in the eaves and realizing that sometimes her behavior was as black and disgusting. She pushed her confused thoughts aside and returned to the job at hand. Digging her fingers in deeply, she pulled out a glob of waste and felt a splash of the black goop hit her cheek. With no free hand to wipe it off, she left it there.

No longer able to reach the debris in either direction, Karen realized she had to climb down to move the ladder.

Part way down the rungs, Eric's voice rose up to meet her. "What in the world are you doing?"

"Not having my tires rotated," she said, gazing down at him. She knew from his expression he recalled his exact comment in the grocery store days earlier.

34

"Okay. You got me," he said. Playfully, he hung his head, as if he was ashamed.

She continued down while he waited. As she shifted the ladder, he took it from her and moved it down a few feet, then turned to face her. "Nice decoration."

"What?"

"That glob on your face."

She lifted her clean hand and brushed away the slime. "I don't expect you to help me."

"I know that. I want to."

Karen lifted her chin, trying to keep her emotions from getting in the way of good sense. "I need to be honest, Eric. After talking Saturday, I really think that—"

"I'm sorry about Saturday. I know I sounded like an unemployed womanizer, but that's not true. Please trust me. When you get to know me better, you'll see who I am. Don't think I'm a bad guy because my grandfather's a little gruff."

She bit back her desire to question his "a little gruff" comment, then had second thoughts. The look on Eric's face and the sincerity in his eyes made her remember God's Word. *Do not judge, or you too will be judged.* She hadn't given Eric or his grandfather a chance. "Why should I trust you?"

"Because I'm trustable." He grinned at his made-up word. "I've done nothing to make you think otherwise."

Shame covered her. "You're right, Eric. You've been nothing but helpful and kind. I'm sorry."

"Glad that's settled," he said. "Now let me get to work." He shifted the ladder, extended it its full length, then grasped the rungs, and headed to the second-story eaves.

Karen watched as he climbed to the top without a qualm. Her knees would be knocking as they were now just watching him. She clung to the ladder rails to support it and waited, praying he wouldn't break his neck. Karen wanted to do that herself if she found out he wasn't telling her the truth.

❦

Karen scrutinized her grandfather raking broken limbs and dried grass into a pile in the backyard. Another rainstorm had hit in the night, and branches lay strewn across the lawn. Karen had suggested he wait a day or two. The wind was still whipping the leaves, and raking seemed a futile task, but her grandfather had gone out anyway. Now Karen felt guilty, watching him.

As useless as the job seemed to be, she left the back porch with the hope she could help him finish the task before he got sick again. "Grandpa, the wind's shifting things around today. It's hopeless. Let's wait until tomorrow."

"It's almost finished," he said, as determined as ever.

"You should have put this farther back, don't you think?"

"This is a good spot. No trees to catch fire."

"Catch fire?" Karen looked at him, then at the pile he'd assembled very close to the Kendalls' fence. "You can't burn this here, Grandpa. You'll start the fence on fire."

"No, I'll watch it," he said.

Before she could stop him, he knelt down and dropped a lit match into the limbs. Dried grass smoldered then spread, and soon the limbs were snapping and sending firefly sparks into the air. Karen watched with dismay as the dark smoke curled upward, then sailed across the fence into the Kendalls' yard, where Lionel was sitting beneath a tree with the daily newspaper.

"I should have known," she said, marching across the grass toward the water hose.

"No, you don't," her grandfather called.

"Yes, I do, and please move out of the way or you'll get wet."

Lionel Kendall was hanging over the fence, shaking his fist, while her grandfather made faces at him like a child.

Lord, help me, Karen pleaded. She cranked on the water spigot and headed toward the flames. As she neared, she turned on the water nozzle, and both men backed up as she aimed the stream at the fire.

Her grandfather strode away, grumbling under his breath, but Mr. Kendall clung to the pickets, still shaking his fist. In a heartbeat Eric came to her rescue. He guided his grandfather back to the chair, returned to the fence, propelled another daring leap, and landed on her side of the barrier.

"Two little kids," Eric said. He walked toward her with his fingers planted in his jeans pockets.

"I'm sorry about this. I'd hoped my grandfather could learn to turn the other cheek."

"You're looking for a miracle," he said, chuckling.

Karen didn't like his laughing at her comment. She was serious. She couldn't work a miracle, but God could, and she'd hoped the Lord might provide it.

"Let me help." He tugged his fingers from beneath the denim and grabbed the rake.

She was too tired and frustrated to argue.

Chapter 6

The breeze rustled the leaves of the huge oak tree in the back woods. The rough bark scuffed against Karen's jeans as she sat on the broad limb and surrendered herself to the quiet and to God's voice. She'd been fighting the desires of her heart, and she wasn't sure if the warning voice she heard was the Lord's or her own worries.

Karen knew better than to link herself with an unbeliever. She'd been wanting to talk to Eric about his faith, but part of her was too afraid to hear the truth. If he confessed he wasn't a Christian, she would have to walk away, so not knowing seemed easier. Yet she knew she was leading herself into temptation. She asked God's forgiveness and strength to do what was right.

No matter how Eric might answer her question, Karen had to admit he reflected many gifts of the spirit. He'd been thoughtful so many times—helping at the stand, cleaning the eaves troughs, coming to her aid with the rubbish fire issue, too many things to list. He'd been compassionate. He'd shown concern over her grandfather's health and showed the same with her job problems and other concerns. Eric loved his family, another important attribute in Karen's eyes. He also gave her the gift of laughter. So many times, when she wanted to be angry, Eric smoothed out her ire by bringing a smile to her face. But Karen wasn't fooled. Unbelievers could show the same attributes. Thoughtfulness and kindness were no guarantee. Still, she enjoyed his company. More than enjoyed it, if she were to be truthful to herself.

The sun sprinkled a patter of speckled light along the path below and made the tree leaves shimmer with its glow, outlining the veins and shapes. Even more had changed to autumn hues. Gold and red dominated the once-green foliage, reminding her that summer was fading and her vacation as well. She'd return to her job and the stress she so disliked.

Maybe she should quit. The words popped into her thoughts and out again in a heartbeat. Karen liked to plan ahead, to know where she was going. Perhaps that's why Eric's admission that he was between jobs set her on edge. She couldn't imagine being jobless, but was being between jobs really so bad?

Lately she'd neglected prayers for herself. Worried about her grandfather, Karen's prayers had been focused on him and on her concerns for Eric, but her employment needed prayer as well. Karen closed her eyes and spoke to the Lord from her heart, and when she said "amen," a calm washed over her like spring sunshine. Her heart warmed, and she knew that God was in charge.

Karen began to hum. Then the words filled her mind. Amazing grace. The Lord saved wretches like her and like so many who walked the earth. How precious was God's grace and love. She felt it shimmer on the summer breeze like a balm.

"Hello, songbird."

Eric's voice made her pulse skip.

"Caught me again." He looked so handsome and refreshing. So often he'd become her spring rain, sprinkling her with drops of humor and reflection. . .and sometimes ruining her picnic, but that was life. If he didn't rile her a bit, she would wonder if perhaps he wasn't a real friend.

"I'm enjoying the solitude," she said from above him.

"Solitude?" He pinched his chin, as if in thought. "Does that mean you're enjoying being alone or being quiet?"

She couldn't help grinning at his question. "Just enjoying."

"Are you coming down, or should I come up?"

Karen had no plans to come down just yet, but she wasn't sure she wanted him in the tree beside her. "If you promise to be quiet." The words slipped out unbidden.

"I can't promise that," he said, grasping a lower limb and boosting himself upward until he settled on a nearby branch. "It's nice up here," he said, his voice breathless from his climb. "No wonder you sit in tree branches. I haven't done this since I was a boy."

She leaned against the trunk. "It is nice and peaceful. You shouldn't let life pass you by. As they say, take time to smell the—"

"You mean take time to climb the trees, don't you?"

"That, too," she said.

Silence settled over them. Only the sounds of the woods—bird calls, whispering leaves, and chirping insects—broke the hush.

"Please don't stop singing. That's what drew me here." His comment interrupted the quiet.

A little uncomfortable at having an audience, she ignored his request, but soon the song hung in her serene thoughts, and she continued the song she'd begun earlier. When she finished the last verse, a ray of sunlight broke through the canopy of trees and fell on her. She narrowed her eyes to keep out the bright light.

"A spotlight for the performer," Eric said, offering his applause.

She shushed him, uneasy with his accolades. She was singing to God, not to Eric.

"Everything's been civil for the past couple days," he said.

"Civil?"

"With our grandfathers. They haven't tried to maim or destroy one another's property. I'm saying that's progress." He sent her an invigorating smile.

"You're right. Good things can happen with time." And patience, she added to herself. Her words were a good reminder. "Anything new in your life?"

"My, um, job offer looks good. I should know what's happening very soon."

His comment surprised her. The last she knew, he was between jobs. "You didn't mention you had an application in for a job."

"You didn't ask me."

True. She hadn't, but. . .

"I don't want to talk about it yet until I'm confident everything's going as I hoped. It's embarrassing to announce a. . .new job and then lose it."

Karen's heart lifted. "I understand." One negative concern had sailed away. He wasn't just a loafer. She cringed with the admission. She knew he wasn't a goof-off already. No matter what he said about himself, Eric had worked hard since she'd met him, and mainly for her and her grandfather. How could she doubt he was enterprising?

As she shifted, Karen's branch gave a groaning creak. Fearing it might break, she clutched at the trunk. "I'd better get off of this before I go down the quick way."

"Right now you're out on a limb, literally," he said, grinning at her, "but I think it's just the old oak's growing pains. Still you shouldn't take chances."

Eric shifted from his branch to get out of her way and lowered his foot to feel the limb below. Karen followed, moving from branch to branch, with Eric below her. When he reached the ground, he raised his arms, grabbed her by the waist, and swung her down from the final limb. He lowered her to the ground, where they stood face-to-face.

Her heart gave a wild thump, and her blood raced through her body as she faced the truth. She wanted Eric to kiss her. Searching his eyes, she saw the same look reflected in his, but too many issues still clung to her reasoning. Harnessing her emotions, she stepped back and won the battle. Still her lips could almost feel the soft, sweet touch of Eric's.

He cleared his throat, tucked his fingers into his jeans as if to tether them, and took a step down the path. Eric waited until she followed. They walked side by side, hands brushing against each other as they went. When they came out of the woods, they crossed a meadow into the apple orchard. Eric stopped long enough to pick two apples from a tree. He polished them on his shirt and threw a shiny orb to Karen. She caught it. Together they bit into the juicy pulp. No words were spoken, but the silence seemed to speak as they headed back to their houses.

Eric said good-bye when they reached the garden. Karen watched his broad shoulders sway with each step. If only he were less evasive, she would feel less confused. As she made her way toward the house, she realized her grandfather was in the garden, picking vegetables. As she neared, he straightened and gave her a look.

"You with that Kendall guy again?" he asked.

She bent down to pluck a ripe tomato from its stem. "His name's Eric. I ran into him in the woods."

"He seems to hang around the woods a lot, wouldn't you say?"

She placed the tomato into the basket sitting beside her grandfather's feet. "I wouldn't call it hanging around. He was passing through and heard me singing."

Her grandfather motioned toward the distant trees. "Why are you singing out there? Singing's for church."

"It's for anyplace the spirit moves me, Grandpa." Teasing, she patted his head. "Don't get yourself in a tizzy, please. Eric's a nice man."

"He's probably a heathen like the rest of them. Lionel raised all his boys that way."

"Are you sure, or are you speculating?"

He gave his shoulder a shrug. "Just makes sense."

"Not to me," Karen said. "Eric's his grandson. A lot of things could have brought him to know the Lord." She said the words but wondered how true her words were.

"An apple doesn't fall too far from the tree. Ever hear that?"

She had, but she wanted to give Eric a chance.

"I'm busy now." Walter crouched down and began gathering the rosy, warm tomatoes for the basket.

Feeling suddenly disappointed, Karen turned her back and walked toward the house. She should have asked him when they were in the woods. Then instead of wondering and worrying, she'd know the truth.

❦

Eric slid from his automobile and climbed the steps of My Friend's Place. He'd volunteered to help paint some of the rooms, a volunteer project his grand-mother's church was supporting. He smiled at the organization's name. A home for abused women and families, My Friend's Place had a genial sound and gave the families who came there a welcome feeling. "I'm staying at my friend's place," they could say, without feeling uneasy.

He tapped on the door, and another church member, Bill Jackson, invited him in. He looked around, surprised to see the rooms without occupants.

"All of the families are on a picnic while we paint," Bill said, apparently noticing Eric's curious expression. "It protects their identity. Some are nervous around men, so they try to go somewhere when we come in to do maintenance."

"Good idea."

"Although I've come by to help with plumbing and they've stayed," Bill said. "With painting, I suppose it's easier for them to spend the day away."

Eric followed Bill through the house, noticing the small bedrooms, some with evidence of young children by the clutter of coloring books or building blocks. His heart ached, knowing that within these walls, women and children had to find refuge from an abusive spouse.

His life wasn't perfect, but he'd come from a loving home. Not much religion came through his door. His father cursed and drank, but he was kind in his own way. Eric had been encouraged in his faith by his grandmother Bea. She'd not been regular at worship, but she'd taught him stories about Jesus, and he followed her examples of kindness and gentleness. He found it hard to believe that some of that sweetness didn't rub off on his grandfather. Eric supposed much of his grandfather's gruffness was for effect and that deep inside he was a loving man who didn't know how to break away from his reputation.

Bill set him up with brushes, rollers, tape, and a gallon of paint, and Eric got busy. He moved the furniture to the center of the room and covered it with plastic sheets, but before he did, he'd noticed a small family photo on the dresser. A slender, tired-looking woman with two children, a boy and girl of elementary school age, he figured.

Eric thanked God for My Friend's Place, but he didn't think it was the best home for children. He knew they were basically confined to the small house and narrow yard—no place to run or play ball, little to stimulate their minds but a couple televisions he'd noticed in the common rooms. If he could only make a difference in a few lives, his purpose would be worthwhile.

❦

Eric seemed to have vanished for a couple of days. Karen missed his unexpected visits and silly grin. She hadn't laughed since she'd last seen him. She disliked the disappointment that she felt and knew that he shouldn't mean so much to her. Soon they would be going their separate ways, and then what?

She dressed quickly and headed down to breakfast. If she didn't hurry, they'd be late for Sunday worship. The service began at 8:00 A.M., probably leftover from an older generation of early risers.

"You look handsome, Grandpa," Karen said, admiring his short-sleeved dress shirt and pressed trousers. His sun-browned arms showed beneath the sleeve hems, giving him a healthy glow.

"You look mighty pretty yourself," he said, wrapping his arm around her shoulder. "Sometimes you remind me of your grandma. She was a strong spunky woman, too."

His image of Karen caused her to chuckle. Maybe she was strong and spunky. She'd never thought of herself like that.

She drove her grandfather to church, preferring to get there relaxed and not on edge, as she felt with her grandfather's aggressive driving. The church parking lot was half full, and the sight disappointed her. Then she remembered summer. People traveled, as she was doing. Her hidden longing was to walk into the sanctuary and see Eric sitting there alone, perhaps, or with his grandmother. Karen recalled Gramma Bea was a Christian woman. Perhaps her faith rubbed off on Eric.

Once inside, she saw that her secret dream wasn't fulfilled. Eric's dark wavy hair and playful smile weren't there.

They settled into what she'd gotten to know as her grandfather's pew. He sat in the same place each Sunday, as if his name were on the bench. It wasn't. She'd even checked once—on both sides—just to make sure, but she had noticed since she'd attended church with her grandfather that many people sat in the same seats.

The service began, and her voice lifted in song while her grandfather's deep-throated mumble sounded beside her. Though his voice wasn't melodic, his spirit was, and that's what counted. They sat for the choir's musical selection and the readings. While she leaned against the pew, her thoughts drifted again to Eric as they so often did. She compared her yearning to a child with a nickel looking into a candy store where everything cost a dime. The looking was useless, and she'd make more progress going somewhere else to spend her five cents.

On the cover of the morning's program was a picture of a vine growing from a stem and winding around a tree, much like one of the large oak trees in the woods. The lesson focused on Jesus as the vine and believers as the branches. The words took her back to her grandfather's garden. She could see the cucumber plants winding their way along the ground, heading in many directions, all from one stem. The pastor's voice rang through the large sanctuary reading from John's Gospel. The words captured Karen's thoughts.

" 'Remain in me, and I will remain in you,' " the pastor said. " 'No branch can bear fruit by itself; it must remain in the vine. Neither can you bear fruit unless you remain in me.' "

Had she stayed in the vine, or had she strayed? In the past days, she'd borne no fruit as far as her grandfather's situation. "No branch can bear fruit by itself; it must remain in the vine. Neither can you bear fruit unless you remain in me." Had this been the reason for her failure? Had she again tried to solve the problem on her own without the Lord's blessing? She'd been out on a limb by herself, disjointed and not connected to the Lord. She needed to cling to the branches of her faith when it came to her grandfather's troubles, her feelings about Eric, and her job indecision. Prayer and God's Word were the way. She'd said it so many times, but too often she spoke the prayer without really connecting to the Vine.

The awareness left her heavy with thought, and when the congregation rose to sing the last hymn, she remained seated until her grandfather touched her arm. Embarrassed at her distraction, Karen rose and grabbed the songbook.

Outside, she stood in the morning sun, waiting for her grandfather, and her thoughts became prayers. Today, she felt connected, and later, when the time seemed right, she hoped to help her grandfather see the analogy of bearing good fruit in his relationship to Lionel Kendall. If nothing more happened this summer, she prayed God would help her make a difference.

Chapter 7

Karen sat on the back porch after church. Her gaze drifted every few minutes to the Kendall yard. She still hadn't seen Eric, and she'd begun to wonder if he'd gone back home without saying good-bye. Loneliness washed over her—a feeling she wanted to escape.

Solitude had never bothered Karen. She'd lived with it for a long time, not because she didn't like to be around people and not because she was afraid to date, but because she felt weighted by her work. She found it difficult to come home to her comfortable apartment and look forward to a life of luxury and social events when daily she saw people who didn't even have the necessities.

With those feelings knotted inside her, Karen gave her all at work, but her all didn't seem to be enough. Now she'd run into another wall. She'd met a man who touched her heart and made her laugh, but it would end there. Instead of mourning over what wasn't, Karen thought about what was. God had given her a few bright days and many cheerful moments. Laughter was good for the heart and soul. She could handle whatever the Lord had in mind for her. Her sacrifice was so small compared to God's gift of His Son, who died for her sins. Her own earthly wants seemed so unimportant.

She drew up her shoulders and headed inside. Dinnertime was coming quickly, and she needed to make decisions. When she reached the living room, she drew up short. Her grandfather sat in his recliner, his gaze directed out the window, his eyes misted, and Karen's heart weighted with his sadness.

Not wanting to interfere, she took a step backward, but he'd noticed her and sat up straighter.

"Are you getting hungry, Grandpa?" Karen asked.

"A little, I suppose."

She walked across the room and sat on the arm of his chair. "Something bothering you?"

He waved away her words. "Just an old man being melancholy."

She placed her hand against his arm. "Thinking of Grandma?"

He tilted his head toward hers. "Always."

Karen wanted to cry. She missed her grandmother, too, but she had no comprehension of how much he missed her, the married couple having spent so many years together day after day. "Anything I can do?"

He pressed his lips together and shook his head. "Not unless you want to organize a pie booth." His sadness melted behind a half smile.

"A pie booth?"

"For the Arts and Apple Fest. The city has one every year, and your grandma always rallied the ladies together from the church and in the neighborhood to set up an apple pie booth."

"For what? The church?"

"No. They selected a local charity each year, and the proceeds went to benefit those who needed help." He leaned back against the chair and stretched out his legs. "Your grandma had a knack for finding the perfect charity that would get the women excited."

"And she made the best apple pies," Karen added.

"She did that, too."

Karen tensed as the thoughts ran through her mind. She was good at rallying people together, and though she didn't know the community well, she could probably locate the perfect charity, but if she had to bake pies, she'd destroy the fund-raiser. Pies and Karen were like oil and water. They didn't mix.

"Let me think on it, Grandpa," she said after a moment's silence. "Maybe I can help. No promises now, but I'll mull it over in my mind and see what I can do."

"You'd do that for me?" His voice lifted with the words.

"For you and Grandma. . .and the charity."

"You're a sweet woman, Karen. Your grandmother would be proud of you."

Karen wanted to stop him. She hadn't said yes yet.

Or had she?

〜

Flour sprinkled the countertop and floor as Karen rolled out a piecrust. If she could handle the pie-making part of the requirement, she would volunteer to do this project that was so important to her grandfather. She feared she'd already volunteered in his eyes.

She winced, eyeing the crust recipe, but gathered courage and followed directions. Making a pie couldn't be that difficult. She had called Eric's grandmother for a recipe, and the older woman offered to do an honest taste test when it was finished. Karen was anxious to go for a visit, since she learned that Eric had not left town but had gotten involved in a volunteer project of some kind. She was curious what that was all about.

After the ingredients were arranged on the kitchen counter, Karen mixed the dough, formed a firm ball, then grasped the wooden rolling pin and began the processes of flattening the dough. She smiled as it spread into a thin circle. But her smile faded when the crust clung to the wooden cylinder as she tried to lift it. A ragged hole gaped in the middle of the perfect circle.

She balled up the dough, kneaded it back together, and began again, but this time her heart sank when the pie dough adhered to the countertop. Trying to keep a positive attitude, she scraped it up and pressed the dough together. Then, using a mass of flour, Karen found success. She lifted the round shape and plopped it into the pie tin, breathing a deep sigh, which sent a gust of flour dust into the air. She waved it away with her equally white hands.

Feeling more confident now, she began the filling. She peeled the apples then added the flour and sugar. She opened the spice cupboard and saw a jar of cinnamon, but no nutmeg. Doubling the cinnamon would do, she decided, and she added two measured scoops. She spread the mixture into the piecrust and added a few pats of butter, and a crumbly streusel topping finished it off before she popped it into the oven.

The sweet scent filled the air, as pride filled her chest. The pie smelled sweet and tangy, if nothing else, and she couldn't wait to take it next door. When it came from the oven, she almost took a sample taste, but the golden crust looked so inviting, she decided to take it next door uncut.

Karen freshened up, then carried the still-warm pie across the grass and knocked on Gramma Bea's door. Her heart rose to her throat, hoping that Eric would answer, but instead, his grandmother stood before her when the door had opened.

"Mercy," she said with a flicker of amusement in her eye, "what do you have here?"

"Apple pie," she said. "You offered to taste test, and here I am."

Gramma Bea pushed open the screen and stepped back. Karen came through, her picture-perfect pie held between two potholders. The woman beckoned her to follow, and they passed through the dining room into the kitchen.

Karen kept her eyes moving like a searchlight, fearing Eric's grandfather would burst on the scene and scare her with one of his booming comments. She could imagine her pie in crumbles on the floor, but he didn't appear. Neither did Eric, to her disappointment.

"Let me have a taste of this," Gramma Bea said, as she dug into a drawer. She pulled out a wedge-shaped utensil with a serrated edge and made a slice, then another, and placed them on saucers. "Here's one for you." She handed Karen the plate.

Karen watched, holding her breath. The older woman produced two forks from another drawer, but before they dug in, Eric came through the doorway.

Karen faltered and lowered her fork.

"This is a surprise," he said.

Gramma Bea's hand stood suspended as well. She lowered it and headed for another plate and fork. "I suppose you want to try Karen's first apple pie."

He gave Karen an amused smile. "Your first. I can't believe it."

"I've never been much of a pie baker, but Grandpa asked me—not accurate— he hinted that he wished someone would take over my grandmother's involvement with the Arts and Apple Fest booth for charity. I opened my mouth."

"Good for you," Eric said.

He accepted the pie from his grandmother and dug in. His face took on a look of surprise, and Karen didn't know if the surprise was he didn't expect her pie to be so good or it was a disaster.

Karen lifted the fork to her lips as Gramma Bea made a choking sound. Karen slipped a piece into her mouth and felt her heart sink to the basement. She longed to spit out the contents, but that wasn't ladylike or polite. "It's awful," she moaned. "What did I do?"

Eric had finally swallowed and set the pie onto the table. "I don't know, but it's hot as fire, and the taste isn't cinnamon."

"It's chili powder," Gramma Bea said. "The jars look alike. I think you picked up the wrong spice."

Chili powder. She remembered seeing it beside the cinnamon, and she'd thought to herself they looked somewhat alike. She could only imagine that not having the nutmeg threw her off. And her crust was like a rock. Embarrassment washed over her, and now she wished Eric hadn't appeared as she prayed he would. That was one plea she wished God had ignored.

"Maybe you should buy your spices in cans," Eric said. "You'll have to read the label and not just look at it."

"Hush," Gramma Bea said.

Karen ignored his comment, but inside she smiled. He was right. Reading the label would have helped. . .except for the piecrust. "Why is my crust so horrible?" she asked, facing that she might as well admit the total disaster.

"Overworked, I'd guess," Gramma Bea said. "The less handling the more tender the crust."

Karen remembered how many times she'd kneaded the dough back into a ball. Overhandling was right. "I'm mortified. . .and it looked so pretty."

"You get one point for pretty," Eric said, sending her a teasing look. "I have to admit the pie was different."

His grandmother gave him a playful swat. "Let the poor girl alone. She did her best."

"I hope that's not her best," Eric said, sputtering a laugh.

Karen opened her mouth to respond, but Gramma Bea beat her to it.

"She'll be the best pie maker in town once I get done with her. You can volunteer to organize the booth, Karen. I'll be happy to help in any way I can."

"I guess the first way is to help me learn to make a pie." The horrible taste still clung to Karen's tongue, and she was sure they were all being polite. "Could I have some water to wash this taste out of my mouth?"

Gramma Bea grinned. "How about some iced tea and some homemade cookies?"

"That sounds even better," Karen said.

"Count me in, too." Eric pulled out a kitchen chair and motioned Karen to have a seat.

She did, and he joined her while Gramma Bea poured the drinks and piled a plate full of goodies. The conversation dwindled while they nibbled. Karen knew the flurry of activity was motivated by her horrible pie. Finally they slowed and settled back to include conversation.

When the talk turned back to the Arts and Apple Fest, Karen brought up her next concern. "I need a charity. I really don't know the needs of the community here, and I know Grandma always had some specific purpose in mind. Any ideas?"

Gramma Bea pursed her lips in thought, but Eric jumped in immediately. "My Friend's Place would be a good choice."

Karen felt her forehead wrinkle. What did his friend's place have to do with a charity? "I don't understand."

Eric laughed. "I suppose that sounded strange. It's a safe haven for abused women and families. They call it My Friend's Place. I've been painting over there the past few days. Volunteers do most maintenance and repairs. The house has been open for a couple of years but hasn't had a lot of backing."

"My Friend's Place," Karen said. "I didn't think in a small community like Gaylord they would need a safe haven."

"Small communities can be the worst. Social life is limited unless a family is church active, and even then, people look for amusements, especially men. The local bar seems to fill their needs. They have a drink and shoot the breeze, then one drink leads to another, and you know where it goes from there."

Karen nodded. "I see so much of that in the city." The whole situation filled her with sadness. "The children break my heart. They're the innocent victims of most family problems."

"I promised to drive back to the shelter with another gallon of paint so they can finish up bright and early tomorrow. If you'd like to ride along today and talk with the director, you're welcome to join me."

She paused a moment, as if uncertain. Eric saw the struggle reflected in her expression. He wondered why.

"Thanks. I think I will," she said, finally. "What time are you going?"

"I'll have lunch now, then go back. How about one-thirty?"

"Sounds good." She cringed, looking at the sample she'd brought over for Gramma Bea to try. "Guess I'd better get my booby-prize pie home and get ready. I'm still covered with flour dust."

"But it looks good on you," Eric said.

"Don't be dismayed, Karen," Gramma Bea said. "We can have our pie-making lesson whenever you're ready. I learned to make them from my grandmother."

Karen's emotions shifted to an ambiguous blend of joyful and sadness. "Wish I could say the same. Grandma made exceptional pies. I never bothered to learn."

"God's giving you a second chance," Gramma Bea said.

Her spirit lifted. "Second chances are great. Sometimes thirds are needed, but let's hope I get a home run on the next try."

❦

Eric couldn't help but smile as he ate his lunch. He recalled Karen's "one shoe on and one shoe off" embarrassment the day they met in the woods for the first time in years, and today she was even more humiliated with the pie. It was horrible. The taste returned to his memory, and he pushed it away. Chili powder had no place in an apple pie.

Pleasure filled him, knowing that Karen had agreed to visit the facility with him. She'd been rather standoffish, in a way, and he'd decided to do the painting project to give her time to stew over his absence. He guessed it worked, because it didn't take her too long to agree to go.

They hadn't discussed the family feud lately, and maybe that was the problem. Perhaps she thought he'd given up or figured he didn't care enough to do anything. He'd tried the best he could. He knew his grandfather and his stubborn nature. Pushing only doubled the problem, and being subtle didn't work either. He needed something in between.

If it wasn't the feud, then he didn't know what it was that kept her at a distance. She said she had no special male friend. He had to believe it was true. Why would she not admit it if she did have someone in her life?

He so longed to tell her about his bid on the property for his market. Only one issue needed to be resolved before the land and building was his. He planned to start small, but if it took off, he could add to the building, expand the stock. His thoughts filled with possibilities. Best of all, he'd be living right back here near his grandparents in northern Michigan farmland, the place he loved.

Chapter 8

Karen was ready when Eric pulled into the driveway. My Friend's Place filled the conversation as he drove her to the facility. He told her he'd called ahead, and the director welcomed her to visit, especially when she heard it involved a possible fund-raiser.

When they parked in front, Eric leaped from the car to open Karen's door. She waited and grinned when she let him be a gentleman. She looked at the house with interest. It was an older farmhouse, not far from the center of town. Like many farms, property sold off to investors, and little by little, the city grew up around once-fertile fields.

Karen stood a moment and studied the wide front porch. At first she wondered why it was empty and not filled with rocking chairs and benches. Then she remembered.

"I suppose they can't sit out front."

"Right," he said. "The back has a few trees and tall shrubs as well as a privacy fence around the small patio. It's not the greatest place for kids. It is safer, though, than when they were living at home."

Karen's jaw tightened as she nodded. He guided her up the sidewalk and rang the bell. The director opened the door.

"Welcome," she said. "You must be Karen. I'm Nadine Smith, the director of My Friend's Place."

"Thanks for letting me visit," Karen said.

"I hear you're thinking about doing a fund-raiser this year during the Arts and Apple Fest."

"My grandmother did this kind of thing for years, and she died almost a year ago. . .so I'm trying to fill in for her." She gestured toward Eric. "Eric mentioned that you have quite a need here, and I thought I'd drop by and talk to you in person."

Eric touched Karen's arm and lifted the gallon of paint. "I'll take this to the basement while you look around."

Karen nodded and watched him go, then turned her attention to Nadine. The woman described the facility and its program, then listed its needs. As she listened, Karen had no doubt the haven for women and children was a worthy benevolence.

She viewed the empty bedrooms, but in the community room, women sat around talking or reading. Then Karen and Nadine came to a parlor turned into an indoor playroom. Inside, one of the women sat at a card table working on a puzzle with her children, a girl Karen figured was about eight and a boy. She guessed he was about nine or ten. The children were pale skinned, and Karen could only believe that sunshine and outdoor play would be a special treat for the boys and girls living here.

The woman looked up and gave a hesitant smile, but Karen saw the sadness in her eyes. The children wiggled in their chairs, as if eager to run free. But where?

Outside, Karen viewed the play area, a small section blocked from view by a privacy fence.

"We have to be so careful with the children. It's important that we shield them from danger or retribution of an angry father. Outdoor play has to be restricted. We even bus them to a different setting for school once it begins. It's impossible to let them attend their home schools."

Karen understood. She'd had a taste of this kind of problem in Detroit. "How could more funds add to the play area?"

"Perhaps you didn't notice, but the lot next door is for sale. We would love to extend a more secure privacy fence, add playground equipment, a slab for basketball, whatever we could fit in the area. We could make the patio area larger with a covered roof, so that in rain or hot sun, the women could enjoy the outdoors." She made a broad sweeping gesture. "You can see the area is too small to do much of anything now, and our privacy fence isn't sturdy."

"And it only covers a small area." Enthusiasm roused Karen as she thought about what the charity could do. The vision gave her motivation to learn to make wonderful apple pies. "I'm thrilled to be part of this fund-raiser, and I hope it's a success."

"Thank you so much," Nadine said, opening the door to the inside.

"You don't seem to have many children here now."

"They come and go. We're always happy when the situation changes so our families can go home. We have only the two children here now. Sad to say, when we have more kids, they at least have someone to play with."

Karen understood that, too. "Do you have one small need that I might do for you now? Anything."

"We always need personal hygiene products—soap, shampoo, deodorant, things like that."

"Then I'd like to help with that. I'll go shopping and pick up a few things for you."

"You've been a blessing," Nadine said. "I've spent a lot of prayer time focused on the needs here, and your visit has been the answer to them."

Karen was touched by her comment. She said good-bye to Nadine and thanked her for her time. Outside, she breathed in the fresh air and praised God for giving her the opportunity to serve a worthy cause. Though pleased that she could buy a few items to make life easier, Karen focused her thoughts on the plight of the children. They needed a place to play and to grow strong. They needed to see the sunlight and not be bound inside a few rooms, but with the situation, she realized that was almost impossible. She grieved for the situation.

Eric stood beside his car, his hip leaning against the side panel and his fingers tucked into his jeans. "Well?"

"This is the place. They have so many needs. I'm going to shop for some soap and shampoo—things like that—and bring them back. They have a great need here, and it's such a wonderful cause."

Eric brushed her arm as if wiping off specks of dirt, but Karen wondered if it was his way of saying he agreed.

"I thought you'd see their plight," he said. "I was touched by their need, too. That's why I volunteered."

"You're a nice man, Eric."

He drew his head back as if her comment startled him, but a silly grin made her know he'd feigned the shock. "You think so?"

Eric wasn't only nice. He was special. Karen had to believe his volunteering at the facility was an unselfish act of kindness. She'd seen his compassion and sensitivity to the predicament of displaced families. "I know so," she answered.

Before she expected, they'd arrived home, and Karen waved good-bye, realizing she'd never worked the conversation into her important question—whether or not Eric was a believer. As she headed inside the house, her grandmother's caution rose in her head. The verse from Second Corinthians flared in her thoughts. "Do not be yoked together with unbelievers. For what do righteousness and wickedness have in common? Or what fellowship can light have with darkness?"

With God's Word echoing in her head, Karen envisioned Eric's playful smile and teasing ways, his gentle kindness. *Lord, give me an opportunity to ask the right question, and if the occasion does arrive, give me courage to ask.* She knew fear held her back from knowing the truth. Ignorance is bliss. But was it? Ignorance was just plain old ignorance. She needed backbone and grit.

Where else could she find such strength, but in the Lord?

❦

Eric headed across the dewy grass to the Chapman roadside stand. He'd seen Karen heading that way and assumed she was there. When he reached the front, he was disappointed to find her grandfather seated there, too.

Walter gave Eric an unwelcome greeting, but Karen's smile made him feel better.

"What are you up to?" she asked.

"Gramma Bea wants some apples to make applesauce." He looked at one variety and then the other. "Which is best?" He aimed the question at Karen's grandfather.

"Macintosh makes the best sauce and pies," he said. "The others are eatin' apples."

"Gramma wants a peck." He lingered there, wanting to talk, but Walter put a damper on the situation.

Walter lifted the peck and set it in front of Eric. "No charge. Tell Bea it's payment for the chicken soup. If it weren't for her soup, I would've had to pay a doctor bill."

"You sure?" Eric asked.

He nodded and lowered himself into the chair.

Eric felt disappointed. He'd longed to talk privately with Karen, but that was impossible with her grandfather here. When he looked at Karen, he sensed she was disappointed, too, but he couldn't linger. He had the apples, and that's partially what he'd come for. "Thanks. Gramma will appreciate it."

"Welcome," the older man said.

Eric hoisted the peck onto his hip and turned away, but before he took two steps, Karen stopped him.

"Grandpa, I'm going to walk over with Eric for a minute."

He heard a harrumph and a grumble, but Karen joined Eric anyway.

"I wanted to talk with you," she said.

"I guessed as much." He gave her a sideways smile. "Anything in particular?"

"My Friend's Place."

Disappointment nipped at him. He'd hoped it might be about them. "What about it?"

"The children. I can't get them out of my mind."

He didn't understand, and her comment caused him to pause and face her. "I still don't understand."

"I was thinking about inviting the two—the boy and girl who were there—to visit the farm. They need a place to run and play. A place to get some sun. They've been cooped up in those rooms. It's just heartbreaking."

The peck felt heavy, and Eric shifted it to his other arm. "But I don't think that'll help. It may just cause problems. One day in the life of those kids won't make much difference."

"It's one special day in their lives."

"But you can't save the world's ills, Karen. I give you credit for trying."

She shook her head. "You're wrong. With God's help, we can do mighty things. Are you a believer, Eric? The Lord can move mountains. Do you have faith?"

Eric grinned. "Sure, but did you ever notice God, who's supposed to be all powerful, can't seem to heal our families' feud?"

Her shoulders slumped, and Eric was sorry he'd teased her. "Don't let me stop you. If you want to bring the kids to the farm, you need to make sure Nadine thinks it's okay, and then you need their mother's permission. If they both agree, it's a done deal as far as I can see."

Karen nodded, but the light had faded from her eyes. "I'm going to pick up some of those products this afternoon and drive over there. I'll ask then."

Seeing Karen's reaction to his baiting her, Eric knew he'd made a mistake. She held her faith too seriously to toy with. "I'm sorry. I was only teasing. Could I go along? I'd like to pick up a few items, too. I'm sure they could use everything we bring along."

She gave a half shrug. "It doesn't matter. If you want, I guess." She motioned toward the produce stand. "I'd better go."

"How about after lunch?"

"Sure," she said. "One o'clock?"

He agreed and watched her walk away. Eric knew he'd messed up good. In the midst of his irritation with himself, he wondered why Karen had asked. Did she really think he wasn't a Christian? The possibility startled him.

❦

Karen looked into her hand basket and eyed the items—soap, shampoo, toothbrushes, toothpaste, and deodorant. That was a start.

"What about combs and hair stuff?" Eric asked.

Karen hadn't quite gotten over Eric's comment earlier that day. She wondered if he was a Christian in name or in his heart. Today, she watched him live the faith he professed as he helped her do the shopping for My Friend's Place. She grinned at his words. "Hair stuff? Like curlers and clips?"

"And those ponytail things and the headbands. Little girls would even like those."

Eric's soft heart caught her up short again. He riled her with his teasing, then melted her to a puddle. "I'm sure they would."

"And lotion. That good-smelling stuff."

Karen followed him along the aisle, adding body lotion and hair stuff, as Eric called it. When the cashier rang up the sale, they looked at each other, seeing the cost.

"No wonder the facility likes donations," Eric said, pulling out his wallet. "Let's split half and half."

Karen agreed, but she still wanted to check out the dollar store. They always had bargains. When they exited the pharmacy, she guided him down a few stores. "They have great bargains here. Nothing more than one dollar."

"Really?" He pulled open the door, and she stepped inside.

By the time they left the shop, they had another plastic bag filled with gifts for the facility.

"Thanks for coming along," Karen said. "The company was nice, and you shared in the cost. I appreciate that."

"I'm glad," he said, opening the trunk and dropping in the purchases, then closing it. They climbed into the car and headed toward My Friend's Place, but before Eric made the turn onto Shady Road, he veered into a roadway park and stopped the car in the parking lot.

"What are we doing?" Karen asked.

"I wanted to talk, and a park seemed more pleasant than sitting in the car." He climbed out and rounded the vehicle to open her door.

He wanted to talk. Her mind filled with questions. What about and why were foremost in her mind. Karen followed him to a rustic picnic bench, and they sat on the same side, their backs against the table.

"First," he said, "I want to apologize for my curt comment earlier. I was joking, but it didn't come across that way, I guess."

"You mean the one about God being all powerful?"

He nodded and pinched his bottom lip. "I thought you knew I was a Christian. I never even considered that you didn't."

His testimony settled over her with a mixture of relief and joy. "How would I know?"

His laugh filled the air. "I'm not sure. I knew you were. I just assumed."

"You've never mentioned praying or going to church, nothing that would lead me to believe you were a believer, and my grandfather said your grandfather is a heathen."

Once the words were out, she saw them for what they were. "I'm sorry, Eric. I suppose your grandfather would be a heathen in my grandpa's eyes if he were part of the clergy."

"I think you're right," Eric said. He rested his elbows on his knees, braced his hands together, and cupped his chin on them. "I don't talk much about my faith. I came from a home where men didn't discuss their feelings openly. . .or their beliefs. Men had to be strong and stand on their own feet. Even if God could give them aid, a man was supposed to handle his own problems."

"Your father's philosophy?"

He nodded. "He was a good dad. He even went to church occasionally, but I don't know if he accepted Jesus as his personal Savior. I learned a lot of that on my own and from my grandmother."

Karen thought of the church. She hadn't seen Gramma Bea there either. "Does she go to church?"

"Most every Sunday. We go to the small Sonshine Community Church. Sun is with an O."

Sonshine Community. The name lifted Karen's spirit and made her smile. "I've never seen you at First Christian. I wondered."

"Gramma likes the simpler service. She's not into crowds too much."

Karen felt ashamed of her judgmental attitude. She'd made an assumption— a bad one. "I'm sorry, Eric. I was afraid to ask, and the longer I waited the more I assumed you weren't."

"Why were you afraid to ask?"

His question hit her bull's-eye like an arrow. How could she explain that away? Reasons came to mind—*because I like you so much I was afraid to learn you weren't a believer* or *because I'd like to spend time with you, and I'm afraid I'll get too attached.* Or the truth? *I'm falling for you.*

The silence hung above them, and she squirmed against the table back. "I—I like you a lot, and I hate to think of you missing out on heaven." That was true, but she felt so much more, yet she couldn't admit where her heart was headed.

His face reflected puzzlement, then he nodded. "Thanks. You can stop worrying."

"I'm glad," she said. "I should have asked you long ago."

"I wish you had."

He rose, and she followed. They walked slowly across the grass saying nothing, and their feet crunched against the gravel in the parking lot. They spoke little as they finished the ride to My Friend's Place. Karen wondered what had happened. They'd talked so congenially, so naturally, until the final question. She'd been too evasive, but a woman wasn't supposed to declare her feelings for a man before she knew how he felt. That's how she'd been brought up.

Karen and Eric, now familiar and safe faces at the shelter, delivered the bags of gifts to a smiling Nadine.

"I can't tell you how wonderful this is," the woman said. "You've been so kind to us, and on top of that, you're planning a benefit for the shelter. God has blessed us more than I can tell you."

"You're welcome," Karen said. She faltered, not wanting to ruin the lovely moment. "I do have a personal question to ask."

Nadine's smile shifted to curiosity. "Yes?"

"Are the two children still here? The ones we talked about? I don't know their names."

"Yes. They're here. Dylan and Hailey." She still looked curious.

"My grandfather has a farm with lots of land, and I wondered if it's against the rules for the children to come there for a visit. I realize they can't be in town, and I'd certainly keep my eye on them."

"That's very kind, Karen. I don't think we have a policy to cover this kind of situation. We do take the families on picnics occasionally, so I don't see anything wrong with that, but you'd really have to talk to their mother, Ada."

"I understand. That's not a problem, but I hate to ask in front of the children in case she says no."

"They're on the patio, I think. I'll call Ada in to talk with you while I keep tabs on the kids."

She stepped away, and in minutes, the woman with the sad eyes appeared in front of Karen. When Karen finished her offer, Ada's eyes filled with tears.

"They'd love to go to a farm, but are you sure you want to handle two rambunctious kids? They've been cooped up here for weeks."

"I can handle them. I can't see a problem at all."

"Praise the Lord," Ada said. "I've felt so badly for them, and this is such a kind offer. When did you have in mind?"

"Tomorrow?"

"I'll have them ready."

Karen shook the woman's hand. "I'll be here after breakfast. They'll have a whole day to enjoy themselves."

"That worked out better than I thought," Eric admitted, as they returned to the car. He'd loved watching Karen talk to the woman. Her excitement was as fresh as newly picked peaches, and the thought tickled him as much as peach fuzz.

"Now I have a million things to do," Karen said.

"Like what?"

"Buy some food kids like, think of activities for them—all kinds of things." She gave him a look as if to ask why he didn't realize she had all those things to do.

"I imagine they'll just enjoy the freedom, Karen. Don't make things so organized they can't just be creative kids." He slipped his arm around her shoulder and gave her a playful squeeze.

Karen laughed. "You're right."

Eric let his arm linger across her back, and his hand brushed the smooth skin on her upper arm. Holding her there seemed right, and he wished he didn't have to let go, but he did. She gave him a questioning look, and he stepped away.

They climbed into the car, and she was quiet. Eric didn't disturb her thoughts. He had thoughts of his own. . .like how much he enjoyed her company and what it might be like to date her.

"I don't have swings or slides—nothing for them to play on outside," Karen said, breaking the silence.

An idea popped into Eric's head. "No slide, but I think we can come up with a swing."

"Really?" Her face lit up like the sun. "How?"

"You just wait."

He ignored her questions, and when they pulled into the driveway, he sent her home, then hurried into the backyard, and opened his grandfather's shed. An old tractor tire leaned against the wall. A tire swing. He hadn't seen one of those in years, and he suspected those kids had never seen one. He searched the shed for rope. Disappointed, he found none. He'd have to go back into town. When he stepped outside, his pulse skipped a beat. Extended behind the shed and attached to a pole was a long stretch of rope, up and then back again. Enough for his purpose.

He looked toward the house and prayed his grandmother hadn't planned to hang out the laundry. He'd buy her another coil when he went into town. She had a clothes dryer, but she always said there was nothing like sunshine.

Eric detached the rope and tossed it over the fence, then hoisted the tire, which took more strength than he'd considered. A large oak tree stood beside the shed where Walter kept his produce, and Eric hung the loop of rope over his shoulder then rolled the tire to the tree.

"What are you doing?" Karen asked, jumping from the top porch step to the ground and darting across the lawn. She grinned when she saw his surprise. "A tire swing."

He nodded. "I bet those kids have never had one of those."

"I haven't, either," she said.

Karen seemed as anxious as a child awaiting Christmas. Together, they strung the rope and tire to the tree. When it was finished, they stood back and gazed at their handiwork.

"Can I give it a try?" Karen asked.

He grinned and helped her slide her legs into the opening. Once she was situated, he stood back and gave the tire a push. The tire spun in circles as it flew backward, while Karen's laughter filled the summer air.

When she'd had enough, Eric caught the tire and slowed it. His chest tightened as he looked into Karen's shining eyes. Her cheeks glowed with happiness, and at that moment, she was the most beautiful woman he'd ever seen.

"Help me out of this thing," she called.

Eric supported her back as she pulled one leg, then the other from the tire. He lowered her to the ground, and she stood so close he could smell the flowery scent of her shampoo. Her lips curved to a smile as she looked up at him, and it was all he could do not to kiss them.

He steadied himself, then stepped back, fighting his longing. Karen needed time to get to know him. If he acted rashly, he'd chase her away like a frightened bird.

This lovely bird he wanted to keep.

Chapter 9

K aren stood back and watched the two children run across the backyard with the freedom of a new colt. Hailey was eight and Dylan was ten, as she had guessed. On the way to the farm, Dylan wanted to know if he could milk the cows. He didn't seem too disappointed when Karen explained the farm was small and had only a garden and apple orchards.

Hailey was excited when she saw Karen's grandfather at the roadside stand as they pulled up. Karen knew better than to allow them to stand in full view on the highway, not knowing who might see them. Instead, she led them to the backyard, and once they saw the space, they galloped around, checking out the produce shed, the vegetable garden, and the tire swing.

"Can we ride on this?" Hailey asked.

"You're too small," Dylan said, obviously wanting to be the first one going for a ride.

Karen moved toward the tire. "I think she can handle it."

Dylan looked as if he wanted to protest, but he didn't. He stood back and helped his sister settle safely onto the swing. He gave a small push, and the tire swayed forward and back, but the second push sent the tire on a spiral ride. Hailey's squeals of joy rang across the grass.

"What's all the noise?"

Karen grinned, seeing Eric at the fence. "We're having fun. Jealous?"

"I sure am," he said, bracing himself on the picket bar and leaping over. "Now don't you try that," he said to Dylan.

The boy eyed the fence as if to question whether or not he was tall enough and strong enough to make it. He apparently decided he wasn't because he turned his attention back to the swing. "My turn," he called.

Hailey gave a whine but gave up gracefully when Karen stopped the swing and let Dylan climb on. This time Eric gave a big push and the tire went spiraling into the air. The boy's delight caused them all to laugh with him.

Karen admired Eric's ability to entertain the children. He organized a flying disc game, and when Hailey got bored, Karen took her into the house to help with lunch.

"Would you like to go to the woods after we eat?" Karen asked. "We can climb trees, and then on the way back, we could pick apples."

"Off the trees?" Hailey asked, her eyes as wide as pancakes.

"Right off the trees. I love climbing in the woods," Karen said. "I sit on a limb and feel close to God."

"Do you go that high?"

Karen smiled. "Not as high as heaven, but pretty high."

"I wish I could climb to heaven." Her face twisted with her thought.

"You do? How come?"

"My real daddy's there."

Karen's voice caught on a knot in her throat. "I didn't know that."

The child nodded, and Karen could only imagine the wonderful "daddy" memories that had become shattered by the acts of Hailey's stepfather. She busied herself, keeping her tears at bay.

No matter what disappointments Karen had felt in her family life, she praised God for giving her a solid home and loving parents.

❦

"How am I going to work off this big belly?" Eric asked, pushing away from the kitchen table and patting his stomach.

The children giggled at his action.

"Karen said we're going to the woods after lunch," Hailey said.

"What's the woods?" Dylan asked, to Eric's surprise.

Eric ruffled his hair. "Trees."

"Can we climb?" the boy asked, his eyes brightening.

Karen rose and began moving the soiled dishes. "What good are trees if we can't climb?"

At the mention of the woods, everyone rose and helped Karen clear the table, and soon they headed across the meadow, carrying baskets to gather apples on the way back.

"There's the orchard," Karen said, motioning to the spread of trees in neat rows.

"I can see one," Hailey piped, jumping and pointing toward the red orbs that hung on the branches. Karen grabbed two and gave one to each.

Once they'd reached the woods, a natural hush fell over the four. Birds chittered, and brush rustled. The children's gazes darted from one spot to another, as they pointed out a chipmunk or squirrel. Eric couldn't believe the simple things he took for granted enthralled them.

"Here we are," Karen said, pointing to the sprawling oak.

"Can you climb up there?" Eric asked.

Both children nodded, but Eric prayed they were right. Karen went first, followed by Hailey and Dylan. Eric stayed below to make sure they were moving safely among the limbs, and when he was confident, he joined them.

Today Karen didn't go as high as she did alone, but it was enough to thrill the children.

"Everything looks different from up here," Hailey said. "And I could see far if the trees weren't in the way."

"That's sort of the way life is," Eric added. He gave Karen a grin, and seeing her smile, he knew she understood.

"This is like an old-fashioned world," Dylan said, "like when people were lumberjacks like Paul Bunyan."

"You know about Paul Bunyan?" Eric said. "That's great."

"I know something," Hailey announced. "It's another old-fashioned place. We learned about it in school."

"What is it?" Karen asked, her face as glowing as the sun that filtered through the tangle of leaves.

"It's called Mack-nack, and it's an island that only has horses and carriages."

Karen clapped her hands. "Good for you, Hailey. The island is Mackinac, but it's pronounced Mackinaw. . .like the city." She spelled out the two locations.

Dylan screwed up his face "Why does it have two names that sound alike but are spelled different?"

"It's very complicated. The area was named by Indian tribes," Karen said. "When the French heard what the Indians called the island, they spelled it like the French language. The letters *ac* in a word have an *aw* sound, but when the British settled in the city across from the island, they'd only heard the name and never saw it spelled, so they spelled it with the *aw*. Is that confusing?"

"Kind of," Hailey said.

"It's even confusing to grown-ups who live in Michigan," Eric added.

Karen laughed. "You aren't kidding." She ruffled Hailey's blond hair. "Did you know that we're only about an hour from Mackinaw City? That's where you get the ferry boat to the island."

"Really?" The little girl's voice was an awed whisper. "I wish I could go there."

"They have bicycles on the island, too," Eric said. "Horse and carriage, horseback, and bicycles. If you don't want to travel that way, guess what you have to do?"

Both children shrugged.

"Walk," he said.

The children giggled at his answer.

"When I first met Karen, she was sitting in this very tree." Eric recalled the day so vividly. He could almost remember their dialogue.

"This tree?" Hailey patted the bark and tilted her head.

"For sure," Eric said. He told them the story, and they laughed at the part about the shoes. "Karen likes to sing up here. . .just like one of the birds."

"Can we sing?" Hailey asked.

Karen sat quietly a minute and pinched her lower lip. "Do you know 'Jesus Loves Me'?"

They both nodded.

Karen began, with the children chiming in after her. Eric listened to their voices drifting through the limbs and wondered what a stranger wandering through the woods might think of three people singing from the branches of a tree.

It didn't matter because he knew the Lord was in heaven, smiling. So was Eric's heart.

🌿

Eric sat at the dinner table, holding back his news until they'd eaten. He'd heard from the Realtor, and the sale had gone through smoothly. He owned the property and the small building. Once the renovations were complete, he'd have his market. He could no longer contain his joy, and before they'd finished, he burst out the news.

"You bought a building?" his grandmother said.

"And the property under it," Eric added, giving her a teasing wink.

"Now what in land's sake are you going to do with a building?" his grandfather asked.

"Open a health-food store. More like a whole-foods market, really, with natural products and health food. Homegrown produce." He pushed aside his grandfather's negative response. That was his way. "I'll be moving to Gaylord, naturally."

"Moving here?" His grandmother leaped from her chair and wrapped her arms around Eric's neck. "I couldn't ask for anything better."

"You mean we'll see you more often?" Lionel's negativity weakened at the prospect. "That'll be okay."

Eric grinned, and when they quieted, his thoughts turned to Karen. Finally he could tell her his plan. No one could change his mind now. The deal was settled. He planned to see Karen right after dinner.

Later when Eric stood at the Chapman door, no one answered. Both cars were in the driveway, so he wandered into the backyard. The shed stood open, and Eric saw the baskets and dolly missing. Immediately he knew where they had gone.

The apple orchard.

He slid his baseball cap on backward and headed across the meadow. White and yellow butterflies skittered along the wildflower tops, and bees hummed in the early evening heat. Already he could smell the scent of drying grass and leaves turning crisp in the late summer sun. Hints of autumn hung on the air, a newness with each season—so much like life.

Ahead he caught sight of Walter, his arms raised above his head, and farther on, he saw Karen standing high on a ladder propped against a limb. As he neared, the sweet aroma of warm apples filled him with a sense of comfort. These fragrances were home.

God had been good to him. Despite his sins and mistakes, the Lord had blessed him with an abundant life—not wealth, perhaps, but richness of the spirit. A tingle of sadness washed over him when he recalled how Karen had thought he wasn't a Christian. He brought that on himself, he supposed. Eric hadn't been a good witness to his faith. He knew it was something he needed to change. . .something to pray about.

"Hi," Karen called, seeing him approach.

Her grandfather gave a brief nod and continued plucking apples from the branches.

"Can I help?" Eric asked.

Karen chuckled and climbed down the ladder. "How about you heading up there, and I'll keep my feet on the ground for a while."

"Happy to," he said, taking her place on top of the ladder.

Karen's grandfather paused and eyed the two of them. "If you're both going to pick, I think I'll take a break."

"You should, Grandpa. You look tired." She gave his arm a pat. "I'm tired, and I'm a little younger than you are."

"I'd say so." He lifted his gaze toward Eric. "Sure you don't mind helping out?"

"I'm happy to, sir."

Walter paused a moment then gave his head a decisive nod. "You're a good man." He adjusted his straw hat and strutted away through the trees.

Eric gaped at him in surprise. When he turned toward Karen, her look echoed his amazement. "Now that's a change." Puzzled, Eric scratched his head.

"Praise the Lord," Karen said. "Wonders do happen." She shook a finger at Eric. "Oh ye of little faith."

He doffed his cap. "I admit it. I was wrong."

Eric picked a few apples, wondering when a good time to talk might be. Knowing his news would require explanation and some apologizing, Eric decided to wait until they loaded the dolly and started back.

The conversation was only snatches of comments and grunting sounds as each stretched for the ripe fruit. Finally, when Eric thought his back would break, Karen suggested they stop.

"I've been thinking about Hailey and Dylan," Karen said, as they loaded the baskets onto the dolly.

"What about them?"

"They had such a great time, I'd like to bring them back again."

Eric settled the final peck of apples onto the dolly. "I see nothing wrong with that, but don't get too attached. One day they'll be gone."

"So will I, soon, but that's life. Things come and go, but while they're here I can offer them some fun."

"I suppose," he said, while his mind adhered to her comment that she'd be gone soon.

Karen grasped the dolly handle then paused. "What I'd really like to do is take them to Mackinac Island. They'd love it."

"You'd be taking on a big job. Two kids, you, and a huge lake."

"Party pooper."

They grabbed the dolly handle and realized they were facing a difficult job pulling the cart along the meadow path.

"We probably overdid it on the apple picking," Karen said, "but if we left them, they'd become bird feed."

"Or worm houses."

"True," she said, a grin spreading over her face.

They unloaded a few pecks and tugged the dolly onto the path. As they walked, Eric told her his news about the property.

Karen's face moved from a smile to surprise to a frown, leaving Eric confused.

"I thought this would be wonderful for the community," he said. "I hinted about this to you in the grocery store the other day, but as I said, I didn't want to give out details until everything was settled."

"It might be fine for the community, but how will this be good for farmers? In my mind, your store will hurt them."

Her comments shocked him. "But I can sell their produce in the store. Like I said, they won't have to worry about cold or rainy weather. No spending time sitting at the roadside. They have freedom."

"Freedom to do what?"

"Well—" He stopped to give that some thought. "Freedom to do what they want to do."

"They want to grow and sell their produce."

"They can, Karen, in my store. I don't understand why you can't see that. I really thought someone like your grandfather would love this." His stomach knotted, and the afternoon pleasure darkened as quickly as the setting sun. "Why wouldn't farmers want to sell their produce in my market?"

"Pride. Farmers are proud of what they grow. They like to show off their wares and compare the size of their tomatoes to the next farmer's. You don't know much about farming, do you?"

"I thought I did."

"I think you don't."

She gave a tug on the dolly handle and quieted. He walked beside her, but he'd lost his spirit and excitement for the new market. He had other products to sell, but one of his personal joys was to help the local farmers. Could he have been wrong?

Chapter 10

K aren set the last of the vegetables onto the stand. She shifted the half-emptied baskets away from her feet and stretched her neck upward to alleviate the tension. Her conversation with Eric settled on her like a semi truck. She assumed Eric had good in mind, but all she could see were the problems for her grandfather. Why stop at a roadside stand when the same thing was available in town at Eric's market?

She heard her grandfather's footsteps crunch in the gravel, and she forced herself to look pleasant. He'd want to know what was wrong, and at this point, Karen didn't want to tell him about Eric's proposed market. He'd been feeling down as it was, and his health had become Karen's major concern.

Walter settled in his chair and eyed her handiwork. "You're setting up the stand like a pro."

She gave him a hug before joining him in a canvas chair. "Thanks. I learned it from the master."

He sent her a warming smile.

The sky above them looked clear and bright blue. The temperature had cooled, and Karen hoped for a pleasant day, despite all her concerns. As the comfortable thoughts ran through her, sprinkles fell against the stand then struck them behind the counter.

Knowing rain was impossible, Karen rose and looked to her right. She eyed Lionel Kendall adjusting his high-powered sprinkler on the edge of his property. The water sprayed across his property line, striking the side of the stand and going beyond where customers would select their produce and in the area they would park.

When her grandfather realized what was happening, he stood and gave a yell, his fist shaking in the air, but Lionel turned his back and strode into the house.

"Sit down, Grandpa," Karen said, more determined than ever to end this foolish, unchristian rift. "I'll take care of it."

Her grandfather crumpled into his chair, while Karen strode around the stand heading for the Kendalls'. But before she took a step, the water halted. She looked toward the neighbors' house, expecting to see Eric. Instead, Gramma Bea stood beside the outside spigot.

She turned and made her way across the damp grass. "I'm sorry," she said, facing Walter. "I can't answer for my husband. Sometimes he goes too far."

"We don't blame you," Karen said, feeling sorry for the sweet woman who had to deal with her husband as if he were a child. Recalling the debris fire in their backyard, she knew her grandfather behaved the same at times.

"Karen's right," Walter said. "Don't go frettin' over it. He'll get his comeuppance when he faces the Lord."

Gramma Bea smiled, probably thinking the same thing Karen was. Both men would have some tall explaining to do. The older woman eyed the bright red tomatoes and slid a quart basket toward Karen. "I'd like these and a half-dozen corn. I'll run the money back later."

"No money needed," Walter said. "Just knowin' Lionel's eatin' my produce is worth all the money in the world."

"You're a rascal yourself, Walter," she said, and waved away his words.

As Karen bagged her corn and tomatoes, Gramma Bea moved closer. "I wanted to tell you how nice I think it is that you're bringing those children over to play. Eric told me."

"I enjoy it as much as they do." Karen set the bags in front of her.

"No matter. It's wonderful. The poor children aren't to blame for their parents' problems and sins, but they sure do suffer for them. You're doing what Jesus tells us to do—open our arms to children and people in need."

"She's takin' them on a trip," Walter said.

"A trip?" Gramma Bea asked.

Karen didn't want to be fussed over. She was doing what she thought was right. "Just up to Mackinaw City and then to the island. They were so curious about a place with no automobiles and so excited telling me what they knew about the island that I couldn't resist. We're going there tomorrow. We'll be leaving early so we have all day."

Gramma Bea frowned. "You're going to handle two children alone?"

"Just them and me. They're good kids." She wondered why Eric's grandmother seemed so concerned. "Keep us in your prayers, though. We can always use the blessings."

"Oh, I will," she said, loading the two bags into her arms. "I'll try to keep Lionel away from the sprinkler. We can both add that to our prayers."

Karen gave her a wave good-bye. Too bad Gramma Bea's good nature didn't rub off on her husband.

Then Karen's thought reversed itself. Too bad she couldn't teach her grandfather something about Christian behavior.

❦

The new building took a big bite out of Eric's time. He had to hire construction workers to do the renovations, and he'd begun contacting whole-food distributors for catalogs of products. He hoped to open the store before Thanksgiving. Though Gaylord wasn't the hugest town, many smaller towns nearby would welcome a new and unusual store to the area, he hoped. Research said he was right.

Though busy, he tried numerous times to talk with Karen, but she seemed to give him curt answers, and her geniality had turned from hot chocolate to a fudgsicle. He'd watched her entertain Ada's children, but she didn't welcome him when he dropped by, so he left, wondering what he had done to upset her.

He knew she didn't like his store idea, but he was giving that thought. She didn't give him a chance to tell her. Grudges. Feuds. He didn't understand them, and he wondered why someone like Karen, who disliked the dispute their grandfathers had carried on so long, was acting very much the same.

As he pulled into the driveway, Eric saw the roadside stand set up to catch the Friday afternoon traffic. He admired the way Karen's grandfather seemed to understand the community. He knew the best times to be outside. Every store owner should have that kind of sympathy for his customers.

When he stepped from the car, Eric headed toward his grandparents' house then stopped. Why was he running away from Karen? If she had something to say, he wished she'd say it. He'd finally made progress with Walter Chapman, and now Karen was giving him a rough time. What happened to her Christian attitude?

Instead of going inside, he backtracked and strode toward the roadside stand. If Karen didn't want to talk with him, he could at least chat with her grandfather. "How's the roadside business today?" He focused on Walter.

"Not bad." He jingled his money box.

"That's good news," Eric said, letting his gaze drift to Karen.

"We'd have done better, except your grandfather turned the sprinklers on us." Her voice was spiked with irritation.

Eric looked at her, then his grandparents' lawn. Sure enough, the sprinkler was set at the edge of the property. "Did you turn it off?" He'd truly hoped she might have eased up by now and understood what he wanted to do with the market.

"Your grandmother did," Karen said. "She came over for some veggies."

He could picture his grandfather eating Walter's produce, and the vision made him grin.

Karen's gaze was aimed at a car pulling alongside the road. Two people left their car and came to the stand. They seemed to be friends of Walter's, and as he chatted, Karen stood with her arms folded across her chest.

Eric took advantage of the moment and sidled beside her. He decided the direct approach would save a lot of time. No hemming and hawing today. "You're angry with me?"

"No. Not angry."

"Upset?"

"Disappointed," she said.

"About the store, I take it."

She backed away from the customers, and he followed her to the corner of the stand. "Do you see my grandfather?" she asked.

Obviously he saw him. He nodded.

"He loves talking with customers and showing off his produce. Think about that when you talk about opening a market. You're being unthinking and selfish."

Eric gaped at her. "Selfish? I thought I was offering a service to the community and to your grandfather." As he spoke, two automobiles pulled to the shoulder.

"I still think you thought wrong," Karen said as she stepped away.

"I'm sorry, Karen, I—"

She made her way behind the counter. "We'll have to talk about this later."

Later? He stepped back without saying any more. As he walked away, he sent up a prayer that God would give him a way to make things better with Karen. . .and a way to fix the problem he'd created.

❦

"Are we almost there?" Hailey piped, her nose pressed to the window.

"About halfway," Karen said, not sure, but her folks always told her that whenever they traveled when she was a child. She figured the answer worked for her. It should work for the children.

She had a difficult time concentrating. Eric filled her mind, and she felt ashamed how she'd treated him lately. Their relationship had risen above the family-feud issue with work on both their parts, but now his market plans disappointed her—not for herself, naturally, but her grandfather. Karen realized she needed to change her behavior. Even if she thought he was wrong, she shouldn't take it out on him, but she felt driven to let him know how concerned she was for the farmers in the community.

"Let's sing again," Hailey said.

The child's request jerked Karen from her thoughts. She turned toward the girl, trying to get her thoughts organized. "You like singing?"

"It was fun when we were in the tree."

"We're not in a tree now, silly," Dylan said.

Hailey's mouth turned down, and Karen knew she'd better jump in. "Not fair to your sister, Dylan. She only meant she enjoyed singing when we were in the tree."

He gave her a glance and mumbled, "Sorry."

Karen thought a moment. "Do you two know 'Jesus Loves the Little Children'?"

Hailey shook her head no.

"We know 'Jesus Loves Me,'" Dylan said.

"We sang that in the tree. How about if I teach this new one to you?"

They both turned toward her, waiting, so Karen began. She had them hum the tune with her and follow the words, and soon they were singing about all the children of the world. Her spirit lifted, and the problems that had pressed against her mind vanished with the children's uplifted voices. Who could be moody when kids were around?

As the sign appeared for Indian River, Karen's thoughts veered to a second adventure. The Cross in the Woods. "Your mom takes you to Sunday school, doesn't she?" She recalled them knowing "Jesus Loves Me."

"When we can go," Dylan said. "We haven't been to our church since we came to My Friend's Place."

Karen's heart ached, hearing him talk about My Friend's Place and knowing what they had been through. "I'm sorry you miss your church, but I thought you might like to stop and see a church in the woods."

Hailey looked at her with disappointment. "But I want to go to the island."

"We're going there," Karen said. "This will only take a few minutes, and I have a big surprise for you."

Her eyes widened. "Surprise?"

"What kind of surprise?" Dylan asked.

Karen gave them a smile. "This church is very different. It's outside, and it has a special cross."

"Is it a wooden cross like Jesus died on?" Dylan asked.

"But bigger," Karen said, looking at Hailey through the rearview mirror.

"Really?" Hailey tilted her head, as if she thought Karen was teasing.

When they pulled into the parking lot, the children's excitement faded.

"I don't see a cross," Dylan said.

Karen shooed them across the parking lot. "You just wait."

When they reached the building, she aimed them toward the side of the gift shop and past the inside chapel toward the woods behind the building. As they descended the stair steps leading to the bottom of the hill, the children let out a whoop. In front of them was a towering cross on a dais. Surrounding its base were bleacher seats arranged in wide rows.

"Do people really go to church here?" Hailey asked, skipping down the stairs.

"Sometimes," Karen said, awed as always by the gigantic structure.

"How tall is it?" Dylan asked.

"Fifty-five feet," Karen said. "It was made from one California redwood tree."

The children skittered ahead of her, their "wows" and "ohs" greeting her as she followed them.

As the children climbed the steps to get closer, Karen sat on a front-row bench and watched. In the quiet, prayerful setting, she bowed her head, this time for the children rather than her own problems. They needed God's care far more than her relationship with Eric or the family feud.

When she could capture their attention, Karen led them to the top of the hill and back to the car. The running did them good, as well as seeing the cross. They settled back, and before they could ask again, she took the I-75 exit ramp into Mackinaw City and drove to the ferryboat dock.

The hydro-jet boat stood at the pier. Karen paid for the tickets and hurried the children on board. Before she could stop them, they darted up the stairway

68

to the open deck at the top of the ferry. Soon the boat began to move, and they took off for the fifteen-minute ride to the island. The children giggled as the warm wind whipped their hair into tangles. The sunshine sparkled on the water, and the waves churned away from the ferry as they skimmed the water.

"The American Indians who lived here called this island Michilimackinac," Karen said. "Do you know why?"

Both heads indicated they didn't know.

"They thought the island looked like a great turtle, and that's what the word means."

"It does look like a turtle," Dylan said, drawing the shape with his finger.

The island drew nearer, and the children craned their necks to see the view. Their excitement bubbled into their voices. "We're almost there," Hailey said, pointing to Fort Mackinac seated on the hillside and the town nestled below it.

"What's that?" Dylan asked, pointing to the long white building gracing the hillside above the town.

"The Grand Hotel," Karen said. "Wait until you see it up close. It's a very famous place."

When the ferry drew nearer, the boat nosed into shore. "Please don't start running until the ferry comes to a stop and it's tied to the pier," Karen said.

They minded, and once the go-ahead was given, the children bounced down the stairs with Karen behind them. She took their hands as they stepped across the temporary walkway onto the long wooden pier. Benches along its edge were filled with people waiting to board, and Karen kept her gaze peeled to her two charges.

Hailey came to an abrupt stop and let out a whoop. "Look who's here," she yelled, then broke loose from Karen's hand, and darted off ahead, her feet pounding against the wooden pier.

Upset and bewildered, Karen followed behind her like a frightened mother hen, until she came up short and gaped.

"Hi. What kept you?" he asked.

Chapter 11

Eric grinned at Karen's surprised expression. The children danced around his feet as if he were the Pied Piper, while Karen seemed speechless. Concerned about a confrontation, he focused on the kids when he spoke. "How was your trip?"

"We saw a cross made out of a redwood," Hailey said.

"You did? You must have stopped at the Cross in the Woods."

Dylan tugged at his arm. "We climbed up and stood next to it. It was taller than you are."

Eric tousled the boy's hair. "Much taller, I'd say."

"I thought they'd enjoy seeing the cross." They were the first words Karen had spoken since she saw him. "So. . .why are we so honored?"

She'd continued down the pier as Eric followed. "I figured you could use some help."

"I'm sure we could have managed very well alone. . . ." She faltered a moment. "But it was nice of you to think of us."

She had been all he'd thought about the past couple of days, but he wasn't about to tell her.

They strode along the pier and arrived on Main Street. The Lake View Hotel spread out before them. Its turret and sprawling white porch with rocking chairs lined in a row added a unique charm to the white building. Bicycles wheeled past and carriages rolled along, their arrival announced by the clomping of horse hooves. Eric scanned the street, still amused by the charm of a town without motor vehicles.

"Ice cream," Dylan called, pointing toward Ryba's Ice Cream Shop.

"Let's wait," Karen suggested. "I thought you might like a carriage ride."

"How about renting bikes?" Eric asked, giving Karen a questioning look. "It's not too far. Just a little over eight miles around the island."

"Bikes," Dylan said. "I vote for bikes."

Hailey looked disappointed, and Karen shifted to her side. "We can take the carriage ride and let the boys ride bikes."

Eric hung on her answer. He had no desire to bike around the island without Karen. That would mess up his plan to give them some time to talk.

Finally Hailey shook her head. "No. I'll go on the bike ride, too."

Karen raised an eyebrow toward Eric. "Bikes it is, then."

She didn't appear totally happy, but Eric was. The children scampered after him to the bike rental shop only a short distance away, and within ten minutes, they were climbing onto bikes. "I still think you're wrong," Eric said. "A bicycle built for two would be fun."

"I don't do tandem," Karen said. "And it's only fun depending on who's sharing the bike."

Though she snipped her comment, he noticed a grin stealing on her face.

"Don't blame me if you get tired," Eric said.

"Me? Tired?" She sent him a facetious laugh.

He wondered if she remembered part of the ride was uphill.

They headed away from the center of town passing the fort above them on the hillside, the Chamber of Commerce building, the marina filled with sailboats, the Visitors' Center, and St. Anne's church. As they rounded the bend, the road began to climb. Eric flew along then realized he was alone. He skidded to a stop and looked over his shoulder. The children were pedaling with all their strength, but Karen had given up and was pushing her bike up the hill.

When she reached him, her faced glowed with perspiration and a frown that would win first prize. "You didn't remind me this was hilly."

"I figured you knew," he said.

The children seemed thrilled and pointed ahead to the limestone rocks jutting above the highway.

"What's that?" Hailey asked.

Eric looked ahead. "It's the Arch Rock."

"Let's go." Dylan jumped on his bike and pedaled away.

"It's flatter here," Eric said to Karen. "And remember, I offered a tandem bike. You said no."

"I made a mistake." Her response caused her to chuckle at herself.

They moved on together until they reached the children, who had paused below the rock formation.

"Can we climb the steps?" Dylan asked.

"Park your bikes at the roadside first," Eric said.

Karen watched the others secure their bicycles as her spirit toppled. She looked upward at the long flight of wooden stairs. "It's a hundred and fifty feet up there. Hundreds of steps. I don't think so."

Eric tousled Dylan's hair. "Sure we can. Last one up is a kumquat."

Karen's back straightened as she struggled for a response. He'd jumped right over what she had said.

Hailey giggled. "A what?"

"Just ignore them," Karen said, watching Eric and Dylan begin the climb. "We can stay down here and wait."

"It's a fruit," Eric called from twenty steps above them.

"I want to go, too," Hailey said, her lower lip thrust forward.

Karen swallowed and looked again at the long flight of stairs. She took a deep breath, lowered the bike stand, and hurried along behind Hailey.

She wanted to be furious at Eric, and part of her was, but the other part reminded her that she needed to stop her uncharitable attitude. She'd criticized the families for the feud, and she'd carried her own misgivings with Eric too far. Forgiveness was the key. She knew the Bible well enough to know she couldn't distort what Jesus had said. If she wanted to be forgiven by the Father, she must forgive others.

Eric and Dylan had vanished, and halfway up, Karen and Hailey stopped to gasp for breath. The view was amazing, and Karen knew the sight from the top was even better. They started off again, and huffing and puffing, they reached the top.

"Look," Hailey said, gasping as she reached the summit, "we could have come here on the carriage ride."

Karen nodded. That's how she'd always viewed Arch Rock before, and that's how she would view it from now on.

Eric and Dylan had been leaning over the parapet as she and Hailey had struggled the last few steps. Karen heard their laughter follow them to the top.

"This is the last time I'm listening to you," Karen said, but she didn't mean it. During the final trek up the staircase, she'd admitted to herself that she'd been pleased that Eric had joined them.

Eric caught her hand. "Bad sport?"

"No, bad friend."

He gave her a quizzical look.

"Thanks for surprising us today. I'm glad you came along." She didn't pull her hand away but enjoyed the closeness. He smelled of sun and fresh air. The breeze on the bluff ruffled his wavy hair, and she longed to run her fingers through it.

"I'm glad I did, too. You know who put me up to this?"

He caught Karen by surprise. "No. . ." Then she remembered Gramma Bea's many questions the day before and knew the answer. "Your grandmother."

"Right." He squeezed her hand. "She wanted to make sure you had no trouble keeping an eye on the kids around the water."

"Good for Gramma." Karen's pulse heightened feeling her hand in his bigger one.

"Let's go," Dylan called.

Karen grinned, understanding the children's eagerness to get moving, but at that moment, she didn't want to go anywhere but into Eric's arms.

The trip down the stairs was easier than going up, and once they'd reach the road again, they unlocked and climbed on the bikes and pedaled ahead. Some bikers flew past them, and some were on foot pushing the cycles up the hill. Along the way, carriages clomped past while tour guides told the tourists the island's history. An occasional horse and rider left the narrower paths and galloped along the road that circled the island.

The water rippled to their right, and distant boat sails fluttered against the blue sky. Even a freighter could be seen against the horizon, making its way through the Great Lakes toward Wisconsin or Chicago.

When they reached Point Aux Pins, Karen announced they were about halfway. The children's eagerness had faded, and she knew they were hungry. "If we go a little farther, we'll come to restrooms and a snack bar."

"Can we eat?" Dylan asked.

"We sure can."

"We'll stay there awhile, too," Eric said.

The news cheered them, and soon they parked their bikes near the snack bar, then made their way to the menu attached to the wooden building. Eric insisted on paying for their lunch. They balanced hot dogs and chips, along with a cold drink, toward the water's edge, where they found an empty picnic table.

Immediately the air was filled with squalling seagulls, landing near the table and hovering over them, waiting for a crust of bread or a lost potato chip. The children gobbled their food then took most of their hot dog buns to feed the birds.

When they were alone, Eric slid closer to Karen. He rested his elbows on his knees and tossed a pebble from one hand to the other. His attention was focused on the children, but Karen sensed he wanted to say something. She decided to make it easier for him.

"I haven't been very friendly lately," she said. "Not just today, but for the past few days. I'm sorry. I let my disappointment get the better of me."

He dropped the pebble onto the ground and shifted toward her. "Don't apologize. I guess you were right. I was so excited about my market idea, I didn't consider the ramifications."

"Shush," she said, feeling guilty for prompting an apology.

"No. Please," he said. "I'm rethinking the idea, and I'll find a solution. Everything else is a go. I've made the deal on the property and building. The work's been contracted out, and now I can give some thought to the other matter. Hopefully I'll find a way to work things out to everyone's satisfaction."

Karen's chest tightened as she watched him struggle to explain. He'd done what he thought was right for the community, and she had been viewing it from her grandfather's point of view only. Maybe her own point of view, when it came down to it. She'd never mentioned Eric's store to her grandfather. "I'm fine with it. I appreciate your trying to make things better."

"Then I'm forgiven?"

"I hope you can forgive me."

He slipped his hand over hers. "No need. Let's forget all of this and enjoy the day."

Karen agreed. When they rose, his hand brushed against hers until he captured her fingers in his. Hand in hand, they walked toward the water and joined the children at skipping rocks and chasing the seagulls.

Watching the sun inch its way lower in the sky, Eric suggested they start back, and on the way they made a detour to admire the majestic Grand Hotel with its seven-hundred-foot veranda that could be viewed with the naked eye all the way from Mackinaw City across the straits. They pedaled past the lovely old Victorian homes then rounded the bend. Main Street was ahead of them.

After returning the bikes, they stopped for the ice cream Dylan had wanted then waited for the ferry to take them back to the lower peninsula. Karen snuggled beside Eric on the bench, her heart lighter than it had been in days. She'd finally heeded God's urging to use wisdom, understanding, and forgiveness, and following His will, she'd gained so much more than her anger had accomplished.

She'd experienced a oneness with Eric. Karen liked the feeling.

❦

Karen scurried down the stairs and into the kitchen. "I'm sorry, Grandpa. I overslept. You should've called me."

"You were tired. Yesterday with those kids wore you out."

She glanced at the wall clock. "Yes, but now we've missed church, or else we'll get there in time for the last hymn."

Her grandfather patted the table. "Have some breakfast. We can go to the little country church not too far away. They have a later service."

"Really? That makes me feel better," she said, throwing two pieces of bread into the toaster. She sent up a prayer of thanks to the Lord for her day on the island and for the food she was about to eat. By the time she'd pulled butter from the refrigerator, the toast was ready.

The previous day ran through her mind like a wonderful movie, one she wanted to see again. She enjoyed the children, and Karen especially loved spending the relaxing time with Eric. Her feelings had grown even stronger as she watched him with the children. He'd make a good father and a good husband.

An alarm sounded in her head. Father? Husband? She tugged the reins of her imagination. She and Eric had a long way to go before allowing that kind of fantasy to spend any time in her mind.

When she finished her simple meal, she and her grandfather hurried to her car while he guided her to the church. The steeple rose about the trees, and after they came around the bend in the road, Karen was pleasantly surprised at the cozy, white church building that appeared.

She parked in the small parking lot, and they hurried into the building. A piano sounded as they came through the doorway, and they found a seat midway down the center aisle. When Karen opened the program, she read the church's name. Sonshine Community. The name struck a familiar cord. Then she remembered. Eric's church.

Karen let her gaze scan the congregation, and to her delight, she spotted Eric and Gramma Bea ahead of them. She grinned to herself, thinking perhaps the

Lord had been at work again. Today eased her concern about Eric's faith. She still didn't know what was in his heart, but she felt compelled to believe he knew Jesus as she did. How could she judge his beliefs? Often her own behavior seemed as shaky as a baby's rattle.

The joyful service inspired Karen. Though a small congregation, the spirit was abundant. The songs rang in the rafters, the pastor's message filled her with God's love, and the offering plate overflowed with the congregation's gifts.

Following the last hymn, Karen held back, waiting for Eric to pass in her direction. His face brightened when he saw her. Gramma Bea gave her a smile then shook her grandfather's hand. When another farmer and his wife greeted the two grandparents, Eric took Karen's arm and guided her outside into the sunshine.

"This is a great surprise," he said.

"I woke up late," Karen admitted. "Grandpa suggested we come here. He didn't tell me the church's name, so I was pleasantly surprised when I realized where I was."

"What do you think?"

"Of the church? It's very nice. Spirit filled."

"It is," he said, tucking his hands into his pockets. "I think Gramma went to your granddad's church, but felt more at home here."

Karen nodded, understanding his grandmother's feelings.

"Walk?"

"Where?" She looked around her, seeing only the gravel parking lot.

"Flower gardens," he said, tilting his head. "They're behind the church."

"Sure, but what about—"

Eric held up one finger. "They'll chat forever. This is social hour, but so you won't worry, I'll run in and tell them." He darted off while Karen waited.

In a moment, Eric returned, carrying two doughnuts. He handed Karen one on a paper napkin. "I couldn't carry two drinks without spilling them."

She laughed. "This is fine." She eyed the cream-filled fattening doughnut and hesitated, but in a heartbeat, she pushed common sense aside and sank her teeth into the sweet cake.

Eric moved along the sidewalk, and Karen followed. Each of them bit into the treat and then brushed away the evidence with their napkins. When they rounded the corner of the building, Karen stopped. "This is a beautiful place. It's a rose garden."

"Roses, but other flowers, too. It's nice in the summer." He pointed to the dried stalks of snapdragons and irises. The remnants of gold and purple yarrow greeted them around a shrub. A garden bench sat nearby, and Eric motioned toward it. "Let's sit a minute."

Karen finished the last of her doughnut, wiped her mouth, and tucked the soiled napkin into the outside pocket of her handbag. She took Eric's suggestion and settled onto the bench.

Morning had passed, and the early afternoon sun had risen above the tree-tops. Karen breathed in the scent of fading flowers, foliage, and a citrus aroma she knew was Eric. He smelled tangy and sweet like lemonade and ginger.

"Yesterday seemed special," Eric said. "I'm happy we resolved a few things. I had a great time."

"So did I." She looked into his eyes, curious about so many things.

Eric shifted and lifted one leg to rest his ankle against the other knee. He adjusted his sock, and Karen sensed he was thinking.

The silence was broken by the hum of a bee among the faded garden.

"Sometimes I'm startled that you didn't know I was a Christian," Eric said. Karen opened her mouth, but he didn't let her speak.

"I'm not blaming you. I'm blaming myself. I'm not good at witnessing. That's an area I need to grow in. . .that and my teasing."

"I love your teasing. I missed that very much when I was upset."

He grinned. "You did?"

She nodded. "Some of the misunderstanding was my fault. My grandfather seemed to think you were all nonbelievers. When I told him that I didn't know about you, he said, 'An apple doesn't fall far from the tree.' I guess I didn't question that. Grandpa was wrong."

"I've been wrong, too, Karen."

"How?"

"In questioning you and your feelings. I've never told you much about me."

Karen's pulse skipped. "You haven't, and I've been curious. I felt as if you were holding something back. You seemed to avoid talking about your faith, and then when you said you were a Christian, I didn't understand why you were so evasive."

"Mixed up, I suppose. I told you not long ago, I ended a couple of years' relationship with a woman, and I've been leery."

"Leery?" Karen asked, listening with mixed emotions.

"The breakup was my choosing. I knew Janine wasn't a strong believer, but I considered her a Christian. I was lukewarm myself when it came to attending church and studying the Bible, but I know Jesus. I know He's my Savior, and His death and resurrection gives me eternal life."

Karen warmed inside at his words.

"What I thought was that Janine also held my values, but the closer I got to giving her a ring, the more I realized we were heading in two directions."

Karen listened as he told her the revelations he'd come to as he saw their lives heading in different directions.

"I love the country," Eric said. "The birds, the trees, the quiet are all gifts to me. My grandparents' farmhouse is a palace, but not to Janine."

Karen's heart filled with joy as she realized that she and Eric shared so many things. They both loved their families, despite all the problems. They enjoyed the country and didn't need a mansion to be at home. Simple and cozy was better than elegant and sophisticated any day.

"We're of like minds," Karen said. "I agree."

"I know you do, and that's what makes me think that the Lord has plans for—"

"Ready?"

Her grandfather's voice stopped Eric in midsentence. She waved to him and rose. Eric stood, too, with a look of disappointment. Karen longed to ask him to finish the sentence, but their grandparents had made their way into the garden, and they didn't have the privacy or the time to finish the conversation.

Eric stepped forward first, with Karen right behind him. Her mind ran over and over his sentence and clung to his last words—*the Lord has plans for. . .*

Plans? Karen longed to know, because she'd begun to have plans of her own.

Chapter 12

Karen hurried to answer the knock. She opened the door, and two strangers, a man and woman, smiled from the other side of the screen door.

"I hope we're not too early," the man said. "Are you the home owner?"

A frown tugged at Karen's face, and she looked for some kind of sales gimmick or a catalog of fund-raiser candy. "No, I'm not. This is my grandfather's house."

The man looked at the woman then returned another genial smile. "Could we speak to him, then?"

Her grandfather hadn't felt well last night, and Karen had let him sleep in. She was about to open her mouth when a noise sounded behind her. She turned, and he appeared in the living room.

"Grandpa, someone wants to talk with you."

He gave her a blank gaze and ambled to the door.

Curious, Karen stepped back and listened.

"Hi," the man said. "We wondered if it's too early to come in and look around your place."

Walter gave Karen a wide-eyed stare before he turned to the stranger. "Yes. It is. Why are you—"

"Sorry," the man said, motioning for his wife to leave the porch. "We'll check back later."

Karen and her grandfather watched the couple head back to their car, their voices tangled in the morning sounds.

"What was that all about?" Karen asked.

"How should I know?" He closed the door. "Maybe they like farmhouses."

While Karen prepared her grandfather's breakfast, her mind jumped between concern about his health and the strangers who appeared on their doorstep.

"Feeling better?" she asked.

"Now don't you worry about me," he said. "I'm just getting old."

Karen couldn't help but worry, but she decided not to let him know. Before she returned to the city, her grandfather would have a doctor's appointment for a checkup. No arguments. She set his breakfast on the table, but before she could sit, she heard another knock at the door.

Carrying her mug, Karen went to the living room. When she opened the door, another stranger faced her. "I'd like to look at the house, if it's convenient."

Karen's mind twisted with confusion. "No. It's not convenient. Sorry. I really don't underst—"

The man looked at her uneasily. "I thought this house was for sale."

"This house?" She laughed. "No. You've made a mistake."

"But I thought. . ." The man made an empty gesture. "Never mind." He turned on his heel and marched away.

Karen watched him go. Something was up. She grabbed the morning newspaper from the porch and flipped it open to the want ads. Someone had made a mistake. Maybe mixed up some house numbers. She carried the paper into the kitchen and plopped into the chair.

"Company?" Walter asked.

"No. Wrong house," she said, not wanting to upset him. She scanned the ads, then let her gaze move slower over the house-for-sale listing. Nothing. She folded the paper.

When another knock sounded, Karen threw the paper on the floor and marched through the living room to the foyer. She flung open the door and faltered when she saw Eric. A puzzled expression covered his face.

"Whoa!" Eric said. "I'm on your side. You look like you're ready to wring someone's neck."

She shook her head. "It's been a weird morning."

Eric's face shifted to concern. "It has? What's going on? Please don't tell me the arguing has gotten so bad between our grandfathers that Walter's going to move."

"Move?" Karen studied his face. His look seemed sincere. "You're not kidding?"

"No." His arm swung backward toward the roadside stand. "I noticed one of those store-bought signs in front. FOR SALE BY OWNER. Is your grandfather really selling the place?"

"No." Air raced from Karen's lungs like a pin-pricked balloon. "So that's it. It must be your grandfather's handiwork." She beckoned him inside and related the visitors they'd had inquiring about the house.

Eric's expression looked as exasperated as Karen felt.

"I'll bring it in." He turned, headed through the door, and jumped from the porch to the ground. In a moment he returned, carrying the sign. "Enough is enough." He handed her the cardboard poster. "I have to talk with my grandfather."

"Wait," Karen said. "Talk does no good. He needs a reason to change."

Eric shifted from foot to foot, looking pensive. "Reason? You've got me." He ran his fingers across his hair. "I've talked to him. Gramma's talked. We've appealed to what Christian upbringing he has. Nothing works."

Karen's mind stretched to a possibility. "Does he know you and I have become friends?"

Eric shrugged. "He knows I talk with you, but—"

"What would happen if he thought. . . ? What if he thought we were getting serious about each other and—"

Eric's face brightened. "And he thinks we might bring the family together by getting married."

"Right." Her words and their meaning struck her. Why had she proposed such a thing?

"It might work." Then his expression dimmed. "Maybe not, but it's worth trying."

Karen began to think nothing would work, and she was about to say so when Eric laughed.

"Funny you made that suggestion." He rubbed his chin and gave her a playful smile. "I'd come over today to see if you'd like to go to dinner. Maybe a movie."

"Why?"

He took two steps backward. "Why? You're kidding?"

Karen wished she'd phrased that more carefully. "I mean we've spent a lot of time together, but we've never had a real. . .date."

"I know. That's why I'm asking you out to dinner. I thought it was time."

His expression made her laugh. "I have a pie-making lesson with your grandmother this afternoon, so dinner tonight would be nice."

"Great. We can set a time later." He took a step toward the doorway. "What should I do with this?"

"Set it on the porch. I'll get rid of it. Thanks."

He did as she asked, then darted down the steps. When he turned toward home, he tucked his hands into his pockets and whistled.

She watched him until he and his whistle had vanished.

❦

Eric closed the passenger door, gave a tap to the window, and rounded the car to climb into the driver's seat. "Ready for this piece of information?"

Karen pivoted her head to face him, a frown settling on her brow. "Something wrong?"

"When my grandfather was in town today, he had two people ask him what he wanted for his truck."

"Is he selling it?"

Eric grinned. "No, but the sign hooked on the tailgate said FOR SALE BY OWNER. He got a taste of his own medicine."

"I can't believe Grandpa did that. I avoided telling him about the sign. How did he know?"

"His hearing isn't as bad as he makes out," Eric said, guiding the car along the state road, amazed at what codgers both men were. "Did you get rid of the sign? I left it on the front porch."

"No. I forgot." She covered her face with both hands. "They both need a good whipping," she said behind her fingers.

Eric laughed, and so did she.

Karen became silent and looked out the window.

Eric watched the trees flash by on both sides until buildings began appearing, scattered along the roadside.

"Where are we going for dinner?" Karen asked.

"The Sugar Bowl. I hope that's okay."

Karen nodded. "I've never been there."

"The place sounds like a dessert spot, but it's not. The menu has all kinds of choices. Everything from whitefish to ribs to Greek food."

"Greek food?"

He nodded. They sank into silence again, and when they reached Main Street, he turned and found a parking place on the street. As they approached the restaurant, Eric gestured to the building. "It looks like an alpine chalet with its half-timbered walls and cedar shakes." His hand touched hers, and he wove his fingers with hers. She didn't resist, and he certainly didn't either.

"Look at the colorful glass bricks," she said, "and the stained glass. It's a beautiful place."

"Wait until we get inside," he said.

The hostess seated them in the Open Hearth room, where a chef was preparing meals beside the diners. A puff of flame shot upward on the far side of the room, and voices hollered, "Opa!"

Karen gave him a quizzical look. "What was that?"

"Greek food. Remember? It's saganaki," he said. "Flamed cheese."

Once seated Karen eyed the unique menu, and after they'd placed their orders, she sipped her iced tea and looked around at the stained-glass window frames and cherry paneling. "This is nice."

"The food is great, too." Eric slid his hand across the tabletop and rested it on hers. "I'm glad you agreed to come. I let my grandparents know we had a date. You should have seen Granddad's face, but he didn't say a word."

She smiled. "Did he get frazzled?"

"Probably after I left."

Their food arrived, and they enjoyed the meal. The conversation was centered around Eric's business matters, and Karen's attempts at pie baking for the Arts and Apple Fest.

"I'll be a real pastry chef when Gramma Bea gets finished with me," she said. "Sometimes I wish that was the only problem I had."

"Something wrong?" He laid his fork on his plate and leaned forward on his elbows, concerned about the stressed look that appeared on her face.

"Nothing serious. You know my vacation is running out. I took extra time for Grandpa, but I'm expected back at work."

His spirit sank. He knew she would leave eventually, but he'd tried to push it out of his mind. "You like your work?"

She tilted her head back and forth. "Yes and no. I realize it's important. Being a child advocate is rewarding and challenging, but it's not the personal connection I like to have with people. I love seeing progress made, changes happening, smiles on people's faces. Even when we try to do what's best for the children, I see too many tears and so much sadness."

"I'm sure it's difficult." He didn't know what else to say to make her feel better. He watched her hand pressed against the tabletop, and he lowered his arm and wrapped his fingers around hers. "You have great credentials. Maybe you need to look for something else, a position that will use your talents, but in a more positive way."

She nodded. "I've just let things ride. The easy way out. . .but not always the best way. I suppose I should look around. Something's bound to be out there that will make me happier than what I'm doing."

He agreed.

The waitress appeared and took their plates, then offered the dessert menu. "We aren't called the Sugar Bowl for nothing," she said, her smile as broad as her frame.

Eric scanned the many options. "What's the specialty here?"

She grinned. "Warm homemade raspberry pie. Everyone loves it, and it's in season."

Karen licked her lips. "Sounds yummy."

"We'll take two orders, and make that à la mode."

"You got it," she said, gathering the menus and moving off.

Karen tilted her head, her eyes brighter than before. "So what's up with your property? Where is it, by the way?"

"It's down the street a ways. Too dark to look at now, but we can come back in the daylight. They're making progress. I hope to open before Thanksgiving."

"That's fast. I'd love to see it."

Eric feared he might bore her, but his excitement motivated him to continue and detail all the changes he'd done to the inside of the building and all the ideas he had for the future. "I have a set of blueprints in the car. It makes great reading on a date."

Karen sputtered a mouthful of iced tea. "Sounds romantic. I'll have to see them."

He loved to hear her laugh, and her reference to romance captured his imagination. What if Karen lived in Gaylord? What if a real relationship progressed? What if. . . ?

So many possibilities. So many windows the Lord was opening for them both.

Chapter 13

The rain seemed unending. Michigan had always been known for its unexpected changes in weather, but the rain clouds had become a daily event. Thunder, lightning, and drizzle. Karen watched her grandfather pace across the living room. He'd pause to gaze into the sky then resume his journey back and forth on the carpet. She figured if the storms lasted much longer, he'd wear out the rug.

"All those vegetables are going to waste," Walter said as he paraded to and fro. "It's a pity. The apples will rot, too, unless I get them into a cool, dry place."

"When the rain stops, we'll think of something," Karen said.

Her grandfather sank into his recliner and snapped on the television. His finger hit the remote, flashing from station to station.

"What are you doing?" Karen asked.

"Looking for a weather report."

The scenes blinked past, and Karen wondered if he would miss the station in his impatience.

A rap on the door caught her by surprise. Who'd be out in this weather? She rose and strode across the room. Through the small window, she saw Eric drenched to the bone. Karen flung open the door. "What are you doing outside in this?"

"Visiting you," he said, stopping on the door rug to slip off his shoes and shake the rain from his hair.

"You must be part duck."

"I'm bored," he said, lifting his hand to acknowledge her grandfather.

"Come inside," Walter said. "But you won't find much to lift your spirits here."

Eric gave Karen a curious look.

"He's depressed because of the produce that's spoiling in the shed."

"And the rest will be drowned by the rain. I've been thinkin' maybe we should consider building an ark."

Eric chuckled at Walter's sense of humor. "Couldn't hurt." He stood near the door and leaned against the jamb. "Sorry about the vegetables. I know this is tough."

"A roadside stand is only as good as the weather. Not much else to do."

Eric's face brightened, and he moved closer. "I don't think I've told you about my new business venture. It could help farmers in situations like this."

Walter's attention perked up. "Sit. Sit. Tell me about it."

Karen cleared her throat loud enough for Eric to hear, but he seemed too bent on talking about his new store, and he missed her hint.

Eric stayed where he was. "I'm all wet, Mr. Chapman."

"Phooey! Wet dries in time. Have a seat."

Walter motioned Eric toward the sofa, but he selected a chair and sat on the edge.

"So what's this about a business venture?" Walter asked.

Eric glanced at Karen, and she did all she could to let him know, in her opinion, he was stepping on sensitive ground. Whether he understood or not, Karen never knew, but whichever, it didn't stop him. Eric began to detail his business dream. To her surprise, her grandfather leaned closer, as if interested in what Eric had to say.

"That would move the produce, at least," Walter said. "I hate to see it go to waste. Rain couldn't close a store."

Karen felt her eyebrows hit her hairline. Her grandfather's attitude startled her. She had been positive he'd be upset. Hearing him made her realize she'd been upset over nothing. She owed Eric a huge apology.

Walter scratched his head. "If I could think of somewhere to send all that food, I would."

Eric sat a moment in thought then snapped his fingers. "Why not the women's shelter? I'm sure they would love to have the fresh produce. It would help their budget."

"And rather than be garbage, it'll serve a purpose," Walter said. "Great idea."

"I'll call Nadine Smith—she's the director—just to make sure," Eric said.

Karen pointed to the telephone then listened to one side of the conversation, but already she knew that Nadine was thrilled. So was her grandfather.

When Eric hung up the phone, Karen grinned. "You don't have to tell me. I know you've made her day."

"That and more," he said. "And it's not me. It's your grandfather." He turned to Walter. "She's really happy about this and wants me to thank you."

Walter brushed off his comments, but Karen knew he was pleased to have been able to do something nice for My Friend's Place. Her grandfather loved the children around the farm. She was sure it helped distract him from missing her grandmother.

Karen found an umbrella in the closet, and she and Eric nestled close together and made a dash for the produce shed.

❦

Eric enjoyed having Karen by his side as they skipped over the puddles. He slid his arm around her back to keep them together under the umbrella, and Eric loved the feeling. Water splashed around their feet, and they were laughing as they hurried into the shed.

Karen shook the water from the umbrella then pulled the door partially closed. Eric pulled a cord that hung from the ceiling, and a small overhead bulb offered them dim light so they could work.

"I'll pull the car closer once we have the stuff packed up," Eric said, searching along the back for a box. He found a couple stacked in the corner. "Maybe the rain will pass and your grandfather will have one good day to open the stand. We should probably leave the freshest vegetables in the shed."

Karen agreed and began filling the boxes. "This was a good idea," she said. "Grandpa feels better knowing the food's not going to waste." She paused a moment, then stopped, and turned to him. "I owe you a big apology. Grandpa didn't mind your idea at all. After I acted like a jerk about it, I realized I was totally wrong."

Eric caught her hand and drew her close to him. "You weren't totally wrong, and you aren't a jerk at all. I admire you, Karen, for having such strong feelings for your grandfather. You were defending his right to his business while I hadn't given it any thought. That's noble of you."

She made a face, as if she thought he was making too much of it. "It's not noble. It's just love. I adore him and didn't want him to get hurt."

His pulse kicked into gear as he lifted his hand and brushed her cheek. "Then I admire you all the more. Love is much more important."

He felt a shudder run through her.

"Cold?"

"No. Just amazed."

He let her comment drop because he had more to say. "I want you to know I still plan to remedy the problem of the store interfering with the outside stands. Something will come to me."

She nodded and tilted her chin upward as if searching his eyes for something deeper.

Her eyes sent his heart on a whirl, an amazing sensation of spinning out of control. He captured her chin in his fingers and brushed one along her lower lip. The feeling was warm and tender. His control skidded to the edge of wisdom and dropped over the edge as he lowered his mouth to hers.

His pulse skipped when she accepted the kiss, her own hand rising to rest against his hairline. Breathless, he eased back. They said nothing but stood face-to-face as he listened to the rhythm of the rain tapping on the roof and echoing the beating of his heart.

❦

Uneasy, Karen sat beside Eric, pondering his kiss. She'd not pulled away but leaned into it. She felt uncertain as to its meaning but that was no surprise. She had a difficult time figuring out her own feelings.

The tender kiss had caught her off guard, but now the memory lingered in her thoughts and sent her pulse scurrying through her. Eric had mentioned his past relationship, and concern niggled her. Could his interest only be a rebound reaction? She sidled a look at his sculpted profile, his firm jaw, and the hint of a dimple beside his smile lines. She'd never noticed them until recently.

"You're quiet," Eric said, glancing her way. He shifted his hand from the wheel and brushed it against her fingers folded in her lap. "Thinking?"

She nodded.

"I hope they're good thoughts."

She realized he'd become apprehensive, probably about the kiss. Karen longed to string him along, but she didn't have the heart. "This wasn't the first time you kissed me, you know."

He glanced at her again, this time surprise on his face. "I hope you aren't angry with me."

"How could I be? I didn't fight you off."

Eric grinned. "No, you didn't." His grin turned to a chuckle. "I remember the first time we kissed. I was seven or eight, and you were a year younger. Where did I get my nerve?"

"Nerve? Where did you get the idea?" She hadn't thought of that incident until recently. "I think you watched too much late-night TV."

"I probably saw my mom and dad kiss. They were very romantic. Properly so."

Karen chuckled. "It's nice when married couples are still in love."

"Do you remember where I kissed you?"

She nodded. "In the cornrows."

"Life was easier then, wasn't it?"

"Much easier." Karen's thoughts slid back to those days. If the grandfathers were disagreeing, she'd never noticed. "Do you remember the feud back then?"

"No, I was too busy chasing the pretty neighbor girl."

"We have to find out what caused it, Eric. I really think God brought us together to solve the problem." She shifted in the seat and adjusted her seat belt so she could face him. "Do you know what I mean?"

He paused a moment before answering. "I'd hoped the Lord brought us together for something more special than smoothing out their problems."

Special? Her heart rose to her throat and choked away her words.

"Not that I don't think we should do something, but I really like you Karen, feud or no feud."

"I like you, too," she said and wanted to say "very much," but she reined in the words. "Still, I'd feel better if we could improve the situation. I think the key is your grandmother."

"Gramma Bea? She can be a hard nut to crack. I've tried."

"We'll see," Karen said, her mind spinning with ideas. If the Lord was on her side, she knew she'd find the answer, once and for all.

When Karen focused outside, she was surprised to see My Friend's Place up ahead. Eric parked, then ran inside for a dolly. As they loaded the boxes, Nadine greeted them with open arms.

"Bless you," she said as they brought the produce inside. "God answers prayers." She shook her head as if awed by the bounty they'd delivered.

"I'm glad you can use the food," Karen said. "My grandfather didn't want to see it spoil, so your need made him feel purposeful."

"We do have need," Nadine said, joining them in unloading the boxes. "We're partially funded by the state, but most of our finances are gifts from people who care. People like you."

"Too bad you can't publicize the facility more," Eric said. "I didn't know you existed until I volunteered through the church to paint."

"That's one of our problems. I'm so busy being housemother and administrator that I don't have time to promote the facility or do fund-raising. I got word a few days ago that one of the groups that supports us is giving us a generous gift to finance a new position here. The board has already approved it, and I'm going to be looking for someone to do those jobs—letting people know we're here and promoting ways to add to our funds."

"That's great," Karen said. "That's the key to a service-oriented program like yours. I'll keep your need in my prayers."

"Thank you," Nadine said. She stood back and shook her head. "This food is amazing. Our families will be thrilled. She buried her nose in the basket of tomatoes. "Nothing smells more wonderful than sun-ripened vegetables and fruit."

"I'm sure my grandfather will be happy to send over some extra things now and then. The season is coming to an end, but until it does, you can count on us."

"These are the gifts that keep us going." She clasped her hands against her chest. "On top of that, we'll benefit from the Arts and Apple Fest pie booth. That's another gift."

"We're excited about helping," Karen said.

"Is there anything we can do here for the booth? Would some flyers help, telling people about our services?"

"Excellent," Eric said. "Every person who knows about My Friend's Place will share the information with people who need to know you're here."

"I'll see you get a stack."

"Thanks," Karen said, but her thoughts had already drifted to other matters. "How are Hailey and Dylan? The rain has kept me from coming back to take them to the farm."

Nadine's face brightened. "I'm so pleased you mentioned them." She held up one finger. "I have something for you."

Questions buzzed in Karen's thoughts, and she gave Eric a puzzled look, but he only shrugged. Within a moment, Nadine reappeared, carrying an envelope.

"This is from the kids," she said, handing it to Karen. "They've gone back home. Naturally they were thrilled, but Hailey and Dylan both said they'd miss you."

A knot caught in Karen's throat. She looked at the envelope. "What happened that they could go home?"

Sadness filled Nadine's eyes. "We were able to help Ada get a restraining order against her husband, and we had enough photographs of her condition when she arrived that the police can prosecute." She shook her head. "I get too emotional over these things. I'm happy for them leaving, but they've been through so much. Life will be harder without his income, but easier on their self-worth and safety. Ada's praying he'll get some help."

"I agree," Karen said, fingering the envelope.

Nadine gave her a nod. "Open it if you'd like."

Piqued by the sealed envelope, Karen peeled back the flap. Inside, she found two drawings, one from each of the children. Her eyes welled with tears as she gazed at them. Words wouldn't come, and she handed Eric the sketches, then brushed the tears from her eyes.

Eric gazed at the pictures, then showed them to Nadine. "Karen took the kids to see the Cross in the Woods, and this one is us bicycling on Mackinac Island."

Karen shifted her gaze to the drawings in Nadine's hand. Hailey had drawn a picture of the majestic cross with two stick figure children standing below it. In the sky a bright sun sent rays in a large circle, but the longest rays touched the cross and the children beneath. Her childish printing read, "I love you. Don't forget us."

Forget them? How could she? She swallowed back the sob that ached in her throat. Dylan's picture showed more talent. Four bicyclists standing beneath the huge Arch Rock. A long staircase worked its way to the top, and in his simple cursive writing, he'd also left a message. "Thank you for the fun times at the farm and on the island." His spelling was perfect, and Karen read the words again as they blurred in her eyes.

"So nice," Nadine said, handing back the drawings. "You've touched two children with your love and compassion. Ada felt the same. She told me to let you know how grateful she was for your kindness." Nadine offered her hand. "I'm grateful, too."

Karen and Eric accepted her handshake, then made their way outside.

As they pulled away, Eric gave her a thoughtful look. "How's that job sound that Nadine talked about? It sounds like something you could do."

"Me?" Karen's heart skipped. "I hadn't given it any thought."

Could this be the Lord's answer to her prayers? Karen leaned against the car seat and let the question wash over her.

Chapter 14

Karen stood by the doorway, waiting for Eric. He'd invited her to see his property, and she had agreed. She knew he was struggling to make things right, and she admired him for that. Even though her grandfather had agreed his store was a good idea, Karen's concern had put questions in Eric's mind. He was a man of his word. Karen had learned that.

Her own thoughts snagged around questions about her work. Eric had raised a good point. She didn't have to go back to the agency in the city. The Lord opened doors and windows, and Karen knew she only had to trust in Him to guide her.

The new position at My Friend's Place banged in her thoughts. She needed to weigh the pros and the cons. Would working in Gaylord be a wise career move? Where could she go in that position? Where did she want to go? Her thoughts churned into a thick buttery mass of confusion. The possibilities lay as a lump in her mind.

Then came Eric. What was going on between them? Were her feelings premature? Had the Lord guided her to something special and lasting with Eric? The family's squabble rose in her thoughts. Maybe a serious relationship between them would make a difference between the grandfathers. As soon as the thought left her, she realized that the Lord didn't bring two people together to fall in love for that purpose. Love was a precious gift requiring commitment and devotion. Was that where her heart was leading her? Eric's image rose in her mind. No, he wasn't an Adonis, but that wasn't what she wanted. He was handsome enough, and best of all, he was filled with all the good gifts the Lord handed out. Eric, despite all her earlier fears, was a true Christian.

Karen heard a noise and looked toward the driveway. Eric had pulled up and stepped out of his car. Before he could reach the door, she moved to the porch and met him halfway.

"You're not that eager to see my empty, half-finished building are you?"

She shook her head. "No, but I have a mind full of butter that needs making into little neat pats."

He wrinkled his nose and squinted at her as if she'd lost her head. "Huh?"

"I'll explain," she said.

He accepted that, and once in the car, she expounded on her thoughts. Karen needed pros and cons before she would even consider applying for the job in town. They tossed out ideas. Pros: She would live near her grandfather; she would have the kind of contact with people that she enjoyed; she would see positive things happening in her work; and she would feel less stress.

"That's a good start," Eric said. "How about the cons?"

"First one is much less money. I'm sure the salary couldn't touch what I'm making now. . .although that's not a fortune."

"How important is the money?" Eric asked.

She shrugged, not certain how to answer the question. "I suppose it depends where I live. In the city, things cost more. If I'm here, my costs are less."

"Then that's not a problem."

His comment took her by surprise.

"Next," Eric said and waited.

"Next?" She thought a moment. "I'd have to give up my apartment."

"And?"

She chuckled. "I wouldn't need it if I were living here."

"You could live with your grandfather until you decided you needed more independence."

"He'd be thrilled. He really misses my grandmother." The words caught in her throat.

"I'm sure he does," Eric said. "I know he's happy you're there, and I think you're relieved to be there."

She nodded. Eric was right again.

"Another con?" he asked.

"Benefits? Would I have insurance coverage? That's important."

"It is," Eric said. "You'll have to find that out when you apply. . .if you apply."

He turned the car into a concrete parking lot. "This is it."

The building was larger than Karen expected. She peered at the trucks and construction equipment, knowing the men were at work. She felt honored to be one of the first to see what he was doing with the building.

Eric came around to open her door, and she paused before leaving the car. "You've given me a lot to think about. I'll never know unless I apply," Karen said. She stepped to the ground, and Eric closed the car door.

"Good thinking," Eric said, brushing his fingers across her cheek.

She smiled, and he captured her hand in his then led her across the parking lot. As they walked, Karen reviewed their conversation. She'd found many more pros than cons in applying for the new position. She needed to pray about her decision and let the Lord be her guide.

Admiring Eric's profile as they walked, she sensed the Lord was leading her in his direction as well. Still, what was Eric thinking? Karen knew she could be a summer fling and nothing more. Could she trust Eric's romantic actions?

The sun slid behind a cloud, and a chill rustled through her. Faith. She needed to put it all in the Lord's hands.

Eric settled onto the back porch, waiting for Karen to bring out some iced tea. Her grandfather had fallen asleep in his recliner, and they didn't want to disturb him. Eric had enjoyed the afternoon, showing Karen the building and his plans. She seemed impressed. The renovations had gone smoothly, and he anticipated the November opening as he had hoped.

"Here you go," Karen said, coming through the doorway with a tray. She carried two tumblers of tea and a plate of cookies.

"Home baked?" he asked, sending her a playful grin.

"Homemade," she said, lifting her nose in the air as if he'd hurt her feelings.

Eric took a bite of the chewing confection. "They're chocolate chip."

"I thought those were your favorite."

"They are. You remembered."

She smiled, then her expression changed, and she rose from beside him. "I have an idea." She hurried from the room.

Eric waited, wondering what thought had come to mind so quickly to motivate her to hurry from the room.

He had the answer in a moment. Karen returned carrying photograph albums. She settled back onto the wicker love seat. After laying the others on the floor, she opened one of the books and flipped through the pages.

"These are the photos I showed Grandpa when he got so moody." She tapped on a couple of pictures. "What do you think?"

He leaned down to look at the faded black-and-white photos. "Interesting."

"I thought so."

He turned the page.

"This is my grandmother," Karen said, pointing to the picture.

Eric chuckled. "Guess who's standing beside her."

Karen pushed her face closer to the photograph. "I have no idea."

"My grandfather."

Her head tilted upward like a shot. "Your grandfather. Lionel Kendall?"

"Uh-huh. I didn't know they'd been neighbors that long."

"Me, neither," Karen said, taking a bite of cookie.

Eric brushed cookie crumbs from the page, and curious, he flipped to another. He scanned the pictures and found one more that included his grandfather. "They must have been friends at one time." He gazed at Karen. "Doesn't it look that way?"

She nodded, her eyes wide and dazed. "I wish I could ask my grandfather about this." She shook her head. "I know he'd go into a tizzy and probably throw these away."

"Hide them."

She chuckled. "He has a nose like a bloodhound. He seems to see and hear everything."

"And smell everything," Eric said, gesturing to the trash cans along the fence as they both laughed. He looked at her sweet, smiling face and drew her against his shoulder. "I love seeing you in a cheerful mood."

"I am. I'm really feeling good and settled. I made up my mind about the job. I have an appointment tomorrow."

"Really?" He sat up straighter.

"Really." Karen shifted and felt her stomach growl. "I'm starving. Are you?"

He nodded, realizing he hadn't eaten in hours except for the cookies.

"How about staying for dinner? We can pick some corn. Think how fresh that will be."

"Sounds great." Picking corn. God couldn't have guided the occasion any better. He jumped up and helped her rise. He didn't let go of her hand as they headed outside, enjoying the closeness and the feeling of her smaller hand in his.

On the way to the corn, they grabbed a basket, and Karen dropped in a few tomatoes on the way. When they reached the field, she ran ahead, and Eric followed. . .just like years earlier when they were children. His heart galloped. When she stopped to pick a ripe ear with deep golden silk, he took the basket from her hand and set it on the dark earth.

She paused then turned to face him. He watched her expression shift from bewilderment to understanding.

"I can't let the opportunity pass," Eric said.

Her gaze locked with his as he drew her into his arms. She tilted her face upward, and he lowered his mouth, touching hers in a breathless wash of memory and delight. Eric eased back.

A tender smile curved Karen's soft lips. "Like a step back in time."

"I couldn't resist."

"I'm glad you didn't," she said.

For a moment they stood so close he could feel the warmth of her body next to his. The scent of fertile earth and plant life filled the air. His own life blossomed like new buds on the branches. He prayed that life had only begun for him and Karen, but he knew better than to rush things. She was a determined woman who had her mind set on how things should be. He wanted to make sure he was part of what she wanted.

❦

Karen pulled into the My Friend's Place parking lot. Nadine had been excited to hear from her and encouraged her to apply. Although the woman didn't have total control over the hiring, Karen hoped Nadine's recommendation would hold some weight. She sensed the woman liked her.

Snapping her thoughts closed, Karen asked God's forgiveness. She'd vowed she would put the ultimate choice in God's hands—she'd get the job or not, but she knew that the Lord knew the future and knew what was best for her. She had to let go of the decision and give God lordship over her life.

She strode across the parking lot, her mind full of purpose. Nadine opened the door as if waiting for her, and she followed the petite woman into her small office.

"Have a seat, please," Nadine said.

Karen sank into the chair and crossed her legs. "I'll be honest. I've tossed the pros and cons back and forth, trying to decide if I should apply. I've wanted to leave my present position, and this one seemed to jump out and grab me. I'm asking the Lord to lead me."

"That's the only way," Nadine said. "Funny that you mention feeling grasped by the opportunity. When I mentioned the position, I had a warmth in my heart, sensing the Lord telling me something. I wondered if it was you He was leading to answer our need." She chuckled. "You've answered it so many times already—unknowingly."

Karen could only nod, awed at the way God worked in her life. "The Lord sort of sneaks up on me and turns me around sometimes."

"Exactly." She flipped open a file and handed Karen a document. "Here's how the board envisions the new position. Take a few moments to read it. You gave me your credentials over the telephone, but I'll need them in writing for the committee."

"Certainly," Karen said, accepting the papers from Nadine, then handed her the manila envelope she'd brought with her. "Here's my résumé. This should cover everything, but if you need anything else, please let me know."

"Great." She pulled out the résumé and scanned it. "I'm sure this will be fine. It's very impressive."

Karen lifted her eyes from the job description and gave her a smile. "Thanks." She returned her gaze to the papers and read. She liked what she saw and sensed the job was perfect for her. Though she'd worked as a child advocate, she had taken classes in college in management and public relations. Karen felt confident she had people skills and could handle rejection. Rejection? Most kinds, she added. Eric's rejection would be something she didn't want to experience.

Fund-raising appealed to her. Talking with people, getting excited about what My Friend's Place had to offer people in need and finding creative ways to solicit funding all seemed to intrigue her. Even the fund-raiser coming up at the Arts and Apple Fest would let people know about the facility. The two jobs worked hand in hand.

"This looks good," Karen said. "I think I could handle this very well." She paused, knowing the sensitive questions were coming. "What I don't know if I could handle is the salary and benefits."

Nadine smiled. "I don't blame you for your concern." She slid a second sheet across to Karen. "Our board is excited about the position, and our benefactors are supporting this need. You won't be rich, but I hope it's something you can live on."

Karen studied the sheet. The salary was lower than she'd been earning, but the insurance looked good, as did the leave days for vacation and illness. She lifted her gaze to Nadine's questioning eyes and nodded. "I can live with this, too."

"God be praised," Nadine said. "We've had two other applicants. I've spoken with one, and I have another interview at the end of the week. I'll take the information to the board as soon as I can, and I'll let you know. I'm sure they'll want to interview our first choice. . .but then, maybe not."

Karen rose, feeling hopeful.

"By the way, I have something for you." Nadine rummaged through her in and out box and pulled out an envelope. She handed it to Karen. "This came a couple of days ago. I figured I could give it to you today."

"Thank you," Karen said, feeling a frown settle on her face as she studied the envelope. She eyed the return address and saw the name Ada Reynolds.

Clutching the envelope, Karen said good-bye, and when she stepped outside, she sent a thank you to the Lord for heading her in this direction. If the board selected her, Karen felt confident they would do so with God's blessings.

She clasped the letter in her hand and didn't open it until she'd started the car and turned on the air-conditioning. Praying the woman was well and having no serious problems, Karen tore open the envelope. She scanned the letter as tears filled her eyes.

Dear Karen,

Thank you so much for your kindness to my children. You gave them many fun-filled hours with new experiences they will never forget.

I'm sure you know that we are back at home and safe from my husband's wrath. My faith was strong during that time at My Friend's Place, but I want you to know that your example of God's love and compassion gave me courage. I have tried to be a forgiving woman, but seeing the joy in my children's faces when they returned from visits with you, hearing the freedom they had running through the meadow and singing in the trees, I realized that we had no freedom with an abusive man. Until he opens his heart to God's bidding and loves us as the Bible commands, our lives are in danger and without fulfillment. Having you in our lives made a difference. I was able to do what I did to protect my children.

Thank you also for sharing your faith with Hailey and Dylan. They returned to the facility singing songs about Jesus, and this gave me such comfort. I pray the Lord guides your life in the ways He wants you to go. I pray that you are washed in God's blessings.

In His love,
Ada Reynolds

Karen let her tears flow. They ran down her cheeks and dripped on her suit jacket. Leaning her head against the steering wheel, she closed her eyes and praised God for giving her an opportunity to witness for Him and the joy of touching lives that made a difference.

She spoke the amen aloud, then shuffled through her purse for a tissue. After she wiped away her tears, a smile settled on her face. *God is in the heavens and all is right with the world.*

Chapter 15

Karen slid on her jeans and an old T-shirt. She needed to pick apples because Gramma Bea had promised to continue the pie-baking lessons so she would be prepared for the Arts and Apple Fest the coming weekend.

Perspiration beaded Karen's hairline as she headed down the staircase. Autumn had taken a step back the past few days and decided to reissue the summer's heat. Today promised to be another scorcher. The scent of coffee greeted her as she reached the bottom step. Her grandfather's coffee was always an adventure, but today it smelled rich and fresh, the way she liked it. Still, she knew a taste test was necessary before she'd drink a full cup.

Her grandfather sat at the kitchen table. He'd pushed his empty plate aside. He seemed content, but his face looked pale. Concern skittered up Karen's spine.

"Not feeling well?"

"It's the heat," he said. "I was restless all night."

She watched him raise his hand to his chest and press against his heart. Her fear deepened. "You need to get air-conditioning in this house, Grandpa. The Kendalls have it." She slammed her mouth closed, realizing she'd opened an unwelcome topic.

"He gives no money to the church so he can afford air-conditioning. I tithe."

Karen shook her head. She knew her grandfather had enough money for his own unit, but he had to put down the Kendalls one way or the other. She elected not to respond.

"Only good thing that came out of that family, besides Bea, is that young man who hangs around here. At least he has a brain, and we saw him in church."

"Eric's a Christian, Grandpa."

Her grandfather's hand hadn't left his chest, and being subtle about it made no sense. "Are you having chest pains?"

He lowered his hand. "I'm fine."

"You're holding your chest like something's wrong."

"Can't a man do what he wants in his house without someone judging every move?"

Karen gave up and pulled out a bowl. She added cereal and fruit then sat beside her grandfather. "I'm going out to pick apples today. Tomorrow I'm making lots of pies with Gramma Bea."

"I'll give you a hand at pickin'," he said. He drained his cup then rose for another.

"It's too hot, Grandpa. I want you to stay inside today. Sit on the back porch in the shade. Hopefully you'll get a breeze there."

"You telling me what to do again?" He gave her a gruff look.

Karen knew this was her grandpa's way. "Yes. I'm taking Grandma's place and telling you what to do."

He waved his hand at her as if her words could be brushed away, but she hoped he listened. When she finished her breakfast, she set her dishes in the dishwasher. "I forgot my hat," she said.

She left her grandfather and headed back upstairs in search of her straw hat. It had been her grandmother's, and Karen had found it shortly after her arrival. The hat not only held many memories, it would serve a useful purpose on this hot day.

She found it on a hook in her closet and slapped it on her head. She glanced in the mirror and chuckled. As she descended the steps again, the telephone rang. By the third jingle, she knew her grandfather wasn't going to answer, so she bolted down the last few steps and caught it.

"Karen?" the voice said.

"Yes, this is Karen," she said while catching her breath.

"It didn't sound like you. This is Nadine."

Karen's chest tightened. "Hi, Nadine. I was out of breath. Any news?" She waited anxiously.

"No news, but I wanted to let you know that I feel positive about things. The last interview didn't go well, and your credentials seem to top them both. I'm meeting with the board on Monday, so we should have some news very soon after that."

Karen let out a pent-up breath. "Thanks for letting me know. I've been wondering."

"I've been praying," Nadine said. "No matter what, we can count on the Lord."

Karen smiled. "Yes, we can."

After her good-bye, she hung up the telephone then went to the kitchen to check on her grandfather. She was concerned why he hadn't answered. When she stepped through the doorway, she knew why. He wasn't there. She poured a thermos of water then went in search of him. "Where are you?" she called.

He didn't answer.

"Grandpa?"

No response. She couldn't find him on the lower floors. An uneasy feeling caused her to ascend the steps again to the second story. No Grandpa. Fear gripped her. Where was he? The half bath downstairs perhaps. She hadn't noticed him there, but it was a possibility. She descended the stairs two at a time, careened around the corner, and stopped. The bathroom door stood open. She hurried to the back porch again. Maybe she'd missed him.

The porch stood empty. Karen headed through the doorway, her gaze like a beacon, shifting back and forth, but she caught no sight of him. When she looked in the shed, the dolly stood against the wall and baskets sat on the tables. Then she noticed a small cart missing. The truth struck her. He'd gone to the orchard in spite of what she'd said.

Karen loaded the dolly with baskets, tossed in the thermos and tugged it all through the doorway. She hurried along the meadow path while the empty baskets pitched and bumped on the dolly. When she drew closer to the orchard, she could see her grandfather high on a ladder. He wore a burlap sack strapped around his neck, and she could see him lowering the apples into the bag. Her prayer rose as she closed the distance.

"Why are you up there?" she called from below. "I asked you to stay inside today."

"I didn't want to," he said. "I always picked apples for your grandmother's pies for the booth. I'm not stopping now."

Her heart wrenched with his words. She could only imagine how much he missed his wife. How could she stop him from doing something so important? Her wisdom fought her emotions, but her heart won the battle.

Karen walked away and grabbed an empty bushel, then headed down the row until she found a tree with ripe apples hanging from the lower branches. She plucked them from the limb and set them into the basket. The heat beat down through the trees, and she paused to take a drink from the thermos. She was certain her grandfather would be thirsty, too.

She left her basket and started down the row toward her grandfather. When she came through the trees, she noticed he wasn't on the ladder. She looked below. He wasn't there, either. Her feet carried her like the wind, and as she rounded the dolly, she found her grandfather sprawled on the ground.

Fear stabbed her, and tears raced to her eyes. "Grandpa!"

He didn't move.

"Lord, please, help him," she cried. She knelt at his side and saw the faint rise of his chest. He was alive. "Grandpa!"

He didn't move, not an eye blink.

Karen dropped the thermos beside him and sprinted through the trees to the meadow. She needed help. She needed Eric. She veered around her own picket fence and raced to the back of the Kendalls'. "Eric!" She pounded on the door.

No sound came from inside.

"Help, please!" she called.

Then she heard sounds, but instead of Eric, Lionel Kendall came to the back door, his face in a deep frown.

"What's all the noise?" He pushed the door back. "Eric's not home. He's at his store."

Her heart sank to her toes. "Grandpa's in the orchard. He needs help."

"Walter?" His frown changed to fear.

Karen had no time to question Lionel's mood or his expression. Her grandfather could be dying. "He's unconscious, but he seems to be breathing. Please. He needs help."

"Use the phone and call 911 while I go and see what I can do."

His last words faded away as he darted across the backyard and into the meadow.

Karen had never seen Eric's grandfather move that quickly. Amazed, she bounded into the house and dialed for help. When she'd given the information, she tore through the doorway and headed back to the orchard.

The heat shimmered off the timothy and tall grasses, now dried from the summer sun, and they tangled around her legs as she ran. When she arrived her heart stopped. Her grandfather was sitting on the dolly drinking from the thermos that Lionel was holding to his lips.

"Grandpa," she cried, racing to his side. "What happened?"

He shook his head. "Last I knew I was climbing down the ladder with a bag full of apples."

"The heat," Lionel said. He aimed a disbelieving look at her grandfather. "You, old codger, don't have a lick of sense."

"You ought to know, Lionel. You left your brain out in the rain, and it shrunk."

"Stop this." Karen's voice rose through the trees frightening the birds. They fluttered from the branches into the sky. Both men halted in mid barbs and gaped at her.

"That's enough from both of you. You've been neighbors forever and friends, too. It's time you acted like men and not little boys." She saw shock on their faces. "I'm sorry, but it's the truth."

She turned toward Lionel. "Thanks so much for your help. Do you think we can get Grandpa up to the house for the EMS."

"EMS," her grandfather said, his face settling into a new scowl. "Now why in the good earth did you call them?"

Karen's fist punched against her hip. "Because you were unconscious on the ground, and your neighbor told me to." She motioned toward Lionel.

"Trying to keep me alive, are you?" her grandfather asked Lionel. "I suppose life wouldn't be as interesting without me to taunt."

"Hush up, old man, and rest yourself on that dolly," Lionel said. "I'm pulling you back to the house."

"Like snow in summer, you are." Walter struggled to rise, but Karen pushed him back and lifted his feet. He finally gave up as the dolly jiggled onto the pathway.

Karen followed, hearing her grandfather carry on that Lionel was trying to break his back or rattle his brain loose. She didn't hear his response, but she was certain Eric's grandfather asked, "Who said he had a brain?"

Eric rapped on the screen door then called. He heard Karen's voice in the distance and stepped inside. She met him in the living room, exhaustion straining her expression.

He opened his arms, and she fell into them, tears warming his chest where they soaked through his shirt.

"Is he all right?" Eric asked, pressing his cheek against her herbal-scented hair.

"Heat and stress, they said. They decided not to keep him in the emergency room, so he's home." Karen tilted her teary face toward him. "Sorry for messing up your shirt."

"You didn't mess my shirt, so don't be sorry. I couldn't believe what Gramma told me when I got back. She'd been away to the church for a Bible study, and she came back in time to see the EMS pulling into your driveway. She said her heart was in her throat."

"Mine, too. You can't imagine how awful it was."

They settled together on the sofa. He listened as she told him the details, and he was amazed at what he heard. "I thank the Lord your grandfather's okay, and I'm praising God for the change."

"What change?"

"You said my granddad ran into the orchard to save your grandfather's life. Now that's change, and if it's not God's handiwork, I don't know what is."

"I was so upset the thought didn't occur to me. How could I have missed that?" Her smile widened. "The Lord heard our prayers."

"Maybe this is the beginning of a new relationship for them."

"Maybe, and speaking of prayers, I heard from Nadine today."

His heart lurched. "You got the job."

"No, but it's looking good. She said mine was the best interview. The meeting with the board is Monday, and she'll call me as soon as she hears their decision."

He grasped her hands in his. "Then I won't stop praying for you. I'm really pleased, Karen. I think you'll be content working there."

"I think so, too, and I'll be closer to Grandpa. He needs family nearby."

"He takes chances, too, like going out to pick apples alone." Eric's mind shifted. "So what about the apples?"

Her eyebrows lifted. "I forgot about those. We have some in the shed, but Grandpa and I both had a partial bushel in the orchard. I suppose I should go back and finish the job."

"We should go back," he corrected. He stood and drew her upward. When they reached the yard, Eric grasped the dolly handle, and they walked side by side back into the orchard.

When they reached the thermos and apple-filled burlap sack, Eric pictured his ornery grandfather standing over Walter Chapman, concerned about his life. The picture warmed his heart, as did the woman standing beside him. God had worked many miracles in the past weeks, and Eric felt certain he should leave things in the Lord's hands.

With the sweet scent of ripe apples on the air, Eric stood beside the woman who'd changed his life in so many ways as he plucked the rosy fruit from the branches. An apple had caused the world to fall into sin, but Eric knew that these apples were bringing him closer to the kind of love God had in store for all of His children.

Karen watched Gramma Bea dust the counter with flour and deftly roll out the dough. She placed it into a pie tin, then heaped in the sliced apples, which had been mixed with sugar and flour. Karen daubed on the butter while Eric's grandmother rolled the top crust.

"It looks so easy when you do it," Karen said.

"Next time, it's your turn." Gramma Bea gave her a warm smile and finished crimping the edge.

Karen's turn came, and she followed directions. This time the flour kept the dough where it was supposed to be, and when Karen lifted it, the circle of pastry rose easily from the countertop. She placed it into the pie tin then Gramma Bea filled it with the apple mixture. The top crust rolled as smoothly as the bottom. Karen couldn't help but smile as she took her turn crimping the edge. She'd made a pretty good-looking pie.

They worked side by side pulling pies from the oven to the cooling racks and starting again. Karen enjoyed the Kendalls' air conditioner, and even with that luxury, the oven warmed the room. Her cheeks felt hot, and she figured they were as rosy as a new apple.

Karen began a new batch of dough. She'd watched the older woman work the shortening into the flour in small pea-sized nuggets, then gently add the liquid, making sure not to overwork the dough. She felt for the familiar consistency and was satisfied. She liked what she felt.

As she began the next crust, Karen took a chance on opening an unwanted door. "I was looking at some of my grandmother's old photographs the other day. I didn't know Eric's grandfather and mine were friends years ago." She paused a moment to watch Gramma Bea's expression.

Her face didn't flinch. "They were good friends for most of their childhood. Even in high school. They were inseparable." She gave Karen a curious look.

Inseparable? That seemed utterly impossible. Karen paused, then decided that since she'd taken one step forward, why not go for two? "So what happened? I can't imagine anything ruining such a strong friendship."

She hesitated then released a long breath. Whatever she'd kept private for so many years appeared ready to be released. Though Karen should have felt victory, instead she felt like a traitor.

Gramma Bea gave Karen a tender smile. "It's all so ridiculous. You know men. They're competitive. They can't give up until they win, and Lionel's the worst. He hates to lose."

"Competitive? Over what?"

As she asked the question, her grandmother Hazel's voice rang in her ears. "Lionel was a poor loser."

Her chest tightened. "Maybe I shouldn't have asked."

Gramma Bea patted Karen's hand with her floured fingers, leaving a white imprint. "You're welcome to ask. Just don't try to make sense out of it." She turned her attention to the pies as she talked. "It's just so silly, it's not worth the breath."

Karen waited, longing to know the truth.

"During high school," she began, "your grandma and Lionel were best of friends. Though nothing had been said while they were young, Lionel had planned to ask Hazel to marry him one day."

"Mr. Kendall and my grandmother?" Karen's pulse skipped as her thoughts flew back to the photographs and her grandfather's reaction. Things began falling into place.

"Yep, that's what he thought, but your grandma was a strong Christian woman"—she gave Karen a grin—"and you know Lionel. He's a believer all right, but he only sets his feet in church for special occasions. I've known him to go on Christmas and Easter. Weddings and funerals. Not much more. But he does read his Bible."

Hearing that he read Scripture made Karen feel much better.

"So getting back to the story," Gramma Bea said, "when the relationship grew more serious with Lionel, Hazel began to have second thoughts. Maybe her parents said they were unequally yoked. Maybe she realized that sitting in church alone for the rest of her life wasn't what she wanted."

Karen listened, her pulse racing with the information.

"Anyway, your grandfather always showed respect for their relationship until Hazel's eyes turned toward him more and more often."

"Grandma was a flirt, I think."

"She was, but in an acceptable sense of the word. She enjoyed life and was playful. Fun to be with and very honest."

"So Grandpa captured her heart."

"Yes, I'd say so." Gramma Bea chuckled. "Lionel didn't let water flow under the bridge for very long. He and I knew each other, too, and within a few weeks Hazel was only a distant memory. Lionel's aunt lived close to my house, and suddenly he appeared in my neighborhood more and more. He'd drop by for a visit, and soon we'd fallen in love. We married and lived in a little apartment until his parents moved to Arizona for their health. Then we moved here—right next door to Hazel and Walter."

"And the feud began," Karen said.

"Not began. The foolishness continued," Gramma Bea corrected. "They'd long gotten over the issue of Walter marrying your grandmother. It became a game of one-upmanship. They were like two little boys trying to get the best of each other. They both acted like blockheads to me."

Karen laughed at Gramma Bea's description. "I think the same." She finished another pie and moved to the next, amazed at how fast she worked when distracted. "What amazed me was when Mr. Kendall came to my grandfather's help yesterday."

"You see. That's why they're so silly." Gramma Bea rested her hand on the countertop and shook her head. "I really think they feel like brothers, but they're just too proud to give in."

"I can't believe it's dragged on this long over nothing. Eric and I have talked about this a lot, and we plan to fix everything," Karen said. "Just you wait."

Chapter 16

Standing inside the pie booth, Karen wiped the perspiration from her forehead with a tissue and tucked it into her pocket. She couldn't believe how many pies they'd sold. Some of the women would bring theirs later in the afternoon so pies were arriving fresh throughout the day. The fund-raiser had been a tremendous success.

"Getting tired?" Gramma Bea asked, dropping by the booth.

"A little. It's hot, and the sun's been beating on us, but it's moved now."

"You should take a break. I think Mrs. Russell will be here to replace you in a few minutes." She glanced at the sheet of paper she'd pulled from her pocket. "Yes. She should take over any minute." She gestured toward the other booths. "You haven't had a chance to look around at all the crafts and food booths."

Karen felt her stomach grumble. Being in charge, she'd felt a responsibility to stick around, but Gramma Bea had truly been the leader, and Karen felt grateful. "I am starving. I've been staring at these pies all afternoon. What I'd love is a tall glass of lemonade or even apple cider." Cider? Why had she agreed to look at anything related to apples? She'd seen too many lately.

"I'll run to get you something, and as I said, Mrs. Russell should be here in a minute."

Gramma Bea moved off, and Karen took a moment's reprieve to rest. She sank into the chair behind the counter, leaned back, and closed her eyes. The sun sent a rosy glow through her eyelids until something blocked the light.

"Apple Annie's tired?"

She jerked upward, hearing Eric's voice. "Where have you been all day?"

"At the building. It's looking good." He handed her a large drink in a plastic tumbler.

She couldn't help but smile, seeing the excitement on his face. She grasped the container and took a long sip. Lemonade. Her cheeks puckered to its welcome tartness.

"I ran into Gramma. She told me where you were and gave me your drink order."

"Thanks." She toasted him with another swallow. "I'm really happy to hear about the building."

"I'm so anxious, anticipating the completion. I feel like a kid waiting to unwrap the gifts his parents have hidden on the floor of their closet."

"Is that where your parents hid them?" Karen remembered her mother kept theirs in the attic.

His eyes sparkled. "You guessed it."

As he spoke the last word, a woman strode to the booth with a smile. "Hi, I'm Wilma Russell. Ready for a break?"

"I sure am," Karen said. She took a moment to explain the procedure then joined Eric on the customer side of the booth. "Someone else should be with you soon. We decided to double up on help later in the day."

The woman gave them a wave, and Eric linked his arm with hers as they moved toward the other activities at the festival. Karen stopped to gaze at a home-made birdhouse and a hand-woven rug. The scent of roasted sausages, burgers, and popcorn hovered on the air as they maneuvered past the crowded aisles between the booths. After they'd had enough of handcrafted gifts, apple and fruit preserves, candy apples, apples of all kinds sold by the peck, face painting, and fake tattoos, Eric stopped beside a food booth.

"How about a hot dog?" Eric asked.

She agreed, and with her hot dog in hand, they moved into the shade. The Pigeon River gurgled beyond the trees, and Eric led her closer through some taller grass where they sat on the bank and ate their snack. He opened a bag of potato chips and held them out for her. She nibbled one, feeling as if nothing could be more wonderful than sitting in the grass beside him.

"I have some news for you," he said, breaking the silence.

She faced him, noting a special tone in his voice, as if he'd solved the world's problems. "Something good, I hope."

"I hope." He bit into another chip then took a sip of his lemonade. "How's this for a solution to the farmer quandary? It's not perfect, but I think it's better than doing nothing."

She sat straighter, realizing he'd given this so much thought, not for himself but for her concern for the farmers. The awareness touched her. "I can't wait," she said.

"What if I give farmers the option of selling their own produce on consign-ment at little stands within the store. The products could be tagged with a spe-cial bar code so they would receive their rightful cut of the sale. Those who don't want to sell the products themselves can have the choice of selling the produce directly to me. I'll have a special locally homegrown section."

She tried to imagine how that might work. "It's great, if you think that's not too complicated."

"I picture small stands right inside the front doors where farmers can sell their wares in any weather. In winter, when their produce is gone, I could hire those interested to work with the produce inside the market, bag groceries, and any other jobs that come along. This will provide a little added income even in the winter months."

"That's a great idea, Eric. People so often give the jobs to high school students and forget the senior citizens."

"That's what I was thinking. They'll have a chance to be with people, keep vital, and have a purpose. Some may not be interested, but people like your grandfather might enjoy it."

She reached out and wrapped both arms around his neck. "You are one of the kindest, sweetest people I know. If this doesn't work, it's not that you didn't try. You're a very special man."

He rested his hands on her shoulders and looked into her eyes. "You're a very special woman. Do you think that's why the Lord decided for us to meet again after our youthful encounter in the cornrows?"

She chuckled at the memory. "Could be." Her own news grabbed her. "I have some news for you, too."

"The job?" Interest filled his face and his eyes searched hers.

"No. Something more personal." She braced herself against the ground to rise. "Let's walk for a while."

Eric leaped up to help her rise, while a curious look covered his face.

Karen stood and brushed the back of her pants, then for the first time, she took the initiative and reached for Eric's hand.

He gave her a tender look as they moved off together along the river.

"What's your news?" he asked. "I sense it's something important."

"It is, and I'm luxuriating in the information."

"You're teasing me. Getting even is what I'd call it for all the times I taunted you." He drew her closer and nuzzled his cheek against her hair. "Come on. Tell me."

She tilted her head upward. "Well. . .I know it wasn't a pig that caused the feud."

He looked surprised. "What do you mean? Did you find out something?" His eyes widened, and an earnest look covered his face.

"I know how it started."

"How did you find out? Who told you? Why didn't you tell me earlier?"

He asked one question after another until Karen had to shush him. "I asked Gramma Bea, and she finally gave up the silence. She told me the story."

"She told you? Tell me."

She grinned at his impatience, but she didn't blame him. Karen told him the story just as she'd heard it from Gramma Bea. Eric's comments echoed her own while she'd listened to the tale, and when she finished, they stood grinning at each other, amazed that the mystery had been solved.

"If we had known, we should have pleaded Psalm 79 to the Lord."

Eric tilted his head. "Sorry. I don't know Bible verses by heart."

"I only remember some, but here's the one I mean. 'Do not hold against us the sins of the fathers; may your mercy come quickly to meet us, for we are in desperate need.'"

"And we were desperate," Eric said, "except you got part of that wrong."

"Wrong?"

"It was the sins of the grandfathers."

"It was."

The river rippled past, mixing their chuckles with its bubbling sound.

"We've come a long way in a short time," Eric said, slipping his arm around her shoulder, then paused, his eyes filled with tenderness. "I hope you feel as I do, Karen."

Her heart jolted, and she studied his face. How did he feel? "I'm not certain what you're thinking, Eric."

"Then I'll tell you, but do you really want to hear this?"

She nodded and held her breath.

"I believe that God has worked wonders in our lives. He's brought us back together—old friends, of sorts, meeting again. He's brought about job changes. Today I'm almost the owner of a specialty market, and you're nearly the public relations person for a women's shelter."

"Dreams come true for both of us," Karen said, squeezing his hand.

"For sure. And the Lord has brought us closer to our families. I'll be back in Gaylord nearer my grandparents, and if this job comes through—and I think it will—you'll be moving nearby, too."

"Probably in with Grandpa until I make other arrangements."

Eric halted and drew her into his arms. They stood face-to-face beside the riverbank. Karen looked into his eyes and saw so many words yet to be spoken.

Eric leaned closer and brushed his lips against hers. "I can offer you some other arrangements."

"Other arrangements?" His meaning didn't register.

"Living arrangements," he said.

She drew back, afraid of what she was hearing. "Eric, I would never—"

"Karen, no." His face paled. "I'm not proposing anything inappropriate. When a man and woman get married, they live in the same house."

"Get married?" The sound of the river hummed in her ears, and she clung to him, unable to believe what he had said.

Dismay and shock flashed to his face. "You don't feel as I do?"

His expression broke her heart.

"I love you, Karen. I thought you understood that, but I was afraid to move too quickly for fear—"

"Never fear," Karen said. "I do feel the same. I think I fell in love with you when I was sitting in that tree, but I didn't want to admit it."

"In the tree?"

"Maybe not that soon, but a long time ago." She smiled, and his face gleamed like sunshine.

"I know this is what God wants," Eric said. "I know it's what I want. We don't have to rush. We'll take time to get to know each other better and to adjust to our new careers."

"You're that confident in me?"

He brushed his finger across her cheek. "I have all the confidence in the world in you. . .and in the Lord who led us to each other."

Karen knew Eric was right. When she finally quit fighting the Lord, He took charge and made all things right. One problem still rose to her mind. "We still have work to do, though."

He seemed to know what she meant and smiled. "The answer is in the Bible," Karen said. " 'If you hold anything against anyone, forgive him, so that your Father in heaven may forgive you your sins.' It's time our grandfathers ask for forgiveness. We know they like each other. Look what happened when my granddad was unconscious in the orchard."

"You're right," he said.

"You ready to go out on a limb with me one more time?" she asked.

"Real limb or figurative?"

"Maybe both, but I'm talking about setting up a plan that'll force those two to shake hands. They have to, if we're going to be together."

Eric nestled her against his chest. "I'll go out on a limb with you anytime."

Karen hung up the telephone and clapped her hands together. Nadine had called to say the job was hers. Her first instinct was to thank the Lord for His loving guidance. Her second thought was Eric. She punched in the numbers and listened to the telephone ring. When Gramma Bea answered, she asked for Eric and waited.

His voice came over the line, and Karen let out a whoop.

"What is it?" he asked, sounding as if he wasn't sure if she were happy or dying.

"Nadine called. I've been hired for the position."

"I knew it," he said, his voice reflecting her joy. "Now what do you have to do? You're still employed by the other agency."

"I'll give my notice when I get back. It'll give me time to pack my belongings and get out of my apartment lease."

"And I'll be here waiting for you."

"I'm not that far away. We'll see each other. I can come up on weekends."

He chuckled into the phone. "I guess you're right. What's three hours?"

"Nothing where love's involved," she said. "Now the job gives me a great reason for inviting Grandpa on the picnic we talked about."

"Are you going to tell him about the new job?"

"Yes, but not where it is. I'll save that for the picnic. Have you said anything to your grandparents yet?"

"I did today. I told them I want to take them to see the store, and then we're going out to eat. The picnic part will be a surprise."

"You're a chicken," she said. "They probably hate picnics."

He laughed. "Just Granddad, but he'll get over it. I love you, Karen, with all my heart."

"Me, too," she said.

When she disconnected, she took a deep breath. Life was amazing. A few weeks had made all the difference in the world. Not only had she fallen in love, but she also had a new job and a great plan to heal a long-standing grudge.

"Grandpa," she said, hurrying to the back porch. "Guess what. I've just heard I've been hired for a new job. I thought we could celebrate. How about going on a picnic tomorrow?"

Chapter 17

K aren opened the trunk and pulled out the picnic basket. She handed it to her grandfather while he eyed her with suspicion. He'd asked numerous times why the two of them were going on a picnic. She gave him a variety of answers. He accepted none.

She lifted out a small cooler, then lowered the lid and led the way to the banks of the Manistee River. Picnic benches sat beneath the colorful trees, and being a weekday, the park was quiet, the way she and Eric had hoped it would be.

When she placed the cooler on the bench, she returned to the car for two canvas chairs. She knew her grandfather would grumble about having to sit too long on a picnic bench.

"It's a beautiful day," she said, trying to pass the time until Eric arrived, but the afternoon was unbelievable—almost perfect. The bright blue sky was feathered with wisps of gentle clouds. A breeze fluttered through the trees, shaking the crisp leaves. Some broke from the limbs and drifted down like orange and gold butterflies flitting to the ground. The humidity had lowered, with a temperature in the seventies. She felt a hint of autumn in the air. Seasons changed, and so did lives. She, Eric, and their grandparents would have so much to look forward to after things settled.

She'd prayed hard all night long, each time she woke, asking God to guide the day and bring about a gentle peace between the grandfathers. She prayed, too, that she and Eric would use their time well to get to know each other and adjust to the many changes they would face. Though she prayed for the Lord's continued blessing, Karen felt certain God would continue to direct her and Eric's path.

Silence lengthened between them.

"What do you say, Grandpa?"

"I say let's eat so I can get back home. I don't like eating with ants or any bug, for that matter."

Karen ignored his grumbles and opened a canvas chair. "Here. Sit in the comfortable seat, and let's enjoy the quiet. We don't get to do that too often." She filled her lungs. "Smell the fresh air. It's nice."

Her grandfather sat, then squirmed in the lawn chair and studied her with narrowed eyes. "You have something up your sleeve, Karen. I just don't know what it is."

You'll know soon enough, she thought. She patted his hand and drew her chair up beside his. "Let's talk."

"Talk?"

She nodded.

"About what? You need a loan?" His steady gaze looked suspicious.

"I don't need a loan. I want to talk about you. How are you feeling?"

"Good," he said. "Better when I'm in my recliner."

"Grandpa, you're hopeless." She leaned closer. "I worry about you. About your health and your loneliness. I hope the time I've spent with you has been nice. I have to go back to the city next week."

Her grandfather's back straightened, and his eyes glinted as if he'd gained some understanding. "So that's it. You're worried about your old grandfather."

He leaned forward and grasped her hand. "I'll be fine, Karen. Losing your grandmother was like having my arm cut off. It takes time to learn to use the other one. I loved having you here, but you have a life, and I can't interfere. I'd love you to live closer. You've been a special granddaughter to me, but we don't always get what we like. We settle for what's necessary."

She nodded, wanting so badly to tell him the surprise. "I'm glad. When I'm gone, I want you to remember that you need to rest and not push yourself. No more climbing apple trees in the heat. Hire some young whippersnapper to do that for you."

He chuckled at her whippersnapper phrase.

Before she said more, she heard a car pull onto the gravel. The motor stopped, and she turned toward the parking lot. Her pulse skipped as she saw Eric climb from the car.

Her grandfather had noticed the sound, too, and chuckled. "So that young man's followed you here." But his voice faded to silence when he saw Lionel Kendall climb from the passenger seat.

Eric opened the back door, and his grandmother slid out. Together, they carried their picnic gear onto the grass while all tension hung on the air until Lionel spotted her grandfather.

"What's this?" he roared. "It's a plot."

"Hush up, you old bag of wind," Walter yelled back.

Eric put his hand on his grandfather's shoulder and said something that quieted him.

Karen watched her grandfather's face grow curious as he followed their every step.

"Hi, Gramma Bea," Karen said, kissing her on the cheek. She nodded to Eric's grandfather, whose face looked as if it had been caught in a vise.

"Everyone sit down," Eric said. "We're having a picnic whether you like it or not, but before we eat, Karen and I have some things to tell you."

Heads swiveled from one to the other. Grumbles sounded from their grandfathers, but Eric stood his ground, and soon the three grandparents had settled into their lawn chairs, their gazes glued to Eric.

"First, we're going to deal with this ridiculous, eternal squabbling." He turned to his grandfather. "Granddad, do you love Gramma?"

The old man drew back and gawked at Eric like he was on the brink of insanity. "What do you think? We've been married for nearly fifty years."

"Gramma, how about you?" he asked.

She gave a chuckle. "I'd be out of mind to stick with him if I didn't love him. Who wants to wake up each day to a grouchy old man who thinks of every childish thing in the book to do to his neighbor?"

"Beatrice!" Lionel swiveled and frowned at his wife, while his cheeks flushed.

"Don't blame her, Grandpa. How do you think the Lord feels with all this foolish squabbling? You've been holding a grudge all these years over which one of you two married Hazel?"

Lionel's back drew upward as straight as a plumb line. "Who told you that?"

"It's a fact. You've been a poor loser, and worst of all, you don't really care."

"Phooey! This has nothing to do with who married Hazel. That was long ago. It's the principle of the thing," Lionel said, pointing to Walter. "He always had to have the last word. Always had to come out on top. I just got tired of it."

Karen touched her grandfather's arm, afraid he'd yell something back. Instead, he leaned forward and shook his head. "You've won the big one, Lionel."

Eric's grandfather drew back. "What are you talking about?"

"We both were winners when it came to marriage. The Lord led the four of us to each other, and we both had wonderful marriages until Hazel died. You and Bea still have many good years ahead. I'd say you came out the winner."

Lionel paused a moment, his mouth hanging open like a Venus's-flytrap. He glanced at Gramma Bea, then Eric, and then Karen before his gaze settled on her grandfather.

"Walter, you're breaking my heart," Lionel said. "I know you miss Hazel. After she died, I held Bea in my arms at night and felt tears in my eyes, knowing how lonely you must be. The feud just seemed to go on, and it got such a habit I didn't know when to stop."

"Neither did I," Walter said. "Guess we made dolts out of ourselves with our foolishness." His pause grew until he chuckled. "I was always amazed at what you could come up with."

"You're pretty ingenious yourself," Lionel said. "I know I'm not a good Christian. I should go to church. I'm just a lazy man, but Bea's told me over and over I had to stop. I just didn't know how to let the feud die gracefully."

Eric put his arm around his grandfather's shoulder. "You know Karen and I have strong feelings for each other, and you two arguing made it hard for us to know how we really felt. We've been praying for this to stop, and we thank God it has."

"We have more news, too," Karen said, giving Eric a nod. "You go first."

Eric detailed his idea to help the farmers in the community. Though Lionel didn't sell produce, Karen watched her grandfather's face brighten as Eric talked.

Walter clapped his hands. "You mean you'll hire me to bag groceries and kibitz with the customers?"

"I sure will," Eric said, his face beaming.

"What about those teenagers?" He eyed Karen. "Those whippersnappers who always get those jobs?"

"They'll have to look elsewhere. I'm employing the old codgers."

Everyone laughed, even Eric's grandfather.

"You've done a nice thing," Walter said. "I can still do my stand if I want and still sell my produce at your market. The best of both worlds."

Eric agreed. "Now it's your turn, Karen."

A lump formed in Karen's throat as she looked at her grandfather. "I'm leaving at the end of the week, but I'll be back."

Her grandfather's face shifted from attentive to perplexed.

"I'm going home to give my notice at the agency and to pack my belongings."

"Your belongings? Why?" His face sagged. "Where are you moving?"

Karen rose and wrapped her arm around her grandfather's neck. "I have a job here in Gaylord. I'll begin in a month, so I'm facing lots of changes. I hope you won't mind if I stay with you for a while." The job details could wait. Right now, his delight was most important.

"Mind? You're kidding. I'd be happy as a pig in mud," Walter said.

"But she can only live with you temporarily," Eric added.

"Temporarily." Walter paused and pinched his lower lip. "Right. Karen'll want her own place, I'm sure."

"Not her own place," Eric said. "She'll be moving in with me."

Heads turned into swizzle sticks as they gazed back and forth, with eyebrows raised.

Eric chuckled. "Stop your worrying. We have good news."

Karen shifted to stand beside Eric. He slid his fingers between hers and raised her hand to his lips with a kiss. She watched the grandparents' faces shift from confusion to smiles.

"We've fallen in love." He held up his hand to hold back their comments. "Since this has been a fast courtship, we're not making any plans right now. Karen will live here with you, and we'll have a chance to get to know each other better. We're putting this in God's hands, but we both feel that the Lord has guided our paths to each other."

"Eric kissed me years ago in the cornrows. We were only children then, but we truly believe that God has brought us back together for His purpose."

Eric squeezed her hand and turned her to face him. "Now I have a surprise for you."

Her heart tripped in her chest. "For me?" She had no idea what he had in store for her. She held her breath.

Eric shifted in front of her and went down on one knee. He slipped his hand in his pocket and pulled out a velvet-covered box.

Karen's pulse raced while her heart thudded in her chest.

"Karen, you've given me such joy. You've strengthened my faith and shown me how God must be the center of my life. I've known of you for years, and now I want to know you better so our future can be side by side. Will you honor me by being my wife?"

Her hand trembled as she accepted the box. Thoughts tumbled in her head. Yes, she'd known that marriage was in store for them, but she had no idea he would ask her today or that he would offer her the token of his love. She lifted the lid and her hands shook with such extreme that Eric chuckled and pulled the ring from the slot.

It glittered sparks of fire in the sunshine. The beautiful diamond sat in a gold setting. Eric slid the ring on her finger and looked into her eyes. "Will you?" he asked.

"You know I will," she said, resting her arms around his neck and gazing into his wonderful, smiling face.

He drew her closer and kissed her lightly on the lips. When they parted, Karen turned her attention to their grandparents, who had bundled together like the best of friends—shaking hands and hugging.

Her grandfather captured her in his arms with a bear hug then stepped away to shake Eric's hand. Eric's grandparents followed. Lionel hugged her close and whispered how happy he was, and Gramma Bea, whose eyes were filled with tears, clasped her to her chest with blessings.

"Let's eat," Walter said.

The group laughed then went about setting out the picnic food. After the blessing, they delved in, and when everyone was full and the food was put away, Eric clasped Karen's hand.

"We're going for a short walk if you don't mind," he said.

"Mind?" Gramma Bea said. "You two deserve time alone. Have fun."

Eric's spirit lifted when he took Karen's hand and led her away from their grandparents' eyes. They wandered along the riverbank then stopped beneath a large sprawling oak. "We're alone."

Her eyes sparkled as brightly as the ring on her finger. "We are."

"I wanted a few minutes alone to tell you how much I love you. I knew when Janine and I split that God had something special in store for me. I felt it in my heart as well as knew it in my head. Then you walked into my life...." He chuckled, recalling the moment. "You didn't quite walk in. You hovered above me on a tree limb then hobbled away, but that day I sensed something special. I asked my grandmother about you as soon as I got back to the house."

"What did you ask? 'Who could the goofy girl be sitting in a tree in the woods?'"

"No, but I was addlepated. Gramma thought I'd had too much sun."

"Really?" she asked, tilting her head upward while the sun sprinkled light and shadows on her nose like freckles. "You never told me."

"Some things you don't confess until you're confident."

"I liked you, too, but I fought it, thinking you weren't a Christian, but we discussed that. No matter how hard we fought, God let me see the Holy Spirit's gifts reflected in you and everything you did. You made my heart happy."

Her words touched him, and he drew her into his arms. "Can I kiss you now like I've wanted to for so long?"

"Please," she said. "I've waited for the same."

His lips met hers, filled with commitment and love. She returned the joy in her response, her arms closing around his neck, her fingers brushing against his hair. When they drew back, Eric caught his breath. "I think we need to keep the rest of these kisses until we're married."

"I agree," she said, a flush tinting her cheeks.

They turned back, but in few steps, Eric spotted a climbing tree, one with low limbs and wide branches. "Want to celebrate?"

"What do you mean? Aren't we celebrating?"

He motioned toward the tree. "How about a climb?"

The nostalgia touched Karen's joy-filled heart, and she ran ahead of him.

Eric watched amazed as Karen scampered into the tree and settled herself on an upper limb.

"Won't be long and I'll be too old to do this."

Or expecting our first child, he thought, but he didn't say the words. They had plenty of time to discuss important things like that.

He joined her, sitting a little closer to the Lord on the limb of an old elm tree.

"We're really out on a limb now," he said.

"Not any more. We're right where we're supposed to be." She took his hand in hers and kissed each finger. "God's awesome, you know."

"He is." Eric's memory flew back, and he turned to her. "Would you sing to me one more time?"

His question spiraled her joy to the treetops. "Do you know the song 'Awesome God'?"

He nodded. "Will you sing that for me?"

"Only if you will," she said.

"Me? I don't sing."

"You will today." She gave him a smile that warmed his heart all the way to his toes.

She began, and soon he joined in, lifting his voice into the trees. He wondered if they were close enough to the picnic area for their grandparents to hear the wonderful words that praised God for all His gifts.

When the song ended, Karen's eyebrows raised to the sky. "You have a wonderful voice, Eric. I never knew."

"No," he said. "You're just hard of hearing."

"You do, and you know it." She gave him a playful push.

As she did, Eric shifted back so she'd miss, but he realized too late. He felt his legs slipping from the limb, and he could do nothing except grab a lower branch as he slid from his perch.

"Eric," she yelled.

He grinned at her, hanging from a branch below, but his shoe had caught in the crook of a limb, and he dangled above the ground with one shoe off and one on.

When Karen saw he was fine, she laughed and started down, grabbing his shoe on the way.

Eric dropped to the ground and lifted Karen from the tree, holding his shoe. "Isn't this where we came in?" she asked, handing him his sneaker.

"Not really." He drew her into his arms and kissed her forehead, then her nose, then brushed a kiss on her mouth. "We've come a long way since that day."

She smiled. "I guess we have."

"And we have a long way to go. . .with God's help," he said.

Karen gazed into his eyes. "A long way to go. . .together."

As they wandered back toward their grandparents, the sun's warmth washed over them like a blessing.

Chapter 18

Two summers later

K aren gazed into the backyard from her bedroom window, enjoying how lovely her grandfather and the Kendalls had decorated it. A large tent covered one side of the yard, filled with round tables borrowed from the church. Gramma Bea had insisted on renting white linens, and she'd arranged vases of flowers from her garden. Beneath the trees two long tables had been arranged to hold the food for the guests—hams, corn from her grandfather's garden, fresh tomatoes, an array of delicious dishes. The chairs had been arranged in neat rows in front of a trellis arch covered with fresh-cut flowers. Karen's heart thundered, knowing the day had finally arrived.

Tears filled Karen's eyes, thinking of her grandmother on this special day—her wedding. As she and Eric had known in their hearts, God had guided and blessed them. Living in Gaylord near her grandfather had added joy to her life and a sense of family she hadn't enjoyed since her parents had moved away. Eric's market had been blessed with tremendous community excitement, and Karen loved her work at My Friend's Place. Nadine had become more than her employer. She'd become her friend.

A rap on her door sent a jolt of jangled nerves through Karen's body. "Just a minute," she said, straightening the folds of her summer satin wedding gown. Her hand rose, touching the pearl-and-beaded bodice then tracing the line of the modest scoop neckline. The whole day felt like a dream as she made her way to the door, feeling like Cinderella, except she was wearing both her shoes and they fit perfectly.

Nadine's smile greeted her. "Your dress is beautiful, Karen, and so are you. Are you nearly ready?"

"You look lovely yourself," Karen said, admiring the pastel peach gown with iridescent beads outlining the bodice. "Could you help me with my veil?"

"I'd be honored." She hurried through the door and closed it again.

Karen motioned to the hem-length veil lying on the bed, with a headpiece of netting and forget-me-nots.

Nadine carried the veil to the vanity mirror where Karen was seated. She worked carefully to attach it firmly then fluffed the netting before Karen stood. "Perfect."

"Thanks, Nadine." She looked in the mirror again and touched the headpiece, then focused on her matron of honor. "Have you talked with Eric?"

Nadine laughed. "He's pacing in the living room. He can't wait to see you."

Karen couldn't wait to see him in his tuxedo, but most of all, she longed to look into his dark, loving eyes.

Another knock made them both jump. Nadine held up one finger and inched the door open.

Karen's mother scurried inside. "You look beautiful," she said, holding Karen at arm's length then kissing her cheek. She eyed the spot her lips had touched and smiled. "No lipstick smear."

Her mother's mood made Karen smile. "How's Daddy?"

"Nervous, but excited. The pastor's about ready if you are."

Karen swallowed her emotion. Her parents had flown in from Florida and Eric's had arrived from Arizona. They were thrilled when they had finally set a date. Karen took one more look from her window at the rows of chairs. Friends from the Detroit suburbs, church family, and neighbors were selecting seats and chatting as they waited. The church's small keyboard had been placed to the side of the arched trellis, and the church organist stood nearby, ready to be seated.

"Looks like most everyone's here," Karen said, hearing a tremor in her voice. When she turned to face her mother, tears welled in her eyes. "I wish Grandma were here."

Her mother embraced her. "Me, too, but maybe the Lord's letting her look down from heaven today."

Karen wasn't sure about that, but it was a nice thought, and she loved her mother for it.

When Nadine opened the door, both women descended the stairs and shooed everyone from the house. Karen made her way slowly, so as not to trip and break a leg. After waiting so long, she didn't want to ruin her beautiful wedding.

From the porch, Karen could see Eric standing near the pastor with a long-time friend who had honored them by agreeing to be the best man. Eric's dark hair glinted mahogany highlights in the summer sun. He stood tall and lean, a bronze tan giving his face a warm glow. Perhaps it was love, instead, shining on his face.

Karen stepped onto the sidewalk as the music began, then she moved to the lawn as Nadine made her way to the front. Karen's father hurried forward, kissed her cheek, then grasped her arm and led her toward the aisle. As the bride's music filled the air, Karen and her father made their way along the white wedding runner rolled onto the grass.

When Karen looked up, Eric's eyes were focused on her. A smile curved his lips, and she felt so much love she thought she would burst. She took one small step at a time, smiling at the guests who beamed back at her.

Her heart rose to her throat when she saw Ada and the two children watching wide-eyed from a row of chairs. Karen's prayers had been answered. Ada's husband had been making progress. He'd been moved to a halfway house to receive counseling and to work, and he'd been faithfully sending financial support to the family each week. God worked miracles, and Karen prayed that Ada's life would be one of them.

Eric shifted to the center as she reached him. Her father relinquished her arm, and Eric's fingers entwined with hers. The pastor's words washed over them with a message of love, commitment, and blessing. "For better or worse, in sickness and in health, forsaking all others. . ."

Eric's hand tightened on hers, and Karen knew that God had given her a special gift. Her life would be filled forever with laughter, joy, love, and faith with the man who'd found her singing in a tree and captured her heart. In the Bible, the Lord said, "But love ye your enemies, and do good, and lend, hoping for nothing again; and your reward shall be great."

Standing hand in hand with Eric, Karen knew God had rewarded her in many ways, but especially with Eric, a husband to have and hold forever.

OVER HER HEAD

Chapter 1

"What do you mean you brought home a man?"

Lana West peeked out the window at the attractive stranger on her front porch, then turned to her younger sister. "Why is he here?"

Barb gestured toward the lawn. "You've been complaining for weeks about the yard work."

Glancing at her wristwatch, Lana noted the time. "Now that I think of it, why are you here?"

"I'm running errands for my boss." Barb grinned. "Fridays are slow. He told me to take my time."

"Friday might be slow. . .but not you." Lana shook her head. "You're worse than a kid. I can't count the number of stray dogs and cats you've brought home. But this is ridiculous." Despite her astonishment, she chuckled. "This time you've brought home a stray man."

"He's not a stray. He needs a job."

"What happened to the Michigan Employment Agency?" Lana asked, half joking and half serious. Barb had always been the most soft-hearted person she'd known.

Frowning, Barb eyed her. "I hope you're kidding."

Lana sent her a halfhearted smile but didn't answer.

"You're always complaining about being too short to reach the upper limbs." Barb stepped toward the window. "Look at him. He's tall and strapping."

Lana had already noticed the man's build. She would have been blind not to, but she took another admiring peek anyway. "I'll grant you that," she conceded, amusement escaping her voice.

Barb lowered her arms in seeming disappointment. "I thought he'd be the answer to our prayers."

Looking at her sister's dejection and conceding Barb had been correct about her dislike for yard work, Lana admitted perhaps the tall, well-built handyman was God's answer to her prayers. The yard needed major spring pruning and trimming, and until school let out for the summer, Lana didn't have time to do anything but correct papers and write exams. Once school closed for the summer, she had a whole list of wonderful plans—things to do for herself. She could forget her students and classwork and luxuriate in her own needs.

Finding a gracious way to admit defeat, Lana shrugged. "Since he's here, you might as well ask him to come around back, and I'll get him started. I know you need to get back to work."

"See," Barb said, "I knew you'd see my side of it." She tossed Lana a teasing grin and hurried out the door.

Watching her benevolent sister dart through the doorway, Lana breathed a deep sigh. If she didn't harness Barb's enthusiasm, her sister would force her into too many unwanted situations like she so often did. Barb had a knack for volunteering for anything while Lana liked to plan ahead—get organized and have a handle on things. Lana's counsel seemed to roll off her sister's back like rain off an umbrella.

Though Lana hated to admit it, she had a fault or two herself. Too often she plopped the burdens of the world on her own shoulders and forgot to let God carry some of the load. She prayed God would teach her how to let go and let God. . .or for that matter let anyone take charge except her. And patience. . . Lana pushed that fault from her mind. Going there would only depress her.

Pulling her thoughts together, she stepped through the side door into the attached garage and pulled out the equipment she figured the stranger would need. When she located all the yard tools, she strode into the backyard carrying a hedge trimmer, edger, and pruning shears.

Planning to supervise the stranger, Lana faltered when she faced the man directly. He had an air of authority that made her squirm, but drawing on her fortitude, she forged ahead. "My sister said you're looking for work."

He didn't respond, instead watching her with his arms folded across his ample chest and a mischievous twinkle in his crystal blue eyes.

His expression addled her. She found it unreadable—somewhere between perplexity and amusement. An uneasy feeling shuffled through her, and she hoped Barb hadn't hurried off to work too quickly. She might need defensive backup.

Trying to assume a look of control, she ignored his stare and motioned to the garage access door. "You'll find anything else you need in there," she said, dropping the pruning scissors and edger onto a garden bench. Feeling a sense of authority, she clung to the trimmer.

He gestured toward the bench. "Looks like you have about every tool a man would need right here."

His rich, clear voice surprised her. For someone who couldn't find a job, the man sounded educated. . .and articulate. Recognizing her uncharitable attitude, Lana cringed.

"So, what did you have in mind?" he asked, stepping toward her.

"If you look around," she said, clinging to the trimmer and motioning toward the tall shrubs while turning one hundred eighty degrees, "you'll see—"

As she swished past him, the man ducked and shot backward.

"Sorry," she said, embarrassed that she'd wielded the gas-powered trimmer like a machete. "You can see why I don't do this myself. I'm dangerous handling anything with a motor."

His eyes crinkled in a warm smile. "Yes, I see that." He grasped the trimmer handle. "Why don't you give me that weapon before you hurt one of us."

Lana relinquished the implement into his large hands. Undaunted, she led him around the yard, explaining what needed to be pruned and shaped, but each time she faced him squarely, his smiling eyes flustered her, and her pulse sputtered like the gas-driven trimmer.

Realizing her earlier fear had been foolish, Lana couldn't help but admire the man. His gentle spirit and good humor surprised her, coming from a person without a job. He commented with familiarity about the shrubs and grasped her instructions. While the yard tour preoccupied him, she used the time to quiet her revving heart.

"What do you think?" she asked, motioning to the work.

"I think I've got it," he said, giving her a polite nod that came close to a bow. "I'll be inside if you have any questions."

Lana made her escape into the sanctuary of the house. What in the world had gotten into her? She felt wildly out of control, like a stampede pursued by experienced herdsmen.

Forcing herself to concentrate on her work, two hours passed before she heard a knock on the back door. When she answered, he stood outside, perspiration and dirt smudges sullying his good looks.

"I'm sorry," she said, thinking of her manners. "Here I am sitting in air-conditioning, and I didn't give a thought to offering you something cold. I can't believe May has had such high temperatures. Would you like something to drink?" She looked beyond his shoulder and surveyed the backyard. Already his work had created vast improvements in the landscaping.

"No, thanks. It's getting late. I'll have to come back and finish. Maybe tomorrow. It's time to call the dealer to see if my car's ready."

"The dealer?" Rattled, Lana played with the top button of her knit top. "You mean you own a car?"

"Sure do. I dropped it off this morning for the six-month maintenance check-up."

No job and a sixth month check-up? "You mean it's a new car?" Her pitch hit the top of a piano scale. Embarrassed, she modulated her tone. "I had no idea."

"Why would you?" he asked. With a soft chuckle, he pushed the amber-colored hair from his forehead.

Struggling to make sense out of their conversation, Lana peered into his face and organized her thoughts. "I don't understand. My sister said you were—"

"A slight misunderstanding, I think." He rubbed the back of his neck. "I'm your new neighbor. . .temporary new neighbor." He wiped his fingers on his newly soiled trousers and stretched his arm toward her. "Mark Branson."

Humiliated, she stood dumb struck. "My temporary new neighbor?" Then, like a sleepwalker, she extended her arm. "I'm so sorry. I'm Lana West."

His handshake felt firm, and the amiable warmth rolled up her arm.

"It's okay," he said, his smile as caring as the Good Samaritan. "I just moved into town, and I'm staying with a long-time friend. Jim Spalinni."

She felt her mouth sag, and she snapped it closed. "You mean you're staying. . .there." She pointed to the neat brick ranch next door.

He grinned and nodded. "Until I get a place of my own. That's my next project."

"I have no idea how my sister let this happen." A headache stole up her neck and throbbed in her temples.

He shifted uneasily and tucked his soiled hands into his pockets. "To be honest, I didn't understand the mix-up at first either. When I sorted out what had happened, I hated to embarrass you." He released a good-natured laugh. "Anyway, I had time to kill."

She circled two fingers along her aching forehead. "I don't understand. I gather my sister got confused somehow."

"Apparently." He appeared to cover an escaping chuckle. "When she pulled up, I recognized her as a neighbor and gave a wave."

Lana listened, confounded while he unraveled the mess-up.

"Your sister. . .what's her name?" Mark asked

"Barb," Lana answered, wanting to scream at her sister's ridiculous faux pas.

"Anyway," he continued, "Barb asked if she could help. I said, sure, thinking she recognized me. When she said, 'Climb in,' I didn't think twice. I didn't have to pay taxi fare."

Lana shook her head. "Why didn't you say something sooner? I feel like a fool."

His face filled with amusement. "I got a kick out of it. Figured it would make an amusing story." He gestured behind him toward the access door. "By the way, I put your tools back in the garage."

Tension rose up Lana's spine. "I'll wring Barb's neck when she gets home."

Grinning, he flexed his palm in protest. "Don't let me be the cause of sibling-cide."

She smiled back despite her irritation. "I believe that's fratricide." She swung around, looking for her purse. Paying him for the work seemed the least she could do.

His eyes leveled toward her mouth. "You should do that more often."

"What?"

"Smile. It looks nice on you."

A burning flush heated her cheeks. She never blushed, and the sensation left her feeling helpless. "Please come in for a minute," she said, opening the screen door.

He stepped inside, and she hurried to the kitchen table and pulled a wallet from her bag. "Let me pay you. . .despite the mix-up."

He wove his fingers together behind him and backed away, shaking his head. "I haven't finished the job yet. At Branson's, we guarantee to please our customers."

She thrust the bills toward him. "No, please take the money. I'm serious."

"So am I. God tells us to treat our neighbors as we'd like to be treated. Maybe someday I'll need a favor, and you'll be waiting there with a willing smile like the one I just saw a second ago."

A favor? She didn't do favors. . .though she knew she should. Discomfort edged up her collar again, and she pulled on the neck of her blouse, hoping the motion might scare away her embarrassment. "You're a Christian? That's nice."

"Sure am," he said, a look of joy filling his face. "How about you?"

She nodded. "I was raised knowing Jesus, but I don't think I've gotten the Ten Commandments down as well as you have. I'm working on them."

Tender humor settled on his face. "We all are. How are you doing?"

"With the commandments?"

He nodded.

"I'm still struggling with the first one."

He ran his fingers through his hair and pushed back an unruly strand while sending a rich, warm laugh into the air. "Me, too."

"I'm serious," she said. "Look at what you did today. I'm usually so busy with my own well-polished agenda, I don't notice other people's needs." She winced, wondering why she was confessing her sins so blatantly. "When I do notice, I'm usually tied up with my own plans." She shook her head. "See. That's just one of the sins I have to conquer."

"If I had time, I'd confess mine." He scanned the room and motioned behind her. "Could I use your telephone? I'll see if the car's ready."

"After you did my yard work, how could I refuse?" She gestured toward the wall phone. "If it's ready, I'll be happy to give you a ride to the dealer."

Mark grinned at the petite woman who demonstrated so much pluck—the woman who'd just mentioned she didn't do favors. "You're not trying to get off that easy, are you?"

A pink tinge rolled up her neck.

He grinned and headed for the telephone. She seemed a paradox—soft inside and hard on the outside like candy-coated chocolate or a child with a toy backhoe trying to move a mountain. Lana had marched him around the yard, instructing him about what he should prune and what he shouldn't. Tucking her short brown hair behind her ears, she'd eyed him with riveting gray eyes. She certainly had supervisory skills, but he liked that.

When she shoved the bills back into her wallet, she'd struggled to maintain a calm exterior, but her embarrassment colored her fair skin, giving her away. He had to chuckle, and though Mark felt a little guilty, he enjoyed seeing her a little tongue-tied and out-of-control.

He pulled the dealer's business card from his shirt pocket while he scanned the tidy, antique-filled kitchen. Though the cabinets and countertops were modern, one wall was covered with baskets, old wooden spoons discolored from age, and antique kitchen implements whose original uses he couldn't imagine—except for an old rug-beater that hung near the doorway.

"Nice place," he said, lifting the telephone and punching in the telephone number.

"Thanks," she said.

Before he connected with the dealer, Lana left the kitchen. His inquiry was answered with speed, and when he hung up, he peeked into the living room, thinking he'd find her there. Instead, the room stood empty. Letting his gaze sweep the room, he enjoyed the cozy feeling. As if in welcome, an antique oak table held a floral bouquet, and near the door, vintage umbrellas with carved handles rested in an antique stand. Everything in place. Everything fitting—so much like the paradox herself.

Not wanting to wander farther, he retreated to the kitchen and called her name.

In a heartbeat, she came through the door. "Everything okay?"

"Someone will drive my car here, and I'll take him back. Thanks for letting me use your phone."

A warm smile curved her full lips. "You're very welcome. I'm really sorry for the confusion. But the more I think about it, I can't help but laugh." She lifted a finger and shook it in the air. "Wait until Barbara gets home."

"Should I hide the weapons?"

"No, I promise I'll be gentle. That's one commandment I've mastered."

Her smile wove through his chest, and Mark sent up a silent prayer. If God willed it, he wanted to get better acquainted with this spirited woman.

"But maybe you could. . ."

Her pause aroused his curiosity. "Could what?"

She'd lost her commanding presence and stood beside him obviously nervous.

"You could. . .drop by later just to make sure I don't do her harm. For dinner, maybe." Her lovely gray eyes widened as she waited.

Her discomfort assured him she'd never asked a man to dinner before, and he delighted in her innocence. "I think that can be arranged." He ran his fingers over his chin in playful thought. "Although you have to understand that one dinner isn't going to pay off this debt either."

"Okay," she said, grinning. "I still owe you."

He loved the idea, and after agreeing on a time for him to arrive for dinner, he stepped outside and calmed himself. Like a schoolboy tripping over his shoelaces, he tethered his excitement and forced himself to behave his age—a man pushing thirty—no matter how joyful he felt.

When Barb walked in from work, Lana barraged her with questions like BB shot. "Why? How? What made you think. . . ?"

"I'm serious. I passed this guy with a poster that said, 'Looking for any kind of work,' and I felt guilty. We're Christians, and I knew we had yard work. . .so I backtracked."

"I'd say so," Lana said, finding her sister's story both amusing and outlandish.

Barb huffed. "When I swung around the block again, I didn't see the sign, but the same guy stood there in jeans and a T-shirt." She narrowed her eyes. "At least, I assumed he was the same guy who'd ditched his sign. I'd only been gone a minute."

Lana tried to tuck away the grin, but it rose on her face anyway. "Barb, where did you think he pitched the sign?"

"I didn't think."

"Precisely," Lana said, marking a victory into the air before teasing her sister some more. "But you're fortunate. I promised not to harm you." She warmed, remembering her conversation with Mark.

"Promised who?" A frown rested on Barb's face.

"Our handyman. . .our neighbor."

"Temporary neighbor." Barb said, her scowl shifting to a toothy grin. "Nice guy, isn't he?"

Trying to contain her chuckle, Lana folded her arms and nodded.

"What's the grin for?" her sister asked, suspicion edging her voice.

"He's sooo nice. . .I've invited him to dinner."

"Dinner?" Disappointment spread across her face. "I'm going out with friends tonight."

"Then, it's your loss," Lana shrugged, sending her sister the illusion of confidence, but a tremor of nervous energy rifled through her. Now she'd have to entertain the man alone.

"Apologize for me, will you?" Barb said as she scooted through the doorway.

"I've apologized for you numerous times," Lana said, staring at the empty doorway. Her response fell into the air. Apparently Barb didn't have time for more chitchat. She had plans.

And so did Lana. A dinner to make in less than an hour. . .by herself.

After she'd offered Mark the invitation, Lana had pondered what to serve. Not knowing his likes or dislikes, she'd settled on chicken. She didn't know anyone who didn't like fried chicken.

Scrounging through a folder of recipes, Lana found one a friend had given her. With flour and herbs blended in a shallow bowl, she added ground peanuts and used the mixture on the chicken with a milk and egg wash. Letting it stand for a few minutes was the secret.

She dashed between the kitchen and the small dining room, setting the table and keeping an eye on the food. When the doorbell rang, Lana had been so preoccupied she'd forgotten to be nervous.

Opening the door, she gave a quiet gasp. Mark looked wonderfully attractive in khaki trousers and an electric blue knit shirt, the color enhancing his light blue eyes. To her delight, he held a single yellow rosebud and a carton of ice cream.

"Dessert," he said.

"Which one?" she asked, hiding her smile.

"The ice cream. The flower is the centerpiece."

She loved his sense of humor and accepted both the gifts with a thank you. "Have a seat, and I'll be right back." She gestured toward the living room.

In the kitchen, she slid the dessert into the freezer—grateful for the contribution because all she had in the house were some store-bought cookies. Then she found a vase on an upper cabinet shelf and placed the flower in water. "Want a soda?" she called, opening the refrigerator door and scanning inside.

"Sounds great," he said so close to her ear that her heart rose to her throat. Swallowing a scream, she spun toward him. "You scared me. I thought you were in the living room." Though the fried chicken sizzled in the skillet and sent out a delectable aroma, Lana inhaled an exotic scent like a rain forest blended with island spices. She looked into his eyes and seemed to sail away to a tranquil Caribbean lagoon. "You smell good," she said.

"Not as good as whatever's in that frying pan."

"It's chicken," she said. But the statement triggered a new thought, and she lowered her arms in frustration. "I forgot to bake the biscuits. It'll only take a minute." She snapped on the oven, then turned down the chicken and pan of rice. Again her delayed manners struck her. "Please get us some soda out of the refrigerator. You scared the thought right out of me."

With a good-natured nod, he opened the refrigerator and pulled out two cans. In a moment the biscuits were in the oven, and Mark handed her one of the sodas. She watched him swig from his can, and so she followed, feeling the cold effervescence cool her throat.

"Let's sit for a minute." She beckoned him into the living room and motioned him to an easy chair. "I'd like to hear more about you. Tell me why you moved to a small town like Holly."

He took another sip and rested the can on his knee. "A new job. I start next week."

"That's great. What do you do?" she asked, curious what type of business would entice a handsome young man to a rural town.

"I'm a youth director. I'll—"

"I work with kids, too." She realized her voice lacked enthusiasm.

"Where do you work?" he asked.

"Holly High School. I'm a social studies teacher. Kids hate history. Sometimes I wish I'd never see another teenager."

His face twisted with concern, and she wished she'd closed her mouth.

"I don't mean that exactly," she corrected. "I suppose most of the time it's their foolish excuses for not doing their homework and their obvious disinterest in learning. Even the brightest ones want to take the easy way out of learning."

"I know," he said. "They can be a handful. . .but not all of them. And even the bad ones are redeemable with a little love and compassion."

His words hit her like a rock. She needed to talk to God about her attitude. "You're so much like my sister."

He leaned forward. "You mean bringing strangers home?"

"Maybe that, too," she said, thinking of Barb and her stray animals. "You and my sister seem to be Good Samaritans."

He leaned back against the cushion and chuckled. "I suppose it's part of the job."

A vague notion rattled through her, and humiliation began to creep up her back. "Don't tell me you're a minister?"

"No. Not a minister." The same mischievous grin she saw that afternoon slipped onto his face.

"What then?" She closed her eyes and tethered her hands from covering her ears.

"I'm a church youth director. Almost as bad, isn't it?"

"Yes. . .I mean no. . .I mean. . ." As his words sank into her brain, Lana had another mortifying realization. "Don't tell me." Why hadn't it dawned on her before? "You're the new youth director at First Church of Holly."

"How did you guess?"

A frown stirred his face a heartbeat before the smoke detector let loose its shrill scream.

"The biscuits," Lana yelled, bounding toward the kitchen with Mark following on her heels.

Smoke rolled from the oven while she turned the knob to off and yanked open the door. Before she could ask Mark to dismantle the alarm, he'd anticipated the need and darted into the hallway.

The noise stopped, and Mark came back holding the battery. "Saved by a long arm. I also opened the side door."

"Thanks," she said, feeling defeated. She grabbed the potholders and pulled out the blackened biscuits. "Remember, I'm a teacher, not a chef."

"I can see that," he said with a chuckle, then looked into the frying pan. "No real harm. The chicken still looks and smells great.

She slid the baking tin into the sink, realizing she hadn't answered his earlier question before the alarm went off. She let the subject drop. If he didn't pursue it again, the answer would be her surprise.

In moments, they were seated at the table. Her golden brown chicken looked like a picture postcard, and to her relief, the rice pilaf had remained moist. Before dishing the salad, they bowed their heads, and Mark offered the blessing.

For once her organization and quick planning paid off. Mark took a second helping of everything, and despite the loss of the biscuits, her meal had turned out a success.

But as they talked, Mark's expression began to concern Lana. A look of discomfort had settled over him. He'd begun to rub his throat and seemed to have difficulty swallowing. His cough worried her more, and concern stabbed through her. Mark grasped the water glass and gulped.

Lana leaned forward, watching panic grow in his eye. "Is something wrong?"

"No. . .yes, it's my throat. I can't breathe."

"You look terrible," she said, being not only honest but concerned. She'd put nothing spicy on the food. Her mind ran over the list of ingredients, her own panic growing.

"There's only one thing I'm allergic to that bothers me like this. . .but—"

"What are you allergic to, Mark?" She held her breath, afraid to hear his answer.

"Peanuts, but I didn't—"

"Yes, you did."

"I did?" As his eyes widened the size of baseballs, his jaw dropped open.

If she could have commanded the floor to open, she would have. "I put ground peanuts in the chicken batter."

He rose like a bullet, sending the chair on a spiraling journey. "I have to get my medicine," he gasped, reaching the doorway before Lana could think.

"I'll come with you," Lana cried, following him outside. She cringed as she spouted her next thought. "You might need me to call an ambulance."

By the time she reached his front door, Mark had vanished. Her heart pounded with fear. "Where are you?" she yelled. The house had the same floor plan as hers, and she followed a noise to the kitchen.

Mark sat on a kitchen chair, an EpiPen stuck through his pant leg. He held the device in place for a few seconds, and afraid to speak, she waited until he withdrew the needle.

"What can I do?" she asked. "I'll drive you to the hospital or call an ambulance."

He concentrated on his leg, massaging the spot where he'd inserted the needle. Finally he lifted his head. "No. . .I'll be fine now."

"Are you sure? It's no trouble." Trouble. She'd caused him the trouble. "Where's Jim? Will he be home soon?"

A faint grin settled on his mouth. "Really. Don't worry. I'm fine."

"But I feel so responsible."

"You didn't know. I should have told you about the peanut allergy." He pinched his lips together and shook his head. "And I should have had the EpiPen with me.

I'm supposed to carry it when I go out. . .but you only live next door and. . ."

Though he still looked flushed, she couldn't hold back a smile. "So, you're not perfect after all."

He chuckled at her comment. "I plead the Fifth."

She stood nearby, wondering what she should do. "We have ice cream for dessert. Do you want to come back and—"

"Thanks. No. We'd better call it a night. I'm fine, but I need to stay put and let the medication do its job."

"I'll wait with you." She pulled a chair out and sat down at the table.

He didn't argue, and they talked for a few moments, but she could see he was uncomfortable. "I suppose I should get going."

He nodded. "This takes awhile, but I'm okay. Really."

She rose and backed toward the doorway. "I'll let myself out. You take care, and I'll call you in the morning. Okay?"

"Sure. . .and thanks for the great. . .dinner."

Guilt crawled up her spine. She gave a wave and spun around, heading for the front door. Reality hit her like buck shot. She'd nearly killed the first man who'd appealed to her in a long, long time.

Chapter 2

T he next morning, Lana sat at the kitchen table, thinking about the horrible evening. She'd told Mark she would call him, but it was early and she thought, since she'd tried to kill him, he might still be in bed.

Being her neighbor made the matter worse. If Mark lived across town, she might see him only on Sundays at church, but now the incident would live in her memory every time she saw his face.

While Lana tucked her cotton robe around her and sipped her second coffee, Barb bounded into the room, fully dressed, and plopped onto a chair. "Hey, Sis, very attractive wrap you're wearing." Barb gave a chuckle and leaned back, eyeing her with a curious gaze.

Lana looked down at the bright yellow-and-orange robe with Flub-a-Dub on the front and smiled along with her. "I found this the other day. Remember when Mom was on one of her memorabilia kicks? The old Howdy Doody television show was celebrating some anniversary, I guess." She poked at the familiar puppet faces grinning from the cloth. "I look stupid, but I tossed my summer robe in the laundry. I ran across this in the things-we-should-throw-away closet."

"Well, between your Clarabell the Clown hair and Howdy Doody robe, you look just great."

"Thanks," Lana said, knowing she hadn't done anything to improve her looks since she'd crawled out of bed.

Barb glanced at her watch and bolted up. "Whoa! I have a dentist appointment in ten minutes. Where did the time go?" She darted away and returned with her shoulder bag.

"Could you toss in the newspaper before you leave?" Lana asked, rising and putting her cup into the sink.

Barb glanced at her wristwatch. "Sorry. I'm really running late." She hurried past Lana and out the side door to the garage. "No one will see you, and if they did," her voice rang with humor, "they wouldn't believe their eyes. They'd think it was an apparition."

Lana followed Barb into the garage and peeked outside toward the mailbox and newspaper holder at the curb. The street appeared empty. She gave one cautious look toward the Spalinni house. Nothing but silence. She ducked beside Barb's car as it backed out of the garage and followed it down the driveway, figuring that it would camouflage her from the view of one particular neighbor. Once she had the newspaper in her clutches, she'd dart back inside, undetected.

As Barb backed onto the road, Lana snatched the paper from the box and turned toward the garage. Her sister tooted a good-bye and headed down the street.

Not taking the time to wave, Lana bounded toward the safety of the house but panicked as she watched the garage door lower into place. "You hit the remote," she yelled, turning toward the road and trying to flag her sister. Why? Why? Why? She gaped at the empty street, realizing Barb had pushed the closure button out of habit.

Lana heard the garage door bump against the pavement, then gave another desperate look down the street just in time to see Barb's car round a corner and vanish from sight. Standing in the driveway, Lana closed her eyes in a silent prayer. *Please, Lord, work a miracle for me.*

Struck by a thought, Lana rushed into the backyard. Maybe she'd left the garage access door unlocked. The possibility seemed good since Mark had put the tools away for her.

When she turned the doorknob, she grimaced. The access door had been locked tight. Mark had done a top-notch job of safeguarding her lawn equipment.

Lana gaped downward at her garish bathrobe. Who would have thought she'd find herself locked outside in this ridiculous garb? Now what could she do?

She weighed her alternatives. Hiding in the backyard until Barb came home from the dentist didn't make much sense. Knowing Barb, she'd probably handle twenty other errands before trekking home. If the situation didn't seem so outlandish, Lana would have cried. But all she could do was gaze at her gaudy reflection in the window glass and laugh.

A small stepladder lay against the back of the garage. She remembered using it to fill the bird feeders, and with trepidation, she carried it to the lower windows to check the locks, but each one she tried was tightly fastened.

Peeking around the front of the house, she eyed the quiet street. One last hope sailed into her mind. The dining-room window. Dragging the ladder, she raced around the house and climbed the two steps to the window. Locked. Her shoulders slumped.

"Howdy, Doody." A friendly guffaw sounded behind her. She propped her body against the ladder to avoid tumbling to the ground. Looking over her shoulder, she saw Mark standing directly behind her with a five-star grin spread from ear to ear.

"Nice get-up," he observed.

"Thanks. I see you lived through the night," she replied, covering her mortification.

"No thanks to you." His voice lilted with humor. "But I do appreciate your efforts to make up for the damage." He chuckled once again. "Where'd you buy that charming outfit?"

Though she had a layer of pajamas beneath, Lana grabbed the neck of her robe and tugged it closed, feeling utterly mortified. "Don't ask. . .and don't say another word."

"Then I suppose you don't want my help either." His voice sang out with amusement. "I have a very tall ladder."

Struggling for courage, Lana gazed at him. "A real tall one?"

"Sure thing. It'll reach the second story." Mark playfully jiggled his eyebrows.

"That would be great. Thanks." She stepped to the ground, clinging to her colorful cover-up.

"Anything open up there?" he asked.

"The bathroom window maybe. While you check, I'll hide in the backyard."

"Right," he said with a straight face.

She took off on a run, his laughter following her around the corner of the house.

Lana waited in a lawn chair under the tree, and in a few minutes, the garage access door opened, and Mark appeared. "You can get in now, Miss Doody."

She rose from the chair like a marionette jerked into action and bolted past him into the house. "Thank you," she called.

Tucked between his distant laughter, she heard his voice. "Don't mention it. . . but you can be sure I will. You owe me now. No question."

Lana and Barb strode into church and slid into a center pew. Lana nodded to a couple students she knew from the school. Sometimes she was shocked to see them in church after watching their behavior in class. She wished she knew how to make a difference in their lives.

The opening music ended, and the congregation rose to join in the first hymn. She scanned the worship area, wondering where Mark was. Saturday, after she'd dressed and calmed down, she'd called him, but no one had answered. She guessed he'd been at the church all day. . .which was probably for the best. Her behavior seemed questionable around him. Never having told him she was a member there, she couldn't wait to see his surprise.

Opening the hymn book, Lana read the familiar words. She loved the music and prayers but often left church with a shard of guilt pressing against her like a minute sliver impossible to extract. She knew the commandments, and she'd read the Bible. Parts, anyway. She just didn't seem to follow it the way a Christian should. Granted, all of God's children sinned, but her sins started with a capital S. At least, that's how she felt. Barb inevitably chattered all the way home about the wonderful message, seeming to feel sinless. Lana knew better.

This morning the pastor rose. "Today we'll focus on Psalm 46," Pastor Phil said, allowing people time to open their Bibles. "God is our refuge and strength, an ever-present help in trouble. Therefore we will not fear, though the earth give way and the mountains fall into the heart of the sea, though its waters roar and foam. . . ."

Lana's mind drifted, and the source of her guilt edged into her consciousness. Her age-old problem. She tried to be her own refuge and strength. Her own help in time of trouble. And she rarely felt eager to help anyone else. What would life be like if she were like her sister, always helping the needy and concerned about others. . .like stray—?

" 'Be still, and know that I am God.' " Pastor Phil's words struck Lana's ears like a jackhammer, as if God Himself had pinned her to the chair. She ruefully recognized that she wasn't still very often. She preferred to direct everyone else's traffic as well as her own. She needed to remember those words. "Be still, and know that I am God," she whispered.

Scowling, Barb hissed in her ear. "Shush. You may think you're God, but don't tell everyone around you."

Lana's heart jolted. Had she said the words aloud? She slid lower in the pew and kept her lips sealed.

Near the end of the service, Lana's distracted thoughts settled on her very empty stomach. Fearing she'd be late for church, she had neglected to eat breakfast. To add to her emptiness, Mark seemed nowhere in sight.

But Pastor Phil came forward, as if God considered Lana's concern, and addressed the congregation. "This morning I'm happy to introduce you to our long-awaited youth director, Mark Branson. Mark is ready and eager to begin working with our young people." He scanned the congregation, a look of apprehension on his face. "Mark?"

Lana's heart sank. Had Mark overslept or, worse yet, died during the night from her dinner?

The pastor's face brightened, and Mark came down the aisle from the back of the sanctuary. When he turned to face the congregation, Lana's heart tripped over itself. He looked terribly handsome in gray slacks and a navy blazer with a gray and navy tie against his white shirt—a dramatic contrast to the jeans and casual shirt he'd been wearing when she first met him.

"Thank you, Pastor Phil," he said, his eyes filled with pleasure as he scanned the worshipers. "I'm looking forward to getting to know the young people of this congregation. Young people are filled with untapped energy and spirit. I think together we can build a strong youth organization here. I ask for your prayers as I begin my ministry."

The congregation applauded as Mark retreated down the aisle. After the final hymn, Lana worked her way toward the exit with Barb on her heels, both anxious to get some food. Before Lana reached the foyer, Mark's voice wrapped around her thoughts like waxed paper on a sandwich.

"If it isn't Miss Doody. Great to see you here. Where's your fancy costume?"

For the second time that morning, she felt pinned to the spot. "At home on a hook." She faced Mark's amused gaze which, at the moment, looked even more appealing than a honey-baked ham. "Surprised to see me?" she asked.

"I am. What are you doing here. . .besides worshiping, that is?"

"This is my church. I've been a member here for years."

He looked puzzled. "You never mentioned it."

"No. I would have except I had to answer my smoke alarm." She rolled her eyes. "You haven't forgotten, have you?"

"Now that I think about it, you did leave me hanging that day."

His taunting eyes ruffled her emotions again. "You mean choking. I tried calling yesterday afternoon to thank you again for opening my door."

He sent her a heartwarming grin. "Sorry I missed your call."

"I still feel badly about that dinner. You look great today," Lana said.

"Don't feel guilty. Like I said, I'm sorry I didn't mention my peanut allergy. You said dinner, so the problem hadn't entered my mind."

"I'll know next time." Uneasy, she focused on the beige tweed carpet.

"Next time? Now that sounds promising." He slid his hand into his jacket pocket. "Did you want to set a date?"

Her pulse kicked like a mule, and she raised her head, hoping she could hide her attraction. "I was speaking figuratively. Right now, I'm on my way to breakfast." She scanned the crowd looking for Barb. "But I've lost my sister, it seems."

"I'm sure she hasn't gone far." He gazed over the milling worshipers, then faced her again. "Breakfast? Sure that's a great offer." He pulled his hand from his pocket and ran it through his hair.

"Offer?" She laughed. "You mean you're coming along?"

"Why not? It sounds safe. No peanuts."

She rested her fingers on his arm. "Will you ever forgive me?"

"You were forgiven when I saw your horrified expression. No words needed."

No words needed. The Bible said God forgave like that. But the Bible also talked about repentance, and until she could lasso some patience and compassion, forgiveness seemed hopeless. "Let me find Barb," Lana said, distracted by her thoughts.

As she walked through the church's front door, Lana spotted her sister in a circle of friends.

"Do you mind if we skip breakfast?" Barb asked when Lana caught her attention. "Jenny invited me to her place for brunch."

"That's fine," Lana said, hoping she could come up with some interesting conversation at breakfast rather than revealing all her idiosyncrasies and flaws. She wished she were a woman worthy of spending time with a kindly, handsome youth director.

"Ready?" Mark asked, slipping behind her.

"Barb's going to brunch with friends," she said.

"No problem. Why not ride with me, and I'll bring you back for your car?"

She nodded and followed him to the parking lot, admitting his safety seemed more guaranteed in a restaurant than at her house. Between the burnt biscuits and peanut poisoning, she'd become a human danger zone.

❦

Mark placed his menu on the table and watched Lana peruse the breakfast choices. He'd never seen her in a dress before. Around the house she wore jeans or slacks and knit tops, but today, she'd donned a dusky blue dress with a navy stripe that accentuated the gray of her eyes—a violet gray like heather.

"What are you going to have?" he asked. "I'm ordering bacon with the mile-high stack of pancakes."

She sent him a wry grin. "That's because you're a mile high. I'm a shrimp, but that's not on the menu." She tucked her hair behind her ear and refocused on the menu. "I think I'll have a two-egg omelet with an English muffin."

"You'll waste away."

"Don't be silly." She slid the menu onto the table and sipped the coffee, her gaze searching his as if she had questions to ask.

"What's on your mind?" he asked.

"Just wondering." Her fingers circled the cup.

"Wondering what?"

"About you. What made you decide to be a Christian youth worker, for example?"

"That's a funny story," he said, rubbing the back of his neck. "I'd planned to be a coach and phys ed teacher. I loved gym class in high school." His mind flew back to his folks' frustration with his low marks in math but straight As in phys ed.

"You must have done well in other subjects since you made it through college."

"I wasn't too bad," he said, "but I worked hard for some grades. . .like math."

"Math wasn't my favorite either." She leaned forward on her elbows and grinned. "You still haven't answered me. Why did you become a youth director?"

"When I headed for college, my parents weren't thrilled with my phys ed choice, but I was determined—do or die. I do have an occasional flaw."

"Really. I can add that to your unwillingness to carry the EpiPen."

"It's the same problem. I'm stubborn at times."

Her face brightened. "Glad to hear I'm not the only sinner."

"Not by a long shot," he said, pushing away the list of his flaws. God knew his flaws, but why admit them to Lana until they were evident? The thought made him smile.

"You're also evasive. Tell me why you became a youth minister."

She'd caught him again, and he grinned. "Like I said, I was determined to go into coaching. You know, be a phys ed teacher. But when it was time to go through registration, I stood in line clutching those forms, and a strange sensation came over me. Something inside me gnawed and pushed until my fingers gripped the pen and filled in my classes without my consent."

"Huh?" She tilted her head, her face was charged with bewilderment.

"I felt the same way you look, Lana. Puzzled. Perplexed. All I can say is God's will pushed my pen that day. I changed my major to leadership and specialized in youth ministry."

She gave him a blank stare. "You mean God filled out your college registration?"

"He pushed my pen. . .but the choice hadn't been mine."

"Are you sorry?" A frown wrinkled her freckled forehead.

"Not one bit. Youth ministry is my calling. God had to hit me over the head a little, but I finally came to the realization that working with kids in a church setting was what I was meant to do." Another truth crossed his mind. "And my career strengthened my faith even more than I could imagine."

Her frown had vanished, replaced by interest. "So how did your parents feel about that choice?"

"They loved it. My folks. . ." He halted as the breakfast fare appeared in front of them. He eyed his huge stack of pancakes and slabs of bacon, then focused on Lana's small omelet and muffin.

"Anything else?" the waiter asked.

"You can refill the coffee," Mark said.

The young man nodded and left.

"Would you like me to say the blessing?" Mark asked, taking each of Lana's hands in his.

She nodded, and they bowed their heads while he thanked God for the food and their friendship. He gave her fingers a squeeze before he released them. Then he eyed his pancakes and picked up his fork.

"Thanks," Lana said, a gentle look in her eyes. She tried her omelet and then cornered him again. "So what about your folks? What did they think about your choice?"

Mark chuckled at her inquisitiveness. "You mean I don't even get one bite?"

"Go ahead. I can wait, but I'm interested."

He forked into the pancakes dripping with butter, then after the first bite, added some maple syrup. The next taste left him with a pleasant sweetness clinging to his lips, and his mind drifted to Lana. . .and her lips. Would her kiss be as sweet? Surprised at his mind's journey, he refocused on the breakfast and pushed the romantic thoughts from his mind.

When he'd satisfied his hunger, Mark washed the syrup away with hot coffee and returned to Lana's question. "My folks were active Christians, so they were thrilled when I decided to focus on church work." He rubbed his neck and chuckled. "I suppose if I'd been a city road worker, they would have been supportive. They've always been that way."

"Where did you grow up?" Lana asked. "Around here?" A piece of English muffin stood poised in her grasp.

"In Michigan. We lived in Warren while I was in high school. Now my folks live in Sterling Heights. You know where that is?"

She nodded. "I grew up in Fenton. My parents are still there, but after college, Barb and I decided to live on our own. I like my independence."

"I suspected that," he said, giving her a knowing smile.

She nibbled on the muffin, then picked up the napkin and patted her mouth. "So how do you know my neighbor Jim?"

"Whoa. Let's talk about you first," Mark said. "What's fair is fair."

"What's that mean?" She eyed him with suspicion.

"What do you mean, what does that mean?" He shook his head. "You made me tell you my life story. Now let's hear yours." He delved into the pancakes again, looking forward to a break.

"I hate talking about me."

"Too bad," he said through his mouthful of pancakes.

"Just tell me about Jim," she countered. "Then I'll talk about me."

Remembering her persistence, he swallowed his mouthful and gave in. "Jim and I met in college. We were roommates for a couple of years until I got my own apartment."

"He didn't move with you?"

"We realized even though we were friends and had some things in common, we had a few things that clashed." Mark felt the sting of his words. He'd been the one to move out, and when Jim had asked about moving in with him, Mark had suggested it wasn't a good idea. Jim had been hurt by his decision.

"How did you clash?" She took another forkful of omelet.

He knew she'd ask. "He has different beliefs than I do. That's the main thing."

"You mean religious beliefs? I notice he doesn't seem to go to church."

"He doesn't, but that wasn't the reason. He drank too much when we were in college. That really bothered me. He seems to handle it better now, but I didn't want to be around it." If he were baring his soul, he needed to tell her the whole story. He studied her serious face for a moment before continuing. "To be honest, my faith wasn't as strong then. I felt myself tempted to follow along. You know, be part of the group."

She looked at the tabletop and nodded. "It's what kids tend to do, isn't it?" She lifted serious eyes to his. "At least you've admitted your failing."

"I felt guilty. . .like I should have been stronger. I am now." He chuckled. Since he was spilling his faults out on the table, he might as well barrel along. "But I'm still not perfect."

"Aha. Another flaw. Stubborn, determined, and not perfect. I'm tallying this in self-defense."

He grinned, but saw her face grow serious again. "So what about now? You're staying with Jim."

"I tried talking to him when we were in college. It never worked. Now I just offer a few gentle comments, hoping one day it'll sink in.

"That's what you have to do, I suppose. If you push too hard, a person pushes back."

She'd spoken the truth. He'd teased her a little about her impatience, but pushing wouldn't do any good. He'd seen it in himself. Anyway, he had a long way to go with perfection. He hid his private grin. If change happened, it had to be the sinner's decision with lots of help from the Lord.

"I'm surprised you and Jim are still friends," Lana said, nudging her plate away and resting her cheek on her propped-up fist.

"That's my fault." He released his tethered smile. "I don't like to make enemies or lose friends. He was upset when I moved out, but he got over it. I think he understood in the long run. When I was called to First Church of Holly, I knew he lived in town. I called him, and he offered me a place to stay. He's a nice guy. . .and like I said, I'm a stronger Christian now. . .even with my faults."

A truth struck Mark that he needed to remember. The teens would grow in their faith as they became adults. Working with them, he couldn't push like he wanted to sometimes. He had to be firm but compassionate.

He pulled himself from his thoughts and focused on Lana. "Okay. I answered your questions. Now it's my turn to ask. Tell me why you became a teacher." He'd wondered about that since she'd mentioned not being fond of teenagers.

"My parents' idea." She blinked a couple times before continuing. "They were willing to help me finance college if I picked a sensible career." She shrugged. "Teaching seemed sensible to them."

"But what about your own interests?" He couldn't believe she'd become a teacher for her parents.

"You just told me God signed you up for church work. Why can't my parents sign me up for teaching?" A silly grin settled on her face. "Just teasing," she said. "When I was younger, I thought I wanted to be a nurse. I suppose all kids do. I felt the qualities of a nurse fit my skills."

"For sure," Mark said. "Organization, authority, details. A nurse with the marines. Am I right?" He playfully patted her hand.

"No," she said, giving him a ferocious scowl, "but it doesn't matter. As I said earlier, my math wasn't great either, and my science was even worse. So I got realistic."

"Realistic?"

"My parents are practical people. Dad is a factory worker in Flint. Automobiles. He worked to provide all our needs, and my mom's a homebody. I needed to study something sensible."

Empathy nudged at his emotions, but her analogy made him chuckle. "So you became a teacher and hate it."

"No, not really. I suppose I sound like I hate it. It's just frustrating. Kids have too many problems and not enough guidance. Mothers and fathers both work while teens are left on their own too much. They want everything handed to them. They don't want to figure out anything. At least that's the way it seems."

"And that's why I'm a youth director. Even Christian kids fall into that rut—like I did. They need to find out no matter how busy their parents are, Jesus is walking along with them. God is on their side. If they need help and they can't talk with their parents, turn to the Lord in prayer. . .or maybe, their youth director."

Lana grinned. "My parents would have considered a church youth director practical and sensible, too."

"What about Barb?" he asked. "What does she do?"

"She went to business school and works in an office. That's—"

"Very sensible," he said.

She laughed, but the lightness faded, and in its place, her face shifted to a more serious expression. "I know I drive people crazy with my organization and details. I was the oldest, and my parents emphasized being on time and always doing my best. It just stuck, I guess. When I was a kid, I wanted to please them. Now I can't seem to forget that need. I'm still trying to please them, but I'm not making myself happy. I get frustrated at my own flaws and inabilities, and I don't like to deal with disorganized, tardy, abstract people."

"Nothing wrong with being on time and being organized." He slid his arm across the table and rested his palm against her silky arm. "You just have to remember that not everyone has those skills."

"Be patient, you mean?"

He nodded. "Patience is a virtue. . .a fruit of the Spirit. And the Holy Spirit's ready to develop more such qualities in your life if you ask for them."

"You think so?"

"Bible says so."

She grinned. "It does. That's true."

Her expression shifted like food in a blender, and Mark suspected she was delving for a comeback.

"Let's see. Stubborn. Determined. So," she said, giving him a mischievous look, "let's talk more about you."

Chapter 3

Clipping off a dead branch, Mark heard a voice and looked up.

"What are you doing?" Lana's face appeared through the kitchen window screen.

"Finishing my job. You hired me, didn't you?"

She flagged away his comment. "Then tried to poison you. So you're back for more?"

He laughed, delighting in her humor. "You don't see me eating anything, do you?" He patted his belly. "Besides I have to work off the pancakes from breakfast."

"Sounds like an excuse. You're just determined."

He grinned and tallied a point for her into the air with his index finger. She'd begun to know him too well.

"It's Sunday. I thought we're supposed to rest." Her face vanished from the open window, and in a moment, he heard the garage access door open. She came through the doorway carrying a rake. "If we're worried about breakfast calories, then I need the exercise, too."

Mark loved watching her expressive face, the way her head tilted and her nose wrinkled—a nose dappled with freckles, and a natural smile that sent his pulse on a gallop. "Don't you have anything better to do?"

"My lesson plans are finished for the week. We have only three days of classes because final exams start this Thursday. After three test days and two more for grading and cleanup, I'm free." She lifted her shoulders in a deep sigh.

"Then let's get busy." Mark motioned toward the fallen twigs from the shrub. "You can rake those in a pile."

Lana eyed the scattered clippings and headed across the lawn, stretching her arms and dragging the debris into a neat pile.

Mark stood a moment, admiring her energy; her slender arms pulling at the rake and her short stature gave no evidence to her bigger-than-life personality. But not a big heart—from what she said.

He wondered why a lovely young woman like Lana possessed such a negative outlook on teens. The attitude just didn't fit. She wasn't that old herself. Probably three or four years younger than his twenty-nine years. He longed to probe but not until he knew her better. Maybe in time she would tell him what bothered her.

Glancing his way, Lana paused and leaned on the rake. "If you're stopping, so am I." She sent him a wry smile.

He shrugged playfully and turned back to the trimming, but she stayed in his mind. The way her gray eyes squinted in the sunshine. The way the sunlight accentuated the red streaks in her light brown hair falling in wayward straggles over her forehead. The way her small stature seemed elfinlike. . .yet delicate and lovely.

When he turned her way, she'd disappeared, leaving a pile of dead twigs and trimmings in a tidy pile along with the rake. Before he could wonder where she'd gone, she reappeared with two shiny red apples. She strode toward him in her purposeful way and offered him a piece of fruit. He took one from her, and his teeth dug into the crisp, juicy Braeburn. The snap of the skin sounded in his ears, and the sweetness rolled on his tongue while the juice ran down his chin.

Lana laughed and pulled a napkin from her jeans pocket. She handed him one. "Always thinking ahead."

Organization seemed her gift and her bane. Details could be part of her problem. She had no patience for those spur-of-the-moment souls who enjoyed adventures in life rather than mapping out each strategy. Just like he'd always been determined to do things his way.

They ate their apples, talking about nothing important, and when they finished, Lana held out a paper towel. "I'll throw the core away," she said, extending the toweling toward him.

Mark grasped the apple fragments. "Toss it into the shrubs. The birds will eat it, and if not, it'll work as compost. It's great for the soil."

Her expression let him know she didn't like the idea.

"You don't have to," he added.

He could see her mentally struggling with his suggestion. Finally she tucked the towel back into her pocket. "If you don't think the neighbors will accuse me of throwing garbage in my yard. . ."

"I don't think so," he said, tossing the apple core into the tall hedge along the fence.

With much effort, she followed his example, and in his heart, Mark congratulated her for doing something spur of the moment. Something unplanned and natural.

Returning to his pruning, Mark enjoyed the smell of the spring loam, rich from the winter's decay. New growth surrounded him, and he suspected Lana exhibited new growth, too.

The word "new" prodded him with another thought. He needed to find an apartment or flat—some place to call home. In the interim, Jim had been gracious to invite him to stay at his place, but he realized his presence limited Jim's way of life—a life that was guided by different values than Mark's. He didn't judge, but he believed God's Word. Mark tried hard to live a life that God would approve.

"Looks good," Lana said, appearing at his side and pulling him from his thoughts.

"It does, if I do say so myself." He grinned at her upturned face.

"So. . .will another dinner minus peanuts cover my indebtedness?" She rolled her eyes and shook her head, faltering.

"I don't think so." Teasing, Mark slid his arm around her shoulder. "I have plans for you," he said, startled by the excitement that rolled through him with his touch.

"Plans?" Her voice sounded suspicious.

"How about letting me borrow your newspaper? I need to do some apartment hunting. Do you think it's too late?" He checked his watch. Six o'clock.

She eyed hers and shrugged. "Maybe a little late."

"Okay. How's this? I'll check the paper, and you can help since you know the area. We'll make a list, and tomorrow you'll go along with me."

She stood in silence a moment, then nodded. "Okay. I suppose I should be neighborly, but. . .what about dinner?"

"Let's order pizza. Easier and safer. I've never had pizza with peanuts."

Lana grasped his arm, giving it a teasing shake. "Then you've never had my homemade pizza."

Enjoying the earlier sensation, Mark slipped his arm around her shoulder as they headed for the house. Unbidden thoughts slithered into his mind. He needed to know Lana much better before allowing his heart to get tangled with hers. Now all he had to do was convince his heart to pay attention to his warning.

❦

Lana did a full turn, scrutinizing the kitchen. Ugly cabinets, little counter space, old appliances. Mark couldn't live in a place like this. She eyed the newspaper ad they'd looked at the evening before. The whole thing seemed full of untruths. "Look, it says right here," she said, pointing to the paper, " 'cozy apartment.' "

Mark clasped the back of her neck, giving it a gentle squeeze. "Some people's cozy is another person's misery."

"But you're smiling," she said, amazed at his optimism. "They didn't tell the truth." She tapped her finger against the want-ad listing. "Right here in the paper."

"They exaggerated," he said. "And remember. . .never believe everything you read in the news."

His good humor nudged at her frustration, shifting it an inch. "Let's try the next place."

"Okay, but don't get your head in a whirl with any preconceived notions." He steered her through the doorway and down the stairs. At the apartment supervisor's door, Mark dropped off the key, then headed to the car.

"The ads are always so disappointing and discouraging," Lana said. "Before we bought the house, Barb and I looked for a rental to share. We were so frustrated."

"You have to take a lot of the details with the proverbial grain of salt," Mark said.

A grain of salt. Mark seemed to do that. He looked at life with an open mind, willing to take whatever came his way with that proverbial grain of salt he'd mentioned, like the day Barb brought him home to clean the yard. He'd done it with a smile.

"Here's an idea," he said, jolting her from her thoughts. He took one hand from the steering wheel and motioned toward the newspaper on the seat beside her. "Read me the next ad. We can speculate what the reality might be."

His good nature dragged a grin to her face. She picked up the paper and scanned the listing until she found the ad. "Here goes. Five-room apartment." She stopped. "Let's see. We can expect two rooms. Right?"

He shook his head. "Four rooms and bath—living room, kitchen, bedroom, and. . .foyer."

She gave him a presumptuous look. "An entry's not a room."

"But it is in newspaper ads."

She poked his arm. "You're being silly." Focusing on the paper, she ran her finger along the column to find the ad. "Good location, it says here. What about that?'"

"It doesn't say good for what, does it?"

Mark was surprised by her laughter.

"What about this?" she asked. "Spotless." She held up her palm, halting him. "Don't tell me." She rested her finger beside her mouth. "Painted only five years ago and adequately clean."

"You got it," he said, pleased that she'd jumped in with the silly definitions. "Now you won't be disappointed." He glanced her way and prayed she could handle whatever they found.

When he saw Oak Street, he turned left and checked addresses. In the second block, he felt pleasantly surprised. Two neat rows of single-story apartments stood face-to-face, divided by a long driveway that led to a carport beside each unit. The grounds were neat, and a small tree shaded each front yard. But behind the buildings, Mark could see taller trees—oaks and elms towering over the rooftops. So far, so good.

He eyed Lana, and her expression looked positive. "A carport's nice. Keeps the snow off."

"And I like the trees," he said, motioning to the tall branches evident behind the buildings. "Wait here, and I'll get the key."

He darted to the first apartment, and when he returned, a gentleman followed along.

"Hello there," the man said, giving Lana a nod. "I'll unlock the door for you so you can take a peek." He gestured toward the apartment on the end of the complex.

Lana liked the wide windows at the front and the building's neat appearance.

"Now you take your time," the man said as he turned the key and opened the door. "You two look like a nice, friendly couple. I hope you like the place."

"We. . .I'm. . ." Lana's voice trailed off, and she eyed Mark, waiting for him to respond. Heat rose to her cheeks.

Mark sent her a toying grin and nodded at the man. "Thanks. We'll let you know when we're finished."

The gentleman nodded his head and turned back toward his apartment while Lana gaped at Mark, confused.

"What's the sense of disappointing him?" Mark asked. "He thought we were a nice, friendly couple."

His smile sent Lana's heart reeling. He was only teasing her. That seemed Mark's way. His crazy sense of humor.

She followed his gesture and stepped into a small foyer with a coat closet. "First room," Lana said with a laugh.

"We'll have to see," Mark said good-naturedly. He walked through the large living room and down a hallway to a fair-sized bedroom and bath, noticing with pleasure the place did look spotless.

Lana followed behind him, but her wary gaze held a new hint of optimism. "The carpet looks like it's been cleaned recently," she said.

Mark agreed. The medium gray carpet seemed fairly new. Inside the bedroom, he opened a large double-door closet. "See. Not bad and an extra big closet."

"Maybe it's large because that's the fifth room," she said, then sent him a teasing smile.

They retraced their steps and entered a roomy kitchen with plenty of cabinets. The appliances looked well kept, and the room had ample table space. But the surprise hit him at another doorway. "Look." He motioned to Lana. "A sun room, and it's heated so it's year-round."

Her eyes widened. "You mean this really is a fifth room."

"Looks like it," he said, thrilled at what they'd found. He gazed out the wide windows at the tree-filled setting. "What a great place to enjoy the outdoors even in winter and still be warm."

"The owners outdid themselves on this place," Lana admitted. "This is really a nice rental."

"You admit you were wrong about newspaper ads?"

"Wrong about one ad."

"Where there's one, there's hope. Just keep that in mind," he said, beckoning her through the front door. "This is it as far as I'm concerned."

"It's great, Mark. Why not give the man your deposit?"

She caressed his shoulder, and a sweet feeling ran down his arm. He loved to see her smile and rejoice with him. Could this be God's direction? He prayed it was.

Lana stood in her classroom doorway and spied Stacy Leonard talking with a friend. Her anger seemed evident, and Lana held back, not wanting to get involved. But Stacy lifted her gaze and saw Lana watching her. The teenager slammed her locker and headed her way.

"What's wrong, Stacy?" Lana asked. The girl looked as if she'd planned to scoot past, but Lana felt compelled to stop her.

"Nothing." She rolled her eyes and looked at the ceiling.

"For nothing wrong, you seem mighty upset." Lana held her ground and kept the girl in direct focus.

"It's nothing that concerns you. You wouldn't understand anyway," Stacy said.

"Why don't you try me?"

"I'm just tired of having my plans goofed up. I had everything organized, then my friend tossed in her own plans and. . .I'm tired of it." Stacy's head lowered, and Lana suspected she had tears in her eyes.

"I'm sorry your friend didn't take your plans seriously. Sometimes two people's ideas clash, and if we want to remain friends, we have to compromise. I'm sure you've heard that before." Lana rolled her eyes and grinned.

A faint smile crept to Stacy's face. "We were supposed to spend the night together at my house, but now she wants to go to the movies first, and unless I lie to my parents about what we're doing, they won't let me go."

"Sounds like you don't want to tell your parents a fib." Lana prayed she was correct.

Stacy shook her head. "If I do, they'll find out anyway. They always do."

"Truth is easier, isn't it?"

The girl nodded. "But now she'll go off with other friends and party while I sit home alone."

"Can you talk with her? Maybe you can suggest something different that your parents will approve. Roller skating. . .or hanging out at a mall." Lana grasped at ideas, hoping she might hit on something that would help.

"The mall? She might like that idea."

Lana could almost hear the girl's mind working through ideas. "You see. Compromise can work. You just have to remove the emotion and think with reason."

Stacy laughed. "If you ask my parents, they don't think I'm very reasonable."

"Parents worry a lot about their kids."

Stacy's face had brightened, and she took a step backward. "Thanks, Miss West. I'll call Julie and see if she'd like to go the mall instead."

"Good for you," Lana said, sending the girl a wave as she sped away.

Lana turned into her classroom. Only the weekend and then three more days before school closed. Her own plans filtered through her mind. This summer she'd decided to redecorate her bedroom. She had some great stenciling ideas for refurbishing her old dresser and headboard. When she finished that job, Lana had plans to tackle the dining room—paint and add a border where a chair molding would be. Her list had grown, and no one could stop her.

She faltered, recognizing Stacy's complaint as her own. She hated people to botch up her plans, and although she'd given Stacy good advice, compromise wasn't Lana's favorite way to solve a problem. Not at all.

❧

Mark left his car in the street and headed into Jim's place. He had a little packing to do, and tonight, he had bowling with the teens. Not his favorite activity, but it was his job. Tomorrow, he looked forward to getting into his own apartment. As he rounded his sedan, Lana came down the driveway toward the mailbox. He gave her a wave, and she returned his greeting.

"Tomorrow's the big day," he said. "My furniture comes out of storage."

"You're moving tomorrow?" Her face shifted through a medley of emotions and settled on an amiable smile.

He strode toward her. "I could use a woman's touch getting settled. . .and I know you don't work on Saturdays."

She fingered her top button and thought for a moment. "Living next door, I'm at your mercy." Her grin looked more natural than the earlier smile. "I'm not good at carrying. I'm too short. . .and weak."

"How about small boxes? You can handle those."

She nodded.

"And unpacking. You can do that if I open the box."

"Got me," she said, giving him a poke. "You sound like you think I'm trying to wheedle out of helping you."

"Aren't you the lady who said you hated doing things for other people?" He sent her a knowing gaze.

Amused, she winced playfully. "Me and my big mouth. I need to learn to keep it shut." She pulled the mail out of the box and shut the lid.

"Too late. I already know that little tidbit of information." He patted her shoulder. "So I can count on you?"

"Why not? My exams are all ready. No papers to grade. The clock is ticking down, and a smile is rising." She sent him a toothy grin.

"Now that you shared that piece of news, I have another idea."

She did a quick two-step backward. "Sorry, I can't hear you." Her feet carried her farther away.

He beckoned her toward him, and she grudgingly acquiesced.

"What?" she asked, tilting her head with a pitiful frown.

"It's this way." He took his finger and lifted the corners of her mouth, forcing them into a grin. "I have to do something tonight I'm not crazy about. . .and I thought maybe you'd like to join me."

Her forced grin grew into a real smile. "Now there's an offer that's hard to pass up." She glanced at her mail, then tapped it against her cheek. "So what not-crazy-about activity are you asking me to participate in? Bungee jumping off a bridge? Sky diving from a jet?"

"Sounds like you aren't crazy about heights."

"That and snakes. Don't ask me to do anything that involves either of those things."

She looked squeamish just mentioning snakes, and her expression tickled him. "No snakes. No heights. You're safe."

"Safe? I doubt that. What did you have in mind?"

"Bowling." He watched her face turn from fear of snakes to disgust. "Apparently you're not fond of that activity either."

"I hate it. What fun is it to roll a fat, heavy ball down a narrow lane and knock down a few wooden sticks?" She rolled her eyes and shook her head.

"Teenagers. They love it. It's not bowling. It's the camaraderie. . .and that's what I need. A friend and, better yet, a friend who knows some of the kids. You'd be so helpful."

"I can't bowl."

"Okay, you can keep score." He gave her his most optimistic look.

He could see her mind conjuring up something important she had to do.

"Your hair looks fine," he said. "You don't need a shampoo." He clasped her free hand, and its smallness sent a sensation skidding through his chest. He gazed at her fingernails. "Manicure looks good." He worked to keep his voice steady. "No excuses."

She covered her face with the handful of mail and laughed. "Wow! You're hard to discourage."

"Come along—please. You'll give me adult conversation, and all you have to do is keep score. I'll show you how." He recreated the pleading look from his childhood that worked miracles on his mother and sent it Lana's way.

She shook her head. "Scorekeeper, and that's it."

"It's a deal," he said.

151

Chapter 4

"Come on, Miss West," Gary said. "You can't just keep score. Everyone bowls."

Lana looked at the lanes of bowlers and sent a pleading look to Mark. "You promised."

He shrugged. "No, I only said it's a deal."

She gripped the black marker and clutched the chair with her free fingers. She wasn't planning to budge. Bowling came right in there next to having her tooth filled without benefit of Novocain.

"Come on, Miss West." Three other teens joined Gary, their pleading voices sailing across the surrounding lanes.

Embarrassed at the attention, Lana dropped the marker. "Fine. I have to rent shoes and find a ball." She strode away, trying to keep a cooperative look on her face, but fearing that she had failed.

With red, white, and blue rented shoes announcing her size five on the back and a ball that seemed far too heavy to lift, she returned to the group and plopped onto the bench. The teens had already begun to bowl, and she watched the pins teetering, then dropping to the floor while cheers rose and shouts of spare or strike reverberated to the high ceiling.

She looked at the alley next to hers where Mark stood poised, the ball clasped in his gripping fingers and resting on his other hand. He crouched down and took four quick steps, swinging the ball back, then bringing it forward and releasing it smoothly onto the highly polished surface of the lane. The black ball sped toward the pins, hooking left just before it slammed into them and vanished into the darkness. Lana watched the white pins tumble to the ground except for one that wobbled and then remained upright.

"You'll get this one," a voice urged. "A spare's good, Mark."

Surprised that the boy had called his youth director "Mark," Lana watched the kids cheer when moments later the single pin went flying. She frowned in thought. Mark—and she was Miss West. But wasn't that how it should be? Respect and authority?

"You're up, Miss West," Susan said.

Lana looked down at her clown shoes and rose, grasping the ball. She stuck her fingers into the three holes, hoping she'd done it correctly, and carried the object as if it were a ball and chain.

She remembered what Mark had done and paused in front of the black line, but before she could move, Mark stepped beside her.

"Back up a little, or you'll step over the line," he said, guiding her by the shoulders.

"I know," she said, taking a couple of steps back. She should have told Mark. Not only couldn't she bowl well, she'd never bowled in her life. Later she would tell him, but not in front of the kids.

"Haven't you ever bowled?" Mark asked, eyeing her.

With his question, he'd saved her the trouble of a confession. She shook her head and whispered, "No. I told you I hate the game."

"Do you want some pointers?" he whispered back.

"No." She sent him a determined look. She didn't want to stand there like a novice while all the teens watched her get a bowling lesson.

"Okay," he said, "just step forward, swing your arm back, and as you swing forward release the ball."

"I know." Telling him she didn't want instructions had been as effective as watering the lawn during a rainstorm.

She grasped her fortitude—along with the ball—took aim, stepped forward, swung back, and released the ball. A thud rang out along with the titters of surrounding bowlers as the ball shot behind her and settled beneath the bench.

"The lane's in front of you, Miss West," Jason called.

She swung around, catching the frown that surged to her face and replaced it with a look she hoped was good-natured.

Jason jumped up and returned the ball. She turned her back, aiming again, but this time clung to the ball with every muscle in her thumb and two fingers. She pranced toward the black line, cautiously swung her arm back, then brought it forward before she released the ball. This time her heart lifted as the blue-and-white beauty spiraled down the lane. But her up-lifted heart sank as the ball took a wide curve and dropped into the gutter.

"Gutter ball," Susan yelled.

She refused to turn around as she waited for the oppressive orb to return. She grasped it again, this time more determined.

"Keep your arm straight and follow through," Mark whispered from the adjacent alley.

She arched an eyebrow, got set, took her steps, swung, and released. The ball went forward. It curved toward the gutter, but this time, it curved back and clipped five pins. Relieved, she spun away and marched back to her seat. How had she gotten herself into this mess?

As her next turn neared, she eyed the score sheet and realized she faced eighteen more opportunities to make a fool of herself—assuming she didn't get any strikes. When she rose again, she uttered a silent prayer. She knew God had more important things to do than worry about her hitting those pins, but she felt utterly mortified, and she hoped the Lord understood. Opening her eyes, she let the ball go, and to her surprise, it rolled down the center of the lane, sending pins flying.

A cheer went up, and when the fallen pins had been cleared away, only two pins remained standing. The ball returned and she grasped it, feeling more confident. She realized it just took a little time to get the hang of bowling. She focused on the spots, and when she released the ball, her ring finger caught inside the grip holes. The ball flew through the air and thudded about halfway down the alley. While she nursed her throbbing digit, the ball knocked the pins into the air for a spare.

Applause and cheers rose behind her, but when she turned around, the sound died.

"What happened?" Mark asked, pulling away and gaping at her swelling finger.

"I don't know. It seemed to stick in the hole."

While a few teens gawked, Mark studied it a moment. "Looks like a sprain. I'll get some ice from the bar." He rested his hand on her shoulder. "Looks like you'll be sitting out the rest of the frames."

Gratitude tangled with her pain. "Seriously?"

He nodded.

"What a shame. I was just getting the hang of it." She sank to the chair in front of the score sheet and clutched her throbbing finger while she hid her grateful grin.

❦

Standing in Lana's driveway the next morning, Mark studied her purposeful expression. "Are you sure?"

"Yes. You drive your car, and I'll follow you with the boxes in mine." She lifted the trunk lid and eyed it. "What doesn't fit in the trunk will go into the back seat."

"I can probably cram a couple more things into my trunk," he said again, sure she couldn't get everything into her small-sized vehicle.

"Remember, I'm Miss Organization. Trust me." She clutched her chest, and her splinted finger jarred his memory. Her eyes shifted from him to her bandage and back. "And if you hadn't manipulated me into going bowling, I wouldn't have a sprained finger. Now I'm working with a handicap."

He bit his tongue, wanting to tease her and say her biggest handicap was her lack of patience and stubborn resolve, but she'd hit upon the truth. Another of his flaws. He did try to direct people and situations. "I'm sorry about your finger. I didn't realize the kids would goad you into bowling."

"Neither did I, or I wouldn't have gone." She turned back to the trunk and shifted a couple more boxes.

He'd never known anyone so set on doing something her own way, but he knew pushing her wouldn't work. He thanked the Lord that she hadn't been the one chosen to lead the children of Israel into the Promised Land. They'd still be wandering, lost somewhere in the Himalayas. He could easily imagine Lana bypassing the Red Sea and trying to part the Indian Ocean instead.

"Okay," he reluctantly agreed, "but let's get going. Jim's already on his way with the moving van, and I have the apartment key." He stood back, watching her shuffle and reorganize until she had each item in a specific spot only a mind like Lana's could arrange.

"What else?" she asked, challenging him.

"Clothes. Things from my closet and a bag of shoes. Things like that, but I'll come back for those." She seemed like an immovable mountain, and Mark could tell she wouldn't budge on the issue.

"They'll fit in here. Why come back?" Her petite frame seemed to grow in size.

Giving up, he shrugged and marched inside with Lana behind him. Avoiding her sprained finger, he loaded her arms with bags of shoes, his travel kit with his EpiPens, and a small box of personal items. Then he gathered up his shirts, suits, and trousers—all the things he hadn't packed in his luggage.

They marched to her car, where she slid a couple items onto the roof, then packed the smaller boxes onto the backseat floor. After she'd arranged most of his clothes on the back seat, she took the final pieces from his arms.

"You go ahead, and I'll be there in a minute. I know Jim's waiting. I only have these last things to pack."

He stood empty-armed, figuring he'd be safe leaving and certain he'd arrive at least a half hour before she would. "Okay. I'll meet you there."

She gave him a wave, and he headed down the driveway. Without looking back, he climbed into his car and pulled away from the curb. What a woman. Why did he feel so attracted to her? A stubborn, impatient woman didn't seem to fit the description of the ideal partner for a youth director. But when he thought of Lana, instead of picturing that determined look, he remembered her casual grace and warm, teasing smile. She made him laugh. Maybe God had given him a challenge so he might learn humility and guidance. . .or maybe Lana would learn something from him. Patience and optimism, perhaps.

He grinned, wondering if God had the patience for either one of them.

When Mark pulled in front of his apartment, Jim was waiting, leaning against the back of the moving van.

"I thought you got lost," Jim said, pulling open the double door of the truck. "Let's unload the furniture first. If I can get this truck back early, it'll save you a few bucks. Maybe enough for a six-pack of beer."

Mark tried to smile. "No six-pack for me, Jim. I work with kids, remember? I need to be a good example." He whacked Jim's paunchy belly with the back of his fist. "Plus I don't want to lose my youthful physique. Before you know it, you won't be able to bend over and tie your shoes."

Jim only grinned, but Mark hoped his words sent a cautious warning into his friend's mind.

Mark joined Jim at the truck, and together they carried in the mattress and box spring, then the rest of the bedroom furniture and the sofa, one piece at a time. While they toted in the boxes, Lana pulled into the driveway.

"We're taking in this load first," he said. Knowing she'd be antsy waiting, he added, "But if you can dodge around us, you can hang the clothes in my closet if you want."

She nodded and opened the back door of the car.

He moved ahead into the house and grinned, watching Lana stay out of their way without a squeak until the truck was emptied.

When Jim left with the trailer, Mark and Lana finished unpacking her car, and after everything was inside, he stood in the living room and surveyed the situation. "Here's what we can do. A woman's comfort zone is the kitchen." Then, thinking of their near mishaps, he laughed. "Let me rephrase that. With your unique skills, I'll let you set up the kitchen. . .and don't worry. I even have a step stool."

"All the modern conveniences," Lana said. "And what will you do? Watch the ball game?" She tilted her head toward the television.

"I'll unpack my clothes and handle the bedroom," he said.

"Sounds like a deal." She headed into the kitchen.

In the bedroom, Mark arranged his clothes in the dresser drawers and listened to the sounds coming from the kitchen. The ting and clang of dishes and pans assured him that Lana was at work. He'd been smart giving her the kitchen task. That's where her skills could shine.

Mark looked around the room for the bag of dress shoes he remembered putting in Lana's car. . .and his travel kit. Besides the EpiPens, he'd tossed his checkbook inside. He suspected they'd never made it to the bedroom and ambled down the hall to look for them. In the living room, boxes still sat unopened, but he saw no sign of the bags he wanted. Concerned, he headed for the kitchen.

"How are you doing?" Mark asked, scanning Lana's progress from the kitchen doorway.

"Good," she said. "You don't have as much junk as I do."

He laughed. "I avoid the kitchen as much as possible." Maybe so should she. He chuckled at his thought.

"What's funny?" She pulled open a cabinet door, and he regarded the inside—the contents were arranged in a much more organized and logical fashion than he would have managed. "Just thinking about you in a kitchen."

"Quiet," she said, hurling a dishtowel across the room.

He caught the towel and carried it back to her. "Have you seen the bag with my dress shoes and my travel kit?"

She turned, a thoughtful look on her face. "Not that I remember."

"Could they still be in the car?" He wandered around the room, nosing into the boxes and searching beneath the table and chairs—anywhere in hopes he'd find them.

"No, it's empty. I'm positive," she said, facing him and leaning against the counter. "The last time I saw the travel kit was when I. . ." Her face paled.

"When you what?" Her look sent his stomach on a spiraling journey. "What?" he repeated.

"When I set them on top of the car." She jammed her hair behind her ear and looked as if she might cry.

Their eyes met, and he studied her anxious face.

"I'd planned to put them on the passenger seat after I finished in the back, but I don't remember putting them there."

Mark rubbed the back of his neck. His dress shoes, his allergy medication, razor, and all his other toiletries. "Are you sure?"

She bit her lip and nodded. "I'm so sorry."

"It was an accident," he said, but he couldn't help but mentally tally the cost of replacing everything, and he could, but what about the checkbook? *God will provide*, he said to himself, not wanting to upset Lana.

"I know, but I seem to be a klutz lately," she said. "What happened to those detail skills you razz me about?"

Though troubled, he aimed to appear lighthearted. "They took a vacation before you did." While he spoke, a hopeful thought settled in his mind. "You know, the things may have fallen off in the driveway. I'll take a ride over and see. You stay here and pray."

"Let's call Barb. Maybe she's already found them. If she did, she wouldn't call here. She doesn't know your telephone number."

"Good idea, but let's pray anyway," he said, seeing concern grow on her face. He tried to cover his own distress. He could replace everything. . .but his checkbook worried him.

She lifted the phone, punched in the numbers, and waited. In silence, she hung up and turned to him. "She's not there. The answering machine kicked in."

"I'd better go over to your place, then, and see."

"That's what I figured. No sense in leaving a message for Barb." She tugged on her top button, gloom covering her face. "I'm so sorry, Mark. It's just another example of my imperfections. I had to do it my way. . .and alone. If I hadn't chased you off, you would have seen the things on the car roof."

He could have given her a lecture, but it wasn't the time. Anyway, it would have done little good. Lana had to learn control and patience for herself. . .and that could only be with God's help. At least she hadn't dashed out to her car so she could solve the problem herself.

Unforeseen, she faced him, then moved toward the doorway. "On second thought, let me go home and look. I'm the one who caused the problem."

Mark's last thought slithered to the floor. "No, I'll do it, Lana. You take care of the kitchen."

She followed him to the door but didn't argue, and he was grateful.

The trip was only a matter of blocks, and as he drove, Mark kept his peripheral vision glued to the road, looking for telltale signs of his belongings. Seeing nothing, his hope lifted, but when he pulled up to the driveway and stopped short of the spot where Lana's car had been, he saw nothing.

He climbed from the car and walked along the driveway. In a crevice between the driveway and lawn, something caught his eye. An EpiPen. If that had fallen there, where was everything else?

He moved in a full circle, wondering if a neighbor had picked it up for safekeeping or worse a child. If his carelessness by not closing his kit had caused a child injury, he'd never forgive himself.

The side door flew open, and Mark jerked.

"Mark." Barb stood in the doorway. "Are you missing some of your things?"

With his heart in his throat, he could only nod.

"The stuff's inside. Come on in."

She pushed the screen open, and he took a calming breath before going inside. "I didn't know you were here," he said, catching his breath. "Lana called, but she got the answering machine."

"I just got in. I'm thankful no one found it." She gestured to the duffel bag and travel kit sitting on the kitchen table. "Can you picture the little kids in the neighborhood playing grown-up in your shoes?"

He unzipped his shaving kit and pulled out the checkbook. "Or writing checks." He gave her a grateful grin.

"Whew! I didn't know that was there. I assumed the stuff was yours. Lana mentioned you were moving today." She pulled out a kitchen chair. "Have a seat. I'll get you a drink."

With his mouth as dry as Death Valley, he accepted the offer. "Let me call Lana first, if you don't mind. I know she's worried."

"Sure thing," she said, pointing toward the telephone.

When he'd heard Lana's relieved exclamation, Mark gave her a quick explanation and hung up. Sliding into the chair, he took a long, cool drink of the iced tea.

"How did your bags get in our driveway?" Barb asked as she joined him at the table.

"Guess," he said, then told her the tale.

"She's a character, isn't she?" Barb shook her head. "I love my sister with all my heart, but she's like a marine sergeant sometimes."

With his mouth full of tea, Mark sputtered. He covered the front of his mouth with his hand in a futile effort to keep from showering the table.

Barb grabbed a paper napkin and slid it across to him. He mopped up the drizzle and shook his head. "I called her something like that a week or so ago."

"How did she take it?" Her smile told him she was joking.

"I think she'd heard it before," he said, remembering when he'd teased her during their after-church breakfast.

"From me." Barb took a swallow of tea and leaned against the chair back. "There, but for the grace of God, go I." She gave him a wry smile. "You know that saying."

Mark nodded. "I'm afraid I admitted my flaws to her—and she won't let me forget them either.

"If we didn't have flaws, we'd be angels or something." She grinned. "Poor Lana got the worst of it since she was the oldest. We have wonderful parents, but our father has always been the kind of man who lets you know what he never had and what you have. Know what I mean?"

Mark nodded again, although not totally sure he understood.

"Dad never had a bicycle, and he spent his life making sure we had a bike. But we always knew to be grateful for it. We spent a lot of our childhood trying to make Dad happy and being the best kids we could be. . .to the point that now I try to save the world while Lana tries to save herself." She lifted the glass and took another drink. "We're a little goofy, I suppose."

"Not goofy. Just unique. But I understand a little better why Lana is who she is."

"She doesn't talk much about herself," Barb said. "Just let her be in charge, and she's happy. It'll get done fast but in her own way."

Mark had seen that demonstrated, but he had to admit that often Lana's way was a good way. He drained the glass and rose. "I'd better get back. Your sister's organizing my kitchen."

"Then you've got it made. She'll put everything on the shelf in alphabetical order. You won't have to guess where to find a thing."

Mark chuckled and gathered his belongings. Thanking Barb for the tea, he headed for his car. So many things made sense now. Lana had good parents, but her well-meaning father expected appreciation. And how does a kid show gratitude? By behaving and being as perfect as possible.

But Barb's words awakened another thought. He also had a problem with trying to direct the world. His father had tried to guide him when he was younger, and he'd fought back. Now he found himself acting like his father—trying to save the world with his will.

Mark closed his eyes as his words drifted up to heaven. *Father, help Lana and me both learn that we cannot save ourselves or anyone. It's only through Your precious gift that we're saved—through Your Son, Jesus. Help us to live that, Lord. . .and soon.*

When he opened his eyes, he turned the key in the ignition and grinned. He'd just given God a real challenge.

Chapter 5

On Wednesday, the last day before vacation, Lana slid a graded exam onto the corrected pile and grabbed another. She didn't have to use the answer key anymore. After thirty exams, she knew the answers by heart. Catching a movement out of the corner of her eye, she looked toward the doorway.

"Come in, Don. Have a seat."

Don Fabrizio stepped through the doorway and ambled across the floor. He eased his long legs beneath a front desk and wove his fingers together.

She rose from her desk and stood in front of him. "I'm sorry I had to throw you out of the exam Monday, Don, but you know you were cheating. I saw you. I don't understand why you did that."

He shrugged and stared down at his fingers clutched together on the desk. "So what do you want?"

"I want to know why you cheated. You're not a bad student. In fact, your grades are pretty good. So what's wrong?"

"I didn't study. I couldn't remember all that stuff."

"Why didn't you study?" Lana asked, watching his nervous behavior.

He responded with another shrug, his focus never leaving the desktop.

"I shouldn't give you another chance, but I'm willing if you are," she said, amazed at her decision.

With her offer, his head lifted, and his gaze sought hers. "What do you mean?"

"Another chance," she repeated. "I'll give you a different exam. I always prepare more than one version since I have three classes that are the same."

"You mean. . .you'll let me. . ." He paused as if disbelieving.

"Yes," she said. "You might not do well, but you know I'll have to mark your final grade down horribly if you don't take it at all."

"I know," he said, his voice distant and sad. "And I'd never hear the end of it."

Alerted by his words, Lana searched the boy's face for a hint of his trouble. If he could only talk and tell her what was wrong, he might have some relief from his problem. Her thought stopped her cold. Once again, she saw her own behavior in the teen. How many times had she avoided telling others the things that troubled her. She knew it would seem so unimportant to anyone else, and the telling made her feel vulnerable. Better to keep her thoughts inside and deal with them privately.

"I don't like to talk about my problems either," Lana confessed.

Again, Don lifted his face to hers, his gaze seeming to beg to believe she understood.

"Look, Don," she said, sliding into the desk beside him. "Here's the deal. You tell me why you didn't study, and I'll give you another exam. Fair?"

His face drained of color, and she sensed he was about to rise from the chair and leave. She watched his arms brace against the desk and his foot shift to stand.

Instead, he caved back against the desk and shook his head. "It's too difficult to talk about my family. And nothing I say will change anything."

Lana heard her own thoughts coming from the boy, and sadness rolled through her. She'd spent a lot of time letting her past—a good past really—get in the way of a full life. At least she'd maintained a sense of humor. Quick wit. That's one thing she loved about Mark. The phrase sizzled through her. Loved about Mark. Had she really meant what she said?

She drew her attention back to Don, his face strained by unhappiness. "No, you can't change your family, but you can change yourself and how you react to the family. That's all I can offer you."

"What do you mean change myself?" He released a bitter sigh. "It's my dad who drinks and acts crazy when he gets home at one in the morning. He wakes everyone up, kicking the furniture or else yelling so loud even God couldn't sleep."

God? Was Don a believer? She struggled to decide where to go with the discussion. She couldn't just tell him to give the problem over to God. She knew how she'd struggled with that and failed. He needed more, but he needed the Lord, too.

"The other night," Don continued, "he came in early. . .but stupid drunk as usual. I was trying to study, and he kept poking at me and grabbing my study notes. If anyone had seen him besides my family, I'd have died. He acted like a nut case. I wanted to scream at him or blast him one, but he's my dad."

Don lifted his face to Lana, and she saw the teen's longing to love his father unconditionally. Hope filled his face, and it tugged at Lana's heartstrings.

"I'm sure that was terrible," was all she could find to say. She'd never known a life like that.

"The worst thing was. . .he t–tore up my study notes." He choked on the words.

"Tore them? Why?" She struggled to keep her face from showing emotion.

"For fun."

His answer settled in her stomach like a mountain. How could she respond to this hurting young man? "You had a bad time, Don. Do you have friends you can study with next time? Go to their house. . .or even the library?"

"I don't have many friends. Who wants to invite someone over to see their dad acting like that? And I can't hang out at the guys' homes without having them over. I just gave up."

She grasped at his earlier reference. "Do you believe in God?" Her silent prayer soared to heaven, asking for wisdom.

He nodded. "My mom taught us about the Bible. She used to read us stories about Jesus, but we don't go to church much."

"I have a friend who. . .he's the youth director of First Church of Holly. Do you know where that is?"

He nodded. "It's not too far from my house."

She felt God's prodding. "Here's an idea. First Church has a nice youth group. They go bowling and. . .all kinds of things." Her mind went blank, and she tried to imagine what else they did. "They don't meet at private houses usually because they have the church. Some of the kids who are members there you might know from Holly High. Why not come to church some Sunday and check it out? You can see what the youth group is doing."

He listened to her without making his escape, and she prayed he'd accept her invitation.

He shrugged. "I don't know. I hate going places alone."

"Well, bring along a friend. And remember that you're not really alone, Don." Mark's words soared into her mind. "Jesus is always walking along with you, and God is on your side." She filled with relief, thanking God for Mark's words. "And you know me, too. I realize I'm old, but I'm still your 'old' friend."

He laughed for the first time. "Thanks, Miss West. I'll think about it."

She gathered her wits and returned to the reason he'd come. "Okay, you kept your part of the deal. So if you want to take a look at this exam, maybe you'll do better than you think."

He nodded and settled into the seat, leaning forward to pull the stub of a pencil from his back pocket.

Lana selected a blank exam from her packet and slid it in front of him. "Take your time. There's nothing tricky. The test is asking you to think more than repeat dates and events. Just use your common sense. . .and a little bit of what you learned in class."

He smiled again and bent his head over the test.

Lana returned to correcting papers and averaging grades. She'd already cleaned her room, stripped the bulletin boards, and stored away her teaching materials. At three o'clock she would be a free woman. . .as long as her grade books and sheets were turned in. She could pick up her paycheck and go home.

Home. She had the whole summer to do the projects she'd thought about. Shame filled her. All she had on her mind to worry about had been summer projects. Don had too many worries for a teenager. She lifted her head and eyed him. She thought she'd led a difficult life. She'd lived in bliss compared to this young man.

Again Mark came to mind. Now that he'd moved, she wondered how often she would see him. Maybe it had worked out for the best. His life seemed so devoted compared to hers—giving his time and his talents to make others happy.

She glanced at her wristwatch. Nearly three. Anxious to turn in her grades and leave, she glanced at Don. To her pleasant surprise, he shuffled his test papers in order and rose. "Thanks, Miss West. I know I didn't get an A, but I don't think I failed it either."

"That's great, Don. Have a nice summer, and remember what I said. If you have a chance, drop by the church. I'm sure you won't be sorry."

He nodded, slid the exam onto her desk, and went through the door. She stared at the vacated space for a moment, praying that God would move the boy to come to the church. With a sigh, she pulled his paper in front of her and began to correct his exam.

When she finished, she tallied his grade and averaged the results. Don had been correct. He hadn't failed, and he'd gotten a C minus. Not great but better than a zero. She piled her grade book, report sheets, and exams into a neat pile to turn into the office.

As she rose, a familiar figure appeared at her doorway. "What are you doing here?" she asked, surprised to see Mark.

"Looking for a pretty teacher with freckles. Know anyone like that?"

She laughed, and the sensation felt wonderful. She'd been tense, listening to Don's story and reliving her own pitiful drama. She thanked God he'd tuned her thoughts back to reality. Her hang-ups were of her own making. Now, the challenge was to dump them.

"Don't know a soul like that," she said, stepping toward Mark. "So tell me. Why are you here. . .really?"

"I thought you'd enjoy a friendly face." He stepped into the room and sat on the edge of a student desk, looking around the room. "So this is where you pour knowledge into youthful minds."

"I try," she said.

"And today's your last day until fall?"

She lifted her pack of papers and grades. "Right here. I turn this in, and it's sweet freedom."

"You looked a little thoughtful when I watched you from the door," he said, his sensitive face acknowledging his suspicion.

"I had to deal with a problem today. It made me think." She told him briefly about Don's situation, but not her revelation. She'd hang on to that in private and see what she could do about the problems alone.

Mark stepped to her side and ran his fingers along the tense cords in her neck. "That was a great suggestion. I'm glad you invited him to come to church. . .especially when he lives so near."

"I don't know if he'll come, but I tried." She touched Mark's arm. "You know what was strange? Something you said awhile back came to me out of the sky. The words were perfect. It was almost as if—"

"As if God put them in your head?" He smiled at her and drew the palm of his hand down her back.

She nodded, awed at the realization. "Now that we're being truthful," she said, sending him a knowing look, "tell me the real reason you came." He had something on his mind. She knew it in the pit of her empty stomach. "I'm waiting," she said, trying to sound blithe.

"I have a youth outing tomorrow morning, and my female chaperone broke her arm."

She eyed him suspiciously. "And who was this female chaperone?"

"Teri Dolan's mother. She tripped over the dog and fell on her right arm."

"And she can't chaperone with only one arm?"

He shook his head. "Not this activity. I need someone to volunteer."

The words, "Not this activity," made her nervous. "I'll pray that you find someone," Lana said with wide-eyed innocence.

He chuckled and touched her skin, letting his finger trail along her arm. "I always appreciate prayer, but today, I'd really appreciate a volunteer, too."

"Would you like me to ask Barb?"

His eyes narrowed to a toying scowl, and he didn't respond.

"Oh, I see, you want me to volunteer." She quieted her heart, fighting the desire to yield to his charm. "I empathize, but my vacation starts tomorrow. During the school year, I'm knee-deep in teenagers. I couldn't bear to spend one more minute with. . ."

She broke off the sentence as his gaze caught her eyes.

"What's your outing? Not bowling, I hope." She tried to bite her tongue, but the words spilled out.

"Not bowling, I promise." A sly grin slid to his face. "Horseback riding."

That did it. She flung her palm forward like a policeman stopping traffic. "Not me. No way. Not on a horse. Carousel, maybe. But not a live horse that gallops and snorts."

"Have you ever been horseback riding? These horses lumber and plod. Trust me." He patted her arm. "Please, I'm desperate. I'm new at this job. I can't take a mixed group of teens on an outing without at least one adult woman chaperone. You know that. And if I cancel, the kids will be so disappointed, not to mention their parents. I hate to start out on the wrong foot."

"I'm sure you can find someone else. Another parent or. . .someone." When she looked at his face, a sinking feeling washed over her.

"I don't know that many parents yet, and I hate to show defeat and bother Pastor Phil with this." He rested his hand on her arm. "Be a pal. I know you don't owe me anything. You've paid your debt." He sent her a beguiling smile. "Please come along. It's only a few hours."

Lana understood he was in a spot. But horseback riding? She and horses didn't speak the same language—or move in the same rhythm for that matter. She'd watched Westerns for years and noticed the smooth, elegant gait attained by horse and rider. The two times she'd had enough courage to climb—and she really meant climb—on a horse's back, she'd felt like the old Scottish folk song, "You take the high road, and I'll take the low road. And I'll get to Scotland afore ye." She went up and the horse went down, and the pain caused when they met in the middle was something she didn't want to remember.

But she looked into Mark's pleading eyes, and her mouth spoke without her brain participating. "All right, but this is the last time."

"Thanks a million," he said, drawing her into a bear hug. "We're leaving about nine. I'll stop by, and you can ride over with me."

"Okay," she said, feeling her cheek quiver like someone facing a firing squad. "Now what can I do to repay you? Name it. I'm yours."

His spirited smile sent her heart flying, but her inner beast came out of hiding. She had a plan. "You're mine? Do you mean that?"

"Sure."

"How do you like to paint?"

"Paint? You mean—" He studied her face, his enthusiasm fading.

"Not by numbers; that's for sure" she said, enjoying his agony. "Walls. Lots of walls. Maybe even ceilings."

"Walls and ceilings," he repeated.

"That's right, and thanks," she said, allowing her finger to ramble playfully up his arm in the same way he'd captivated hers. "I'm so pleased you've volunteered for my project."

Mark stepped from the car but didn't have to go far. Lana came out the side door dressed in jeans and a knit top. He noticed her sturdy hiking shoes and felt gratified that she at least knew how to dress for horseback riding.

"Good morning," he said, expecting her to respond, "What's good about it?" Instead she yawned. "Good morning."

He grinned, pleased at her attitude. "I'm sure it feels nice being on vacation."

She sent him one of her looks. "My first day off, and I had to get up at the same time I always do."

"Sorry," he said, opening her door and watching her climb in. "But think of the good deed you're doing."

She arched one of her eyebrows and remained silent.

Relieved, Mark saw the hint of a smile flash for a heartbeat and knew she was teasing.

Leaning against the headrest, she closed her eyes, and Mark let her relax. She'd have a workout, he knew, but he appreciated her pinch-hitting. He'd wanted to ask her to come along from the beginning, but he'd watched her misery bowling and had decided to give her a break. Instead, Mrs. Dolan had experienced a break. . .a real one.

At the church, Lana stayed in the car while Mark made sure his fourteen charges were seat belted up with licensed drivers. He set the ground rules, prayed with the teens, and climbed back into his car, relieved that he had enough teens to drive so he could make the trip with only Lana in his car.

They drove like a caravan, Mark leading the way, and when they parked at the stable, he steered them toward the building where men were saddling horses.

"I'm Mark Branson," he said to the dude in the cowboy hat. "I called last week. Fourteen teenagers and two adults." He eyed Lana and realized she looked as young as the kids.

The ranch hand only grunted and waved his arm toward the horses waiting to be mounted.

"This way." Mark beckoned to the group, and they followed, each attaching themselves to a horse as the stable crew gave them the animal's name and helped them mount.

Mark returned to Lana, hoping he could encourage a little enthusiasm. "I'll tell them to make sure they give you a mild-mannered mare." He slipped his arm around her shoulders and gave her a squeeze.

"Mild-mannered? Listen to that guy," she said. "Those plow horses have names. Charger, Buck, Titan, Cyclone, Gringo. Let me know when he comes to Sleepy, Dopey, or Bashful. That's my kind of horse."

"Don't worry," Mark said, patting her shoulder. "They give them spirited names to give the riders a thrill. They can go home and tell their friends they spent the day riding Avenger. Sounds more exciting than Daisy."

"You think so? Give me Daisy or Dandelion any day."

"Notice I said it sounds exciting." Mark tried to read her expression. At this point he wasn't sure if she were joking or serious, but either way he should have been more thoughtful and asked Pastor Phil to help him find a volunteer. If he really cared about her, he'd been stupid to force her to come along. . .even though he enjoyed her company. Why couldn't he stop being like his father, trying to push everyone into doing what he wanted?

Mark looked at Lana's tense face and hoped to ease her worry. "These poor animals have been up and down these paths so often they don't have to think. But it's fun for the kids. So here we are."

When the time came for her to mount, he followed Lana to the horse. "This one's docile, I hope," he murmured to the stablehand.

The man with the cowboy hat gave him a peculiar look and nodded.

Mark felt foolish asking the question, but he wanted Lana to feel secure. He boosted her up, and she managed to swing her short leg over the horse's rear. She grabbed the reins looking like he'd asked her to ride a bucking bronco. She towered above him, and he tipped his imaginary hat. "I'll be up on your level in a jiffy," he said, slipping his foot into his saddle's stirrup and swinging his leg over the saddle. "Nice weather up here."

"Are you kidding? Nothing's nice up here." She sent him a faint grin.

He patted the horse's mane. "Howdy, Fancy. You and I are going to be pals for an hour or so."

"Fancy?" Lana gave him and the horse a dubious look. "What kind of a name is that? Did you hear what they called my horse? If I need to plead with him, I'd like to address him by his first name.

Mark chuckled and tried to remember what the cowboy had mumbled. "Furry, I think. Sounds tame."

"Furry? That sounds like something they'd name a gerbil."

He grinned and looked ahead at the other riders. "Looks like they're moving out," Mark said, watching the dude with the cowboy hat wave them onto the trail. "Hang on."

Chapter 6

Hang on? Lana sent Mark a look with the power to turn a dew-glistening grape into a raisin. Hang on! That's what she had been doing. And tight. Feeling the shift and sway of the horse's back, Lana watched the teens ahead of her as they plodded toward the wooded path. Fat-rumped horses lumbered along, their reeking odor growing stronger in the morning sunlight.

Mark rode beside her, looking comfortable and tall in the saddle. His blond hair glinted like gold in the sunlight, and his friendly eyes sparkled even brighter.

With the clip-clop of the horse's hooves, a peculiar urge rose in Lana to sing some sentimental western song, like "Get Along Little Doggies" or "Tumbling Tumbleweed." Instead the words, "Don't bury me on the lone prairie," intruded into her thoughts, barging through her mind like a guitar-strumming posse.

The teens had moved ahead down the shadowed path, and though she'd moaned about the horseback riding, she enjoyed the quiet of the woods. Bird songs and the snap of twigs beneath the horse's hooves sounded crisp and friendly in the dappled sunlight.

"We'd better catch up," Mark said, coaxing his steed into a trot.

As he bounced forward, Lana stayed behind, clinging to the reins and avoiding giving even the flick of motivation against her horse's back. Her caution was unwarranted. Furry and Fancy must have had a thing for each other, because Furry didn't want to be left behind. He shifted into passing gear, and the horse and Lana flew past Mark at a ragged clip—her up, the horse down, and then the painful meeting in the middle.

As she tugged on the reins, Mark caught up with her. "Sorry, Lana. Usually these old nags barely move."

"Furry's spurred on by the smell of my perfume, I think," she said, grasping for any comic relief she could muster. "And I'd give a lot for one whiff of eau d'cologne instead of the whiff I'm getting."

A grin stretched across Mark's face. "Just know that you're a lifesaver. The kids are having fun, and I think these first outings will bring them closer together so we have a friendly, cohesive group for summer camp."

"Summer camp?" Her chest vibrated with each step as she smacked against the ironclad leather beneath her and felt the chafing of the horse's ballooned sides against her legs.

"Church camp. It's the first time our church will have camp for the youth. I think it's a great way for teens to learn about nature, themselves, and God.

Camping knits people together. They'll have memories they'll never forget."

She understood exactly what he meant. Her experience on this horse's back would cling to her memory like chewed gum to a shoe. Her bones rattled with each clop. "This horse and I aren't in sync. I think I've jarred my teeth loose," Lana said, wishing for a bathtub filled with warm, soothing, bubbly water.

"Gallops are natural and easier. Let's try."

Before she could protest, Mark dug his heels into Fancy's sides, and with the flick of the reins, he was off. Lana grabbed hold, knowing that Furry wasn't about to be outdone.

Sure enough, Furry gave a snort, and Lana sailed past Mark, clinging to the reins with one hand and the saddle horn with the other, but Mark had been right. She and the animal moved with the same up-down motion, and the ride would have been exhilarating except Lana realized that somehow the saddle hadn't been tightened properly. She felt herself slipping sideways. Seeing the woods from a vantage point parallel to the ground had not been part of the deal. She clung to the horse's scruffy mane for dear life, praying the saddle would stay put.

She'd caught up with the teens, but Furry had the zeal of a winner and had no plans to let another horse get in the way of the winner's circle.

With the thud of hooves and her beating heart, Lana galloped past a group of teens.

"Look at her go," Dennis called out.

"No fair," Susan grumbled. "How come she gets the best horse?"

An old adage with a new twist careened through Lana's thoughts. "Best is in the eye of the beholder," she yelled into the air. She would have willingly traded horses with the girl and thrown in a twenty-dollar bill to boot.

No more complaints met her ears, only a pitiful titter as she struggled to stay mounted. For the first time in her life, she understood the true meaning of sidesaddle.

About the time she thought she could bear no more, the path turned, and to her relief, the stables loomed straight ahead. But as Lana uttered a grateful sigh, Furry spotted the stable, too. Apparently ready for lunch and a nap, the horse gave a resounding snort and whinny, then seemingly sprouted wings and bolted forward with momentum just short of a Concorde's.

"Look at Miss West," Gary echoed behind her. "I wish I was riding Fury."

Fury? Her heart rose to her throat. She distinctly remembered Mark calling the brute Furry. And forget the well-worn path. Whether Furry or Fury, she and the steed left the others eating dust. As they flew across the field, her life ripped past in fast-forward.

The horse stopped before she did, and when woman and beast finally focused on each other, face-to-face, Lana found herself sprawled in his dinner on the floor of a stall.

Mark tore in behind her, waving his arms in panic. "Are you okay?" He stood over her, his face pale and pinched with concern. When he saw she had survived, his fear shifted gears to the familiar laugh that she'd grown to know too well.

"Put a muzzle on it," she said, rising to her feet and pulling straw from her hair. "Or you'll be eating this stuff."

She lifted an eyebrow, but the picture was too much even for her. Lana's laughter joined Mark's, and as she walked away from the stable, she had to admit her pride hurt much worse than her backside.

❦

By Monday, Lana could move her stiff, sore legs with greater agility. The "horse-side" ride, an apt name, lingered in her thoughts like an abscessed tooth. Yet if she were to admit it, the time spent with Mark gave the outing its pleasurable moments.

When the doorbell rang after dinner, she eased herself off the chair and went to the door. Mark stood on the porch with a sheepish grin and a bouquet of flowers.

"I should have gotten these to you earlier." He thrust his flower-laden hand toward her. "Accept these with my deep thanks and condolences." He made a gallant bow.

Lana grinned and swung the screen door open. "You look too humble. It doesn't suit you at all. Come on in."

He stepped past her into the foyer, and she swung the front door closed against the hot sunlight. Turning, she eyed his broad chest and recalled how handsome he looked on horseback. And how tender he'd been after his laughter had subsided.

She buried her nose in the bouquet, then looked into his eyes. The sparkle gave her heart a flutter, and she turned away before admiration rose to her face. "Let me get these in water."

"Good idea." His voice rang with playfulness behind her.

"You can have a seat." She motioned toward the living room and continued her journey to the kitchen.

Opening a cabinet, she pulled out a vase and filled it with water. She unwrapped the florist paper and drew out the baby's breath from the bouquet. Touched by Mark's lovely gift, she nested their stems into water, then added the miniature carnations, daisies, and lilies.

"Looks good," he said.

She turned and found him standing in the doorway. "Thanks. They're beautiful."

"Not as pretty as you, though," he said, his gaze riveted to hers.

Startled by his comment, she faltered for a moment before finding something to say. "Now I know you're trying to wheedle me into something."

He smiled, but she feared she saw disappointment in his eyes. Trying to epair the damage, Lana carried the bouquet to him and tiptoed to kiss his cheek. Thanks. I haven't had anyone give me flowers since. . . See? I can't even remember the last time."

He rested his palm on her arm. "You're more than welcome."

"I'll put them on the table," she said, beckoning him into the living room.

He followed her and plopped his tall frame into an easy chair, then stretched his legs out in front of him. "How are you feeling? I notice the limp is fading."

She sank onto the sofa. "My hobble's disappearing but not the memory. I've ended my cowgirl career. Not even your pleading tears will ever move me to agree to a venture like that again."

He squirmed with a grin. "How are you with canoes?"

Her head zoomed upward. "Why?" She narrowed her eyes, hoping the look pinned him to the chair.

"Just making conversation." A wry look filtered across his face.

Her stomach tightened. "Like pig's wings. Tell me the truth." Gazing into his face, she felt herself weakening—with or without his pleading.

"I'm teasing." He leaned forward, elbows on his knees. "I'm working on the Christian camp activities. I think it will be fun."

"Some people's idea of fun isn't healthy," she said, enjoying his puzzled expression.

"But camping is. Fresh air, nature, exercise, and God."

"Great. I had my rebuttal planned, but you ruined it. How can I say anything negative when you included the Lord in your list?" She folded her arms across her chest.

"I know you can't. That was my plan."

She unfolded her arms and sent him a sweet smile. "Want to know my plan? What I've been thinking about—while sitting here wounded and in misery?"

"Okay. What?" he asked, rising and sliding next to her on the sofa. "Tell me. Maybe it's the same thing that's on my mind."

She caught an innuendo in his comment, and it rattled her. She liked him— a lot. But Mark seemed too perfect for her. Too optimistic. Too expecting. He presumed she experienced his enthusiasm for life and his penchant for helping others. On the other hand, life did seem more exciting when he was around.

"Why so quiet?" he asked.

"I'm thinking about what might be on your mind, because I doubt if it's paint and wallpaper."

He collapsed against the sofa back and groaned. "You mean you haven't forgotten that project?"

"I haven't forgotten the project or your offer." She moved her face closer to his and looked him straight in the eyes. "I believe it went something like, 'Name it. I'm yours.'"

He inhaled, and the zesty scent of mint filled the space between them.

"I recall hearing someone say that." He pressed his palm against her cheek. "You don't really want me to paint. I'll drip the stuff all over the place."

Flustered by his closeness, she eased away. "I use drop cloths. No problem."

"I suppose I owe you this," he said, standing and eyeing the walls. "Are we painting this room? It looks good to me."

"No. The dining room and my bedroom. . .plus I'm doing stenciling in there." She rose and showed him the decorating plans she had for the summer. "And I want to buy border for the dining room to go around at the height where you usually find chair molding."

"Okay. I give. You're about as manipulative as I am."

Lana grabbed his waist from behind and guided him into the kitchen. "Hungry?"

He turned and faced her. "Starving, but I want to take you out to dinner for a change."

"Don't trust me?" she asked.

"Sure I do, but the flowers were only part of my apology." He shook his head, his face earnest. "When I saw you sprawled out on the stable floor, I—" His laugh started with a chuckle.

"You laughed. I know." She poked him in the ribs. "So listen here, Mr. Nice Guy. Not only do you buy me dinner, but we're picking out paint samples. Maybe even the border."

"A—all that for a little. . .laughter?" he sputtered.

Lana gave him a nudge. "He who laughs last, laughs best. You'd better remember that."

Music spilled out into the air as Lana climbed the steps to the church entrance. Since Barb lagged behind, Lana didn't wait and headed inside. She'd missed church the previous Sunday, unable to sit on the hard pews, and now she dreaded to face the teens who'd watched her make her sidesaddle debut on a horse named Fury.

When she entered the vestibule, Mark waited for her and waved in greeting.

"The kids have been asking about you," he said.

"Did you tell them I survived the ordeal with minimal scars?"

He hooked his arm through hers. "I told them you were wonderful. Do you mind if I sit with you?"

She scanned the congregation, wondering what people might say. "If you think you can deal with the gossip."

"No gossip in here. It's a sin." With a grin, he released her arm but walked beside her to the middle of the sanctuary, then motioned her into a row.

"Keep an eye out for Barb." Lana turned, looking over her shoulder for her sister. She spotted her a few rows back, seated with a man Lana didn't know. She turned back to Mark. "Never mind," she whispered, "she's with a friend."

Playfully, she wiggled her eyebrows.

"Really? Let me check him out." Mark glanced behind him.

Lana shifted and gave another subtle glance, but instead, her eyes focused on a young man sliding into a back pew. She swung back toward Mark. "The boy from my class is here. The one I invited to visit the church. Remember? Don Fabrizio."

"He is? Where?" He twisted in the seat and glanced over his shoulder.

She turned again. "In the third row from the back. He's wearing a blue knit shirt."

"I wonder if I should send one of the kids over to sit with him." He shifted and faced the front. "I could probably ask Gary."

"I don't think so. Don might feel uncomfortable. Let's wait until after the service."

As Mark nodded, the organ began the introduction, and they rose to sing the first hymn.

As the service continued, Lana wondered how Don felt worshiping alone in an unfamiliar church. She didn't want to turn around so she kept her eyes forward, but her thoughts stayed with the young man. When Pastor Phil rose and began his sermon, Lana's pulse heightened as she listened to the verses he read from Ezekiel 18:

> The word of the Lord came to me: "What do you people mean by quoting this proverb about the land of Israel:
> " 'The fathers eat sour grapes, and the children's teeth are set on edge'?
> "As surely as I live, declares the Sovereign Lord, you will no longer quote this proverb in Israel. For every living soul belongs to me, the father as well as the son—both alike belong to me. The soul who sins is the one who will die."

Pastor Phil laid his Bible down and looked at the congregation. "Today we will focus on what God expects of us. In these verses, we learn that we must learn to follow Jesus' call without worrying about our family's failings. We do not take on the sins of our father. What we do is follow Jesus and let Him rule our lives."

Lana let the words wash over her. She knew God's Word could give Don hope. He could throw off the weight of his father's sin. His task was to follow Jesus. But could the teenager do that? Her own past dragged through her mind. How long had she tried to prove herself to the world to make herself worthy of the gifts she received just as she struggled to show her father appreciation? But her gratitude now was not to a single person or the world. She had nothing to prove and would never be worthy except by the grace of God through Jesus.

Bathed in that thought, she settled back and prayed Don had also been touched by the message. She felt Mark's hand resting beside hers on the pew. She longed to cover it with her palm, to feel his pulse beating beneath her fingers, but she pushed the thought away.

They rose for the last hymn, and when the service ended, Lana clutched Mark's arm and hurried them through the departing worshipers to reach Don. "Hello," she said, grasping the young man's arm. "I'm so glad you came."

"I–I surprised myself," he said. "I woke up this morning, and something made me get up early. Next thing I know, I'm walking to church."

Lana gave Mark a knowing look, recognizing how God had worked in the teenager's life. She grasped his arm. "Don, this is Mark Branson, the youth director I told you about."

"Hi," Mark said. "I'm pleased you accepted Miss West's invitation." He extended his hand, and the young man grasped it in a firm shake.

"Like I said, I surprised myself," Don said. He shifted his eyes toward a group of teens as if looking for someone his age.

Lana gave Mark a desperate look.

Thinking quickly, he flagged one of the nearby teens, and Gary joined him with a smile.

"Hi, Don," Gary said. "What are you doing here?"

Mark chuckled. "Same as you probably. Worshiping the Lord."

Gary looked embarrassed. "I knew that. I meant I've never seen you here before," he said, addressing Don.

"Miss West suggested I visit some Sunday." He tucked his hands in his pocket and lowered his eyes. "And here I am."

"Glad you're here," Gary said. "Hey, what about tonight? We're having a planning meeting for summer camp, but it's a pizza party, too. What do you say?"

Don grinned. "Pizza sounds good."

"And the church pays for it," Mark added. "That makes it extra special." He gave Don's arm a friendly shake. "After our meeting, we usually have a Bible study."

Don nodded. "I have a Bible."

"Then bring it along," Lana added.

"Will you be there, Miss West?"

She wanted to sink into the ground. "Well. . .I. . ." Mark's gaze riveted to her face, and she read the message in his eyes. "I–I'll be there. Sure."

Mark's hand slipped to her arm and gave it a squeeze.

Somehow either Mark or God or both were involving her in things she had no intention of doing—just like Barb had done over the past years. Lana paused, letting the thought wash over her. She was strong willed and purposeful. If she really didn't want to do these things, why would she agree? Had she been led because that's what she wanted to do in her heart all along?

Chapter 7

Lana plucked a pepperoni from her pizza wedge and dropped it into her mouth, enjoying the spicy tang. She chewed and swallowed, then took a full bite of pizza. The zesty sauce and rich creamy cheese lay on her tongue, and she licked her lips to capture every morsel.

"Good, isn't it?" Don said, sitting beside her.

"Sure is," she said, watching Don's expression as he chowed down a large slice.

"We don't get pizza at home," he said. "My dad wants meat and potatoes."

"Then this is a treat," she added, not wanting to say more in earshot of other teens.

He nodded.

Although Don seemed a little uneasy, the kids he knew from school had been sociable and welcoming. Lana prayed this would be only the beginning for her student.

The pizza vanished quickly, and while Lana cleared up the boxes and paper plates, Mark started the meeting. She heard only snatches of the conversation, and when she settled down with the group, they had turned to the topic of the camping trip's purpose.

Dressed in khakis and a blue-and-beige knit top, Mark stood beside a podium and addressed the teens with his usual patience and good nature. "Sure, camp is for having fun," he said, obviously not wanting to embarrass the girl who'd offered fun as the trip's purpose, "but besides fun, what else can we accomplish?"

Like any classroom, the answers varied—exercise, a good tan, appreciation for home cooking—but eventually more serious answers evolved.

"Friendship," Gary said.

"Good answer," Mark said, focusing on Gary. "What do you mean by friendship?"

The teen scowled, appearing uncertain how to respond. "Well, getting to know each other better."

"And care about the other campers," Teri said.

"We'll learn things we have in common," Jason called out.

"Great," Mark said, smiling as the answers flew. "Anything else?"

"Learning new things," Don said, "you know. . .like archery maybe."

Mark nodded.

"Or canoeing."

"And canoeing helps us learn something else." Mark looked over the faces

175

and grinned. "How about cooperation?"

"Right," Gary said. "You can't canoe without that."

"So we can learn cooperation. What else?" Mark asked.

"Compromise," Lana added. "How to split the difference."

A quirky grin appeared on his face. "Miss West is right. Sometimes we have to know when to give a little."

"Cooperation means teamwork," Susan added.

"Now we're getting somewhere," Mark said, "because teamwork is one of our major focuses on our trip. Think about teamwork. What's part of teamwork? We've already mentioned cooperation and compromise. How about another C word? Communication."

"You can't cooperate if you don't communicate," Dennis called out.

"Excellent. You're right. If we don't communicate, nothing happens. We're at a standstill."

"Trust," Don said. "We have to trust people to do their part when we work as a team. . .like in football."

"That's so true, Don. Trust is a vital factor in all kinds of relationships— employer-employee, child-parent, romance, marriage, and God."

"How will we learn about trust at camp?" Susan asked.

Mark laughed. "That's my surprise. You can expect a lot of challenges as well as a lot of fun."

"And a lot of learning," Lana added, thinking about the types of activities Mark might use to teach the teens teamwork. . .and trust.

Mark pulled a Bible from beneath the podium. "Speaking of trust, let's take a look at God's Word. Do you all have Bibles? If not, share. Okay?"

Shuffles and murmurs rattled in the air while they opened their Bibles and agreed who would share with whom. Having heard about the Bible study, Lana had brought hers along and waited for Mark's direction. When a hush settled over the crowd, Mark began.

"Open the Scripture to Matthew 11:28. Follow along with me: 'Come to me, all you who are weary and burdened, and I will give you rest. Take my yoke upon you and learn from me, for I am gentle and humble in heart, and you will find rest for your souls. For my yoke is easy and my burden is light.' " He stood a moment looking out over the teens. "What does Jesus mean in these verses?"

A hush settled over the room, and Lana watched the teens' faces, twisted with bewilderment or eyes lowered to avoid being called upon. As always, Mark waited with patience. Lana filled with admiration. He had a way with young people—not a friend exactly, but like a counselor, probing and challenging, but without judgment.

When Lana could no longer bear the silence and wanted to send out a response herself, a girl raised her hand, and Mark nodded toward her.

"I understand the easy part," she said. "Jesus invites us to give our problems to Him rather than try to handle them all by ourselves."

Mark nodded and sent the girl a smile.

Silence weighed on the room.

Lana noticed Don squirming as if wanting to speak. Finally, he lifted his hand, and Mark gave him a nod.

"I'm not sure I understand that second part," he said. "The part about take my yoke on you." A frown settled on his face. "A yoke is like a harness that holds two oxen together, right?"

"That's right," Mark said. "Oxen or any draft animal. Horses, too."

"So Jesus isn't just telling us to dump our problems on Him and split."

When the group giggled, Lana cringed, fearing Don would be offended, but Don grinned along with them.

Mark pushed the subject forward. "What is Jesus telling us, Don?"

"That He'll share the weight of our problems?" His face filled with anxiety.

Mark gave him a thumbs up. "Absolutely, Don."

The teen's expression switched to pleasure.

"Okay, someone else answer this," Mark said. "What's the problem with sharing the weight of a heavy load with someone?"

Murmurs rose from the teens, but no one responded.

"It's teamwork, right? You need to communicate," Mark said, prodding them to think.

"Don't you need to trust that someone's carrying their half of the load?" Gary asked.

"Aha. We're back to trust again," Mark said. "That's right, Gary."

Lana listened to the discussion on trust and thought about her own trust issues. Was she so afraid to trust others she had to be in charge to make sure the job was done right? Did she look at God's promises in the same way? Why would God be willing to bear her burdens?

Her thoughts drifted to her own petite stature. Too short. Too unsubstantial. So many things she couldn't carry or reach by herself. Family and friends always had to pitch in and help her. She realized Jesus made the same promise but about things that were bigger and more serious. He offered to bear the load and give His children rest.

By the time she'd tuned back into the conversation, the topic had shifted from trust to summer camp. The students raised questions, and Mark shot back answers.

"We'll have at least two parent chaperones. Maybe three," Mark said. "Each of them will be responsible for a cabin."

"You, too?" Gary asked.

"Sure thing. I'll take a cabin."

"I want to be in Miss West's cabin," Susan said. "Okay?" She looked at Lana. Lana sank into her chair, wishing she could vanish. After listening to their conversation on trust and cooperation, how could she tell the girl she had no interest in being a camp counselor?

Mark's amusement was blatant. A grin stretched across his face from sideburn to sideburn. "What do you say, Miss West?"

"Lana," she said. "I feel like someone's grandmother with the 'Miss West' tag." The crowd hooted and laughed.

She'd avoided the answer, and the topic turned in another direction as she sighed with relief.

"I'll be calling a meeting with all of the parents so we can set down the ground rules," Mark said. "Any questions?"

Heads shook no, but Dennis asked if there was any more pizza. That line got another laugh, and finally, the group rose and began their trek to the door.

Lana stood off in the distance, fearing Susan might corner her again about being a camp counselor. When the last teen vanished through the doorway, Lana released a panicked gasp. She eyed Mark across the room, a smile still brightening his face.

"Trapped," he said. "I saw you squirm. The kids want you to come along."

"No way. I have teens under my feet all year, remember? And I hate camping."

"Teens under your feet all year means you're skilled. Don't forget, you have two weeks to get prepared."

"Prepared?" She crumpled into a folding chair. "What about my paint and wallpaper?"

"You've got me. I'm your handy-dandy painter man. We'll have that job licked before we leave."

Looking at his kind face and good-humored smile, her arguments sounded weak. "But I detest sleeping bags and bugs. Not to mention snakes."

"I won't mention them—not once. Promise." He crossed his heart with his index finger. "The job's not bad," he added, his voice soft and convincing. "You'd only have to sleep in the cabin to keep an eye on them and help with a couple group activities. That's it. No horses. I promise. The rest of the time you'd be on your own. Like a mini-vacation."

"About as mini as you can get." She disliked camping and bugs more than she could say, but the look in his tender eyes tugged at her heart. He was all a woman could want—sweet, funny, handsome, and truly filled with the fruit of the Spirit. She liked that.

"What are you thinking?" he asked.

She felt her frozen determination thawing.

He didn't push her, but waited, his patience overwhelming. He fiddled with his cuticle, giving her an occasional cursory glance as if too much motion would refreeze her block of resolve.

As her resistance puddled at her feet, she turned to soft mush. "How long is the stay at camp?"

His head triggered upward. "Two weeks."

"Two weeks." The words rumbled from her in a moan. "What happened to all the one-week camping trips?"

"No good for our purpose. Team-building, Bible study, and fun—two weeks works best. We'll leave on a Saturday and come back a week from the following Friday."

"You're making two weeks sound like a short time," she said, recognizing a con job when she saw one.

"I know, but think about this. Not only would I appreciate your coming along, the Lord will, too."

"Did you ask Him?" She sent him a half-hearted grin. "Do you promise to never darken my door again with another request?"

A lengthy silence filled the room, and the look of guilt settled over his face. "I. . .I don't want to promise never. But how's this? I'll really try to never ask you for a favor like this again."

"That makes me feel much better."

His chuckle joined hers. And though she hadn't agreed, they both knew she'd go.

❦

Mark climbed down the ladder, then examined the ceiling. It looked good to him, but he was also aware of Lana's high expectations. Good to him and good to her could mean two different things. "What do you think?" he asked as he rested his brush across the edge of the paint can.

Lana turned toward him, and when he saw her face, an amused grin tugged at his mouth.

"What?" she asked. Her eyes narrowed, and her head tilted at a questioning angle.

"The ceiling." He looked upward, admiring his work. "What do you think?"

She gave her head a quick shake. "Not that. What's the silly smile for?"

"One thing at a time," he said, closing the distance between them. He guided her head upward. "The ceiling? Good or bad?"

"The ceiling looks great." She tugged her chin to its normal position. "Now, why the grin?"

He touched her cheek. "The war paint. It looks great on you. . .but then, most things do."

The feel of her soft, warm skin sent a sweet sensation down his arm, and his pulse did an unexpected jog.

"War paint?" She fingered her cheek and backed away through the dining-room doorway.

Mark watched her go, grinning at the splotch of hunter green latex on her cheek. He moved the ladder and eyed the can of paint the color he'd admired on

Lana's face. She had a long way to go to finish the walls. He needed to wash his brush and join her on that project.

In a moment, Lana returned, the paint splotch missing. Where it had been, only a rosy tinge remained, evidence of her vigorous scrubbing.

"Too bad," he said. "You look good in green."

"So will you. . .when I pour this can over your head." She sent him a teasing smile.

"Before I tackle the walls with you, how about a break?"

She glanced at her hands, now clean from her face scrubbing. "I suppose. . . before I'm speckled again."

Mark wiped the rim of his paint can with a rag, then tapped the lid onto the can with a rubber mallet. Lana did the same with the green latex, then straightened and headed for the kitchen.

"Want a sandwich?" she asked over her shoulder.

"Sure," he said, surveying his painting clothes before he settled into a wooden kitchen chair.

After swinging open the refrigerator door, Lana pulled open the meat drawer and lifted out ham slices and a wrapper of cheese.

"Can I help?" Mark asked, standing up. Lana handed him the packages, which he placed on the table, and as she pulled out lettuce and condiments, Mark got down two plates from the cabinet.

Lana poured iced tea into glasses, tore open a bag of chips, and settled at the table across from Mark.

He concentrated on building a sandwich, and after the blessing, he took a bite, enjoying the blend of meat and cheese. . .but even more Lana's company. He wondered if she felt the same. Her face looked content and relaxed, and lately Mark sensed they had both grown comfortable with each other.

"Thanks for helping me with this project," Lana said. "Ceilings are so difficult for me."

"I'm enjoying the challenge." Mark dropped a few potato chips onto his plate. "And you've certainly gone the extra miles for me and the teens."

She sat a moment in silence, her lips pursed in thought. "Odd you mention me and the kids. I've been giving that some thought myself."

"What? Going the extra mile?" And she truly had when he considered bowling, horseback riding, the meeting, and now her silent agreement to be a camp chaperone. The whole transition amazed him, and he definitely saw God's hand working the miracle.

"That, too, but. . .no, it's more than that." Her gaze lowered, and she stared at her plate a moment before looking up. "I'm really enjoying the kids at the church. Maybe the difference is that it's not my job. I'm not responsible for hammering knowledge into their heads. At the pizza meeting the other night, did you hear them?"

"Sure. . .but what do you mean exactly?" The comment stirred individual responses in his head—Gary, Susan, and the new boy Don.

Her eyes widened. "They were thinking." She pushed a strand of hair behind her ear. "Sure, you prodded a little, but they were expressing ideas on their own. And even better, they showed interest and asked meaningful questions. Why can't I teach like that?"

"Don't get down on yourself," Mark said, letting his hand slide across the table to capture hers. "We were dealing with a topic close to their hearts—the Lord and their relationships to Him and to each other. I wasn't trying to get them to put a comma in the right place or remember who was at the Alamo and what happened there."

"I suppose," she said, a thoughtful frown settling on her face. "I was so pleased when Don jumped in with his comments, and then I felt terrible when the kids laughed at him."

"Not at him. With him. There's a big difference, and laughter is a wonderful medicine. Do you realize how much healing takes place when we can laugh at our own failings and problems?"

She nodded, and a faint grin curved her lips. "Lately, I've had to admit some of my own ridiculous idiosyncrasies."

He squeezed her hand and longed to carry it to his lips and kiss the soft, smooth flesh that left him feeling addled. "They're not ridiculous. Not at all. Those qualities are what makes you you. They make you dear to my heart. They make me smile."

"So. . .you're laughing at me," she said, a lovely glow brightening her face.

"Laughing at humanity. What about my foolishness?" He winced waiting for her list.

"You aren't foolish at all."

Her response startled him. "Sure I am. What about making jokes all the time. . .even when I should give a serious answer? What about manipulating? Not the first time, but after that, I allowed things to progress, hoping to motivate you to come along with me and the teens. . .against your will."

"I don't know about that, Mark." She leaned forward and rested her palm against his fingers. "I thought about that the other day. You know how bullheaded I am."

Teasing, he nodded with an extra measure of enthusiasm. Again he was taunting when he should have been serious.

"Don't overdo it," she said, shaking her head at his silliness. "I started thinking about my response to stimuli. If I'm so set on doing things my own way, then why am I allowing myself to be manipulated?" She lifted her thoughtful face and locked her gaze with his.

Mark considered what she'd said. Was she saying she chose to be maneuvered? Did she want someone to take charge and control her? He couldn't quite believe that. "Maybe you don't have the patience to fight off people's exploitation." Hating to admit the truth, he meant himself.

She chuckled. "Patience. Now that's another problem. No, I wonder if deep in my heart I know what is right and really want to be more thoughtful and generous. Maybe it's just difficult to change the way I've functioned for so long. Sort of a pride issue. Do you understand?"

"You mean you have to keep proving to the world that you're tough and you can do it your own way?" He eyed her, wondering if he'd hit anywhere near what she was thinking.

"Right. Something like that. God wants me to be humble and hear His will." She turned her attention to the sandwich, lifted it to her mouth, and took a bite.

Feeling almost as if she were talking about him, Mark let the conversation fade and concentrated on his lunch. Yet curious, he wondered if she were telling him she felt she had changed. Change seemed to sneak up on people. It did on him. . . that day at college registration he'd learned when God wanted to improve him, He didn't sound the trumpets. Things just changed.

Lana rose, slipping the final chip from her plate into her mouth, and carried her dish to the sink.

After Mark finished his sandwich, he brushed the crumbs from the table to his plate, then followed her. Standing behind her at the sink, he let his gaze explore her petite frame, her slender arms busy beneath the tap, rinsing the dishes with a soapy sponge. He eyed an unruly strand of hair that wanted to be noticed, and on a whim, he lifted his finger and pushed it behind her ear. . .like she did so often.

She glanced at him over her shoulder, surprised yet smiling.

He longed to turn her around, to hold her in his arms and feel her slender body against his, but a warning harnessed his behavior. Let God's work continue in both of them. When the time seemed right, Mark would know in his heart—and most important, he would know God's will.

Instead of reacting as his heart desired, he lowered the dishes into the sink and backed away, wrapped in the scent of herbal shampoo and lemony dish soap. A prayer fluttered through his mind. *Keep my direction steady, heavenly Father, and guide me in the way that You want me to go. In Jesus' precious name.*

A sense of wholeness settled over him, and he followed Lana back to the dining room, readying to paint the walls while God coated his spirit with joy and insight.

❧

A warm summer breeze filtered across Lana's arms and ruffled her hair. She lifted her fingers and pulled them through her short locks, catching a glimpse of herself in a storefront window. Her heart skipped a beat, eyeing Mark beside her, his broad shoulders and impressive height dwarfing her in the reflection.

Lately, she'd felt smaller than usual, but not just physically. The expanse of Mark's heart had knocked her down a peg. The knock had been her own doing. Mark's generosity and kindness would never allow him to belittle her, but she measured herself against him as a person and found herself humbled by the experience. No, she'd not become perfect, but she sensed an improvement for which she felt grateful.

"I hope we have nice weather like this at camp," Mark said. He'd gained a healthy looking tan while playing basketball and volleyball with the teens in the church yard after school, getting to know them better.

"Me, too," Lana said. "I suppose we have to be prepared for everything."

Mark chuckled. "Not snow. But rain and cool evenings. Bring a sweatshirt and a poncho if you have one."

His helpful advice left Lana with less confidence about two weeks at camp, but she'd promised herself to focus on the bright side. "I have one."

She paused beside him at one of the few streetlights in town. While she waited, Mark's hand brushed hers, and to her delight, he wove his fingers through hers, giving her a hopeful glance.

Lana didn't hesitate, but tightened her grip to let him know she approved. She avoided looking at him for fear her emotions would show on her face. Instead, she kept her focus on the shop windows.

"Hungry?" Mark asked.

"Not really," she said, knowing the relationship she longed for couldn't be satisfied with food.

"How about some lemonade or maybe a dessert?"

"Lemonade sounds good," she said.

"Let's try the Holly Hotel," he suggested.

"Good idea. They might not be busy this time of day."

They crossed the street, and Lana ascended the steep steps, then waited while Mark opened the door to the historic hotel where Carrie Nation, the suffragette, had taken her axe to the hotel bar. Once inside, Lana admired the carved wainscoting and enjoyed the air-conditioning that cooled her arms. In a few minutes, the hostess seated them near the front windows covered with lace curtains that filtered the view of the street.

Lana declined dessert and sipped her lemonade while Mark dug into a slice of cheesecake with cherry sauce. She watched the red syrup escape the fork, and he licked his tongue across his lips, giving her a warm chuckle.

"I'm like a little kid. I can't stay away from the candy jar."

In her heart, Mark seemed far from a kid. He was all the man Lana wanted, even with his boyish behavior. She remained silent, enjoying the antique surroundings and the pleasant cool air while she watched him finish the dessert.

He pushed the plate aside and took a drink of iced tea. "I've been wanting to get your input," he said, leaning forward on his elbows, "about some of the team activities I could use. I have a couple ideas, but I thought you might have some others since you spend so much time with teenagers."

She shook her head. "I work in a classroom, and most of their activities are individual. They have group projects once in a while, like a report or panel discussion, but that wouldn't work in a camp setting."

He remained silent, his eyes focused on the white linen tablecloth. "I'll need an ice breaker on our first night. Something fun, but an activity that needs cooperation."

"How about a scavenger hunt?" she suggested, remembering the parties she'd attended in her youth.

"No neighbors here. Don't they have to knock on doors and ask for things?"

"You could list items they can find in the woods. Better yet, make it like a road rally where they have to decipher puzzles to figure out where to look for the next clue."

"I've never been on one," he said. "Guess I've missed something."

She chuckled. "Nothing life shattering. Let's see. A clue could be hidden near the canoes. Then you need to set up clues to lead them to the canoe. You might have five questions that need answers, and each answer begins with one of the letters that will spell out the location of the next clue."

"That sounds confusing. Give me an example."

She sighed. "Okay, let's take the canoe idea. First question. What thing a day keeps the doctor away?"

"Apple."

"Right," she said. "That gives you the letter A. Now where are Christians on Sunday morning?"

"Church," he said.

"Now you have the A and C. They know they're looking for the first letter of each word. After five questions, they'll have all the letters spelling canoe, and they shift them around until they know where to look."

"I get it. So what do they find at the canoe?"

"At the canoe, you'll have another puzzle for each team to solve. Each team figures out the solutions at different times, so usually one team is already gone before another one arrives. Road rallies are fun."

"And what do they get at the end?"

"You'll have a prize for the winning group. A special treat or reward of some kind."

"I like it. Could I count on you to organize that one for me?"

He gave her one of his sweet smiles she couldn't resist, and he knew it.

"I'll see what I can do," she said.

"Thanks." He sipped the iced tea, his finger brushing away the condensation. "My goal is to teach them to trust and have faith in each other but also to learn that they can trust the Lord, confident His direction is unfailing."

His direction is unfailing. Lana considered Mark's words, knowing that she really needed to listen to God's instruction. She knew she was falling in love with Mark, but even if he loved her in return, could she offer him the support he needed or be the partner that God commanded her to be?

Chapter 8

L ana glanced out the rear window of Mark's car and saw the large bus bounding behind them. They'd left the main highway, and now the washboard road rattled Mark's newer model car like a pair of maracas. For once her small stature seemed a blessing since she'd noticed Mark's head occasionally smack the roof of the car when he hit the bigger potholes.

Lana felt her fast-food lunch flipping around in her stomach. "You'd think they'd grate this cow path, wouldn't you?" she asked.

"They probably don't want campers to get too hopeful," Mark said, rubbing the top of his head from the previous bump.

"Too hopeful about what?" Though she asked the question, fear settled into her well-shaken stomach.

"Not to expect too much luxury," he answered.

"But what about necessity? A car's axle is not what I'd call a luxury."

"Good point," he said as he hit another jarring hole. "Camps have low budgets, I suppose. Church camps are funded by congregations' generosity."

Lana shifted in her seat. "Let's pray that the First Church of Holly will become a generous donor."

He grinned and gripped the vibrating steering wheel.

Looking behind her, Lana spied the sway and bounce of the bus and felt grateful she'd been able to ride with Mark. Two parents had volunteered for bus duty, and Mark had said one car was needed for an emergency. Emergencies were now on Lana's thankful list.

"There it is," Mark said, pointing through the windshield off to the right.

Lana strained to see a group of smaller log cabins nestled in a wide semicircle beside a larger building. "That must be the office," she said.

"Office, cafeteria, game room, and meeting rooms, I imagine. I've been to a few camps in my day. They're all about the same."

But as they drew closer, Lana cringed. From a distance, the rustic cabins had looked truly rustic, which made her nervous. When they pulled into the camp grounds and stopped, "from a distance" had become the best view of her two-week accommodations.

She stepped from the car and watched the teens spill from the bus, carrying sleeping bags and duffel bags. The driver opened the rear and unloaded suitcases, boxes, and overnight bags.

While they gathered their belongings, Mark spoke to the camp director, and soon everyone had gathered to receive their cabin assignments. As the director called names and assigned a cabin, the campers moved to the side.

Lana waited for hers while one of the parents beckoned a group to follow her to a cabin called Running Deer. Another counselor herded a group toward Sleeping Bear. With her obvious inexperience, she feared her bunkhouse might be called Dying Hawk or Wounded Possum, but she smiled when she heard her cabin assignment: Little Flower. Now that name she liked. In moments, Mark led his crew across the grass toward Soaring Eagle, and Lana eyed the log cabin in the opposite direction and assumed it was hers.

When she stepped inside, a dank, mildew aroma greeted her, and Lana remembered Flower was the skunk's name in the children's tale Bambi. Grasping for optimism, she told herself that mildew was better than skunk smell any day.

As she peered at the log-walled room with only a narrow walkway between bunk beds, she questioned her sanity. Even a self-respecting mouse would avoid the drafty, damp interior for some cozy nest in a knothole.

Just like the rodent, Lana wished for such a sanctuary. Instead, she herded eight chattering teenage girls into a twenty-by-sixteen-foot space, no closets, and a makeshift nightstand void of even a candle, let alone a lamp. Five grimy windows and two glaring overhead bulbs served as the only sources of light.

Forcing her too large suitcase beneath her cot, Lana panicked. Where was the bathroom? With one door at the back and another at the front, the answer to her question did not seem promising. She folded her arms as a war cry sounded in her head. Mark had called this a mini-vacation with a wonderful natural setting. No bathroom was too natural for Lana. She darted outside, ready to wring Mark's neck.

The other cabin stood across a stretch of grass and dirt, and Mark stood outside herding in his charges. Catching his eye, she strode toward him, but he turned and appeared to be heading in the opposite direction. "Wait up, Mr. Youth Director," Lana called.

Mark stopped while Lana watched his grimace tug into a Cheshire Cat smile that didn't fool her. "I didn't know," he said before she could say a word.

Her fists jabbed against her waist. "You mean you didn't check the place out first?"

His arms flailed out from his sides. "I read their brochures. It sounded typical to me. Rustic cabins, sandy beaches, canoes, hiking, archery. What more could a person want?"

"How about walls without cracks, a lamp on the nightstands, a hook for clothes, and a door that leads somewhere other than outside."

Mark moved toward her and wrapped his arm around her shoulders. "Sounds like you've never been camping."

She nodded her head voraciously, hoping he sensed her sarcasm. "You can say that again. And what about a restroom?"

"About fifty yards that way," he said, his finger aimed at a small, gray building. "I hope you remembered a flashlight."

She arched a brow. "And shower?"

His mouth curled to a sheepish grin. "The camp director said there's only one shower." Mark lifted a half-hearted finger toward another less-than-eye-catching building about one hundred yards away. "That means we need a schedule. Women shower at night and men in the morning."

"Dandy." She gave him her best evil eye.

Mark squeezed her shoulder reassuringly. "Hey, cheer up. Once you get into the spirit of it all, you'll think camping's fun. And things could be worse."

"They could? How?"

He tweaked her cheek and spun on his heel toward his own home-away-from-home. Before Lana took a step, a shriek pealed from her cabin. She raced back and met two teens exiting as she attempted to enter. "What happened?" she asked as she studied their ashen faces.

"A mouse. . .with wings," Susan screeched.

"Bats," Teri corrected her in a pitch that didn't sound as confident as her response.

Wrapping her arm around her hair—just in case—Lana darted inside. As she gaped toward the ceiling, she saw what had panicked the girls. A frightened bat had awakened from its rest in the rafters and was dive-bombing the bunks. Recalling her line about no self-respecting mouse, she realized she hadn't thought about a lowly bat. Apparently they didn't care at all where they lived.

But she did.

Though she wanted to be a good sport, a bat in her bunkhouse wasn't acceptable. She spun around and marched outside. With one sweeping view of the area, she headed for a building marked "Camp Office." She would give them a piece of her mind—maybe two pieces while she felt in the mood.

❦

Mark looked around the quiet cabin and took a full breath. Along with the stale, damp odor, he smelled relief. He'd gotten his nine young men organized and sent them out to enjoy the scenery. The two parent counselors had finished setting up their cabins, and most everyone had drifted off in various directions.

Though the cabins were a disappointment, he'd spied the water and headed that way, praying he'd find the wide beach he'd admired in the brochure along with a few sturdy canoes and rowboats. Usually optimistic, he smiled when he saw the narrow sandy shoreline. At least one thing in the pamphlet appeared to be somewhat accurate. Canoes and a couple rowboats had been piled along the grassy bank, and he eyed them, looking for telltale holes. Seeing nothing but solid wood, his optimism grew. If they could survive the beyond-rustic cabins, the two weeks might prove to be enjoyable.

Already teens were sitting cross-legged in the grass, talking, while others waded through the cadet blue water. Some he'd seen heading in the opposite direction, he assumed to investigate the wooded paths and discover where they led.

Alone for a moment, Mark eased himself down on the grassy bank and stared across the sun-specked water. He hadn't told Lana the whole story of his struggle with his career. Someday he would. Even today, he wondered sometimes if the job suited him. He enjoyed the teens—cared about them with all his heart—but that was the problem. Would he be a good role model? Could he allow them to grow on their own terms without manipulating them?

He'd struggled against his parents' will for the sake of being an individual. Could he allow the students their individuality and still guide them in God's Word? The responsibility awed him, and he feared it. How much easier to be a coach. To list rules on sportsmanship and not be directing someone in God's rules. He didn't feel worthy. Maybe he should have forced his hand to register for the gym teacher and coach classes.

Why did he question God's will? Sometimes he wondered if God was forcing his will or if his own need to stay close to the Lord motivated him. Other times, he felt assured that God had led him for His own purposes. With his debut as a youth director at First Church of Holly, Mark prayed that the Lord would validate his decision.

Lana's image rose in his mind. He'd pushed her to the limit, but this too he sensed was God's direction. Since the day he'd watched her strut across her yard, wielding the hedge trimmer, he'd recognized a woman with spirit and a sense of humor. He loved both of those attributes. And despite her sometimes focusing on herself, he believed a compassionate heart beat within her. Obviously, Lana had embraced Jesus and was a true Christian—but a Christian, he feared, who had allowed one of her "fruits of the Spirit" to spoil on the vine. He grinned at his imaginative speculation, wondering how much of his own fruit was decaying.

He focused heavenward as a feeling of God's presence washed over him. The sunlight pierced through a billow of cumulus clouds like a heavenly beam striking the rippling water, almost as if God's spotlight stirred the lake and pinpointed the horizon. Could this camping experience be part of God's design? He'd already seen Lana change more than his teasing and pushing could have caused. And he felt his own heart moving closer to the Lord. Would being here bring Lana and him new insight into their relationship?

"Fancy meeting you here." Surprisingly good-natured, Lana's voice surged behind him.

A warm prickle rose on his neck, and he glanced at her over his shoulder.

"At least the camp manager apologized," she said, plopping down on the grass at his side. "He promised he'd make sure the bat found another cave to sleep in. . .since I can't." She tilted her head and shifted her body to view his face.

Mark touched her arm. "I'm sorry, Lana. The place isn't quite what the brochure said, but for our purpose, I pray it works. God's here as well as at the Ritz Hotel."

Lana covered his fingers with her own, her voice gentle. "To be honest, I prefer this to the Ritz." She shook her head and gazed around as if stunned. "I can't believe I said that."

"I hope you meant it, because I feel the same way." Her face shone in the warm sunlight, and his heart skipped, sensing their nearness.

"In some ways, I do. Though I admit a convenient bathroom would be awfully nice."

He agreed wholeheartedly, but he'd never utter the words or else he'd be rewarded with her I-told-you-so smile.

"Just be grateful," he said, knowing his comment had a cryptic element.

"Grateful for what?" She leaned forward and a scowl settled on her face.

"At least these flush."

Her chuckle rose on the quiet breeze. "I didn't think about that."

His attention turned toward the heavenly glow rippling on the lake. "We'll have our first Bible study after dinner tonight. When we're finished, I thought you could introduce the team activity you planned. If they're still not worn out when it's over, we'll end with a campfire and sing-along."

"That sounds safer than horseback riding." She turned her head slowly toward him. "I think." With her last comment, she rose.

"We could roast a few marshmallows," he said, as if that made it even safer.

She only grinned. "I'm heading back to check out the rest of the facilities. I need to know what else I'm in for."

❦

As Lana approached her cabin, the sound of youthful voices carried across the grass from the activity building, and in the open field, she saw a volleyball game in progress. The playful cheers and boos sailed to her ears and, for once, sounded inviting. Expecting the cabin to be empty, she faltered when she stepped inside. A dark-haired teen Lana didn't know raised her head from the pillow and looked at her, then lowered it again. The girl's eyes looked red rimmed, and Lana hesitated, wondering how the girl would react when she approached her.

"What's wrong?" she asked, then waited in silence for the teen to respond.

A muffled "I'm fine" rose from the sleeping bag.

Lana wandered to her own cot and sat, gazing at the girl two bunks over. "Doesn't sound like it."

"Doesn't really matter," the girl said.

Lana rose and slid onto the next bunk, facing her. "Sure it does." She waited a moment before she spoke again. "Sometimes having someone listen helps," Lana offered again.

"My parents say I have eternal PMS." Her voice muffled in her pillow.

Lana chuckled but couldn't help the pull of emotion as she looked at the bundle of sadness lying on the bunk. "It's good to have a sense of humor."

With apparent curiosity, the young woman lifted her head.

Lana smiled into her amazed, wide eyes. "I often laugh at myself. It's better than crying. . .and much better than getting angry."

The girl rolled on her side and propped her cheek against her fist. "I usually get angry. . .at myself. I rarely let other people know I'm upset. It doesn't do any good."

"What's the use of getting angry at yourself? Laughter's lots better." She moved closer to the teen. "For some reason, I haven't met you before. I'm Lana West."

The teenager paused, then nodded. "Janet. Janet Byrd. Or 'Bird the Nerd' as they call me." Her voice rang with sarcasm.

When she heard Janet's comment, Lana's stomach twisted with disappointment. So many times at the high school, she'd heard the taunting remarks of teens to one another. Sometimes they could be so cruel. But she expected Christians to behave better. "Do you mean one of the kids from church called you that?"

"No. I usually hear it at school." She stared at her pillow and then added, "My parents insisted that I come here. It wasn't my idea. Not at all."

Lana shifted and sat on the foot of Janet's bunk. "Ah, I can hear it now. 'Janet, it'll be good for you.'"

The girl sat up cross-legged, then grinned for the first time. "Right. I heard that when I was a little girl. 'Janet, this spanking hurts me more than it hurts you.'" She giggled.

"I remember hearing the same line. Do you think God programs that sentence into parents?"

"Could be," she said, taking a strand of hair and twirling it around her finger. "I guess I'm feeling sorry for myself. I've always been a loner. I don't come to the youth activities at church, so I don't know these kids."

"That makes it hard," Lana said, knowing now why she'd never met the girl.

"We moved to a rural area last year. I go to Fenton High, and most of the kids from church go to Holly or Davisburg."

"It's hard to get to know new people, isn't it? Especially if you're not involved in the activities. You attend church, though?"

She nodded. "But that's it. I don't drive yet, and my parents don't want to drop me off and pick me up for teen Sunday school and things, so. . ." Her voice faded away.

Lana gathered her thoughts. "Even though you don't know them well, Janet, you share something important with these kids."

"Not school." A look of frustration crossed her face.

"No, not school. Something much better and more important."

The teen's expression shifted to curiosity.

"Jesus. That's much more important than everything. Give the kids a chance, Janet. I can't promise you miracles. You know as well as I do that teenagers can be great or they can be unkind, but hopefully, the kids at church camp will be an improvement over the high school students. The problem is you have to give a little, too."

"They seem to look past me," she said, stretching her legs out and lowering her feet to the floor.

"It's because they don't know you, and when you look away or look uneasy, they protect their own feelings by not taking a chance to talk with you."

With a thoughtful look on her face, Janet shrugged.

Before Lana could pursue the subject any further, noise sounded outside the door. In a heartbeat, Susan and Teri bounded into the cabin and came to a screeching halt.

Teri looked from Lana to Janet. "Are you sick?" she asked Janet.

Janet gave Lana a nervous look, then turned her attention to the girls. "No. Just lazy."

"Lazy? That's better than being sick. I hate to be away from home and get sick." She plopped onto her bunk. "You should have been out with us. Then you'd really be nauseated."

Susan laughed. "Our volleyball score was terrible."

Teri eyed Janet from head to toe, then narrowed her eyes. "How tall are you?"

Janet looked at her long legs and stood. "Five-nine. Why?"

"Can you play volleyball?"

Janet nodded.

Teri turned to Susan and motioned to Janet. "The next game, huh?"

"For sure," Susan said.

Shifting her attention back, she folded her arms over her chest and looked at Janet. "Promise you'll be on our volleyball team tomorrow. Okay? We need someone tall like you."

With a sheepish grin, Janet looked at Lana before giving her answer. "Sure. Promise."

"Great," Teri said, crossing to her side and lopping her arm over Janet's shoulder. "Next time, we'll beat the pants off them."

Chapter 9

With Mark's help, Lana spent part of the afternoon trying to hide clues for the camp road rally without anyone seeing her. She'd dodged the campers numerous times, tucking eight clue packets into the haystack at the archery range, hiding another set in one of the canoes, hanging a plastic bag holding the next set in the shower, and putting the last ones in a coffee can behind an unoccupied cabin.

When the dinner bell sounded, Lana headed for the dining hall, praying for something tolerable. If the meals were as rustic as the setting, she'd beg Mark to find a small town nearby with a fast-food restaurant. As she stepped into the dining hall, the aroma of grease and hot dogs filled the room. What else should she have expected but frankfurters and French fries? While the fare may have pleased the teenagers, Lana hoped she'd brought along some antacid.

Mark signaled to her from across the room. She joined him and slid onto the bench at one of the long plank tables. When all the teens were accounted for, Mark rose. "Before we eat, who'd like to ask the blessing?"

No one spoke. "Okay, tonight I'll take a turn, but someone else can be ready tomorrow. Let's join hands."

Lana rose and was amazed as table after table of teens joined together until they had formed one big zigzag circle around the room.

Mark bowed his head, and his pleasant, resonant voice filled the room. "We thank You, Lord, for our safe journey here today, and we give thanks for the food prepared by our able chefs. We ask You to bless our two weeks together. Help us to learn to give up our own control over situations and trust solely in You. In Jesus' name we pray, amen."

"And patience, Lord," Lana whispered, inserting her personal need into the prayer.

When the teens moved forward to fill their plates cafeteria-style, chatter, and the clink of dishes filled the room. Lana sat and waited with Mark, unmotivated by the menu, yet hungry.

"Before you all go back for seconds," Mark said as a general announcement, "please let the camp counselors have some food, too."

Laughter and taunting echoed around the room, and when the clamor faded, Lana rose and followed Mark to the food counter. After taking a healthy portion of salad, for which she was grateful, Lana accepted a hot dog and a portion of soggy fries. She decided to forgo dessert.

"Think you'll survive?" Mark whispered once they sat.

"Your guess is as good as mine," Lana answered, "but if I don't, bury me somewhere quiet. . .like in the woods." She sent him an eye-rolling grin.

"You're a good sport, Lana," he said, then opened his mouth and filled it with a bite of a hot dog and bun.

When the meal ended and the dishes were cleared from the table, Mark announced the Bible study. Lana watched Bibles appear from everywhere—back packs and shoulder bags. Some campers pulled small New Testaments from their back pockets.

"Since we're going to learn about teamwork and trust, let's look at one promise Jesus made," Mark said. "Open your Bibles to Luke 6:27."

Pages rustled and then silence.

Mark read the verses. " 'But I tell you who hear me: Love your enemies, do good to those who hate you, bless those who curse you, pray for those who mistreat you.' "

Lana heard the teens mumble among themselves, and finally they turned toward Mark.

"So what does this have to do with us?" Mark asked.

Questions flew. How can we love our enemy? Does God really expect us to bless people who curse us? Though they'd heard the words before, the teens' disbelief resounded.

The discussion continued, and Lana watched Janet. She knew the girl had felt alone, and she'd wondered how the teen would handle this discussion topic.

"Jesus does this every day," Sara said.

"Huh?" Jason grunted.

"Jesus forgives us all the time for our sins and expects nothing in return," Sara responded. "If we're to follow Jesus, then we have to do the same, no matter how hard it is."

"That's right," Mark said. "Listen to this in verses 35 and 36: 'But love your enemies, do good to them, and lend to them without expecting to get anything back. Then your reward will be great, and you will be sons of the Most High, because he is kind to the ungrateful and wicked. Be merciful, just as your Father is merciful.' "

Lana let the meaningful discussion settle in her thoughts. She recalled the teens at her high school, wondering how many of them went to church and if they were eager to learn about Jesus like these teenagers seemed to be.

The vision, however, gave her hope. Maybe her attitude had been as much of a problem as her students themselves. Had she really given them an opportunity for input? Had she excited them in the same way Mark seemed to do about studying God's Word? Looking at her teaching in a new light sent a flutter of anticipation through her. Maybe next year things would be different.

"The important thing," Mark continued, "is to look for nothing. Don't expect a reward here on earth. Instead you'll find those treasures in heaven." He closed his Bible and ended with prayer.

"Campfire?" Gary asked from a front table.

"Later, maybe," Mark said. "First, we're going to have fun."

Groans filled the hall, and Lana couldn't hold back a smile.

"Lana's going to tell you about our camp version of a road rally. Remember our focus here is teamwork—cooperation, communication, and caring about others. Now it's time to break up into eight groups of four, and before you get too far away, make sure you all grab a flashlight. This rally may last until dark. "

Lana listened to the scraping of bench legs against the plank flooring as they rose. She watched in fear, praying that one teen wasn't left unselected and feeling unwanted, but in moments, she eyed the room and saw eight groups of four. Her focus first settled on Janet. Next she eyed Don, thrilled to see him among the campers. Both previously isolated teens stood with three others, looking animated and happy. Her heart lifted at the sight.

"Lana," Mark said, "tell them how this works."

Though an experienced teacher, Lana stood in front of the group feeling her own kind of apprehension. A classroom was her territory, not a camp meeting room, but she looked at the eager faces and began. After explaining the procedure, she watched enthusiasm grow in the room. "Does everyone understand before I give you the first puzzle?"

"What's the prize?" Susan asked.

"If we win, what do we get?" Jason echoed.

Mark laughed. "Now if you were listening to our Bible study, you wouldn't expect any reward on earth."

The room filled with laughter. Yet Mark had made a point.

"Let's not worry about the prize for now," he said. "The objective is to come in first with all of the puzzles solved."

The buzz of voices faded without an argument so Lana continued. "Select a team captain, and send your leader up for the first puzzle."

Following a chaotic moment, Lana distributed the clues, and the teams scattered, heading through the two screened doors to the outside.

"You did great," Mark said, sliding his arm around her waist. "What's the first clue?"

"You want to be on a team?" she asked, giving him a sly grin. "It's a bag of elbow macaroni with a note that says, 'Use your noodle.'"

"I know noodle means to use your head, but I'm sure it has another meaning. Right?" He grinned.

"Inside one of the elbows is a little note telling them where to go next."

"Not bad," he said. "Should we follow?"

She shook her head. "We'll probably get there before they will. But here's a question for you. What's the prize?"

"You're as bad as the kids," he said. "The camp administrator went into town, and I had him pick up a pizza. I'll pop it in the oven in an hour or so."

"Pizza?" Her stomach growled at the thought. "I love pizza."

"We don't always get the things we love," he said. "Not right away, anyway. Sometimes we have to wait."

His tender eyes sent her on a whirlpool journey to her heart. She sensed his words had a deeper meaning, and the reality fluttered through her like butterflies. Lifting her gaze to his, she couldn't speak.

Mark clasped her arm and guided her outside beneath the dusky sky. "Let's go check out the fire pit. I'm sure they'll want a campfire before bed."

She walked beside him, and he wove his fingers through hers as they made their way toward the sandy fire ring. The scent of pines and earth sailed on the air, and Lana inhaled the aroma, feeling that God had given her a reprieve from everyday experiences—even though she had fought the opportunity. She fought so many things. The concept weighed on her mind. Would she ever give up the fight and let God take control?

She looked up at Mark, admiring his strong profile against the setting sun. Could Mark be part of God's plan? They'd known each other such a short time. Maybe two months. Yet Lana felt close to him and comfortable. Her heart fluttered at the touch of his hand, and her pulse skipped like a child at recess when he gazed into her eyes.

"Why so quiet?" Mark asked.

"The quiet sounds nice, doesn't it?"

"You're thoughtful." He squeezed her fingers. "Sorry you came?"

"Never. I'm learning more than the kids are."

He gave her a surprised look. "What do you mean?"

"About my teaching style. . .and my attitude. I know I have a long way to go, but maybe it wasn't you who motivated me to come here. Do you think it might have been God?"

His smile brightened the shadowy surroundings. "God works in mysterious ways."

She nodded, enjoying the conversation and the feel of Mark's arm brushing against hers.

Close to the lake, they found the fire pit. Fallen logs formed a wide circle around a sandy hollow piled with kindling and fire wood. A generous supply of split wood stood nearby.

"Looks good," she said.

He nodded, then slipped his fingers from hers and guided his arm around her waist. Turning toward the lake, Lana stepped along with Mark, and when they reached the narrow strip of sand, he paused.

"Nothing like a sunset on the water," he said. "When I see beauty like this, I wonder how anyone can doubt God controlling the order of things. Such systematic detail can't happen by chance."

Lana looked across the multicolored lake, rippling with orange, gold, and coral splotches. "I think people are afraid to believe because they think they'll lose their free will, like God will take over their lives. They don't understand. Even with God, we make choices and decide the path we follow. Trouble is, some of us make bad choices and follow misleading paths." She released a disheartened chuckle, knowing she'd made many bad decisions in her life.

"Do you have someone specific in mind?" Mark asked, his voice teasing.

"Not a soul," she said, understanding he knew better.

He glanced at his watch and turned away from the lake. "I'd better get that pizza in the oven or our winning team will have a cold prize."

When they returned to the activity hall, it stood empty. Mark headed for the kitchen, and Lana checked her clue list, guessing how far the teens had gotten in their solutions. She'd left the canoes for last, and since no one was at the lake when she and Mark were there, she figured it would be awhile longer before the winners arrived.

To her surprise, only fifteen minutes passed before the winning team came through the door, bursting with conversation and laughter. "Did we win?" Janet asked, scanning the empty room.

"You sure did," Lana said. "Congratulations."

The girls let out a squeal, and Mark came to the kitchen doorway. "Your prize is almost ready."

Sniffing like bloodhounds, the four girls hurried toward the kitchen while giggles and noise sailed through the doorway.

Lana heard the screen door open and turned, watching another group file inside. Seeing the empty room, their faces broke into grins, then faded when they saw the girls coming from the kitchen with the pizza.

Despite their disappointment, conversation rolled with stories of how they'd followed the clues and where they'd made mistakes. As each team arrived, they watched the girls scarfing down the pungent pizza, and soon they wanted no more watching.

"How about a campfire?" Gary said. "At least we can eat marshmallows."

At the word campfire, conversation hummed. Mark gave the go-ahead, and the door swung open and slammed closed as they darted outside. Voices raised with comments about finding a stick to whittle and heading back to their bunks for their stash of marshmallows.

"Ready?" Mark asked. "The girls can finish that pizza alone." He gave them a wink.

"Save us a seat," Teri called.

Mark nodded and turned to Lana. "We'll get our flashlights and head down."

Without hesitation, Lana agreed. The scent of the tangy pizza had stirred her appetite, and she had considered mugging the girls for one little piece.

Mark clasped her elbow as they stepped outside, and as always, Lana liked the cozy feeling. She sensed his enthusiasm for the whole day, and she admired his Christian love for his work, his youthful charges, and the Lord. Mark seemed the epitome of trust. Lana had no question that she loved God, but she prayed the rest of Mark's qualities would rub off on her even a little.

Clutching flashlights, she and Mark headed for the wooded clearing. When the fire blazed, everyone scooted forward with anticipation, awaiting the perfect moment to toast their marshmallows over the glowing coals.

One of the boys brought along a guitar and strummed some familiar camp-fire tunes. Little by little, voices joined in singing.

Mark sat beside Lana with a jackknife, whittling pointed ends on long sticks for the marshmallows, and as he passed them out, the marshmallow bags were opened, and the white puffs of sweetness were skewered to the ends.

Lana marveled at the blackened, flaming globs they pulled off the stick ends and ate. She sat near the fire and, with great patience, rotated her stick, holding it the proper distance for the golden brown version she preferred.

"Here, Lana," one of the boys said, thrusting a coal black ash in front of her. "See it's perfect. You can have it."

"Thanks, Bernie," she said, "I'm doing fine."

Bernie eyed her with curiosity while she continued to rotate the spear, admiring the golden, swelling puff. Perfection. "There," she said, "now this is what I call a toasted marshmallow."

As she pulled the stick forward, the soft confection lost its housing and dropped into the fire and burst into flame.

"That's what I call garbage," Jason chortled.

"How about making me one just like that," Gary joked. The group nearby tittered as they watched her golden masterpiece burning in the fire pit.

Purpose rose in her, and she thrust another one onto the end and again pivoted the stick slowly at the perfect height from the coals, watching the deepening bronze. With great pride, she pulled the marshmallow forward—more carefully this time—but a passing teen bumped her stick, and her prize marshmallow fell to the ground. She scowled at the teen and snatched another white orb from the bag.

Mark laughed. "Is it really that important?"

"Yes," she muttered. "I'm demonstrating the art of toasting a proper marshmallow."

"Look," one of the boys called and waved his stick toward Lana to show off his near perfect exhibit. But the loose, gooey mass flew from his skewer, and the confection sailed through the air and tangled in Lana's hair. A gasp rippled around the circle.

The young man gaped at the empty point on his stick then at the others around him. "Hey! Who snatched my marshmallow?"

While the teens tittered at his distrust, Lana pulled away the gooey lump now decorated with strands of her brown locks. "Here you go," she said, extending the mess toward him.

His eyes widened. "Wow! I'm sorry, Lana. But do you see how perfect it is?"

"Was," someone called out.

The crowd laughed him into embarrassment, and Lana gazed at the sticky goo. "Sure thing. That's what I call perfect."

With the mess smeared on her fingers, she rose. "I guess I'd better beat the girls to the shower so I get dibs on the hot water." She leaned toward Mark and sent her most satirical voice his way. "I'm glad the ladies have the night shift." She sent him a sweet wave and pattered down the path toward the cabin.

Though she'd joked, Lana winced at her behavior. *It's my way or no way.* Like Mark said, did it really make that much difference about the marshmallow? She'd begun toasting it for fun—as a challenge to herself and to demonstrate what a really great glob of golden perfection looked like. Instead, she'd frowned and behaved like an idiot. Mark deserved so much more than a woman with her pitiful amount of self-control.

After the shower when she crawled into her sleeping bag, Lana relived her last disillusionment of the day. Needing a schedule to share the same shower stalls seemed bad enough, but no one had prepared her for the other news.

Ice cold water.

Chapter 10

Mark relaxed. Two days had passed without incident. Serious incident, he corrected, thinking of the bandages, bruises, and narrow escape when two teens at the archery range decided to play William Tell.

He savored the time with Lana. Though he still caught her familiar grimace on occasion—like the night of the first bonfire—she'd grown, and so had he. He no longer struggled for courage to slip his arm around her shoulders or grasp her hand as they walked. Those actions had become natural. But he'd not kissed her, and the desire banged around in his head like the cabin bats and made his pulse pick up its pace.

Should he? The question soared through his mind. If he kissed her, would things change? If Lana resisted, would it build a barrier between them? They'd known each other such a short time in contrast to the age-old feelings that wove through his heart. Mark felt certain he loved her. Not for her pretty face and shapely figure—and definitely not for her stubbornness—but for her wit, her intelligence, and her humanity. Though she fought it, her compassion had blossomed like a spring flower.

But Mark felt uncertain. How could he know for sure how Lana felt about him? At first, he figured she found him amusing. Maybe a challenge. But lately, she accepted his friendship without question and didn't pull away when his arm wrapped around her. He suspected she enjoyed it. He even noted a softer, more intimate whisper when she spoke, avoiding the ears of the teens that surrounded them most of the time. But was his interpretation correct or only wishful thinking?

Feeling upbeat, he roused himself early on the third day of camp with a happy heart. Today he'd planned another team activity. The first had been successful, and he hoped while they had fun and a sense of competition among the teams, they were learning those attributes he'd discussed with them.

With a light heart, he stepped outside and confronted the director heading toward him. The director's desperate expression slowed Mark's upbeat spirit to a dirge.

"Sorry," he said. "This is bad news. The cook and her assistant have both come down with the flu. The twenty-four-hour kind, they've both assured me, but. . ."

Mark heard his lengthy hesitation, and his heart sank. "But?"

"I haven't found anyone able to prepare the day's meals. I even asked my wife, but she has a commitment she can't break. The cook said if she can drag herself here later for dinner she would, but we still have breakfast and lunch to worry about."

"So what should we do?" Mark asked, hoping the man had some ideas.

"We have some cold cereal, I think. Maybe we could look together," the man said.

Mark's culinary interests slipped into first gear. All he needed was a helper. "Let me see what I can do."

The director nodded, his expression grateful.

Mark's mind whirred in thought. Breakfast he could handle. Sandwiches would get them through lunch, and he prayed by evening the cook would recover enough to scrounge up a feeble dinner. He stood for a heartbeat gazing heavenward. *Lord, I need a little guidance here.*

His body involuntarily shifted, facing Lana's quiet cabin. He glanced into the clouds again, closed his eyes for moral support, and forged across the grass. She slept near the window, and he rapped gently on the shuttered glass and pressed his lips close to the pane. "Lana." He rapped again and waited.

No sound came from inside. His knuckle plinked the glass again. "Lana, I need to talk with you."

A slight rustle moved behind the shutter. He waited. A weary face peered from the narrow space between the door and frame. "What?" she whispered. "I have eight sleeping girls in here. What's wrong?"

Her expression changed when she opened the door a hair-breadth wider. "You look like someone stole your bicycle. What is it?"

The words tumbled from his mouth, and he watched her shoulders tighten beneath her sweatshirt, then droop like a receding tide.

She shook her head. "I suppose I'm in this thing for the duration." A rattled sigh escaped her. "Give me a few minutes. I'll meet you in the kitchen."

His own relieved sigh rippled through his chest, and with a confident wave, he darted across the dewy grass to the back door of the dining hall. The building was lighted, and the camp director, his mouth agape, stood between the large work counter and huge iron stove, pivoting in a slow circle like a weather vane caught in a strange wind. "I don't even know where to begin," he groaned.

"Leave," Mark said. "I'll take over breakfast, but I expect a generous refund on this venture." He stood his ground until the man nodded.

"I suppose it's worth it," the director said and hustled through the doorway like a man newly paroled.

Mark stared into the refrigerator. What would be quick and easy? Cereal, he thought, but today was their big canoe day. The teens needed energy. Scrambled eggs? With cheese? Fast and easy. Add toast, and he had his breakfast menu.

By the time he'd hauled out the ingredients, a blurry-eyed Lana stalked through the door.

"Okay, Betty, what can I do?"

"Who?" He squinted at her, trying to decode her thinking.

"Crocker. Betty Crocker," she enunciated. "What can I do, Chief?"

He laughed. "That's chef. Isn't it?"

"We'll see about that, won't we?" She gave his arm a poke and stepped up to the food-laden counter. They worked side by side, cracking dozens of eggs and beating them into a foamy mass. Then he grated cheese while she buttered bread.

When she slipped the big crock of butter back into the refrigerator, she stood, staring inside. "We ought to do something interesting. Give the eggs a little zip."

"Zip? What are you talking about? Kids don't like zip. They like plain, regular stuff. Things they know."

She didn't move. "I've heard of adding mayonnaise to eggs."

"Forget it, Lana. Let's stick with cheese."

Before he could stop her, she swung around and unleashed the cap from a bottle. "Here we go. Just a dash for added flavor."

He attempted to shift the mixing bowl, but the bathtub-sized container made shifting more challenging. She caught the edge with her zip before Mark could read the label. An enormous splash appeared, and the eggs swam with a dark red liquid.

She pulled back, staring at the bottle. "Oops." She eyed the label, her face paling.

Mark froze like a Thanksgiving turkey. "What do you mean, oops?"

"I thought it was a shaker bottle." She hid the label behind her back like a little kid caught in the cookie jar. "I meant to grab the Worcestershire sauce."

"So what is it? What did you put in the eggs?"

She swung the bottle around to face him. "Hot sauce."

He cringed. "Hot sauce. Wonderful."

She shrugged sheepishly. "Okay. . .so what do we do now?"

"We?" He narrowed his eyes and allowed a scowl to settle on his face. "I'm going to announce you threw hot sauce in the eggs."

"Come on, Mark. Think. We can call them Mexicali eggs. Teens like tacos and things."

Biting her lower lip, Lana scanned the room with a look of desperation until she lurched forward and snatched up a half-empty bag of corn chips. She squeezed the bag, and the crunch and crackle sounded through the room.

Panic rifled through Mark's mind, but again, his body reacted more slowly than Lana's. She pulled open the bag and dumped the crumbled chips into the eggs.

"What are you doing?" Mark asked, his imagination flying.

Grabbing the whisk, she swirled the hot sauce and chips through the eggs. "Voila!"

"That's French. How about 'Vaya con Dios'?" He felt his shoulders sag and his spirits with them.

"Don't be a bad sport." She spun toward him, looking like a mountain climber reaching the top of Everest. "It may be delicious."

"May is the operative word." He leaned against the counter for support. If she ruined breakfast, what would he do?

Lana turned her back on him and tore through the cabinets looking for the proper-sized pans and griddles. Gigantic seemed to be the smallest. He took two huge frying pans from her and divided the mixture, pouring half into each.

Lana had grown quiet. She covered two burners with a wide griddle and tossed the buttered bread on top.

When the clock hands reached seven-thirty, Lana rang the breakfast bell and returned with speed to set out the jugs of milk and the pots of water for hot chocolate. The first comer burst threw the doorway and came to a screeching halt.

The boy's eyes opened nearly as wide as the plates sitting in a pile on the serving table. "What are you two doing here?"

Mark chuckled at the teen's expression. "I've always wanted to be a cook. Let me know if I should change careers." *But not with this meal,* he thought, wondering how the boy would react when he tasted Lana's concoction.

"I'm an innocent bystander," Lana added.

Mark sent her one of his sternest looks but made no comment.

The parents and teens piled into the hall, and after Gary said the blessing, the huge mound of cheesy eggs and grilled toast nearly vanished. To Mark's amazement, the breakfast received rave reviews. Lana pranced in the kitchen like she'd won a blue ribbon at a bake-off.

Before the campers scraped the bottom of the serving dish, Mark put a couple of spoonfuls on a plate and eyed the scrambled mess. He dipped his fork into the mixture and slid a bite into his mouth. He grinned and took two more tastes. The creamy cheese sauce blended with the hot sauce and chips, leaving a spirited flavor in his mouth. Lana had been right. The Mexicali creation tasted like real Mexican cuisine.

Disappointment slithered over faces when they came back for more and found an empty bowl. When the scraping forks quieted, Mark slipped out of his discolored apron and joined his charges in the dining room. "We'll have our Bible study this morning since today is our canoe trip and tonight we have another team activity."

Cheers and voices rose above his, and he quieted them before continuing. "Hold on, pals. When we're finished with our lesson, we'll meet at the hut by the beach. Pair off before you get there. We'll be heading for a park a few miles downstream. When we arrive, we'll have a picnic, and the bus will bring us back. The camp director will take care of the canoes."

"You mean we don't get to canoe back?" Sara asked.

"No," Mark said

Moans and groans hummed around the hall.

Mark shook his head, realizing they knew little about canoeing. "You'll thank me. Did you ever try to canoe upstream?"

From the teens' expression, Mark knew they had no idea about upstream or downstream, and he realized a quick canoeing lesson would be a must before they paddled away later in the morning.

"Open your Bibles," Mark said, "to Romans 15:13–14. Look over the verses. I'll be right back." He hurried to the kitchen, realizing he had to break the bad news to Lana.

"We have a problem. . .as you know," he said, eyeing her in dishwater up to her elbows. "I have to lead the Bible study so I'll see if the other counselors will come in and help you. Okay?"

"What if I say no?" Her arms hung at her sides, and water dripped onto the plank floor.

"It's only two jobs. Finish the dishes, and make sandwiches for the canoe trip. And you can bring along some of those apples, too," he said gesturing toward the peck of fruit on a counter. He ducked as a soggy dishcloth flew through the air, missing him by a soap bubble. He gave her his sweetest smile and escaped back into the dining room.

The parents cooperated, and with the magnified sounds of dishes being washed and put away along with a few door-bangs and muffled groans coming from the kitchen, Mark began the lesson.

He opened his Bible and faced the group. "You've had a chance to read these two verses. What do you think Paul means, and what does the message have to do with us? Listen again: 'May the God of hope fill you with all joy and peace as you trust in him, so that you may overflow with hope by the power of the Holy Spirit. I myself am convinced, my brothers, that you yourselves are full of goodness, complete in knowledge and competent to instruct one another.' "

The discussion got underway, and Mark prodded and encouraged their understanding of hope and trust in each other as well as in God. "When you get in the canoes a short time from now, some of you might be experienced and some not. These verses remind us to listen to your partner's knowledge and learn from his or her instructions. Don't think you know better. Remember, we are all full of goodness—which means cooperation and concern for each other."

With his final words, Mark sent the teens and parent counselors on their way to dress for the canoe trip, then bolstered his courage to face Lana. When he slid into the kitchen, she was alone. He watched her for a moment before she noticed him. "Hi, Camperella. Where are your helpers?" he asked.

Perspiration glistened on her nose, and mustard decorated her fingers. "Camperella?" She gave him a quizzical look. "Oh, I get it," she said, with a slight smirk. "They went to the ball without me." She stuck her foot toward him. "Where's my glass slipper, Prince Uncharming?"

He looked at her tiny feet clad in damp, food-stained sneakers. Seeing her at work—work she'd agreed to do to bail him out—touched him. He sidled next to her, sliding his arm around her waist. She turned her shiny face upward, and he grabbed a paper towel to daub the moist droplets sitting on her nose. "My poor friend, I've worked you way too hard."

"It's hot when you're up to your elbows in dishwater."

"I know." A strong urge soared through him to kiss her upturned lips. Like a magnet, the attraction drew him forward, and without thinking, his mouth met hers in a sweep of tenderness. To his joy, she didn't pull away, but tiptoed upward and returned the touch with such gentleness it might have been a dream. But he knew better, and so did his heart, hammering like a woodpecker.

When he eased away, Lana lifted her eyes to his with a look of surprise. But her expression shifted to acceptance, then pleasure. His joy soared, and he longed to return to her sweet mouth, but caution waved a flag in his thoughts. He'd wait for another time and another place.

With a hint of embarrassment, she lowered her eyes. "Everything's ready," she said. "The sandwiches and sodas are packed in the two coolers. I put the apples in this box." She gestured to a carton sitting beside the coolers.

"Then we'd better get ready, too," Mark said, wishing he could do something wonderful for her kindness.

They closed the kitchen, and as they headed out the back door, the director flagged Mark.

"The cook is still sick, but I have good news," he said. "I found a replacement for dinner tonight."

Mark stepped toward him. "That's a relief." He motioned toward the kitchen. "The coolers and box of apples are ready to go."

"Good work," the man said. "The bus should be there long before your group arrives."

"I hope so," Mark said, beginning to wonder if any more catastrophes might occur.

Outside, Mark and Lana headed in the direction of their cabins to slip into clothing suitable for the canoe trip. Both ready, they crossed the lawn together and headed to the lake. When they arrived, most of the teens were waiting and immediately started egging him to get going. The canoes had been lined up on the shore, and Mark glanced at the map and instructions, praying for a safe outing.

While Mark checked to see who still seemed to be missing, Lana motioned each pair together and assigned them a canoe. She surprised him when she moved to his side and whispered. "Problem, I think."

"What?" he asked.

She gave him a subtle tilt of her head.

He surveyed the groups of twosomes and spotted the problem. "Janet?" he whispered back.

Lana nodded. "She's been great since that first day. She and Teri hit it off, but I think Teri's paired up with Dennis."

Mark eyed the boy and girl, standing together. "What happened to Susan?

Weren't they all friends?"

"She's not feeling well and asked one of the parents if she could stay in the cabin."

Mark eyed the situation. "So what do you think we should do now?"

"You'll canoe alone, and I'll tell Janet I don't have a partner."

"Or we could include her in the rowboat with the two fellows."

Lana's raised eyebrow told him that wasn't the answer. He unwillingly conceded. "Okay, but I thought you've never canoed before."

She gave him one of her how-dumb-do-you-think-I-am looks. "It can't be that hard to learn," she said, one hand on her hip.

"It's tricky, Lana. You have to be—" He was talking to himself. Lana had bounded away and returned dragging Janet, wearing a smile on her lips.

Janet's face seemed a mixture of relief and embarrassment, but Lana rattled on as if the choice were hers, not caused by Janet's obvious exclusion from the other pairings.

Mark's caution about canoeing had fallen on Lana's deaf ears. Knowing Lana, she would do as she pleased. He decided to let it go and gathered the others for a review of canoeing instructions. "Now when you climb in, step to the center, and do it carefully." Fearing the worst, his eyes sought heaven.

"And remember," he continued, "follow each other, and don't try to play hero. Remember, we have the rowboat handy for emergencies." He paused whispering up another plea. "And no silliness. When we reach the park, pull over to the shore. You'll recognize it by picnic tables and a big bus."

They all laughed, and when he finished, the teams clambered into the canoes, some nearly toppling at the shoreline. Within minutes, the caravan of canoes floated out to the center of the lake. Mark signaled for them to take the sharp turn into the narrower branch of the river where they would be pulled downstream toward a larger lake.

The rowboat stayed behind, keeping an eye out for toppled canoes, and Mark, navigating alone, lingered midway, watching the progress of the eager teens. His heart sank when he viewed Lana and Janet zigzagging their way far behind most of the canoes. Janet appeared to know a little about canoeing, but his instinct suggested that Lana was doing her thing. The teen didn't have a chance.

Despite her stubbornness, he was proud of Lana. Though her attitude about teens seemed to have been tarnished by her teaching position, she had given it another try and had succeeded. He admired the way she'd worked with the campers. He'd been touched by her sensitivity to Janet and her earlier response to Don. Lana might think she didn't like teens and teaching, but she seemed a different woman since they'd arrived at camp.

The rowboat passed him by and, concerned about Lana, Mark slowed and looked over his shoulder. Instead of continuing, he held back until her canoe drew closer. "How are you doing?" he called.

She gave him an exaggerated thumbs-up, but from the look on Janet's face, Mark guessed they weren't doing as well as Lana's thumb indicated.

When they came closer, Janet gave him a pitiful look. "She's worse than a teenager, Mark. She won't listen to a thing." Janet grinned, but the girl had pinpointed reality. Lana had grown so much, but at times, she slid into her old ways and needed to be in charge.

Mark viewed Janet's paddling skills and noticed Lana would have been better in the back, working as the rudder. Maybe because of her petite size, her oars hit the water with uneven strokes. Janet's long arms and taller stature could shoot them through the water while Lana's dragging paddles seemed to slow them down. Before Mark could stop himself, he'd uttered his thoughts aloud.

"Then we'll trade spots," Lana said, standing in the canoe and shifting her weight toward the back.

Mark let out a cautionary yell while Janet grabbed the canoe's sides and struggled to keep it upright. But in Lana's case, the struggle failed, and she tumbled from the canoe along with the paddle. When she resurfaced, Lana and the paddle had parted company.

Mark fought to turn his canoe back, but the current pulled him forward. He saw no way for Lana to climb back into either canoe without tipping them over. If he dived in to help her, he'd lose his own canoe. The logical course seemed for him to charge ahead for the rowboat.

"Swim to the side, Lana," he called, "and I'll get the rowboat to pick you up." He dug his paddle deep into the water, moving the canoe downstream. As he flew forward, Lana's paddle bobbed up and floated past. Leaning over with caution, he grabbed it before the paddle vanished into the debris along the riverbank.

Mark plunged his paddle from side to side at a racer's pace until he sighted the rowboat ahead of him. Yelling and waving to capture their attention, Mark moved forward, but his mind backed up, returning to the rubble swirling along the river's edge. He prayed a water snake hadn't chosen Lana's bank to sunbathe.

Finally, the teens in the rowboat spotted him and turned around. He thanked the Lord he'd had the forethought to prepare for an emergency. The boys gave Mark an acknowledging wave, reversed course, and sailed past on the way to Lana's rescue.

Mark back-paddled, waiting and praying Lana didn't panic. Janet came by with panic etched on her face. "I'm sorry," she called as the current pulled her past. "If I'd realized what she was doing, I'd have—"

"Not your fault, Janet. You can't stop a freight train."

She nodded knowingly and skimmed by on her way to join the others.

Holding his position, Mark stroked backward as the current pulled him forward. Finally, he heard the rowboat's splash behind him, and Mark turned to spot a wet and scowling Lana, her hair straggling over her forehead like seaweed.

"Nice job," he teased, hoping he'd get a smile.

"I was waist-deep in frogs," she called. "Great big ugly things."

"Could have been worse," he said, following alongside the rowboat.

"Worse? Explain that to me." Her arms flailed in a wild gesture.

Though he tried to control his amusement, Mark grinned, seeing her dripping and madder than—he chuckled at his appropriate imagery—a wet hen. "Better than snakes."

Panic covered her face.

"You could have landed in a nest of water snakes."

"You mean to tell me there are snakes here?" She clung to the wooden side and stared into the dark, rolling water. For a heartbeat, she lifted her gaze toward Mark, then returned her attention to the water. "You aren't kidding, are you?"

His voice reverberated into the trees. "Come on, Lana. Would I kid you?"

As his canoe skimmed past her, Lana scowled darkly.

Chapter 11

Lana pulled her legs underneath the rowboat bench and glowered. She felt utterly humiliated. Of all the boaters, she had been the only one to fall into the river. . .and only one of the two adults who had ventured out in the canoes.

As the boat brought her closer to shore, the teens stood around their canoes moored in the sand and gaped at her. Her clothes clung to her like plaster, and her wet hair sagged around her face.

When the rowboat beached, Janet ran toward her, her face filled with apology, and Lana felt swamped by guilt. She had caused her own spill, not the teenager. Hoping to calm the girl, Lana pushed a grin onto her face.

Without seeming concerned about getting wet, Janet threw her arms around Lana's neck. "I'm so sorry. I tried to stop you, but it was too late."

"Janet, it wasn't your fault. I did it to myself." She patted the girl's arm to calm her.

"I know but—"

"But nothing. You'd have fallen over yourself if you'd done anything else." Lana stepped back from the girl, now nearly as wet as she was. "Thanks for trying to stop me. I'm not what you'd call a sailor."

Mark slid next to them. "That's a little fishy." He grinned.

Lana lifted an eyebrow, acknowledging his corny joke.

"Now, now, don't be a wet blanket," he said.

Both eyebrows flew up while the campers grinned at their interaction.

Mark rested his arm against her damp shoulder. "Better yet, we've all heard of the Frog Prince. We could crown you the Frog Princess?"

Lana took a playful poke at his arm. "Watch out, or I'll turn you into a wart."

The teens cheered at her comment. Lana thrust her nose into the air and turned on her heel as she snagged Janet by the arm. "We're not appreciated here, Janet. Let's find better company."

Janet grinned as they headed toward the picnic table where the hungriest campers were unloading the coolers.

A small group of teens gathered around Janet, and Lana couldn't avoid hearing their conversation.

"Great save," Teri said.

"You really know how to keep your canoe from flipping," Don added.

Sara poked Jason in the side. "Next time, I vote for Janet in my canoe. You

209

nearly flipped us twice."

"I did not," Jason said, looking indignant.

Don shifted forward and moved to Janet's side. "Next time, Janet can be in my canoe. . .if you'd like," he said to her. A faint tinge of nervousness slid up his neck, but he stood his ground.

"Sure," Janet said, her own flush rising to her cheeks. Her gaze fastened to Lana's as happiness settled on her face.

"Let's eat," someone called.

Lana smiled, watching Janet being pulled along by the chattering teens, and she was touched by Don's interest in the girl. She raised her eyes heavenward and sent up a prayer of thanks. Looking toward the picnic table, Lana noticed that Janet had melted into the crowd. She herself longed to melt into the earth in her sodden, river-smelling garb.

She waited until the crowd had settled on the grass with their fruit and sandwiches until she wandered to an empty picnic table to slip off her water-logged sneakers and socks. The air felt warmer on her water-soaked feet. Leaning her elbow on the plank tabletop, Lana rested her cheek against her fist, scrutinizing the noisy, fun-loving teens. Though hungry, her appetite had been squelched by the frogs.

The days she'd spent at camp skittered through her thoughts like mice in a cheese factory. Mark's kiss lingered in her mind, the tender warmth that left her heart jogging. Other memories were not so pleasant, like her marshmallow drama or the spill in the river. But through it all, she'd learned a lesson. When things went wrong, she seemed to be at the helm. Breakfast could have been a disaster—God had graciously gotten her out of that one—and her fall from the canoe could have left her or someone else injured.

Why did she always have to take over? She needed to work on that. Even more, she needed to pray about it instead of tackling it alone.

Lana looked around for Mark and saw him near the rowboat. She felt alone and wondered why he hadn't come to talk with her. She feared he was angry with her foolishness.

With that concern still in her thoughts, she heard Mark's voice. Did he call her name? She glanced around to see what he wanted. He stood away from the others, holding a dark green plastic bag and beckoned to her. She rose and walked to him, dragging her bare feet through the grass.

"Hey, Pal," he said, brushing her damp hair away from her cheeks. "How would you like some dry clothes?"

She looked at him, wondering what he meant. "Where would I get dry clothes?"

He held out the plastic bundle. "I came prepared."

She opened the bag and peeked inside. "What's this?" She fingered the garments. "Your clothes?"

"Just a pair of jogging shorts and a T-shirt. The shorts have a drawstring. I threw them in at the last minute—just in case."

"You figured I'd do something stupid. Right?"

"It could have been anyone. I thought you'd prefer to be dry."

She accepted his explanation and was touched by his thoughtfulness. "That was nice of you. Thanks."

Lana looked around, wondering where to change, and spotted a wooded area nearby. She flagged Janet.

When the girl arrived, Lana showed her the plastic bag. "How about standing guard while I change?"

Janet's face brightened. "I've been wishing I could do something since you fell in. This is easy."

She followed Lana toward the wooded area, and while Lana hid behind a tree, sliding out of her clothes and into Mark's, Janet watched for intruders.

"I'll be dressed in a minute," Lana said, dragging the clinging, wet clothes from her body.

"I don't mind," Janet said. "I've wanted to talk with you alone anyway. This gives me a chance."

"Oh?" Lana said, curious what the girl had to say.

"I wanted to thank you for talking to me when we first got here. You don't know how much it meant to me," Janet said.

Lana stopped a moment, wanting to run over and hug the girl, but her state of undress held her back. "It wasn't me, Janet. When the girls came in and saw you upset, their concern let you know they cared. And that changed you. I'm thrilled it happened."

"The best part is I feel better. I'm not afraid to be who I am. . .even at school. I know it'll still hurt me when kids act bogus, but I'll know I have friends at church and, best of all, I know I have a friend in Jesus. . .like you said."

"What you just said couldn't make me happier." Lana thought about Don and wondered if she should bring up the subject.

"And then Don's been so nice," Janet added

Lana's smile blossomed behind the girl's back. "I wanted to say something about that but hesitated. He's a nice boy. And sensitive."

"I know. He's told me about his family. It's great to have someone to talk to. Wait until I get home and tell my parents how glad I am I came here."

Dropping her soggy clothes into the plastic bag, Lana stepped from behind the tree and slid her arm around the girl's shoulder. "Isn't God awesome?"

"He sure is," Janet said.

With private grins, they headed back to the others.

Lana returned to the picnic table, and after she gathered up her shoes, Mark arrived with two sodas in one hand, three sandwiches in the other, and apples bulging from his pockets. "You feel okay?"

She saw no silly grin on his face for once, only his tender gaze. "I'm drier now. Other than that, my ego's a little injured, but I'm fine."

"Here." He offered her a sandwich, then set everything else on the table. "I'll say a blessing before we eat."

Earlier Lana had watched others around the park doing the same, bowing their heads in prayer with their hands joined. She liked the custom. She'd never prayed that way before the camping trip, and the act filled her with a sense of Christian fellowship. Maybe that's what she'd never experienced—a true sense of the communion of saints.

Mark slid onto the bench and took her hands in his. They bowed their heads, and Mark quietly prayed, giving thanks for the food and the day. Before he ended, he added a postscript. "Oh, and Lord, thank You for Lana's safety. And Father, could You help this woman learn that You are the captain of the ship? Teach her to trust in others and in You."

Saying amen, he squeezed her fingers, then grabbed a sandwich from the table and tore off the wrapper. "I'm starving." He bit into the bread, then paused and peered at her. "Not hungry?"

"Thinking, I guess." With an effort, she pulled herself from her thoughts. She took time unwrapping the waxed paper she'd folded so carefully around the bread and meat earlier that day.

"Thinking what?" Mark asked.

"What you said about teaching me to trust others, because the same idea sailed into my mind a few minutes ago."

"Lana, you're a sweet lady—"

"But with a few minor flaws," she said, tucking her damp hair behind her ear.

"But only a few," he said. "And very minor."

❦

Exhausted, Lana stood in her cabin, pleased the one-shower schedule gave the women's cabins priority to use the facility in the evening. On the ride back from the canoe trip, her frazzled thoughts had focused on taking a shower. She slipped off Mark's damp clothes, wrapped herself in her robe, and darted the few yards to the shower building. Even the cold water running over her tired body felt good, and when she dried and dressed in clean clothes, she felt human again.

Outside, the campers gathered on the grass, waiting for the dinner bell and reliving the events of their afternoon canoe trip. Lana noticed Janet sitting with Don and enjoyed being a witness to their blossoming relationship. The excitement on the river had made Janet more popular among the group, and little by little, she was coming out of her shell.

Mark joined Lana, smelling of herbal soap and wearing clean clothes. Though he'd been deprived shower privileges, she knew he'd done his best to freshen up.

"You look good," he said, sinking onto the grass beside her.

"I feel better. And look," she said, nodding slightly toward Janet.

"A budding romance. That's nice."

"They're two people who need each other," Lana added.

Mark's fingers slid over hers resting in the grass. "I know two other people in the same boat."

"You mean canoe," she said, making a joke to hide her pleasure.

"Now who's the one joking about something serious?" He squeezed her hand.

The dinner bell rang, saving her from admitting he was right, and Mark rose and helped her from the ground. They joined the campers heading inside and took their seats in the dining hall. A wonderful aroma drifted from the kitchen.

"I wonder if it really smells that good or if I'm starving?" Lana asked

"Both, I think." He leaned over close to her ear. "But you smell best. Fresh, soapy, and wonderful."

"Probably because I reeked earlier."

"Never," he said, brushing his finger over her skin.

The sensation filled her with simple pleasure. Never had she had such a sense of partnership and sharing.

When almost everyone had arrived, Mark stood and surveyed the group of upturned faces. "Thank you for the safe and fun day. I'm proud of all of you. You followed the rules, and we're all back in one piece."

Lana heard a few titters and knew they were aimed at her.

Mark glanced down at her, and the laughter rose a couple decibels. "I should say most everyone followed the rules."

The room rang with laughter until Lana's voice brought a hush. "I plead the Fifth," she said, which revitalized the clamor.

Mark quieted the group. "Okay," he continued, "whose turn to say our blessing?"

When Janet raised her arm, Lana held her breath.

Mark's eyes widened, apparently as surprised as Lana. "Great. Janet volunteered."

He extended his arm toward Lana. She took his hand and offered her other hand to the person on the her right while the teens did the same, linking the entire room. To Lana's surprise when everyone bowed their heads, Janet began to sing. Her sweet, clear voice filled the room, and before she reached the second line, others had joined her.

They began a second verse, and by the end, even those who may not have known the song joined in the last line. Compliments filled the room when Janet finished, and Lana sent her own silent thanks to heaven as the girl graciously thanked those around her.

Lana studied the young people, different in many ways from her high school students. What made the difference? The answer struck her like a dart in a bull's-eye. God made the difference. These teens weren't afraid to demonstrate their faith. They acted out what God expected. Then she turned her thoughts inward. Did she? After these new experiences, Lana knew she had a place to start, and that would make the difference in her.

The Lord is good to me, Lana thought. *So good. And I don't deserve any of it, and that's what makes me all the more grateful.*

❦

Mark lay in his bunk and thought about the past week. The camp outing had helped him to become acquainted with the teens, and watching them grow in their relationships with Christ and each other had filled him with joy. What could be better in life than to be part of that experience?

With each new day, serving the Lord filled Mark with greater joy—a joy he couldn't explain—and feelings washed away his inner concern that he had made a bad career choice. God had strengthened his confidence.

To his great happiness, he'd gotten to know Lana even better. She brought smiles to his face with her abundant energy. . .though often that energy was aimed in the wrong direction. Somehow Mark sensed that God had directed him to her. Since they'd arrived at camp, he knew both he and Lana had changed in miraculous ways.

Struggling to fall asleep, Mark reviewed the ups and downs of the first week, reminding himself the last half of their stay began the next morning. After one silly prank in his cabin—a frog hidden in Jason's duffel bag—he had given the entire group a lecture on shaving cream in the sleeping bags and plastic wrap on the toilets. He'd planned ahead and prayed he'd thought of everything. At least, he hoped he had. Mark finally closed his eyes, looking forward to a fun-filled day the next morning.

During the night, the sound of heavy rain awakened Mark. Grateful that the camp had indoor activities if needed, he forced his eyes to stay closed, but within minutes, the heavens disturbed the silence. Cracks of lightning and the rumble of thunder jarred Mark again. Slipping out of his bunk, he tiptoed to the cabin window and peeked outside between the shutters.

A grand lightning display played above the soggy grass and rugged buildings. The dirt paths had turned to muddy rivers, and he wondered what the morning would hold.

"What's happening?" a voice asked from the darkness.

Mark heard the shuffle of a sleeping bag and then the patter of feet as the boy approached him.

In the light zigzagging through the window, Mark recognized Don. "Can't sleep?"

He shook his head. "At home noise like this is too familiar."

Though Lana had told Mark the boy's story, he shook his head as if he didn't understand.

Don explained about his family problems in a hushed whisper, limiting facts but getting the point across. "Coming here has been great." He leaned his back against the wall. "I needed friends, and when Miss W. . .when Lana invited me to come to church, I sloughed it off. But like I said before, something made me get up that morning, and I'll never be sorry."

"I'm glad," Mark said. "You've been a great addition to the camp."

"Thanks. I've made a lot of friends."

Mark nodded, giving the boy space to talk.

"You know what's really nice?" Don asked.

Mark rested his back against the wall and shook his head.

"Janet."

"Good company?" Mark asked, thinking of his feelings about Lana.

"That, too, but she understands my problems. I guess that means more to me than anything. . .except the Bible studies. They've helped me focus on what's really important. Things won't be perfect at home, but I think I'll be able to handle it better."

Mark clasped the boy's shoulder. "That's the important thing, Don. You have friends and you have God. That makes life different."

The teen yawned and stretched. "Thanks," he said. "I've been wanting to say that."

"You're welcome," Mark said.

The boy smiled and then ambled back toward his bunk.

Mark stood in the window for a moment longer, and when fatigue pressed against his eyes, he returned to his bunk and drifted off to a restless sleep.

When dawn's light peeked between the shutter slats, Mark pulled himself up and sat on the edge of his bunk. The teens snored and mumbled in different stages of sleep, and he hated to rouse them to face the gloomy morning. He slid into his jeans and sneakers, then pulled a T-shirt over his head and crept toward the door. Moving in silence, he opened the door and slipped outside.

The rain had stopped, but the trees continued to drip, and rivulets of water ran where the pathway should have been. Across the sodden grass, Lana's cabin door opened, and she stepped outside, pulling the door closed behind her. From her expression, Mark knew without question that she had endured a difficult night.

When she saw him standing outside, she riveted her gaze to his and stepped from the wooden porch. Her hushed voice pierced the morning stillness as she headed toward him. "Latest on the home front. The roof leaks. Can you believe it?"

Mark opened his mouth to warn her about the slippery ground, but before he could act, Lana stepped from the grass, and her feet hit the sodden path and skidded in the muck. Wavering backward and forward like a child on her first ice skates, Lana struggled to retrieve her balance. With caution, Mark maneuvered through the mire, hoping to stop her fall, but before he'd taken three steps, Lana lay sprawled in a pool of mud. Her cry ricocheted through the trees, sending a bevy of birds flying heavenward.

When Mark reached her side, she looked like a chocolate-dipped bonbon. Mark sputtered between concern and laughter. "I tried, Lana." Fighting his amusement, his chuckle won out.

She glared up at him from her pitiful, prone position. "Don't just stand there. I'm up to my armpits in mud."

"I noticed." His chuckle gave way to a full laugh.

"Not funny, Mark." She extended her arm toward him for help.

Mark gripped her slippery fingers with a heave-ho, but instead, his feet did a heave-ho of their own, and he joined her, landing on his knees in the oozing muck. Facing her at eye level, he gawked at her soiled face. "Trying a mud pack? I hear they're great for a beautiful complexion."

"Really," she said, sending him a grin. "How about trying one yourself?" She lifted her muddy hands and dragged them across his cheeks.

They gaped at each other, and their laughter disturbed the quiet morning.

"Guess I fixed you," she said in her playful, cocky tone.

"Not as much as I fixed you."

"Fixed me?" Her face shuffled through a medley of confused expressions.

"It's morning. Men are scheduled to shower now. You'll have to wait until tonight, Missy." He raised himself, semi-covered in mud and helped Lana to stand.

"Please don't make me wait," she whined. "I can't go all day like this. You know—"

"Stop your pitiful moaning." He touched her nose with the tip of his finger, putting a daub of mud on one of the few spots that had remained unsullied. "Grab your clothes, and I'll stand guard."

"I could kiss you," she said. "Thanks."

As the words left her mouth, he watched surprise widen her eyes. "Not now, you can't," he said. Playfully, he stepped away from her mud-speckled form, yet longing to kiss her anyway, anytime. "Besides, I'm only doing this in hopes of getting another glimpse of your Howdy Doody bathrobe."

"Sorry," she said, wading back to her cabin, "that's at home in my treasure chest."

Chapter 12

C lean again, Lana headed for breakfast. With a new appreciation for the cooks, she stopped complaining about the food and enjoyed listening to the conversation, jumping in when she had something to add. After the meal, the teens opted to stay in the activity hall until the sun dried the footpaths. Mark agreed, and the two parents offered to keep a watchful eye on the campers while they played Ping-Pong, darts, and board games.

Lana grinned at Mark, who looked cleaner and brighter than during their earlier meeting, and they slipped outside for a rare moment of free time. Wiser after their morning misadventure, they kept a watchful eye for slippery mud patches. As they headed toward the lake, Mark let his fingers brush against Lana's, and enjoying a rare moment alone with him, Lana eagerly slipped her fingers into his.

Enjoying the serenity, Lana regarded the rain-washed world—leaves and grass a shiny green. When they arrived at the lake, even the water rippled with a malachite glow. Ignoring the damp wood, Lana dropped to the park bench near the water's edge. In the glorious silence, neither she nor Mark spoke, but her mind drifted, and her heart thumped a tom-tom rhythm. She had fallen in serious "like" with the stray man her sister had dragged home only weeks earlier.

Though her heart drummed, Lana felt at peace. She'd been unhappy with herself for too long. Discontented at work and with her life in general, she'd looked at her sister with envy and irritation. Barb had learned an easy acceptance of herself and others long before Lana had even a vague understanding of what such an outlook meant. But now things were different. Since she'd met Mark, a new feeling had emerged—a comfort with her faith and a completeness she'd never known before.

"Five bucks for your thoughts," Mark said, resting his arm along the bench back. His fingers played along her upper arm, and his touch sent tingles through her chest.

"Not worth a penny." She stopped herself. "Is my nose growing?"

"Only a little, Pinocchio."

She tilted her head and nodded. "My thoughts are worth a million dollars."

"Want to share?"

She did, but how? How could she say all that was in her heart without making herself uncomfortable and very vulnerable. He liked her, but did he feel the same as she? "It's hard to put my feelings into words. So much has happened these last few weeks." She gazed into his eyes. "Especially this past week."

"I've seen the difference. Felt the difference. Not only in you, but in me. I think God had His hand in our first meeting—as silly as that day was. Now that I think of it, you haven't attacked me with one power tool in the past couple of weeks."

Lana grinned. "Do you think God has a sense of humor?" The question sailed from her lips without her thinking, and she grimaced, fearing she had made light of the heavenly Father.

"I sure do. He made you. . . ."

Her head jerked upward, but her scowl faded when she saw his smiling face.

"And me," Mark continued. "We humans are a silly lot. I'm sure God gets a good laugh over our antics."

"And hurts with our pain," Lana added.

He nodded. "The Bible says Jesus wept."

His words wrapped around her heart. Jesus laughed and cried. The Lord knew human feelings and understood. The reality seemed overwhelming. "I've learned some things about myself at the camp." She tucked a lock of her hair behind her ear. "I'd like to think I'll be a better person one of these days."

"I'd like to think so, too." He grinned at her.

She gave him a poke.

"You know I'm teasing. I have no right to judge anyone."

"What do you mean?" she said.

His playfulness faded, and he clasped her hand in his, caressing her knuckles with his free hand. "I spend a lot of time taunting you about being flawed and needing improvement, but I'm as flawed as anyone—and definitely need God's grace and guidance."

Her pulse skipped a beat before mounting to a trot. "I don't understand."

"I told you how God guided me to sign up for youth ministry classes."

Holding her breath, she nodded, fearing what he might tell her.

"I have spent a lot of time doubting God's wisdom, Lana. Even though I signed up for the classes and took a youth ministry job, I still questioned God. Still thought He'd made a mistake. Still figured I was unable—even more, unworthy—to guide young people." His gaze left hers and turned toward the blue water winking with sunshine.

She longed to respond, to tell him he was wrong, but wisdom guided her to listen.

"I learned something here, too." He shifted his face toward hers, his gaze seeking the depths of her understanding. "I finally realized I don't have to be perfect. . .because God is perfect. All I have to do is help the teens struggle with that truth just like I have done all my life."

A deep sigh shot from Lana's chest. "It's that easy?"

"It's not easy," he said, grinning. "But it's the hard truth. If we give God the best we can by listening to the teens and speaking from our hearts, then we can't go wrong. Since I've been working with them these past months, I've always tried to ask myself how a Christian should handle the situation. In these past few days, I've questioned myself over and over."

She couldn't keep back her smile at seeing him so serious, but she loved seeing that side of him. "You make me laugh, Mark, and now. . .you've made me want to cry."

"Cry?"

"Because what you've said is so beautiful. . .and true."

"It's God talking, not me."

While she laughed, he slid his hand into his pocket and brought out a small package.

"Here," he said, handing it to her. "I bought you a little present before we left home."

Her heart skipped as she reached for the tiny paper bag. "Why did you do that?"

"I wanted to."

She slid her fingers into the sack and pulled out a thin, woven bracelet that displayed four letters: WWJD. She had no idea what it meant. Radio call letters was all that came to mind. "Christian radio station?"

His laugh filled the quiet. "You're kidding. Haven't you seen these? Teens wear them."

She shook her head, embarrassed that she'd never heard of the bracelets that apparently were popular with Christian teenagers.

"The letters stand for 'What would Jesus do?' I thought—"

"I can guess what you thought." She gave him a knowing smile and gazed at the bracelet resting in her fingers. "Thanks. Would you hook it for me?"

"Sure thing." He grasped the two ends and connected it around her wrist.

She studied the four letters. "This will be a great reminder. Lots better than a tattoo on my forehead. I know I'm not perfect, but I'm trying, and you've been a wonderful example for me."

"Me?" He shook his head. "You're looking at me through love's eyes."

The words startled them both, and their gazes locked.

Mark's tethered breath escaped him. "At least, I hope that's true."

His gaze drifted to her mouth, and Lana touched her bracelet and waited suspended as he leaned toward her. Eagerly, she lifted her lips to meet his, anticipating his kiss.

"Hey, there you are." A voice shot from the distance.

They jolted backward. Lana's heart tripping in expectation and disappointment like a ride on a roller coaster that climbs to the very edge of the first steep slope and stalls.

Looking as if he'd swallowed a chili pepper, Mark's face reddened, and he turned his head toward the voices. Behind them, two of the teens waved wildly, totally unaware they'd put a headlock on what Lana had hoped would be a very romantic moment.

Mark's rigid shoulders sagged. "Drat," he said. Then like a spy movie, before the teens arrived, he whispered in her ear. "I'll meet you after the team activity tonight. Behind your cabin. Nine o'clock."

Lana chuckled and pointed to her wrist. "Should we synchronize our watches?"

Playfully, they pushed their wrists together and compared minute and hour hands with a dramatic nod.

"Tonight," she murmured. "Nine o'clock."

When they lifted their eyes from their wrists, the teens had landed.

The sun grew warmer as the day went on, and soon the grass no longer held traces of the morning's rain. After lunch, Mark began the Bible study. "Tonight we're taking a deeper step in our studies. Two days ago, I tied you together with string, and you learned, I hope," he said, looking around the room at the grinning faces, "about cooperation. Without that, you'd still be strung together in knots."

The teens chuckled and groaned as they remembered their feeble attempts to avoid breaking the string while getting untied.

"Tonight we have two events, one with string and one without."

Moans were quickly followed by applause.

"Before I tell you about tonight's activities, let's open our Bibles to Luke 6:39–40. Jesus has been answering questions, and we know how Jesus often explains his meanings."

"Through parables," Gary said.

"Absolutely, and after Jesus told the questioners a parable, this is what he said." Mark looked down at the Bible and read: " 'Can a blind man lead a blind man? Will they not both fall into a pit? A student is not above his teacher, but everyone who is fully trained will be like his teacher.' "

An intense discussion followed. Some wondered how it would feel to be blind, and others tried to comprehend how they could be a student, yet a teacher.

"Tonight you'll find answers to both these questions," Mark said. "Give it some thought as you enjoy your day."

With the day growing hot and sunny, just about everyone gathered at the beach that afternoon, though Lana had no desire to swim in what she considered frog- and snake-infested water. The young people splashed and bounded in the lake while the adults watched from the shore.

When the two parents headed for the rowboat, Mark slid next to Lana. "What time does your watch say?" he asked, a silly grin playing on his face.

"Two-thirty. How about you?" Lana's pulse tripped at his smile.

"Same." He leaned his head sideways and pressed it against hers for a fleeting minute.

She longed for the hours to pass so she could experience their comical secret rendezvous.

Mark looked back out toward the water. "Only four more days and we're heading home."

Lana's heart sank like a stone. Though crawling into her own cozy bed at home sounded wonderful, she would miss the special time they'd shared here. "You sound disappointed," she said, hoping to hear he felt the same.

"Disappointed? Not at all." He didn't flinch but stared ahead.

Lana struggled to keep her disappointment hidden.

Slowly, he turned to face her, his expression taunting. "I'll have my own bed to sleep in and get back to my everyday, lonely routine. No irritable woman to ruin my scrambled eggs or knock me into the mud."

"Right. And no more leaky roofs, canoe disasters, or creepy, crawling, slithering things."

His teasing eyes softened. "I'll miss being together like this."

A sigh ruffled through her. "Me, too," she admitted.

"I know we don't live too far apart, but it's not quite the same. Life gets busy, and you'll probably find excuses to avoid me."

"Avoid you? Not me." She paused. "If I did, you'd probably miss my antics."

He caressed her fingers. "You make me laugh."

"At or with?" she asked.

His forehead wrinkled in a thoughtful scowl.

"Laugh at me or with me?"

His expression shifted to a grin. "Aren't they the same?"

She gave him a poke. "Not in my head they aren't."

His gaze sought hers and hung there, suspended. "You're learning to laugh at yourself, and I'm learning to care so much for you."

Her heartbeat did a Texas two-step and then galloped ahead like her wild ride on Fury, leaving her breathless. She could only nod, acknowledging the truth. She'd changed in the past few days. More than she could ever imagine.

All Lana thought about the rest of the day was the evening's private meeting with Mark. Why, she wasn't sure. So far, their best intentions had turned to lumpy oatmeal, but her pulse raced in anticipation anyway. After dinner she ambled outside, wandering alone while Mark explained the team activities.

When the teens gathered on the grass, Mark blindfolded four at a time and gave them a lengthy piece of string tied at the ends. "Your job is to form this string into a square."

"How?" Don asked, peeking from beneath the cloth binding his eyes.

"No peeking," Mark said, tugging the fabric in place. "The first step is to discuss the solution between yourselves. Then move around until you think you've accomplished it." He turned and looked at the others watching. "No hints from the crowd, and avoid sounds—especially laughter. Let them do this on their own."

The group agreed. The four teens stood in the middle while the others formed a large circle around them. Those blindfolded pondered and discussed how to shape a square. Each one tried to convince the others his way was best. Finally they settled on a system and moved into position.

Lana grinned, seeing the lopsided shape they'd formed.

"Take off the blindfold," Mark said.

When they removed the covering from their eyes, all the teens joined in the laughter.

"It's impossible," Jason said.

Mark shook his head. "Wait. Let's see if it is."

They discussed where they went wrong, and four more blind-folded teen-agers set out to learn from their fellow campers' mistakes. The result was not much better.

Lana watched with interest, impressed by how Mark had set up the exercise.

The next four had help—a group of teens who had already discussed the best way to accomplish the task. While the four held the string, blindfolded, Teri, serving as the group captain, called out instructions about where each should move and when. The result was a near perfect square.

After the cheers quieted, Mark stepped into the center. "So what's the lesson?"

"Don't try to accomplish things on your own. Ask for help," Gary said.

"When you do ask for help, listen to instructions and follow them," Susan added.

Don raised his arm. "Sometimes we can't accomplish things alone because we're knocked over by the problems and blind to the solutions. But someone else, who can see what we can't, can help us."

The meaning became clear, and the teens talked about their need for Jesus' friendship and for the Holy Spirit's guidance.

Lana contemplated the discussion. *Sometimes we can't accomplish things alone because we're blind to the solutions.* Don's words reverberated in her mind. She needed to say the phrase over and over until it stayed with her.

When the team lessons were finished, the teens had free time until lights out. Mark and Lana ambled away and headed for their cabins, waiting to make sure the teens were occupied before their rendezvous.

Dusk had settled over the woods, and darkness was not far behind. When Lana's wristwatch read nine o'clock, she slipped outside and rounded the corner for the darkest area behind her cabin.

The heat of the day had melted into a pleasantly warm evening. In the moon-lit darkness, the heady scent of decaying undergrowth enveloped her. She listened for Mark's footsteps, but only the lone hoot of an owl and distant croaking of the frogs broke the stillness.

Finally, a rustle of brush drew her attention, and she waited hidden in the shadows. A familiar silhouette rounded the cabin.

"Lana?"

"I'm here." She moved toward him, feeling giddy. "This is silly, isn't it?"

"Oh, I don't know. Getting away from this pack of kids isn't easy." He paused a moment. "Let's take a walk toward the archery range. We should be alone there. Notice I said 'should be.'" He drew her alongside him.

Lana moved with careful steps in the dark to avoid turning her ankle in the rutted underbrush. "Do you feel like a Hardy boy out on a caper?"

His chuckle sounded rich in the quiet night. "More like Davy Crockett sneaking up on the Indians."

"And I'm an Indian chief's daughter," she said, joining his game, "like—"

"Princess Summerfall Winterspring."

She cringed. "Please. Not back to Howdy Doody!"

He slid his arm around her shoulder, drawing her closer. With a spurt of courage Lana wrapped her arm around Mark's waist. The hay bales used for targets at the archery range appeared as silhouettes in the moonlight, and when Mark and Lana reached them, he lifted her into the air as easily as a downy pillow and set her on top, then scooted up next to her and placed his arm around her waist.

She nuzzled close to his side. "This camping thing has been wonderful, and so many things about it. Enjoying the setting, the Bible study. . .and you."

He drew her closer. "It has been special." His voice sounded husky in her ear.

She loved being nestled in his arms. "And the kids," she added. "I've really enjoyed getting to know them."

"It's obvious you care about the teens. Remember the things you said when we first met?"

She shook her head. "I bet you wondered what kind of a horrible person I was."

"No," he remained thoughtful. "I realized that you needed to focus on God's will and ask the Holy Spirit for help. It worked. Look how you were with Janet. You forgot about your own needs and helped her when she needed a friend."

"She's like a new kid in just over a week. Almost a miracle."

"It's not the amount of time, Lana. It's the heart. And it's God working in that heart. That's what makes the difference."

"And that's what's changed me."

"God working in your heart?"

For a moment, she could only nod. Tears pushed against the back of her eyes, and she wiped them away, glad that the darkness hid her emotion. "I've been a Christian most all of my life. A Christian in name, that is, but I need to work harder to live my life the way God expects."

And so did he. With his arms around Lana's shoulder, Mark felt tension rifle through her. She gazed at him in the moonlight, and moisture glinted in her eyes. He shifted and kneaded the tension in her neck.

She flexed her shoulders and moved her head from side to side. "That feels so good."

He harnessed his emotion. If that line wasn't the perfect lead-in, nothing was. "If you think that feels good, this should feel wonderful."

He guided his fingers from her neck to the tip of her chin and tilted her mouth toward his. Her lips looked firm and inviting in the creamy moonlight, and he moved his palm across her hair as his lips touched hers.

Their unison sigh rose and met like voices blending in harmony. . .and Mark loved the song they sang. He eased his mouth tenderly from hers, and as he spoke he felt the feathery touch of his lips near hers. "I've wanted to kiss you like this all day."

"And I've wanted—"

"Mark. Lana. Where are you?" Voices shot through the darkness, turning their melody into caterwauling.

"I know they came this way," a female voice muttered.

Instinctively, Lana and Mark dove from the hay and crouched behind the bales. Mark inched along, staying low to the ground, and Lana followed. They crisscrossed their way back into the trees through the tall grass like video-game characters.

"They're great kids," Mark muttered, "but I wanted just a few moments alone with you."

"I know."

Youthful voices swept across the field. "Did you see them?" asked one teen. "Over that way," said another. "Hey, let's leave Mark alone," hissed a different voice.

Mark lowered himself into the grass, then inched his way into the woods. Lana followed behind him. "I'm the youth director," he whispered over his shoulder. "What am I doing?"

When the night seemed quiet again, Mark stopped, leaned his back against a tree, and pulled Lana to him. "Aren't we terrible? I feel like a kid hiding from my parents."

Lana shook her head. "I know. I feel guilty—like we've done something wrong."

Turning her around to face him, Mark clasped her to him. "Instead we've done something right."

Hand-in-hand, they wandered the long way back and arrived at the shimmering lake drenched with moonlight. Sitting on the bench, Mark brushed her cheek with his fingertips. "We won't forget this night, will we?"

"Never," Lana said, with a loving sigh.

Chapter 13

In the middle of the night, Lana realized the words she'd said earlier in the evening had been the absolute truth. She would never forget that night. Yet there was more than Mark's wonderful kiss that woke her in the darkness. Her legs and arms itched as if they'd been attacked by a herd of mosquitoes in a roundup. She pointed her flashlight beneath the sheet and witnessed the telltale blisters dotting her lower legs and arms where she'd crawled through the underbrush.

Though irritated with herself, she couldn't hold back a chuckle, thinking of Mark scratching himself into a tizzy in his cabin. She reviewed what she might have brought along in her luggage to stop the stinging. Nothing came to mind. *Great planning, Miss Organization!* Yet somewhere in the cabin she recalled seeing some pink lotion.

She tiptoed from her bed and crept along the rows of bunks, gazing at the window sills. That's where she'd seen it. Sure enough, the silhouette of a bottle glowed in the moonlight, and stealthily she pulled it from its narrow sill and eased her way outside.

She headed for the bathroom, where a light glowed, and inside she gawked down at her red blistered limbs. Smoothing the pink fluid onto her arms and legs, she wondered whose parent had been wise enough to send the healing balm along. After sealing the bottle, she whipped outside and, in the darkness, missed seeing the hurtling body who charged into her, leaving her breathless.

She stood for a moment to catch her wind, and Mark gazed down at her, dumbfounded. "I'm miserable. I've been itching for hours," he grumbled. Then he glanced at her arms sticking from beneath her T-shirt. "You, too?"

She nodded with a guilty smile. "Up to my neck."

He yawned and gaped at her. "What should we do now?"

"Want to borrow some of this lotion? I found it on a window sill. I feel better already."

"I suppose. Anything is better than this. I'm a mess," he grumbled.

Lana opened the bottle and daubed some of the soothing lotion on the spots bubbling up on his arms and legs.

Unexpectedly, Mark pulled away from her. "Wait a minute," he said, staring at the thickly coated spots. "I can't wear pink. Pink's for girls."

Lana sputtered. "You can't? Well, sorry, but this doesn't come in blue. Pink is the fashion color of the season."

"Then go easy. Not such big globs."

To taunt him, she made the next spots bigger than before. He grimaced but didn't complain.

Lana screwed the lid closed. "I don't know whose lotion this is, but I'll explain in the morning."

"Do you think you could leave my name out of it? We'll look a bit suspicious with our arms and legs covered in pink goop."

"Don't be a baby, Mark. I'll tell them a masked bandit crawled through the poison ivy with me." She gave him the once-over and snickered. "You can sneak a second coating under your clothes in the morning. Stop whining." She tiptoed and gave him a teensy kiss on the lips.

With the pretense of drama, he staggered backward. "Now that makes this all worthwhile." His mouth curved into his sunny smile.

Lana smirked and ignored his comment. Without a word, they turned back toward their individual cabins and waved a silent good night.

❦

Mark returned to bed and had to admit that the lotion did ease the terrible itching. He envisioned the scene and chuckled to himself. They did make a silly sight, each of them dotted with pink spots covering their blistering skin. He should have known better than to creep along the ground. Poison ivy and poison oak were the first plants he'd learned about in Camping 101. But at that moment, he'd been desperate. Stifling his overtired snickers, he tried to close his eyes.

But his thoughts returned to Lana. They'd almost had time to talk about things that were important until his youthful charges interrupted them. Mark longed for some quiet time to share his dreams and hopes with the woman who'd barreled into his heart. The sensation had caught him way off guard.

Still amazed, he relived how his feelings had run away with him. He was no kid anymore. He'd be thirty on his next birthday. Then his mind drifted, wondering at what age wisdom became one of God's gifts. Or if he might ever be wise. But tonight—except for his telltale blisters—he felt a little smarter.

For the first time in his life, he knew positively that he'd made the right career decision. He felt at home with these teens. Sure, he wanted to have a moment of quiet, but he loved what he was doing. Each day, he grew stronger in his faith and worked to improve his weaknesses. He felt blessed to be given the task of touching their young lives with pure, clean enjoyment and with Bible study and fellowship, despite his personal flaws.

Those experiences still lived inside him from his own youth. He prayed that these teens would come away from the experience with memories that made a difference. With Lana on his mind and his itching limbs soothed, he finally drifted off to sleep.

The early morning sun shot through the window and pressed against his eyes. The itching had roused itself as morning neared, and Mark jumped out of his bunk, slid on his clothes, and darted across the grass. He needed some of Lana's medicine. And he needed it before the whole camp awoke.

With only a light tap on the window, Lana heard him and tiptoed to the door. She opened it a crack and poked the bottle outside. "And hurry up. I don't want to wake the girls."

"What's wrong, Lana?" One of the girls' voices mumbled, as she lifted her head and gaped through the doorway.

"Nothing, Sara," Lana whispered back. "Go to sleep."

"Is that Mark outside?" the girl hissed.

"Shush, I don't want you to wake the others." Lana warned her again.

"I'm already awake." Janet's voice sailed through the doorway. "What's wrong?"

"Nothing," Lana said, hoping they'd go back to sleep.

"Then what's all the commotion about?" Susan asked.

🌾

Janet leaned over her bunk and peeked through the chink in the door. "Mark's using calamine lotion. Poison ivy?"

Lana held her finger to her lips to silence her and nodded. Janet's gaze traveled down Lana's arm, staring at her telltale blisters also caked with the pink lotion. A grin rose on the girl's lips. "I think you two better find a safer place to chat than in a poison ivy patch."

A loud yawn traveled along the bunks. "Who has poison ivy?" Teri asked.

A muffled voice rose from a sleeping bag. "Lana and Mark. Our fearless leaders."

A snicker traveled the length of the room.

Lana shook her head. "Don't call me your fearless leader. This is the first camping trip of my life, and I don't plan to go on another one—ever."

"Oh, you'd better not say that," Janet murmured. "Mark's a youth director. He'll have lots of camping trips to take in his lifetime. And I think he'll want you right there at his side."

Lana felt a flush cover her cheeks. "Hush." But the truth was she wanted to be at his side—forever.

Girlish giggles filled the cabin.

"Look," someone snickered. "She's blushing."

Mark stuck the bottle through the gap in the doorway.

Instead of taking the container, Lana flung the door open wide. "No sense in being subtle, Mark. They're all in here laughing at us hysterically."

He gaped at them helplessly and then grinned. "Okay, but one word from any of you, and I'll. . .I'll. . ."

"You'll what?" Lana asked.

"I'll think of something."

"It's cute, Mark," Janet called from her bunk. "You and Lana look really great together. Especially with both of you decorated in pink."

Mark raised his eyebrows and glared at the girl. "The lotion doesn't come in blue, Janet. I asked."

Eight girls sat up in their bunks and joined in a full-bodied laugh as he spun on his heel and headed back to his cabin.

Mark leaned against a bench near the dining hall, waiting for the lunch bell. He felt hungry. In fact, more than ready to eat. "These two weeks have turned me into a trash compactor. I'm never full."

"Nervous energy," Lana agreed. "Keeping an eye on thirty-two teens isn't cotton candy."

"No, but they sure tried to stick to us as if we were." Mark let loose a chuckle, thinking of his analogy, then glanced at his drying blisters. "Three days with that lotion and we're lookin' good." He beamed a smile her way.

Lana surveyed her arms and legs. "I thanked Sara for the calamine. Glad her mother thought ahead. But I worried we might spread the infection all over the place."

Mark grinned. "No, but we did an A-one job on ourselves."

"And taught everyone an important lesson at the same time. Don't walk through underbrush in the dark." She gave him her teacher expression. "Always remember to turn your bungled activities into a positive experience."

"I suppose when you put it that way. . ."

Lana pulled herself into a ramrod pose. "I'm the master of bungling."

Mark laughed at her confession. "No one could argue that."

As the words left his mouth, the lunch bell rang, and the crowd appeared like a tidal wave and filled the dining hall. With a clatter of forks and knives, the campers finished lunch, and before they scattered, Mark knew he'd better review their final day.

"Quiet, everyone." His voice resounded through the room, and little by little, the din dwindled. "Free time this afternoon to enjoy yourselves. But remember we leave tomorrow so you may want to gather your things together and not leave it all until morning. After dinner, we'll have our final Bible study and then our farewell bonfire. So when you're done here, you're free to go. . .but stay out of trouble."

Amid their hoots and chuckles, an arm shot up. Mark pivoted toward the teenager. "Dennis?"

The teen's discomfort was evident as he squirmed in his chair. "Teri didn't show for lunch. I wondered if anyone's seen her."

Mark recalled seeing the pair as a constant twosome, so the young man's words sent a minor charge through his chest. "Anyone? Girls? Is Teri still in her cabin?"

Lana touched his arm. "She wasn't there just before I came outside. She bunks in my cabin."

Mark's pulse picked up pace. "Anyone?"

The teens stared with blank expressions toward him. As they rose to leave, Mark figured he'd better get down to the facts. "Hold up, Dennis."

Before he headed toward the youth, Sara stepped up. "I heard Teri say earlier she was going down by the lake."

Lana pressed the teen's shoulder. "Thanks, Sara, we'll have a look."

Dennis came forward, guilt written over his face, making Mark more than curious. "What's up, Dennis?"

He shrugged. "Teri and I had a little argument this morning, and she huffed off. I thought she'd get over it and I could talk with her at lunch, but—"

"But she's not here, so you're worried." He lifted an eyebrow at the teen.

Dennis nodded.

"Mark," Lana said, "did you hear Sara?"

He turned his eyes toward Lana. "The lake?"

Lana nodded.

"Then we'd better check it out."

The three rushed down toward the lake and met Sara heading back. Before they reached her, she called to them. "She's not there, and the rowboat's there so she didn't take it out."

Jolted by nervous energy, Mark gathered his wits. He had prayed nothing would go wrong on this trip. Now, on their last day, he looked heavenward. *Lord, keep each of these kids safely in Your care.* He eased his rigid shoulders back, letting God's promise filter through him—*Ask, and you shall receive.* Mark struggled to let go and receive.

He looked into three tense faces. "Okay, let's think logically and then spread out. Lana, check your cabin, toilet, and shower. Sara, you check the other girls' cabins and the activity hall. Dennis and I will cover the archery range and soccer fields, then the hiking trails. We'll meet back here, hopefully with Teri. Okay?"

❦

As Lana darted into the cabin, her mind flew. What does an angry teenage girl do? Usually something dramatic, she remembered from her own youth. The cabin was quiet, as were the two outbuildings. Dramatic? What was dramatic?

She spun around. She might pin herself to the archery bull's-eye, but the guys were checking there. Lana closed her eyes. The lake made sense, and Lana raced back to the water's edge. It made a great setting for moping and feeling sorry for one's self. She'd done it herself as a teen.

Lana's legs prodded her to the lake almost faster than she could run.

Disappointment washed over her when she skidded to a stop. No one. The rowboat sat empty at the shoreline. She sat on the bench, resting her elbows on her knees, and thought. A canoe? Teri wouldn't go out alone in a canoe. Dramatic, yes. But foolish.

Her heartbeat charged to a sprinter's pace, and Lana rushed to the far side of the boat shed. The door gaped open, and a deep rut had been cut through the loose sand where a canoe had been dragged to the water. Sure enough, the foolish, lovesick teen had gone off alone in a canoe. Lana looked back toward the cabins far in the distance. Should she waste time looking for help or go on her own? The question surprised her. Her take-charge attitude faltered.

A "no time to spare" intuition ran through her, and she pulled at a canoe, amazed they were heavier than she expected. She tugged it with amazing strength to the water's edge, then darted back for two paddles. She pushed the canoe carefully into the water. Where it rested against the sand, she stepped into the center, remembering as many of the rules as she could. This time, not standing up, she crouched and worked her way to the middle. But at that moment, she faltered.

She should leave Mark a message. She glanced down at her bracelet. WWJD. If she left that on the bench, he'd know where she was. With caution, she stepped from the canoe and darted across the sand to the bench. She tugged on the bracelet, then paused. What would Jesus do? The question slowed her thoughts. Jesus would pray. . .and He'd look to His disciples for help. The awareness struck her.

What had Mark been teaching the teens during the two weeks? Teamwork. Cooperation. Not depending on yourself but turning to others and to God. Though she knew God would be with her, she couldn't go alone. If she'd learned one thing during these two weeks, she'd learned to listen to others. She had to be patient and get help.

Lana pushed her feet through the sand, then reached hard ground where running came easier. In a moment, she saw one of the teens heading toward her. "Gary," she waved her arm. "Tell the others she took a canoe. Tell Mark I'll start out and for him to follow."

He gave her an understanding wave and spun around, heading back toward the cabins.

Thanking God for reminding her to rely on others, Lana turned back and climbed into the canoe. Once settled, she dug the canoe paddle into the water and tugged with her short arms. Slowly she moved into the lake and finally caught the river current. If she hadn't left word for Mark, she would have no idea how to get back to camp, fighting against the current's surprising strength. Now she knew Mark would be on his way to help her.

"Oh, help me, Lord," Lana called out aloud. "I need Your guidance. Teri's in deep trouble." The words might have made her smile another day, but at this moment Lana saw nothing to grin about. Her skills at people-saving had never been tested.

The current helped her move along, and the lessons from the earlier canoe trip had apparently found a home in her brain. She moved the paddle from one side to the other, pushing the water past her, digging deep, and gaining speed.

Lana glanced over her shoulder. The lake was far behind, but she thought she saw a speck where the beach area had vanished around the bend. Mark. Her head leaped with hope. Ahead, she saw nothing but water and sky and the shoreline on each side of the fast-rolling river. Approaching a parcel of trees along the shore, she recognized the place where she'd fallen into the water days earlier. She steered clear of the spot, but around the next bend, her heart lurched. A canoe paddle lay captured in the tangle of tree branches.

"Teri! Teri! Are you there?" She searched the bank for evidence. Tears rolled from her eyes, and she launched fervent prayers to heaven. Along the bank, she spotted an overturned canoe. Her senses jolted as a young voice sailed to her over the water. "Here. I'm over here."

Lana looked ahead and caught sight of the teenager, waving wildly from the bank a few yards ahead. She looked behind and saw the distant form growing larger. A mixture of relief and fear plummeted through Lana's chest. *What could have happened, Lord? But You kept her safe. Thank You.*

"I'm coming!" Lana called. Calling out words of assurance to the teenager, her voice rose on the breeze as she pulled herself toward the shore. But Lana's panic remained. If that speck behind her wasn't Mark, what would they do? She had no idea.

Teri hung over the bank and grabbed the end of the canoe. "I was so stupid," the teen uttered over and over. "Just because I was upset at Dennis. And it was so silly."

"He's already forgiven you, Teri, and he's scared to death."

"He is?" she asked, clinging to Lana's side.

"He sure is."

Lana held the shivering girl in her arms, hoping her own tremors would go unnoticed. She looked down the lonely stretch of river, wondering how she'd had the stamina to get this far and praying that Mark's strong arms would bring him to her quickly. Then her eyes lifted to heaven, and peace filled her.

Chapter 14

Mark's chest tightened as fear gripped him. They'd searched everywhere. When the campers reassembled to compare notes, everyone gathered except Lana and Gary. Now his panic heightened. Others had joined the hunt to no avail. He closed his eyes, trying to imagine where the two had gone. As independent as Lana was, he had no way of guessing what she had done.

Before he could calculate what to do, Gary appeared, running toward them. "She took a canoe. Lana's on her way and asked you to follow."

Following Gary, the group ran toward the lake. Mark's mind whirred, praising God Lana hadn't gone off without asking for help.

"Okay, the rest of you wait here. Keep your eyes open while Dennis and I take the rowboat."

The parents gathered the teens around them in animated chatter as Mark and Dennis rowed away from shore.

The boat glided along quickly, picking up the river current. With powerful tugs of the oars, they sailed past the shoreline, eyes peeled for any sign of either canoe. As they rounded the bend, a canoe paddle bobbed among the debris at the bank, but they pressed forward.

Mark saw them before Dennis and waved his arms wildly. Relief charged through him when both women waved back, and their shouts of encouragement bounced across the water.

When they reached shore, Mark jumped to the sand to moor the boat, and before he reached Lana, she froze in place, and her piercing scream sent a bevy of frightened birds fluttering from the trees.

His heart lodged in his throat, and he charged toward her while Lana's face paled in horror.

"It's only a snake," Teri yelled, tugging on Lana's arm.

Mark masked his grin. Lana had met her nemesis. She shot across the grass like an arrow and, in a heartbeat, clung to Mark's chest.

He wrapped his arm around her shaking frame. "You're okay now. It's gone. You scared the snake worse than he scared you, Lana."

"Are you sure it's gone?" she asked, her head buried in his shirt.

"Positive." He chuckled silently. "You're safe from snakes and being marooned."

She lifted her head from his chest. "Praise the Lord you found us. I had no idea what to do," Lana whispered, her body still trembling.

Mark tightened his embrace. "You did the right thing. You ran for help." He tilted his head lower to gaze into her eyes.

"I was positive Teri had taken a canoe, and I almost left without sending word to you." Her face flushed with her guilty admission.

"But you didn't. You asked for help and then went after her. Two weeks ago you'd have suggested someone else look for Teri."

Lana's eyes widened. "You're right. I probably would have done just that." A sad grin tugged at her mouth. "You know what did it?"

"Did it?" He studied her face, wondering what she meant.

"What reminded me to go for help?"

Whatever it was, he thanked God for the blessing.

She lifted her arm. "The bracelet. WWJD. I started to leave the bracelet on the bench, thinking you'd find it, but instead, I thought of the meaning. This gift means more to me than you'll ever know."

A large lump caught in Mark's throat. He hadn't cried in years, not since he was a kid, but maybe tears weren't so bad. If they were good enough for Jesus, they were good enough for him. He wiped the moisture from his eyes and sent an inner prayer of thanksgiving heavenward. A prayer thanking God for the women's safety and for Lana's growth.

❦

Mark looked over the crowd after dinner, their faces a blend of emotions. In the morning they would return home to the comforts they enjoyed, and the good times they'd shared would be only memories. Mark felt the same. His gaze settled on Lana's thoughtful face. He'd given thanks so many times during the day for Lana and Teri's safety. Lana had changed his life.

The activity hall seemed warm, and a breeze had risen outside. Rather than keep the campers inside, Mark suggested having Bible study around their last campfire. The teens accepted his idea with eagerness.

While the evening was still light, they ambled in, two and three at a time, and gathered around the fire pit. As he scanned their faces, his gaze settled on Lana in the dusky light, looking up at him from the log, her face tanned and her tousled hair streaked with sunny highlights. His chest burst with happiness.

He opened the Bible and scanned the verse, sensing the message was a perfect way to end the camping trip. "First let's think back over our two weeks together. As I watched you these past days, I've seen the closeness and warmth that have happened in the short time we've been together. Imagine if we could reach out to the world with the same zeal. How wonderful the earth would be."

Murmurs of agreement drifted across the open space.

"We've worked on communication and cooperation, all part of teamwork. And I hope we've developed a bond with each other and an even greater one with the Lord. When we go home, keep what you learned in your thoughts. The enjoyment and experiences will soon be only memories, but I hope the lessons we learned have planted seeds in your hearts."

His eyes shifted again to Lana, her sweet face gazing at him with open admiration. He loved her, and all he needed was the courage to tell her so.

He turned again to the Scriptures and eyed the waiting teens. "For those who have their Bibles, open them to Galatians 5:22–25. The rest of you can listen. I hope you will take these verses with you and keep them close. They will serve as a personal motto for each of us as we return home: 'But the fruit of the Spirit is love, joy, peace, patience, kindness, goodness, faithfulness, gentleness and self-control. Against such things there is no law. Those who belong to Christ Jesus have crucified the sinful nature with its passions and desires. Since we live by the Spirit, let us keep in step with the Spirit.'"

Rather than discuss the passage, he asked the teens to think quietly about what he'd read. After a few minutes of silence, he closed with prayer.

To his surprise, the teens had prepared their own words of thanks. Gary rose, and as he reminisced their two weeks together, his wit and good spirit infected everyone as quickly as the poison ivy Mark and Lana had endured. Laughter lifted as high as the smoke from the bonfire.

"If you're having marshmallows tonight," Lana added, "please don't show me your perfect specimen." She sent out a warm smile and was greeted with more merriment.

"How's your poison ivy, Mark?" Don asked.

"And how's yours, Lana?" Janet teased.

Lana grinned, but Mark nailed them with his witty remark. "If all of you had learned to leave a man and woman alone for a few minutes so they could have a serious conversation, no one would have poison ivy, and who knows what special moments might have happened?"

Kissing sounds echoed around the campfire and ended only when the sound of guitar music filled the air. The campers joined in with familiar camp songs while Mark settled beside Lana, and in the dark, they clasped hands. Scanning the teens, he noticed Janet sat close to Don, and once again, Dennis and Teri smiled at each other, their squabble resolved. As the moon rose and the fire died, Mark sent the teens back to the cabins, herded along by the two counselors. Standing in the silence, Mark looked at Lana and drew in a deep, relieved breath.

"Should we douse the fire?" Lana asked, feeling a surge of comfort wash over her.

Mark nodded, and he shoveled sand onto the smoldering ashes while Lana raked the coals that had drifted away back into the pit.

As she pulled on the rake, Lana looked down at her blue and white WWJD bracelet—what would Jesus do? Mark couldn't have given her a more appropriate gift. The bracelet would help keep her on track.

With a final bucket of sand sprinkled over the charred wood, Mark stepped back and caught Lana's hand. "So this is it? Tomorrow, we're home."

Courage and honesty rushed through Lana's thoughts. "I'm home right now, Mark." His moonlit smile brightened the darkness, and her heart swelled with complete joy. "This has been some camping trip."

"Lana, I wish I could tell you what it's meant to me. You've been a partner through it all. A difficult partner at times, but a perfect partner. I thank God for bringing us together."

She grinned. "Maybe we should thank Barb, too. She brought you home."

"When we first got here, I figured we'd leave after two weeks with you not speaking to me. Instead, I've fallen in love with you. I hope you know that."

She tried to speak, but her voice caught in her throat, and she only nodded.

He slipped his arm around her and drew her closer to his side. "I think of all the crazy things that happened. You were up to your elbows in soapsuds, waist-deep in frogs, up to—"

"Up to my neck in poison ivy." She gazed into his glowing, moonlit eyes and smiled. "And now I'm over my head in love." She looked into the spangled sky and sensed God's blessing.

Mark's gaze embraced her. "I love you with all my heart, Lana, and there's nothing better in the whole world than to be loved."

As naturally as the sun rising, their lips met, and Lana's heart soared over her head and up toward the stars. Like them, she glimmered with happiness, and she silently praised God for His generous blessing—the gift of love.

SEASONS

Prologue

The icy February wind penetrated her body. The canvas flapped overhead, and a distant voice drifted in and out of her hearing. She felt numb, numb through to her heart. The canvas flapped loudly again. Suddenly the voice stopped. A hand reached under her elbow to help her from the cold metal chair. The heel of her shoe turned in a rut in the frozen earth. Her legs buckled.

"Are you okay?" someone asked, grabbing her arm to steady her.

Even in the icy cold, the heavy scent of dying flowers caught on the wind and filled her nostrils. Her stomach churned. Well-wishers patted her arm, her shoulder. Words, sad words, floated into her consciousness—*so sorry. . .with God. . .deepest sympathy*—words she didn't want to hear.

She didn't want sympathy. She wanted Tim. She wanted to scream out, to close her eyes so it would all go away. She tried to make it go away continually, ever since she received the call. *Michigan State Police. . .accident. . .hospital. . .serious.* These, too, were words she didn't want to remember.

Someone nudged her back, or was it the wind? She wanted to strike out and cry, "Let me alone. I can't leave him here." Tears rolled down her icy cheeks—warm tears, the only warmth left in her.

"Come on, Sally. It's too cold to stand here. Let's get into the car," her brother's voice urged—softly distressing her. She knew he was trying to help, but no one could.

She found herself moving through the patches of crusted snow toward the sleek black limousine. Heat met her face as the door opened, and she leaned over to slide in. The door closed. A gust of cold air announced the opening of another door. Bill, her brother, and his wife, Sue, climbed into their seats. The door closed. Sally felt the vehicle move slowly along the gravel road, heading back to the church for a luncheon prepared for the mourners. She was a mourner, but she didn't want to eat. She wanted to stay here with Tim.

Her eyes were drawn back to the flapping canvas, the mound of flowers, the hard earth camouflaged with artificial grass, and the bronze box holding inside her love. Her husband. Her heart.

Chapter 1

E nough is enough."

Sally Newgate chided herself as the church steeple loomed into view. She shook her head, bringing herself back to the present, and turned her coupe into the parking lot of Holy Cross Church. Each week old memories tugged at her as she participated in the support group. At her first session, Jack Holbrook opened the program with a reading from Ecclesiastes, "To every thing there is a season, and a time to every purpose under the heaven." She hadn't believed it at first, but now, she'd begun to.

When Sally entered the Fellowship Hall, she searched the rows for a familiar face, and spying one, she slid in next to the woman, pulling a notebook from her handbag. "Ready?"

The woman flashed her own pad and pencil. "Sure am." She turned an embarrassed grin toward Sally. "Before I started these meetings I thought I was the only one with troubles."

Sally grinned. "You're not alone. You're surrounded by multitudes." She gestured toward the growing crowd sitting around the large hall. As her gaze followed her arm's sweep of the room, her smiling face lifted, and she looked into the friendly chocolate-brown eyes of Brad Mathews.

He stood above her, his ashen hair falling in a soft wave with one curl dipping to his forehead. "Thanks for the welcoming smile." He looked amused. "It was for me, wasn't it?"

Sally felt a blush creep along her hairline. Mesmerized by his sparkling eyes, she stared at him without a word. Brad had edged his way into her thoughts since the day they met. For so long, memories of Tim filled every moment of her day. But lately, the pain had softened and settled into acceptance.

"Sorry," he said finally. "I was trying to step by without disturbing you—to sit there." He pointed to the chair next to Sally. "Now I'm waiting, hoping you'll invite me to join you."

Sally fluttered. "Goodness. You don't have to ask. Please join us." Words tumbled out, and she swallowed to gain control of a rush of emotions. From the first session, Sally had found him attractive. But tonight, dressed in beige slacks and a heather green pullover, he looked strikingly handsome. His gaze stayed connected to hers, and she felt her flush deepen.

His full lips curved into a bright smile. "Thanks for the invitation." He stepped past her and slid into the chair.

The chatter subsided as Jack stepped to the microphone. "Tonight our topic is 'A Time to Keep and a Time to Throw Away.' For each of you, the time of grief is different. Some of you have made changes in your lives. Some haven't. It doesn't mean you love more or less than the next person. It only means that your adjustment to the change has proceeded more quickly or more slowly. That's all."

His words flooded into Sally's memory. She recalled a year and a half earlier when she wasn't ready to remove Tim's belongings from her bedroom. She had wandered to the closet, cradling his clothing in her arms like a baby, her face buried deep within the cloth. She was stronger now.

When Jack finished his presentation, she headed for the refreshment table, and Brad joined her. Thoughtfully, he pulled a cookie from the tray as if lost in thought. "I wish my kids understood what Jack said. It's difficult to explain to two young children why their mother died. She was active and healthy, and in less than two months, she was gone."

Sally twinged.

"I tried to be brave for them," he continued, "and I suppose the charade was good for me. My kids—that's another story."

"It doesn't matter how old you are," Sally said. "I still miss my mom, and she died ten years ago when I was twenty-four. How long has it been since your wife died?"

"Just over a year. I know it takes time."

Brad's gaze caught hers, and her heart skipped double-time.

The conversation continued into the small group discussion, and when the session ended, Sally headed toward the exit. Brad's long strides brought him to her side, and they left the building into the crisp night, the fall leaves smoldering piles along the curb.

As they ambled down the sidewalk, Sally glanced at him. "I wonder if you should talk more about your wife to your children instead of avoiding it. They'll see you haven't forgotten her, and it gives them permission to talk about her, too."

He slowed to a stop, his hands deep in his pockets, his head bowed. "I do avoid talking about Janet. I'm always afraid I'll make them sadder than they already are." His gaze rose to hers. "What you said makes sense. Thanks."

They continued through the parking lot and reached Sally's car. Brad stood by her side as she opened the door. She paused uncomfortably before sliding in. "Well. . .good night."

His hand rested on the handle. "Thanks for the idea. Good night." He closed her door, hurrying toward his own car.

❧

The telephone rang, pulling Sally from a near nap. She dragged herself in a daze across the living room and picked up the receiver, her "hello" a near whisper.

"Sally Newgate?" a glib masculine voice asked.

"Yes. May I ask who's—"

"Hi, it didn't sound like you. This is Steve Wall."

An uneasy feeling ran through her. Steve Wall? From work? Why was he calling?

"Did I wake you?" he asked.

No way would she admit she had fallen asleep on a Saturday afternoon. "No, I was daydreaming, I guess."

She heard a slight chuckle. "That's why I'm calling. I've been daydreaming about you."

Daydreaming? What? His words sent a chill through her. She hardly knew this man.

"Is something wrong? Did I call at a bad time?"

"I'm sorry, Steve," she muttered. "I'm not sure I understand." She clutched the receiver with icy hands. Since Tim's death, the only men who called Sally were related or old, not a man daydreaming about her.

"I'll be blunt. I wondered if you'd have dinner with me sometime. How's that for being more direct?" His voice lifted with good humor. "Next Saturday?"

Sally blanched. She took a deep breath, calming herself. This was ridiculous. "Sorry, Steve. I have plans next weekend." Her niece, Carrie, was to spend the day with her. Though her alibi was real, she decided to be blunt. "I'm rather new at being single, Steve. I'm not dating yet."

Steve's tone took a sarcastic edge. "Mine won't be your only invitation, I'm sure. I can't believe I'm the first to ask you out. You're a lovely woman, Sally. Some other time then?"

Sally hesitated. She pulled the telephone away from her ear, but she stopped herself from hanging up. "Perhaps," she heard herself say, not believing her own voice.

"All right then." His toned brightened. "See you at work."

Sally clutched the telephone, startled more at her reaction than at the call. Placing the receiver on the cradle, she thought of her meetings. She felt terribly disappointed in herself. Shouldn't she be beyond the point of pure panic by now?

Two years had passed. But she still struggled at times feeling Tim let everyone down, dying at thirty-seven. For so long, Sally felt angry at him. Really, she had been angry at everyone—the drunk driver, Tim, and even God. Eventually, her anger turned to sadness, then to loneliness, and now to a periodic dull ache.

She turned and caught her pale reflection in the hall mirror. Steve had called her attractive. "Lovely," in fact. She studied her reflection. Her weight-loss, after Tim's death, defined her cheekbones. Her chestnut hair, then lifeless, had recaptured its natural sheen. Tim had often told her she was beautiful. She hadn't heard that word in a long time—or the word "lovely" for that matter.

On Monday, Sally pulled into her driveway after work and found her neighbor Ed Washburn with a wheelbarrow full of compost, mulching the perennials in her flower beds. Sally parked her car and ambled across the grass toward him. He leaned on the shovel, his white hair contrasting with his leathery skin.

"Ed, you did this last year for me. I certainly didn't expect you to do it again."

Ed's hazel eyes crinkled at the edges. "Decided to have the fun myself." He brushed his white hair off his brow with the back of his gloved hand. "Really, I finished mulching and had compost left in the barrow."

"Well, you're the best friend in the world. Thanks."

Sally eyed her flower beds, now tidy with mounds of the dark earth protecting the lifeless foliage. "You're almost finished?"

"Yep. This is the last rosebush."

"Come in for a cup of hot tea. I might even find a snack for you." She elbowed him playfully.

"You know how to get to an old man's heart." Ed grinned.

Ed moved the wheelbarrow and shovel to the edge of the driveway, then followed Sally to the back door and into the kitchen. He thoughtfully removed his shoes and draped his jacket on a chair as he sat at the oak table by the bay window.

Sally reached for the dish of scones sitting on the counter as Ed eyed the plate.

"Baked some biscuits, did ya?" Ed asked.

"Griddle scones, like my grandma used to make. They're like a sweet biscuit, browned on a griddle. I made these with dried Michigan cherries. I'll warm them for you."

As she talked, she heated the scones and made tea. "Ed, you're a man. Let me ask you something from a male's point of view about being single—dating, actually."

Ed cocked his head, an amused look on his face. "I might be a man, but remember, I'm an *old* man. That's different."

She grinned over her shoulder. "You still had to face being single again after all those years of marriage."

"That's true, but it took me a long time. Alice is the first woman who caught my fancy. Before Alice came along, I still felt married to Mildred. But when I met Alice, I knew. My feelings stirred, and I came alive again."

Sally slid the warm scones and mug of tea on the table. "Here we go."

Ed grabbed up a knife and smoothed butter over the warm pastry. He took a big bite. "These are great."

"I don't make them often. They're too good to be healthy."

Ed laughed and attacked another scone. Sally stood at the counter, sipping her tea, and watched him with pleasure. Sally was amused by the blossoming friendship between Ed and Alice Brown, her elderly church friend. Alice had come to Sally's rescue after Tim's death, full of energy and love, packing and boxing, cleaning and listening—especially listening.

Sally's thoughts drifted back to her question about dating. She looked through the window. The sun's setting rays spread purple and orange across the sky. "A man who works with me called with a dinner invitation, and I fell apart." She refocused on Ed. "You said it earlier. I still feel married."

"When you meet the right man you'll know. You'll feel it inside." Ed tapped his chest. "In your heart. You don't need to look for it either. It'll happen." He chuckled, licking his fingers. "Now, do you need any other words of wisdom from an old man?" He wiped the crumbs from his lips with a napkin.

"No, but thanks." She gazed at his warm smile. "By the way, I've finished decorating my room."

"Well, I'll be. You mean I don't have to listen to you and Alice discuss wallpaper and quilts for a while?" He rose on stiff legs and brushed the crumbs from his lap. "The other day I had a thought. Maybe you'd like an old quilt stand for your room. I could look in the attic. I think there's one there, and you could have it."

"A quilt stand? I'd love to buy one."

"Buy? You already paid me. Those scones were worth a million. The stand belonged to my grandmother. It'll sit up in the attic 'til I die."

"But. . .give it away?"

"What do I want with that old thing? If my son were living, maybe he'd like it, but since he's gone, I'd like you to have it more than anyone."

"Son?" His statement jolted her. "Ed, I had no idea you had a son. How did he die?"

"In Vietnam." He remained silent for a moment. "It was so hard on Mildred. He was our only child."

"You've talked about Mildred, but never about your son."

"I try to think about the good times."

"I wish I'd do that. I'm always moping because we never had a child, and here you had a child who died. That's worse."

"I had him for a time, Sally. I knew him and loved him—and I have memories."

"Memories," Sally repeated, plopping down at the kitchen table. "Memories can be bad."

Ed rested his hands against a chair back. "They're bad at first, maybe. Later on you'll concentrate on the good things."

"Life can be so ironic. I may never be a mother."

"You're still young. You have a whole future ahead of you."

She gazed at his gentle face lined by his own hurts and sorrows. "Do you go to church, Ed? Funny, I don't think I've ever asked you."

A tender grin flickered on his lips. "Mildred and I went every Sunday. After Mildred died, I got out of the habit, I guess. Too lonely. Wouldn't go to bed at night, though, without reading my Bible. It gives me perspective."

"Perspective, that's what I need." She rose and pressed her cheek to Ed's. "You are an amazing man."

"Well now, I think that's a compliment."

❦

Brad stood near the refreshment table, focusing on the wall clock. Sally hadn't arrived yet, and disappointment trudged through him. His recurring thoughts of her seemed to be a mixture of pleasure and guilt. Since he first heard her speak in the small group sessions, he couldn't get her out of his mind. What captivated him were her warm, sensitive eyes, the brightest moss green he'd ever seen.

He hadn't looked that deeply into a woman's eyes since Janet died. And he supposed this was what caused his guilt. Janet had always been a sensible woman. If she could speak to him now, she'd say, "Brad, you can love my memory, but you can't love me. So don't be foolish. Make a new life for yourself and for the kids. What are you waiting for?" His lips curled into a private grin at the thought of her.

"And what's causing that little, secret grin?"

He looked down into Sally's eyes. She stared at him with curiosity. Again, her gaze left him flustered.

"Just life, I suppose."

Sally remained riveted to him. "Life can be amusing."

"To be honest, I was thinking about Janet." He couldn't admit he was also thinking of her. "If Janet were here, she'd be sending me down the road to get on with it. 'Things will never get better if you just think about them.' Maybe not that exactly, but. . .she'd say my life's on hold."

"Tim, too," Sally said, with a knowing look. "He'd go with the flow, as they say. Not me. I get in the canoe and tip over." Her full, bright lips parted to a smile.

"You do have a gift for words. I've lost my oars many times, too. Especially going over the rapids."

The microphone squealed, and Brad turned to see Jack waiting for the room to quiet. "I suppose we should grab a seat."

Jack opened the meeting with prayer and introduced his topic, "A Time to Seek." Brad felt rattled by Sally's nearness. He recalled about nine months after Janet died, his cousin Darlene invited him to dinner. She hadn't told him she'd also invited a divorced lady friend. He'd made the best he could out of the situation, but in his heart, the evening was a disaster. At work, women dropped hints here and there they were available and interested. The problem was, he wasn't— until now.

Concentrating on the presentation proved difficult. Brad couldn't keep his eyes from Sally. She followed Jack's every move. Her expression reflected Jack's words, her head nodding, her mouth curving into a fleeting grin.

Suddenly, she turned toward Brad with a questioning glance, her skin tone rising to a shy schoolgirl pink. Tender sensations surged through him. Before he could force his attention on Jack, the presentation concluded.

"Jack's right," Sally said. "It's what you said. You can't sit around waiting for life to happen, you have to find a new life, make new friends and new traditions. Sounds easier than it is." She rose, and Brad followed.

"I couldn't help but think of my cousin's good intentions at playing matchmaker. A horrible experience. I wasn't ready at all. Haven't been, yet. Not one date."

Sally's eyes brightened. "Nice to know I'm not alone—and it's been longer for me. A coworker asked me to dinner, and you'd think he asked me to eat worms. I panicked. I disappointed myself."

"Maybe he wasn't the right one." His pulse fluttered as a faint ray of hope rose inside him. "One day it'll happen for both of us." He gazed into her lovely eyes, and his mind filled with images. *Maybe someday you'll like to have dinner with me.*

She smiled, and his stomach took a dive. He prayed he hadn't spoken his thoughts aloud. "Did I say something?"

She grinned. "No, but you sound like my neighbor. He said when the right one comes along I'll know it. In my heart."

"And how old is this neighbor?" His question jokingly hid a real fear.

She looked at him slyly. "About a hundred, maybe."

Chapter 2

B rad sat in his cousin Darlene's living room, sipping coffee after dinner. Her words filled him with nostalgia, not that their situations were the same, but the loneliness for both of them was real. "Divorce is a little like death, Darlene. I can understand. The loneliness seems endless. Then one day, you realize unless you make a move nothing will change."

Darlene curled her legs beneath her on the sofa. "I know, Brad. But the world marches around in twos. I'm always a third wheel. No one to go with anywhere. I've been out of the loop since Phil and I separated. Now I'm facing divorce, and I prayed so hard we'd work things out."

"Keep praying, Darlene, but don't tell God what you want. Ask Him to do His will."

She pushed her curls away from her ears. "Easier said than done."

"I'm in a dilemma, too. I've met a woman in my group."

Darlene leaned forward, raising her eyebrows, and her face relaxed for the first time that evening. "One woman in particular? Doesn't sound like a dilemma at all. Sounds wonderful, Brad."

"Thanks. It's brand-new. No dates, only talking, but I sense something special. I haven't felt that way since Janet—"

"I know, Brad. I can only imagine how I'll feel when my bitterness fades, and I spot that special someone."

Brad rested his elbows on his knees. "But along with the pleasure and anticipation of being with her, I feel guilty."

"Guilty? You knew Janet better than I did, and I know she'd laugh at you. You can't bring her back. And she'd want you and the kids to be happy."

"It's the kids that bother me. Kelly's having an awful time."

"I can't help you there. I know nothing about kids. Wish I had a couple. They might make my lonely world a little fuller."

"And much more painful," Brad added, shaking his head. Kelly and Danny's hurt faces soared through his mind.

"I suppose you're right."

"Well, anyway, getting back to my new friend. She's witty, compassionate, pretty as a picture, and a Christian. I'll never forget that night, remember, when you invited me for dinner—"

"Please, let's forget that. I felt terrible. Now I know how you felt. I pushed too hard." Her face twisted with the memory.

"Don't feel bad. Look at me now. I'm mooning over a woman I haven't even dated."

"But you've spent time together."

"We have, and she's been helpful with the kids." He paused in thought. "She doesn't have kids herself. I don't know why."

"Maybe she can't. Or thought life was easier without them."

Darlene's words sent an uneasy feeling through him. He couldn't imagine her not wanting kids. "I doubt. . .I suppose I'll find out one of these days." The thought lingered in his mind.

"I'm sure she has her reasons," Darlene said. "I'm glad you met someone, Brad. But if I were giving advice, I'd suggest you move slowly, especially where the kids are concerned. Let them get used to her little by little."

Brad shook his head. "I came over to give you a little support, and instead, you're helping me. I didn't mean that to happen." He leaned against the chair cushion.

Darlene shifted uncomfortably. "Actually, you could help a lot." She paused as if trying to phrase her sentence. "A gal from work invited me to a party, and I hate to go alone. I've sort of hinted my life is normal—with dates. I didn't really lie, but I never admitted I'm a dud."

"You're not a dud."

"No, but I'm alone."

"So you want your old cousin to be your escort, is that it?"

She gave him a flushed smile. "Yeah, and I feel embarrassed. I've never asked a man out before—even my own cousin."

"I'd be happy to take you. And one of these days you'll have lots of dates."

"I'd feel awful if anyone found out who you are." She looked miserable.

"I promise, I won't tell a soul we're related."

"Thanks, pal." She hurried to his side and gave him a hug.

❦

On Thursday at Davidson Electric, Sally sat with Darby in the lunchroom eating a spinach and bacon salad. "I didn't want to say no. Jim so rarely asks me to work overtime, but I don't like working weekends."

"What's up in your department?" Darby wiped her hands on a napkin.

"We're doing some changeovers on our accounts. It's a big job." Sally buttered her roll, glancing around the lunchroom. "I'm so uncomfortable since Steve called. Every time I see him I shudder."

"Don't worry about it."

"I know." Sally finished her salad and slid back the plate. "I want to feel normal, Darby." She paused. "Whatever that is."

"Don't ask me." Darby shrugged.

Sally tapped her fingers on the table. "I wonder if Jim would mind if I work overtime tonight instead of Saturday?"

Looking at her watch, Darby jumped up. "Wow! Speaking of overtime, our lunch ran overtime. We were due back five minutes ago." They jumped from their seats and hurried back to their desks.

That evening as others left for home, Sally, with Jim's approval, remained behind her computer. When her stomach growled, she looked at the clock, surprised at the late hour. Finishing the final account, she closed the program and turned off the computer.

As she gathered her belongings, a noise resounded in the hallway outside the office. Curiously, she inched open the door. She bolted as a hand darted through the opening to grasp hers. "Aha, so you're here late, too."

Sally recognized Steve Wall's smooth, syrupy voice. She tensed. "Steve, you scared me." Sally forced a casual tone. "You're being dedicated, too, huh?"

"I'm not sure it's dedication. It's a necessity for me. If I want to keep my promotion, I work late occasionally."

"If we're confessing, I don't want to work Saturday." She shrugged. "So much for dedication." She hoped to end the conversation. "Well, I'm off. Need to get home and eat. I'm starving." Immediately, she was sorry she set herself up for an invitation.

He took advantage of her lead. "Would you like to stop somewhere? No sense both of us eating alone, is there?"

Sally hesitated. She'd acted like an idiot on the phone and needed to overcome her fears of being single. But she stopped herself. "No, I need to get home, Steve, but thanks."

"Hey, it's only a dinner. No big deal."

Sally ignored his comment and passed him by, heading for the elevator. But he followed. She punched the button and waited.

"I'm sure it's been difficult for you," Steve sympathized. "A woman needs a man around the house for companionship."

He put his arm around her shoulder and Sally shrugged it off. "Most people don't choose to be alone," she stated matter-of-factly, "but I make the best of it. I've learned a lot."

The elevator arrived, and the door slid open. They stepped inside.

"But it's lonely," he whispered, leaning too close to her, "those long nights all alone."

The door shut, and Sally tensed. She felt trapped. "I manage." Her hands trembled, and she placed them in her pockets so he wouldn't notice. "You adjust." Her voice edged with irritation. She lifted her hand, pushing her hair from her face. He moved closer to her, pressing her into the corner. "I'd love to spend some of those lonely nights with you." Steve reached out and grasped at her fingers before she tucked them away. "You're a special woman."

She jerked her hand away from his as the door slid open. Panic rose in her, and she pushed past him into the parking garage. Words tumbled out of her mouth. "I need to get home. I have a busy day tomorrow."

"How about the coffee? Maybe we could. . ."

Sally wanted to run to her car—to get away from him.

"No, really, I need to get home." She backed away, fear soaring through her.

"Listen, is there some misunderstanding? I didn't mean to chase you away."

Sally halted. "Steve, I'm not looking for a companion. And I'm not desperate for attention. I'm going home."

She turned and darted to her car. She never, ever wanted to be alone with a man again. But as she slid into the driver's seat and locked the door, a gentle, handsome face flashed through her mind.

❦

The following week Brad stood in the foyer of Holy Cross Church and watched Sally hurry through the parking lot. The northern winds blew against her back like an angry crowd pressing her forward. As she reached for the handle, he pulled open the door. She paused, her surprise aimed at him. His heart lurched, and he felt foolish.

The force of the wind whipped against the door, and he propped it open as she literally blew into the foyer.

He waited for her to catch her breath. "Now that's what we old sea captains on the Cape call a 'nor'easter.' "

She gasped, holding her chest. "I was thinking more of Dorothy and Toto." She ran her fingers quickly through her wind-tossed hair. "You can give me a 'southwester' any day. I assume that's the opposite."

He grinned and walked alongside her as she headed down the hallway. "I suppose you noticed I was waiting for you." His heart thundered with his confession.

She pivoted toward him, her face a sudden pink. "Not really," she said. "But I'm glad you were there."

"I wanted to catch you to say thanks for your idea to talk with the kids about Janet. I've started slowly, but already I see a difference."

"I'm glad."

"I didn't want to confuse them by saying too much, but when it fits, I mention things about her."

"Taking it slow is a good idea."

"I see a look in their eyes now, especially Kelly."

"I suppose not having kids makes it easier for me. But sometimes, I still wish I had one."

Her words brought a smile to his thoughts.

Outside the door of the Fellowship Hall, Brad glimpsed at the easel. "A Time to Heal." The topics always seemed to fit his needs. And fate had nothing to do with it. God knew when he needed a boost.

They wandered in, and Sally gestured toward the refreshment table. "Coffee smells good. I'm chilled through to my bones. Let's have a cup, and I'll tell you about my latest terrible experience."

She headed for the coffee urn, and Brad followed, wondering what she meant. Filling her cup, she began her story, telling him about her experience with Steve in the elevator.

Brad's protective nature rose, but another emotion stirred in him. Jealousy. He didn't want other men forcing their attention on Sally. "Being single again is scary and difficult. The guy's uncaring. He doesn't deserve a second glance."

She shook her head, discouragement showing on her face. "I know, but I feel like a naive school girl. And I guess I don't feel single." She looked directly into his eyes. "But I'll tell you, if I did, I guarantee I wouldn't date Steve."

Her words danced through him. "I suppose, you can't blame the poor guy for trying—especially with a woman, not only attractive, but also intelligent and sweet. He couldn't help himself."

He saw her flush shyly, and he couldn't believe himself. The words poured out of him like a leaky bucket. He could have said *attractive* and stopped there. No, he had to add all the other glowing adjectives. She'd assume he was acting like Steve, coming on to her. His thoughts came to a skidding halt. He *was* coming on to her—not very successfully, but that's what he was doing.

Her flush lessened, and she gave him a simpering pout. "He couldn't help himself, hmm? Well, now that you put it that way, I feel sorry for the poor dear. Next time he asks I'll jump at the chance for a date."

He dove in. "You don't have to go that far. I really think the man's a cad." He laid his hand on her arm, and a pleasant sensation ran through him. "Seriously, Sally, don't be hard on yourself. People plug along with grief in stages. But being ready for dating and falling in love—I don't know—that's different."

She nodded. "Maybe I'm afraid to think about love, because I can be hurt again. Sort of guilty and frightened." Her eyes widened.

She'd put her finger on his feelings.

She looked into his eyes. "I think that's it, exactly," she said, seemingly pleased with herself.

Brad put his arm around her and gave her a quick hug.

She patted his arm, and it wasn't until they found their seats that he realized what had happened—how natural their responses had been. No guilt. No embarrassment. Only warm friendship.

Chapter 3

Sally stood in her bedroom admiring the quilt stand she and Ed had located in his attic the Saturday before. She had draped it with an old quilt belonging to her mother, and the colors added just the right touch to her newly decorated Victorian room. She smiled remembering last Saturday. Ed wanted to give her the whole attic. From the bottom of a steamer trunk, he had pulled out an old photograph album, bound with a gold clasp and covered in moss green velvet, embossed with darker green vines and small pink blossoms. Sally almost had to stomp her foot to refuse the lovely gift.

She was procrastinating again, she knew. She spent the good part of the morning in her bedroom, rummaging through her closet and wondering what to wear to Darby's birthday party. She discovered a simple teal blue dress in the back of her closet. *Tolerable.* She prayed the same word described the party.

Forcing herself into the car, she drove the few miles to Darby's apartment. She felt awful going to her first real party without an escort. Throughout the day she wished she would've had the nerve to invite Brad—like a friend, someone to give her confidence a boost. But she hadn't. The idea was a bit late in coming.

When she arrived at Darby's, she took a deep breath. The door flew open, and a stranger welcomed her in to the spacious, yet crowded, apartment. Darby saw her at the door and hurried across the living room to greet her.

"You're here," Darby said, giving her shoulders a squeeze. "I'm glad you came. You know lots of people." Darby gestured in the direction of her guests.

Sally nodded, smiling at familiar faces from the office.

The elegant apartment was highlighted by the black teakwood furniture. An abstract art piece in ebony and a copy of a vase from some oriental dynasty caught her eye, displayed in an elegant etagere. As Sally gazed into the cabinet, Eric Farmer, Darby's longtime boyfriend, joined her.

"Hi, Sally."

"Eric, you're so sweet to give Darby this party."

"Can't help myself," he said, guiding her to a table overflowing with hors d'oeuvres. "Can I get you something to drink?"

"Do you have a soft drink?" Sally asked.

"Sure do. I'll be back in a minute."

While Sally waited for him to return, she surveyed the room until she found herself staring into a familiar face.

"Hi, remember me?" he asked, "Ron Morton. We met a long time ago."

"Sure, I thought you looked familiar." Sally gazed again at the handsome man with friendly, deep brown eyes.

"So, how have you been?"

Eric returned with a filled glass, eyeing them together. "I see you two recognized each other."

Sally nodded. "Yes, but it's been a long time."

Eric handed Sally the glass with a wink. "Don't let me interrupt. I'll leave you two alone."

Before Sally could respond, he walked away. His innuendo prompted her to feel self-conscious. They stood, looking at each other in uncomfortable silence.

"I'm not often at a loss for words," she said finally. "Tonight, I'm making my debut as a single—a nervous single."

"Darby mentioned it's your first party." His pleasant smile revealed a mouth of straight white teeth. "You're doing fine."

Another lull caused Sally further discomfort. "I didn't mean to put a damper on our conversation."

"You haven't, by any means. In fact, I was going to invite you to join me across the room." He gestured to a couple of empty chairs near the fireplace.

Darby swept past them, and Sally's gaze was drawn to the door as she welcomed two latecomers. Sally recognized Darlene Elmwood from the personnel department. But her heart skipped a beat as Brad stepped through the doorway. He greeted Darby with his generous smile and surveyed the room fleetingly. Sally expelled her halted breath. He hadn't seen her.

"Is something wrong?" Ron asked.

Sally pulled herself together, her pulse galloping. "No, I'm fine."

The strange expression on Ron's face forced her to return to their conversation. Moments later, as Darby changed the hors d'oeuvre table to a buffet spread, she excused herself, needing time to regroup.

Sally crossed the room to where Darby was covering a dessert table with a linen cloth. "Can I help?"

Her friend gave her a look of thanks. "The buffet's nearly ready, but I could use help with this table." She handed Sally a pile of plates and silverware. "When you're done with that I have all kinds of goodies in the kitchen."

"Fine, but," she whispered, "do you know the guy who came in with Darlene?"

"No," Darby said, glancing toward the couple. "Why?"

Sally hated to tell her. "He's the man I mentioned from my group meetings."

"Hmm? Nice-looking. Darlene has good taste."

Darby apparently hadn't understood. Sally laid out the dinnerware, pleased to have the distraction, and headed for the kitchen for the dessert trays. She returned with the large platters as Darby made room on the table.

When Sally finished, she searched the crowd for Ron, but her eyes lit on Brad approaching her.

"I couldn't believe it was you." His face beamed, and she melted with his smile. "What are you doing here?"

She wanted to ask him the same question. "Darby's a friend of mine." She forced her mouth to curve into a halfhearted smile, trying to be genial. But what about Darlene? "I saw you come in. I had no idea you knew Darlene."

His eyes widened, and he paled. "Oh, she's just my c—my friend." He shifted uncomfortably from one foot to the other. "We've known each other forever."

His gaze clung to hers, a strange expression creeping across his face. Sally's heart sank. Obviously he had lied to her. *Never dated before*, he had told her. He and Darlene looked comfortable with each other. This was no first date, she felt positive.

Disappointment wrestled with anger inside her. He'd lied. Why? For sympathy or camaraderie? She didn't know. She'd been fool enough to tell him about Steve as if he would understand. Brad had played her for a fool, too.

"So, how do you know the hostess?" Brad asked, his pleasant expression wavering. "Or are you here with someone. . .too?"

He swallowed nervously, and she realized his faux pas had dawned on him. "No, I'm alone. I told you I hadn't started dating yet, remember." She stressed the words so forcefully, she felt embarrassed.

"Me, either," he said shifting uncomfortably, "until Darlene asked me to be her escort. She's separated and hated to come alone."

"I understand how she feels." She raised her eyes to his and saw his expression fill with frustration. Despite her anger, she felt sorry for him. He looked miserable.

Before he responded, a hand pressed her shoulder. She turned to face Ron. "I saved your chair if you'd care to join me." He pointed to the empty chairs across the room.

"Thanks, Ron. That would be nice." She wanted to gloat like a hurt child. Brad scowled.

"Oh, Brad, this is Ron Morton, a friend of mine. Ron, Brad Mathews." She eyed Brad to see his reaction. The scowl remained.

Ron stuck out his hand. "Nice to meet you, Brad." He flashed a look of embarrassment toward Sally. "I hope I didn't interrupt anything here."

She forced an artificial chuckle from her throat. "No, not at all. Brad and I were just chatting." She turned to Brad. "Well, I'll see you next Tuesday, I suppose."

Brad stood wide-eyed. "Right. Tuesday." He turned trancelike and returned to Darlene.

Sally hustled over to the table spread with cold meats and salads, crusty dinner rolls, and pastas. The food looked tasty, but Sally's appetite had vanished. She spooned a few items on her plate and followed Ron across the room. But her mind and eyes were focused on Brad and Darlene.

Brad felt weighted by frustration at the situation. At first, when he saw Sally walking into the kitchen, his heart lifted. He wanted to run to her, pleased he'd agreed to escort Darlene. Then he realized the ramifications.

The horror of the situation struck him when he looked at Sally's face. She thought he had lied to her. He was sure of it. And he was stuck. He promised Darlene he wouldn't tell anyone she was his cousin. In fact, he'd almost slipped earlier. Darlene turned to him and frowned. "Something wrong?"

"Sort of," Brad said, staring toward Sally. "The woman from my grief group is across the room. The one I told you about." He gestured discretely toward Sally and Ron seated cozily in chairs by the fireplace.

"Well, I'll be," Darlene said. "That's Sally Newgate. She works in accounting."

"I never knew where she worked. I told her I hadn't started dating yet. And now here I am with you. She thinks I lied to her."

Darlene gave him an odd look and shrugged. "She's with a date. What's the problem?"

Brad shook his head. "No, he's not a date. She told me she's alone. I think they just know each other or something."

Darlene chuckled. "Brad, it'll work out. In fact, maybe she lied to you. Maybe he is her date, and she's embarrassed that you caught her. Don't let it ruin your evening."

Her words startled him. "Yeah, maybe," he said, covering his shock. *Sally wouldn't lie to me, would she?* His stomach somersaulted.

Darlene didn't understand. How could she know his feelings? Thoughts of Sally had brightened his days lately and filled him with hope. When Janet died, he believed his world had ended. He knew now he could love again.

He avoided watching her, but when she stopped by the dessert table, he couldn't take his eyes from her. Within minutes, she walked away and headed for the door, pausing a moment to speak with Darby. His stomach lurched when Ron followed. But worse than that, his heart sank when Ron followed her out the door. He had been so certain Darlene was wrong.

When Sally woke Monday morning, the autumn leaves that cluttered the ground were disguised by a thick coating of frost. Sally shivered, realizing winter lurked around the corner. Her thoughts were as icy as the weather. Brad weighed on her mind. She wanted to believe he hadn't deceived her, but she created one scenario after another, and nothing made sense. She longed for Tuesday when she would see him face-to-face.

That evening when she reached home from work, she grabbed the mail from the box and darted into the house, carrying it into the kitchen. The cozy room with its golden oak cabinets and country wallpaper in blue and white print reminded Sally of the kitchen from her childhood when cookies baked in the oven and homemade soup simmered on the stove.

She dropped the mail on the table as the telephone rang. She was greeted by Ed's hearty voice.

"Alice and I plan to see a play at the community theater, and we thought maybe you'd like to join us? We haven't seen much of you lately."

"That's because you only have eyes for each other," she teased. "A play sounds like fun. Thanks for the invitation."

"I'll try for Saturday. Is that okay?"

"Count me in."

Pleased at their thoughtfulness, Sally placed the teakettle on the burner for tea and sat at the table, shuffling through the mail. An unusual postage stamp caught her eye—Africa. A letter from Tim's sister, Beth. Sally tore it open, anxious to hear from her sister-in-law. Beth had been out of the country for a long time doing research for a university. Tim's death had been difficult for her. The two had been very close.

The teakettle whistled, and Sally poured the hot water over a tea bag in her mug. Reading the letter, Sally wondered if she should have encouraged Beth to come home for the funeral. Her trip from Africa would have taken at least a week. At the time, Sally wanted no delay to the horrible nightmare of burial. Beth had listened to her and missed the funeral. Now, Beth's grief was still fresh. First she'd lost her father, then Tim. Now the letter explained her mother, Esther Newgate, was seriously ill.

After Tim's death, Sally felt herself drifting from Tim's mother. The painful memories seemed to be too much for his mom. Though Sally pursued with calls and letters, Esther seemed different. Now Sally wondered if it was her growing illness.

As the tea brewed in the cup, Sally grabbed a table knife from the drawer and slit open the other envelopes. She read the newsy letter from her longtime friend, Elaine Miller. She and her husband, Mark, moved away. Of late, they rarely talked, and she wondered how a thing like that could happen to such close friends. Sometimes life seemed filled with losses.

Chapter 4

On the last Tuesday in November the weather turned bitterly cold, and Sally prepared to face her group meeting. She'd been asked to work overtime, but instead brought home a pile of reports to proofread. If seeing Brad hadn't been so important, she would have stayed at the office.

When Sally arrived at Holy Cross Church, she hurried into the foyer, pulling off her woolen scarf and gloves. She glanced around for Brad, but he wasn't there. Finding a seat, she stared at the clock, wondering if he would come at all. Maybe he was too ashamed.

Though she felt apprehensive, she wanted to talk to Brad about the incident Saturday. She prayed the situation had a reasonable explanation. She glanced toward the doorway one last time as Jack stepped to the podium.

Coward, she thought. But suddenly the children came to mind and she worried. Perhaps one of them was ill. She felt distracted, glimpsing around the room again, until she finally gave up, deciding he wasn't coming. A sense of loss showered over her.

Jack's words flowed from the microphone. "Open your heart to those new gifts of friendship, experiences, and love. Allow yourself to heal." His thoughts marched through her head. Brad had stepped into her life, and they had helped each other. But her healing wasn't complete, and she wondered how much time it would take. The utter loneliness was gone. Hope had returned, but she had lost confidence in herself and her judgment.

During the worst times she turned to God, believing He had a plan for her, but lately, she wondered. Even tonight, she realized God had given her a little taste of hope with Brad, then took it away.

When Jack concluded, she rose, and as she headed toward the refreshment table, Brad rushed through the doorway toward her. The expression on his face made her heart skip a beat, whether from fear or joy she wasn't sure.

❧

Brad had stood in the doorway watching Sally before she noticed him. When the presentation ended, he hurried to her side. "Sorry I'm late. I wanted to talk to you so badly. Of all things, I had to work overtime. The new designs have to be ready by the end of the month, and you know what that means for the engineering department." He was rattling, and he sensed her coolness.

"I thought maybe one of the kids was sick."

Her tone sounded icy. "No, just work." He hesitated, glancing around the room. "Could we talk privately? I thought maybe we could go for coffee after the meeting. I told the baby-sitter I might be a little later than usual."

"Sorry, I can't. I brought home a ton of work so I didn't have to stay in the office tonight. I didn't want to miss the meeting."

Disappointment washed over him. Was she avoiding him? He didn't blame her if she was. "I've got to talk to you. I need to explain."

She didn't respond, but glanced around the room.

People were already gathering into the small group sessions.

He felt desperate. "Could we at least find a quiet spot in the hall. Anything?" He stepped toward the doorway.

Relief filled him when she followed. He led her to the hall and the door of a small, unoccupied room stood open. They entered. Before they sat, he blurted, "I wanted to explain about Saturday. I was really happy to see you at the party. But I hadn't considered what you might think. . .until it was too late. I was in a spot." The words tumbled from his mouth.

"Yes, we were both uncomfortable."

"You thought I'd lied to you." Her face reflected her feelings. "And I couldn't explain. I'm breaking a promise now talking to you, but our friendship is more important. Darlene's my cousin."

"Your cousin?" She looked at him quizzically.

"She's separated and was uncomfortable going to the party alone. We both know how that feels."

She balked. "She really is your cousin?" Embarrassment swept across her face. "Brad, I'm sorry. I thought—"

"I can imagine. You opened up to me, and you must have thought I was playing games with you, sort of like—"

"Like Steve. Yes. That's what I thought. I was so hurt. Not so much you were with Darlene. . .but you'd deceived me."

She hesitated. She was hurt? Had she been jealous?

"I know. And I'd promised Darlene I wouldn't tell a soul. She'd be so embarrassed if people knew she went to the party with her cousin."

Sally took a finger and crossed her heart. "Promise I won't tell, Brad. I'll keep the secret forever." A deep breath quivered through her. "I feel like a fool."

Brad looked toward the door. He longed to ask her about Ron, but he didn't want to push his luck. Instead, he took her hand, giving it a squeeze. "Friends?"

Her smile overwhelmed him. "Friends," she said.

They returned quickly to the large room where the small group sessions were beginning. Tonight they remained quieter than most evenings. For the first time since he attended the sessions, he felt no need to speak. Talking to Sally and looking into her understanding eyes, seemed all he needed. When the session ended, Brad drew to her side and whispered in her ear. "I wish you could go for coffee."

Her face revealed her disappointment. "Some other time."

Sally's positive response was all he needed. "Great."

Helping her with her coat, they walked to the parking lot together, huddled against the powerful wind whipping everything in its path.

❧

Saturday evening, Ed and Alice picked up Sally for the play at the community theater, and they arrived with only enough time to be ushered hastily to their seats. With sides aching from laughter, the final curtain lowered and they edged into the narrow aisle. As Ed went ahead to get their coats, Sally faltered, hearing a familiar voice.

"Well, well, look who's here."

She gazed wide-eyed into Brad's bright smile. She flushed, being caught off guard. "Well, hello." Pleasure galloped through her, but in a pulse beat, she filled with apprehension and eyed the lobby.

Brad answered her question as she searched the crowd. "I'm here with my friend, Larry, over there." He pointed to a man across the lobby. "He and his wife have season tickets, but she had other plans, so I'm his date."

To her embarrassment, Sally let out an audible sigh of relief. Her face reddened, again. But he didn't seem to notice. She blurted, "I'm here with friends, too."

He looked pleased. "Larry and I drove separately. So, maybe you and your friends would like to go for some dessert and coffee."

Sally's heart fluttered. Tonight, she had no reason to say no, and she responded eagerly. "I'd love to, but let's check with them."

She eyed the crowd, searching for Alice and Ed, and in the lull, she calmed her giddy feelings.

She saw them by the coat check. Sally's coat lay over Ed's arm. With Brad in tow, she hurried to their sides. "Brad, I'd like you to meet my friends, Alice Brown and Ed Washburn. You've heard me mention them in group discussion, I'm sure. They've been my guardian angels, like a mom and dad to me." She turned to Ed and Alice. "This is Brad Mathews."

Ed and Alice beamed at Sally's introduction. "It's so nice to meet you," Alice said with her soft drawl, thrusting her hand forward. Her ladylike manner reminded Sally of a grand Southern lady, like Melanie Wilkes from *Gone With the Wind.*

Brad spoke without hesitation. "It's nice to meet you. I asked Sally if you'd care to join me for some dessert?"

Ed glanced at Alice, and then his gaze rested on Sally's face. "No, I think not, but thanks for asking." Gesturing to Alice, he continued, "I need to get this young lady home before her driver falls asleep at the wheel, but why don't you young people go and enjoy yourselves?"

Sally wanted to hug him. "You're sure you don't mind?" The sentence caused her to grin. "But I suppose you two really don't need a chaperone, do you?"

Ed glanced at Alice. "*We* don't." He squeezed Sally's elbow as he helped her with her coat. They walked together to the parking lot, each couple heading in their own direction.

❦

Not far from the theater, Brad spotted a cozy little storefront restaurant still open. A sign in the window advertised Homemade Pies.

They ordered and the pastry, they agreed, did taste homemade.

"I told you I was hungry," Brad said, shoveling a forkful of the nutmeg-scented apple pie and vanilla ice cream into his mouth.

"I noticed," Sally teased.

They dug into their tasty desserts and washed them down with the steaming coffee. Brad's mind spun, trying to decide how to broach the subject of Ron. He set his coffee cup on the table, the words tugging at his heart. "The other night we talked about Darlene, but I'll be honest, I saw you leave the party with the fellow you were talking to, and I wondered about that myself."

Sally's surprised eyes raised from her forkful of raspberry pie. "What do you mean?"

"I noticed you were with him all evening. You said you were alone." He hoped he didn't sound like a pitiful wimp.

Her eyes widened. "You're right. I suppose you wondered like I did." She tilted her head, looking sheepish. "Ron's just Darby's friend. I'd seen him before a couple of times."

Brad's stomach tumbled, and the pie sat like a brick. "But he left the party with you." His mind swirled out a million unwanted pictures. He waited for the bomb.

"He did?" Her brow furrowed. "You're right. He walked me to my car. I had parked down the block, and I suppose he was being a gentleman. That's it. I thought he went back inside. Didn't he?"

Brad felt embarrassed for his suspicions. "No. I'm sure I would have noticed."

She shrugged. "He must have decided to leave. He tried to put me at ease all evening, knowing it was my first party alone."

Brad wanted to kick himself. Naturally, she was uneasy being alone, and then to have him walk in with a date. He sighed. "I'm sorry, Sally. I hadn't thought about that. I suppose the evening was strange for you."

She shook her head. "It was."

"I wish you'd asked me to go. I would've gone with you like I did with Darlene." He shriveled. *That wasn't what I meant to say.* "I mean, I would have *enjoyed* going with you."

She raised her eyes to meet his, a faint grin turning the corners of her mouth. "Thanks. I wish I had asked you."

He gazed at her, tongue-tied. After a lengthy silence, he recovered. "The kids seem to be doing better. Not perfect, but really improved."

"You're blessed to have two nice children." She paused as if struggling with herself. "Lately, I've been sorry we never had a baby. If we had a child, I'd feel like a family. Someone to lavish my love on." She stopped, looking away. "But I see the problems you've had. Then I wonder."

"It's hard, but they're a blessing." He studied her face and unanswered questions stalked through his thoughts. He pushed his fork around on the plate in silence. Then he lifted his eyes to hers. "Didn't you want children?"

Her head jerked upward. "Oh, yes. We both wanted a child." She glanced away. "I had a miscarriage. I felt guilty—as if there was something wrong with me that I couldn't carry the baby to term."

"I'm sorry." His response seemed feeble, in relationship to the sadness on her face.

"It's odd how things work. We were going to try again, but Tim was killed. . . Well, anyway, the doctor said I had nothing physically wrong. Miscarriages happen sometimes."

Brad reached across the table and laid his hand on hers. The sensation rocked him. He yearned to hold her against his chest. "I've always believed that God has reasons for everything. We don't always understand though."

"So many things we don't understand." Sally paused. "I don't know what's gotten into me, telling you all this stuff. Anyway, I suppose we should talk about something more cheerful."

He wanted to tell her how much her words meant to him, to know she liked kids and wanted them in her life. Instead, he opened his heart, and told her about Janet's illness and death, the grief for himself and his children.

She listened, and his sorrow reflected in her eyes. She raised her hand to wipe a tear from her eye. Their past swept before them, and Brad emptied his bottled emotions into a river of hope. His hand still lay on hers. Her warmth helped him feel alive again.

"I'm glad you told me about Janet. It helps to talk about things, doesn't it?"

"Sure does." He could bear no more and took the opportunity to change the subject. "Tell me about the couple you were with tonight."

Sally chuckled. "They're wonderful. I played cupid. I introduced them. Alice goes to my church and really helped me after Tim died. I felt so alone and she offered to sit with me in church to keep me company."

Brad listened, her animation raising his spirits.

"Ed lives down the block," she continued. "He was always a good neighbor. If we needed anything, he was there. He gave Tim a lot of gardening tips. Ed's a wonderful gardener, and he's helped me so much. You should see my garden in the spring."

"I'd love to." Brad's candid comment amazed him.

Sally flushed. "Are you saying you'd like an invitation in the spring?"

"Or sooner." Her smile delighted him. "Maybe you could teach me something about flowers. Janet was the gardener. I tried to keep things growing, but I don't know beans about flowers." They snickered at his picturesque phrase.

From that point, they talked easily, telling each other about their childhoods, their hopes, their dreams, and, after more refills of coffee than Brad could remember, he drove her home, delighted that the evening had moved their relationship a step beyond friendship.

Chapter 5

On Thursday evening Bill telephoned. "Listen, Sis. Could you do us a big favor?"

"Sure, as long as it's not a loan," she teased.

"No, this is worse than a loan. It's a really big favor. I have to go up to Grand Rapids on Saturday for a business meeting. Sue and I thought we could make it a little trip for us, too, and stay overnight, but we have one small problem."

"Is the small problem a size six?"

"Exactly." Bill chuckled. "We could take her along, but having a night on the town, a romantic dinner, well. . ."

"Say no more. Carrie and I'll get along fine."

"Thanks so much, if you're sure you don't mind."

"What are sisters for?" Ways to entertain Carrie marched through her mind. "Does she have ice skates?"

"Sure does."

"Bring them along."

"She'll be thrilled. The neighbor girl takes her on a little pond, but she spends a lot of time sitting, not skating."

"Don't laugh! I'll probably do the same, and I have much farther to reach the ice than Carrie."

Bill's hearty laugh echoed through the phone.

"Let's not mention the skates, in case I chicken out."

"No problem. I'll bring her by early on Saturday."

"Bring her on Friday night. That'll make it easier." *Easier for you,* she thought as she hung up the receiver. She rolled her eyes. Even if she found her skates, she wasn't sure she could stand on them.

On Friday night, Carrie arrived, and Bill slipped Sally the ice skates, hidden in a large paper bag. The evening was filled with baking chocolate chip cookies and storybooks. Finally, at bedtime, Sally listened to Carrie's prayers, and then pulled the blanket around her shoulders. Kissing her cheek, she left the door ajar with a relieved sigh.

By the next morning, a light dusting of snow had fallen. The sun was bright, glinting on the white powdery flakes. After breakfast, three puzzles, and two more storybooks, Sally surprised Carrie with the day's plan.

"Ice skating," Carrie moaned, "but I didn't bring my skates."

"Sure you did." Sally displayed the paper bag holding her shiny skates.

"Your daddy brought them."

Carrie squealed and clapped her hands.

Sally grabbed the heavy wool sweater from her room and bundled Carrie into her ski pants, sweater, and jacket. With scarves, knit caps, mittens, and ice skates in tow, they hurried out into the bright, crisp morning.

The dusting of snow had begun to melt with the morning sunshine before they arrived at the recreation center. Families glided along the mirrorlike surface of the outdoor rink.

Sally walked, and Carrie flew to a bench near the ice edge. She dropped her skates on the bench and pulled off her boots before Sally could catch her.

"Hold on there, eager beaver. Don't get your feet cold and wet before I can help you." Sally sat beside her on the bench and retrieved her boots from the snow. With speed, she pushed Carrie's feet into her skates, lacing them tightly. Finally Sally laced her own.

"Okay now, are you ready to help your old aunty to the ice?"

"Are you old, Aunt Sally?" A quizzical look crept across her face.

"Just a little bit. Nothing to worry about. Are you ready?" Sally's question was foolish, for Carrie tugged her toward the ice rink.

Hand in hand, they edged onto the ice, gliding cautiously. When they gained courage, they joined the others circling the smooth, steely ice. Before long they skated together, moving in rhythm.

Sally's courage overtook her wisdom as she pivoted to face Carrie. Instead, she and Carrie found themselves sprawled on the ice in a heap. They sat on the cold surface and laughed, embarrassed, but unharmed. Sally, trying to stand, tripped herself again. Suddenly two arms reached down, grabbed her by the waist, and helped her rise.

"Is this a new skating technique? I've seen the double axel, but this is a new one."

Her heart leaped as she looked into Brad's glinting eyes, his cheeks glowing from the cold. A knitted half-cap covered his ears, and a lock of hair curled on his forehead.

"Brad, I didn't know you were coming here." She clamped her mouth closed, hearing her exuberance bubbling without control.

"I'm glad I did. You can meet the kids." He turned and waved at two young skaters, carefully heading his way.

"Kelly, Danny, I want you to meet Sally Newgate. She's in the group I go to." The two children looked up at Sally, shyly. "Can you say hello?" Brad urged.

"Uh-huh." Danny nodded, but Kelly only looked at her and then at Carrie.

"Well," Sally said, "I'm glad to meet you. Your daddy talks about you all the time. This is my niece, Carrie. Her mom and dad are out of town."

Brad leaned down, resting his hand on Carrie's shoulder. "Hi, Carrie. Your aunt has told me about you, too."

"Did she tell you that we made cookies last night?" Carrie asked. "They're chocolate chip."

"No. She didn't. I imagine they're delicious. Kelly loves baking cookies, too." He glimpsed at his daughter, but she remained silent. Brad looked at Sally with frustration. He darted to a new subject. "Been here long?"

"About an hour. It's a perfect day. I wasn't sure if I'd remember how to skate. And I wasn't doing too badly. . .until I fell."

He grinned. "The kids are just learning, so we try to get here at least once on the weekend."

"Daddy, let's go and skate." Kelly pulled at his jacket, urging her father toward the skaters. "Come on," she insisted.

"Kelly, in a minute. I'm talking. Skate with Danny."

She folded her arms across her chest. "I don't want to skate with Danny. I want to skate with you." Her young face puckered in anger. Danny waited, silently.

Brad's shoulders drooped. "Please don't be rude." He gestured them forward. "Let's all skate together." He dug his skate in the ice and glided along next to Sally. Carrie joined Danny and Kelly.

But Kelly stopped, facing her father. "I don't want to skate with other people. I want to skate with you."

Brad's expression shifted between defeat and embarrassment. "I'm sorry, Sally. She's usually not a rude kid."

"I'm not a kid. I'm seven." Kelly's young voice became strident, and she looked ready to cry. Brad stared in confusion.

"Brad, we're getting ready to take a break. The three of you go ahead, and I'll talk to you later."

Brad offered a grateful nod. Sally watched as they skated back toward the circling crowd. Sally and Carrie headed for a small refreshment stand where the aroma of coffee and hot chocolate drifted on the air. With a hot chocolate in their hands, they navigated to the benches near the ice rink.

"How come that girl wasn't nice?" Carrie asked.

"Well, she's confused, Carrie."

"Was she mad at us? She acted mad at *us*."

"No, I think she's a little jealous of us taking her daddy's attention. Kelly's mommy died, and she needs lots of love and attention right now. So we should forgive her."

"Okay. Let's forgive her." Carrie quickly changed the subject and sipped her hot chocolate. Sally listened to Carrie's chatter only halfheartedly. Her thoughts were preoccupied with Brad and Danny and the very unhappy young girl between them. The last she noticed them, they were heading toward the parking lot.

❦

After church on Sunday, Brad scurried off to the bedroom and pulled Sally's phone number from his wallet. He punched in the numbers, looking over his shoulder like an accomplice to a crime.

When the ringing stopped, he heard a young voice say in a very business-like voice, "Newgate residence."

"Hi, Carrie, this is Brad. I met you skating yesterday." He heard nothing and figured she was shaking her head. "Would you tell your Aunt Sally I'm on the telephone?"

"Okay." He heard a clink as she placed the telephone down, and she called out, "Auntie Sally, it's for you. It's that skating man." Then in a nearly inaudible breathy whisper, she added, "The one with the rude girl."

He couldn't help but smile.

In a flash, Sally greeted him. "Hi. How did you make out yesterday?"

Brad cringed, remembering. "I'm really sorry. I thought we'd made progress, but I was wrong. After we left, she clammed up, so I just let it go, rather than make it worse."

"Probably for the best. When Carrie and I went for hot chocolate, a thought crossed my mind." She stopped speaking for a minute, then her voiced lowered. "But now isn't the time."

He imagined Carrie nearby listening to the conversation.

Her volume raised. "I'll tell you when I see you."

"You can see I need help." He glanced over his shoulder again. "I guess I'd better get off the phone before they get suspicious. I let Kelly and Danny make cookies, and I sneaked off to the bedroom to call. Who knows what mess I'll find?"

She chuckled. "Are they chocolate chip, by any means?"

"What else? Kelly talked cookie-baking since she heard Carrie say she had made some. Kids! Don't you love them?"

"Actually, I do." Her voice smiled.

"I know you do." His heart raced, thinking how important her statement was to him. "See you Tuesday."

"Have fun and eat a cookie in my honor."

❦

At their Tuesday meeting, Sally and Brad stood near the back, waiting for the presentation to begin. "So, what did you want to tell me?" Brad asked.

"Well, when I took Carrie to the zoo a few weeks ago, she asked me questions about dying. Carrie and I hadn't talked about Tim's death before. I was shocked when she asked if I wanted to die to be with Tim. It tore me up. She hugged me and said she was afraid that I'd die like Uncle Tim." Sally ached, remembering the day clearly.

Brad's eyes widened. "You think the kids are worried that I might die and leave them like Janet?" Confusion etched his face.

A sigh raked through her. "Something like that. They lost their mother and don't want to lose their father—to death *or* to someone else. Now, it's all the same to them. Kelly wants your full attention. She doesn't want to share you."

"I give the kids extra time, but maybe that's not enough."

"I don't think it has to do with time as much as fear. They need to be assured you won't leave them—in any way."

Brad placed his hands on her shoulders, searching her eyes. "You make it sound simple."

"It's easy when it's someone else's problem. I don't see my own solutions at all. I don't think people ever do."

He dropped his hands, shifting from one foot to the other uncomfortably. "Listen, I wanted to talk to you tonight about something else. I may as well fess up."

Sally held her breath, wondering.

"And promise you won't compare me to that guy at work."

"Hey, you convinced me, it's hard for a man to keep his hands off a wonderful, delightful person like myself." She teased, fluttering her eyelashes. Her pulse raced.

"That's true, but I'll try. My company holds an annual hayride—or sleigh ride if there's snow, and I'd love you to come along." He rested his hand on her shoulder. "And if you agree, I'll be a perfect gentleman. "

Her heart pressed on her vocal chords. She steadied herself, not wanting to sound like an overanxious teenager. "I haven't been on a hayride in years. It sounds like fun. Is it for families?"

"No, adults only. A real date. I'd love you to come."

"When is it?"

"Saturday." He looked sheepish. "I've waited a long time to ask you, but I've felt as nervous as a schoolboy."

She grinned, feeling as nervous as he. "How can I resist?"

As they headed for their seats, her hands trembled so badly she put them in her pocket so he didn't notice.

❦

The night of the hayride fresh white snow covered the ground. Tonight Brad's heart sat on his sleeve and lay on his tongue. The words and thoughts had skittered around in his mind—*romance, love, commitment*—but he hesitated to lay them out in the open. If Sally rejected him, he couldn't deal with the hurt—not yet. But the desire to speak his emotions tripped on his tongue, and he swallowed to hold them at bay.

As couples jumped and hoisted themselves to the wagons, they found a space and settled in. With a jingle of bells, the horses shuddered, the wagon lurched, and they were on their way.

"Warm enough?" Brad asked, hoping for the opportunity to move closer.

"A little chilly."

"Then, let's move back," he said, scooting back from the edge of the wagon and onto the hay. She followed, and they nestled together in the chilled air.

Before they had moved around the bend into the woods, the first wagon's passengers burst into song, and their group joined in. Sally's sweet, full voice rang in Brad's ears, and he wanted to yell to the world that he was falling in love. Soon the third wagon added their voices. Old campfire songs echoed through the woods.

Time passed and a light snow drifted down, its presence glistening in the moonlight. Brad slid his arm around Sally's shoulder, feeling foolishly shy. "Warm enough? I felt you tremble."

"I'm fine—cozy. I think it's the bumpy ride."

But Brad looked into her eyes, sparkling in the moonlight and sensed a different reason. Sally shifted, resting her hand on the straw next to his, and even through their gloves, he felt her nearness. He covered her fingers with his, searching her eyes for approval. She flashed a shy smile in his direction, and he filled with utter joy. Lifting his eyes, he looked toward heaven, confident that God had sent her to him.

But the peaceful moment ended. Without warning, a wad of hay flew into Sally's hair, and she tossed a handful back. Then, more hay flew past like a school cafeteria food fight.

"Can't get away with that," Brad called, grabbing a handful for himself, and as he threw the wad of straw through the air, the wagon lumbered into a clearing. The lights of the lodge glowed before them, and the wagon lumbered on with a trail of hay dropping to the ground and voices echoing with laughter. Though Brad joined in the merriment, he yearned to keep Sally wrapped in his arms.

❦

When Sally saw the lights of the lodge, she felt a twinge of disappointment. She wished the ride would go on forever. Nestled in Brad's arms, his hand on hers, she experienced feelings that had lain dormant deep within her far too long. She had questioned God about her life and where it was going. Was this what He'd planned for her?

The wagon came to a halt, and immediately snow missiles replaced the hay. Couples scurried from the wagons, skittering through the white glistening drifts, chasing one another with yells and giggles.

Sally snickered to herself as she slid from the wagon, intent on joining the fun. Her heart thudded, as she scooped up a ball of snow. When Brad jumped from the wagon, she drew in a deep breath and barreled him with her cold, white weapon.

She skirted away from his attack and darted past him, heading for the lodge. But he was hot on her trail. As she veered around the wagon, her boots slipped beneath her. She gasped and tried to maintain her balance, but Brad caught up to her, grabbing her in his arms with a handful of snow.

Her heart pounded with the childish fun, and she bolted away, until they both tumbled to the ground, laughter and breath bursting from their chests. Sally lay on her back, defending herself from his white icy weapon, her pulse racing from his nearness. He lifted himself on an elbow, his face inches from hers. Her racing, joyful heart soared, as their laughter died away, and his gaze sought hers with longing.

"If I hadn't guaranteed I'd be a gentleman, you'd be in deep trouble." His voice sounded breathless—from the chase or from their nearness, she didn't know.

At that moment, she wished he hadn't promised. The words "forget the promise" rose to her lips, but she forced herself to make light of the situation. "Should I call you Steve?"

His lips paused an inch from hers. The warmth of his breath brushed her face, and the aroma of sweet, fresh spearmint invaded her senses. Her heartbeat raced in anticipation. Brad hesitated. "No, but you can call me stupid. A promise is a promise." His lips touched her cheek tenderly, and he raised himself from the ground, leaving Sally with a sense of longing.

As he helped Sally rise, she struggled to gain composure. Brad took her hand, and they headed into the lodge. Her cheek tingled where his lips had pressed, and she longed to kiss his full, tender mouth. Yet they'd known each other only a few months. They had time—*a time for every purpose under heaven.* She'd wait for God's guidance.

Chapter 6

On Thanksgiving Day, Sally attended worship. For once, she could lean back and enjoy the service, not worrying about the oven timer or reviewing the list of tasks to complete when she returned home. This Thanksgiving Sue's parents were visiting from Florida, and Bill and Sue had invited her for dinner. Her only responsibility was to bring coleslaw and a cranberry mold.

After dinner, they sat around the living room, fighting sleep and wishing they had pulled away from the table sooner. Bill stretched out on the floor and propped his head on a pillow. "Okay, Sis, give."

Sally scowled. "Give what?"

"You've been scarce lately. I've called you and so has Sue, and you're never home. Something's happening in your life." He rolled over, eyeing her.

Knowing Bill, he would drift off sound asleep in a few minutes. But the question had been posed. "Overtime, grief group, church, that's about it." She felt uneasy. Bill was too observant and too opinionated. Though nearly two years had passed, Tim's death seemed fresh in everyone's mind. She wondered if he and Sue would understand about Brad.

"Okay, okay. Forget I asked." He rolled over on his back. "I just want to make sure you're not running around. I know you're lonely, but you have to be careful. That's all." Within a minute, his deep breathing announced he had fallen asleep.

Sally forced herself to chat and grin, but inside she felt irritated and guilty. She didn't like Bill's comment. "Running around" sounded terrible. On top of that, she'd avoided the truth. She could hear her mother's words, echoing from their childhood. "Children, one lie leads to another and another. Oh, what a tangled web we weave when first we practice to deceive." She forced her attention back to the conversation. It hadn't been a lie exactly—perhaps more, the sin of omission. But his words stayed in her head. Was their relationship a mistake?

A few days later, Brad called with a favor. He wanted to give Kelly another try and invited Sally to join them for an animated Christmas display at the mall. His voice pleaded, and Sally didn't have the to heart to refuse.

When Sally opened the door, she knew she was in trouble by the expression on Brad's face. "Problems?"

His head nodded slowly. "Sort of. We'll have to work on it. I'm sorry to put you through this again. I hope once we're on our way things will change."

Her heart dropped like a weight against her stomach. "No problem. What are friends for?" Another fib. She saw the spider weaving the webs her mother warned her about.

She zipped her jacket and followed him to the car. Kelly and Danny sat in the back seat. Danny eyed her as she climbed in, leaning forward with curiosity, but Kelly sat, arms folded across her little chest, pressing herself as far in the corner of the seat as she could.

Sally smiled into the backseat. "Hi. This should be fun. Did your daddy tell you where we're going?"

Danny looked with half-lowered eyelids and nodded. "Uh-huh. To see some fairytale people."

"I can't wait." She turned to Kelly. "Are you excited, Kelly?"

Kelly stared out the window, her lips pressed tightly together. Sally thought she would get no response at all, but without looking, Kelly mumbled, "No."

Brad glanced at Sally helplessly. She signaled him not to say anything and turned back facing the front. Maybe if they ignored the problem it would go away.

They drove in silence with only an occasional comment about traffic or some unimportant topic. Sally knew they were both preoccupied with Kelly's behavior and her sadness.

The Summit Place Mall parking lot overflowed. Shoppers—the courageous warriors out to grab up their first Christmas bargains—scurried in and out of stores. Brad found a parking spot and squeezed in with little room to open their doors. Sally eased out, and Danny followed behind her without hesitation. But Brad stood helplessly on the other side of the car, door open wide, with Kelly refusing to leave the backseat. She continued to sit, arms folded and eyes closed.

Brad pleaded. "Kelly, we're all looking forward to the display. I can't let you sit here by yourself. I wouldn't be a good daddy to do that. You'd be cold. Please come along."

She didn't respond.

Sally's heart ached as she watched the scene. Many parents might have dragged her out by her arm, threatening untold punishments. But Brad knelt down by the door and spoke softly to her. An occasional word drifted from the open door, "understand. . .okay. . .love." Finally, Brad rose, pulling back the seat, and Kelly exited the car, still silent, but walking along beside them.

Though Kelly warmed to the animated displays, she kept Sally blocked from her view. Sally pondered what to do. She had little choice but to accept the situation. God had given her a taste of joy, but she felt it sinking into the mire of despair.

When they stepped outside to the mall parking lot, the snow blew horizontally from the force of the wind, and Brad struggled to clean his windshield. Snow mounded against anything stationary. With effort, he pulled out of the lot.

Salt trucks rumbled in front of them on the road, and the snow plows headed in every direction across the city. Brad drove slowly, finally arriving at Sally's door.

❦

Brad gazed at Sally, knowing he had to talk to her privately for at least a moment. With his eye on the children, he walked her to the door, stepping into the foyer for a moment.

"I'm sorry again, Sally. What can I say? I'd really hoped today would be better." Frustration tore through him. "I know it takes time, and I have to be patient."

Sally rested her hand on his arm. "One of these days, she'll understand that someday you're going to fall in love. But first, she has to know that you still love her."

Her words gave him hope, but part of the comment troubled him. *Someday you'll fall in love.* Didn't she sense that he had tremendous feelings for her? Each time they parted he wanted to cling to her.

So many people he'd spoken with about Sally treated his feelings like puppy love. He recalled some of Darlene's comments. Everyone reminded him they had only met a few months earlier. They reminded him Sally was the first woman he'd been out with since Janet.

Everyone made jokes about hormones and urges. Yes, he was human. He wanted to hold a woman again, to feel her body next to his, but the woman in his thoughts had a face. A lovely face. Sally's. But his feelings were far more than hormones.

Brad squelched the desire to talk with Sally about his feelings. He needed time to understand things himself. His hormones and urges might cry out for release, but an outlet for passion wasn't the reason for his attraction. Brad felt sure, positive, that she was the one to make his life whole and complete again.

Sally gazed at him. "You'd better go. The kids are waiting, and the snow's getting worse." She laid her hand on his arm.

Brad covered it with his own. "If the snow's too deep tomorrow, don't try to clear it yourself. If I can get out, I'll come over and help you."

"Don't worry about me. You get home." She tilted her head with a grin. "But would you call me? So I know you're okay."

"I sure will." He was touched by her worry. When she closed the door, he wished he had acted on his instinct. He longed to slip deeper inside the house, away from the children's eyes, and kiss her good night. Instead, he settled for her wave from the doorway and headed home, feeling lonely.

❦

The city officials declared a snow emergency that evening, and the next morning schools and businesses were closed for the day, including Davidson Electric. Sally stared outside, seeing the huge drifts of snow against the garage door and knew she was housebound unless she attacked the white prison.

With relief, Sally found the shovel on the back porch. And as always, Ed came up the drive with his snowblower. He worked on the heavy white mounds while she shoveled at the garage door. Before he finished the driveway, Ed turned off the machine to give Sally a hand, and in the lull, she heard the telephone ring. She slipped and slid back to the house.

"Hello," she said, panting to catch her breath.

"How are you doing?"

She beamed hearing Brad's voice. "Pretty good. I tackled a snowdrift against the garage door, and Ed showed up with his snowblower to clear the driveway. We're nearly done."

"I hoped to get over, but it took me forever to dig my car out. The kids are having a wonderful time. You should see the snow angel and snowmen. . ." He paused. "Anyway, I have to run a couple of errands. And while I'm out, what if I pick you up and bring you here for dinner?"

Sally heard apprehension in his voice. One thing about Brad, he never gave up.

"Maybe if Kelly gets to know you, she'll perk up a little bit. You can see what an optimistic fellow I am."

"I like optimism, but don't get your hopes up. Still, I'd love to come to dinner."

"Great, I'll be there around five."

"I'll be waiting." She felt as if she'd burst. How could her heartstrings tangle so quickly around his? In wonder, Sally returned to the yard to retrieve the shovel from Ed and finish clearing the snow.

When Brad arrived, Sally saw him through the window. He tooted the horn and stepped from the car, encouraging Kelly to move to the backseat where Danny already sat. Kelly slumped further down in the front seat, shaking her head no.

Sally eyed Kelly as she approached the car and smiled. "How about if I ride in the backseat with Danny?"

Brad looked at her, gratefulness reflecting on his face. Kelly sidled a glance at Sally. A glimmer of thanks shone for a moment, but was quickly covered.

Sally greeted the children and climbed into the back, fastening her seat belt. "Well, Danny, your daddy tells me you made a wonderful snowman in the backyard."

"Uh-huh. We made two, one for me and one for Kelly."

Kelly inched back against her seat, her ear tilted toward them, straining to hear their conversation over the noise of the automobile.

Sally grinned to herself. "Did you give your snowman a top hat like Frosty?"

"Nope, but one snowman has on Daddy's cap, and they both have scarves." Before Sally could speak, he changed subjects. "Did Daddy tell you I helped Kelly bake cookies?"

"Yep. I hope I can try one."

"Sure. You can have two."

"Thank you. You're very generous." Pleasure filled her. Danny's usual shyness seemed to have vanished.

The ride to Brad's house was short. The attractive homes in the small village of Huntington Woods had been built of dark red brick with gray slate roofs, and thick ivy, clinging to the chimneys, added charm. Beveled glass windows glinted from stairwells and doorways.

Brad pulled into the driveway, and the door rose, giving them access to the large attached garage. In the back hall, they hung their coats on hooks in the hallway, and the children placed their boots on a boot tray next to the back door, impressing Sally by their neatness.

Her first view was the cozy kitchen with rich cherry cabinets and a butcher block island. "This is lovely, Brad." Janet's feminine touches were everywhere.

She passed through the dining room, decorated with a small floral beige and raspberry print wallpaper extending from the cove ceiling to the chair railings. Below the chair railing, the wall was painted in rich raspberry. A long fruitwood table stood in the center, and a china cabinet filled with lovely old dishes covered one wall.

Sally gazed into the cabinet. "You collect antiques."

"Janet did, but I like them."

The living room impressed her with a floor-to-ceiling French pane bay window looking out on a sprawling backyard now covered with snow and guarded by two winter-garbed snowmen.

The room stretched from the front of the house to the back. A stone fireplace on a side wall formed a conversation area around the stone hearth. She could picture Brad and a faceless woman sitting there on cold winter nights, and she felt a twinge of melancholy.

"Beautiful, Brad. And a wonderful setting."

"Thanks."

He opened his mouth as if to say more, but Danny returned with a selection of storybooks and headed directly toward Sally.

She gave Brad a secret smile as Danny scampered beside her on the love seat. "Well, Danny, what kind of books do you have there?"

He offered her the stack of books.

She skimmed over the titles. "Let me see, *The Little Engine That Could, The Wooden Soldier,* and here's one about you, *Danny Goes for a Ride.*" She held the book toward him.

Danny nodded his head.

"Would you like me to read you this one?"

"Yep," he said, and they began.

❧

Brad occupied himself building a fire in the fireplace. He watched Sally nestled on the cushions with Danny, and his thoughts drifted to Janet. A wave of sorrow washed through him, not only for himself, but for the children. Sally's presence in the house brought back a surge of memories.

Kelly returned from her room and sat with her eyes focused on Sally. Brad knew, from Sally's occasional glance, she hoped Kelly would join them. "Do you like to read stories, Kelly?"

She sat at a distance, swinging her legs. "Yes, but my books are more grown-up." Her eyes stayed riveted on Sally. Brad's heart ached for his child.

"That's because you're older," Sally said. "You're seven, aren't you?"

Brad watched the interaction with awe.

"Uh-huh. I was seven in October."

Danny chimed in. "My birthday's in July. I'll be six."

Brad hid his grin, watching them vie for attention.

"Then I can go to school for a whole day."

"That's great," Sally said. "You'll learn to read by yourself, and you'll be nearly as grown-up as Kelly."

Brad eyed Kelly, and she beamed when Sally called her "grown-up." Brad marveled at Sally's way with the children.

"Then I won't have to do everything for you, Danny," Kelly said, rising from her chair and wandering to the arm of the love seat nearest Sally. "You'll be able to do things all by yourself."

Brad felt a weight lift from his shoulders. Sally would make a wonderful mother. But Janet loomed again in his thoughts. He imagined Sally living in this house, changing things, and he wondered if he'd ever be free of the guilt that hung in his thoughts.

Though he needed to prepare dinner, Brad longed to stay and watch the children with Sally. Before he tore himself away, Kelly asked if they could watch television. With the young ones in front of the TV, he invited Sally to join him in the kitchen.

She stood next to him at the counter and breathed a sigh. "I think I made some progress, but I'm exhausted."

"I couldn't keep my eyes off of you. You're wonderful. You handled Kelly so well." He patted her back lightly, fighting himself from taking her in his arms.

She poked his ribs, and he flinched.

She wrinkled her nose. "Didn't think I could do it, huh? To be honest, neither did I. I amazed myself."

They talked while Brad worked on the steaks. Sally cleaned the green beans, putting them in a steamer. While Brad set the table, Sally volunteered to make the salad and busied herself with washing and slicing the vegetables.

With the food ready, they sat around the table and bowed their heads. Brad thanked God for their blessings as emotions tugged at his heart. Through half-closed eyes, he caught the image of Sally in Janet's seat at the table. His heart lurched, and he swallowed to hold back the tremor that moved through his body. They joined in the "Amen," and Brad added a silent postscript to God, asking for guidance.

"This is great," Sally said, running the knife through the tender steak. "You're a gourmet."

"What's a gourmet?" Danny asked. "Are you one, Daddy?"

Brad set his face with a serious expression. "If Sally says I am, then I guess I am." Danny looked quizzical.

"A gourmet is a very good cook—like in a wonderful restaurant," Sally explained.

"My daddy is a gourmet," Kelly agreed.

Brad and Sally controlled their laughter.

"Well, then I guess that's that," Brad concluded.

Kelly was in charge of dessert. She brought out ice cream and proudly displayed a plate of her homemade cookies, that Sally duly complimented.

Brad walked in a dream through the evening, thrilled, grateful, and confused. The emotions that sneaked into his consciousness bothered him. New fears and questions arose, but he tucked them away, praying time would smooth them into nothing.

Before the children's bedtime arrived, Brad arranged for the neighbor girl to sit with the children while he drove Sally home. They finished a final game of Candyland, and Brad tucked the children into bed and listened to their prayers. When Katie arrived, Brad and Sally headed for the car and the ride home.

In her driveway, Sally lingered for a moment. "It was a wonderful evening, Brad. Thanks for inviting me. Your home is lovely, and you really are a gourmet."

"Thanks." He shifted in the seat to face her. "Seriously, Sally, I enjoyed having you there. I was proud of Kelly. She seemed more like herself. You did a great job with her."

"They're wonderful, Brad. When I sat with Danny reading the storybook, I realized how much they must miss their mom."

Words hung on his lips. He wanted to release the thoughts that hammered in this head, but he couldn't say it all, not yet, not until he understood it himself. "Some of the same thoughts went through my mind."

"Maybe it was good for them to have a woman in the house."

Brad placed his hand on her cheek, and his eyes searched hers. Did Sally understand how he felt? Did she sense his own needs? "It was good for them and for me. You're the first woman in our home since Janet—a woman who isn't family, I mean. It seemed. . .strange. But nice." He felt the longing move through him, not for Janet, but for Sally. He caressed her cheek, then his fingers nestled in her chestnut curls. She shuddered, and he returned his hand to her cool, soft skin. He wanted her to be his at that moment, but instead, he leaned forward, placing his lips on her cheek where his hand had been. "I can't

276

say in words what this evening has meant to me."

Her gaze sought his. She placed her hand over his. "Next time, it's my treat."

Her words lay on his ear. Before he responded, she squeezed his hand and opened the car door. He couldn't let her go like this. He touched her arm, urging her back. Leaning forward, he pressed his lips tentatively to hers, then drew away.

She pressed her fingers against her lips, her eyes searching his. Then she slid from the car and hurried to the porch. She waved from her foyer, and he backed out of the driveway, heading home to the children with anxious thoughts careening like bumper cars through his mind.

The next morning Sally awoke with the previous evening's memories swirling in her head. The kiss happened so gently and with such haste she had wondered if it were only wishful thinking, but when she looked in a mirror, she knew it had been real. The emotion overwhelmed her. She recalled Ed's words. *It will happen. You'll feel it for sure.*

Her feelings for Brad were growing rapidly—too rapidly, perhaps. Apprehension rose in her. Sitting in his home, she had felt Janet's presence. She tried to block the thoughts from her mind, but they lingered throughout the evening. Could she risk being hurt again?

Janet had been gone for a little more than a year. Was that enough time for Brad to know his heart? He cared for her. She saw his struggle as she felt her own—the passion, the longing. Time was the answer. They needed to move slowly. But saying the words didn't stop the race pounding through her heart.

Chapter 7

The days flew by. Sally approached the holidays as joyful as the colored lights and the decorated buildings. She and Brad grew closer each day, and for Sally, Christmas this year promised to be special. Yet amid the joy and thrill of their blossoming relationship, fears nudged her. Kelly was yet far from total acceptance of her, and Sally had yet to tell Bill and Sue about Brad. Their comments at Thanksgiving left a tainted memory in her mind. Yet keeping him a secret put a damper on her happiness.

The grief sessions were drawing to a close. This evening, everyone gathered around the large hall filled with holiday spirit.

Following Jack's presentation, Brad took her arm and whispered in her ear, "Who knew coming to these meetings would be so important? I met you."

Sally avoided looking into his eyes for a moment. She fought back the tears that edged their way into hers. Some people couldn't express their feelings, and Brad sharing his with her meant nearly as much as the words he said.

"I feel the same, Brad." Sally struggled to contain her emotions. "I think about *you* now, instead of feeling sorry for myself."

He put his arm around her, pulling her close, and she flushed, realizing that others were watching them.

Instead of the small group sessions, they celebrated Christmas with an elaborate spread of snacks and desserts. Later, one of the facilitators played the piano, and everyone gathered around and sang carols.

Brad and Sally mingled with the others. She beamed at Brad as she listened to his excellent baritone voice resounding, "Oh, come let us adore Him, Christ the Lord." When the party neared an end, the pianist concluded with "Silent Night." Brad took her hand in his, and her eyes misted as they stood together, singing her favorite carol.

When Brad pulled into her driveway, he nuzzled her in his arms and drew her to him. His warm, tender lips touched hers and lingered, filling her with a sweet sense of completeness. He leaned back, searching her eyes. "I've wanted to kiss you like this for a long time."

"And I've wanted you to."

Embracing her, he kissed her hair and her forehead. His body trembled as did her own, and their lips met again, softly, yet completely. "You are so beautiful," he said.

Tears slid from her eyes. She had not heard those words since Tim said them to her so long ago.

Sally sat at the computer, a pile of accounts in front of her. The approaching holiday also meant the year-end inventory. She squinted at the screen, her eyes aching, and a headache edged its way up the cords of her neck. She wondered if she were catching a cold. Glancing at her wristwatch, she hoped the hand was nearing five o'clock, but the hour hand rested only a hair past the three.

She massaged her shoulders and ran her fingers along the tension below her hairline. She lowered her hands and refocused on the numbers spread across the computer screen. Without warning, warm fingers kneaded the tension in her neck, and she spun on her chair in surprise. She gasped when her eyes focused on Steve, a slack grin formed on his lips.

"What are you doing?" Sally drew back from his hands suspended before her.

"Helping you relax. I saw you rub your neck. It's much more enjoyable when someone else massages those tender spots."

"I don't think so." Her words swung at him like a whip.

He backed away from her angry words. His hands flexed defensively, as if to hold back her verbal daggers. "Sorry. I thought I was doing a good deed. You looked like you could use a little relaxation."

She wished she could erase the moment and start again. Anger solved nothing. "Look, Steve, I'm sorry I snapped, but you surprised me. Please don't do me any more favors. Okay?"

Her kindness, apparently, came across as encouragement. Steve seated himself on the corner of her desk with a wink. "Okay. You're right. Next time, I'll ask permission first."

"There won't be a next time." She slid her papers closer to the computer and faced the screen. He didn't move and watched her. She pivoted her chair a fraction in his direction. "Did you want something?"

His grin broadened into a leering smile. "You don't have to ask, do you?"

She shuddered. "If you have nothing serious to say, I'd like you to leave. I'm in the middle of inventory, and I need to concentrate."

He rose from the desk as if in slow motion, and as he passed her chair, his finger traced the line of her arm. Sally closed her eyes and remained still. Any word and she would only encourage him. He didn't seem to understand what she said. Yet at the moment, she had no desire to explain herself to him. Maybe Darby could give her a tip about discouraging unwanted attention. She didn't seem to have the knack. Not one iota.

Two weeks before Christmas, Brad paced in his living room, knowing he had to call with news that would dampen Sally's spirit. He wanted to phrase it right, to let her know he was disappointed, too. When he had his words in order, he trudged to the telephone. "I dreamed of us spending some of the holiday together, but I've had an unexpected change in plans."

"What is it, Brad?"

He heard anxiety in her voice. "My mother convinced us to fly to the Cape for the holidays. I hope you're not too disappointed."

"Why? What happened? I thought you said she was coming here."

This time he heard disappointment. "She was under the weather for a couple of weeks and said she doesn't feel up to traveling during the Christmas rush. I'm really sorry—and disappointed."

"I was looking forward to the holiday, but I know your mother must love having you all there." Despite her bravado, he could envision her downcast eyes.

Brad felt torn by her disappointment. "She loves having us there, but I think she's disappointed, too. She hoped to meet you."

Her voice softened. "I'm sorry to sound like a baby. I'm disappointed. Will you spend the whole holiday there? Maybe you could come home between Christmas and New Year. We could still have some time together. How about New Year's Eve?"

Desperation coursed through him. Would she understand what he had to tell her? "I'm sorry, Sally. When I agreed to go to the Cape, Mother planned a full agenda, and I've already made arrangements."

"Oh, and they can't be changed?" Her voice dwindled to a murmur.

"I had a difficult time getting airplane tickets so I added vacation days to the regular Christmas holiday. We're leaving earlier and returning later than most travelers. It worked out best that way."

"Oh."

Her utter disappoint ricocheted in his thoughts. "I'm sorry."

A sigh rattled from her. "I guess I understand."

✿

When they disconnected, Sally felt ashamed. Normally, she behaved better. But today, her emotions wavered between anger and disappointment. Tears rolled down her cheeks. She was being selfish. If her mother were alive, Sally would visit her for the holiday without a second thought—especially if she'd been ill.

Her disappointment doubled as she thought it through. He'd be gone, but most of all, he hadn't asked her to come with him. She shook her head. She knew the answer. Their relationship was too new. Asking her to join him wasn't appropriate. Though she said the words, the hurt and disappointment stayed.

Sally struggled with the situation, sorting it out in her mind. A new romance offered both ups and downs. She opened up and felt the joy of being wanted again. But giving her heart to Brad made her vulnerable. Her own emotions hung by a string. Sally feared losing him. She wanted to keep him in her sight, to guard him. Now, she'd acted like a thoughtless child.

Sally dug deep to locate her compassion. Christmas would be difficult for Kelly and Danny. Being with their grandmother would ease their sadness. What would ease her sadness?

Distraction was what she needed, something to get rid of her disappointment. She delved into her work at Davidson's and the final preparations for Christmas. Then on Sunday after church, she walked through her back door to the ringing of the telephone. Without taking off her coat, she grabbed the receiver.

"Hi, Sally, this is Ron."

"Ron." Her heart skipped a beat, and she flushed with discomfort. She hadn't spoken to him since Darby's birthday party. "It's been a long time."

"Sorry I haven't called you sooner, but I've been working long hours on a new training program. I'm thankful it's about over." He paused. "But I've thought about you a lot."

Sally hadn't thought about him at all. "Things are happening around here, too." Brad had happened—that was more truthful. Then, she tensed, wondering why he'd called.

"Eric asked me to make some calls for him. He's planning a surprise for Darby next weekend. It's one of his brainstorm ideas, so it's short notice. He thought you'd like to be there."

"Surprise?" Her curiosity was piqued.

"Yep—a surprise party."

"It's not her birthday. We just celebrated that."

"No, it's not her birthday—but I'm sworn to secrecy. He's having a small dinner party on Saturday. Can you come?"

She hesitated. Was he asking her for a date or only telling her about the party?

"I'll pick you up. Eric has a private dining room at Aunt Fanny's. . .on Woodward."

Picking her up? But what was the occasion? "Come on, Ron. Give me a hint. I wouldn't miss a special party for Darby, but. . ." Sally thought for a moment, and then the party's purpose dawned on her. "Ron, are they engaged? He's going to propose to her, isn't he? It has to be that! Am I right?"

"I never told you a thing, Sally," he chuckled.

The excitement prickled up her arms. "I wouldn't miss it for the world. But I'm just around the corner from Aunt Fanny's. I'll drive there myself. Thanks anyway."

"It's no problem, Sally. Why take two cars?"

She felt foolish arguing with him, and she didn't want to tell him about Brad on the telephone. In person seemed better. Yet, guilt marched through her. Would Brad's mother plan a date for him in her plethora of scheduled activities? Jealousy inched into her thoughts, and she shuddered. "What time, Ron?"

"How's seven? And don't say a word, I'll pick you up."

She bit her lip, wondering how she would keep the excitement out of her face when she talked to Darby.

Brad looked into the embers of Sally's fireplace and then returned to her eyes. Her disappointment clung in his thoughts. If the situation were reversed, he'd feel the same way.

She stared toward the sparking fire. "I need to apologize to you. I behaved like a pouty, pleading child. I hope you forgive me. I know it's important for the kids to be with family. I'm sorry I sounded so pitiful."

Her chestnut hair glinted red highlights in the glow of the flames. "If you didn't care about me, you wouldn't have cared. How's that for a sentence?" He grinned and rose from the chair, crossing to the love seat.

He sat beside her and slipped his arm around her shoulder, nestling her head under his chin. She lay against him, and his fingers brushed her powdery skin. "You know I'll miss you."

She snuggled closer, and he yearned to keep her there forever. But tonight was his turn to be honest. "In fact I'll make my confession. I would've asked you to join me on the Cape, but I haven't told my mother how I feel about you. I made our relationship sound casual when we talked. I thought telling her in person was better. Can you believe it? I'm ashamed of myself."

A pink flush rose up her neck, and she raised her head to face him. She pressed her hand to his cheek. "If this is confession night, let me join you. I haven't mentioned you to my brother and his wife. Their attitudes have been a little strained, and I'm waiting for a better time to talk to them."

Neither of them knew how to handle all that was going on. Brad surveyed Sally's face. She looked so fragile tonight, her long dark lashes lifting shyly to reveal her glistening green eyes. He lowered his lips to hers and raised his hand, caressing her cheek. Then he glided his hand to her delicate neck where his fingers tangled gently in her shining, soft hair.

When he felt ready to burst, all control crumbling around him, he forced his aching lips to leave hers and curved his arms around her, feeling her heart beating in rhythm with his own. "I'd better stop right now, or I won't stop at all."

"I don't want you to stop." She raised her lashes, uncovering her misted eyes. "But I know we must."

Brad forced himself to rise. For distraction, he grabbed the poker and jabbed at the glowing logs. He waited until his emotions had ebbed, and then he turned back to her. "I'd better get going. We leave early tomorrow, and I have lots to do."

She rose and returned to his arms. He felt her slender body blend into his own, and he wondered how one person could cause so many sensations to tear through him. She hugged him freely and, for the first time, kissed his eyelids and the tip of his nose, before placing her soft lips against his.

The kiss was gentle and fleeting, but she offered it eagerly. She stepped back, leaving one arm wrapped around his back. "Listen, have a wonderful time, and I'll be right here when you get back."

"You'd better be. I don't want some handsome man plying you with his charm." He stood before her, their hands joined.

"I don't know any handsome men but you."

With shivers of yearning, he opened the door, promising to call her, and hurried to his car.

Chapter 8

When Brad walked out the door, Sally wanted to kick herself. She knew her mother would be rolling over in her grave if she heard her. Another fib. Ron was a handsome man—but not one Brad needed to worry about.

For the next few days, she relived their parting, and she asked herself over and over why she avoided mentioning the surprise party and Ron. Guilt? Fear he would think she was being vindictive? A ball of uncertainty bounced back and forth in her head.

Yet after all her worries, the party for Darby's engagement was wonderful. As always, Ron was a gentleman. On the way home, she casually told him about Brad during their conversation, and though surprise showed on his face, he listened with quiet acceptance. Why hadn't she been as honest with Brad?

Feeling sorry for herself wouldn't help a thing, and on Sunday after church, Sally solicited Ed's help to put up the Christmas tree later in the week with the promise of pizza and homemade cookies. He eagerly accepted.

Sally stopped by a tree lot and selected an old-fashioned balsam with sparse branches leaving spaces for large bulbs and other tree ornaments. Then a couple days before Christmas, she lay on the floor with Ed standing above her, gripping the sticky tree branch.

"Okay, hold it steady," Sally instructed, as she wound the screws of the stand tightly against the tree. "There. Let go, and see if it's okay."

As Ed removed his grip, the tree moved only slightly, and Sally breathed a sigh. "I think it's fine."

She crawled from under the tree and stood up. When they stepped back, Ed's guffaw filled the room before Sally burst into laughter.

"Looks like that leaning tower of Pizza," Ed chortled. The tree tilted noticeably to the right.

"That's *Pisa*, Ed, as if you didn't know." She gave his shoulder a poke and crawled beneath the tree for the second time, and after much readjusting, they gave up.

"This tree's a little like me, Sally. It has a mind of its own." He clamped his hand on her shoulder. "I think we ought to give the thing its rights."

"Rights," Sally said, arching her eyebrow. "It sure does have its *rights*."

The tree with its predominate tilt stood proudly, and with Christmas music playing in the background, Ed helped her haul out the decorations and she trimmed while he chomped on pizza. When the decorating was finished, Ed nibbled on a cookie while she admired the room lit only by the delicate lights of the Christmas tree.

Ed's sudden voice jolted her from her reverie. "So, where's your friend?"

"On the Cape. His mother's ill and couldn't travel."

Ed's knowing eyes studied her. "Thought you seemed a little down."

"It's that and more, Ed. His daughter Kelly hasn't quite warmed up to me yet. And my brother's so wary of me meeting anyone, I haven't told him about Brad. I keep praying and God isn't listening." She blinked the tears back behind her eyes. "Guess I have the holiday blues. Feeling sorry for myself."

"One thing I learned in my old age, Sally. You can't force the issue. Things have a way of working out, and you need patience. And don't go blaming God. He's hearing those prayers, but maybe His answer is 'no' right now. Parents don't always agree with everything their children want. Sometimes, they know that things are worth waiting for." His kindly blue eyes sought hers. "Remember?"

She nodded, thinking of too many times as a child when her parents said no to her pleas.

"You just keep praying and listening. God's hearing you. And if I know fathers, after awhile, they give you what you want just to shut you up." His laughter filled the room again.

His words brought a smile to Sally's face, and she gave him a huge bear hug. "Ed, what would I do without your sage wisdom?"

He chuckled, "Sally, you're getting along mighty fine. Just takes you a little longer, maybe." He patted her arm. "Don't lose hope—or faith. Things take time."

❧

The following Monday, Sally trudged to Davidson's, eagerly awaiting the Christmas holiday. In the morning, she came upon Darby in the copy room, concentrating on the pages flipping from the machine.

Sally put her arm around her friend's shoulder. "Hey, the engagement party was wonderful. You looked so surprised."

"Surprised! There's no word to describe how I felt. Astounded, maybe. We'd talked, but. . .flabbergasted, now there's a word." She laughed. "And speaking of flabbergasted, I was surprised to see you with Ron."

Sally faltered. "I wasn't really with him. He offered a ride and I tried to explain, but he wouldn't take my 'no.' I finally gave up. I did tell him I was seeing Brad."

Darby stared at her. "Was he disappointed? He often asks about you. I think he really likes you."

A soft flush rose on Sally's face. "I like him, too, but as a friend. I suppose I should confess that Brad's stolen my heart, Darby. We've no plans, no commitments, but he's all I think about. It feels so good, Darby. I'm feeling happy again."

"So, is this serious?"

"Too soon. I don't know. We're getting to know each other. We have fun. We're comfortable. Our values are similar—family, children, God. He makes me laugh and feel alive."

"Then enjoy it, Sally, but be careful. Keep an eye on your emotions. Remember what happened to Cassie Bellows in marketing?"

Sally's enthusiasm faded. She hadn't expected Darby to caution her. "What do you mean? I don't remember."

"You don't? She met some guy at a singles' club. Fell head over heels in love, and. . ."

Sally's heart fell. "Now I remember. They got married less than a year after they met and divorced in a shorter time." Sally scowled. "But I didn't meet Brad at a singles' club."

"I'm not saying you did. I mean, sometimes when we first tumble, we don't keep our heads on straight. You're no fool, Sally. You have lots and lots of time. What will be, will be. I'm happy for you. If Brad makes you happy, enjoy it. Just don't use Ron to make Brad jealous."

"I'm not." Sally snapped her response. "I've never used a person to hurt someone else. All I know is how I feel with Brad—safe and cared about. It's wonderful."

"Then be gentle with Ron. He's a good friend. I know you won't hurt him on purpose, but think before you act."

Sally tensed. Darby wasn't listening. "I said I told him about my feelings for Brad. I was honest with him."

"Good. If he realizes you're out of the picture, he'll find someone else. He's handsome."

"And nice, I know. There's a girl out there who'll love him. It's just not me."

Confusion rattled through her. Why wasn't anyone thrilled for her when she mentioned Brad? All she heard from her family and now her friend were warnings. She was still hiding her feelings. What was wrong with her? If she truly loved him, wouldn't she sing his praises to the sky?

Returning to her desk, Sally found an envelope with her name printed on it, tucked under the computer keyboard. She lifted the flap and pulled out a note handwritten in a bold flourish. She scanned to the bottom, her pulse pounding. *Steve.*

Immediately, her hand trembled. *Why? What have I done?* The words blurred on the page.

What a scamp! You told me you aren't ready for dating. Tell the truth next time. I saw you at Aunt Fanny's. Don't tell me the guy's your brother. Save a little of that romance for me.

The note dropped from her trembling hand. She stared at it lying on the floor, picked it up. Wadding the offensive paper into a ball, she threw it in the wastebasket. She had to do something about him.

On second thought, she retrieved the note and tucked it into her pocket. Hurrying down the hall, she entered Darby's office. Though preoccupied, as Sally flew into the room, Darby looked up.

"I know you're busy, but look at this." Sally handed her the note. Darby smoothed out the wrinkles and scanned the paper.

"Yep, he's weird." She faked a grin.

Sally pulled up a chair and sat beside her. "I don't know what to do about him. Most anyone looking at the note would think I'm silly. He isn't threatening me, but he makes me nervous. I have to get him to leave me alone."

"Talk to Jim. He can force Steve's hand. It's sexual harassment, I would say."

"It's only right I talk to Steve first. I can't say he's harassing me if I don't let him know how I feel. I just have to get the courage."

She paused for a second, her thoughts racing. The Bible said if you're offended by someone, talk to them. She had to work up the courage somehow. Being single was the pits.

Sally looked back at Darby. "I wish I understood him. I'd think a million women'd die for a chance to date him. Why me?"

"Because you don't want him, probably. Some people like a challenge. Chase him. He'll probably run like a rabbit."

"I'd rather be miserable."

Darby snickered and returned the note.

Sally crumpled it for the second time and tossed it into Darby's wastebasket. "That's what I think of Mr. Wall's little memo. Thanks for listening. I needed a shoulder to cry on."

"Anytime," Darby called after her.

Sally hurried back to her desk, thinking about Steve's note. Since Davidson Electric would close for the holiday, she decided to talk with him after the new year. Cowardice was becoming her specialty.

❦

On Christmas Eve after the worship service, Sally invited Alice and Ed to come for hot cider and desserts. Ed acted like a child when it came to the Christmas gifts. For the past two years they had exchanged small gifts. This year he saved hers until the end. It was larger than the rest, and although she knew it was from Ed, she was sure that Alice helped him wrap it. The gift looked elegant in deep green foil tied with a large plaid Christmas ribbon.

"Guess we know who this one is for." Ed chuckled and handed Sally the package.

She took it from him and gently slid off the beautiful ribbon. She removed the paper and lifted the box lid. "Oh, Ed. I said you should keep this. It's so pretty, and it holds all your family photos. You shouldn't have."

Sally looked down at the charming old photograph album in the delicate greens and pinks that Ed found in the trunk of his attic. Her eyes welled with tears.

Alice patted her hand. "Ed knew you'd like it, Sally."

"And don't you worry. Alice and I went to a little shop in town and found a replacement, not nearly so pretty, but it'll hold some of my old pictures. I wanted you to have this one, and I even left a few old photos in it. For the life of me, I have no idea who the folks are, so it will add a little authenticity to the album."

As always, Ed made Sally laugh. "I love it." She leaned over and kissed him on the cheek.

"See," he said to Alice. "It was worth it, right?"

Alice gave him a poke.

Sally looked through the leafs of the album, examining the shapes and sizes of slots for the pictures. "You know, if I remember correctly, I have a few old pictures from my parents' memorabilia in my attic. I haven't looked at them in years."

The album gave her a new idea. She could spend Christmas Day rummaging through the attic. She had no idea what she might find there. And best of all, she could pass the time waiting for Brad's phone call.

❦

On Christmas Day Sally attended Christmas worship and, later in the day, plowed through the attic, looking for the old photographs. In the memorabilia, Sally found an old doll, her report cards in a manila envelope, and a packet of wonderful old letters tied with a traditional blue ribbon. She spent the rest of the afternoon reading the old letters and gazing at the tintype photographs.

Sally felt apprehensive, waiting for Brad's call. She kept her eye on the clock, and the clock hands pointed to seven in the evening when the telephone rang. She jumped with anticipation and hurried to answer it.

Chapter 9

M erry Christmas."

Brad closed his eyes when he heard her voice. "Merry Christmas, Sally.

"I'm so glad you called. How's your visit? How are the kids?"

She sounded happy, and his tension faded. "The kids are great. Mother coddles them, and they need the attention. It makes Janet's absence easier. At least, it seems that way."

"I hoped it would. So, how's your mother?"

"Fine. She's sorry she didn't get to meet you."

If it hadn't been for the children, he might have avoided telling his mother about his growing feelings for Sally. He feared she'd think he got involved with a woman too soon. But Danny blurted out Sally's name over and over with Kelly coming in second, and his mother didn't miss a word. To his delight, she sounded pleased.

Yet her enthusiasm also carried the usual mother's caution. "Just don't rush into anything, Brad. You've been lonely. Don't mistake passion for real love." He was sure he hadn't, but he would keep her warning tucked somewhere in his subconscious.

He'd spent a lot of time thinking while he was gone. They needed to deal with their fears if they were ever going to make their relationship work. He was as guilty as Sally.

"I really miss you, Sally. A lot."

"I miss you, too," she whispered.

The urge to get back to her overwhelmed him. "We'll be here a few more days. Mom's kept us busy, but I'm looking forward to getting home."

"I'm anxious to see you."

He didn't care what anyone said. How could these feelings not be love?

"Brad, you'll never guess what happened since you've been gone. Darby and Eric are engaged."

"Engaged. Great. They're a nice couple."

"I knew before you left, but I was sworn to secrecy."

"You knew about what?"

"Eric planned a surprise dinner party for close friends and family and proposed there. In front of everyone. It was nice."

Disappointment edged through him. Promises aren't meant to be kept from. . .from who? Boyfriends? Husbands? What was he to Sally? "Sorry I wasn't there to go with you."

"Me, too," she mumbled.

Sally's voice sounded strange. He had to ask, but he wasn't sure he wanted to hear the answer. "You didn't go alone, did you?"

He heard her inhale. "Ron Morton helped Eric make the calls. He offered to pick me up. You remember him, don't you?"

Naturally, he remembered. "Sure. From Darby's birthday party."

"Uh-huh." She rushed on. "They made me promise I wouldn't tell Darby. I had a terrible time keeping quiet."

"I bet you did." He sensed tension between them, but he didn't know if it were his or hers. "I'm glad you had someone to go with. It's more fun."

The line was silent until he continued. "Well, I don't want to say good-bye, but I better get back to the family. I really miss you. I'll call as soon as we get home."

"I can't wait, Brad. Have a safe trip. . .and give my best to your mom and hug the kids for me."

When he hung up, he felt irritated. The tension that filled the empty airwaves made talking impossible. His hair bristled when she casually mentioned Ron.

If she were trying to make him jealous, she had done a good job, but he didn't like that either. He rolled his shoulders, feeling the tension move from his neck down his spine. They would have to talk when he got home.

When Bill and Sue returned from Florida, they invited Sally for dinner. Carrie talked incessantly, listing every gift she received and detailing every event.

Sally enjoyed the evening until Sue asked if she had plans for New Year's Eve. "I'm staying home." She needed to introduce the subject of Brad, and Sue's question gave her the opportunity. "I would have plans except the man I'd like to be with is—"

Bill, who was only half listening, cut her off. "I'm glad you're taking it easy, Sis. Sue and I think you should take your time getting back into the social whirl. Too many people jump into relationships while they're still grieving and make big mistakes."

Sally winced. "But Bill, I'm not—"

"Right," Sue said, "and you know what men want, Sally. Many of them just want to take advantage of your loneliness. Getting involved with someone now could lead to nothing but trouble."

Sally froze. How could she tell them about Brad now? Better to keep it quiet than hear their disdain.

"Darby's warned me about the plight of single women." She hoped the comment would halt the subject. "And speaking of Darby, she and Eric are engaged. He invited a few friends for a surprise dinner and asked her in front of the whole crowd."

Bill laughed. "Wow, how embarrassing if she'd said no."

"He must have been pretty sure she'd say yes, silly," Sue said, "or he wouldn't have asked her that way."

Sally sighed, relieved she'd sidetracked them. She'd wait a long time before she'd mention Brad.

The conversation didn't return to New Year's Eve, but their words kept coming back to her, and Darby's warning came to mind. *Remember what happened to Cassie Bellows in marketing? She fell head over heels in love, and. . .* Her thoughts would remain private from now on. She would savor the pleasure and deal with the pain alone until she knew she could handle everyone's negative attitudes. Was there one person who'd be happy for her?

🌿

Sally sat alone on New Year's Eve, watching the ball drop in Times Square and thinking about Brad. As always, thoughts of him warmed her. Still, icy fear crept in to cool her spirit. She lost one love. Would her relationship with Brad be a blossoming flower that also died on the vine?

The more she thought, the more troubled she became. Brad had children, and they added problems. How could he get on with his life when the children hadn't? The situation was frustrating and mind-boggling. The answer seemed to rest on time.

On January third, Sally returned to work, facing the year-end inventory and knowing that she must talk to Steve. She had put the confrontation off long enough. Looking for a neutral location, she settled on the company cafeteria.

When she entered the lunchroom, Steve was alone at a table. She wanted to get the whole thing over with. She breathed deeply, harnessing her courage, and marched forward bravely. "May I join you?"

Before he spoke, he examined her from feet to face. "My pleasure." He rose, pulling out a chair. His unusual attempt at chivalry embarrassed her. Steve returned to his seat and stared at her until she flushed. He appeared amused.

Sally bolstered her courage. "I've been wanting to speak to you since I found your note."

"My note?"

She had no desire to play games with him.

"Oh, my note. It was so long ago I nearly forgot."

"Steve, I'm asking you to please understand that I'm not interested in seeing you socially. I prefer keeping my work separate from my private life."

"I bet you do." His mouth curved into a smirk, and he leaned across the table. "I like to see you with fire in your eyes," he said in a breathy murmur. "It looks good on you. Real spunky." He slurred his words.

Sally felt her courage failing. "There are many women who'd probably enjoy your attention, Steve. I'm not one of them. I don't appreciate it at all."

"*He* must be quite a man. I admire him."

Sally frowned, confused by his comment. "What are you talking about?"

"The friend you were with at Aunt Fanny's. He must be quite a man to keep you happy. You're a little spitfire."

Sally rose, her voice an angry whisper. "Listen, Steve, I wanted to be civil, but you don't understand. I'm not interested in you. I never will be. You're harassing me, and if you don't leave me alone, I'll be forced to do something about it." She spun around and darted from the lunchroom.

❦

When Brad arrived home on Tuesday, he dropped the luggage and rushed to the telephone before he unpacked. "It's good to know you're only a few miles away instead of hundreds," Brad said. "How about dinner? I can't wait to see you."

All her feelings melted away and a smile spread across her face. "I'm ready now."

"Do you mind if I bring the kids? Or I can get a sitter. Maybe that would be best."

"No, please bring the children. I've missed them."

Her words filled him with joy. "Great. They're anxious to see you."

Amazing, he thought. The tension seemed gone. She'd forgiven him for missing Christmas with her. "Great. I'll pick you up about five and then drop them back home before the meeting."

Their "welcome home" dinner was filled with the children's chatter, and Brad hardly had time to say a word. He controlled his own eager greeting, knowing he and Sally would have to wait until they were alone. But after dinner, Sally handed the children gifts she'd purchased for them, and then opened their package to her. She pinned the guardian angel pin to her lapel, and tears glistened in her eyes.

❦

Near the end of January, Sally and Brad headed for their last meeting of the grief group. The participants clustered together in talkative groups like graduation day, reminiscing about their first meeting and the progress they'd made. For Sally and Brad, the memories held special meaning.

Jack ended with the topic, "A Time to Love." Brad held Sally's hand, squeezing lightly as he listened to Jack's words. "Love does not have limits. Think of God's love for us. It never runs out. God loves us with fullness and completeness. No one is loved more than another. We are loved equally. So we may love again, not diminishing the love we had, but a new love—equal, full, and complete—may grow in your lives."

Jack's words rattled through Brad. He remembered feeling guilty when Sally first came to the house, as if he were cheating on Janet by sharing their children and home with another woman. But that had changed. His love was boundless and growing daily.

Jack finished, "Our loved ones helped create the persons we are. A new love is only an extension of the love we had. Our departed loved ones continue to live in us as we live in God and in each other. May our love for one another and God's love shine through us always." When Jack finished, the room thundered with spontaneous applause.

The discussion group session flew by. Telephone numbers were exchanged, prayers were offered and requested, and finally, hugs and good-byes were given. Brad and Sally walked out together into the surprisingly mild January night.

Waving to others, they ambled toward the car. Brad held Sally's hand and leaned into her shoulder, feeling familiar and loving. When they slid into the car, he wrapped his arm around her, caressing her shoulder. "I know our relationship is only months old, Sally, but I want you to know you make me feel whole again."

Sally looked into his eyes without speaking, but when Brad lowered his lips to hers, he needed no words. Their lips met tenderly, breathlessly, like a compelling love song. She yielded to the kiss, returning freely what he gave to her. The kiss lay gentle and sweet on his lips and on his heart. Brad lingered, brushing kisses on the end of her nose and her eyelids. She raised her lips to meet his once again, and his former worries melted away.

Her voice came like a whisper. "You mean so much to me, Brad. I've been trying to sort through it all. I didn't think that I could feel this way again. In many ways, it seems I've known you for a lifetime."

He nestled her within his arms, holding her as if he would never let go. When he relaxed, easing against the seat cushion, he gazed steadily into her eyes that glistened with tears. "I love you, Sally."

"I've been afraid to call it love, Brad. Whatever it is, it's wonderful—but it scares me."

He didn't tell her he felt scared at times, too. "We have time. All the time in the world."

Headlights from another car flashed past the window, and Brad noticed two men standing next to their cars, watching them. He pointed to them. "If we don't leave soon, we'll have a crowd volunteering to give us a push. I imagine they think my car won't start." They laughed as he started the car and drove from the lot.

Chapter 10

O
n February first, Sally dealt quietly with the second anniversary of Tim's death. She climbed into her car alone and drove to the cemetery, her thoughts stirring inside her head. On her lapel, she attached the guardian angel pin, the Christmas present from Kelly and Danny. In her gloved hands, she carried a piece of German chocolate cake. In a way, the cake seemed foolish, but Tim loved German chocolate cake and she could think of nothing else to bring to him on a cold, wintry day. She traversed the frozen grass and stood over his grave.

The stone was free of snow, and she read the inscription. *Loving Husband, Timothy Ronald Newgate, April 7, 1958 to February 1, 1996.* Sally bent down, tracing her finger along the letters carved into the gray granite, for once controlling her emotions.

Feeling foolish, she placed the cake on the grave. "Well Tim, my love, you may think a piece of cake is rather silly. I realize this isn't a celebration—and not exactly a regular party, but it's a gift from my heart. I know heaven is filled with wonderful things, but I'm not sure if heaven has really good German chocolate cake. I know how much you love it."

Her eyes puddled with tears, and she pushed them back, closing them for a moment to gain her composure.

A large pine tree stood nearby, and Sally wandered over and leaned against its sturdy trunk. She spoke aloud, feeling comfort in the sense of real conversation. In her memory, she could see Tim grinning at her when she did something silly.

"Tim, I need to talk to you. I hope you know I'm okay. In fact, I'm doing pretty good now. That's what I want to tell you about. I never thought it would happen, but I've met a really wonderful man—with two children, a girl and a boy, Kelly and Danny."

Her lips trembled, and she stopped speaking to calm her emotions. "Brad means a lot to me. Love is what I think it is, and I want you to know. I cherish the years we had, but I have a lot more love to give—enough, even, for those two lovely children who need a mom. Knowing you, I imagine you're happy I've found someone. I know I'd have wanted you to fall in love again. . ."

She swallowed to stem the sorrow creeping into her voice. ". . .and have the children we never had. Oh, Tim, I think that was the second worst part, not having even one little piece of you with me."

This time she let the tears fall, rolling in warm rivulets down her cheeks until they turned to icy dampness beneath her chin. "I'm not going to stand here and cry like a baby. I feel sorry for myself. And I'm scared."

She walked back to the grave and patted the headstone. "I'm going to go before I get too morbid, but I'll leave the cake, and I want you to know that I love you." She turned away and hurried to her car.

In the beginning of March, Sally received a surprise telephone call from her old friend, Elaine. It had been months since she had heard from her. The hurt still lingered over the distance between them following Tim's death, and when Elaine invited her out to dinner, Sally was pleased.

But the dinner and friendship felt different and strained.

When they returned to the house, Sally made coffee, and their conversation turned to children.

Elaine stared thoughtfully into her coffee cup. "Mark and I are hoping to have a baby soon, did I mention that?"

"No, but it would be wonderful." Sally pushed back her pangs of envy. "Tim and I decided to try again—just before the accident."

"Sally, I feel so bad. I know this has been so hard for you, and I haven't been a good friend."

Sally wanted to agree and say, *Right. You haven't been a good friend to me*, but she couldn't. Attacking Elaine served no purpose but to create guilt. Guilt wasn't productive, but sharing was. If anyone should be happy for her, Elaine should.

"You've been away, Elaine. And I've made new friends." Sally took a deep breath, bolstering courage. "One has become really special, a widower from my grief group with two little kids. He's wonderful, and I care about him and his children. Kelly's seven and Danny's five. They miss their mother dreadfully."

Elaine glared, and her voice took on an edge. "You seem to know him well. Is this serious?"

An icy sensation shivered through Sally's body. "I don't know, Elaine. It's a fairly new relationship. He loves me, and I. . .I love him."

Elaine's voice sliced through Sally. "I'm surprised at you, Sally. Tim hasn't been gone that long. I can't believe you're involved with someone already!"

"Elaine, I didn't say I was involved—not the way you make it sound. We're good friends. We understand each other. We share feelings and dreams." Sally clenched her fists, her nails digging into the palms of her hands. "I didn't die, Elaine. Tim did. It's been two years. I've felt dead long enough. I need to live, and I'd think you, of all people, would want me to."

Sally couldn't believe that she was saying these things to Elaine. Anger and frustration boiled inside her. Tears clung to her cheeks. She raised her gaze heavenward, remembering what God expected of Christians. A renewed peace swept over her and her anger subsided like a leaf caught on a dying gust of wind. She loved Elaine. No more hurt was needed for anyone. There had been enough for a lifetime.

"Oh, Elaine, I'm so sorry. I can't believe I talked to you like that. It was hard, Elaine, and I needed you so badly. You were always my best friend, the person who I could tell my deepest thoughts—and you always understood. I don't have you anymore. You're too far away, and my other best friend was too far away, too—he died."

Elaine looked on, pale-faced, mouth agape as Sally brushed the tears from her eyes. "I've made new friends and picked up the pieces of my life. I can't sit in the house and die, too. I'm young. Tim wouldn't want me to die. I know he wouldn't."

Sally tried to compose her voice and her emotions, but her body quivered with depths of stored, repressed feelings. They were unleashed like wild animals. Her honesty and hurt bounded across the space between her and Elaine.

Elaine covered her face in her hands and wept. "Sally, please forgive me. How could I say that to you?" Pulling a tissue from her handbag, she dabbed at her eyes. "You're right. I've been sitting in Bay City with my husband and my new life. You've been here alone. I am so sorry, Sally. I wish we had talked long ago."

When she rose to leave, Sally held her arms open, drained and weary, and they clung together like the old friends they had always been. Though their differences had been settled, Sally faced the truth. Few people understood her feelings for Brad. People measured her feelings based on their concept of time and their measurement of love. Sally wanted to scream to heaven, *Lord, answer me. Tell me what is right. You're silent when I need to hear Your voice. You've said everything has a season and a purpose under heaven. Lord, when is my season?*

❦

Easter came early in April. Sally took stock of the situation. If God wasn't going to help her, she needed to help herself. She'd allowed everyone's opinion to guide her, and she'd hidden Brad from Bill and Sue. The time had come to deal with the issue. She invited Brad and the children to her home for Easter dinner. Brad and her family needed to meet.

Yet, despite her resolve, the words of family and friends banged unpleasantly in her thoughts. Elaine, Bill and Sue, and Darby, people who should want her happiness offered her only fears. She remembered Darby's comments. *Sometimes when we first tumble, we don't keep our heads on straight.* Is that what had happened? Was she throwing all good sense out the window?

Easter morning when Sally rose, she looked through the bay window in the dining room to study the weather. A beautiful day appeared with a sky clear and the sun like a bright golden ball.

Her mother always told her the sun danced for joy on Easter morning. As a child, she hoped to awaken early enough to watch the sun dance, but she never did. She smiled, remembering her mother and her childhood Easters. Might the sun dance today in her brother's eyes when he saw her happiness?

Brad took the children to their own church for Easter services while Bill and his family joined Sally at Good Hope. The Easter music soared with of the strains of "Christ Has Arisen! Hallelujah!" Choirs sang and a brass ensemble added their festive sounds to the hymns and anthems. But Sally felt empty of the joy and looked to the cross, wondering why God ignored her prayers.

When Sally arrived home, the sweet spicy aroma of the ham baking slowly in the oven drifted through the house, whetting everyone's appetite. Sally offered coffee and bagels to everyone and then distracted Carrie with a new picture book. She took advantage of the quiet moment to prepare Bill and Sue for Brad and the children.

Bill's face soured. "It's your life, Sally. You do what you want. But a man who's only been alone for a year doesn't seem like a wise choice. You'll step into his life and mess his kids up good. They haven't adjusted to their mother's loss yet. Then you come along and leave them. Seems pretty tacky to me."

Sally's voice caught in her throat, and she struggled to keep tears from her eyes. "I'm not planning to hurt the children. I'm very fond of them, and—"

"No one said you've planned it, Sally," Sue said. "Children get used to you being around and then when you leave, there's another hole in their lives. You certainly don't think this will be a lasting relationship with this man, do you? You know he's a new widower."

Her eyebrows raised, and Sally felt herself sink into the chair cushion, beaten back by their words. "I don't know where this is leading. We're giving it time."

Bill's voice rose, and Sally noticed Carrie looked at them with curiosity. "Well, I should hope so. You had a great marriage to Tim. I sure don't want to see you land in divorce court a year or two after you marry this guy. Use your head."

Shocked, Sally's anger rose. She and Bill rarely had words, and today it was the last thing she wanted, but she snapped her response. "Divorce? Never. I'm sorry you don't approve. I'm not planning to jump off the deep end with any decision. And I *have* used my head." *And my heart,* she added to herself.

Sue watched, her gaze darting from one to the other. "Let's not get riled here. We'll make the best of it. Bill, it's Sally's decision, not ours."

"All I ask," Sally added, "is that you make Brad and his children feel welcome."

Sue turned to Sally. "This is your home, Sally. We'll certainly be cordial, won't we, Bill?"

Bill nodded his head and shrugged. He rose and snapped on the television to a golf tournament.

A noise sounded in the driveway, and Carrie rose from her book, glancing out the window. "Your company's here," Carrie called out as she ran toward the door.

Sally watched Brad and the children come up the walk to the porch.

Beneath her coat, Kelly was donned in a sea-green dress, the same color glinting in her eyes, with a floral print ruffle at the hem and neck. Danny, looking the image of his father, sported gray slacks and a navy blue sport coat.

Sally's aching heart lurched with love, and she ushered them in, trying to hide the fear that spread through her. With the introductions, Bill shook hands halfheartedly and turned his face back to the television set. Carrie seemed shy for a moment, but when Danny noticed her new storybook, she showed him the pictures, and they sat together on the floor. Kelly stood back and watched in silence.

"Kelly," Sally said, "would you like to help me in the kitchen? I could use an assistant."

Kelly shrugged, giving the other children a sidelong glance. "I guess so." She followed Sally into the kitchen. "I'm more grown-up than Danny and Carrie."

Sally agreed, then gave Kelly the silverware for the table and the child headed off to do her job. As Sally pulled the ham from the oven, Brad walked into the kitchen.

"Smells wonderful. Much better than the unpleasant aura in the living room." He placed his hands on Sally's lower neck muscles and massaged. "You're as tense as a wound-up spring."

"I know. I just told Bill about you today. Sorry, I should have done it sooner, but I'm a terrible coward. He promised to be civil."

"Good. And I promise to do the same." He stepped back as she pulled the ham from the oven. "And time for a taste test."

Sally gave him a quick grin, setting the roaster on trivets. "How about if you maneuver the ham into the stand there?" She pointed to a metal holder. "You can be in charge of slicing."

"I'd be delighted. With the knife in my hand, I'll know it's not headed for my back." He gave her a teasing smile. She grimaced and he quickly added, "Just kidding."

Kelly returned to the kitchen and hesitated for a moment in the doorway and then continued into the room. "I'm an assistant, Daddy. I'm setting the table."

"Let me see." He wiped his hands and followed her into the dining room. Sally heard him talking to her from the other room. "You've done a very nice job, as always—like Mom taught you."

When they returned to the kitchen, Kelly's face reflected she was pleased he had compared her to her mother. Kelly continued her tasks, as Brad sliced the ham, garnishing the dish with pineapple slices. Sally placed the potato casserole in a protective wicker basket and dished up the vegetables.

When the table was ready, she called the family. Bill and Sue wandered into the dining room, cordial as they had promised, but restrained. They gathered around the table and bowed their heads for prayer. Though conversation seemed stilted, they ate with relish, and Sally was grateful.

After dinner, the children were eager for an activity and sat on the floor looking at the Candyland game that Kelly had brought along. When Alice and Ed arrived to join them for dessert, their presence eased the tension, and conversation flowed more freely.

When the pies were eaten, Sally carried the dishes and leftover desserts into the kitchen. She was at the sink rinsing dishes when Brad walked up behind her, putting his arms around her waist. He kissed her hair, and she turned to face him.

"You smell just as good as that cinnamon apple pie," he murmured.

"I take that as quite a compliment."

He slid his hands up and down her arms, looking deeply into her eyes, then embraced her, lowering his lips to hers with a kiss, deep and loving. Brad moved his arms tenderly along her back, and she felt wonderful being near him. When their kiss ended, she remained enfolded in his arms with her head resting on his shoulder.

Brad's voice was hushed. "Sally, I want to tell you. . ." Before he could finish, a sound stopped him, and when he swung around, Kelly stood in the dining room doorway, a game piece from her hand rolling across the floor. She stared at them, unmoving.

Chapter 11

Brad rushed toward Kelly, but she pivoted and ran into the dining room. Brad followed her and held her in his arms as she sobbed. "Kelly, Sally my friend. She's helping all of us from being so sad. We have fun again like a new—"

But Kelly's words shattered the silence. "But she's not my mother. I don't want a different mother. I want my own."

Brad's heart lurched, tears filling his eyes for her pain. "I know, sweetheart, but. . ." What could he say to ease her fears and sense of loss?

They'd been so careful, doing everything to avoid upsetting the children. How could he have been so thoughtless today? He knew Kelly was nearby, but in his emotions, he had forgotten.

When Kelly quieted, he looked into her face. "Wait here a minute, and I'll get our things so we can leave." Brad left the dining room feeling tense and drawn. He returned to the kitchen where Sally waited, staring at the doorway, her eyes wide and filled with the evidence of tears.

"I'm so sorry, Sally," he whispered.

"Me, too. Is she okay?"

"She will be, but I think we'd better go. I hate to leave on such a note, but it's best. Would you call Danny in here so we can leave through the back? You can explain after we're gone and give my apologies to everyone."

"Brad, I feel bad, too, but isn't sneaking away a bit dramatic? Danny's having fun, and—"

"Sally, I don't want to upset Kelly any more than she's already upset. It's better if we leave quietly."

"But won't leaving so quickly give her the impression we're wrong to care about each other? We've tried to be thoughtful, Brad. How long will it take for them to accept me?"

"It will take as long as it takes. I'm sorry you feel that way. Please ask Danny to come in here."

Sally's face registered shock, but she did as he asked. Brad hurried back to the dining room and, protectively, guided Kelly to the kitchen as Sally returned with a confused Danny.

"Why do we have to go, Daddy?" Disappointment filled his face. "We're playing Candyland."

"I know, son, but Kelly doesn't feel well. We have to go home now. You can play the game another day."

Danny pouted as Brad herded the children out the back door. Sally stared after them, pale and silent.

✺

Monday at Davidson's, Sally was in the midst of chaos. She couldn't get Brad out of her mind. She knew the children needed time for adjustment, but that's what she thought they were doing, moving slowly and cautiously. How much time did it take? She felt impatient. She wanted to show her feelings for Brad openly. Yet, now, they'd hurt Kelly.

She expected Brad to protect his children. But yesterday, she felt alienated from him, as if he were ashamed of their feelings for each other. As the thought trudged through, she remembered her own delay in sharing her feelings with Bill. She realized her error.

Along with her personal worries, Davidson's was involved in a company inventory and a buyout transaction. Moving quickly was important. Sally agreed to stay late to help complete the information necessary for negotiations.

When her telephone extension buzzed in the afternoon, she controlled the irritation in her voice. The caller was Brad.

"Hope this isn't inconvenient," he said cautiously. "I've been thinking of you all day and didn't get a chance to call last night."

"How did things go?" Their first real argument lingered in her mind, a mixture of hurt and frustration.

"First, I want to apologize, Sally. I acted like an idiot. I should have considered your feelings, too. We've done everything we can to help the kids adjust, and I don't know what else to do."

"I didn't mean to sound cold and unfeeling, Brad. I'm sorry that it happened, too. Later I thought about Bill and Sue and how I've behaved. We have our own problems accepting the changes in our lives, worried about what others think. Then we have the children's problems. I'm beginning to think our problems will never end."

"Please don't be discouraged. We'll work things out." Brad paused a moment. Sally wondered if he believed what he said. Then Brad broke the silence. "When I got home last night, I got Danny distracted with his toys. He was upset because he had to leave your house. With him busy I explained things to Kelly. I said you and I are good friends—that you care about all of us. I stressed *all*. I told her you made me happy and helped me get over my sadness. When I said that, I saw the fear in her eyes—like I had already forgotten her mother. I assured her that I would always love Janet."

"Did she understand? Even if she did, I'm sure she felt betrayed."

"I imagine—in her eyes, I betrayed her and her mother by kissing you. Oh, Sally, this is so difficult. I feel terrible. Last night, I didn't think about Kelly being in the next room. I looked at you and did what my heart told me to do. I kissed you. Now, we have a mess again. I feel like you do. I'm losing patience." His sigh echoed over the phone line. "It'll work out."

"I know. We had made good progress—until yesterday."

"Could we get together tonight or tomorrow night? I can get Katie to baby-sit. We need to talk and decide where we go from here—what we do next. I need ideas. I want to help the kids, but I can't stop living, Sally."

"Brad, I'm working tonight and probably tomorrow night. We have some complicated stuff going on here. Maybe I can get off by eight tomorrow. We could have a late dinner together."

"That would be great. I hate to put you in the middle of my family problems, but. . ."

"I *am* in the middle. You didn't put me there. I joined right in, so I'm responsible, too. I care about the kids, Brad."

"I know you care, or I wouldn't ask you. Maybe tomorrow we can think of something."

❦

Sally and Brad agreed upon a plan—quality time for her and Kelly, just the two of them. Sally suggested taking her to lunch and asking her to help select a birthday gift for Carrie. A few days later, Brad had eased the idea into Kelly's mind and following a personal telephone call from Sally, Kelly agreed.

The child waited at the door when Sally pulled into the driveway the next day, and they headed for Kelly's restaurant choice, Big Top Burger. The fast-food restaurant offered special meals packaged for children with a surprise toy inside, and Kelly was collecting the miniature dolls. With their meals ordered at the counter, they found seats.

Sally had used every piece of parenting technique she could muster, praying she would move cautiously. "Do you like to shop, Kelly? Your daddy says you are very helpful."

"Uh-huh, my mom liked me to shop with her. I pushed the cart at the grocery store. And put things in the basket."

"That was helpful. Your mom was smart to think of taking you along."

She nodded, her bright curls bouncing. "My mom was smart."

"I've never had a girl to help me shop before. I'm glad you came with me. When I was your age, I liked to help my mom."

Kelly's gaze drifted to Sally's. "Do you help her now?"

"No, I can't anymore, Kelly. My mom died, just like yours."

"She did?" Kelly eyes widened in surprise. Then she frowned. "Did she get real sick, like my mommy did?"

"Yes, she did. My mom died about ten years ago. I really miss her."

"You do?" Again Kelly's eyes widened, this time with a question. The look washed over her face until finally she spoke. "Did you forget what she looks like?"

Sally was stunned at Kelly's question. Now, she fathomed the depth of Kelly's fears. "No, I'll never forget, Kelly. I have lots of pictures that I look at to remind me. I can even hear her voice in my head, telling me to eat so I don't get sick."

Kelly nodded as she listened. "My mom said I should eat all my vegetables." A silence settled over them. She looked at Sally, searching her face, soliciting trust before she confessed in a voice like a whisper, "Sometimes, I'm afraid I'll forget what she looks like."

Sally's heart ached. "You have pictures of her at home, don't you? Ask your daddy to give you a picture of your very own to put in your room. On your night-stand, maybe. Then you'll see her face before you go to bed at night and when you get up in the morning. That would be nice."

Kelly nodded. "Then I won't forget."

Sally heard her audible sigh of relief. "Oh, Kelly, sweetheart, you'll never forget. Moms are very special. No one takes a mom's place. No one would ever want to."

Kelly looked at Sally quizzically, her pretty green eyes searching Sally's face. Then, as if it were a new day, a smile curled on her lips, and she changed the subject.

They finished lunch and continued on to stores where Kelly pointed out games and clothes she thought Carrie might like. Sally made her purchases. As they left the department store, Sally eyed a display of small padded picture frames covered in delicate floral fabrics, perfect for a snapshot.

She led the petite child to the display. "Kelly, do you like these?" She pointed to the frames. "You could pick one out for your mom's picture. I'd like to buy it for you."

Kelly's gaze riveted to the bright cloth frames. Taking her time, Kelly looked at each one, questioning if it were a design and color that her mother would like. Finally she made her selection. The clerk placed it in a bag, and Kelly carried the purchase herself, holding it against her chest like a precious gem. "Thank you for the present."

"You're very welcome." Sally said, giving her a hug. Kelly responded by hug-ging her back. They were friends again. "I have an idea. Let's go to my house. We can call your dad and Danny and have them come over for dinner. We could order pizza and make a salad."

"Okay. I'll call Daddy when we get to your house. And then we could play a game after our pizza. It's still at your house, isn't it?"

Sally could only nod. A lump formed in her throat. She looked at this dear child so recently sorrowful, now clinging to her parcel and jabbering about pizza and Candyland.

❦

Summer weather came quickly. In late May, the temperature stayed in the eight-ies. The beaches opened Memorial Day weekend, and Sally was packing a picnic lunch to take to the beach when the telephone rang.

"Sally, this is Elaine. I wanted to tell you in person, but I can't wait. We're expecting a baby."

"Oh, Elaine, I am so happy." Sally winced involuntarily, ashamed that she thought of herself. The feeling passed quickly, and her joy for Elaine and Mark returned. "Mark is ecstatic, I'm sure."

"Oh, you would think he did it all by himself. I get no credit." Silence hovered for a moment before she continued. "I'm still feeling bad about what I said, Sally. I hope you've forgiven me."

"Elaine, we all say things we wished we hadn't. You know I've forgiven you." She hadn't forgotten, however, and she wished she could. "Let me know if you're coming down this way again, and if I'm coming yours, I'll let you know."

The conversation ended on a congenial note, yet Sally rolled her shoulders to relieve the tension. Forgiveness was something she could give. Forgetting wasn't as easy, and she longed to erase the memory of that day from her mind.

❦

Brad arrived with the children early, eager to be on their way. If they were early enough, they could lay claim on a table in a choice location. The beaches were popular with the warm temperature, especially on Memorial Day weekend.

They found a parking spot that would be protected by shade later in the day. Gathering blankets, food basket, cooler, and swimming paraphernalia, he loaded up Sally and the children, and they headed for the picnic tables closest to the water.

The water felt cold even in the heat of the day. Danny walked in timidly, uncertain and cautious. Everyone but Brad yelled out and shivered as the icy liquid rolled up their bodies. He forced himself to be courageous, a bit of masculine pride, he admitted to himself, and he was the first to dive in, stifling his screams of icy anguish. Kelly followed, but didn't hold back from admitting the water was cold. Brad looked back toward the shore, and grinned. He'd left Sally in the shallow water to wade with Danny.

After lunch, Brad sent the children to play in the sand. He wanted to speak to Sally in private. She spread a blanket on the ground next to the picnic table and leaned against the bench. He spread out on his back looking at the fleecy wisps of clouds overhead.

"My friend Elaine called to tell me she and Mark are expecting a baby. Naturally, I'm thrilled for her, but I have to admit I had a twinge of jealousy."

Brad gazed at her face glowing in the sunlight and longed to say something to bring her peace of mind. They'd had difficult times dealing with their personal sorrows and struggling with Kelly. But things had finally begun to fall into place. Someday Sally would be a mother herself, and he prayed he would be the father of that baby.

He lay on the blanket in thoughtful silence, then grinned at her. "One of these days when you're waddling around with your belly out a mile, you'll wonder why you ever felt jealous." He rumpled her hair. "And I'm planning to stand by your side and laugh at you."

Though she attempted to act casual, a look of amazement crept across her face. "Thanks for your vote of confidence."

"No problem. In fact, I'm looking forward to it."

A blush rose on her cheeks, and he quieted his beating heart.

"You know, Brad, I probably never told you the whole story, and it's something that's caused me so much grief. I suppose I'm ashamed of myself."

Icy fear darted through him. "What, Sally?" *Nothing could be that bad.*

"When I had the miscarriage, Tim begged me to try again. He didn't just ask me, he begged. And I refused. I had no faith, and I was terribly ashamed of myself. Like I was inferior, even though I knew better."

He rested his hand on hers and felt the tremors race through her.

"After Tim died, I felt such shame and loss, not only for him, but for the child we might have had. I longed so much for one after he was gone. But then, it was too late."

He pressed her hand beneath his. "But it's not too late now, Sally. Forgive yourself. We all do foolish things we wish we could erase. You've grieved enough."

"I know, but I wanted to tell you."

"I'm glad you did." They sat in silence, and as the tension eased from her body, Brad continued. "So, let me tell you my news. I'm taking my vacation in July." He paused, looking for the children on the sand. Seeing them playing safely, he turned back to Sally. "I wanted to talk to you about your vacation. Do you have any plans yet?"

"Nothing yet." She eyed him, and he thought he saw a glimmer of hope reflected in her face. "What are you planning?"

"Well, that's what I wanted to talk to you about. I'm taking the kids to Cape Cod to visit my mom. She loves it when we come. It's wonderful there in the summer—the ocean, the quaintness." He saw he had piqued her interest. "I'd like you to come, too. I'll be gone nearly a month, but I'd like you to come for whatever time you can arrange. I've been talking to Mom about you, and she's anxious to meet you."

"Oh, now that's scary. You're taking me home to meet your mother?"

"Isn't that the first step?"

"That's what I'm afraid of."

Though she joked, Brad noted the heightened color in her cheeks and a sparkle in her eyes. She was pleased with the invitation.

"I could arrange a week, I imagine. It would give me time with the kids—and with you. I'd love it."

"A week would be wonderful. The kids and I'd be really happy, and it would make my mother happy, too."

"Well, let's not disappoint your mom." She gave him a coy smile.

The next weeks flew by, and Brad stopped by before he left for the Cape. His mind hammered with things he wanted to share with Sally, but couldn't yet. He had to prepare her for them. He'd talk to her on the Cape.

"Brad, is something wrong? I feel like you're going to give me bad news or something."

He took her hand in his, rubbing her cool skin with his warm fingers. "Nothing's wrong. We haven't talked about us lately, and I guess I've been wondering where we're headed. Where do I stand in your life?"

"What brought this on?"

"Oh, I don't know. Maybe I'm getting melancholy knowing that I'm going away, and it'll be a couple of weeks before I'll see you again. I'm taking you to meet my mother, and I suppose I want to know if you care as much about me as I do about you."

She pressed his hand with hers. "Brad, you have no reason to wonder. I care about you more than any man I know. We've shared so much. We've helped each other through terrible times. Our lives are intertwined. No one is as important to me—just you and the kids."

"I wanted to hear you say that. I love you, Sally. I know you're a worrier. You wonder if we've known each other long enough to be sure about our feelings, but I don't think it has anything to do with time. It has to do with people. People who open themselves and share everything that's important." He looked deeply into her eyes, longing to read her mind.

She gazed back at him, this time her eyes more assured. "I am a worrier, I can't deny that. One day long ago, I asked Ed about being single after years of marriage, and he said something that's stayed with me. 'When the right person comes along, you'll know it. You won't ask questions. You'll know it.' And I do. I do love you, Brad."

A question lay on the tip of his tongue, but all he could force himself to say was a hint of his real concern. "Enough to go to the ends of the earth with me?"

"Well, I'm not sure about that far." She laughed and tousled his hair. "Now, you're the worrywart."

Her response wasn't what he wanted to hear. Why hadn't she responded with a resounding yes?

He saw a quizzical expression on her face. Then she chuckled. "I think you have the jitters, taking me to meet your mother."

"Maybe that's my problem." He tried to be jovial, but he knew that wasn't his problem at all.

She shook her head at him.

He said no more, but embraced her warm, loving body, and they stood together quietly. Then he pulled himself away, kissing her good-bye. He felt disappointed in himself. He so wanted to tell her what had been pressing on his mind for days, but he couldn't. He feared her reaction and didn't want to ruin her visit to the Cape. He'd wait until the end of her stay.

❧

On Friday morning at the Barnstable County Airport on the Cape, Sally came through the gate. Brad waited for her, alone, and she wondered if it were the children's choice or his.

"Hi. How was your flight?" he asked, putting his arm around her and kissing her quickly as they walked through the terminal.

"Not bad at all. By the time they served the coffee and breakfast, I thought we'd land before I finished."

"Alice and Ed drove you to the airport?"

"Yep. They're great. They said they'd keep an eye on the house, plus my garden will look better with Ed in charge than with me keeping it up."

"Mother is planning a welcome luncheon. I hope you didn't fill up too much on that wonderful airplane breakfast."

"No problem. Where are the kids?"

"Oh, Mom convinced them to stay with her and let me pick you up myself."

"I've missed them. I've missed you, too."

His arm encircled her shoulders as they walked to the baggage claim area. When they arrived, the luggage was already circling on the conveyor, and they headed for the car.

The traffic moved steadily along as they headed toward South Dennis. As they turned toward the ocean, they passed through the lovely village of Dennisport situated on Nantucket Sound. Gray and steel-blue clapboard cottages with shuttered windows rose before them on narrow streets. Patches of flower gardens, ragged and wild, tossed in the ocean breeze behind the weathered houses.

Turning down Old Cape Road, Brad announced they were nearly home. Soon the clapboard cottages became sprawling colonial homes on spacious landscaped grounds. Sally gaped, wide-eyed.

"Many of these places were built by wealthy sea captains," Brad said. "Wait until you see our own widow's walk."

"You didn't prepare me for this." She certainly had not contemplated that Brad's mother would live in a mansion.

"Here's our place now." He turned the wheel and the car headed down a tree-lined drive. Sally was astounded.

Chapter 12

Near the end of the driveway an old carriage house stood, covered in white clapboard and sporting window boxes filled with pink and white ivy geraniums and alpine strawberries. At the end of the driveway, a charming three-story colonial house appeared with white clapboards and slate-blue shutters. At the top of the house, Sally saw a small windowed room looking out to the bay with the widow's walk that Brad had mentioned. White and pink hollyhocks, lavender foxglove, and purple yarrow grew in abundance around the wings of the old house.

Her voice caught in her throat, gazing at the splendor of the lovely home. "Brad. It's beautiful."

"Thanks. It is nice, isn't it?" They left the car in the driveway, and Brad opened the trunk to retrieve Sally's luggage. As he lifted it out, children's voices echoed from the entrance.

"Daddy, you're back." Danny came running out of the door toward them. Kelly was close behind. "We made brownies while you were gone."

"Are they still warm? I love warm brownies," Brad said.

"Yep. Sally can have some, too."

"Why, thank you, Danny. I love brownies."

"We're gonna have lunch on the terrace," Kelly announced.

"This is a perfect day for it," Brad said.

As they approached the entrance, Brad's mother appeared at the doorway. She transcended her petite stature by her generous grace and refinement. Her green eyes, the same color as Kelly's, sparkled, and her white hair curled softly around her pleasant face. She stepped forward with her hand extended in greeting.

"Good morning," she said cheerfully. "Welcome to Cape Cod. I hope your flight was pleasant."

Sally stepped forward, taking her hand. "Yes, it was very nice. I'm so happy to be here. What a lovely home you have. And bursting with history, I'm sure."

"Yes. I wish it were our family history, but it is not, you know. Brad's grandfather bought this home, many years ago, from the original family, Captain Jack Slater. It was built in the early nineteenth century."

Brad's mother entered the foyer first, her peach and green print cotton skirt swirling ahead of them, a mint-green cardigan draped from her shoulders. The grand foyer was elegant with its wide, open staircase leading to rooms above.

A parlor on the left connected to the foyer with opened French doors. A dark mahogany fireplace, surrounded by the same dark paneling, lent an air of masculinity to the room. The tall windows looked out to an expanse of rolling green lawn.

On the right, the library housed rows of bookshelves filled with thick volumes and an expansive desk sat to one side. A library table stood on the wall below a large window, affording a view of the stately elms and the carriage house. Two large upholstered chairs were arranged in front of the rugged stone fireplace.

Awestruck, Sally stared at the rooms. Brad headed for the staircase. "Let me carry your bags up to your room."

"Yes. Show Sally her room, Brad," Mrs. Mathews said. Then she turned to Sally. "Take your time. Come down when you are settled, and we will have lunch on the terrace. We are ready when you are."

"Thank you, Mrs. Mathews."

"I will have none of this 'Mrs. Mathews,' my dear. Please, call me Amanda. Mrs. Mathews sounds so stuffy."

"Well then, thank you, Amanda." Sally smiled.

Sally followed Brad up the stairs. The guest room sat in the front of the house, affording a view of Nantucket Bay and the ocean beyond. Sailboats dotted the water, triangles of white against the ever-changing green.

A quilt of dark green and pale lavender print covered the four-poster bed, and a huge armoire stood against one wall. The fireplace and plank flooring covered with large Persian rugs created a cozy feeling.

Brad set her luggage on the bed. "I'm glad you like antiques. The house is loaded with them."

"I love it. Everything's wonderful."

"The kids love it here on the water, and Mother is thrilled to have them."

The children's excited voices echoed outside the windows. Sally looked down and saw the terrace below her window, a large area of stone and cement circled with urns of fuchsia and ivy geraniums. In front of the terrace, roses grew in a patch of garden bordered with colorful Sweet William and clusters of white feverfew. Brad looked out and, catching the eye of the children, waved.

"I'll leave you alone so you can get your things put away. When you're ready, come down, and we'll have lunch."

She walked him to the door where he embraced her and kissed her lovingly. "I'm so glad you're here." He turned and headed back down the staircase.

Sally hung her clothes in the armoire, refreshed her makeup in the bathroom mirror, and ran a comb through her hair. She then returned to the first floor where she knew they were anxiously waiting.

She heard the voices coming from the front of the house as she reached the bottom of the stairs. She turned toward the open door next to the staircase.

The dining room stood directly in front of her, connected to a vast living room by an open archway. An elegant glass vase held an arrangement of fresh flowers from pink to burgundy—foxglove, yarrow, and delphinium—obviously picked from the flower gardens around the house.

The windows from floor to ceiling looked out to the terrace and the bay beyond. Voices drifted in through the French doors, and Sally caught sight of the children playing on the grass near the water's edge as she stepped onto the sunny terrace.

❧

Brad saw Sally immediately as she came through the doorway. Amanda turned, also, and rose from her chair where she and Brad were talking. "Well, you found us," Amanda said. "I hope your room is comfortable."

"Oh, it's wonderful. Every room is beautiful."

"Well, thank you. If you look closely, things are beginning to wear, but it does have charm. Come to the table, and we will eat."

Brad rose as Sally joined them at the patio table beneath a large blue umbrella. He was sipping a tall, frosted glass of iced tea and quickly poured a tumbler for her.

"Children," Amanda called, waving her arm. "Come up to the house. Lunch is ready." She walked back toward the kitchen.

"How does your mother manage this house?"

"She has a day lady, Naomi. She comes in the morning and goes home after dinner. For years we had a couple who lived over the carriage house."

The children's voices drew closer, and by the time Amanda returned from the house, they had reached the table.

"Grandma, there's two big white birds on the water. Are they swans?" Kelly asked, bursting with excitement. "They have long necks."

"Well then, I imagine they are."

Naomi brought a large tray to the table and laid before them a basket of crusty rolls, a plate of sliced fresh vegetables, and crab salad. Leaving, she returned with a bowl piled with fresh fruit and a second frosty pitcher filled with lemonade.

"Thank you, Naomi," Amanda said as the woman headed back to the kitchen. "Brad, would you say the blessing?"

They bowed their heads, and Brad offered thanks for the food and for Sally's safe journey. Without hesitation, they filled their plates. Brad studied his mother's face as she chatted with Sally. If she had any concerns, they didn't show.

Sally seemed relaxed and dished salad for the children, speaking to them as if they were important to the conversation. The children's response filled Brad with pleasure. He had wondered if the day would ever come that he could feel this kind of joy.

Finally Danny burst into the conversation. "Let's take Sally to Chatham and see the fish boats."

Brad chuckled. "You do like to watch the fish boats."

Danny nodded. "I like to watch the fish go down the slide and see the big pile of fish heads."

Amanda grimaced. "Oh dear, Danny, I am not sure fish heads is a good topic for our lunch."

"Danny, you're making us all sick," moaned Kelly.

Brad, trying not to smile, spoke to Danny. "Okay. No more fish talk until after lunch, either of you. I promise we'll take Sally to Chatham. If nothing more, she'll enjoy the Chatham Light."

Later that afternoon, they followed the highway to Chatham. The ride took them through little fishing villages nestled along the bay. They headed first for the Chatham pier to watch the fishing boats come in, bringing their catches for the day. Vessel after vessel pulled up to the fish chute, emptying their cleaned, headless catch to be weighed. Seagulls wheeled overhead, landing on the pier and soaring off again, confiscating a tasty morsel for themselves.

Danny clapped his hands as the fish slid down the chute, pointing as he saw the great container of fish heads sitting on the boat deck. Kelly claimed it was disgusting, but her glowing face attested that she enjoyed the excitement, too. Leaving the pier, they drove to the lighthouse itself, standing tall over the vast sandy beach stretching out on the peninsula below. The sun glowed behind the towering building, creating a vibrant silhouette.

"Tomorrow we can drive up to Provincetown. You'll see some great lighthouses on the way. Some of the oldest on the Cape."

"Let's take our bathing suits," Kelly said. "Sally wants to swim, don't you?"

Her expression hungered for a positive answer, and Sally didn't disappoint her. Brad wanted to hug her in front of them all.

"Swimming it will be," Brad said. "There are good beaches along the way." He chuckled at his own excitement. "Sally Newgate, we'll certainly show you the whole Cape in the week you're here." Then he remembered, and he knew he would show her more than the Cape. He prayed she would be thrilled.

❧

That night Sally slept well, and in the morning, she awoke relaxed and ready for the day. Her window opened onto the bay, and she could hear the sound of waves crashing on the shore and the call of the seagulls. A breeze blew in through the window, and the thin curtains billowed and fell with its motion. Hearing no sounds from below, she showered and dressed quickly and quietly, not wanting to wake the others.

To her surprise as she entered the breakfast room, the whole family was seated around the breakfast table.

As she entered, Danny's voice boomed. "Good, now we don't have to be quiet. Daddy said we had to be quiet until you got up."

"He did?" Sally chuckled. "You must have done a good job. I thought everyone was still in bed and I was the first one up."

"We surprised you then, didn't we?" Brad winked. "You look bright and chipper."

"Did you sleep well, Sally?" Amanda asked.

"Oh, very well, thanks. The sound of the waves on the beach is like a lullaby."

"Good, I am pleased. Now, help yourself, there, on the buffet. Naomi has made a lovely breakfast for us."

Sally ate her fill, and after breakfast, they set out on their trip to Provincetown. At the Coast Guard Beach in Eastham the frothy waves rolled in from the ocean, and Brad parked the car. When they unloaded their gear, they trudged to the beach.

The water was cold coming in from the ocean, and the children chose to play in the sand and walk the water's edge rather than swim. Brad and Sally swam near the shore, wanting to be close to the youngsters.

Back on the hot sand, they lay on blankets, feeling the warm sun on their backs, the ocean breeze offering a false sense of coolness.

"You know, I think I'm getting a sunburn," Sally said, pulling on her top. "We'd better check the children."

She rose and walked to where the children were playing in the sand. "Are you starting to sunburn?" She reached down and touched Danny's shoulders. "How about you, Kelly?" she asked.

Kelly, engrossed in her sand castle, didn't look up. "No, Mommy, I'm not sunburned." As the words left her mouth, a look of confusion and embarrassment covered Kelly's face. Sally knelt in the sand to comfort her, but the child jumped up, tears streaming down her cheeks, and ran toward Brad, throwing herself into his arms.

"What happened, sweetheart?" He hadn't heard her mistake. She didn't speak, but buried her face in his shoulder. Brad looked questioningly at Sally. She didn't want to embarrass Kelly any more by telling him what happened.

Danny hurried to his father and provided the details. "Kelly called Sally *mommy*. Wasn't that silly? She's not our mommy." Then he leaned over, looking into Kelly's face. "Why are you crying, Kelly?" He patted her shoulder. "It's okay."

Brad looked helplessly at the children.

Sally also didn't know what to do. She picked up Kelly's blouse and handed it to Brad. "Here's Kelly's blouse. I do think they're getting a little sunburned." Then she turned to Danny. "Let's put this shirt on, or you'll look like a lobster and people will try to have you for dinner."

Danny giggled, oblivious to the tension around him. Brad helped Kelly into her blouse.

Sally took Danny by the hand and wandered down the beach, chattering about the seagulls and the sand castle.

"Why did Kelly call you 'mommy'?" Danny asked as they splashed through the water's edge.

"She made a mistake, Danny. She was so busy with her sand castle, I think she got mixed up. She'll be fine." Sally squeezed his hand, and they continued down the beach. Later Brad and Kelly joined them, and the four strolled along the shore, feet dragging through the foamy water. They walked until they saw the Nauset Light with its bright red roof on the rocky slopes above them. Nothing more was said about Kelly's slip of the tongue.

Chapter 13

Sunday morning they piled into Amanda's station wagon and headed for Beautiful Savior Church to attend worship service. When they arrived, Brad stood with Sally outside the typical picture-postcard New England church as she admired its wide white planks and a tall spire rising high into the sky.

The belfry housed a great iron bell, and as they entered the church, the bell ended its deep resonant toll and the small pipe organ sounded, filling the air with its sweet tones. Amanda glowed as she nodded to her friends and acquaintances, especially when she introduced Sally to some of her closer friends. Amanda obviously hoped Brad had found a new wife and mother for the children.

That evening Naomi stayed with the children, and the three adults drove into Chatham to the Old Chatham Inn where they enjoyed dinner in an elegant eighteenth-century captain's mansion overlooking the bay where sailboats glided along the dark green waters, leaving white foamy trails in their wake.

Amanda's warm feelings toward Sally pleased Brad. After talking over the menu choices, they gave their orders to the waitress. She returned shortly with bowls of chowder, thick with clams. By the time they had eaten the salad, they only nibbled at the entrees now in front of them.

Amanda stared out toward the sea. Low in the sky, the sun spread its palette of warm colors across the darkening water. "Do you remember when we came here a couple of years ago?"

Her question jolted Brad. "Sure, we've eaten here many times."

"Janet sat where Sally is sitting. I remember the sunlight streaking through her hair like gold and red flames. Her hair was very beautiful."

Discomfort shifted through him, and he glanced at Sally as she squirmed in her seat. She avoided looking directly at Amanda or Brad.

"Janet's hair was beautiful, Mom. Why would you mention that?"

"Seeing the sunlight glinting in such fiery colors on the water, I suppose. I look at the children and feel so badly for them sometimes."

"They're adjusting, Mother. It takes time. They've made progress."

She lowered her eyes. "Yes, I suppose they have."

Brad gazed at Sally, hoping she accepted his silent apology. "Let's talk about something else."

Amanda looked up, her eyes widening. "I am sorry. I didn't mean to offend you, Sally."

Sally placed her hand on Amanda's. "You don't need to apologize. I understand loss. I've gone through more than two years of it myself. It's not fun. Brad's right, though. The children have made real strides since I first met them. They'll be fine." Sally patted her hand and placed hers back in her lap.

Amanda sat in silence and then changed the subject as quickly as she had mentioned Janet. "What do you have planned for tomorrow?"

Brad felt a mixture of irritation and sorrow, sadness for his mother's pain but anger that she had brought this up in front of Sally. "Would you like to join us ferrying over to Martha's Vineyard?"

Amanda lifted her sad eyes to his, her apology evident. "Yes, I would like that. Perhaps we could have dinner on the island."

When they arrived home, Sally and Brad sat on the terrace alone. "Sally, I'm sorry about my mother today—bringing up Janet. I don't believe she meant to hurt you or compare you to Janet."

"I know that, Brad. You and the kids live with your loss day in and day out. Your mother only sees it when you visit. She can push it out of her mind in her day-to-day life, but when she's with you, the emptiness clangs in her head like a buoy out on Nantucket Sound. She needs more time to adjust. She's hurting for the children—and for you."

He looked into her eyes. "Thanks for understanding." He rose. "How about a walk?" He offered Sally his hand, and she clasped it. They walked to the darkened beach. The sky shimmered with stars and a crescent moon reflected on the waves rolling onto the shore. They looked silently across the water.

Brad thought about the past days, about Kelly's error calling Sally "mommy" and Sally's gentle message to his mother. The time together knitted them like a family—joy, sorrow, frustration, and love. He pushed his fears aside. *She'll accept my proposal,* he thought. *She must.*

❦

Sally felt as eager as the children when they climbed into the car the next morning to go to Falmouth for their trip to Martha's Vineyard. But she felt frustration, too, wishing she and Brad had more time alone together. She sensed Brad had thoughts he wanted to share with her, but time and proximity hadn't worked well in their favor. In the few minutes they had alone, a deep conversation didn't seem appropriate.

At the pier, when the great doors of the ferry opened, they drove onto the lower deck, and leaving the station wagon, they made their way to the upper decks for their departure.

The children begged to be on the top deck where they could sit outside in the sun and feel the ocean breeze. But when they reached the open water, the air felt too chilly for Amanda, so she and Sally returned to a closed cabin where they had their first opportunity to talk privately.

"Sally, I want to apologize for my reminiscence yesterday. It was terribly rude of me to speaking of Janet in front of you."

"Not at all, Amanda. Janet was very much a part of your life. We can't forget people we love."

"Janet's loss was terrible, certainly. She was a fine daughter-in-law, but that's not my grief, really. The children need a mother, and Brad needs a wife."

Sally's chest tightened, and her stomach knotted. "Yes, that's true."

"I am so pleased that Brad asked you to come for a visit. I am sure you are aware how much you mean to him."

Sally opened her mouth to speak, but Amanda continued.

"It broke my heart to see him in such pain, and the little ones were like tiny boats tossed on the wind—so insecure and frightened. You have been good for all of them, Sally."

Sally looked into the older woman's sincere face. *Is this what she was getting at?* Sally's thoughts had rumbled in her mind earlier, thinking perhaps Amanda disliked her. "Brad and the children have been good for me, too. I thought I was doing okay, and then, little things threw me off kilter. When I became ill after Tim died, I finally agreed to attend a grief recovery program. That's where I met Brad, you know. I thank God for having met him."

"I want you to know how much I have enjoyed your being here. I do not want to interfere in your relationship. I loved Janet. She was a wonderful wife and mother, but she is gone. I do not want the children to be without a mother—nor Brad, for that matter, to be without a wife who loves him. I believe you do love my son. Please forgive me if I am out of place. We have not been alone so that I could tell you these things."

"Yes, I know," Sally said gently. "Brad and I care very much for each other. We both have dealt with terrible changes in our lives—losing our mates. The children have had a difficult time, too. And you're right. Brad and the children mean a great deal to me."

Amanda took Sally's hand in hers. "They mean 'a great deal' to you, but do you *love* them? Watching all of you, I think you do. I pray you love them. I do not want to see them hurt. You seem like a wonderful woman, and whatever feelings you have, I thank you for all you have done for my son and my grandchildren. They are smiling again, and they did not do that for a long time."

"I'm smiling again, too. They've done that for me."

As she finished her sentence, the children came bounding forward with Brad in their wake. They were oblivious to the conversation they interrupted, but Brad, with knowing eyes, saw Sally's hand in Amanda's and knew they had been talking.

"Daddy said we could have lunch in the snack bar," Kelly said. "Would you like something?"

"Certainly, we would," Amanda agreed, and they rose to find the snack bar.

Sally looked at the family—now seeming like family of her own—and a myriad of emotions bubbled inside her. The time they had spent together seemed to be a mixture of beautiful moments interrupted by exuberant children. She would have loved each second, except for a gripping fear that clung to her thoughts.

❦

Brad watched the days pass quickly—too quickly. The thought of Sally leaving left a rift in his life. He longed to keep her by his side. In the middle of the week, he took the entire family on a ride to Providence, Rhode Island—an hour and a half drive. They questioned his sanity, but he didn't respond. He had his reason, but he wanted to wait and share the lovely town with them first before he told them everything.

They drove through the city, passing the bustling business area and admired the restored eighteenth-century mansions winding through the old city.

When they visited the Roger Williams Park, the children scampered from the car, eager to get their legs free from the confines of the backseat. They had sat patiently for the long ride, Amanda between them.

"A zoo, Daddy." Danny pointed ahead, and they followed behind the children.

The animals provided their usual antics, producing delighted giggles from the children. Amanda hugged Danny and Kelly periodically, and Sally watched her with a smile of approval. As the children skipped off toward the monkeys, Amanda held back and waited for Brad and Sally to catch up.

"This is pleasant, Brad, but I do not understand why we came here. It is a long drive to look at monkeys and old buildings."

"I thought you'd enjoy the day, Mother. It's different, isn't it—and a charming city."

"Obviously, I cannot deny that, but I am still confused."

Sally added her floundering thoughts. "I've wondered myself, Brad. The Cape has so many lovely places, I'm not sure why we're here."

"You two," he said, trying to cover his ruse. "Can't a guy take his two favorite women and children to see a nice city?" He had done his best to show them everything he could in the area.

They shook their heads, but didn't ask any more questions.

When Brad woke on Friday, he felt restless. Not only was it Sally's last full day on the Cape, but last night he had rehearsed in his mind the thoughts that had been tossing in his brain since before she arrived. Tonight had to be the night for his confession.

Brad wandered down for breakfast, knowing he had to face the day with a smile. The children and Amanda were nearly finished, and when Sally entered the breakfast room, he sat alone waiting for her and reading the morning paper.

Sally stood in the doorway, her face glowing as she looked at him. "Where is everyone? Is this the first morning I beat the rest out of bed?"

Brad regarded her with a smile. "Sorry. You lose. Mom and the kids are out in the yard."

"I don't understand why I sleep so soundly here. It's embarrassing." She wandered to the buffet and poured a cup of fragrant coffee.

"It shouldn't be. It means you're relaxed and enjoying yourself. I take it as a compliment."

Sally carried the cup to the breakfast table. "Well, good, I hope your mother does. She might think I'm lazy."

"I doubt that, but then, what if she does? Perhaps it's the truth." He grinned at her over the top of his newspaper.

Sally grabbed the napkin from her place setting and threw it at Brad. He ducked, and it sailed over his head as Amanda entered the room. "Well, am I walking in on a quarrel? I think not, since you are both smiling."

Sally grinned and returned to the buffet. "Your son is taunting me—he said I was lazy, which we all know is not true." Sally filled her plate with apple pancakes and a patty of breakfast sausage and carried the contents to the table. "Plus, this coffee is wonderful, and don't tell me—it's something cream. . .aha, vanilla cream. Am I right?"

"Yes, indeed, and anyone with such keen taste buds cannot be lazy, as my son has suggested."

Brad faked a pout. "Oh, fine. Gang up on me. I can take it. And my own mother, too!"

"Take what, Daddy? Take what?" Kelly asked as she twirled into the room, carrying a plastic bucket overflowing with flowers from the garden.

"I need help, Kelly. Your Grandma and Sally are ganging up on me. Protect me."

"I can't Daddy, 'cuz I'm one of the girls, you know. We girls stick together."

Brad threw his hands over his face in a dramatic gesture of defeat. They laughed and applauded. Brad, enjoying the levity, rose and took a deep bow. Danny darted into the room, apparently thinking he missed something. Brad grabbed him under the arms, swung him up in the air, then brought him to his chest. "My only real friend. Right here." He gave Danny a loud, smacking kiss. Danny giggled and squirmed until Brad set him down.

"Do that to me, Daddy." Kelly giggled and, setting the bucket on the floor, jumped up and down in front of him. Brad knew it was impossible to play with one and not include the other, so he picked her up and repeated the motions until she too laughed and wriggled to be released. "Before I let you go, Mary Quite Contrary, where did you get those flowers?" He nodded toward the bouquet of flowers jutting from the bucket where she set it.

"Grandma and I picked them. Aren't they pretty?" She bent down and retrieved the container, showing them to Brad. "We're going to put them in a vase for the living room. But I have a special one for Sally." She reached into the bucket and, moving the flowers around, brought out a perfect rose, delicate pink fading to white edges.

Chapter 14

Kelly handed Sally the lovely rose. Sally looked down at the slim blond girl beaming up at her, and tears gathered on the rim of her eyes. She reached down, taking the rose and gained time to control herself by taking a deep smell of its fragrance. Then she knelt and kissed Kelly's soft, cool cheek.

"Thank you, my princess." Sally's voice was a whisper, barely audible. Kelly reached around her shoulders and hugged her.

Amanda, realizing it was an extraordinary occasion, broke the solemn silence with an air of business. "We had better get those flowers in water, Kelly. Flowers need water to stay fresh and lovely. Come with me, and I will give you a bud vase for Sally's rose." Kelly followed her grandmother through the door with Danny running behind them.

Sally was grateful for the intrusion. Brad gazed at Sally in amazement. "And we were worried." His voice, too, broke with emotion. He walked to Sally, taking his handkerchief from his pocket and wiping the tears which were still clinging to her lashes. She lay her head on his shoulder for a moment, allowing herself to savor the precious memory of Kelly's gift. She stepped back, her eyes drinking in his joy. "You have wonderful children, Mr. Mathews."

Later in the day, as Sally dressed for evening, she gazed at the delicate rose in the crystal bud vase. She thought again about the week she had spent with Brad's loving family, and she bowed her head, thanking God for the gift.

Dinner and a performance at the Cape Playhouse was Brad's special treat for her. Since her arrival, this was the first evening they'd shared alone. Not too distant from the Cape Playhouse, they ate in Yarmouthport at the Old Colonial House Inn where she delighted in a meal of baked fish stuffed with lobster, crabmeat, and scallops. The play proved to be amusing. The entire evening was a memorable ending to a special week.

When they left the playhouse, the moon glowed, bright and clear, and a soft, warm breeze gently stirred the leaves. Instead of heading back to Dennisport, Brad turned down Beach Street to a quiet stretch of sandy shore. He pulled the car off the road, and opening Sally's door, he helped her out. A salty breeze drifted in from the bay, ruffling her hair against her cheek. Brad took her hand in his as they walked to the sand.

A large boulder protruded from the ground. They sat against its rough surface and looked out at the dark waters of Cape Cod Bay. Brad held her hand in his and caressed it gently, in silence. Sensing they had come here for a reason, Sally waited nervously.

Brad finally spoke. "You know that I want to talk to you, and I don't know quite where to begin. I have so much to say."

Sally's hands became clammy, and her legs trembled against the stone. Though the week had seemed so perfect, full of love and companionship, something foreboding had hung on the air. An icy fear streaked through her.

🌿

Brad had sensed Sally's nervousness all evening. She sat against the rock, her hands folded like a knot resting against her lap. His own heart pounded within his chest so loudly he thought she might hear it. "First, I want to tell you that I love you. I have no question, no doubt. I love you with all that I have. I've prayed and asked for guidance, and I believe this is good."

Sally touched his arm. "What, Brad?"

He shook his head. "I know we haven't known each other for very long, although it seems to me it's been forever. Time isn't important when you find someone who shares your faith, your interests, and your love."

"Brad—"

"Please, Sally, let me have my say. I have it memorized." He smiled, hoping to see a smile in return.

A faint grin appeared on her lips.

"I know that you love the kids, and that's very important to me. Most of all, I believe you love me as I love you. We've said all along that we have plenty of time to get to know each other and assure ourselves that our feelings are real. We said there's no rush."

He paused and looked into her eyes, seeing her concern. "That's where I'm adding a complication."

He heard Sally catch her breath. The time had arrived to say what he had to say. He stood up and walked away from the rock and turned back to her and knelt in the sand. "I've been offered a promotion. I say *offered*, but it's more like a command. If I turn this down, it will end my chances to advance in the company, and I can't do that to the kids, to myself, and God willing, to you."

In the moonlight, Brad saw Sally's face register confusion. He took her tightly knotted hands in his. "The promotion means that I have to leave Michigan. Our sightseeing trip to Providence had an ulterior motive behind it. The corporation has a branch office there, and that's where my promotion will take me. It has its advantages, besides the expected raise in salary and position in the company."

What he feared, Brad saw now in Sally's face. Confusion, anxiety, panic. But he had to go on. "It brings us closer to my mom who, despite her good health, is getting older. She loves the children and misses them, and we miss her. She'll never leave her home on the Cape, and I'd never ask her to move. Living in

Providence means that we can see her more often."

Brad raised Sally's hand and kissed her cold fingers. "I am asking you to come here with me—marry me, and we can make a new home together."

Brad held his breath, his gaze riveted to hers. Moving, he thought, would solve some of the problems. Sally and he would have a new home, one without old memories. They could start anew and fresh; her, not sitting in Janet's chair at the table and him, not hanging his clothes in Tim's closet.

Sally gazed at him, still on his knees in the damp sand. She raised her hand to her chest and closed her eyes. "Oh, Brad, we said we had time. . ." When she opened them, Brad saw tears mist her lashes, then run down her cheeks, dripping on his hands as they held hers.

He rose, and wrapped his arm around her. He felt her tremble against him and his own sudden fear joined hers. "I showed you the beauty of this area and a little of Providence. I know it means giving up your job, but there are many jobs in Providence, and Sally, I want us to have a baby—our own little boy or girl. Kelly and Danny would love it, I know."

She opened her mouth to speak, but he silenced her. "Please don't answer me now, Sally. You need time to make your decision, I know." He placed his cheek against hers and pressed her close. "I know we thought we had all the time in the world, but the situation makes it different. That's why I wanted you to think about this while I'm here on the Cape.

"I haven't told Mom or the kids about the move yet. I wanted to talk to you first. When I get back to Michigan, I'll put my house up for sale. I have to be in Providence by the first of September. It'll work out best for the children because they can start their new school at the beginning of the school year. It doesn't give us much time, I know."

She hadn't spoken but clung to him. He placed his lips on hers and tasted the salt from her tears. He felt her mouth yield to his and his kiss deepened, his desire for her crying with a silent voice into the night sky. When their emotions were drained, he unwrapped his arms from around her, and they walked in silence through the sand to the car.

❦

Sally awoke with a headache and was very tired. She had lain awake much of the night, thinking about Brad's proposal. Instinctively, she wanted to say "yes, yes, yes." Though fears and concerns prodded her *yes* to *I don't know* to *I am afraid*. She felt a horrible pressure in her chest. All the words of caution filled her— Elaine, Darby, Bill, and Sue. The truth was they had known each other less than a year. She remembered other couples she knew—like Cassie who thought she was in love—whose marriage ended so quickly. Christian marriage was "until death," and she couldn't make a mistake.

With Brad, her life seemed joyful, but she wanted their relationship to be right. Questions circled through her mind. Was she ready for a new husband? Did she have the courage to leave Michigan? To leave her friends, family, Carrie? Her whole life was there.

Sally sat in frozen silence on the edge of her bed, looking at her half-packed suitcase. Her world spun in her head. How could she answer his question? She loved him. This week validated and assured her that she loved him and the children, but was it a love that would last? Was it what God wanted for her? And moving? Could she do that? Tears rolled from her eyes. Yet, how could she say good-bye to them?

Then her thoughts soared back to Jack Holbrook's talks. Love is not spread out or divided. It grows. Why did she fear this love that lived in her heart? She knew Brad loved her. The kids were growing to love her. Amanda liked her. Then why was she so afraid? She rose and stared outside, the thoughts stirring in her mind—tossing to and fro like the rhythm of the waves lapping the shore outside her window.

She forced herself to confront the day. In the mirror, her face looked tired, creased with lack of sleep, eyes streaked with red. Even after showering and putting on lipstick and blush, she looked pale and tense. In a hotel, she would have called room service, but here she was forced to descend the stairs for breakfast and appear normal. She did not feel normal.

Amanda and Brad were alone in the breakfast room when Sally entered. Brad was startled by Sally's expression, and his hopes fell.

Amanda's face registered a look of concern. "Sally, I hope you are not ill. Did you sleep poorly?"

"Yes, I'm afraid so." Sally attempted to sound casual.

"That is just the way it is. Whenever I travel, the night before I leave for my trip and the night before I return home, I lie awake much of the night. It is very irritating."

"Oh, I'll be fine after some coffee."

Brad listened to the conversation, observing Sally cover her distress. He watched her in disbelief. Though he realized the possibility, he had thought his proposal would be received with joy, not grief. He knew the move to Providence might seem difficult, but wouldn't it solve so many problems? That's what he had thought. Apparently he was utterly wrong. "I'm sorry you didn't rest well. Tonight, you'll be home in your own bed. Maybe you can sleep in tomorrow." He knew better, but he had to say something.

"I'm fine, Brad. Thanks."

Sally filled a cup with coffee, glancing at the choices on the buffet table, and then sat down without taking anything. Amanda observed the tension and rose from her seat. "I had better check on the children. Will you excuse me?" Before anyone could reply, she left the room.

"Sally, my proposal last night has upset you. I'm so sorry. I didn't mean to end our wonderful week on such a bad note."

"Please, Brad. It's not a bad note—confusing, scary maybe—but not bad. It's me and my crazy mind. Thoughts jumped back and forth, up and down, and I couldn't get them to rest. I've many things to think about, and I want to think with a clear, rational mind. I want my answer to be the best for all of us."

"I know, Sally, but don't be too rational. Let your heart speak, too."

"Oh, my heart has spoken, Brad. I love you. But marriage means so many changes. I don't know how many changes I can handle. And do we really know each other well enough? Marriage is for a lifetime. Please be patient with me." *A lifetime.* Her thoughts drifted back to her few years with Tim.

"I'll be patient—as patient as I can be, anyway." He smiled and placed his hand on hers, moving his thumb across the softness of her skin.

Loud footsteps tromped in the hall, and both children burst into the room, squealing. Brad released Sally's hand.

"Kelly found a frog by the water. She said she was going to teach it things and put it on a leash, Daddy." Danny's eyes sparkled with delight.

"Frogs might make good pets," Kelly pleaded. "They're quiet, Daddy."

"Not real quiet. They spend the night croaking. I think we'll leave the frog here with Grandma. You can visit it when you come again."

Kelly's lower lip dropped to a pout.

"Sally, we're going to the airport with you and see your plane fly," Danny chattered. "You can look down from the sky, and I'll be waving at you."

"That'll be nice, Danny. You probably won't be able to see me, but I'll be waving back."

Brad had forgotten his promise to the kids. He and Sally needed to talk. But when? "I told them when you arrived that if they stayed home with Grandma, I'd let them take you back to the airport. Leave it to them to remember."

"That's fine," Sally said softly.

"Aren't you hungry?" Kelly asked, noticing Sally's empty place mat. "Are you sad to go home? You look sad."

"I am sad to be leaving all of you, but adults have to go to work. In fact, I need to get the rest of my things together, or I'll miss my flight." She rose and took a step toward the door, then paused. "It won't take me a minute." She continued down the hall and up the stairway.

Amanda didn't join them at the airport. They said their good-byes outside the lovely old house. Sally took Amanda's hand, but to her surprise, Amanda leaned over and kissed her cheek. Sally returned the kiss.

The children were excited at the airport, pressing their noses against the observation windows and watching the planes pull into the gates. When it was time to board, they each gave her a big hug and to her surprise, a kiss. She was moved by their genuine, simple affection, and felt her eyes brim with tears. She quickly wiped away the tears with the back of her hand without being obvious, at least to the children.

The children looked at Brad. "Say good-bye, Daddy," Kelly said, watching his every move. Sally's heart lurched, wondering how he would respond. Then, she knew. He stepped forward and embraced Sally as the children had done, then kissed her quickly and gently on the lips. When their gaze returned to the children, Kelly and Danny looked at them with nothing more than a loving smile on their excited faces. At that moment, joy swept over her, despite her strained departure.

"I'll call you tonight," Brad said, as she started down the ramp to the plane. She nodded. The children waved, and she turned and waved back at them before rounding the corner. When she was out of sight she allowed her tears to flow freely down her cheeks.

❦

On the plane, Sally closed her eyes and thought, holding back her tears. After Tim's death, she knew her life had ended, but little by little, she had carved a new life out of the rock of despair and sadness. Then she met Brad. New joy blossomed in her life, but with her joy came new heartaches, Kelly's unhappiness, and the concerned comments from family and friends.

For so long, she had prayed for God to guide her, and she'd been angry when no answer came, nothing to give her a sense of God's will. Now, a new life was hers for the taking. Brad and the kids loved her, and he offered her a new beginning.

So why was she clinging to the past? Her house, her job, family, friends, and her familiar world? Her faith had been so strong after Tim died. Through those hard times, she felt God's hand guiding her along. But then time went on and she waited. She waited for God to give her the promised time under heaven, her season. *Is this it, Lord? Tell me? I've known Brad less than a year. Do I leave all I've ever known with the hope I'm following Your will? Lord, I'm waiting to hear Your voice.*

When Sally arrived home, she walked through the lonely rooms, then sat with her face in her hands and wept. That night she dreamed. She was there on the Cape with them all, watching whales leap into the sky and dive deep into the vast unknown of the dark blue waters.

❦

When Brad returned from the Cape, his stress was evident. He had the difficult task of putting his home up for sale and packing his belongings. His firm assisted in the move by locating homes fitting his needs. All he needed to do was fly to Providence and make a decision. Within three days, he placed a bid on a house in an excellent location with an elementary school only two blocks away.

Sally was grateful he didn't push for an answer. He waited. But September was at hand, and his move was imminent. Two weeks before he moved, Sally invited Brad for a quiet evening at home. After dinner, she sat next to him on the mauve and gray living room sofa and gave him her answer.

Chapter 15

I can't marry you, Brad." Tears ran down her cheeks and dripped on her hands knotted in her lap.

Brad's heart fell—his world fell at his feet. The fears that had filled him were now a horrible reality. He took her soft, cold hand in his and listened.

"I've prayed. I need time. I don't know why you're so certain, and I'm not. I know I love you, but I'm...I wish I could sell this house and throw my arms around you and walk away to a new place and a new life, but I can't—not now." Her downcast eyelids raised, tears clinging to her lashes. "Yet, I can't say good-bye."

Brad opened his mouth and heard his husky, unsure voice. "I suppose I expected you to tell me this. I prayed that you wouldn't. I don't want you to marry me unless you know it's right for you. I want to share my life with you—forever. I want to share Kelly and Danny with you, and I want to have a child with you. But most of all, I want you to want that, too, and until you do, I'll have to wait and pray."

He paused, fighting back the tears that stung his eyes. "I can't stand being without you. The last two weeks on the Cape were horrible because I knew you left confused and uncertain. I can't tell you the happiness I felt when you were there. I don't know how we'll manage without you." He slid his arms around her, wanting to bury his face in her neck and sob. His body trembled as wildly as hers.

"Brad, I know. Life's wonderful when I'm with you, and I missed you the weeks you were away. I don't know what I'll do when you're really gone."

Suddenly his despair turned to anger. He sat clinging to her, his mind screaming out his love, but she couldn't offer the same. She doubted her own feelings. He couldn't comprehend her fears. "You've answered my question. Let's not dwell on it. I'm leaving in a couple of weeks, and I'd like our last days to be pleasant memories." Sarcasm and irony sizzled in his voice.

🍃

Brad dragged through the week, struggling with the loose ends on his job and working late hours. His last days with Sally exhibited feeble attempts at light-heartedness. They lived a lie. Their last dinner together lay in a lump at the bottom of his stomach. His body knotted with tension, and his best attempts at acting were a failure.

Sally's lips trembled as she spoke. "Brad, you and I met at a very difficult time for both of us. We were hurting, both of us reaching out to have questions answered. We needed support. We needed people who understood our loneliness and our grief. You needed someone to help you pull the children through their sorrow. We've been there for each other, and I guess that's why we met."

Astounded, he gaped at her. "That's how it began, Sally. We needed support, and we got it from a lot of people, including each other. So, what does this mean?"

"It means that's why God brought us together. Maybe that's all our meeting was meant to be. I wonder if your move is God's way of telling us to let go, to get on with our lives, wherever that leads us. You should be free to find someone to be a mother for Kelly and Danny—someone to love." Tears edged their way down her cheek and dripped from her chin, but she sat staunch and erect.

The anger he'd pushed below the surface tore through him. Heat rose to his face, and his hands balled into tight fists. "What are you saying? Have you found someone else? Is this your way of telling me?"

She shook her head, her voice quivering without control. "No, Brad, I have no one but you."

He rose, towering over her. "Then are you telling me that God doesn't want us to love each other? How can you say that, Sally? How can you sit there with tears pouring from your eyes and tell me you don't love me?"

"I'm not saying I don't love you." She swallowed, and a sob tore from her throat. "I've prayed and prayed, Brad, but I can't seem to let go of my life here. You and the kids have become a huge part of it, but I've asked God to give me strength—to give me an answer. I don't feel it, and I don't hear it. I think God's silence is the answer. It's over."

His body quivered uncontrollably, and the words shot from him. "Over! I thought you were a sane, rational, loving woman, but tonight, you've gone mad. Do you think that I can turn off my feelings for you by your words, 'It's over'? You tear my heart out suggesting such a thing. Are you waiting for trumpets and a fanfare from God? What are you expecting for an answer? Can't you listen to your heart? Doesn't your heart speak of love and happiness with us?"

He paced in front of her, his fist pounding in the palm of his hand, his heart pounding as loudly in his chest. "You've certainly fooled me, Sally, if this were a practice session for getting on with your life; I'm not practicing. I'm *loving* you— here and now. You can go ahead and forget about us if you can, but I'm not forgetting about you. I'll pray God brings you to your senses."

He swung to face her. She sat frozen to the sofa cushion, unmoving, tears dripping to her skirt. His dreams crashed around him. He turned and bolted from the room, and for all he knew, from her life.

❦

Following Brad's move, the weeks dragged by. Sally filled her days, but nothing had meaning. Each time the telephone rang, she jumped, her nerves like frayed edges of a hem trailing noticeably behind her. Beth's call from Los Angeles saying she had returned from her hiatus in Africa brought with it sad news of Esther Newgate's steady decline. Work was her only reprieve, distracting her from all that mattered.

Elaine, near the end of her pregnancy, called, and her apology hung in Sally's mind. "Don't let the thoughtless, irrational words I blurted months ago make you doubt Brad and the love you share. This could be a match made in heaven."

A match made in heaven. That's what she wanted to hear from God, not Elaine. But she'd told Brad to go, and their parting had left only hurt and anger.

❧

The third week in September, Jim Davidson purchased a block of tickets for the Renaissance Festival held in the rural town of Holly. The activity took the place of their annual company picnic. Sally was in no mood to attend, but Darby and others prodded her to go. Finally, she agreed, but her heart wasn't in it.

She wandered with Darby and Eric through the milling, boisterous crowds in the fifteenth-century setting, listening to minstrels play on their lutes and recorders and hearing the sweet sounds of dulcimers echo on the breeze.

After their picnic lunch, Darby halted in front of some bales of hay formed into a large circle. "Looks like the Renaissance Players are doing a skit. Want to stop?"

"Sure," Eric said, glancing at Sally.

The thought of a lighthearted play left Sally cold. Darby and Eric had welcomed her along, but she felt like an extra shoe, and she needed to get away. "If you don't mind, I think I'll take a walk back to the vendor stalls. I'd like to get one of those elfin dolls for Carrie—remember those cute gnome characters?"

Darby paused. "We pass that stall again when we leave, don't we?"

But Eric answered the question, "No. I think it's in the other direction."

Darby shrugged. "I guess you're right." She squeezed Sally's arm. "We'll wait here for you, okay?"

Sally agreed, and following the festival map, she headed toward the vendors' booths. Along the way, she was cut off by a parade of the King and Queen and their court, and as she waited, she felt a hand rub across her back. She swung around and gaped into Steve's grinning face. She tensed. Earlier, she'd seen him watching her, but she ignored him, and he left her alone.

"What's a lovely young woman like you doing wandering alone?" The words slid from his lips.

She stepped forward, and his hand dropped from her back. "I'm heading back to the huts." She nodded in the direction of the vendors' stalls. The parade passed by, and she continued toward her destination with Steve on her heels.

"Maybe I'll follow along and see if there's anything I'd like to pick up before I leave." Steve smirked as he moved into step with her.

She ignored him and hurried ahead. The stall she sought was located down a narrow walkway behind a row of thatched huts. She darted through the area that opened to the sun and crowds of people. She glanced behind her, relieved that Steve had stopped to talk to one of the vendors. She kept moving, hoping she'd lost him.

When she located the stall, she examined the delightful, gnarled faces of the dolls and selected one for Carrie. *Why not get one for Kelly? I'll find something for Danny and mail them.* Loneliness tore through her, and she swallowed her sorrow.

She selected another doll, and with her package in hand, she turned and began the trek back toward the picnic area. Stepping into the narrow stretch between the stalls, she heard footsteps behind her. Sharp fear shot through her and she swung around as Steve grabbed her arm, jerking her toward him. "Well, now I finally have you all to myself."

She struggled to free herself, but he held her pinned against a stall. His hot perfumy breath swept over her face. Screaming seemed foolish. He wasn't a stranger. "Quit playing games, Steve." Her stern voice feigned confidence. "Let go of me. I've had enough of your silliness."

He forced her back like a prisoner. "Silliness? You think I'm playing games? That's what you're playing. You're lonely, and here I am."

His mouth pressed roughly against hers. She could taste the strange scent. She jerked her arm forward and heard her sleeve tear. Quickly she jammed her head upward, bumping his mouth, and a trickle of blood ran down his chin.

He jerked away. "Why, you spitfire," he said.

"Take your hands off me! Don't touch me again!" Her voice resounded in the enclosed area. A hut door banged open, and a young man rushed out to help her.

"Take your hands off the lady!" The young man bellowed, rushing toward him. Others heard his angry voice. More people rounded the corner, and Sally pulled from his grasp, holding her torn sleeve with her hand. She'd dropped the package of dolls and reached down to snatch them from the ground. As the young man confronted Steve, she maneuvered through the crowd and, on shaking legs, hurried back to the picnic area.

❦

The next couple of days at Davidson's were tense. Sally looked for Steve around every corner, in the workroom, and lunchroom, everywhere she went in the building. Then one morning Jim Davidson called her into his office. She went apprehensively.

When she entered, he sat behind his massive walnut desk. As the secretary closed the door, to Sally's surprise, she and Jim were not alone.

Jim gestured toward a chair. "Have a seat, Sally. You know Steve."

She glanced at Steve, sitting rigidly in front of Jim's desk, his tension obvious. Glancing from Jim to Steve, she edged hesitantly to the empty chair and sat. Darby must have talked to Jim.

Jim continued, "We have a problem, and I want to get this cleared up. Steve has something to say to you, Sally." Jim leaned back in his chair, eyeing Steve.

Apprehensive and unsettled, Steve rose and paced across the room, then found sanctuary again in the chair. "As you see, I'm nervous." His eyes pleaded with Sally. "I came in to talk to Jim this morning. I realize that I have a problem, and before I lose this job—a job I enjoy and I'm good at, I told him what I had done. I want to apologize to you, Sally, for what I did at the Renaissance Festival. It was rude and uncalled-for. I treated you badly."

His confession gave Sally a start. Reality struck her. The informer *wasn't* Darby. Trying to understand, Sally studied Steve. "I don't know what to say, Steve. These past couple of years have been bad for me. Apparently, you have some problems yourself."

Steve sat in the chair staring at his shoes. He turned to Sally slowly, his voice a whisper. "I'm an alcoholic, Sally. I've finally had to face it. I had too much to drink at the Festival, and I've been drinking here at work."

Sally turned to ice. Her hands trembled. Her thoughts tore backward in time, remembering a drunk driver had taken her husband's life. Alcohol destroys people. It destroyed her life, and it was destroying Steve's. For a moment, anger filled her. Then she calmed.

She wanted to punish Steve, telling him about the drunk driver who killed her husband—to make him hurt, the way she had been hurt, but she knew what God wanted her to do. Hurt was not the solution. The answer was love. Forgiveness held a new meaning. "I know it was difficult for you to come in here—to tell Jim and me. I'll pray for your recovery. . .and I forgive you, Steve." The words soared like a weight rising from her shoulders.

Steve's face colored, but for the first time, he looked directly into her eyes. "Thank you, Sally. Believe it or not, I respect you. You don't deserve any more problems in your life. One day I was thinking about you, and I remembered your husband died because of a drunk driver. That reality struck me and knocked some sense into my head. I just wanted you to know that."

Steve stared again at his shoes. "I asked Jim for a leave of absence while I get treatment. I'll succeed. I have to. I can't stand myself anymore."

As his words formed meaning, her heart thudded in her chest. He did know about Tim, and he asked for help. In her act of forgiveness, a calm washed over Sally. Somewhere in her heart, she'd also forgiven the drunk who killed Tim. Though symbolic, the act was complete and sincere. For the first time in over two years, she felt a resolved peace.

Jim came from behind the desk, placing his hand comfortingly on Sally's shoulder as he passed. Steve rose. Jim shook his hand, and taking Steve's arm, he walked with him to the door, talking quietly.

When Steve left the room, Jim returned to Sally. "Thanks. I know this was hard for you, but part of Steve's healing will be to face his problem and ask for forgiveness from those he's hurt."

Sally rose. "I didn't know about his drinking. I should've told you about the situation myself, but I felt guilty for some stupid reason—being a single woman, I suppose. I thought I was another statistic."

"Sally, you were happy as a married woman. Some people aren't meant to be single. I hear a lot of things through the company grapevine, and to be truthful, I'm surprised you didn't accept that young man's proposal. Single women bring out the worst in men."

Sally tensed, and pain shot through her shoulder blades. Was he saying she was partially to blame?

"You belong married. It's safer that way. If I were in your shoes, young lady, I'd pack my bags and run to the arms of that young man of yours. If you don't, some other woman will catch him, and you'll be sorry you let him go."

Sally was startled at his comment and his attitude. She looked at Jim, and all she could think to say was "thank you." She left his office and returned to her desk. The thought of using Brad for security and safety left a bitter taste in her mouth. But to her sadness, his words bore a horrible truth. If she couldn't accept Brad's proposal, someone else would.

Chapter 16

Brad had dealt restlessly with his final moments with Sally. Her words had shocked him when he left for Providence. Yet he missed her terribly and loved her deeply. After a month settling in, the days dragged and weighed on his spirit. Another month passed as he struggled with indecision. He'd prayed she would call him, but he heard nothing. And if he called, would she hang up? Finally, he blocked his fears and called her. His heart lifted when he heard her voice.

"Is everything all right?"

He heard her concern. "Everything's fine. I needed to hear your voice."

Her tone softened. "It's nice to hear yours. How are the kids?"

"Better than me, I suppose. They like school. Danny's so proud he goes full-time. Kelly loves her teacher. She says she reminds her of. . .you." His voice caught.

After a pause, Sally whispered, "Tell her I think about her every day."

Her words left him frustrated. How could she think of them, yet reject them? He pushed the thought from his mind. "The house is a real family home. So much room for the kids to play." He hoped she heard the word "family." But the house felt empty without her.

"It sounds nice. I'm happy things are going so well."

When he hung up, the call left him drained and empty. But it gave him hope. They had talked. He sent her photographs of the house and the children. But now he felt lonelier than ever before. And a week later, he called again, then two days after that.

"Did you get the photos of the house?"

"Yes, a couple of days ago. It's beautiful. And I love the yard with the gazebo and flowers," she said. "And the kids. They look. . .wonderful." Sadness echoed in her voice.

"We found a church with all kinds of family programs, uplifting worship, and a wonderful Sunday school."

"The kids are in Sunday school, then?"

"They really look forward to Sundays. You should see them."

"I should."

Brad's heart skipped a beat. Did she mean it? "Did I tell you about my neighbors? And my new position?"

"Yes, the last time you called."

Tell her how lonesome you are. He hesitated. "Everything's great, Sally, except one thing. You're in Michigan, and I'm in Rhode Island. I miss you more than I can say. The kids talk about the Cape when you were there, and I was surprised the other day when Kelly remembered the first time she met you. She asked me why she had treated you and Carrie so mean. She's really growing up."

"I know. They grow up too fast." Sadness filled her voice.

"The neighbors remind me of Alice and Ed. Millie and Chet love the kids. It's like having grandparents right next door." He waited for a response, but he heard nothing. "How are Alice and Ed?"

"They're fine. Full of good advice, as always. Sometimes I wonder when I'll listen to them." Her voice trailed off.

Listen to them, Sally, his mind pleaded. "Do you know how much I miss you?" Desperation flooded through him.

"I miss you, too."

Her words lifted him like a flight of swans. "Then come, Sally. Come for a visit. No pressure, I promise. I'm so anxious for you to see the house. Millie and Chet have a guest room, and they said you were welcome anytime. What do you say? Come for a week, a weekend, a day, just come."

He held his breath, waiting, listening to the lengthening silence.

"Let me think about it, Brad. I'll call you. It would have to be a short visit."

Air shot from his lungs, and his pulse hammered in his temples. "Whatever you can arrange, call me then. I'll take time off. Sally, I can't wait to see you. Please come."

❦

Ridiculous. The single word described Sally's life. Her separation from Brad and the children was absurd. Despite her confusion and fear, she would only be complete when she was with them. She longed to tell Brad what she'd come to realize, but not by telephone. She made arrangements for a trip to Providence for Thanksgiving.

The days straggled along, waiting for the holiday. Only her work and daily responsibilities kept her focused. One afternoon Alice stopped by and asked her to cochair a Mission Project for the Christmas season called the Gift Tree, a clothing and toy drive for children from the County Foster Care Center. Sally readily agreed. Helping to brighten a child's Christmas sounded wonderful, and the activity would fill her lonely, anxious days.

On November 16th, the telephone rang late in the evening. Elaine's husband proudly announced the birth of their son Timothy. He invited her to a celebration party near the Christmas holiday. Sally's invitation to Darby and Eric's December 21st wedding had already arrived, and though she looked forward to the wonderful occasion, she would be alone. Each event helped her pass the time. As Thanksgiving approached, Sally counted the days until her trip to Providence.

Two days before she was to leave, a different providence came into play. Sally received a distressing call from Beth.

"Sally, Mom died this morning. I wanted you to know."

Sally's heart lay heavy in her chest. "Beth, I'm so sorry."

"She died in her sleep. And, Sally, she really didn't know me any more. She thought I was a nice lady. Occasionally she asked if I were her sister. I could hardly bear to see her that way."

Tears burned in her eyes. "Beth, it's so sad."

"I hate being alone through all of this."

Sally's heavy heart fell and she knew what she had to do. "I'll come to California if you'd like. The holiday is here, and I have the time off. I'll try to get a flight."

"Would you, Sally? I was hoping you'd say you would. I'd love to see you and have you here for a couple of days, anyway."

"I'll make arrangements and call you back, Beth."

Grief for Beth—and for herself—wound through Sally. She longed to see Brad and the kids, but she couldn't leave Beth alone now. The whole situation overtook her. God had to be keeping her and Brad apart, or else, why did this happen now?

Each moment away from Brad made her more certain she was meant to be *with* him, but God was showing her the opposite—that their love wasn't meant to be. With a numb heart, she called the airline, then called Brad and broke the news. Disappointment filled his voice, but he said he understood.

❧

The next day, in a little more than five hours, Sally walked down the gate ramp at the airport.

Beth stood amid the crowd, and when their eyes met, Beth darted forward, throwing her arms around Sally's neck. "I'm so glad you came. It's been so terrible."

She choked back a sob, and Sally held her tightly, and calmed her before they followed the signs to baggage claim.

A half hour drive through heavy traffic led them to Beth's apartment in Santa Monica. Though nondescript, the building stood near the Santa Monica pier and Beth's apartment on the top floor was charming. From the open doors of a small balcony, an occasional ocean breeze drifted through the living room. Sally breathed in the fresh, salty air.

"I've missed you, Sally," Beth said, standing beside her at the balcony door.

"Like old times, Beth. Sometimes I remember when I came to your house to see Tim, and you and I sat together talking and giggling. Tim got so mad at us."

"He did, didn't he? This isn't quite like old times, though. You and I have a lot more problems now than we did then."

"When you're young, everything seems wonderful. I'm really glad I came, Beth. I didn't realize how much I missed you." She wrapped her arm around Beth's shoulder.

"You'll make me cry, Sally," Beth said, wiping away a tear. "I thought we could grab a sandwich, and then go over to the funeral home. I don't expect many visitors, but Mom did have a few old friends and a couple of elderly cousins. The funeral's tomorrow."

"I wish I could've come earlier to help you, Beth."

"You're here now. That's what's important to me."

❧

The funeral service was held at the church in Esther Newgate's old neighborhood, and the voice of the pastor echoed in the nearly empty sanctuary. With few mourners and no funeral luncheon, by noon Sally and Beth were seated in a small oceanside café eating salads and looking out at the gray foamy waves dashing on an empty shoreline. The hazy sky offered no hope of sunshine. The sun hid behind the thick, equally gray, cloud cover—a day appropriate for mourning.

Beth, sitting across from Sally, looked up from her salad. "So now, tell me what's really going on in your life."

Sally stared at her plate. The past year flew through her mind. The ups and downs, the positives and negatives. What would Beth say? Could Sally bear to hear Beth's possible biting words about Brad? Yet she'd hid things far too long.

Sally looked out at the empty beach and then back at Beth. "A lot and nothing. How's that for an ambiguous response?"

Beth scowled, obviously confused.

Sally sighed. "I have so many things inside me, I don't know where to begin."

"Start at the beginning, as the song goes."

With Beth's full attention, Sally told her about Brad and the children, the proposal, and Brad's promotion and move to Rhode Island.

Beth's eyes widened. "Sally, I'm thrilled for you. I've waited to hear this wonderful news. But I don't understand your hesitation. Don't you love him?"

Her response shot through Sally like a cannon. Of all the people who should feel differently, it was Beth. Her pulse tripped through her veins. "Yes, I do—and the kids. But we've only known each other a year. I felt so lonely after Tim died, and then Brad stepped into my life. I don't know if I can trust my feelings. Sometimes I feel God doesn't want us together. And I've struggled with leaving Michigan. Moving to Rhode Island means leaving my home, my family, my friends, my job. It means leaving the years I had with Tim. It means taking a chance." Her voice faded to a whisper.

Beth leaned forward, her hands knotted in front of her. "So, what's happening now?"

"That's where the *nothing* comes in. Nothing. I'm doing nothing. Brad moved and started a new life in Providence and I am just sitting in Michigan."

"But why? Why are you doing that? If you love him and his kids, why wouldn't you marry him? Would God have brought the two of you together if

He didn't want you to fall in love?"

"I felt that way at first. But so many people cautioned me about the illusions of new romances. A year isn't very long. I've been afraid."

"Time doesn't measure love, Sally. Don't miss out on a new, wonderful life. I'm Tim's sister. I should be the first to protect the memory of my brother's marriage. But Sally, Tim is gone. Here's a man, living and breathing, who loves you and wants to marry you. And his children love you. If you love him, don't hold back for other people. Your friends are your friends. Your family's your family. Sally, you and I rarely see each other, and yet it doesn't diminish our relationship."

Sally heard her words and remembered hearing them so long ago. How had she forgotten them?

Beth touched her hand. "We still love and care about each other. Bill and Sue and Carrie will never stop loving you if you move. They're family. But, Sally, how long can you love someone long-distance with no commitment? Brad may love you deeply, but if you don't love him enough to go to him, how long do you expect him to wait for a dream? If God's given you another chance for love and happiness, take the gift. Don't let it go."

Beth had touched on the heart of the matter, and her words rang in Sally's ears. Though Sally's fears were foolish, they were real. She loved Beth for opening her eyes and her heart. Had she closed them to God's wishes, too? Now she would deal with them, and Beth was right. How much longer would Brad wait?

❦

A smile spread across Brad's face simply hearing Sally's voice. As they talked about the funeral and their lonely Thanksgivings, what he really wanted to talk about was them.

"So when will I see you, Sally?"

"Soon. I've done a lot of thinking, and we really need to talk, but face-to-face, not on the telephone."

A chill ran through him. "Is something wrong?"

"No, nothing's wrong. We've been through so much, and I feel. . .I guess, I'd rather be together when we talk."

"The Christmas holiday's coming."

"I know. That's what I'd hoped, and I can't wait. I talked to Ed. He has room for you, and the kids can stay here with me. What do you say?"

She bubbled her plans, and disappointment flooded through him. "Sally, I can't. I'm visiting Mom on the Cape. As always, she's prepared her usual calendar of activities. And I'd planned to ask you to join us when you came for Thanksgiving. I'm anxious for you to see the new house, but that can wait. It's you I want to see. Can't you go with us to the Cape?"

Before she spoke, he knew her response from the long, uncomfortable pause. He froze. Were empty promises and weeks apart all their relationship had to offer?

"Brad, I can't stand this any more. Nothing works out. I have the party for Elaine's new baby and I'm going to Darby's wedding. And the mission project with Alice, remember? I can't let her down again. She's done so much for me."

"I suppose. What's another month or two?" Frustration and sarcasm sounded in his ears. "You know, Sally, I've tried to be patient. I'm sorry."

"I'm sorry, too."

When Brad hung up, he sat in silence. Sally had drifted further and further from him. Fear sent an icy chill through his veins, freezing his heart. He'd reached the end of patience. His love wasn't enough to make her love him in return. And the children. Dragging things on would only hurt them more. It had to end.

He sank into a chair and stared through the window at the leafless trees and the death of summer. He was through. No more. No matter what. The pain hurt too much.

Chapter 17

The phone call with Brad left Sally devastated. She'd pushed him to the limit. She'd been thoughtless, filling her calendar with commitments without thinking of him. At first, everything seemed to keep them apart—people's comments, Kelly's jealousy, schedules, job promotions, but, mostly, her own fears.

She had been praying daily for reassurance that Brad was the man God meant for her. But Beth's words were true. Why would God lead her to Brad if there was no reason? For the first time in months, she felt determined. She faced it head on. *I love this man with all my heart. I love his children. I want to be his wife. I want. . .*

Sally stopped and listened, listened to the deafening silence. She looked around the room at what had been her home for many years. She realized her life was missing something—nothing material, nothing she could buy. She was missing the man she loved. It wasn't too late. Her heart told her everything would be fine. She would visit Brad *before* Christmas and tell him she loved him and wanted to be his wife. Everything would be wonderful.

She hesitated. Should she call him tonight? She breathed deeply and dialed Brad's number, praying she'd hear jubilation when she told him.

She heard the click, and Brad's hello.

Her heart thundered. "Brad—"

"Please, Sally, don't apologize. You're right."

She froze. *Right?* She was wrong. Absolutely wrong. "But—"

"Sally, please don't say anything else."

She clung to the telephone, her breath like ice burning through her. The pause grew in length.

"I've been thinking since we hung up, Sally. And you're right. I've been beating my head against the wall, praying and hoping. But I don't want to drag this on any longer. We've both had enough of stress and empty hopes."

Gooseflesh covered Sally's arms, her knees buckled beneath her. She grabbed the edge of the table and sank into the nearby chair. "No, Brad, no. I've been thinking. I wanted to talk to you when we're together. I. . ."

"You've been thinking for a long time, Sally. Talking and thinking isn't the solution. Loving is. I don't think our love is strong enough to carry us through all of the problems. You made me see things clearly. I was blinded by my feelings. But you've said it all, Sally. It's over. I can't bear to go through this anymore. No more promises or wishes or talking."

A growing lump pressed against Sally's vocal chords, allowing nothing but silence. Her chest ached with the pressure of her thundering heartbeat, the pain knifing down into her stomach. She hung her head, tears dripping on her hands and running across her paled lips. "It's over?" she finally asked in a whisper.

"It's for the best. For both of us. And for the kids."

The empty line stretched into dead silence. A whispered good-bye left her lips, and her trembling hand placed the receiver back onto the cradle. She raised her icy fingers to her face and wept until her tears dried to racking sobs.

She wandered into the bedroom, tossing her clothes in a pile and pulled a nightgown over her head. She lay across the bed, fighting the tears that again burned on the edges of her eyes. Why had she been such a fool?

Her ear was tuned for the telephone, praying he'd rescind and call her back. She surveyed the objects around the room, things that meant nothing without Brad. When her gaze drifted to the nightstand, she spotted her Bible, unopened for months. She remembered the day with embarrassment when she had asked Ed if he attended church. His answer was candid and insightful. *No, but I read my Bible every night before I go to bed. It gives me perspective.* That's what she had missed. Somehow along the way, she had lost perspective.

Sally rose on her elbow and grasped the Bible in her hand. She opened it, turning to Jack's lessons from her grief group, Ecclesiastes 3:1. Glancing at the page, she carried the Bible into the living room. She leaned her back against the chair, staring at the page in front of her, running her fingers across the black leather binding of the book. Her eyes focused on the passage. *To everything there is a season, and a time to every purpose under the heaven: a time to be born, and a time to die.* "A time to be born and a time to die." The words tore through her. Yes, death was also a season. She searched the page. *A time to heal; a time to break down, and a time to build up; a time to weep, and a time to laugh; a time to mourn, and a time to dance.*

She'd experienced all of these feelings. She had mourned and wept. With Brad, she had healed and laughed. And her heart had danced. She again focused her eyes on the page. *A time to get, and a time to lose.* But this couldn't be her time to lose. She'd already lost Tim. She didn't want to throw away the love she felt for Brad and the children. She had taken so long to realize the truth. With them, her lonely life was full and complete. A new tear formed on the rim of her eye. And she sought the words. *A time to speak; a time to love.*

Sally looked up from her reading. Her throat tightened. Her heart pounded in her chest. Here was the answer she had sought all along. God had given her the seasons of her life, and she had faced them. She reread the words. *To everything there is a season, and a time to every purpose under the heaven.* How could she question God's purpose for her? She had been given a loving man who wanted her for a wife. And two beautiful children—children she'd longed for—needing a nurturing woman in their lives.

Sally placed the Bible on the table and rose from the chair, crossing to the telephone. God had answered her prayer. The problem was she hadn't listened. She hit the redial button. The telephone rang. Three rings. . .four. . .five. . . No one answered. She looked at her wristwatch. Ten o'clock. The children would be in bed by now. He had to be home. Reality struck her. Brad knew she was calling back, and he didn't answer the telephone.

She placed the receiver on the cradle. She felt dizzy, and her heart ached. Shaken and weak, she fled to her bedroom. Flinging herself on the bed, tears flowed, burning down her cheeks. *Heavenly Father, I've fought You. I haven't listened to Your message. I've blamed You, and all the while, You were handing me a gift and I had my eyes closed. Forgive me. You've opened my eyes to Your will.* She closed her eyes, whispering her prayer until she fell asleep.

❧

All those things that seemed so important marched past Sally like a blur— Darby's wedding and the party for baby Timothy. She worked on the mission project, and on Christmas Eve Day, the packages were delivered to the County Foster Care Center. Her heart ached seeing the parentless children, and their image blurred into the sweet faces of Kelly and Danny.

One surprise arrived as a Christmas card. The return address caught her eye, Old Wharf Road, Dennisport. The handwriting, precise and flowing, was familiar, and she knew it was from Amanda.

With trembling fingers, Sally tore open the letter. It began casually with the typical Christmas greeting. Amanda thanked her again for the lovely vase Sally sent last summer and wrote about her Thanksgiving visit with Brad.

> *I was sorry you could not be with us for Thanksgiving. It was wonderful to be with Brad and the children, but I sensed that things are not as joyful as they were when they were on the Cape last summer. I must attribute that to your absence. I do not want to be a meddling old lady, but I felt you and Brad had a relationship based on mutual respect and caring for one another. Therefore, I do not understand why Brad is alone in Providence, and you are alone in Michigan.*

Sally's hands trembled as she scanned the ivory stationary. The words blurred in her eyes.

> *Despite all my concerns, I respect your reason, whatever it may be, not to accept my son's proposal. You brought much happiness into the lives of Brad and the children, and I thank you for that. I ask you to forgive an old woman's meddling. I wish you blessings and much peace and happiness in your life.*
>
> *Fondly,*
> *Amanda*

Sally sat unmoving, staring at the letter. *You aren't meddling, Amanda. You really love me and you love your family.* Pangs of shame swept through her. Kelly and Danny needed her to care for them and love them. She could never replace Janet, but she could love them. And she did.

Brad had not told Amanda about their terrible, final conversation, and she grasped on to that piece of information with hope. She hoped he would call her, but the hoped-for call didn't happen.

After Christmas Eve worship service, Alice and Ed arrived, smiling foolishly, with a package under Ed's arm. Before they were seated, Sally couldn't contain her question. "So, what's all the grinning about?"

Ed wrapped his free arm around Alice's shoulder. "I've asked Alice to be my wife, and she accepted."

"God's blessed us a second time," Alice said. "I never thought I'd marry again and neither did Ed, but we enjoy each other's company, we share the same faith, and best of all, we love each other." Ed leaned down, kissing her gently.

Sally stared at them in wonder. "I'm thrilled." Yet her happiness for them was stifled by her own self-pity. She looked from one to the other, still standing in the foyer. "I suppose I can invite you to sit down now."

They laughed as they moved to the living room. But before they were seated, Ed, as eager as a child, plopped a gift into Sally's arms.

Sally eyed the package. "What is this?"

"You'd know if you opened it," Ed said, a twinkle in his eye.

"Okay, but help yourself to some cookies and coffee." She pointed to the table covered in a red and green cloth and filled with Christmas goodies.

With the first turn of the package, Sally heard a tinkle from inside. "It's a music box, isn't it?" She tore off the paper. When she raised the lid, her heart skipped a beat. A miniature castle with turrets and towers stood on top of the music box, and winding the key, the castle turned, sending out the airy melody "Someday My Prince Will Come." She hadn't told them of her situation with Brad. Tears crept into her eyes.

Alice's knowing gaze rested on her. "You can't be sad, Sally. Your prince has already come. We love you dearly, but we wanted to say something. You need to be in Providence. There's a man and two children who love you very much. You'll move away, and we'll visit you. Distance doesn't end friendships. But distance ends romance."

Sally looked at the two of them. Her eyes glistened with tears—too many tears lately. She held the lovely music box in her hand. "It's too late. I finally realized I can't live here anymore without Brad and the kids. But I've messed things up badly."

Alice rose and walked to Sally's side. Like a mother, she turned Sally's face to hers. "Have faith, my dear. I'm sure you haven't."

Sally was sure she had, but how could she explain the whole thing to Alice?

On Christmas Day after worship, Sally forced herself to prepare dinner as she'd planned. Sally lit the logs in the fireplace, and as the fire reached a rosy glow, she heard a car in the driveway. In seconds, the front door burst open, and Carrie ran into the room, throwing her arms around Sally's waist. Bill, Sue, and her parents from Florida followed close behind as Sally met them at the door.

Hiding her feelings through the hugs and Christmas salutations, Sally used the meal to keep herself busy, and she controlled the emotion building inside her.

After dinner, Sue and Sally cleared the dishes and stored the leftovers while the others visited in the living room. Carrie brought along a new game, and as Grandma Meier read the rules at the gateleg table, Carrie played with the music box. Its tinkling tune played again and again. The sound drifted into the kitchen.

"If I hear that tune one more time. . . ," Sue said, scurrying to the living room.

As Sally prepared the coffee, Bill wandered into the kitchen, and she grabbed the moment. Despite what had happened between her and Brad, she had to let Bill know how much his words had hurt her. "Sit down for a minute, Bill. I need to talk to you."

He tilted his head in question and slid uncomfortably into a chair. "What's up?"

"This is important. I know you weren't happy about my relationship with Brad. And I'm sure you were relieved when he moved away. Things are probably hopeless now, but you should know that I love Brad and his kids."

Bill raised his hand to halt her speech. "Listen, Sis, you don't have to explain your life to me. Maybe I was a fool. You haven't been the same since he left. A couple of years ago we expected you to be depressed and lonely. Then you seemed happier again, but now all you do is moon around. That's not a life. I want you to be happy."

She looked directly into his eyes. "Brad proposed last summer and I refused because I didn't want to leave Michigan—my family and friends, my job. But I've been miserable. I listened to so many people cautioning me, telling me my relationship with Brad was too new to mean anything. I was so caught up in my own worries I didn't even listen to God. Now that I realize my foolishness, it's too late. I'll never listen to anyone again, Bill—except my heart and God."

Bill looked at her in silence. "I'm sorry, Sis. I didn't mean to hurt you. I thought I was protecting you, but I was probably being selfish. I didn't give him or your relationship a chance. Your happiness is all I care about."

He rose and Sally stepped into his arms, her head on his shoulder. "Thanks. If I have another chance with Brad, I'll not refuse again. I love him too much, and I believe he and the kids are what God planned for me." She took him by the hand. "So come into the living room with me. I want to tell everyone the news. Last night, Alice and Ed told me they're getting married. And if God gives me another chance, so will I."

Brad carried the dinner dishes into the kitchen. As always, his mother had given Naomi Christmas Day off to be with her family. They had warmed the turkey Naomi prepared the day before in its deep brown gravy. Their meal seemed quiet. The children ate slowly, tired from the excitement of gifts and special treats. Amanda eyed him throughout the meal, obviously knowing he wasn't himself.

When Brad talked to Sally before Christmas, he knew then she didn't love him as he loved her. Though her words of love seemed real, her actions spoke differently. She filled her life with commitments, never once thinking of him. Then maybe he did the same.

But he couldn't bear the pain anymore, not for himself nor the children. She meant too much to them. That's why her words had cut him deeply when she called the last time. He felt as if he were an afterthought. Now he knew he'd let foolish pride destroy their relationship. Life would never be right if he didn't try one last time.

With thoughts chasing through his head, he rinsed the dinner dishes, and grabbing a cup of coffee, he returned to the living room where Amanda read to the children. Brad sat in a chair, listening to his mother like he did when he was a child, and pondered what to do.

Her voice jolted him from his wandering thoughts. "Did you hear me, Brad?" She held a stack of Christmas cards in her lap. The children had gone to their rooms to get ready for bed without him noticing.

"Sorry, Mom. I guess I was thinking."

She nodded, her eyes reflecting her concern. "Did you read Darlene's card?"

He shook his head no.

"She is going with a very nice man, she says in her note. They are talking about marriage. She sounds very happy."

"I'm glad. She deserves to be happy." His voice sounded bitter, and he flinched.

Amanda tossed the cards on the end table. "Brad, what are you going to do? You cannot continue on like this. You've been in a terrible state far too long."

"I know. I want her, Mom. But I told her it was over."

"You did what?"

"It's a long story, but I told her on the telephone we were through. Her indecision hurt too much. I couldn't take it anymore, and I worried for the children. They've grown to love her."

"Yes, they talk about her all the time."

"I didn't tell them. I didn't have the courage."

"Brad, you must do something."

"I thought telling her would end it, but I love her."

"I'd hoped you and Sally would marry. Whatever you do, be decisive. This has gone on long enough."

Brad rose from the chair. "You're right. I know what I have to do."

Chapter 18

Sally rose the morning after Christmas feeling as if she'd carried heavy loads up a hill, over and over. Her body ached, and her heart ached. She struggled into her robe. This Christmas seemed worse than when Tim died. Death was forever. Brad and the children were only distanced by earthly miles. If they loved each other, miles should make no difference.

She wandered into the kitchen and made coffee then carried it to the living room. She sat in the recliner, staring at the unlit tree and the pile of neatly stacked gifts beneath it.

How could she expect Brad to wait? Why had she allowed foolish fears and worries to control her decision? She had expected God's assurance to stomp through in heavy boots. Brad had reminded her that sometimes God can answer prayer softly. Her mind had been so filled with fear, she hadn't heard the Lord's soft, gentle assurance.

Sally sat back in her chair, staring out the window. Fluffy white flakes drifted down, swaying and looping on the wind, pressing against the windowpane and melting into tiny rivulets of water like tears. She watched one float on the air, drift down, and cling to the branches of a shrub outside her window. She felt like that snowflake, drifting and clinging. Where was her faith?

She returned to the kitchen, pouring a fresh cup of coffee and toasting an English muffin. She sat at the table, staring at the snow. God had been with her all along. In her struggle, she had forgotten to trust in the Lord, to know that God guided her steps.

The snow floated down, heavier now, and lay on the branches of the shrubs, no longer clinging, but resting on the limbs. She had been clinging to fear and sadness, but no more. Today, she rested on God's promise, on the Lord's assurance.

Finishing the simple breakfast, she showered and dressed. There was no point in calling Brad today. She'd give him time. In a few days, she'd call him, then go to him—plead with him. She couldn't give up. It took her this long to hear God, not in the blare of trumpets, but in a gentle whisper.

She returned to the living room and lifted the Bible, seeking the solace. The snow slowed and finally stopped. She rose from the chair, needing to do something invigorating. Throwing on her coat, Sally headed outside, strengthened by the icy air as the Word strengthened her spirit.

Before she stepped from the back porch, the telephone rang, and her heart leaped. *Brad*. She rushed inside and snatched the receiver, only to hear Ed's nervous voice.

"Sally, would you come down for a minute?"

"Is something wrong?"

"No, nothing's wrong, but I need to see you. Could you come down now?"

Her chest tightened. Something was wrong. "What is it?"

"Just come down, Sally."

His persistence concerned her. He and Alice broke their engagement. Or something as bad. He didn't want to tell her on the telephone. "I'll be there."

Hurrying back outside, she raced down the block, and as she climbed Ed's porch, he opened the door.

"What's wrong, Ed?" she gasped as she stepped in. He looked at her strangely. It was bad news. He took her coat and laid it on the chair near the door.

"Go into the living room. I'll be there in a minute." He turned down the hall toward the kitchen.

Her mind raced. What could it be? She turned into the living room, and in the dusky light of the snowy morning, her eyes were captured by the colorful lights from a small tabletop tree reflecting in the windowpane. The colors diffused like fireworks. She turned toward a chair, then stopped. Her heart thundered, and she couldn't believe her eyes. "Brad! You're here."

❧

Brad saw Sally coming up the walk, her face pale and drawn. But when she saw him, her face glowed, and she raced into his arms, clinging to him, trembling. His own heart beat next to hers, his own tears flowed with hers.

"Brad, I can't believe you're here. I wanted to see you so badly. I needed to. . ."

He leaned down, silencing her with his lips. Her own lips yielded to his, breath bursting from their lungs as they parted.

Her eyes searched his. "I don't understand. I'm so happy you're here, but. . .I don't understand."

Brad led her to the sofa. He sat her down, sitting next to her. "I made a decision, Sally. I don't want to lose you. I love you and need you. The kids love you. Even my mother loves you. I'm here to beg you from the bottom of my heart to give our love a chance."

Sally laughed and cried at the same time. "Please, Brad, don't say anymore. I was so afraid I lost you. When I finally came to my senses, you told me we were through. I thought it was too late."

"It's not too late. I love you too much." He encircled her in his arms, looking down into her tearstained face, tears brimming in his own eyes. "Sally, I don't have enough words to tell you the feelings inside me. You make my life complete. And you bring joy to the children. Will you marry me?"

She grasped his hands with her icy, trembling fingers. Her eyes said everything he needed to hear. "Yes, I'll marry you. I love you with all my heart."

He held her to him, shaking with relief and the depth of his love. Her eyes, though teary, glowed with happiness. "I love you, your children—and your mother." A smile spread across her face, relaxing the stress, and Brad's own tense mouth curled to a grin.

Applause resounded from the hall. Alice and Ed peeked around the corner, beaming with their own joy. They rushed into the room with kisses and handshakes. When the congratulations subsided, Sally sank exhausted on the sofa. "Someone, please explain this whole thing to me. Where are the children? When did you get here? How long—"

"Slow down, my love." He took her hand in his. "I'll explain everything, but first, I want to give you your Christmas present. It's long overdue."

He raised a package from the end table and handed it to her. She looked at him with question and unwrapped the box. When she lifted the lid, she brought out a beautiful leaded-glass box decorated with pressed flowers. "Oh, Brad, it's the box I saw on the Cape—the antique box I loved so much."

"Open it, Sally."

She lifted the lid. Inside was a smaller, hinged jewelry box. She glanced at him, then raising the lid, she smiled. She held her arms out to him, and he wrapped her in his arms, knowing that his prayers had been answered.

He released her and, taking the box, lifted out a glimmering solitaire diamond ring.

"Brad, it's beautiful!" He lifted her left hand and slid on the ring, threading his fingers through hers.

"You see, dear," Alice said, "it fits. It's amazing what I can find out when I need to."

Sally glanced down at the ring, fitting perfectly on her finger. "Alice, you knew this all along?"

"He bought the ring long ago, my dear. He's been waiting for you to say yes."

Sally wiped her moist eyes.

"Now, to answer your questions," Brad began. "The kids are with my mom. I flew out standby last night. I thought it would take forever."

"This is like a dream. Does your mom know about—"

"They all know why I'm here. Mom's overjoyed. Kelly and Danny are thrilled, and they are all praying that you will say yes."

"But Brad, why didn't you tell me you were coming? I called you back the night of our argu—of our talk and you didn't pick up the phone. I thought you were avoiding me. I—"

"We went out after your call. I couldn't bear to sit in the house. I really thought you didn't love me. Then I decided to try one last time. I called Alice late last night. I knew you talked with her, and I wanted to know the truth."

He glanced at Alice's glowing face, and she nodded. "She assured me that you loved me and you'd accept my proposal. So I rushed to the airport and waited for a flight. I needed to ask you in person, not by telephone."

She put her hands to her face, laughing and crying. But he knew the tears were joyful. Embracing her, he kissed her hair and pressed his cheek against hers. He felt lightheaded—giddy. He leaned back, tilting her face toward his, their eyes glazed with love. "When I asked you, I wanted to look into your eyes."

Sally's heart overflowed. "And you are," she whispered. Her mind ruffled through the pages of their lives the past months. Today she felt complete, filled with love and faith. She rose, taking his hands in hers, and tugging him upward. "Now, let's telephone the children."

SCONES
(Griddle Cakes)

Here are the scones that Sally made for her neighbor Ed Washburn. They are cooked on a black iron griddle, heavy fry pan, or electric fry pan.

1 ½ teaspoon baking powder
½ teaspoon salt
½ teaspoon ground ginger
2 cups all-purpose flour (plus extra for dusting)
½ cup granulated sugar
¾ cup unsalted butter, cut into small pieces.
1 cup sultanas (golden raisins) or any dried fruit, such as cherries, cranberries, or diced apricot.
2 large eggs
3–4 teaspoons milk

Sift dry ingredients in bowl and stir in sugar. Rub butter until the mixture is like fine bread crumbs. Stir in the dried fruit. Beat the eggs and add them. Stir in just enough milk to make a firm but sticky dough. Turn the dough onto a floured board, sprinkle with flour and roll it to an inch thickness. Cut into rounds. Re-roll the trimmings and cut more rounds. Brush heavy fry pan with oil and heat over medium. Fry cakes for about 5 minutes on each side until they are well browned. Serve warm with butter or preserves. Also good plain. You may store and eat them cold as well.

SECRETS WITHIN

Chapter 1

Laine Sibley closed her eyes and drew in a ragged breath as she pressed her ear to the telephone. As her sister's voice came in tired, hesitant gasps, tears pressed against the back of Laine's eyes.

"You're okay, then, Kathleen?" Laine asked, controlling her quaking voice.

"Mavis is here. Don't worry."

Laine closed her eyes, thanking God for Mavis Dexter. The woman had become Kathleen's second mother, tending her and Becca with untiring hands. Laine couldn't imagine what it would be like to give that much time and concern for someone else. Looking up, she stared through the window and focused on Moon Lake's sun-speckled ripples a few yards from her front door. "Kiss Becca for me, and I'll see you both later."

Laine sat suspended for a moment, then pulled the phone from her ear as an afterthought and placed it on its base. Her sister's illness seemed more than she could bear.

Laine's thoughts filled with images of Kathleen's five-year-old daughter, Rebecca. With her dark waving hair and ivory skin, the child was the image of her Irish father, who had been killed in a plane crash. Picturing Becca's sad blue eyes, Laine ached for the child and for her own desperate sorrow.

Guilt lay heavily on Laine's chest, and she wished she could erase the terrible feelings of anger and envy she'd felt too often in years past. Her bitter, jealous words aimed at her younger sister weighed on her shoulders like a hulking beast.

Pushing the memories aside, Laine rose from the chair and drained the last swallow of her cold coffee. After setting the cup in the sink, she turned, braced her back against the kitchen counter, and again regarded the golden flecks of sunlight blinking on the lake. Air is what she needed. Fresh air and a few moments to calm her pulsing heart.

A rowboat tied to the small wooden dock bobbed in the morning sunlight. Why not? Since she'd moved back to Michigan and into the condominium a week earlier, she hadn't gone near the water except for the day she was guided through the rental by the agent. Adjusting to her new position at Artistic Interiors and organizing her belongings had taken all her time. On her first free Sunday morning, she could use a distraction, something pleasant like a few relaxing moments on the lake.

Pulling her makeup bag from her purse, she glimpsed in the hall mirror and dashed frosty orange lipstick along the bow of her lips. Scrutinizing her appearance, she decided she'd do. Who would she impress this early in the morning anyway? People with any sense at all were still dawdling on the edge of sleep.

Stepping onto her screened porch, she locked the condo door and dropped the key into the pocket of her walking shorts. The oars lay along the porch wall, and she grabbed them and maneuvered the pair through the doorway and down the two steps to the outside. As she marched toward the path leading to the dock, she heard the screen door swish closed behind her.

When Laine reached the water, a warm June breeze curled along her bare skin, and her sneakers gripped the rough dock boards with a punctuating thud. The small rowboat appeared safe enough, so she slid the paddles into the oarlocks. Grabbing the side of the boat, Laine slipped off the rope tethering the stern, then holding the boat fast, she inched her way forward toward the front mooring.

As she clutched the dock pole, she edged one foot into the dinghy, but the momentum shifted the rowboat from the pier. With a gasp, she clutched the mooring to no avail. The dinghy continued its journey while her yell echoed across the quiet water and she clung to the piling with her left foot on the dock and her right foot in the drifting boat.

As the inevitable rose to meet her, a strong masculine voice struck her ear. "Hang on."

But his encouragement came too late, and she belly-flopped into the cold, sea-weedy water. As she bobbed to the surface, smiling hazel eyes greeted her, and she heard the same full-throated voice. "Good morning. Decided to take an early dip, I see."

"Decided isn't quite the word," Laine muttered as he reached out to her. She grasped his hand, and with one heave, he lifted her, dripping with water and greenish-brown seaweed, to the dock.

When she had the courage to look at him, his amusement sent her mortification packing. She laughed at herself and her wasted effort, recalling the feeble swipe of lipstick moments earlier.

"Nice to see you have a sense of humor," he said. But his expression became serious as he eyed her from head to toe. "Anything hurt?"

"Only my pride." Laine extended her brackish hand. "Thanks for the save. I'm Laine Sibley."

"Laine. Nice name." His lightly stubbled square jaw returned to its friendly smile. "I'm Jeff. Jeff Rice, your neighbor."

With her humiliation in check, Laine focused on the good-looking man standing beside her. A rust-colored knit shirt stretched across his broad chest and hung partway down his beige-colored swim trunks. A full head of tawny hair lay in casual waves that framed his square face. Raising her eyes to his, she caught a flash of curiosity.

"Well, that's it for a relaxing drift on the lake," she said. "The algae and I should go rinse off."

He caught his belt loop with his thumb and glanced across the once-again undisturbed lake. "Why miss the boat ride? I'll wait while you clean up and keep you company. . .unless you'd rather go out alone." He paused.

Laine took a faltering step backward. "No, I'll—" She glanced toward the condo. "I'll be only a couple of minutes." She swung around and dashed up the walk.

❦

Jeff grinned as the attractive blond trotted up the walk, leaving a wet trail behind her. Despite the mermaid disguise, her beauty was evident. When he'd come to her rescue, her peacock blue eyes caught him off guard. When she bobbed to the surface, his heart skipped a beat. Add to those eyes her smooth creamy skin and bowed lips, and her face resembled the antique China doll he'd found in his mother's attic after she'd died.

The memory tightened his belly, and he pushed the thought aside and refocused on the woman he'd just met. Delicate featured, yes, but he sensed she was no fragile toy. Her broad shoulders tapering to strong legs disclosed the body of a capable athlete. Swimmer, he guessed.

Admiring her, he jolted when she turned around and darted back down the path.

"My key," she called, pointing to the lake.

A moment passed before he understood. When her foot sounded on the wooden boards, he was already peering into the dark water, hoping to catch the glint of her key in the shadows.

"How stupid." She knelt beside him, squinting into the water. "See anything? I had it in my pocket."

His vision sought the murky lake bottom. "Only a key?"

"On a chain," she answered.

Something pale glinted beneath the surface. "Is there white on the chain?"

"Uh-huh. Do you see it?"

"I think so." He hadn't anticipated jumping into the shore water, preferring the clearer water by the raft, but how could he ignore a woman in distress? He rose and tugged the knit shirt over his head.

As if understanding his action, she bolted up. "No, I'm already wet and dirty. Show me where, and I'll get it."

He ignored her plea, but before he could stop her, she leaped into the murky water with him. Grabbing the key chain from the sludgy bottom, he rose to the surface. Below in the water, her honey-colored hair splayed about her like silken threads.

When she bounced upward, she peered at him, then at the chain dangling from his fingers. "Why did you do that? I didn't want you to get wet."

"No problem." He forced a gallant pose. "I'd planned to swim anyway, but from the raft." He stared off at the sparkling water further out in the lake, then handed her the key with a chuckle. "Now, if you'd still like to go for that boat ride, I'll meet you back here in a couple of minutes."

❧

The dip of the oars rippled the deep green water and broke the silence. Laine studied Jeff's iron-clad midriff as it tensed and relaxed with the pull of the oars. He wasn't a tall man, under six feet she guessed, but he was strong and solid. Yet his kindness—more like chivalry—was what she found most appealing. Gentle control. His bronzed body flexed, and her curiosity won the battle. "Do you work out?"

He squinted toward her into the sunlight. "Not much. You?"

"Me?" She chuckled. "Not really. I jog and swim, but that's about it. My stationary bike makes a great clothes valet."

"You, too?"

"So then, what do you do to keep yourself in shape?"

His face flashed surprise but in a heartbeat shifted to a grin. "My job, I suppose."

Wondering what made him flinch, she asked, "What do you do for a living?"

"Troubleshooter," he said, staring off in the distance. "Computers."

"Troubleshooter, huh? I'd guess something more exciting and dangerous."

Jerking his head back toward her, he grinned. "Like alligator wrestling?"

"No." Laine laughed, but she had to admit to herself that wrestling seemed more like it. Computers didn't fit. "More like Superman."

Jeff shook his head. "Nope. I'm much more boring than Clark Kent. So how about you?"

"Commercial interior design. I moved here from Chicago last week to work with a Bloomfield Hills company. We design decor for businesses, restaurants, hotels, corporate offices."

"You're from Chicago, then?"

"Not really. Michigan's my home."

"Come clean. You were homesick. Am I right?"

His comments dragged her stifled feelings to the surface. "My younger sister's ill, and. . .I thought I should be nearby."

Shifting with discomfort, Jeff let the oars drag in the water. "I'm sorry. It's serious?"

"Cancer." The word knotted in her throat. "Both our parents died from the same."

Silence hung on the warm breeze. A dog's bark echoed across the water, and in the distance, the rumble of a motor swept in, then drifted off on the air.

He averted his eyes, gazing somewhere beyond her. "Mine are both dead, too. I'm it." He shrugged and gave the oars a hefty pull. "What you see is what you get."

His words rattled in her thoughts, and she glanced at her wristwatch. "I'd better get back. I promised Kathleen I'd stop by, and she's probably looking for me—not to mention her daughter, Becca. She's my cutie of a niece."

"How old is she? Your niece, I mean." Without question, Jeff pivoted the rowboat back toward shore.

"Just turned five. My heart breaks thinking about what she'll face if something happens to my sister." *When something happens.* Laine swallowed back the thought and focused on the shoreline closing in on them. "I'm sorry I got morbid. I've had all this pressing on my mind."

"No problem. That's what ears are for—to listen. Once in a while I've wished someone had listened to me."

His mouth closed, and she didn't have the nerve to ask what he meant. When the boat thudded against the dock, they climbed out and tied it to the pilings, then parted, each going in their own direction. But as Laine dressed to visit her sister, Jeff's image remained in her thoughts.

🌿

Laine heard Becca's eager squeal before she saw her.

"Auntie Laine." The petite, fair-skinned, dark-haired child darted through the doorway. The bang of the screen door echoed as Becca bounded into Laine's opened arms.

"Hi, sweetie." Laine nuzzled her face in the child's silky cheek. "I've missed you."

"Me, too. Mama's waiting for you."

"I know."

Becca snuggled a battered rag doll against her chest, but she grabbed Laine's hand and led her into the pleasant Cape Cod, its white siding trimmed with dark gray shutters.

Inside, Kathleen lay propped against a pile of colorful pillows on the living-room sofa. Her gaunt skin looked the color of bleached ash, a sad contrast to her bright surroundings. Her attempt at a smile broke Laine's heart.

"How you doing, Sis?" Laine asked, leaning over to kiss her sister's cheek. "I see Mrs. Dexter got you all gussied up." Laine crossed the beige carpet and plopped into a nearby chair.

Kathleen shifted her gaze toward Laine. "I don't think 'gussied' is the word, but she tried." A meager chuckle followed her words.

Laine struggled to keep her voice steady as she noticed her sister's glazed eyes. "It's good to see you dressed and out of bed. Did you have lunch?"

Kathleen nodded. "Mavis fixed some soup, but Becca wouldn't eat. She said you'd take her for fast food." The last words faded like the end of an echo.

Laine forced a cheery laugh, but inside her heart cried. Her sister couldn't last much longer. The look seemed too familiar. Her memory took her back to her parents' deaths—each different, yet each the same.

"I'll take Becca to lunch in a little bit. I thought I'd spend a few minutes with you for a change." A few minutes. How could she cover so many years in minutes? Thinking back, so much had happened. And so much more would happen now—with the horrible illness pulling Kathleen's world apart. They had so much to talk about, but for Laine, facing it gave the future too much unwanted reality.

Every time they were together, Laine hoped she could ask the right questions and get the needed answers. Her first concern was Becca. What did Kathleen have planned for the child's care? What about Becca's paternal grandmother, Glynnis Keary? Had Kathleen contacted her? And finally, how much money had Kathleen been able to rescue from the man who'd walked into her life after Alex's tragic death? The queries tore through Laine, striking the brick wall of her cowardice. And worse, she faced her own need to ask Kathleen's forgiveness.

"I'm so glad you have Mrs. Dexter, Kath," Laine said. "She's a real godsend."

"Like a mother." Her words faded.

Laine studied her face, seeing the evidence of pain pulling at every muscle. "Is it time for your medication? Where is it?"

Kathleen tilted her head toward the table, and Laine grabbed the pills and poured water into a glass from the pitcher. She rested her sister's head in her arm and eased the water between her dried lips until Kathleen swallowed the pill.

Desperation washed over Laine. The time had come. Now or never. She saw it in every detail of her sister's appearance. But how to begin.

"Remember when we were kids?" Laine said, delving into her memories. "We had some good times. I often think of the vacations we had. I always smile when I think of the cottage Dad rented. I suppose that's why I moved into a condo on the lake. Such great memories." For a moment, her grief dissipated as nostalgia bathed her in warm thoughts. "Remember fishing, Sis? Dad would take us out in the boat. . .and before your worm hit the water, you were asking if you'd caught a fish." Laine grinned with the reminiscence. "Then when you finally caught a bluegill, you were so excited. We'd have thought you'd caught a whale."

A faint grin stirred Kathleen's mouth. "A–and your first. . .date, remem. . ."

Laine sank with the ache that lodged in her heart. "How could I forget? You pouted because you had to stay home." The scene rolled in as tears rimmed Laine's lashes. "My date. . . What was his name? Mike Bennett, I think. Anyway, he thought you were so cute." She touched Kathleen's arm. "I never told you, but he said you could come along with us." The confession triggered her shame. Everyone thought Kathleen was cute—beautiful when she matured. And Laine had been envious. Always.

"C–Christmases," Kathleen whispered. "R–remember. . .my doll?" She struggled to speak while anguish rifled across her face.

Covering her despair, Laine pushed a chuckle from her chest. "I do. I told Mom and Dad I was too grown-up for a doll, but when Christmas arrived. . .I wanted a doll just like the one they'd given you."

Kathleen nodded. A tear dripped from her lashes and rolled down her cheek. "Good times, Laine."

Laine studied her sister's face. *Tell her. Tell her before it's too late.* She closed her eyes, begging for a way to empty her mind of guilt and sorrow. But who was she begging? God? God had faded from her life so long ago. A ragged breath escaped her lips. "Kathleen, can you hear me?"

Her sister's eyes opened and closed. A faint nod answered her question.

"I need to talk with you before. . ." Laine paused and tried again. "For so many years I've been weighted with guilt, I don't even know where to begin."

Kathleen shifted her hand toward Laine's, her mouth opening and closing in silence.

Laine covered her sister's icy hand. "Don't try to talk, Sis. Just listen." Once more, Laine dragged strength from somewhere inside. "I've spent my life envying you. You were more beautiful, more talented, and worst of all, luckier. Blessed, Mom and Dad called it."

Kathleen's eyes fluttered, focusing for a heartbeat before they closed.

"I seemed to struggle for everything, while you. . .seemed to be covered in good fortune. . .and I prayed, Kathleen, that you'd learn a little about suffering."

Laine's voice broke, and tears spilled from her eyes like the shame that overflowed her heart. Without stopping, she whispered the story of her jealousy, the prayers for retribution, the guilt when Kathleen's husband died as if a vengeful God had answered her prayers. She'd even begrudged Kathleen her baby daughter. "I can't ask for your forgiveness. What I felt all those years is unforgivable, but if I could go back and erase the past, I would. I've missed you so much, but my bitterness and envy. . .and then my shame kept me away."

Kathleen's eyes opened. Mingled in the pain, compassion shone through. "N–no need to for–give. I've al–ways loved—you."

Despair knotted Laine's chest and weighed against her stomach. Grief rose in her throat like bile. She longed to embrace her sister, to hold her against her chest, to crush away the pain Kathleen had lived with for years. Pain? Laine didn't know pain. Today she saw it—the agony of death—in Kathleen's face. "I love you, Sis."

They sat silently for a moment until Kathleen struggled to open her eyes briefly as she whispered words Laine didn't want to hear. "It's time for hospice, Laine. They'll help all of us." Her eyes drifted closed again, and Laine stood above her, watching her even, shallow breathing.

With Kathleen resting, Laine wiped the tears clinging to her lashes, then peeked into the kitchen where Mavis Dexter entertained Becca. "I gave Kathleen her pain medication, and she's sleeping. I think Becca and I'll go have some lunch."

She sent a tired grin to the elderly woman who was sipping from a cup clutched in her gnarled hands.

"Good. The child's been waiting for you all day." Mavis's pale blue eyes looked as weary and spent as Laine's tethered emotions made her feel.

Becca jumped from the chair and wrapped her dainty fingers around Laine's. "Burger Barn, okay? And I'll bring Penny, too."

"Burger Barn it is, Becca. And you know your dolly's invited."

Becca tucked her rag doll under her arm, and they tiptoed past Kathleen and headed out the front door. Laine glanced one last time over her shoulder at her sleeping sister, wishing she'd had the courage to talk long ago. Now they would have to fit a lifetime of communication into a few final hours.

Chapter 2

Sitting across from Becca at Burger Barn, Laine studied her niece's deep blue eyes, pale with sadness. Though the child bubbled with talk about the toy she'd found in the fast food's special Kiddie's Lunch Bag, Laine recognized an underlining fear that found its way into the child's face.

Love filled Laine's heart as she regarded the lovely child. Her dark curls haloed her fair face, and Mavis had dressed her in a yellow-and-blue-striped top that gave her a cheery look, belying the trying times she faced.

What could she do for this little girl? She'd asked herself the question too many times since she'd left Kathleen's side. Becca would soon need someone to offer her love, support, and understanding when her mother was gone. Worry and sadness pushed behind Laine's eyes, and despite her attempts to control them, tears clung to her lashes.

"Did you get something in your eye, Auntie?" Becca asked, studying her face with a child's curiosity.

Laine brushed away the moisture with her fingers. "I think I did, sweetie." She and Becca needed to talk. Though only five, the child would soon face adult decisions—changes in her life no little girl should have to deal with.

In the silent lull, Becca's expression shifted to sadness. She tilted her head up, looking into Laine's eyes again. . .for tears perhaps. Studying the child, Laine wondered if Becca wanted permission to shed her own tears.

"Are you worried about your mom?" Laine asked, reaching across the table to hold the child's hand.

Becca nodded. "Mommy tells me not to worry. She says Jesus is always by my side to help me."

The child's words rolled through Laine's thoughts. "Then you should listen to your mom, Becca."

"Jesus is by your side, too, Auntie. Mom said He's like our shadow. Wherever we go, we have a friend who goes with us."

A shadow. God had been a shadow to Laine for many years. Not Becca's kind of shadow, but a dark, undefined shape that she could never touch. "That's a nice thought," she said, wishing the shadow offered her the same comfort it seemed to give Becca.

"I have a picture book with Jesus holding open His arms to all the children. Know what He says?" Her face brightened.

Laine remembered the story from her own childhood.

" 'Suffer little children to come unto me, and forbid them not.' Is that right?"

Becca smiled and nodded, but Laine's thoughts settled on the word "suffer." She had suffered for years, and now Becca would suffer. What kind of God causes little children to suffer? As the question rose in her mind, her thought flew to the end of the verse: *Whosoever shall not receive the kingdom of God as a little child, shall in no wise enter therein.* Becca accepted God's Word just as Laine had done as a child. Had that been her flaw these past years? Had she been seeking explanations and answers that a finite mind couldn't understand? Had her heart closed to accepting God without question. Sadly, she knew the answer.

She harnessed the pressing questions and drew her attention back to Becca. "I'm glad you can turn to Jesus, Becca. We all need someone to turn to when we're confused or—"

"I don't want Mommy to be sick."

Her statement jolted Laine's emotions. "I don't either, sweetheart. I'd give so much if your mom was well."

"Auntie," Becca said, looking like a child who'd been caught doing mischief. "Even though Jesus is my friend, I want my mommy to be with me, too." Her voice caught in her throat. "Sometimes, I'm afraid."

Laine squeezed her hand, wondering if she should tell the little girl her own feelings. "I know, Becca. I wish I could tell you things will be all right, but—"

"Is Mommy going to die?" Fear filled the child's eyes.

Laine's heart sank. She couldn't lie. . .yet she didn't want to frighten her niece any more than she was already. "Only God can answer that," she said, surprising herself by alluding to the Lord.

"I asked God to take care of her," Becca said. Her face twisted with a new thought. "God takes care of my daddy in heaven. That's what Mommy says."

"God's children live with Him on earth and in heaven, Becca, so you can be sure that He'll take care of your mom." God's children? Laine heard the words and wished she felt like one of God's children instead of like an unforgivable sinner.

Pulling her thoughts away from her selfish concerns, Laine focused on Becca. How could she help the child through the grief she would soon face when her own sorrow covered her mind like a shroud? "No matter what happens, your mom will be with Jesus. . .and no matter what happens, you have people who love you."

Becca studied the trinket from her lunch bag, then lifted her head. "You love me, and Mavis does, too."

Her heart in her throat, Laine moved around the table to be closer to the child and wrapped her arms around her thin shoulders. "Everyone who knows you loves you, sweetie. Mavis loves you. . .and I love you more than words can say." She rested her head on Becca's soft, dark curls, commanding her tears to stay behind her eyes.

Today she could not worry about her own sins or faults. Today her concern as for the child. A child who had more confidence in and understanding of God than Laine had gained in a lifetime.

❦

The visit with Kathleen and Becca had drained Laine. Emotionally overwrought, she sat staring across the tranquil lake. Not one wave ruffled the water, and the still water washed her in a gentle calm.

Bitterness that lay bound in Laine's heart for years had tied her spirit in knots, causing her to question so many things about herself and her worth. Since appearing back in Kathleen's life, Laine had let the bitterness seep away, and today her confession had loosened her guilt—not released it totally so it could drift away but eased it so that only slender threads linked it to her soul.

She'd longed for forgiveness. But today, a new reality overwhelmed her. Though Kathleen had whispered her forgiveness, Laine could not accept the gift and forgive herself. She prayed in time she would, but the longing seemed like a vague dream.

The peacefulness of the lake washed over her thoughts, calming her in its silver stillness. The outdoors beckoned, and remembering her earlier dunking, Laine headed for the bedroom to change. A real swim might relax her.

After slipping into her apple green swimsuit, she grabbed a towel and headed outdoors. She studied the rowboat, wondering if she could maneuver it this time without another catastrophe. With greater care, she successfully climbed in and rowed to the wooden raft resting on four large empty oil drums a hundred yards from shore.

She tethered the boat and climbed onto the raft. Tossing her towel on the wooden planks, Laine dove into the deep green water. For a moment, a chill ran through her, but by the time she surfaced, the water felt pleasant and refreshing in the late afternoon sun.

Like a fish, she glided along in the water, her arms cutting through the quiet tracing ripples. When she slowed and sighted the raft two hundred yards behind her, she jackknifed her legs and headed back. After she lifted herself up the two wooden steps, she dabbed the towel on her damp skin, then spread the terry cloth out like a blanket. Stretched out on her belly, she rested her head, using her hands for a pillow, and breathed deeply, sensing the water's calming effect.

The raft gave a sudden dip and bob. Laine opened her eyes, startled by the movement. A shadow fell across the wooden planks, and she lifted her head to see a pair of powerful arms gripping the ladder top. In one smooth motion, they pulled a solid torso of bronzed muscle to the wooden deck. Jeff stood above her, his hazel eyes reflecting the green of the water. "You're doing it right this time, huh?"

She raised herself on her elbows. "Right?"

"Bathing suit, towel, the works."

Laine grinned and rolled on her side, pulling her legs around to a seated position. "This is a comparison test. I want to see which method is best."

"And?"

The sun glinted over his shoulder, and she squinted up at him. "I haven't quite made up my mind. But I'm leaning toward a planned dip."

"Good thinking. Mind if I join you?"

His grin ruffled her pulse, and if she were candid, she'd tell him he was the best thing that had happened to her that day. "Raft belongs to everyone. But I enjoy the company."

He lowered himself beside her on the bare wood and ran his fingers over his stubbled chin. "Bad day with your sister?"

Laine nodded. "It's heavy stuff. Weighs on the heart, you know, watching her suffer and seeing Becca's fear. And I'm such a coward."

"Coward?" His smooth forehead wrinkled with question. "Why?"

"Because we need to talk. So many things to discuss and so much I'd like to say, but I just can't bring myself to do it."

He stared at his feet. "I don't think you're a coward." He lifted his gaze to hers. "You're human. I'd feel the same way."

Something about his manner calmed Laine, an understanding or compassion she didn't see often in others, especially a near stranger. But his manner soothed her, drew her out, and she fought to keep her emotions in check. She felt a strong desire to pour her burdens out to him like a patient would to her doctor.

She studied his interesting face, noting the facial hair that had caught her attention earlier. "Is that beard coming or ready to take a hike?"

He chuckled good-naturedly. "Coming, but I'm thinking of ditching it. Thought I'd give it a try, but maybe summer isn't the best time."

"I suppose." She studied his jaw, envisioning him smooth shaven. "In case I don't recognize you if you decide to shave, yell out your name, okay?"

"I'll do that." A grin played on his lips.

"The swim felt good," Laine said after a lengthy silence. "Relaxing."

He didn't respond; instead he studied her face. "You look more relaxed than earlier today."

She sensed he wanted to say something further, but he remained silent, and she struggled to think of something to talk about. Silence wasn't golden to her. But before she'd come up with a new topic, he spoke.

"Swimming always feels good. But you know what else would feel even better?"

Laine's head jerked up, and she stared at him. Her stomach knotted in disappointment. A come-on. It hadn't entered her mind. "No, what?" She heard the tension in her voice.

A smile curled his lips as if he read her mind. "A nice steak dinner. I just happen to have a couple of thick, juicy T-bones waiting for two hungry swimmers."

She felt a heated flush rise up her neck to her cheeks, and watching him expression, he hadn't missed its journey. "Two steaks?" She shook her head. "Sorry. My thoughts were way off base."

"I noticed." His chuckle was hearty. "I'm not your local masher. Really. I'm a pretty nice guy when you get to know me."

"I'm surprised you'd want to know me after detecting my evil thoughts."

"Hey, a girl has to protect herself. A steak is what I had in mind. Grilled any way you like it."

"How about medium rare, sort of the shade of pink my face was a few minutes ago?"

His laughter drifted to her ears like music.

❧

Jeff closed up the grill and carried the last of the dishes into the kitchen. He'd filled Laine's glass with iced tea, and she sat on a canvas chair on the front lawn, facing the vanishing sun. Grabbing a drink for himself, he joined her, and they sat silently focused on the golden ball as it dropped behind the trees, leaving purple and orange tails tangled in the distant foliage like the remnants of a kite.

A soft sigh touched his ear, and he turned with interest to the gentle sound. "Now did I keep my word?"

"Better than your word. Great steak and friendly conversation. Couldn't ask for more."

"That's the way it should be."

She shifted in her chair and turned toward him, wrapping her fingers around the honey-colored tresses that curled to her shoulders. With a gentle motion, she flicked the hair behind her and tilted her head. "So you've heard pieces of my sad story. Tell me about you."

"You'd be bored out of your mind."

"That's what I need. Maybe I'd have a good night's sleep, reminiscing about our conversation."

Her teasing smile tickled him, and for once, he wished he could be honest and tell her about his life. But that wasn't possible.

He pushed the real Jeff back and instead told her a mixture of truth and fiction. "Oh, after some college and. . .special training, I started work, but a desk job didn't interest me. I needed something more lively. So when the troubleshooting opportunity came along, I took it. I guess that's it." He paused, though her face disclosed she wanted more.

"Marriage? Children?" she asked.

"Neither fit into my plans really well." He looked away, uncomfortable, but she'd asked, and he felt compelled to answer. "I was engaged for a while to a nice Christian woman, but her needs and mine sort of hit a fork in the road. It seemed for the best."

Her face brightened with his words. "You're a Christian?"

Squirming at her question, he shrugged. "I believe in God. I know Jesus died for my sins, but I guess it bogs down there. Too many things in my life that I question. Not who God is, but why God lets things happen. Haven't quite resolved it all yet." He looked into her eyes. "Does that disappoint you?"

She gazed across the water in silence. When she finally answered, her tone said more than her words—telling and sad. "Not disappointment. You've echoed my own feelings. I believe, but I've drifted, too. I grew up going to church and Sunday school. I know Jesus came to earth to save sinners and offer forgiveness. But somehow I feel. . .I need to forgive myself first." Her gaze drifted to his. "Remember the Lord's Prayer? How can I ask to be forgiven if I haven't done the same?" Her lovely blue eyes were heavy with questions.

He considered her words. What did she mean, "forgive myself first?" For what? He wanted to make some kind of statement, but the words tangled in his mind.

"Don't try to answer. I have to do that for myself."

He closed his mouth. She'd guessed right. Words from years back jumped to his tongue ready to exit, but he tucked them inside. The Bible said to repent and be saved. As far as he was concerned, if anyone were repentant, she surely was.

"Enough about me," she said. "Back to you. What happened to your parents?"

Her question bunched inside his head like knotted threads, and he pulled strands of memories apart to find an answer. "My father died ten years ago when I was twenty-four. Heart attack. My mom. . ." His throat constricted, and he swallowed. "My mom died suddenly four years later." His thoughts lifted heavenward like a prayer. *No details, please.*

"That was pretty close together. My dad lived about ten years after my mom," Laine said. "He was twelve years older. She was only thirty-nine when she died."

Slowly, she sipped her tea, then staring at the glass in her hand, she circled its rim with her index finger. "There must be something more pleasant we can talk about." She glanced at her wristwatch and rose. "But. . .I'd really better get going." She set the glass on a small wooden folding table. "Tomorrow's a workday, and I don't know about you, but I'm under the gun learning the quirks of a new company." She grinned. "They call it protocol."

Jeff controlled a nervous chuckle. She'd struck closer to home than she knew. "I've been under the gun myself a few times."

She turned to him with her hand extended. "Thanks for the great dinner, Jeff, and the company. I needed a lift today."

As he grasped her hand, she sputtered a laugh. "Especially this morning. Thanks for giving me a lift twice."

His thoughts sailed back to the morning when he'd first glimpsed her peacock blue eyes set in a very surprised and wet face. "Anytime," he said, fighting the desire to touch her soft cheek in the dusky light.

※

Becca hung on to Laine's porch door, her nose pressed against the screen. "When can we go swimming? You promised. Remember?"

Laine's spirit lifted, seeing her niece focused on play. "Where's your patience?"

"What?" Becca asked, releasing the door and turning to face Laine.

"Patience," she repeated. "Your. . ." She grasped for a simple definition and found none. "Your ability to wait a few minutes." Looking at the child more closely, Laine chuckled and walked across the room to brush the mesh-shaped patch of dust from the end of Becca's nose. "And with a smile."

Becca ran the back of her hand over the same spot, then sent her a silly grin. "I can smile."

"But can you smile and wait?"

Giggles burst from Becca's throat.

"Remember? We just had lunch." She gave Becca a hug and patted her belly. "Didn't your mom tell you to wait an hour before going in the water?" As soon as the question left her, Laine wished she'd not mentioned Kathleen.

Becca shook her head. "We don't have water at our house."

Relieved the girl hadn't been troubled by the reference to her mother, Laine ran her hand along the length of Becca's curls. "How about this? You can get on your bathing suit and play outside."

"Yippee!" she squealed.

Laine tilted Becca's chin and aimed her eyes at hers. "But on the hill, not by the water."

"I promise," Becca said, skipping toward the guest room, where she had dumped her sack of toys and a clean change of clothes.

Laine returned to her job in the kitchen, and when Becca passed on her way outside, she reminded her to stay on the hill. When she'd loaded the dishwasher and wiped the countertop, Laine grabbed a soda and headed for the porch to check up on her charge.

Having a child around the house seemed strange. But a good kind of strange. Becca's chatter and inquisitive nature kept Laine on her toes, always trying to stay one step ahead of the child's imagination.

In the living room, Laine heard Becca's voice through the open door. *Talking to the rag doll*, Laine thought, recalling that the worn-out toy always seemed anchored to Becca's side. Where she went, Penny followed.

When Laine reached the porch, Jeff's voice rose from beneath the screen windows.

Pressing her nose against the screen, Laine peeked below the sill. Jeff sat cross-legged on the grass, deep in conversation with Becca.

"I wondered who she was talking with," Laine said.

Jeff tilted back his head and grinned. "We're discussing important things. Care to join us?"

Laine pushed open the screen door and stepped outside. "Becca, this is my neighbor, J—"

"Jeff," Becca said, in a tone that told Laine she considered herself in control of the situation. "We introduced ourselves."

"Ah, you introduced yourselves. That's good manners." Controlling a grin, Laine folded her arms and gave Becca a wink. "Becca's spending the day with me."

Jeff rose and brushed the grass from his beige shorts. "You're a lucky woman. I can tell already that Becca's a special young lady."

A grin spread across his face as he lifted his finger and brushed a smudge of window-screen dust from the end of Laine's nose.

"Dirt?" she asked.

He nodded.

"You'd think I'd have learned."

His puzzled expression caused her to explain.

"Becca tells me you're going for a swim," Jeff said, giving Laine a stealthy wink. "Good fun. . .and a healthy distraction."

Laine nodded, knowing he remembered Becca's predicament.

"What's a distraction?" Becca asked.

"You are, my pretty," Jeff said, clasping her under the arms and swinging her in the air.

"Me?" she giggled.

When he lowered her to the ground, she gazed at him with admiration. "Can you swim with us, too?"

"If your aunt invites me."

"Auntie?" she pleaded, her eyes widening.

"Why not?" She gave Jeff a poke. "Keeping my eye on two kids shouldn't be any harder than one."

The joke flew far above Becca's head while Jeff gave Laine's arm a playful squeeze.

"I'll run back and put on my trunks." Facing forward, he moved away from them in a backward trot. "And maybe we could take out that old rowboat. I bet Becca would like to give it a spin."

The child's head bounced like a buckboard on a corduroy road.

With a contented sigh, Laine stepped back into the house, more than grateful for Jeff's kindness. With his tender disposition, Jeff seemed like a man who should have kids of his own. He'd be a great father.

❦

The thick carpet hushed Laine's footsteps as she entered her office the next morning. She yawned, standing beside her desk. During the night, sleep had evaded her. When her mind hadn't been weaving through questions about Becca's future, it had been riveted to thoughts of her neighbor's warm, friendly eyes.

Noticing the time, Laine gathered her folders and headed for the conference room. Since starting this new job, she'd learned she could count on the company's traditional Monday morning strategy meeting.

When she slipped into the room, she greeted her new acquaintances and slid into the same chair she'd used the first Monday she'd been with the company.

Hanging on the periphery of casual conversation, Laine doodled on her legal pad before the meeting began, but the random scrawls transformed into a list of the questions and concerns that had lingered in her thoughts during her sleepless night. Though she'd confessed her past issues with Kathleen, she vowed today they must deal with other pressing concerns. Especially her worry about Becca's future.

The meeting began, and Laine struggled to keep her mind alert to the various topics as the discussion bounced around the room. As the meeting drew to a close, the door inched open, and a secretary tiptoed into the room and slipped a telephone memo in front of Laine. The word "emergency" leaped from the pink paper, and without a word of explanation, she gathered her folders and left the room, her heart pounding in her ears.

At the first available telephone, Laine listened to Mrs. Dexter's narrative of Kathleen's condition. Within minutes, Laine had left the building and headed for St. Joe's emergency room. Her fingers gripped the steering wheel, and tears blurred the traffic lights as she maneuvered her way through the late-morning traffic.

Arriving in ER, Laine followed a nurse's directions to Kathleen's bedside. She stood above her sister, who had been wired and tubed to flashing machinery and dripping bags, and chastised herself for waiting too long.

When Kathleen's groggy eyes drifted open, her whisper rose to Laine's waiting ears. "I'm not going anywhere, Laine, until we talk."

Unable to speak, Laine could only squeeze her hand.

"Don't say. . .a word. Just listen," Kathleen murmured. Drifting in and out of sleep, she dragged sentence fragments from between her lips. "I've put your name on my bank account. . .and as beneficiary to. . .everything." She dragged in a breath, her face twisting in agony. "What's important. . .what I must know is. . .if you'll take care of Becca." For a heartbeat her clouded eyes cleared, their look piercing Laine's.

Laine swallowed the emotion that rose to her throat. Becca? She loved the child, but how could she care for her? Her work often meant late hours. Yet the look on her sister's pain-wracked face knifed through her, and she nodded.

"Say it, Laine. Promise me."

Laine couldn't remember the last time she'd prayed, but her heart lifted in prayer, begging God for wisdom. "I promise, Kath. I love Becca with all my heart."

Kathleen's rigid shoulders sank into the pillows, and her face filled with peace. "Thank you."

Laine backed into a lone chair next to the bed and collapsed, her knees shaking from the weight of her promise. If God could work a miracle, she'd give anything to have Kathleen rouse and heal. But reality smacked her between the eyes.

Gazing at her sister's tired, illness-strained face, Laine's thoughts drifted back to when Kathleen's rosy cheeks and sky blue eyes captured the hearts of every man she met. While Laine was plowing through her senior year of college, Kathleen had hired in as a secretary at Keary Investments, and within a year, she'd swept the young heir apparent off his feet.

Despite the Keary family's disapproval, Kathleen had eloped with Alexander Keary, only their witnesses in attendance at the wedding service. They'd shocked not only Laine and her father, but they'd also destroyed the dreams of the Keary family. They'd expected their son to marry someone with their social prominence, not a naive teenager who'd graduated only from high school.

Laine had struggled with her envy for years. Though she had been born with some of the family's good looks, her sister seemed to float above the world on ethereal loveliness and good luck. Without struggling through college, Kathleen had gained a rich and handsome husband, a beautiful home, and then a beautiful baby daughter.

About the time Laine had graduated from college, her father died, leaving a few bills and no inheritance that mattered. Laine lived in her cramped apartment, working her way up through the ranks of commercial designers, fighting her way through the backbiting world of work, wishing her sister knew a little pain.

Laine's wish rose like a dragon when Alex was killed in a small plane crash on the way home from a business trip. Kathleen was left with a young child and a large inheritance. Yet Laine had envied her the child and the money. And then the dragon's hot breath had seared Kathleen's life again in the form of Scott Derian. Scott had charmed his way into Kathleen's life, swindling her out of much of her fortune. As mysteriously as he'd sailed in, he'd sailed out again, leaving her with little, from what Laine could calculate. Kathleen was reluctant to admit much of anything in the aftermath of that relationship.

And now, once again, Laine looked into Kathleen's face and wished with all her heart that she hadn't allowed bitterness and envy to keep them apart.

"Laine."

Laine pulled herself from her thoughts. Had Kathleen spoken or had it been a dream? "Kathleen?"

Her sister's eyes fluttered. "I must tell you. . ." Her voice faded, drifting back into a drugged sleep.

Laine focused on the lights flashing around her sister's bedside and listened to the steady pump and hiss of the machinery. The bedsheet rose and fell in imperceptible, uneven flutters. Laine slid her hand to Kathleen's cold, still fingers, covering them with her own and closing her eyes.

What must Kathleen tell her? She watched her sister through a blur of tears, wondering what she could do for Becca. The child needed time and attention, and all she had to give her was love. Her mind flew to Glynnis Keary, Alex's mother. She should be told about Kathleen's illness. She would want to give Becca the best. This subject was the final thing Laine needed to discuss with Kathleen.

"Kathleen," Laine whispered. Her sister didn't stir, looking at rest. More peaceful than Laine had seen her in days. Then Laine's focus flew to the straight line on the monitor and the still, unmoving white shroud that covered her sister's withered frame.

Behind Laine's eyes the torrent gathered, pressing into the corners and along the rim of her lashes, then dripping to her hands. Laine lifted her blurred vision to Kathleen's peaceful face. Her heart stood still for one breathless moment as reality knotted within her.

Becca.

Chapter 3

Heavyhearted, Laine slid another carton onto the stack and wandered through the empty house. Even with the furniture removed—sold to a used furniture store—the house still radiated Kathleen's personality. Laine scanned the rooms, admiring the flowered borders rimming the ceilings and lending a hue to the painted walls. Color and cheer. She envisioned the joy that had once been Kathleen's before Alex died.

Painfully, she'd boxed Kathleen's clothing. Mavis's church sent a van to pick up the donation for their distribution center. Laine had only kept trinkets, jewelry boxes, and other personal items that she thought Becca might be pleased to have when she grew older.

Laine had wept as she and Jeff had dismantled Becca's bedroom and loaded it into a rental truck to move to her condo. What would Laine do now? Could she handle the needs of a five-year-old girl when she barely had a grip on her own emotional demands?

Again Mavis had been a blessing. She'd taken Becca into her home for two days while the contents of the house had been packed and dispersed. Though she was grateful to Mavis, Laine worried that Becca would again feel abandoned since she wasn't there for the child. But the work had to be done, and allowing Becca to watch the dismantling of her home seemed even worse to Laine.

Though Kathleen's death had been horrible for Becca, her mother's funeral had added to the toll. The utter finality of the service left the child despondent and overwrought.

And Jeff. What would Laine have done without him? He'd been more than a friend. Jeff had stood by her side, giving her support and strength.

During a rare moment, Laine had longed to lean on the God she knew as a child, but fear or confusion had blocked the road. She'd turned her back on the Lord years ago. How could she come to Him now with a heavy heart and expect His mercy?

With the last items boxed and packed in the truck, Laine gave a final look, locked the door, and slipped the key into her pocket. Proceeds from the sale of the house would become a small investment for Becca's future.

She looked up at Jeff. His eyes reflected his sorrow, and he wrapped an arm around her shoulder as she headed for the rented truck. Sliding onto the seat, she brushed the tears from her eyes and waited for him to start the engine. As he pulled away, she looked back one last time at Becca's past and then turned forward to face the future.

Sunday traffic was sparse, and soon Jeff was backing the trailer down her condo driveway. Knowing Mavis would bring Becca back in the middle of the afternoon, Laine and Jeff hurried the boxes into the basement. The child needed no added stress, seeing her mother's belongings packed away. Someday, when the time was right, Laine and Becca would share memories of Kathleen. The thought sent Laine's memory back to the day a week earlier—one of her last days with Kathleen—when the two sisters had reminisced about their childhoods. Becca couldn't spend time with her mother as she grew to be an adult, but Laine would share a wealth of her own memories with the orphaned girl.

"What do you think?" Jeff asked, setting the last screw into the shelving unit. "Becca should like all this storage."

"I want to get her books and some toys on them before she gets here." Laine felt her throat constrict with emotion. "Make it seem more like home. I hope bringing the furniture and bedding from her old room will make it seem more familiar."

Jeff braced his hand against an empty shelf. "You've done all you can, Laine. Every little thing helps."

"Nothing will help," she said, feeling her sorrow rise to the surface. A sob escaped, and tears rolled from her eyes.

In a heartbeat, Jeff reached her side, his arms drawing her close, his shoulder a sponge for her grief. Soothed by his quiet compassion, Laine pulled herself together, wiped the moisture from her face, and tucked back her shoulders. "Thank you. I'm glad I got that over with before Becca arrives."

"God gives you permission to cry, Laine. You and Becca. Tears are cleansing."

I don't want God's permission, Laine thought. *He took Kathleen's life and made Becca an orphan. I blame God. . .so why ask His approval?* Her bitterness fell like lead against her heart. Struggling, she pushed the hostility away. She recalled the verse her mother had so often quoted: *There is a time for everything and a season for every activity under heaven.* Laine shook her head. What purpose could a merciful God find for allowing this to happen?

"Okay," Jeff said, rubbing his hands together. "Let's get these shelves filled. It's almost three o'clock."

Surprised at the lateness of the hour, Laine let her thoughts shift to action. As she pulled books and knickknacks from the boxes, Jeff placed them on the shelves; and when they were finished, Laine added a few stuffed animals to the room and bed, then tossed the leftovers in Becca's toy chest bench and surveyed the room.

"What do you think?" she asked. "Presentable?" She jolted, hearing the door slam.

Jeff grabbed the last two boxes from the floor and carried them into the hallway.

"Toss them in my room," Laine said, rushing down the hallway toward the front door.

Reaching the kitchen, she found Becca standing by the table, clutching Penny in her arms and holding a duffel bag.

Laine opened her arms and knelt as Becca hurried toward her and pressed her head against Laine's shoulder.

"Did you have a nice visit?" Laine murmured, afraid to speak any louder lest her own sadness spill into her voice.

Mavis watched them from the doorway, then gave Laine a wave as she turned toward the driveway. The sound of her car's motor and the crunch of wheels on the gravel followed. When the sound faded, Laine pulled herself up. "Are you okay?"

Becca nodded. "Are you?" she asked with wisdom beyond her years.

"I'm okay. About like you," she said, wanting to be honest. "Jeff and I fixed your room, but you can move things around the way you like them."

"Where's Jeff?" she asked, her head turning toward the doorway.

"He's in the other room." She took Becca's hand. "Want to say hello?"

The child didn't answer but moved toward the hallway, and Laine stayed back, letting her pass through the doorway first.

Jeff's voice sailed down the hall. "Hi, angel."

"What are you doing?" Becca asked, her voice carrying down the hall.

"I'm admiring your bedroom," he said, his tone filled with encouragement.

Laine waited a moment, letting Becca survey her new bedroom with Jeff before she headed down the corridor. When she reached the doorway, Jeff had Becca in his arms, and they were sorting through the top shelf.

He looked over his shoulder and grinned. "She likes the books in a special order."

"I like things in order, too," Laine said, walking toward them and watching Becca shift the volumes on the shelf. "I'm looking forward to reading some of your books."

"We can read them together," Becca said.

Laine sent her a smile. "Sure thing."

"And I like puzzles. Do you like jigsaw puzzles, Jeff?" Becca asked, squirming in his arms.

He lowered her to the floor. "Love 'em," he said, wagging his eyebrows at Laine.

Becca surveyed the room then headed to the toy box. She dug inside and pulled out two puzzle boxes. "This one has kittens in the picture. See." She tilted the box for Jeff.

Jeff nodded. "Do you like kittens?"

She grinned. "Kittens and puppies. . .and puzzles. Will you help me?"

"Only if your aunt will cook us some food while we put them together." He folded his arms and eyed Laine.

"Right," Becca said, imitating Jeff's stance to perfection, "only if you make us dinner."

Laine's aching heart exploded with love. "I'd like to do nothing better."

Becca giggled as she piled the puzzles in her arms and headed through the doorway.

Jeff sent Laine a tender smile.

"Thank you," she said. The words sounded so simple in comparison to her depth of gratitude.

He nodded and hurried out the door to do Becca's bidding.

When she reached the kitchen, Laine opened the refrigerator and stared inside. What would Becca enjoy? Thinking of possibilities, she stepped into the living room but halted as she overheard their conversation from the porch.

"You know what?" Becca asked

"What, angel?"

"I miss my mommy." Her voice wavered with loneliness.

"I know," Jeff said, "Just remember that. . ."

Unable to listen, Laine took a step back and fled to the kitchen, her eyes brimming with tears. Pressing her knotted hands to her heart, Laine caught her breath and hugged the silence. With her life spinning like a top, she closed her eyes and whispered another thank-you, grateful for the handsome man who'd willingly joined her and Becca on the wild, whirling ride.

❦

Though the sunlight glinted through the window, Laine felt wrapped in gloom. Clearing the last of the breakfast dishes, she looked out to the screened porch. Like a tiny robot, Becca sat at a table with a box of crayons and a coloring book, her cheek resting against her left hand. Penny lay beside the crayon box, always close to her side.

Becca's emotions rolled like the tide. One minute, she acted like the happy child she'd always been, and the next, she bottled her emotions as tightly as she usually clutched the rag doll. Laine had no idea how to proceed. Jeff's influence proved invaluable. When he appeared, Becca's sadness often skittered out of sight like a shy kitten.

Mavis, too, stuck by Laine's side. She'd been Kathleen's longtime neighbor, a good Christian woman who'd often tended Becca when Kathleen went out. When Kathleen became ill, Mavis had become more than a baby-sitter. She'd become a caregiver. Now Laine could ask for no better friend than Mavis. The woman's greatest gift was her willingness to stay on to care for Becca.

When Laine first approached her about caring for Becca while she was at work, Mavis smiled. "I've watched Becca grow from an infant to a little lady. How could I say no? I love her as if she were my own." Laine felt overwhelmed by her kindness.

Laine had no knowledge of Kathleen's other friendships except for one lady who'd appeared at the funeral and later at the house. Becca called the woman Aunt Pat, and any concern Laine had about the stranger melted under the warmth of her niece's familiarity with the woman. She had been a poor sister for years. Kathleen certainly had needed a friend and apparently had found one in Pat.

A motion caught Laine's eye, and she turned toward the doorway and spotted Jeff at the door.

"It's unlocked," Laine called, heading toward him.

He pulled the door open and stepped inside. "All that sun outside, and you two are stuck in here. How about a boat ride or a walk on the beach? Becca, I saw some pretty stones washed up this morning. I think they have diamonds in them."

Becca raised her head and looked at him. "Real diamonds?"

Jeff flashed her a bright smile. "Well, maybe not real ones, but they're sure pretty."

The child swivelled in her chair and faced him. "My momma had diamonds." She lowered her head as if surprised at her own memory. "She said they were for me."

Jeff gave Laine a curious look, then turned his attention back to Becca. "You're a lucky young lady."

"Uh-huh," she agreed with a nod. Pausing for a moment, she turned to Laine. "Where are my diamonds, Auntie?"

Laine's heart sank. "I'm not sure, Becca. Hopefully, we'll find them someday." She knew where they were: in a pawnshop, most likely, or with some stolen goods dealer—wherever Scott Derian had unloaded them. Anger sizzled in her chest.

Becca gazed back at Jeff. "We'll find them someday," she repeated.

"That's great," Jeff said. "But until then, let's go check out those rocks. Okay?"

"Okay. Can we go, Auntie?"

Laine's heart lifted. Jeff did wonders for her and Becca. "Don't know why not."

She tossed the dish towel in the sink and slipped on her sandals. Becca grabbed Penny and headed through the doorway.

When they reached the beach, Laine slipped the sandals from her feet and tossed them on the dock, and Becca did the same. Dragging their feet in the shallow water, Laine and Jeff walked along the sand with Becca bounding off in front of them. Periodically, the little girl reached down to grasp a stone, then darted back to show them her prize before slipping it into her pocket.

Suddenly Laine caught sight of Becca and let out a gasp. Darting forward, she grabbed poor Penny, who hung precariously close to the water. She tucked the doll under her arm with Becca's permission, and they continued on their way.

"You look pretty cute carrying your doll there, lady," Jeff teased.

"If I had anything to say about it, I'd pitch this poor thing and get her another. But if I harmed Penny, I'd be in deep trouble. Becca always loved this pitiful thing, but since Kathleen. . .died, she won't go anywhere without it. I don't know what I'll do when school starts in September."

"Hopefully she'll be doing a little better by then. Kids are resilient."

"I hope so." Moments of silence hung between them, then she added, "I've been meaning to thank you so much for helping me with Kathleen's things. I hated to do everything so fast, but it seemed easier that way."

"No problem. I'm glad I could help. You've got a lot on your mind right now, I know, and Becca's going to need a lot of love."

"I love her with all my heart, but she needs more than that. She needs time and attention, and with my new job, I don't know what I'm going to do. Her dad's mother can give her every chance in the world that I can't."

"This is none of my business, but you know what I think. Love is the most important thing anyone can give her."

Laine knew he was right, yet how could she close her eyes to the opportunities, college, travel, social position—all those things the Keary family had to offer? "I don't disagree with you, Jeff, but I'll have to do what I'm led to do."

They continued in silence with their only interruption being Becca's shouts of glee when she found another "diamond" rock. Soon the child's pockets were weighted with pieces of stone.

Laine and Jeff filled their own pockets with the debris gathered by Becca since Laine didn't want to stop her. This was the first time the child seemed like herself since the day her mother had died.

Eventually, the three turned back toward the condo, and as they neared the neat, red-brick dwellings, Laine saw a lone figure sitting on the edge of the dock. As they drew closer, she detected a woman's form, but Becca was the first to identify the visitor.

"Aunt Pat," the girl called, skipping along the sand.

"Hi, kiddo."

As they approached, Pat rose and met them. "I hope you don't mind my dropping by. You said 'anytime,' so I took you at your word."

Laine had given that invitation in an attempt to be hospitable to Kathleen's friend, but she'd expected a telephone call first. "I see you found us without trouble," she responded.

"Yes, your directions were clear." Pat eyed Jeff. "I don't believe we've met."

"Jeff Rice," he said, extending his hand.

"Pat Sorrento." She gripped his fingers, her eyes riveted to his.

Jeff cleared his throat and extracted his hand. "Well, I suppose I'd better get home." He eyed Laine with a curious look. "See you later." Turning on his heel, Jeff headed home.

Pat watched him walk away. "I hope I didn't interrupt anything."

"No. We went for a walk along the beach." She gave a tiny head nod toward Becca. "A little distraction this morning. Becca's been holed up inside too long."

"Ah, yes. I'm sure things haven't been fun."

"Would you like to come in?" Laine offered, not really wanting the woman's company. Yet guilt rippled through her thoughts. Pat had probably been closer to Kathleen than Laine had been, and the woman needed time to heal, too. Becca's enthusiasm clinched it. She needed contact with her mother's old friends.

Laine guided Pat into the condo, and though she indicated a seat on the porch, the woman followed her into the house.

"Nice place," she said, gazing around the room. "Great the way you have a view of the water from the living room and the kitchen."

"I like it. How about some iced tea or soda?" Laine deposited the rag doll on the table and opened the refrigerator.

"Iced tea would be great."

As Laine poured the tea, Pat leaned against the doorjamb. "I'm sure things have been difficult for you and Becca. Even though Kathleen was sick for a long time, she seemed to go so quickly—it was almost as shocking as when Alex went."

"I know," Laine said. She handed Pat the glass. "Let's sit on the porch. Did you know Alex well?" she asked, glancing over her shoulder.

"Not really." The woman followed behind her. "Kathleen and I became friends after the plane crash."

Laine sank into a wicker chair, gesturing for Pat to sit. Silence hung on the air. As Laine pondered what the woman wanted from her, Pat finally spoke.

"You finished cleaning out the apartment, huh? Everything's gone?"

Laine nodded. "All, but a few mementos." Then Laine recalled why the woman had come. "Ah, yes. You'd asked for a remembrance. I'm sorry I forgot. Most everything's packed in the basement. Did you have something special in mind?"

Pat thought for a moment. "Nothing particular. A trinket. Maybe a piece of costume jewelry. She had a pretty pin she wore occasionally. Green stones, if I remember correctly."

"I don't recall it." How could she? For years, they'd barely been in contact. "If you can wait a minute, I'll run down and see if I can find a couple of the jewelry boxes." Laine eyed the woman, hoping she'd decline.

"If it's not too much trouble, that'd be nice."

Laine released a noticeable sigh, but Pat ignored it. She left Kathleen's old friend chatting with Becca and traipsed down the basement stairs. Reading the box labels, she finally located the one that held the velvet-lined jewelry boxes. Nothing of value had appeared to be inside when she gave it a cursory glance while they were packing, but she lifted the two boxes and carried them up the stairs.

Pat and Becca were coloring a picture when Laine returned, and she set the boxes on a side table and waited. In a few moments, Pat returned to her chair, and together the two women opened the jewelry boxes and peered at the brooches and earrings inside. Pat studied the pieces, tossing them back into the box while Laine waited.

"See anything you'd like?"

"I thought maybe something would catch my eye. You know, a favorite of Kathleen's, but I'm not spotting anything."

"This is all I remember, Pat, unless there's one more box down there I didn't notice. Give me your telephone number, and if I find another box, I'll give you a call."

Pat fingered a small gold brooch inset with a blue stone. "No, that's silly of me. This is pretty, and it was Kathleen's. I'll just take this one, if you don't mind."

"No, not at all. Take two if you'd like."

Pat closed the lid on the box without giving another glance at the other jewelry and then gazed down at the pin. "Thanks. This one is fine." She sighed as she rose. "I've taken enough of your time. Thanks, Laine." She turned to Becca. "Kiss Aunt Pat good-bye, kiddo."

Becca jumped up and planted a kiss firmly on Pat's cheek.

Pat turned back to Laine. "I appreciate your kindness, but I'd better get."

Laine followed her guest out to the driveway, and as the woman drove off, Laine gazed after her, sensing something but not knowing what.

Later that afternoon, Becca wandered into the living room and leaned her cheek against Laine's arm. The child broke her heart. Feeling helpless and confused, Laine wrapped her arm around the girl. "You okay?"

Becca didn't answer. She lifted her lovely blue eyes to Laine's. "Is tomorrow Sunday?"

"It sure is. Why?"

"Will you take me to Sunday school?"

Her question caught Laine off guard. "Sunday school?"

She nodded. "Mama always took me. But when she was sick, I went with Mrs. Dexter."

Laine felt her chest tighten. She had no idea Kathleen had kept up her church attendance. "Did she drop you off?"

Grasping the nearby rag doll, Becca pulled it into her arms, hugging it against her chest. "No, she went to church. Sometimes she went to Sunday school for big people."

A sinking sensation hit Laine's stomach. Now what? She didn't know what churches were nearby. But how could she deprive her niece of this tradition when the little girl obviously needed some things in her unsettled life to remain constant? She'd check the Yellow Pages or maybe call Jeff. He'd lived in the neighborhood longer. Maybe he'd know of a nearby church.

Laine focused on the child, who gazed up at her with curious eyes and a look of expectation. "Sure you can go to Sunday school." She smiled encouragingly. "We'll go tomorrow."

Becca's face brightened, and Laine sat with her for a few moments before she made an excuse and scurried to the telephone, hoping Jeff was home. When he answered on the second ring, she breathed a relieved sigh.

"Church?" A lengthy pause hung on the line before he continued. "Sure, let's see. There's Bloomfield Community Church and Christ Church. They're nearby. And then up on Long Lake is the First Church of Farmington. What's your pleasure?"

"Did you ever go to any of them?" Laine wrinkled her nose, expecting a negative response.

"Actually, I have. Christ Church is friendly. They seem to have a lot of young families with kids. Probably a good Sunday school program, if that's what you're looking for."

Laine nodded, surprised at his answer. "Well, Becca asked about Sunday school. . .and I promised."

"What about her own church?" Jeff suggested. "You could go there."

"It's quite a distance, and I'm afraid it might bring back sad memories. I guess I'll check out Christ Church tomorrow."

"If you'd like some company, I'll join you. Makes it easier if you have a friend."

"You would? You're kidding."

"No problem. Certainly can't hurt me." Amusement brightened his tone. "In fact, it might do me some good."

"But I thought you said you weren't a practicing Christian."

A chuckle came over the wire. "I don't have to 'practice.' I know how," he said. "I just don't."

She voiced a feeble "oh," not knowing how else to respond.

"I suppose you're wondering why I said I don't go to church, and now I'm telling you I go occasionally."

"I guess that's what was going through my mind."

"Once in a while the urge hits me. . .like tomorrow. I have the urge to go with you."

"I'm glad," Laine said. "Thanks. I'll check the times and call you."

When she replaced the receiver, she stood for a long time staring at the telephone. The man seemed to meet every need she had. Strange but nice. She'd leaned on him during the tragedy of Kathleen's death, yet she barely knew him. Sometimes she felt as if God provided for her needs in the strangest ways. Goose bumps rose on her arms at the thought.

Chapter 4

G et up, Auntie," Becca called.

Laine opened one sleepy eye and gazed at the smiling child leaning against the bed, her chin propped against the pillow. The smiling part surprised her. She opened her arms to Becca, and the little girl climbed onto the bed and kissed her cheek.

"Time to get up, Auntie. You promised we'd go to Sunday school."

Laine's pleasant expression flattened. She'd do most anything for Becca, but this request wasn't easy. She hadn't been in church for years. She'd even arranged for Kathleen's funeral to be held in the chapel at the funeral home, rather than face an hour or two in church where guilt stabbed at her. But today she had little choice.

She swung her feet over the bed and sat next to Becca. "You're really going to make me get up out of this wonderful bed, aren't you?"

Disappointment edged Becca's face, and Laine felt sorry she'd said anything at all. "Did I tell you who's going with us?"

Becca swung her saucy dark brown curls back and forth in a dramatic "no."

"Jeff." Laine stood and put out her hand for Becca to join her. "So I think we'd better hurry and get ready before he comes."

Becca hurried off toward her room. Laine let a heavy sigh drain from her. She had to be more careful how she spoke to the child.

She showered quickly, and since Becca had bathed the night before, the five year old was nearly dressed when Laine found her in her room. The little girl sat on her bed, talking to Penny.

Laine's thoughts darted around her promise to Kathleen, wanting what was best for her niece. She needed to make contact with Glynnis Keary. As the fraternal grandmother, Mrs. Keary had a right to know about Kathleen's death. Though they'd been estranged, Laine believed Becca's grandmother should have some input into Becca's future.

As the thought filled her mind, she wondered if her desire to talk to Becca's grandmother was based on a lingering hope that the elderly woman might insist on taking the child. As the reality of the idea jolted her, for the first time she resisted it. Could she really let Becca go away? Despite the child's sad and sudden arrival in her life, Laine adored her, and Becca was all the family she had left.

A knock signaled Jeff's arrival, and when Laine pulled open the door, she stood transfixed for a moment until her embarrassment forced her to close her mouth and invite him in. Dressed in a suit and tie, his stubble shaped to a short, neat beard, he rattled her emotions like a dune buggy on a bumpy back road.

"It came, I see," she said.

His face creased in question as he surveyed her face.

"Your beard," she said with a chuckle. "I see it arrived."

He grinned back. "I'm just giving it a try. Hair today, gone tomorrow." He grimaced playfully. "Sorry. I couldn't help myself."

"Doesn't look bad at all, really. Adds a little character."

"Hmm? Sounds a little like a backhanded compliment."

Her words hadn't come out as she meant them. He had too much character, but the beard protected her from his firm square jaw and distracted her from his full, soft lips. She didn't want to tell him that. "A compliment. I'd never in this world accuse you of not being a character."

Before he came up with a rebuttal, Becca wandered from her bedroom, ready to go.

"Look what we have here," Jeff said with an admiring gaze. "And who might this lovely young lady be? A princess?"

Becca giggled. "It's me."

"You?" He tickled her under the chin. "I guess I should have known. But you look bright and shiny in your Sunday school clothes."

She looked down at her royal blue dress with the pink trim. "It's new. Aunt Laine bought it for me. . .for my mommy's funeral." She lowered her head, her voice fading.

Jeff clapped his hands together uncomfortably. "Well then, I suppose we'd better be going. Can't be late for church."

Laine grabbed her shoulder bag, relieved that he had moved them along and changed the subject. But with each step toward the door, she grew closer to another difficult moment. Church. Her chest tightened, causing her to feel breathless.

❦

Laine stepped from the car, hesitant and concerned. Becca's early morning enthusiasm had continued during the ride to church, but Laine hoped the child would not be disturbed by memories of her mother once they were inside. Facing the truth, Laine's own dread knifed through her. With apprehension, she waited for Jeff by the passenger door. When he rounded the car, she and Becca joined him, and the threesome approached the red brick building.

From the church's classic design, Laine assumed it had been constructed long ago. The rectangular shape, topped by a tall steeple, took Laine back in time, and she fought the nostalgia that swept over her.

Entering through the double doors, she stood in the foyer and held her breath. Rather than facing the curved sanctuary or center altar of modern structures, she viewed an old-fashioned church like the one in her youth. It featured a center aisle flanked by long wooden pews. Ahead of her, stained glass glinted with the morning light, its colors spread like paint on the soft gray carpet.

Laine concentrated on the carpeting rather than the image created by the colorful glass. She could not confront Jesus' anguished face spotted with blood from His crown of thorns or His outstretched arms offering her solace and mercy. She deserved no mercy.

A deep ache reached to every limb. She pushed away her memories in an attempt to soothe her wavering spirit and turned from the sanctuary. Looking at the foyer walls, she spied an arrow pointing toward the Sunday school rooms. With Becca at her side, Laine took the stairs and located the woman in charge of new-student registration. When she'd completed the form, Laine followed along to the preschool class. She kissed Becca's cheek, and after promising to meet Becca when church was over, Laine forced herself back up the steps.

Jeff waited by the inner doors. He motioned her toward the sanctuary as the first hymn began. When they were seated, Laine longed to make an escape, but the weight of her sorrow nailed her to the hard wooden pew. Why could she not raise her head? With Kathleen's forgiveness, she should feel a sense of relief, a desire to move on. But her guilt clung to her like an insect in a spider's web.

A dark blue hymnbook stood in the rack, and Laine pulled it out, checked the song board, and thumbed through the pages. When the first verse began, the congregation rose, and she pulled herself up on quaking legs. Why had she allowed Becca to drag her here? She glanced at Jeff's calm profile, his pleasant voice singing the words to the familiar song. Apparently sensing her attention, he turned and smiled, his appearance comfortable and accepting.

The song of praise filled the room, and pulling her attention from the blurred words, Laine garnered courage and focused on the stained-glass windows. Not one image but many. Surrounding a lily-entwined cross, Laine viewed scene after scene of Jesus' miracles—healing a leper, turning water into wine, raising Lazarus, opening the eyes of the blind man.

Fighting her emotions, a sound reverberated through her mind—a voice as strong as thunder: *Laine, why do you wait to open your eyes? Why do you wait to be healed?*

❧

"How are those pancakes?" Jeff asked Becca as they dawdled over their after-church breakfast.

"Good." She turned her reticent blue eyes toward his.

What had made the difference? Jeff wondered. She'd clammed up after Sunday school. In fact, after they left church, Becca and Laine had become a silent twosome. Laine's discomfort had struck him as soon as they'd entered the building. Tension ticked in her jaw. Her lithe body looked rigid as if she were a soldier standing at attention. No smile, only dread filled her eyes. She'd mentioned one day that she'd drifted from her faith and needed to forgive herself, but her cryptic statement remained a secret. And he didn't have the right to ask.

Silence hung over the table, and he shuffled his feet, pushing back his dauntless curiosity until he lost the battle. "So, Becca, what did you think about Sunday school? Were the people nice?"

She moved her head up and down slowly, taking a sip of milk and wiping off the mustache it created. "They were nice."

"But it was different, huh?"

She nodded again. "I like my old Sunday school best. . .with my mom." Her eyes glistened with moisture.

Jeff swallowed back his own surprising emotion. He was tough. How could those two blue eyes wring such empathy from him? "You know what?"

Her head lifted, and she fixed her gaze on his.

"Change is hard for everyone, especially when it's sad," Jeff said. "And it's okay for you to feel very sad sometimes. I'm sad, too, once in a while. I'm sad when you are."

A look of interest rose on her face. "Did your mom die?"

"Yep, that was sad for me even though I'm a grown-up."

"When I get big, I just want to be happy."

Even Laine grinned at the child's statement.

"Well, I'll tell you what. I pray you get your wish." He turned his head to catch Laine's eye. Her face revealed a multitude of emotions—sadness, longing, amusement, pain. She slid her hand across Becca's shoulders, and the child looked up at her, wide-eyed, then relaxed. So did Laine. She shifted her gaze to Jeff. "Thanks for coming along with us this morning. And for suggesting breakfast."

"You can always count on me to think of food."

Amusement played on her lips. "The way to a man's heart."

"Among other things." His own cryptic message soared out before he harnessed it.

Laine tilted her head but didn't comment, and he felt relieved. These two ladies had carved a niche in his heart, a niche he'd never before allowed to occur. But he'd lost control. Like Laine's Superman, he wanted to rescue them from hurt and carry them away to a brighter day. But for now, that was impossible.

He eyed Becca coddling the rag doll. They'd convinced her to leave it in the car during church, but like a little mother, she insisted the raggedy thing join them for breakfast.

His gaze shifted from Becca to Laine. "So what exciting things do you have planned for this bright Sunday afternoon?" A shadow washed over Laine's face, and he was sorry he'd asked.

"I have a phone call to make—one I've been dreading."

"Oh?"

"To Becca's grandmother."

Becca's eyes shifted upward, listening intently.

"Have you talked to her at all since—?" Jeff lifted the coffee mug to his lips.

"No, but I must. I'd like to meet with her. I think we need to talk." She dropped her napkin on the table with a sigh. "But I dread it. I'm not sure what I want to say or do."

"Worried or confused?" Jeff asked, returning the mug to the table.

"Both, I suppose. I'd thought a lot of things. . . ." She paused, gazing down at Becca's curious stare. "But I'm thinking differently now."

Her gaze moved back to him and then to her niece, making it clear she couldn't be specific with the child's ears so tuned to the conversation. He watched as she reassuringly slid her arm around Becca's shoulders and caressed her cheek with a finger.

"It's probably best if you take your time. Let me know if you need anything, okay? If you want to see her today, I'll be happy to. . .have Becca as my guest for a couple of hours." He hoped he'd said the right thing. He assumed Laine would prefer to speak to Becca's grandmother alone.

"Thanks. Mavis would keep Becca, too, I think."

"No need, though. Becca's one of my favorite girls."

The child lowered her head with a giggle, and her smile lifted his heart. Her delicate face looked too strained for someone so young.

"Thanks. I'll see what happens. I might lose my nerve today. Though I know the sooner the better."

"I'd say. The longer you wait, the more strain you'll put on your meeting." He wondered how much involvement Becca had had with her father's family. Apparently little. Then he wondered why. He sipped from his empty coffee cup, amused at his preoccupation. A carafe stood on the table, and he grasped the handle, holding it toward Laine.

"Just a warm-up, thanks," Laine said.

Jeff poured a measure into her cup, then filled his own. He sensed a larger story here than Laine had offered. Was it a secret or details she didn't want to burden him with? How could he help to lift the pressure from her lovely shoulders? He closed his eyes, knowing he had burdens and pressures of his own he couldn't share with her—secrets that made loving someone too difficult.

Chapter 5

Laine sat outside the large red-brick colonial and stared at the well-manicured lawn, trimmed hedges, and pruned trees. The inside would be as immaculate. Wealth oozed from the mortar of the stately dwelling.

The telephone call had been disjointed and brusque. Glynnis Keary withheld an invitation until Laine admitted Kathleen had died. She'd hoped to tell her in person. The only sound was an intake of breath shivering through the otherwise silent phone line.

What did she want from this visit? Money? No. Sorrow? No. A home for Becca? She gazed again at the opulence. Though her heart said no, reality suggested otherwise. Would the child be better off with this elderly woman who could give her time, advantages, and, she hoped, love? Her head and heart wrestled for an answer.

Laine pulled the key from the ignition, gripped the handle, and pushed open the door. Her legs weakened as she approached the entrance on the neat brick walk. The bell chimed, and she held her breath.

When the front door opened, her heart came to a standstill. She'd expected a servant to answer, but instead a neatly coiffed woman wearing tasteful makeup faced her. They'd never met, and the image Laine had created in her mind shattered. Instead of the haughty and detached countenance she'd expected, a strained, sad face stared at her.

"Laine?" The older woman's voice was rich and full, like a mezzo-soprano, yet the hint of vibrato revealed her advancing years.

"Yes," she said, extending her hand. "And you're Mrs. Keary."

The woman nodded in acknowledgment as she stepped back, allowing Laine entrance to the foyer. Mrs. Keary's simple, yet elegant shirtwaist dress of burgundy silk swished around her upper calves. Her low, dark pumps moved silently on the carpeted floor. Laine gazed at the wide staircase leading upward, and beside the wide arch, an ornate table, holding an array of fresh flowers, reflected in the gilt-framed mirror on the wall behind it.

"Please come in." The woman led the way, and Laine followed.

Glancing down at her simple cotton skirt and plain blouse, she felt underdressed in the woman's company. With the wave of her hand, Mrs. Keary indicated a seat, and Laine lowered herself into a brocade chair facing a pair of French doors.

"Thank you for seeing me, Mrs. Keary. I didn't want to tell you about Kathleen on the telephone, but—"

"I left you no choice," she said, seating herself in the chair across from Laine. "I'm sorry. I hadn't heard from Kathleen in nearly three years, and. . .well, I certainly wasn't prepared for your news."

"She'd been sick, off and on, for a long time. I wish she'd let you know."

"Yes, I wish she had. And Rebecca? She's with you?"

Laine nodded, studying the woman as she mentioned Becca's name. A sad tenderness washed across the woman's pale face, leaving Laine with a greater ache. "Kathleen made me promise to take her before she died. I questioned her wisdom. I work long hours, and I'm single. But Kath insisted."

A lengthy hesitation sent a wave of discomfort edging through Laine. She waited for a response, a comment, something, wondering if one would come.

"And what would you have preferred?" the elderly woman finally asked.

Laine drew in a deep breath of courage. "At first I thought Becca should be here. . .with you."

The woman leveled her with her eyes. "At first?"

"You have time, money, benefits you can give her that I can't. But. . .I love her with all my heart, and she needs me. And I need her." Laine's eyes ached from holding the other woman's gaze, and she looked down to her cold trembling hands tucked in her lap.

"Who needs whom the most, I wonder?"

She wasn't sure if Mrs. Keary expected an answer. And she didn't know if she could respond. "Mrs. Keary, I—"

"Glynnis, Laine. Please call me Glynnis. I imagine, under the circumstances, we'll be seeing each other relatively often, and the less formality the better."

Her comment jolted Laine, the meaning lost somewhere in her confused thoughts. "Thank you." She organized her words. "Does this mean that you'd like to spend time with Becca?"

"I'm her grandmother. And you're correct. Time and money, I have in abundance. But. . .I must decide what's best for the child and for me. I need to develop a relationship with her. She doesn't know me at all. She was less than a year old the last I saw her."

"Yes, I know. After Alex's death, Kathleen didn't make any effort to stay in touch with his family. But you didn't either, from what I understand." Her words were sharp but true, and they needed to be spoken.

"I can't deny that. We were desperately disappointed in Alexander's choice for a wife. We'd expected much more. Though your sister was beautiful and sweet, she lacked—"

"Breeding, status, money. Rather shallow things, Glynnis. You never gave her a chance."

"We never gave each other a chance." Glynnis's sharp, blue eyes nailed Laine to the chair. "I realize I had the upper hand, but if she'd put forth an effort, we would have relented, you know. We loved Alexander. And we could have learned to accept Kathleen, too. According to my son, she was a loving wife. Apparently, she made him happy."

Tears pressed behind Laine's eyes. "And he made her happy. He loved her dearly. I'm sorry you didn't see it. After his death, she was terribly alone. Lost, except for Becca. She didn't have anyone to comfort her or give her support." She lifted her eyes to the woman's eagle gaze. "I let her down, too."

Empty space hung between them. They sat, immobile. The heaviness pressed on Laine's chest, aching, her breathing painful like pneumonia. She forced her gaze to remain locked with the other woman's. Each needed to face their selfish, loveless actions.

This time Glynnis averted her eyes first. "And then the con man stepped in." An unmistakable shudder rippled through her. "Everything Alexander worked for she lost to an evil, sweet-talking man."

"Yes, I think he took most everything. I haven't forgiven myself for allowing it to happen. I don't know what either of us could have done. Maybe something. But we weren't there, and Scott Derian was."

"And where is this man now? Do you know?"

"I have no idea. Kathleen did nothing about it. She was embarrassed and felt used. When I realized what had happened, I tried to convince her to tell the police. But she refused. She said he'd get caught someday, swindling some other lonely woman. I'm sure he will."

"We hope."

Laine edged her gaze upward. "I pray." The word "pray" had distanced itself from her vocabulary for a long time, but in the current situation, it seemed the only fitting word to use. She needed to pray that Scott Derian received just punishment for his crime, for hurting Kathleen, but most of all, for hurting Becca.

"I'd like to see her," Glynnis stated without fanfare.

"I'd hoped you'd say that," Laine replied. But now that she'd heard the words, she wanted to embrace the child, protect her, keep her safe. Could she give Becca to this reserved, prim woman? Jeff was right. Becca needed more than money and time. She needed love and laughter. Could she find that here in this rambling, luxuriant house? "I'll bring her for a visit."

"I'd like to see her alone. I'm afraid, without meaning to, your presence would influence our relationship."

🌿

So much time had passed since Laine had prayed. But today, as she sat in the car next to her condo, she lifted a prayer. If God didn't want to bless her, He would surely have compassion for Becca. Laine needed guidance. Had she made a grave error contacting Glynnis? Even the thought of losing Becca made her feel helpless and alone.

When she turned off the motor and opened the door to the warmer outside air, Becca's laughter sailed across the grass. She tugged at Jeff's arm as he sat in his yard, shaded by a tall elm. But Laine's pulse missed a beat when she noticed a woman also sitting beneath the tree. As she eyed the situation, Becca spotted her and came running across the grass to her arms.

"Auntie," she called as she ran.

Laine engulfed the petite, delicate child, wanting to hold her forever. She looked again at the two adults in the shade of the tree. "Who's with Jeff?"

Becca tilted her head. "Aunt Pat. She came to see me."

"Ah," Laine said, trying to sound pleased, but a strand of apprehension slithered through her. With their hands clasped, she followed Becca across the lawn, planting a smile on her face. "Pat. What brings you here?"

Her first words, though spoken to Laine, were aimed toward Jeff. "I just wondered how you both were. . .and if you needed any help." She finally faced Laine. "I'd be happy to take Becca off your hands for a few hours. Or come to your place if you need me to stay with her sometime."

Laine tensed, not understanding why she experienced this strange reaction to Pat. "We're doing great, Pat, but thanks. Usually Mrs. Dexter sits, but today was rather spur of the moment and Jeff offered." Why did she feel it necessary to apologize or explain her business to this woman?

Pat shrugged. "Well, the offer stands."

Pat's focus drifted back to Jeff, and her gaze dragged across his broad chest to his trim waist, then up again. Laine's hands knotted, and she forced them to relax. She was acting like a jealous girlfriend. . .and she had no right to feel that way.

Jeff turned toward her, his eyes like aspen leaves turning autumn hued. "So how did you make out?"

She had no desire to talk about the situation in front of Pat. "Fine." Her tight-lipped response clearly let him know how she felt.

He understood and asked no more. "So how about an iced tea, Pat?"

The woman shook her head, obviously sensing something was amiss. "No, I'd better be on my way." She stood next to the chair a moment, then shifted toward Becca. "Okay, kiddo, Aunt Pat has to get going. How about a kiss?"

Becca planted a quick kiss on her cheek, and with a wave, the woman strode toward the street where she'd left her car.

Embarrassment crept up Laine's neck. She had blatantly shown her jealousy toward the woman. She hoped Jeff hadn't noticed. Sinking into the vacated chair, she stared at the sun-drenched water. "So what was that all about?"

"Well now," Jeff said, "you tell me."

"What do you mean?" She squirmed under his gaze.

"Do I really have to tell you? You don't like her, and I'm not sure what bothers you." He tilted his head, waiting for her to respond.

"I don't know, either." She checked Becca to make sure she wasn't within hearing distance. "She makes me nervous. Like she has an agenda that I'm not sure about."

"Agenda?"

"I'm not talking about you either, Jeff. Some other agenda. I know I'm talking in riddles, but I sense something."

Jeff chuckled under his breath. "I understand." His gaze also drifted toward Becca and then back. "Tell me how you made out with the grandmother?"

Laine sighed, a long, unsteady breath, and told him about the encounter and her latest fears.

"I don't want to pry, but what's this all about? Why doesn't she know Becca? Obviously, Kathleen and she held bad feelings, but what happened?"

Laine laid the story out for him. She needed to talk, and he offered a willing ear. Most importantly, she needed someone with understanding and wisdom to help her weigh her decision.

Jeff rested his elbows on his knees, hands folded in front of him. "You mean they never relented. Even after Becca was born, no one gave in."

"She was only a few months old when Alex died. Maybe in time they might have, but. . ."

He waited while she sorted through her options for the right words.

"But Kathleen got involved with a man. Too soon, really. About a year after Alex died." The tears she'd kept under control sought release and rimmed her eyes. "I wasn't there when she needed me. No one was. Kathleen was totally alone with a new baby. She turned to Scott Derian."

He nodded as if he understood. "And where's Scott Derian now?"

"He split."

"Split? You mean he dated her for a while, then walked out on her, too?"

"Worse than that. He used her. Alex left her with a tidy sum of money. Scott was a con man, I guess. He wheedled his way into her life and walked out with most of her money and jewels."

Jeff tensed as his gaze locked with hers. "Money and jewels? What was his name?" He slid to the edge of his seat.

"Scott Derian."

"You don't have any idea where he is now?" Jeff asked, his eyes searching hers. "Did you suspect what he was doing?"

"I'd never met him, but from what Kathleen told me, I didn't like him at all. He seemed too slick and sleazy for me. His presence gave me an additional excuse not to see Kathleen."

Jeff leaned forward. "And your sister never reported this to the police?"

"She thought he loved her. . .and maybe she was embarrassed. After he split, I told her to call the police, but she refused."

"Refused?" Jeff caved into the back of his chair, letting a burst of air escape his lungs.

"What? Why are you so upset?"

Jeff corrected his posture and relaxed. "I'm sorry. I can't bear men who prey on women. It happened in my own family, and it doesn't set well with me, that's all."

"Really? In your family?"

He closed his eyes, and she could barely hear his response. "My mother."

"Your mother? You're kidding."

He flashed a fiery look her way.

"I'm sorry, Jeff. Obviously you wouldn't kid about that." She sighed. Her energy had been sapped away with so much happening—Glynnis, Pat, the retelling of her story, and then Jeff's statement. Too much.

She saw the pain in his face and couldn't ask him anything else.

❦

In the middle of the next week, Laine came home from work with a thudding headache. All day she'd thought about Becca's visit with Glynnis. She'd agreed to drop her off for her first visit on Saturday, and though she knew the child should get to know her grandmother, fear filled her. What would she do if Glynnis wanted Becca? She had to decide what was best for the child and not what was best for her own needs.

Massaging her temples, she opened the garage entrance of the condo. She heard Mavis working in the kitchen and Becca talking to her at breakneck speed.

When Laine entered, the woman swung around as if she were jerked on a chain. Her face paled, and her hand rested against her chest. "Oh, it's you." Relief sounded in her voice.

"Is something wrong?" Laine asked, wandering deeper into the kitchen and laying her handbag and attaché case on the counter.

Mavis's eyes shifted to Becca, then back to her. "No, I didn't hear the garage door open. That's all."

Something more than that had caused her ashen face, but Laine understood her comment. Becca was within hearing distance. "Is that for dinner?" She noted the bowl of greens the woman had rinsed and placed in a wooden bowl.

"Yes, I have chicken breasts marinating in the fridge, and I thought you might enjoy a salad. It's such a hot day."

"Thanks so much. How many breasts?"

"There's extra. Four or five, I think."

Laine nodded and eyed Becca. She needed the child out of earshot. "Becca, would you go out to the front and see if Jeff's car is in the drive? Or maybe he's in the yard."

"Can he have dinner with us?"

"Maybe. If he'd like to."

The child slid off the chair, leaving her coloring book behind, and headed toward the front.

"What's wrong?" Laine asked. "Something's frightened you."

"Oh, I'm probably being foolish. I noticed a car drive up and down the street a few times. It slowed each time it passed, and once Becca was in the back. I called her, and when I did, the car sped away."

"Did you get a look at the driver?"

"No, he had a baseball cap pulled down low on his forehead. And my old eyes aren't what they used to be. He was too far away."

"You're sure it was a man?" Pat came to mind. She couldn't help herself. The woman made her nervous.

"I saw the cap," the older woman said. "I suppose I assumed it was a man. Probably someone looking for an address, and I got myself all jumpy."

"Probably. But I appreciate you being watchful of Becca."

She nodded, her eyes focused on the salad fixings.

The front screen slammed, and Becca's pattering footsteps bounded through the living room. "He's coming," she called.

The words no sooner left her mouth then a knock sounded from the doorway. Laine leaned toward the front window that looked toward the water. "Come in, Jeff." Threading her way around the table and Becca, she stepped out to the screened porch. "Hi."

Jeff grinned, looking comfortable in cotton slacks and a sport shirt. "What's up?" he asked.

His smile, as always, wrapped her emotions like a soft blanket. She glanced into the kitchen through the porch window to make sure Becca was preoccupied. "Thought you might like some dinner. Grilled chicken and salad."

"Sounds great. And I just picked up some cookies at the bakery. Could be dessert."

"I think we have some ice cream, too."

His perception was keen, and a questioning look stole over his face. "So what else is up?"

She glanced again toward the window. "I might need a listening ear again, if you know of one."

"No problem. I know two good ones." His eyes crinkled, and he winked. "And very willing ones."

"Thanks. But after someone goes to bed." She tilted her head toward the inside. "Dinner's in an hour, okay?"

"Sure thing. I'll get home and slip into some shorts. See you in a bit."

Jeff meant every word, and following dinner and spending an hour amusing Becca before her bedtime, he became Laine's listener. With the back door locked and bolted, they wandered outside, and sitting on the dock's edge, they dragged their feet against an occasional wave as they talked.

Laine opened her heart about Becca, her feelings and fears, and once those words settled on the quiet evening, she told him of Mavis's concern. "Like she said, the person may have been looking for an address, but I'm getting a little suspicious."

"It's always good to be careful. Did she get a license number? Or a description of the car?"

"She didn't say. She thought the driver was a man. He had a baseball cap pulled low on his forehead. I was thinking maybe a woman could easily hide under a cap."

"Any particular woman in mind?"

She raised her head at half speed and gazed into his teasing eyes. "Okay, so I've already admitted Pat makes me nervous. I don't know why."

"Look, maybe I can check her out." He paused. "At least I can try." He stared down at his hands folded in his lap.

"How can you check her out? Who do you know?"

"I have friends. I know a guy who might be able to find out something. Don't be so nosy," he said, grinning at her. "You know I work with computers."

She eyed him, wondering if he was planning to do something illegal. "You mean you have secret ways to get into records and things?" Her hand gripped the edge of the dock.

He unfolded his fingers and caressed the tension of her hand clamped to the dock. "There are ways to find out lots of things on computers, if you know how. That's the only secret."

"Illegal?"

"Would I do something illegal?"

His smile sent her pulse racing. "Maybe. But I'd like to think you wouldn't."

"Then think I wouldn't." He shifted her shoulders around toward the lake. "Instead, take a look at that sky." He pulled her back against him and supported her with his chest.

She gazed above the tree line, and a sigh stole from her lips. The blue horizon shimmered with a soft lilac glow. Filaments of orange and amber wove through the periwinkle backdrop like spun threads, and a velvety cloud lay in a pool of liquid gold. Within seconds the panorama melted to misty violet, deepening to magenta and plum, and a sliver of an early moon, like a slice of melon, slid from behind the cloud.

Jeff's even breathing faltered, and he slid his hand over her shoulder and feathered her cheek with his finger. "Quite a show, huh?"

As she turned to face him, their gazes locked, and she saw the blaze of swirling colors of his hazel eyes. His focus slid to her lips, and like a bee hovering on the edge of a flower, he lowered his mouth to hers in a warm, sweet, unexpected kiss. He drew back, seeking her approval, before he found her lips again, this time lingering longer and sweeter than before. A tremor of pleasure shimmered through her core.

He lifted his hand and tilted her chin. Gazing at her, he studied her face.

"I've wanted to do that for a long time. And my imagination wasn't anywhere near as wonderful as reality."

For a pulse beat, her muffled voice hesitated. "You've taken my breath away." Her words were reality, too. He'd thrilled her with his unexpected, gentle affection.

They sat for a moment longer before Laine rose on quivering legs and suggested they return to the house. Though Becca was safe inside, a lingering fear hovered in her mind. With Jeff's hand wrapped around hers, they ambled up the path to the house.

Chapter 6

O n Saturday, Laine reviewed for the twentieth time where they were going and why, but the explanation was more for herself since Becca seemed to understand already. Shortly after lunch, they climbed into the car, and Laine drove the few miles to the Keary residence.

When they pulled into the driveway, Becca stared at the large, impressive structure. "Is this a castle?" Her head tilted as she peeked under the windshield's upper frame to see the three-story colonial rise in front of her.

Laine's hands felt icy against the steering wheel, though the warm sun beating through the glass was barely cooled by the air-conditioning. "This is your grandmother's house, Becca."

"It's a big, big house," Becca said, grabbing the canvas bag filled with books and small toys. She looked toward Laine, her small fingers clamped on the door handle.

With her nod of approval, Becca flung the door open and slid out into the hot summer air. Laine followed. No way would she send Becca to the door without leaving the youngster with a final kiss.

After pushing the bell, they waited. Again, Glynnis opened the door herself and stood transfixed, gazing down at Becca, who stared back at the stranger who was her grandmother. The woman was again covered in a soft, silky dress, this time a deep-hued paisley print. Her gray hair lay in short, soft waves around her pale face—the only color, her penetrating, midnight blue eyes.

She opened the screen door and stepped aside. Becca looked at Laine for approval to enter. She nodded, and the child stepped into the foyer.

"Don't forget my kiss, Becca." A strange peal of fear, perhaps panic, lifted in Laine's voice, and she cleared her throat to cover the emotion. She lowered herself to the child's level for the kiss.

As Becca turned, Glynnis halted them. "Please come in, Laine. We can have some tea before you leave. Let Rebecca have a moment to get to know me."

Laine closed her eyes, thankful for the older woman's thoughtfulness, and followed them into the elegant foyer.

Becca stood in the middle of the room, pivoting like a ballerina on a music box, as she gazed at the winding staircase and the crystal chandelier that sparkled high above her head.

A look of amusement washed over Glynnis's face, then she placed her ringed hand on Becca's shoulder to halt her turning. "Rebecca, you don't remember me.

I'm your father's mother, Glynnis Keary."

Becca's mouth drooped, and her eyes lifted to the full-voiced woman, looking down on her. "Are you my grandmother?"

"Yes, I am your grandmother. Is that what you would like to call me? Grandmother?"

Becca's gaze flew to Laine's and then, as quickly, returned to Glynnis. "Grandma," she said with certainty. "I'll call you Grandma."

"All right." Glynnis's face colored to a soft pink, but she accepted the child's decision.

Laine stifled a grin. Glynnis and "grandma" didn't make a good match, but she was pleased the woman hadn't tried to stop Becca from using the less formal title.

"Let's sit in here." Glynnis gestured toward the living room, and Becca followed behind her, lugging her canvas bag. Laine stayed behind, observing the situation.

Glynnis pointed to the same chair she had offered during the previous visit, and Laine sank into the seat. Becca backed up and leaned against her, showing a new shyness.

"Becca, show your grandmother the toys and books you brought from home. She'd like to see what you have in the bag."

The little girl stepped forward, tripping over the edge of the cumbersome sack, and emptied the contents onto the floor. Glynnis controlled what appeared to be a grimace.

Becca shuffled through the items, then handed her grandmother a torn page from the coloring book. "I colored this picture for you. You can put it on the refrigerator and see it when you cook dinner."

Glynnis accepted the jagged page, giving it due attention. "This is lovely, Rebecca. Thank you. I'll certainly find a nice place to keep it."

Laine chuckled to herself, knowing the housekeeper might enjoy the refrigerator location, but Glynnis would probably never see the picture there.

As the child dug for a book from her pile of belongings, the housekeeper entered the room with a tray. She stepped around Becca and slid tea things onto the low table. She turned and left as quietly as she'd entered.

After pulling a book from the hill of toys, Becca slid it into Glynnis's hands. The child stood beside the chair as her grandmother flipped through the pages. "I'll read this with you later. Would that be all right?"

The child agreed.

"Would you like some milk and cookies, Rebecca?"

A hint of a smile rose on Becca's lips, and she sat on the floor and scooted up to the low table. Penny appeared from the pile of toys, and she sat the raggedy doll in her lap as she waited.

Glynnis stopped, the cookie plate suspended in air, and gazed down at the doll. "Oh my, Rebecca, do you still have that old doll? That's the first present your father bought for you. I remember when he showed it to me. I thought of all the lovely dolls in the world, why did he buy you a rag doll?"

"She loves it," Laine offered. "She takes it with her everywhere."

Glynnis blinked her eyes as if awaking and turned to Laine. "She does? I am surprised."

"The doll means a lot to her. Memories, maybe."

"Yes, perhaps that's it." Pulling herself from the nostalgic moment, Glynnis sat the glass of milk on the table nearest Becca and offered her cookies on a napkin.

Laine accepted her cup of tea. With her hand trembling faintly, she moved the cup to her lips, then breathed a deep, cleansing breath, hoping to relax.

While the goodies distracted Becca, Glynnis turned to Laine. "I've been wondering if anything is left from Alexander's estate. Money or the gems? The whole situation breaks my heart. At least I would like Rebecca to have something from her father's inheritance."

Laine lowered her head, not wanting to be the one to disappoint the woman. Her voice caught in her throat, and she swallowed the hard knot that pressed against her vocal cords. "A small amount of savings was left. I'm the beneficiary, but naturally the money is Becca's. Nothing else that I've found."

"Nothing? The emeralds that had belonged to my mother? The diamonds?"

At the word, Becca turned to her grandmother. "My mommy had diamonds for me. Where are they, Auntie Laine?"

Laine squirmed with discomfort. "We haven't found them yet, but we'll keep looking." She looked helplessly at Glynnis.

"Yes, do keep looking. The diamonds were priceless. And the emeralds. . .were my mother's." Her words faded to a sorrowful murmur.

A sinking sensation slithered through Laine's body. What could she do? She had no idea what Scott Derian did with the gems. How could she ever find them?

❦

As she pulled into the condo driveway, Laine hit the garage door opener and parked the car. Since hearing the disturbing news of the strange car that week, she'd bolted the front and back doors before leaving. The only easy access to the house was from inside the locked garage. Anxiety was an uncomfortable emotion, and like a new sliver, its presence was felt every moment.

Glynnis offered to bring Becca home later in the evening, so Laine headed for her bedroom and slid into a pair of shorts and tank top. Sun and air might revive her and relax her tensed nerves.

She stopped in the kitchen and filled a tall glass with ice cubes, then poured herself some bracing tea. Returning the pitcher to the refrigerator, she glanced at its contents, knowing she'd eat dinner alone. Her stomach knotted in confusion, and she closed the door. Right now, food was her last concern.

Carrying her drink, she unbolted the door and stepped onto the porch. The midafternoon sun had ducked behind a cloud, and a refreshing breeze wafted through the open jalousie windows. She grabbed a canvas chair and reached to unhook the screen door. Her breath slammed against her heart as she stared at the hook and attached eye hanging from the doorjamb. Someone had forced the door open.

She dropped the chair and set her glass on the narrow sill. Swinging around, she eyed the front door. A gouge in the wood jarred her. Someone had tried to force open the door, but the deadbolt had discouraged them. Yet the two windows were intact. Why had they stopped at the door? To avoid the noise of breaking glass? Or had someone scared them away?

Her heart pulsed wildly. Had she perhaps halted the break-in? Did the sound of her car pulling into the garage frighten someone away? Her legs quivered beneath her, and she sank to the nearest chair. She needed to look around, but first she had to get a grip on herself. Why had this happened? What did someone want? The question seemed foolish. She knew the answer. Something of Kathleen's—it had to be. The whole mess began after she moved Kath's stuff to the condo.

But what? She'd gone through everything. Her sister had nothing left. One thing was certain: Someone else didn't know that. She leaned forward against the screen, looking toward Jeff's. Was he home? She'd rather he be with her when she looked around the house. Just in case.

She rose, her legs still jellylike, and went to the telephone. After four rings, the machine answered, and she left a simple message, "Could I see you when you have a minute?"

Her thoughts of relaxation marched away through the damaged door. Instead, she sipped the tea and waited. Questions shuffled through her mind. Scott Derian had split. If he'd hoped for more from Kathleen, why did he leave so abruptly? Staying by her side, he could have swindled the rest of her inheritance. Unless something happened. Had Kathleen become suspicious? Had she confronted him about how he handled her money?

From what Laine knew, Scott had supposedly advised her on investments. She entrusted her inheritance to him, bit by bit. He presented her with monthly investment reports. All bogus, she had learned after he vanished.

Laine closed her eyes, a deep, aching nausea rising within her. If she'd only been there to see what was happening. Love could blind a trusting person. And Kathleen had loved him—or maybe had needed a friend. Whatever, she'd trusted Scott.

"Hi."

Laine jumped at the sound. Jeff paused outside the door, his approach so silent she hadn't heard him.

"Thanks for coming over," she said, rising. "Open the screen and look at the hook and eye."

As he swung the door open, his gaze lit upon the doorjamb, and he paused. "What? Someone tried to break in?" His brow furrowed deeply as his eyes sought hers.

She nodded. "That's the only thing I can imagine. I took Becca over to her grandmother's earlier. I was gone maybe an hour. Hour and a half at most. It was like this when I got back."

"Anything missing?"

She shrugged. "I waited for you. Too afraid to look on my own. But I don't think he got in. See the front door. Either he gave up or was interrupted. He could've easily broken in through the windows."

Jeff studied the gouges in the wood, then wandered from one window to another. "How about the other doors and windows? You didn't check?"

"No, but I suppose we should." She turned and led him through the outside door. They circled the house, finding nothing disturbed. No prints in the earth beneath the windows. Next they returned to the house and searched through each room. Nothing. Whoever had tried to get in had failed.

Laine faced him. "This has to be connected with Kathleen. I've wracked my brain, and that's all I can imagine." She told him the thoughts that had gone through her as she'd waited for him to come home. "Does that make sense?"

"As much sense as anything. But you're telling this to the wrong person, you know."

"What do you mean?"

"The police, Laine. You need to call the police and report this."

"But nothing happened. He didn't get in."

"Do you want to wait until he does? Call them. Don't be foolish. That's what they're there for."

"Will you wait with me?"

He glanced back toward his house. "I have some things I need to do." He put his arm around her shoulder. "You can do that by yourself, can't you? Just call the number and tell them what happened. They'll send a car out. No problem."

Disappointment edged through her. Jeff always seemed to be around to offer support, but she was an adult. And she certainly didn't want to be another Kathleen. She'd criticized her sister for not reporting her situation to the police. She gazed at Jeff with a beseeching gaze, but he only chuckled.

"Listen, when's Becca due home?"

She shrugged, having only a vague idea. "Sometime this evening, after dinner."

"Well then, here's the deal. You handle the call, and I'll go over and come up with something for our dinner. How's that?"

"Suppose that's better than you holding my hand for a phone call."

"I knew you could do it."

"You've spoiled me, that's all. Whenever I need you, I find you nearby. Thanks for checking the place out with me."

"No problem. And when the police finish, come over. I'll be fixing you something wonderful for dinner."

He gave her a wink and hurried through the door. She watched him cross the lawn, pleased he'd thought about dinner plans, yet wishing he'd stick around while she dealt with the police.

Chapter 7

After dinner at Jeff's, Laine sat alone on her porch and listened for the car bringing Becca home. While she waited, the events of the past few hours dragged through her mind. The police had arrived quickly, checked the house just as she and Jeff had done, then jotted down a report and asked a few questions.

Finally, she did what should have been done long ago. She told her sister's story. Though the version was brief, she related everything. She noticed sidelong glances when she got to Scott Derian's role. Obviously, they'd heard similar stories.

Leaning her head against the wicker love seat, her thoughts drifted back to Jeff. Once again his cooking surprised her, grilled salmon fillets with herbs and bread crumbs, a salad, and fresh raspberries on vanilla ice cream. She closed her eyes, reliving his arm pulling her to his side and his kiss as tender as the last.

He seemed so different from other men she'd dated. They'd pressured and connived for more than kisses, but she'd always stood her ground. Their scheming turned her off—not on—and had pushed her right out of the dating scene for a while. Laine was tired of the wrestling match.

Though her faith had taken a shaky turn, her Christian morals and upbringing had apparently carved a deep set of values in her heart. As the faintest desire rose in her mind, an image of Jesus rose even brighter, then her mother's watchful eyes filled her heart. So her suitors left her side disappointed.

To her surprise, temptation had taken a new twist after meeting Jeff. He seemed to follow her same moral beliefs. Yet never before had she fought such a fierce battle against her own passions. But Jesus, like her guide and shield, lifted in her mind, and her struggle faded.

A noise sounded outside, and her heart raced with anxiety. Becca's excited voice drifted through the open window, and she relaxed. No burglar. And Becca had weathered her first visit with her grandmother successfully. At least so it seemed from the sound of her exuberant voice.

Laine met her at the door. Glynnis stood outside the car with watchful eyes. Becca, dragging a bulkier canvas bag than when she'd left that morning, took Laine's hand.

"You had a nice visit?" Laine asked the child, already knowing the answer.

She nodded. "Grandma bought me a new doll."

Laine's heart gave a tug. Poor Glynnis didn't understand. A new doll would sit in Becca's room. Nothing replaced Penny. She released Becca's hand and stepped toward the automobile. "I see Becca had a wonderful time," she said, approaching the woman.

"Yes, we both enjoyed the day. She's a lovely child. Kathleen did a good job raising her." She lowered her eyes for a heartbeat. "I wish I'd been able to tell your sister."

"I wish you had, too. But wishes are just that. So. . .what do you have in mind as far as Becca is concerned?"

"Perhaps an overnight stay. Rebecca seems willing. I did mention it to her."

Laine's stomach quivered like an aspen leaf. "If Becca is willing, I have no problem." Her heart thudded to her toes with her lie. She had a problem, but the concern was selfish and hers alone.

Glynnis returned to the car, and as the headlights faded, Laine returned to the house, planting a smile on her face for Becca.

❦

Sunday morning, the alarm rang, waking Laine and making her want to bury herself under her covers. But Becca's gentle reminder of Sunday school had arrived as she'd tucked the little girl into bed the night before. Laine was sorely tempted to turn off the alarm, roll over, and forget about her promise, but duty nudged her. Forcing her legs over the edge of the bed, she rose and dressed.

Less than an hour later, as they neared the church building, Laine initiated her plan. "I have some things I need to do this morning, Becca, so I'll drop you off at Sunday school and meet you outside right after, okay?"

As she slid Penny onto her lap, Becca lifted her eyes to her. "You aren't going with me?"

"Well. . .I thought you wouldn't mind." Her voice faded as disappointment settled on the child's face. "But if you really want me to, I'll stay with you."

Becca ran her hand over Penny, patting the pitiful looking doll. "Mommy went with me. Sometimes she stayed in Sunday school for big people, and sometimes she went up for church. You could go to the grown-ups' class."

A deep sadness rolled through Laine's chest, and tears she'd nearly conquered rammed against the back of her eyes. "I'll do that, Becca." She drew her hand down Becca's arm, resting it on her small fingers clutching Penny's cloth body. "I won't leave you, sweetheart."

The child's tensed shoulders eased against the seat back, and they rode on in silence, each in her own thoughts.

At the church, they headed for the Sunday school rooms. Laine's dawdling left them with little time to spare. The church service had already begun, and the organ's deep pipes sent faint vibrations along the oak floorboards.

The classroom hummed with children wriggling in nearly every seat, and Laine's feelings tugged at her, eyeing the teacher who had to handle the overrun of active students. The woman smiled as she entered and pointed to an empty chair near the front.

Becca hesitated, peering at all the faces turned to her. Laine pushed her forward down the zigzag row of chairs, then backed away as the girl took her seat. But Laine's own retreat was not made quickly enough.

"Excuse me," the teacher said, edging around a child and approaching her. "Are you headed to the service? Or could I prevail on your kindness?"

Laine's eyes widened as she sensed the woman's problem, and she squinted, then plastered a pleasant expression onto her tensing face. "You need something?" Her question was ridiculous. Obviously the woman needed help, but Laine decided to play dumb.

"Well. . .I wondered if. . .the girl who usually helps me left a message that she's ill this morning, and as you can see, I have quite a group here. I could use some help. . . ." Her eyes lifted to Laine's. "Especially during the activity after the story."

Her request reflected in her wide, blue eyes, and Laine couldn't say no.

The woman's shoulders relaxed with a sigh. "I'm Sue Barker, by the way. And your daughter is so pretty. I thought so when she came last week."

"Thanks, but she's my niece. Her mother passed away recently, and she's living with me." She offered her hand. "I'm Laine Sibley."

Sue's face reflected her shifting emotions. "Oh, I'm so sorry." Her gaze darted toward Becca. "Thanks for helping out."

She pointed to a chair, and Laine worked her way around the throng of children and tucked herself into the space and folded her hands. Looking around the room at the eager faces, she ended her inspection on her niece. Becca's eyes glowed.

Laine grinned and leaned back, washed by nostalgia when she saw the woman's teaching material. An easel standing to the side held a large surface covered with black velvet. Flannelgraph. How many years had it been since Laine had heard a Bible story told on flannelgraph?

Animated and collected, Sue faced the children. "Today we're going to hear a wonderful story about forgiveness. Now who can tell me what forgiveness is?"

Laine watched as hands flew in the air. Four- and five-year-old children defined a word she'd struggled with for too long. The time flew as Sue marched the cloth figures through the story of the paralyzed man who walked away after Jesus' forgiveness. Her own heart leaped and tugged at the message.

When the story ended, each child received a paper bearing the picture of a heart with the word "forgiveness" arching inside its shape. The youngsters took the red magic markers provided and colored—some neatly and some with wild abandon.

Laine helped clean the red from their eager hands and, with round-ended scissors, guided some and cut for others the heart-shaped pictures. With small safety pins, they attached the red hearts to each child's top. Sue offered one to Laine and pinned another on herself.

The lesson ended with the children singing an a cappella rendition of "Jesus Loves Me" as they placed their hands over their hearts. Laine joined them, but beneath the paper adornment, her heart tumbled and throbbed with the story of the forgiven man and her own need for forgiveness.

❦

Sunday afternoon, Jeff wandered outside, wondering where Laine had been all day. Becca sat in the grass and called to him. "Aunt Laine's my new Sunday school teacher."

"Is that right?" Jeff stammered, amazement barreling through him. "That's nice." He felt sure there was more to Becca's statement. Looking for Laine, he swivelled his head toward the enclosed porch.

Laine appeared at the window screen. "Not quite right. I gave the teacher a hand today since her assistant was sick." She turned toward her niece. "Now don't get your hopes up, Becca. That was only for today."

Sitting on the grass, Becca lifted her gaze to Laine. "But you could be, Auntie. She would let you come every week."

"I'm sure she would. But I'm not making any promises. And you can forget that hangdog look of yours, too."

Becca looked at Jeff. "What's a hangdog?"

He ran his hand across his mouth, playfully wiping away his grin. "She's teasing, Becca. Hangdogs aren't really anything."

"Oh," Becca said with a smile. "Hangdog sounds funny."

"It does." He flashed a secret smile toward Laine. "And what did you and your auntie learn in Sunday school?"

Laine peered at him through the screen and muttered, "Don't push your luck."

Becca looked up to the sky, ignoring Laine's comment, and thought for a moment. "I learned about a man who couldn't walk, and people put him through a hole in the roof to see Jesus." She paused, her eyes squinting in concentration. "When it rained, did the people get wet with the hole in their roof?"

Laine opened her mouth to explain, but the thrust of the story took hold, and the child continued.

"And Jesus was so happy that the man wanted to see Him, He forgave his sins."

"Wow! That's a good story, so what did—"

"But wait, there's more," Becca said, her hand on her hip. "The man who couldn't walk stood up and carried his bed away when Jesus forgave him."

Jeff staggered backward. "Wow! That's even better. So what did that story teach you?"

Becca scowled and lowered her eyes, then a bright smile lit her face. "When Jesus makes you better, He makes everything better."

"That's a pretty important lesson for all of us, I think," Jeff said, nodding slowly and grasping his bearded chin. He sidled a glance toward Laine. She had mentioned drifting from church and needing forgiveness. He hoped the lesson had made an impact.

He faltered, remembering how he needed to deal with forgiveness issues, too. For so long he'd lived with revenge motivating his life, wanting to get even for his mother's humiliation and loss from a con man like the man who had exploited Kathleen. Like the paralyzed man from Becca's Bible story, his life was handicapped by the driving force of vengeance. If Jesus forgave him his sin, maybe he could walk again without feeling the burden he'd carried for so long. He. . .and Laine, too.

"Step on your tongue?" Laine asked.

He lifted his eyes as Laine strolled from the porch.

"You got pretty quiet there, Mr. Not Very Subtle."

"Sorry. Guess I was thinking of my own situation. I have no room to judge anyone. I have my own problems."

She sauntered his way, but the expression on her face told him she'd been thinking about the lesson. And hearing Becca's simple words was definitely something to focus on. *When Jesus makes you better, He makes everything better.*

Chapter 8

During the week, Laine thought about the attempted break-in, and the idea that it might be connected to Kathleen's belongings stuck in her mind. Could something be there that she'd missed? Maybe if she went through the things once more, she'd feel certain.

With Becca at Mavis's, she waited until Jeff's car pulled into his drive and called him. "Wonder if you'd like to do me a favor."

"Hmm? Let's see now," he teased. "What's in it for me?"

His chuckle made her smile. "Pizza and possible adventure."

"Adventure? You know I love pizza, and you're tempting me with the 'adventure' idea. Explain."

She told him the thoughts dashing through her mind.

"I think I can handle that."

"Thanks. Mavis took Becca to her house for the night. Her grandchildren are spending the night, too. I thought it would be easier for Becca rather than rousing up her sadness."

"Good idea."

"We should have plenty of time to scout through the boxes again, just to make sure."

"No problem. So when's pizza?"

She gave him a time, and after hanging up, she rested against the chair, wondering how things would be without Jeff in her life.

Within a half hour he arrived, and following a meal of pizza and salad, they headed down the stairs and halted in front of the pile of boxes.

"I'm probably foolish to hang on to so much of this, but I know Becca will want the photo albums and Kathleen's high school memorabilia when she's older. I can't quite bring myself to throw some of this away."

"You don't have to, Laine. Becca can sort and decide for herself when the time comes. It doesn't hurt anything sitting here."

They each opened a box, flipping through photo albums and scrapbooks and making a pile on the floor ready for repacking when they finished.

"Look," Laine said, pulling out a small white New Testament. "This looks like one of the Bibles we got in Sunday school when we were kids." She turned the white leather binding in her hand and opened the book, gazing at the pages. "She's underlined verses and written in the margin. I had no idea Kathleen read the Bible. Studied the Bible, the way it looks." Instead of putting it on the pile, she slipped it into the oversized pocket of her blouse.

When they tackled the jewelry boxes, they sat side by side, looking for secret drawers or hidden compartments, but all their pushing and probing resulted in nothing. "I didn't think so," Laine concluded. "They look like plain old inexpensive boxes to me."

"I'd say so," Jeff agreed. "All this stuff looks exactly like 'stuff.' Nothing worth much to anyone but you and Becca." He rested his hand on the nape of her neck, kneading tenderly. "But like you said, if Scott Whatever-his-name-is thinks he left something behind, he might still be looking." He slid his hand gently down her back and turned his attention back to the box top. "If the guy was smart, he'd stay clear of you."

"I'm not sure about his 'smarts.'" She grimaced. "But he sure got away with this scam. Do you think he's still wandering around free?"

Jeff shook his head. "If we knew his real name, we could check it out."

"You and your 'check it out.'" She shook her head. "By the way, did your friend find anything on Pat?"

"Nothing yet. Pat did say her last name is 'Sorrento,' didn't she?"

"Uh-huh. Do you think it's an alias?"

"Could be. I'll talk to him again and see if he's come up with anything."

They reloaded the last boxes and piled them again in the same corner of the basement. Before they walked away, Laine paused in front of the few boxes that held her sister's life, and a wave of grief washed over her. Jeff pulled her close, and she rested her head on his shoulder, drawing strength from his presence.

"This is hard on you, Laine. In a way it's good you've been busy with Becca. It makes Kathleen's death and all your other problems take a backseat. But I'm sure tonight, plowing through the boxes, brings it all out again."

She nodded, unable to speak without sobbing.

"Ready?" He eased her away from the corner and moved her toward the stairs. "Let's go up."

"I'm okay. The truth just gives me a kick once in a while. I feel lonely. I have Becca, and that's it. In the whole wide world, she's my only family."

"I know it's not much, but you have me, too."

Standing at the foot of the stairway, he tilted her mouth to his and kissed her lightly, pressing his palm against her cheek.

She raised her arm and laid her palm against his hand, caressing his sturdy fingers. Then she touched his face, drawing her fingers across the prickly hairs of his new beard, feeling his strong jaw tensing beneath the hair.

When they inched apart, their eyes met and held for a moment, and she drank in the depth of longing evident in his gaze. When she could take no more, she shifted toward the stairs, and they climbed with slow, easy steps, their hands tightly clasped together.

After Jeff left, Laine prepared for bed and found the Testament in her pocket. She placed it on the nightstand, and when she crawled beneath the sheet, she opened the white leather Bible and thumbed through the pages.

She halted at a dog-eared page where an underlined passage from John caught her eye: "Peace I leave with you; my peace I give you. I do not give to you as the world gives. Do not let your hearts be troubled and do not be afraid."

She imagined Kathleen's fear after Alex had died. Or maybe the fear that rose in her when she'd realized Scott wasn't all he'd led her to believe. Laine's heart weighed heavy, and she flipped a page or two before another verse from John stuck out from the page: "I have told you these things, so that in me you may have peace. In this world you will have trouble. But take heart! I have overcome the world."

These words of Jesus had offered Kathleen comfort, and now the same words filtered through Laine's consciousness. She turned further through Acts and then to Hebrews. "So we say with confidence, 'The Lord is my helper; I will not be afraid. What can man do to me?' "

She repeated the words aloud. " 'I will not be afraid. What can man do to me?' "

Lovingly, she closed the small Testament and slid it onto the nightstand. If she read a little each night, she'd learn more about Kathleen. And perhaps something about herself.

❦

The weekend approached, leaving Laine apprehensive. Becca was to spend Saturday night with her grandmother, and Laine dreaded the event. Her thoughts swarmed like bees in and out of their hive. Would Becca be frightened or unhappy staying overnight with Glynnis? Worse, would she love it? What thoughts did Glynnis have for the future? Did she want Becca permanently? If she did, Glynnis would have to fight for her. That was certain.

But as the thoughts drummed through Laine, guilt rose as well. Glynnis could offer Becca so much—time, money, travel, education, luxuries, everything she would need to give her a good life. Then Jesus' words drifted from the back of her memory. What if a person gained the whole world and lost his soul? Were money and luxuries really that important? She thought about Scott and what he did to Kathleen, all for money. Money meant nothing if love and faith weren't the focus of a person's life.

The dreaded Saturday arrived quickly. As she waited for Glynnis's car, Laine hovered around Becca, like a mother hen over her chick. "You'll have a nice time, okay? I'm sure your grandmother has some surprises for you. And I'll see you tomorrow."

"Grandma said she'd take me out to lunch."

"That'll be fun." Laine was sure Becca had Burger Barn in mind. But Glynnis and fast food didn't jibe. A country club sounded more like Glynnis's choice for a restaurant. Laine closed her eyes, pushing away the envy and fear that jabbed at her like a bee sting.

When Glynnis arrived, Laine stood by the door and watched Becca join her grandmother without a backward glance. Penny was tucked under the little girl's arm, and Laine wondered what Glynnis thought of Becca's devotion to the raggedy thing instead of to her new doll. But Laine didn't care what Glynnis thought.

Selfish fear rose in her, and the words she'd read in Kathleen's Bible sailed through her thoughts like a banner behind a small airplane. "Do not let your hearts be troubled and do not be afraid." She needed to listen to those words.

Shortly after Becca's departure, Jeff called to rescue Laine from loneliness. "Let's enjoy the day," he said, his friendly voice filling the phone line. "How about an afternoon on the water? And then I'd like to take you to dinner. Sound okay?"

"Okay? It sounds wonderful."

"I'll meet you on the dock in a half hour."

As soon as she hung up, Laine dressed in her bathing suit, grabbed a towel and her cover-up in hand, and returned to the first floor. She had started paying more attention to security issues since the attempted break-in, and out of habit, she bolted the back door and waited for Jeff on the porch.

A burglar alarm came to mind. She'd procrastinated on getting one, though Jeff had suggested it more than once. The expense seemed foolish. Yet she'd hate to have her condo ransacked. She had little that anyone would want. But. . .

As thoughts marched through her head, Jeff appeared, heading for the dock.

Locking the repaired screen door, Laine entered the house, and after bolting the door, she exited through the garage, taking the remote opener with her. Such a fuss to protect mementos, but she didn't know what else to do.

A few minutes later, the two seated in the boat, Jeff pushed off into the glinting water. They sat in silence, soaking in the sun's warmth and listening to the soft splash of the oars dipping into the blue-green water.

Jeff's muscles tightened as he pulled the oars, sending them out into the lake and around a small island sitting near the middle. Admiration spilled into her thoughts as Laine viewed his strength, like a stanchion against all that could hurt her. Finally, she drew her attention to the small cooler he'd set into the boat, and she grinned.

"Bring your lunch?" She gestured toward the container.

"Our lunch," he corrected her. "Not lunch really but snacks. I take care of my girl."

My girl. The words rippled through her as sparkling and sunny as the tiny sun-flecked waves that danced in her eyes.

A pleasant breeze riffled through her hair, and a calm settled over her as she watched the shore drift by in the distance. In the quiet, they chatted about commonplace things, eventually heading back to the raft.

Jeff tied the boat to the mooring, helped her out, then hoisted the cooler onto the wooden platform. Spreading out a wide terry beach towel, Laine sat down, claiming one side. Without a moment to adjust to the water's temperature, Jeff dove into the lake. When his head bobbed above the water, he called to her. "Hey, it's wonderful. Trust me."

She laughed, certain the water was frigid. But she didn't argue and joined him, knifing deeply into the green lake.

To her surprise, he was telling the truth. The warm, clear water wrapped around her, and her hands cut deeply through its surface.

They laughed and played like dolphins, diving down into the opalescent shimmer of light and shadow, then rising to the surface, arms clinging, lips touching. Their voices echoed on the water's surface like children in bathwater.

When they tired, Jeff climbed the ladder and reached down to pull Laine to the raft. Sitting on the terry blanket, he stretched his legs, then lifted the cooler lid and offered her a soft drink, fresh baby carrots, cubes of cheese, and green seedless grapes as sweet and juicy as an apple.

"Not bad, kind sir. This is wonderful." She nibbled on the welcome snacks and swigged a refreshing drink of the soda.

He watched her, a pleased grin spreading across his full, sweet lips. "You look refreshed and beautiful. I worry about you. Tension is terrible, and you've had too much of it lately."

"Thanks. I feel good right now. Like I don't have a care in the world."

She flopped back on the cloth and stared into the wispy blue sky. "Not a care or a cloud. Perfect."

He lay beside her, his hand brushing her arm. "You're perfect. Well. . .almost."

She chuckled and swatted him away as if he were a fly. "I've been tense, I know. Hopefully, things will calm down. Once I know Glynnis's plans, I'll feel better. I worry she'll want to take Becca." She brushed her hair from her forehead. "I don't think I could bear it."

"Your sister wanted you to raise her. You have that on your side."

"But. . ." She rolled over on her stomach. "No one heard that but me. It's my word against Glynnis's. What if—"

"Hey, don't worry about what-ifs. They don't change a thing." His eyes sought hers, deep and penetrating, and lingered. Hesitantly, he spoke. "While we're on the subject, can I ask you a personal question?"

His words caught her by surprise, and she flinched before she could stop.

"Sorry, Laine. I'm not trying to upset you. I've wondered some things for so long and—"

"Ask me, Jeff. You've done so much for me you deserve to have your questions answered." Despite her statement, tension crept through her.

Jeff seemed to sense it, for he gently caressed her back and shoulders as he talked. "You mentioned a long time ago that you had to forgive yourself before you could be forgiven by God. I've often wondered what you meant. Whatever it is, I know it's pulled you away from your faith. . .and I'd like to understand."

Lying on her side, she propped her cheek on her hand and gazed at the lake, mesmerized by the flickering light on the water, then told him everything—her envy, her anger, her hurtful words. She sat up and crossed her legs, then told him about her sorrow and grief. "When Alex died, I felt that God had answered my prayer in the most horrible way. I'd always wanted Kathleen to know rejection and hurt. Things always seemed to sail to her on a breeze. And I. . ." She slowed, feeling the pain of grief ramrod through her body.

Jeff lifted her hand to his mouth, giving it a tender kiss. "My dearest Laine, God doesn't punish us like that." Jeff heard his words and faltered. He'd done the same, allowed his hurt and anger to heap him with sin and guilt.

She gazed at him. "But still I wasn't satisfied, you know. Even though Alex was dead, she had Becca, and there was Alex's inheritance. She didn't have to struggle to save a few dollars or get up each day to drag herself to college or to a thankless job, praying for a promotion or commendation, anything to put her up one more rung on the ladder of success."

Tears glistened in her eyes, and he rested his palms on her cheeks and wiped the tears away with his fingers. Her pain was his. He bent forward and pressed his lips on her eyelids, kissing the salty tears that clung to her lashes and wanting to let his own tears flow and cleanse his painful thoughts.

"I'm sorry," she whispered. "I don't mean to ruin our beautiful day."

"Sorry? Don't be. I asked, and you're answering. It's what I wanted. . . needed. . .to know. Thanks for telling me." Shame darted through him at questions he'd allowed to surface. Had Laine somehow been involved with Derian? He knew better, but his mind was programmed to question and search for answers. Troubleshooter. Another arrow of guilt struck his conscience.

She continued speaking as if he hadn't said a word. "The last slap was Kathleen's illness—as if God wanted to pound His punishment into my brain. I ache so badly when I think about it. My evil desires hurt my sister and Becca worse than I could ever imagine. My sin."

He forgot his earlier fears. Laine's pain weighed heavily on him. Feeling close to helpless, he sought something comforting, something hopeful that he could give her. God's love was what filled his thoughts. Forgiveness. He needed to understand and accept himself. He struggled to collect his thoughts, to organize his words, but Laine gave him what he sought.

"Remember the New Testament I found in the basement?"

He nodded.

"That night, I read some of Kathleen's underlined verses. And I've read some every night since then. The answers are there in that little white book. Forgiveness is nothing you earn. It's a gift. God's gift to us because we believe that Jesus is His Son and was sent to save sinners." She looked into his eyes, and he sensed the depth of her struggle.

"And if ever there's a sinner, it's me," she added.

"You're my angel," he said, drawing her to him. Her lips trembled, but he halted her tears with his kiss. Then he tucked her head on his shoulder and held her, his own thoughts reviewing the words she'd said. He still had so much to tell her, truths that he wasn't able to share yet. Someday he could let her know the darkness of his own anguish.

As he held her in his arms, a quivering breath eased from her, and soon she calmed, looking at him with sad but clearer eyes. "Let's not waste any more of this wonderful water," she said. "Swim?"

He nodded and helped her rise, and together they dove down into the translucent, cleansing water.

Chapter 9

Jeff drove them to a quaint, quiet spot with dim lighting and soft music. She nibbled on pâté and crackers, then enjoyed a special chicken entrée with capers and artichoke hearts on a bed of angel-hair pasta. The pasta took her back to Jeff's words—*You're my angel*—and she wrapped his loving thoughts around her.

Dinner that evening brought back Laine's smile. She tucked her sadness away, feeling cleansed and relieved. Filled and satisfied, they made their way home. Laine studied Jeff's profile in the dusky light from stores and street lamps that flickered past, grateful for his company.

"Thanks for filling my day. I kept Becca from my mind most of the time, and tomorrow she'll be back home. You've been a great friend."

"No problem. That's what I want to do always, Laine. Fill your days—our days—with good things. You know I care about you."

She nodded. "Me, too." She knew she had more to say and that he did, too; but they held back, each for their own reasons, she supposed. Time was one factor. They'd only known each other for a couple of months and under the worst conditions. She didn't want to misread her heart.

They rode in silence. He parked in his garage, then walked her across the grass to her condo. The moon streaked across the black water like a splash of creamy white paint. Its brightness dimmed the surrounding stars.

She hesitated as she neared the condo. A small basement window glowed in the darkness. She didn't recall being down there, not since they'd checked the boxes, and that had been a few days ago. She knew the light had been off.

"Something wrong?" Jeff halted at her side.

"The basement. There's a light on. I'm sure I didn't leave a light on down there."

"Don't start worrying already. You're getting jumpy." He slid his arm around her waist and continued toward the house. She hit the remote, and the garage door opened. Then turning the key in the inner lock, she entered.

Jeff put his hand on her back and moved around her, taking the lead. She followed him, scanning the room, but nothing seemed touched.

"It's the basement I'm wondering about." She headed toward the basement door, but again Jeff halted her. "Let me go down first, Laine. I know you're nervous."

"Thanks," she said. "For some reason, I'm really scared."

He stroked her cheek and moved around her to the top of the stairs. Halfway down, he paused, glancing back at her. "You were right. Someone was here."

"Oh, please, God, no." She darted down to join him. Kathleen's boxes were dumped and strewn in a pile, her brooches and earrings scattered on the floor, and the jewelry boxes seemed to be missing. The contents of Laine's own few cartons were also scattered around. Storage drawers were open, shelves emptied.

Laine and Jeff raced up the stairs. Her bedroom was in shambles, drawers emptied and tossed, her clothing thrown on the floor. Her own jewelry boxes were scattered on the bed. Becca's room was a jumble, toys tossed about. Her new doll lay in a heap, her dainty dress torn as if someone had stepped on it.

"I'll call the police, Laine," Jeff said as he left the room.

Entering her small office, she found desk drawers emptied in a pile. Her file cabinet was open, its contents strewn on the floor. A ragged breath tore through her. What were they after? Why the whole house?

In a minute, Jeff found her. "They're on their way." He paused, gawking at the room. "What a mess! Whoever did this came through the front window. You'll need that boarded up."

She stood frozen, surrounded by the contents of her previously neat drawers. "I don't know where to begin."

"Well, nowhere until the police come. As soon as they're here, I'll go over and check to see what I have in the garage to board up that window. I need to check my place, too."

They wandered down the hall, and in a few minutes, a noise sounded in the back. Laine peeked through the kitchen door. "Looks like the police."

"Good. Then I'll run on over and see if my place is okay. I'll be back shortly." He turned and headed to the front door.

Laine's shoulders tensed as she watched the officers climb from their car. In a matter of days, she'd had to call them twice. What next? A burglar alarm, she supposed—and thought of the old saying: closing the barn door after the horse got away.

By the time Jeff returned, the police had written their reports and were gone. He brought with him a large piece of plywood and nailed it over the broken window. "We'll get this fixed tomorrow. I'm sure I can find a hardware store open somewhere."

"Thanks again. Anything wrong at your place?" Laine asked.

"Nothing. I didn't think there would be, but I didn't want to assume anything. Did the police have anything to say?"

"No. They just asked the same questions as last time. I told them about the attempt a few days ago. I suppose I need to get an alarm system."

"Maybe, but if it's not random, at least whoever did this knows now that nothing's here."

"I suppose." She shook her head, still confused and trying to understand. "I can't let Becca come back to this mess. Either I have to ask Glynnis to keep her longer or get this cleaned up as best I can tonight."

With his thumb and finger beneath her chin, Jeff tilted her face toward his. "I don't suppose you want Glynnis to keep her longer than necessary."

He always seemed to know her heart. "No, I don't."

"Then I guess we have our work cut out for us. So let's get busy."

She noticed he'd changed to a pair of jeans and a T-shirt, and she grinned. "You're way ahead of me, I see." She gestured to his clothes.

"Didn't want to waste time. I'm not going to let you do this by yourself."

"I'll be a minute. . .that is, if I can find something to put on in that mess." She turned to leave, but he touched her arm.

"What can I do here while you change?"

"Oh, thanks." She looked around. "If my files aren't too messed up, you can stack them in a pile, and I'll put them in the drawers later. When you finish there, toss the pencils and stuff back in that top drawer. Then come up, and we can tackle Becca's room."

She hurried up the stairs, changed, and gathered her strewn clothing from the floor. When she had things folded and partially in drawers again, Jeff appeared at the doorway.

"Not perfect, but I have the folders in piles. I'll start in Becca's room."

She finished taking care of her clothes and tossed her jewelry into the boxes. Hers hadn't vanished like Kathleen's. Whoever took the other boxes must have thought that maybe one had a hidden compartment.

When she joined Jeff in Becca's room, her heart sank. He'd folded most of the little girl's clothing, but her toys were a mess. With a needle and thread, Laine sat on the bed and stitched the doll's torn dress.

"Why would they tear up a child's room?" she asked, frustration flowing from her tone. "It makes me sick."

"No screaming, just keep sewing. Hopefully, she'll never notice." He rested his hand on her shoulder. "Who knows why people do crazy things?"

"God knows," she said. "God knows everything. Now, if I knew, we could get somewhere." Her hands busied themselves with the needle as her mind raced, trying to put the pieces together both literally and figuratively.

❦

Becca didn't seem to notice the torn doll dress or anything else amiss when she returned from her grandmother's. She bubbled and chattered about what they'd done and where they'd gone, and Laine felt like the custodial parent who'd sent her child off to Dad's for weekends where she was entertained and coddled and then sent back home spoiled and unhappy. She pushed her jealousy back and took time each night to read the little white New Testament.

Two weeks passed with no news from the police, but no new problems raised their ugly heads either. Other than dealing with her fears about Glynnis, Laine relaxed. Then Glynnis called and asked to meet privately.

"Leave Becca with me," Jeff suggested. "It's only an hour or two. We always have a good time together. And stop worrying. It's not necessarily gloom and doom."

"I know, but I can't help it. I relax, and bang! Something else goes wrong. I'll go and get it over with, I guess. I'll call her back and arrange it for the weekend."

Glynnis agreed, and Saturday Laine walked Becca, clutching Penny to her chest, to Jeff's, then drove to Glynnis's with her heart beating in her throat. Fear gripped her, wondering what Glynnis had in mind. Though they'd cooperated with each other so far, Glynnis had money to fight Laine in court, and Laine still struggled with the difficult question: What was best for her niece?

The imperious house rose in front of her, and with trepidation she climbed the three brick steps to the fanlight door. The housekeeper greeted her and guided her in. An air of formality hung in the foyer, and Laine's breath tripped inside her as she headed for the familiar living room.

Glynnis sat in her usual chair, like a queen on her throne. A tray of scones and carafe of tea or coffee lay waiting for her arrival. "Good morning, Laine," Glynnis said as her guest entered the room.

Becca's grandmother rose and gestured to the chair where Laine had sat on her other visits. Laine eyed it questioningly, looking for the straps to tie her down and gas pellets to end her life. An ominous feeling clung to her—whether reality or fantasy, only time would tell.

"How are you, Glynnis?" Her voice caught, and a telltale tremor gave it an alien sound. She sat on the edge of her chair across from the elderly woman.

Glynnis looked older than usual. Though a tasteful hint of blush colored her cheeks and her hair neatly framed her face, something seemed different. Perhaps the look in her eyes.

"So," Laine said, directing her gaze. She crossed her leg, but it trembled so obviously, she lowered it again. "You had something to discuss?"

"Yes, but first have some coffee and a scone. They're fresh and very delicious."

The last meal. Laine couldn't swallow a scone if her life depended on it, but she accepted the coffee, controlling her quaking fingers until the cup rested at her side. The woman's gaze penetrated hers, and Laine sat rigid and waiting.

"I've been giving Rebecca's situation a great deal of thought. I realize we've avoided the topic, but school begins in a few weeks, and we should have things settled by then."

"Yes, we should." The words exited her in a whisper.

"Rebecca is all that I have left of my son. Yet I realize that your sister placed her in your care. I want us to do what is best for the child."

"We must, yes," Laine agreed, but the edging fear nailed her to the chair. She heard the beginning of a discussion she hoped she would never hear.

"I have the means to provide Rebecca with many good things. Though I'm elderly, I can hire a young nanny, and I can provide the best schools. Rebecca seems comfortable here. I enjoy her company. She's a lovely, well-behaved child." Her eyes softened. "Kathleen, I must say, was an excellent parent."

"Thank you. I know she was." Laine swallowed hard, forcing back the emotion rising within her. "But please remember that Becca is all I have left of my family—sister, parents. Becca is all I have."

"I know." She paused, lowering her eyes to her dainty china cup. "But we must think of what's best for her." She looked at her again, filled with new energy. "I realize you're young. You have vitality and stamina that I don't have. But you work every day. I'm here. You'll marry and have children of your own. That day is long past for me."

Laine closed her eyes, pushing back tears of reality that struggled for release.

"I believe that Rebecca would benefit from living here," Glynnis continued. "You would certainly have her for weekends, time in the summer, whenever. I'll be happy to share our time. I know you love her and want what is best for her. What I am asking is that you think about what I'm saying. We need to decide soon—before school begins. Whatever we do, I hope it will be in cooperation, rather than in opposition. I'm asking you to think about this."

Laine couldn't speak, and though she struggled, tears hedged from her eyes and tickled down her cheeks. "I have been doing just that, Glynnis. Over and over. But I can't bear the thought of losing her."

"You are not losing Rebecca. You'd be sharing her with someone who loves her as dearly as you do." A faint grin lifted the corner of Glynnis's mouth. "We had lunch at a fast-food restaurant last week."

Laine's heart dipped and rose, and a laugh burst from her, bordering on hysteria. She snatched it back quickly, controlling it to a chuckle. "It's hard to imagine, but I understand what you're saying."

"Will you give some thought to what I've said?"

Laine's shoulder lifted in a desperate sigh. "Yes, I will, and I have. Oh, dearest Lord, I have." Her words were her prayer.

Chapter 10

L aine tossed all hope of control aside when she reached her car. The love and fear she'd struggled to keep buried burst like a dam, pouring anguish and desperation through her. With blurry eyes, she drove back to the condo. Thoughts and questions piled in a precarious mound in front of her, waiting to topple and bury her beneath their confusion.

How could she look at Becca without grabbing her in her arms and holding her in a death grip? The impending feeling of loss and loneliness washed over her. She had to do what was best for the child. She needed to think clearly. She needed to pray.

Pulling into the garage, she saw Jeff across the lawn visiting with someone. She needed time to sort through her problems and longed to speak with Jeff alone. She closed the garage door, entering her condo through the kitchen. She needed to get a grip on herself before she went to him.

She changed her clothes and ran a cold cloth over her face and eyes, then adjusted her smeared makeup. She looked stressed but presentable. If she could only stay that way.

As she crossed the lawn, her heart sank. Pat sat in a chair beneath the tree. Becca leaned on the arm, apparently chattering as she often did. Why was Pat here again? And always when she wasn't home? Pushing a pleasant expression to her lips, she continued forward but knew her eyes told the truth.

Becca darted across the grass to meet her. Laine drew the child into her arms, struggling to keep her grip natural. When she reached the chairs, she added a congenial lilt to her voice. "Pat, how are you?"

"Fine, but how are you?"

Her face looked concerned, and Laine wondered if Jeff had told her about the meeting with Glynnis. The thought irritated her. "I'm okay. Why do you ask?"

"Jeff told me about the. . .to-do the other evening." She glimpsed at Becca. Laine relaxed slightly. "Yes, I've recovered just fine."

Becca swung her head from one woman to the other, appearing to know they were talking over her head. Laine ruffled her hair and sat in a chair beside them, her arms around Becca, who leaned against her.

Pat glimpsed at her watch. "Well, I hadn't heard from anyone and was passing this way, so I decided to stop and see how everyone was." She tilted her head and smiled at Becca. "I can't believe you're starting school in a few weeks. You've grown up too fast."

At the word "school," Laine's heart twisted. Memory of her conversation with Glynnis jolted through her. "She is, isn't she?" Laine said. "Becca and I have to do some shopping for school clothes in a few days."

"Yippee!" Becca said, clapping her hands. "I get new clothes, and you said a schoolbag."

"Sure thing," Laine agreed. "What's school without a schoolbag?" She sensed she was being overly exuberant. Jeff gave her a questioning look.

Pat rose and stood in front of the canvas chair. "Well, I'd better be on my way. Nice talking to you, Jeff. And good to see you, too, Laine." She smiled down at Becca. "Hey, kiddo, give me a kiss, huh?"

She leaned down, and the child planted a kiss on Pat's cheek. With a wave, the woman headed for her car, parked in front of Jeff's condo. Becca skipped along with her to the sidewalk.

❦

Jeff saw the pain and hurt in Laine's eyes but waited for Pat to leave before asking what happened. "Didn't go well, huh?"

"No. She wants Becca."

He saw her swallow back the tears, but the battle was lost, despite her efforts, and she wiped them away with her fingers.

"She wants us to cooperate and asked me to think about it." She lifted her brows, her eyes widened. "As if I haven't thought about it a hundred times."

"At least she's taking your feelings into consideration."

"Her arguments are good ones, Jeff. But I don't know that I can do what she's asking. I'm trying to think of Becca, but my own selfish needs stab at me. I can't bear it."

Her grief stirred his own sadness. He rose and knelt by her side. "Listen, I wish I could be with you tonight. I just got a call awhile ago, and I have to get back to work. Let's take time tomorrow to think this through clearly and logically. Okay?"

Silently she nodded, and he understood. If she spoke, her sobs would take over. Seeing Becca heading their way, Jeff touched Laine's hand. "She's coming back, so get yourself under control." He shifted back into the chair and grinned at Becca.

Becca bounded back, waving currency in her hand. "Look what Aunt Pat gave me. Ten dollars! For school clothes."

Jeff opened his arms, giving Becca a hug and giving Laine time to get a grip on herself. "Wow! You are a lucky girl to have so many people love you."

"I'm lovable. That's what my grandma says."

Laine's grin looked feeble. "Everyone thinks you're lovable, sweetheart."

Becca spun around and gave Laine a bear hug, kissing her cheek. "Would you hold my money so I won't lose it?"

Jeff only half-listened to the two chatter. His mind was distracted by the information he'd learned from Pat. So many questions were answered. So many new questions were formulated. What would he do now? Things were moving in, and what he'd kept hidden weighed him down. He wanted so badly to speak the truth to Laine, but he wasn't free to do that. Not until it was all over.

❧

That evening, Laine curled on her bed, tears running from her eyes. If only Jeff were there to listen. Yet she held the white Testament in her hand, seeking its comfort. Kathleen's underlined words had become hers. Over and over, she read Jesus' words found in John: "Peace I leave with you; my peace I give you. I do not give to you as the world gives. Do not let your hearts be troubled and do not be afraid."

She flipped through the pages, going back to a verse in Matthew. When she saw Kathleen's underline, she halted, running her finger along the sentence—a sentence that meant more than anything at this moment: "If you believe, you will receive whatever you ask for in prayer."

Laine closed her eyes and prayed fervently. She needed strength and courage to do what the Lord wanted her to do and freedom from the fear of the stranger who wanted something she didn't understand. She feared for Becca and for herself. When she whispered her "amen," a quiet peace drifted over her. She laid the Testament on the table and snapped off the light, letting sleep engulf her.

When the morning light peeked through the window, Laine woke with a gasp and sat on the edge of the bed. She'd slept the night through without waking. Though she needed the sleep, she worried if she would have heard anything if something had happened, if someone had broken in again. She would have, she was sure.

She reached toward the Testament and opened the pages, her eyes scanning the words Kathleen had marked, but she read further. Verse after verse, God's Word was renewing her lost faith. She finally grasped the meaning of forgiveness, and she better understood human weakness. As her flaws became clearer, she faced the need to forgive herself. But she knew in her heart, God had forgiven her already.

Her fingers slid along the inside of the back cover, and for some reason, she opened the Testament to the back page. She'd never noticed before. Kathleen had written down an Old Testament verse from Isaiah: "I will give you the treasures of darkness, riches stored in secret places, so that you may know that I am the Lord."

Why? What did this verse mean to Kathleen? Riches stored in secret places. The words tugged at Laine and made her wish she could search through the jewelry boxes for secret compartments again. . .but they were taken during the break-in. Below the verse, Kathleen had written two Bible references—one from 2 Corinthians and one from 1 Peter. She riffled through the thin pages, looking for the first reference.

"Aunt Laine," Becca called from the hall. "I'm hungry."

She stopped and glanced at the clock on her nightstand. If she didn't move immediately, they'd miss Sunday school. She laid the Testament back on the stand. Later, she'd find the verses. Now she'd better get some food in Becca and get them both ready for church.

❦

Arriving at the church, Laine pushed Becca toward Sunday school, but the child's fingers clutched hers, half-dragging her toward the classroom. She caught on in a heartbeat. Becca wanted her to help again in Sunday school.

As they came through the door, Sue smiled at them, focusing first on Becca, then lifting her questioning gaze to Laine. "Did you want to help me again today?" she asked.

Laine opened her mouth to say no, but before she could utter a sound, Becca shot out her answer. "She'll help. Okay, Auntie Laine?" The child looked at her with pleading eyes.

Wondering if she was making a big mistake by letting Becca manipulate the situation, Laine had no real time to reach any conclusion. She was caught in the middle. "If you need help, I'll stay," Laine said, pushing a pleasant grin to her face. "But only if you really need the help."

"I can always use help." Sue hesitated, then her expression crumbled. "Actually, you're saving the day. My helper has decided coming to Sunday school and church takes too much effort, so I'm really shorthanded. I could use a permanent assistant."

"Permanent?" Laine felt the guillotine pressing against her neck.

Sue's shoulders lifted shyly, and the look of chagrin reflected on her mottled cheeks.

Laine glowered down at Becca. But the child's face glowed with happiness, and suddenly Laine's scowl melted to a grin. How could she say no to either of the pleading faces that gazed at her?

"I can only give it a try," she said.

Sue's dismal expression broke into a smile. "Thanks. What a relief!"

Laine shuddered a sigh, lifting her eyes heavenward. She assumed the Lord, as well as Becca, was at work. With the situation out of her hands, Laine delved into her first day as an official Sunday school assistant.

❦

Arriving home from church, Becca claimed she was starving. Laine acknowledged that breakfast had been skimpy, to say the least. So as Becca headed in to change from her Sunday clothes, Laine remained in the kitchen, still dressed in her silky shirtdress and pumps. As she cracked the first egg into the bowl, Jeff's voice called from outside the porch. "Unlock, I'm here."

She hurried to the screen door, unhooking the latch, and Jeff stepped in, blurry eyed but smiling. "Sorry I couldn't be here for you yesterday."

Laine shrugged. "Work is work. I just wondered why you had to go in on a Saturday night."

He draped his hand on her shoulder. "It was a hot job. You know how that is. How are things going today?"

"Okay. Trying not to think about it." She forced a halfhearted grin. "We just got home from church."

He paused and gazed at her for a moment as if seeing her for the first time that morning. "You look better than okay. You sure look great."

"Thanks," she said, "but you aren't going to sweet-talk me. What do you really want?"

He didn't answer, instead slipping his arm around her waist as she guided him back to the kitchen. Stepping through the door, Jeff gave her a squeeze. "I arrived at a perfect time, huh? Breakfast."

"I should have guessed what you wanted. You can smell something not even on the stove yet?"

"I know. It's a man's thing, I guess. We have a seventh sense."

"Scents—s-c-e-n-t-s—is right! But seventh? What happened to the sixth?"

"Women seem to have that." Playfully, he bumped her with his hip. "Let me do these eggs. You go change your clothes, and then do whatever else needs doing."

She bumped him back and hurried from the room. If she didn't change, she'd have grease stains on her clean dress, for sure.

When she returned, Jeff was beating eggs, and she opened the refrigerator for the sausage links. Working side by side, a sense of completeness washed over her. Becca changing clothes in her room, Jeff helping her in the kitchen, it felt right and good, the way God meant life to feel.

"Jeff!" Becca squealed, darting into the room.

Her noisy entrance sent Laine's thoughts out the window.

"Aunt Laine is my pernament Sunday school helper."

Jeff lifted at eyebrow and gazed at Laine. "You? The pernament helper, huh?"

"That word is 'permanent,' Becca." She turned the sausages in the pan.

Becca repeated her. "Permanent."

"Right." She glowered at Jeff, letting him know he'd better not make a single comment, and with a dramatic thud, she popped bread in the toaster and pulled out two mugs.

Jeff ducked playfully and didn't say a single word.

Already the scent of fresh coffee filled the room, and Laine's appetite finally returned with a vengeance.

The meal vanished in less time than it took to think about making it, and Becca wandered off to play. As soon as she left the room, Jeff's hand grasped Laine's. He pulled it to his lips with a kiss, then held it tenderly. "So let's talk while we have a moment. You look so happy, I hate to bring it up. But things need to be said."

He was right. Pushing the problem away while he was there was foolish. Happiness surrounded her now, but later in the day when she was alone, the thoughts would haunt her again. She told him, as calmly as she could, the details of her conversation with Glynnis, her logical thoughts, her sorrows and fears.

His gaze caressed her face as tenderly as his fingers brushed the skin of her hand. She sensed his own emotions as he listened. Nuances of feeling moved across his strong, manly face, and though tears didn't pour from his eyes, she sensed them puddling in his heart.

"I hear everything you're saying, Laine. But I wonder about the priorities. Money doesn't give a child everything she needs. A nanny is one thing, but a mother substitute—a loving aunt—is another. Glynnis is her grandmother, yes. But how long will she be around to stand by Becca's side?"

"I've thought of that. But none of us know how much time we have, Jeff. Look at Kathleen."

He grimaced. "I guess you're right. We don't know for sure. I have no doubt Glynnis loves her deeply. Wherever Becca is, she won't be without love."

"I have a hard time separating Becca's needs from mine—knowing what's best for her rather than what's best for me. I've been reading Kathleen's New Testament over and over. I'm wearing out the pages."

"That can't hurt." He squeezed her fingers gently. "Maybe God used this awful situation to reel you back in, Laine."

"I've thought of that, too." The little Testament stayed in her thoughts, and she remembered Kathleen's penciled references on its back page. "Wait a minute. I want to show you something."

She rose and returned quickly with the New Testament. "Look at this verse Kathleen wrote from the Old Testament. What do you think?"

He read her scrawled words and frowned. "I'm not sure. Maybe she realized Derian was after her money and jewelry."

"That could be it. What I saw was the reference to 'hidden in secret places.' I thought about us searching for hidden compartments in her jewelry boxes weeks ago."

He tapped his fingers against the tabletop. "Right, and so did whoever broke in here. He must've had a similar idea."

"Anyway, there's more. See, she's written references here." Taking the book from Jeff, Laine turned to the first verse Kathleen had noted. They scanned the words together. Phrases jumped out at Laine: "do not lose heart. . .wasting away. . . being renewed day by day. . .momentary troubles. . . eternal glory that far outweighs them all."

She pointed to the words. "Kathleen knew she was dying. There's no question." She ached for her sister's lonely suffering.

Pressure pushed against her throat, but as she continued reading the verse, the last words caught her attention: "So we fix our eyes not on what is seen, but on what is unseen. For what is seen is temporary, but what is unseen is eternal."

Things unseen? Earlier she'd read "stored in secret places." "Look at these words, Jeff. Was Kathleen saying something? Or is my imagination too vivid?"

"I don't know, Laine, but I see what you're saying. It makes you wonder. But don't get your hopes up. 'Things unseen' refers to God's grace and mercy—salvation."

"I know, but it's the particular words that makes me wonder. " 'Things unseen.' I just can't help thinking it means something." Her pulse raced as she hunted through 1 Peter, the next reference. "Listen to this: 'Your beauty should not come from outward adornment, such as braided hair and the wearing of gold jewelry and fine clothes. Instead, it should be that of your inner self, the unfading beauty of a gentle and quiet spirit, which is of great worth in God's sight.' "

She heard him take a deep breath. "Are you thinking what I am? The jewelry? The diamonds? Is there a connection?"

Jeff rubbed his hand along her arm. "Maybe she's saying she got rid of the jewelry. Or she might mean nothing at all. If she knew she was dying, perhaps she was reminding herself that her faith and beliefs were more important than a jewel in God's sight. That could be all she's saying."

Laine stared at the words. While Jeff had a point, in her heart, she believed Kathleen was sending her or someone a message.

Chapter 11

When Laine arrived home from work on Monday, she did everything except call Glynnis. Jeff's words sat in her mind, and like the scale of justice, she piled one set of possibilities on one side and another set on the other. The balance was precarious. It could be tipped either way by a breath of wind.

School was fast approaching, and shopping was a needed and useful escape. After dinner, with Becca in tow, Laine entered the nearest mall. They headed for the popular department store where a "school sale" banner draped across the entrance. Wandering down the aisles, Laine felt distracted, but Becca skipped along, excited to be shopping for her first school clothes.

Laine knew school shopping was a dreaded task for many a parent, but Becca was so young. Shopping with a five year old, she thought, couldn't be that difficult. But it wasn't long before she was gaping in amazement as Becca turned her nose up at one outfit after another. She didn't like the color. This dress was for little girls. Stripes going sideways looked silly. She didn't like tops that were tight around her neck—one problem after another. Though Laine tried to be firm, Becca's distinct fashion style made her grin. Her niece knew what she wanted.

After trying on numerous mix-and-match pieces, they'd only agreed on two sets. Laine gave up on outer garments and found undergarments an easier sell. A new pair of shoes was added to their purchases, and finally, they found their way to the book bags.

Here, Laine gave Becca free rein, and she enjoyed every minute, trying them on, checking the pockets, selecting the color, and unzipping, unsnapping, and unhooking everything. Laine snickered at her antics until, with bright smiles, they headed to the checkout counter.

"Could we have a treat?" Becca asked as Laine signed the charge-card bill.

"Treat? What do you call all this stuff in these bags?"

Becca giggled. "School clothes and stuff."

"Ah, and you want a food treat."

She nodded her head, a sly grin on her lips.

"I thought we just had dinner a short time ago. How about a soft drink?"

"Is that all?" A playful pout pulled on her bottom lip.

Laine gave her a wink. "We could have an ice cream."

Becca's head bobbed up and down like a paddleball.

Balancing her bulky packages, Laine clutched Becca's hand and guided her through the mall. As they headed for the small snack bar, her heart lurched. She faltered.

Turning quickly away, she blocked the view and rounded a corner. Becca noticed everything, and her questioning gaze swept over Laine's face. "What's wrong? The snack place is that way." She pointed back through the mall.

"I know, but I have to sit for a minute and get organized." Laine slumped to a nearby bench, her hands trembling. Becca's perceptive eyes watched her, but she asked no more questions.

Laine opened her sacks, putting smaller parcels in larger bags, anything to pass time while she thought. She had seen Jeff seated inside the coffee shop around the corner. Pat sat across from him. They leaned together talking, looking deeply into each other's eyes. What did it mean? No matter what the answer might be, she decided it wasn't what she wanted to hear. She couldn't believe they were dating secretly. But she remembered Pat had focused an admiring eye on Jeff the first day they'd met. She'd stared at him with interest. But who wouldn't? Laine had passed it off.

Suddenly, Laine viewed Pat's visit with Jeff and Becca a few days earlier differently. If Pat had come to see Becca, why had she parked at Jeff's? When Becca had run to kiss the woman good-bye, Laine recalled distinctly that Pat's car had been in front of Jeff's condo, not hers. Laine's heart hammered.

So what did it mean? Were they working together? Partners in some kind of con game? Lately she'd become suspicious of everything. She couldn't believe they were the people who'd broken into her condo looking for Kathleen's jewelry or money that Laine wasn't even sure existed. She'd felt uneasy around Pat from the first day when she'd showed up unannounced at her house. She'd never understood why, but that's how she felt.

Yet she hadn't suspected Jeff. He was different. He'd been helpful. He'd even told her his friend would check on Pat. Was that only a cover-up? Laine closed her eyes, feeling betrayed and forsaken. She didn't know where to turn.

Jeff had spoken of God and forgiveness. Was it all a lie? Was his affection for her a lie? Was she another Kathleen, blindly trusting a man because she needed a friend? Needed someone to love? Her mind swirled like a raging river, and she was caught in the swift, surging current.

"Auntie, let's go," Becca urged.

Impelled by Becca's pleading, she rose on trembling knees and retraced her steps toward the small snack stand near the parking entrance. What would she say to Jeff? If he were lying, whom could she turn to?

Whom could she turn to?

All the way home through Becca's chatter, Laine sorted out her thoughts. She didn't want to see Jeff. How could she avoid him? A plan began to formulate. She needed time to think. When she arrived home, she'd call Mavis and see if Becca could spend the night. Mavis could bring her home in the morning.

Then what? She didn't have a friend in the world except Jeff, and now. . .now she didn't have a friend in the world. She had to stay away from the house, away from him. At least until she could make sense out of what she'd just seen.

She forced herself to move calmly so as not to frighten Becca. She made the call first. When she hung up from talking with Mavis, she called Becca. "Guess what?"

Becca shrugged.

"You're going to spend the night with Mrs. Dexter."

Her face wrinkled with a scowl. "Why?"

"Because I have some things to do, and I know you don't want me to drag you all over town. You'll have lots more fun at Mrs. Dexter's. Okay?"

"I guess." She shrugged again, looking disappointed.

"Let's throw some PJs in your new backpack."

The backpack idea cheered Becca up. After tossing clean clothes and pajamas into the canvas bag, Laine had the little girl gather up a couple special toys, and she slipped into her own room.

Glancing through her closet, she looked for something to put her clothes in. The last thing she wanted to do was scare Becca by leaving with a piece of luggage. She found an old duffel bag, and pulling it from the closet, she packed what she needed for work the following day. She'd stay away tonight. She was being overly dramatic maybe, but she couldn't handle anything more tonight.

At the last minute, she placed the New Testament into the bag, zipping it closed. Laine looked around her bedroom one last time to make sure she hadn't forgotten anything. She rubbed her neck, planted a pleasant look on her face, then hurried toward the kitchen. As she came through the doorway, Becca skipped toward her with a white envelope in her hand.

"What's that, sweetheart?"

Curious, Becca turned the paper over in her fingers. "I found it pushed under the porch door."

Laine held out her hand, her hopes lifting. "It's probably from Jeff." Becca handed her the note, and she slipped open the sealed envelope. She prayed there was an explanation from him, something to explain his meeting Pat, something that would make her present plan seem foolish and stupid. Instead, a gasp shot from her without thinking.

Becca's face paled, and she grabbed Laine's skirt. "What's wrong?" She clung to Laine's arm.

"I'm sorry, sweetie. The note surprised me, that's all. Nothing's wrong." She glanced at the child's face, realizing that her false words had only lightened Becca's fear. The girl's grip on Laine's forearm remained uncomfortably tight.

Laine shoved the note into her pocket, hoping she appeared casual. "It's from Jeff. He has to work again tonight. I just feel sorry for him."

"Me, too," Becca agreed, accepting her explanation.

"Well, we'd better get going. Mrs. Dexter's expecting us."

Laine moved calmly, though her heart raced as if she were in a high-speed chase. The note might have been from Jeff, but it certainly didn't match what she had told Becca. It was an ominous threat. No demands. No ransom. Nothing. Only the words: "You or the kid knows where the diamonds are. You can't hide them much longer."

Was she right? Were Jeff and Pat in this together? Even as she considered the idea, her heart screamed no. The whole thing made no sense. She knew nothing. Becca knew nothing. What was she to do?

After she planted Becca safely at Mavis's, Laine headed for the police station. Without Jeff's guidance, she couldn't ignore the message. And now, she couldn't trust Jeff. Stating her business, she was directed to an officer she recognized as one of the men who'd come following the break-in.

He read the note and looked at her. "No idea where this came from then?" he asked.

"My niece found it tonight on the porch, slipped under the screen door. Naturally, my first thought was that it came from the man I told you about the night of the break-in."

He scanned the report he'd pulled from the file drawer. "Scott Derian, huh?"

"Yes. He conned my sister out of a great deal of money. I explained that before."

He nodded. "I see it here in the report." He eyed her. "Why didn't your sister notify the police about this?"

Laine shrugged. "I don't know. Afraid of retribution? Humiliated? Ashamed of her gullibility? Your guess is as good as mine."

"You should have insisted."

"Yes, I suppose. But I lived far away then." Excuses. How could she tell him she'd harbored bad feelings toward her sister then? That she'd avoided contact with her?

"So what's your second thought?"

She frowned, squinting at him. "What do you mean?"

"You said your first thought was Scott Derian. What was your second thought?"

Had she really said 'first thought'? Jeff or Pat or both was her second thought. "I'm not sure what I meant. . .exactly."

His eyes narrowed. "Could you give it a try?" He folded his arms and leaned back in his chair, staring at her.

Was he interrogating her? All he needed was the spotlight. "What do you want me to say? I didn't write the note myself."

"Answer my question. What's your second thought? We can't help you if you don't give us all the information."

A pain shot up her neck from her tensed shoulders. She flinched and closed her eyes. When she opened them, his penetrating gaze remained locked on hers. "My neighbor, I suppose. And my sister's friend. . .a Pat Sorrento."

Her heart aching, she told him about Jeff and Pat, her suspicions, her fears. With each word, her heart grew heavier, the sense of loss overwhelming. She'd grown to depend on Jeff. He'd become her best friend, really her only friend since she'd returned to Michigan. Though she had coworkers, they remained just that. She hadn't shared a moment with them outside the office. With Kathleen's death, Becca's arrival, and all the complications, Jeff had stepped into her world and been her mainstay. Without him, she felt lost.

The officer scribbled the information on a form, asking an occasional question and appearing bored. When she finished, drained and depressed, he tossed the clipboard on his desk. "I guess that's it for now. If we have any other questions, we'll contact you at one of the numbers you gave us."

When she stepped out into the muggy August evening, her heart felt as dark as the night sky. A sense of sadness pervaded every step, every thought. Not knowing what to do, she headed for the highway closest to her office, searching for a motel. She'd spend the night there. If she went home, Jeff might try to talk to her. She couldn't handle that tonight.

Once in her rented room, she struggled to make sense out of everything that had happened. Pieces of the puzzle began to fit together. Why hadn't she noticed that Jeff always vanished when the police arrived at her condo? One day she'd questioned him about doing something illegal, and he'd beguiled her just like Scott had beguiled her sister. "I wouldn't do anything illegal," he'd said, and she'd believed him.

Fool. Silly, gullible fool. The problem was genetic. How could she criticize Kathleen for falling in love with a con man when she'd done the same thing?

Awareness shivered through her like ice. Could it be? Was Jeff in with Scott Derian? Was he part of the gang who preyed on innocent women? She remembered the sadness in Jeff's eyes when he spoke of his mother. Was that a fabrication? Did he think she'd trust him, believe him, after she'd heard his tale?

She sank into the cushion like a pin-pricked balloon. She had believed him. She'd even hesitated to ask him for details about his mother, fearing she would only cause him more pain. Laine knew she'd been a fool.

A lonely fool. Sorrow pressed against her heart, and she felt empty.

An indescribable loneliness filled her. Then she recalled the New Testament, and pulling it from the bottom of the duffel bag where it had settled, she lay across the bed, searching the pages for words to give her courage and strength.

Then it came to her—the answer. Here was her friend. In all of her new faith awareness, at the moment of crisis, she'd forgotten what she'd learned. Jesus was her friend. A friend she could count on. Her prayer began, and before the "amen" was uttered, she felt sleep weighing on her eyes.

In the light of morning, Laine woke with new thoughts. She didn't have the answers, but she had to move forward. She dressed, then grabbing coffee and a bagel at a small café, she headed for work.

But that morning work didn't hold her thoughts. She spent more time doodling and struggling to keep her fears pushed away. When the telephone rang, she jumped and grabbed the receiver, identifying herself.

"This is Sergeant Dickson. Are your sure the woman's last name is 'Sorrento'?"

"As far as I know. Why?" She frowned into the telephone.

"I'm just verifying. We'll keep checking."

She put down the receiver, sensing what she'd suspected all along. "Sorrento" wasn't Pat's real name.

The phone's shrill peal caught her off guard again. She waited for the third ring, then lifted the receiver.

"Laine, this is Jeff. Where have you been?"

Ice ran through her. "I had business to take care of."

"But it's not like you. I've been worried."

"Sorry. I was in a hurry." Her voice sounded monotone and lifeless.

"Something's wrong. I can tell by your voice. Can't you talk? Is someone there?"

Her stomach tightened. His game nauseated her. "I can talk, Jeff. I have nothing to say."

"Please, Laine. I know something's wrong. Meet me for lunch. Tell me what's frightening you. What's going on?"

His voice pleaded, but she wouldn't fall for it. She'd let him con her before but not this time. "Jeff, I'm at work and busy. I really can't talk now."

A lengthy pause stretched across the phone line. She heard his sigh. "I can't make you tell me, Laine. I'll see you tonight. Please, don't do anything you'll regret."

The telephone clicked, and she sat immobile. *Don't do anything you'll regret.* Was this another threat? Her hand trembled as she replaced the receiver. What was he planning? What did he want of her?

Chapter 12

All the way home, Laine thought of Becca. More and more, reality stared her down. Becca wasn't safe with her. Glynnis had the safest haven, the greatest advantages, the most logical home for the little girl. The pressure weighed on Laine's shoulders, and her head pounded with the truth. All she could offer Becca was love. Her grandmother could give her that and much more.

Though sorrow spilled from her with the force of Niagara Falls, her decision was made. She prayed Becca would understand that the reason she was giving the little girl to her grandmother was because of the things her grandmother could provide that Laine simply couldn't. Glynnis had said Laine and Becca could have weekends together, time together. The thought didn't soothe Laine. Tears rolled from her eyes, dripping to her hands, which clutched the steering wheel. Laine had lived before without Becca in her daily life. She'd learn to live again.

Somehow.

Entering the house, silence struck her. She smelled food cooking, so she knew Mavis had to be somewhere close by. Hurrying into the living room, she saw Mavis sitting in a chair.

The woman looked up in surprise. "Oh, sorry, I didn't hear you come in." She folded her magazine. "I have a chicken casserole in the oven."

Laine felt as if she were in a trance. "Where's Becca?" Her gaze darted around the room, her ears searching for the child's voice.

"She's outside playing. Is something wrong?"

"No. I'm sorry. I'm not feeling well." She glanced toward the screened porch. "Thanks, Mavis. I'll feel better later."

"If you're sure." The woman eyed her.

"I'm sure," she said, not wanting to talk about her fears.

"Don't forget the casserole." Mavis glanced at her wristwatch. "The timer should go off in about twenty-five minutes or so." She studied her again, finally turning toward the kitchen.

"Okay, thanks," Laine called after her.

She heard the back door close and hurried out to the porch. Scanning the front, she couldn't see Becca anywhere. Then she heard her laughter coming from the next yard. She stepped from the screened porch and saw Becca with Jeff. The child giggled, tugging on his arm. Then she let go and ran from him as he chased her in circles, her screeches and giggles soaring across the grass.

Laine flew through the yard toward them. Jeff looked up and stopped, frozen. She heard herself screeching Becca's name. The child halted in mid-laughter. Jeff and Becca peered at Laine, their mouths gaping as if she'd become some wildcat bounding toward its prey.

"Becca, I said come here," Laine yelled.

Though Becca faltered, she turned and ran toward Laine. "What's wrong?" she questioned, fright sounding in her voice.

"Nothing's wrong. I need you at home." She jerked her by the arm and tugged her across the grass.

Jeff yelled out and raced toward them. "Laine, stop. What in the world is wrong with you?" He reached out and caught her by the arm. "Please stop."

She tugged without success, trying to break free from his powerful grip. "Let go of me."

"No, tell me what's wrong with you."

Becca's sobs brought Laine to her senses. She looked down at the child, wiping her eyes with her hands, tears rolling down her face. She knelt down and wrapped her arms around the frightened girl, ashamed of the scene she had caused and the fear she had created. "It's all right, Becca. I'm sorry. I didn't mean to frighten you."

Jeff knelt beside her. His pleading voice whispered in her ears as she comforted Becca. And her mind heard a swirling mixture of her voice and his.

"What is it, Laine?" he whispered. "What's wrong?"

Laine swung to face him. "Not now. I'll talk to you later. Becca is more important."

She stood, holding the child against her skirt, and they hurried across the lawn and into the house with Jeff staring after them, unmoving.

Inside, shame filled her as she held Becca in her arms, trying to conjure up a reasonable explanation to soothe her. She'd had a bad day at work. Something happened on the way home that had scared her. She was sorry, and she loved her. Laine rocked Becca, clasping the child against her heaving chest. Her own fear and confusion mounted with each moment.

At last Becca calmed down, and when the buzzer sounded, Laine guided her to the kitchen. Hunger had deserted her, and she pushed the chicken casserole around on her plate. Becca nibbled but ate little. How could she blame the child? She'd created a mess with her hysteria. She had to get a grip on herself and think logically.

Distracting Becca with games and stories, the two hours before the girl's bedtime passed quickly. But tucking Becca in brought a new dilemma. Penny was nowhere to be found. Finally, Becca recalled taking her to Jeff's.

"Sweetheart, she'll be safe with Jeff, and we can get her tomorrow. Okay? It's too late now. Let me give you Grandma Keary's doll."

Shaking her head, Becca whimpered, "But I want Penny."

Laine had to stand her ground. "It's this dolly or none. Penny won't be home until tomorrow."

The child rolled over without the new doll, and Laine tucked her in, kissing her on the cheek. Laine snapped off the light and tiptoed out.

She sat in the living room, wishing she'd listened to Jeff, but how could she believe him now? Indistinctly, she heard a noise coming from the porch. The hairs bristled on her arms, and she froze, her hands clinging to the arms of the chair.

"Laine. It's me. Please let me in."

Jeff's whisper drifted through the screens. She relaxed, hearing his voice, but tension surged again, remembering. Not wanting him to disturb Becca, she pushed herself up from the chair on trembling legs and walked to the doorway.

"Not tonight, Jeff, please. I'm very upset, and I'll say things I might regret."

"If I did something, you owe me an opportunity to explain or apologize, please. I'd never do anything to hurt you. I know you're angry, but please tell me what it is. How can I help you if I don't know what's wrong?"

His pleading only confused her further. She didn't know which course to take or where things were headed. But one thing she knew, if she were to trust God's Word, she owed Jeff an opportunity to speak and at least ask her forgiveness for his lies. "You can come on the porch, Jeff, but only for a few minutes."

She unhooked the latch, and he entered, keeping his distance. In his eyes, she saw the desire to take her in his arms, and she had to admit her natural desire was to go to him.

"You can sit if you want." She gestured to a chair.

He slumped down, staring up at her, and she sank nearby and focused on the darkness outside, avoiding his face.

The air was heavy with silence until his ragged sigh broke the stillness.

"Laine, please just say it. What's wrong?"

What could she tell him? If he were plotting against her, she'd make herself even more vulnerable. But if not, then he'd hurt her anyway with the truth about Pat.

"Laine?"

"You're lying to me, Jeff. One way or the other, you've been lying to me."

"Lying? How?"

Though he spoke calmly, she sensed concern in his voice. "I was at the mall yesterday and passed the coffee shop."

In the silence, she heard his intake of breath. "Oh."

She waited, wanting to look at him but afraid of what she'd see.

"I wish you hadn't seen us. It makes things more difficult."

His words pierced her like a dart. "Yes, truth is difficult when you've lived a lie."

"But it's not the lie you expect, Laine. I'm sure of it."

Piqued by curiosity, she lifted her eyes to his, a mixture of anger and confusion. "What does that mean?"

"It means you think I'm having a relationship of some kind with her. A secret romance."

"That's one possibility."

His head drew back, and he appeared to stop himself from moving toward her. "No, no. You don't think I'm involved in this terrible situation, do you? The break-in or plans to hurt you or Becca? I love you, Laine. You and Becca. I love you with all my heart."

She peered at him, swirling in her confusion and doubt. *Beware,* her mind told her. *Con men are smart. They can beguile you to believe anything.* "You love me? Come on, Jeff. I might be gullible and naive, but I'm not stupid. Too many things are involved here. I'm not a—"

Before she could stop him, he was on his knees at her feet.

"Yes, I love you. I love you both. It's a long story, and to tell you is a breech of my job and dangerous for you."

"Troubleshooting computers?" she questioned in frustration. Tears rolled down her cheeks. She could take no more.

"No, I'm an undercover cop, Laine. I had to lie to you. Especially now that I find you're involved."

"Me? What? This burglary? Please don't confuse me."

He took both her hands in his, kissing her fingers. "I don't want to give you details now. We're so close to the end of the investigation. How would I know that you'd move next door to me, and I'd be getting into the situation from both sides?"

"What does that mean?"

"Because I must be sensible and calm. But I care so much about you and Becca, I'm having a difficult time keeping my feelings under control. I want to go wild and do things that could endanger the investigation and your lives. Trust me for now, Laine. I've told you all I can."

His words stuck in her brain like scattered pieces of a puzzle. Was he telling her the truth? She wanted with all her heart to believe him. "But you lied to me. Now you're telling me you're a policeman?"

"Yes, I work undercover. I'm sorry, Laine, but I couldn't tell you."

"But if you're really a policeman, I should have realized."

"Think. Have you noticed that both times when you called the police, I left. Didn't you wonder why? I didn't want any of them to give away my cover accidentally. I was out last night, not troubleshooting computers. I was working on the case. It's not just local anymore. The FBI is involved. The situation's big and dangerous."

Could he be making this up? She couldn't imagine it. "But what about Pat? Who is she?"

"I can't give you details, Laine. And I really didn't know at first who she was. Remember when I slipped up? I nearly gave myself away saying I could investigate her. But she's not your enemy. Can you trust me?"

Could she? She stared at him. "I turned both your names into the police last night." Her heart pounded with the thought.

"You did what?" His eyes narrowed, and he peered at her. "Explain."

"I got a note yesterday—pushed under the screen door there." She pointed to the spot. "Becca found it."

"What kind of note? Why didn't you tell me?"

"Because for all I knew, you wrote it. It said something about Becca and me knowing where the diamonds are and that we can't hide them for much longer."

His face paled. "Dear Lord, no." He closed his eyes as if in prayer. "What did you do?"

"I turned it over to the police and told them my suspicions."

"And I was your suspicion?"

"Not exactly. I'd first thought of Scott Derian. Then the officer asked me what my second thought was. I avoided the questions, but he pressured me. Then I told him about you and Pat."

"They'll have ruled us out, I'm sure, once they realized who we are."

He opened his arms to her and guided her from the chair. "Oh, Laine, you've been so frightened. I'm sorry. I wanted to tell you, but I couldn't. And I can't."

She believed him, maybe foolishly, but she did. She fell into his arms, feeling all the fear and loneliness drain from her. In his arms was where she longed to be. He held her close, his chest pounding against her beating heart.

Then he tilted her chin with his finger and lowered his lips to hers. "You heard me earlier, Laine. I'd wanted to say it at a better moment, but I mean it with all my heart. I love you and Becca. You're precious to me."

"I love you, too, Jeff. But I was so hurt and confused."

"You don't have to tell me. I understand."

For a long time, they stayed in each other's arms in silence except for the lapping of the water against the wooden dock and the pulsing of their hearts.

After Jeff went home, Laine crawled into bed, and with light streaking the edge of the horizon, her eyelids finally closed. When the alarm rang, she pried herself from bed, dragging her tired body into the shower.

Once Mavis arrived, Laine explained about the missing Penny, knowing it would be the first thing on Becca's mind. She sneaked in and kissed the sleeping girl on the cheek, then hurried off to work.

Worried about the note and the youngster, she called home later that morning. "Is Becca okay?"

"She's moping around," Mavis said. "I think she's tired, but she's whining about Penny, too."

"The doll wasn't at Jeff's?" Laine frowned, wondering where it had gotten to.

"I don't know. It may be there, but he was gone before I called."

"Well, tell her we'll be sure and get her later after he gets home."

"Don't worry," Mavis assured her. "We're fine here."

Laine disconnected, wishing somehow she could erase the preceding days and begin again. Somewhere in the past hours, truth had hung before her like a fragile cord, and she wanted to grab on to it without breaking it. She wanted to bind it to her and cling to a shred of what her life had been like before all the fear and secrets began.

❧

Jeff struggled the night away, thinking of the hurt he'd caused Laine. As he reviewed the situation, he ached thinking that for a while she'd feared him. Yet why wouldn't she after seeing him with Pat? With the pace at which events were taking place, the other secrets he'd kept from her would soon come into the open as well, but he worried that by explaining about Pat's role before everything was resolved, he had put Laine at risk.

He had to be careful. If Laine figured out too much too soon, she and Becca could be placed in real danger. He was on Darren Scott's tail, and that had to be his priority. When Pat laid out her part of the investigation, things fell into place. He was a cop. How could he have been so ignorant?

He rose before the sun, and after draining a pot of coffee and mulling over his thoughts, he dressed and left for the police station. At last the department was getting somewhere, and the sooner the better.

In the briefing room, he sat with other members of the investigation team working on the Scott case and listened to the briefing. Scott Derian. Darren Scott. Why hadn't he caught on earlier? The two men had to be one and the same.

Over the years, Scott had conned Kathleen and other rich widows out of money and gems. The con had begun as common larceny—fraud—but somehow Scott had also gotten involved in the purchase and sale of illegal drugs. What had started simply as an investigation into a larceny complaint had led to the discovery of a drug-trafficking operation that spilled out across state lines, and therefore required the involvement of the FBI.

The detective leaned back in his chair and lit a cigarette. "From the bureau source, we know Scott's feeling the pinch and running scared. He's blown his cover, but we can't pick him up yet. We've got the suppliers at our fingertips, and that's what we're waiting for. Scott's going to make his move. Then we get 'em both—Scott and the drug suppliers."

Jeff scowled. "What do you mean, 'He's running scared'?" His thoughts raced to Laine and Becca's safety.

"Promises he can't keep. He's getting sloppy. We know he's been hanging around the Sibley place. He left a note there yesterday. The FBI agent sees two possibilities. He either knows for sure Kathleen Keary had more wealth hidden, or he's picked up on the wealthy grandmother. Whichever is the case, he's obviously out for more. And he's scratching the bottom of the barrel to cover his drug debts. He's desperate."

"Desperate? So what are we doing about it?" Jeff asked, attempting to appear calm. Hearing the detective use words like "running scared" and "desperate," his pulse had already kicked into full gear.

"Don't panic. We're on it. After the break-in, we put on surveillance 'round the clock."

"Surveillance? We can do more than that!"

"Look, you know the routine. We need the names of Scott's contacts, and then we need to catch him in the act. Hard evidence. We can't bring him in until we have both. Scott's con game is chicken feed. The drug suppliers are our meat and potatoes."

Jeff closed his eyes. Chicken feed? No way. When it came to Laine and Becca's safety, the con wasn't a game or chicken feed. He knew he had to stay cool and in control, but a man like Scott, afraid for his life, acted out of desperation. He wouldn't care whom he hurt. And the people he could hurt included people Jeff loved. If Darren Scott was heading for Laine's, he had to do something.

Jeff thought of what Pat Sabin had told him. He remembered how shocked he'd been to learn Pat was an undercover FBI agent. Using the last name "Sorrento," she'd befriended Kathleen to get closer to Scott Derian. Through that friendship, she'd been able to keep an eye on his con game and gather information for the bureau.

But her mission had backfired. Pat had been touched by Kathleen and Becca, especially after witnessing their struggle following Kathleen's illness and death, and Pat had fought her emotional involvement, recognizing that she couldn't allow her friendship to get in the way of the investigation.

Jeff understood her problem. Laine and Becca could easily get in his way. But he couldn't interfere. The police chief assigned his job. Surveillance was someone else's responsibility. If he botched this, someone could get hurt. And that someone could be Laine.

He wrestled with his fears. The people running this job knew what was best—or did they?

Concentrating was nearly impossible for Laine. Over the past few weeks, focusing on a new firm, new clients, and new designs had become nearly impossible. It was time to face her decision about Becca's future head on. She had to talk to Glynnis and explain everything. Even the thought, uttered in the silence of her mind, bored through her nerves like a dentist's drill. The pain was too deep and too excruciating to bear.

For her problem was no longer simply concern over Becca's future. The anonymous note she had received told her the present could be dangerous as well. Jeff had given her hope. The police were closing in, but until they were all safe, she couldn't let down her guard.

Strangely, the tribulations that kept pouring through her life had led her back to her faith—not a perfect faith, but a beginning. But why when she had turned back to God, back to her Savior, did He allow new fears and worries to enter her life? Was it a test? A trial of some kind? What more could happen to measure her endurance?

When the telephone rang at three in the afternoon, she sat unmoving. Fear rose in her, a cold, icy terror like the feeling that follows the call announcing a loved one has died. She lifted the telephone, barely able to understand Mavis's frantic message.

"What are you saying, Mavis? I can't understand you." Laine's pulse roared in her ears.

"Becca," Mavis repeated. "She's gone."

Laine's heart stood still. "Becca? Gone? Where? What are you talking about?" Her limbs trembled, shaking out of control.

"I don't know. First, I heard a woman's voice and Becca's laugh. Then I heard a car drive off. She's gone."

"A woman's voice? Did you see her? What did she say?"

"I heard her say, 'Hi there, kiddo.' I headed for the door, but she was already gone."

Kiddo. Pat. Laine's heart pounded, hammered like a war drum. "Call the police, Mavis. Tell them Pat Sorrento kidnaped Becca. I'm leaving now."

She slammed the telephone on the receiver and darted from her office. Job, no job. She didn't care. She had to find Becca. She trusted Jeff, and he'd told her Pat wasn't her enemy. But why did the woman take Becca? Why?

Jeff. She needed Jeff, and she needed him now.

Chapter 13

When the surveillance call came in that Darren Scott, alias Scott Derian, had made his move, Jeff knew Becca was safe. Pat had taken her away before any danger might come to her. Mavis, hopefully, could take care of herself, but they needed to protect the child. Pat warned the department of Darren Scott's kidnapping plan. With Becca's abduction, he could demand money from Glynnis or the missing fortune he seemed to think Kathleen had hidden from him, or both.

Now with Becca in safety, the police were closing in on Scott. With the goods on him for the first breaking and entering, along with the other attempted B and Es and kidnapping, they had him where they wanted him.

Pat Sabin had provided the key. After Scott split with Kathleen's property, she'd made contact with him, threatening to turn him in to the police unless he took her in as a partner. For a share of the take, she offered to be his liaison with other rich widows whom she would befriend, setting him up for another con job, and she worked her way into Scott's confidence. Over the months, she learned where he stashed his stolen cash and jewelry. Once the heat was off, he would sell the gems to a fence, then use the cash to foot his drug business. But this time, they had cornered him red-handed.

And most important, the department figured he'd squeal and turn state's evidence if they offered him a plea bargain. Scott was a small boat in a large sea. And they were headed for the luxury liner—the drug-trafficking kingpin.

Though Becca was safe, Jeff feared for Laine and Mrs. Dexter. Knowing the police were on their way to nab Scott, Jeff raced toward the condo as fast as his unmarked car allowed.

❦

Laine's heart thundered in her ears as she tore into the driveway. No squad car. The police should have arrived by now. Then she caught sight of an unmarked car standing cockeyed at the curb in front of the condo as if someone had barreled up and rushed into the house. A detective, she prayed.

She bolted from the car and snatched open the back door, her pulse racing. Fear tore through every nerve. "Mavis!" she yelled. Before she could take in the scene in the kitchen, someone grabbed hold of her shoulder. Jerking her around, a stranger glared at her, his eyes narrowed and his mouth pinched in anger.

"Who are you?" the man bellowed.

In confusion, she glanced around the room and saw Mavis cowering against the wall across from her, terror written on her face. "Laine Sibley," she said in a whisper. "What are you doing here?"

"Shut your mouth," he barked. "I'm asking the questions." He jammed her against the wall, pinning her by the throat. He snarled into her face. "Where's the kid?"

She tried to speak, but the pressure of his powerful hand choked off the sound.

"I told you," Mavis said, her voice wavering with fright. "She's been kidnapped."

He shifted toward her and snarled. "Shut up, you old hag. You don't know what you're talking about."

He released his grip a fraction, and Laine coughed, trying to find her voice. "Really," Laine gasped. "Someone took her. A woman. What do you want with her?" Tears blurred her vision.

He glared at her, lowering his red, glazed eyes until they were nose to nose. The veins pulsated in his temples, and his jaw muscles flexed like a tic as he growled into her face, "A woman? You think I'm a fool?"

Laine turned her head, avoiding his crazed eyes.

He jabbed at her again, sliding his hand toward her throat. "Do you think I'm a fool?" he thundered again.

"It's true. A woman," Laine rasped. "Pat Sorrento." She choked out her name.

He flinched as if he'd been hit with a mallet. A sneer covered his face. "That dirty double-crosser," he screamed. "I'll kill her."

He released Laine with a vicious shove and spun toward the door. Before he had one foot on the porch, a police officer spun him around and yanked his hands behind his back. Noise rose from the yard. Laine cringed against the wall as the shouts and clamor continued. She noticed that Mavis had crumpled into a chair and sat with her face in her hands. As Laine turned toward the elderly woman, a commotion sounded outside the door.

❧

Jeff sped into the kitchen, fearful of what he might find. As soon as he saw Laine, he drew her into his arms. Both Laine and Mrs. Dexter looked ashen and shaken but unharmed, and a ragged breath tore from him as Laine's quaking body clung to him.

"Are you all right?" he asked, burying his face in her hair to hide his own trembling fear.

She nodded, and in her swallowed sobs, she questioned him. "Becca?" She lifted her tear-filled eyes to his.

"Becca's okay. Don't worry. They didn't have time to call you. I'm sorry."

"But where is she?"

"She's with Pat."

A bewildered look filled her eyes. "I knew it was Pat. Remember when I told you I had a strange feeling about her." Covering her face with her hands, she paused, then wiped her eyes. "But why did she take her?"

"To keep her safe. Pat Sabin's with the FBI, Laine. They wanted her out of the way when they knew Scott was heading here. It was the best thing they could do. Pat and Becca are probably somewhere having an ice-cream cone."

"Ice cream? Pat Sabin?" Laine looked confused.

"Sabin's her real name."

"It's all too confusing." She buried her head on his shoulder, her tears soaking through his shirt.

"Pat'll bring Becca home soon," he said, hoping to calm her. "She'll check with the station to make sure the danger's past. Becca's fine."

He turned his attention to Mrs. Dexter. "Are you okay?" His question seemed foolish as he stared into the elderly woman's death-white face.

Mavis gaped at him with a dazed expression and mumbled with quivering lips, "I don't understand. What did the man want? He asked for Becca."

"Scott Derian planned to kidnap Becca, hoping to get some more money. . . either from Glynnis or from you, Laine."

"Me?" She stared up at him. "I don't have anything."

"He apparently thinks you know where the rest of Kathleen's jewels and money are."

"But I don't know anything. For all I know, he took it all."

He nestled her to his chest. "Well, Scott thinks you do."

"That evil man was Scott Derian?"

Jeff nodded.

"I. . .we were so frightened, Jeff." She lifted her desperate, tear-filled eyes to his.

"I know." He caressed her golden hair, soothing her fears as best he could but concerned by how weak she felt in his arms. "You need to sit, Laine." He grabbed a chair that had toppled to the floor and set it upright, then eased Laine down next to Mrs. Dexter. Crouching beside her, Jeff patted her tensed arm. "Were you home when he got here?"

"No." She shook her head. "Just Mavis, I guess."

The woman peered at them with a look of amazement on her pale face as if she only then realized what had happened. She sighed weakly.

"It must have been terrible," Laine said, her voice filled with sadness. "What happened before I came?"

Before Mavis could answer, a rap on the back screen door drew their attention. An officer stepped into the kitchen.

"I need to finish this report, Jeff. Okay?"

"Sure," he said, rising from his crouched position next to Laine. "We'd just asked Mrs. Dexter what happened. She was here alone when Scott got here."

The officer lifted the clipboard and stepped closer to Mavis. "Ma'am, what's your name and your relationship to the Sibley family?"

She lifted her eyes to his. "Mavis. Mavis Dexter. I sit with Becca. . .Rebecca, Miss Sibley's niece."

He scribbled on the form. "Ma'am, could you tell me what happened as best you can remember?"

"I'm not really sure what happened myself," Mavis said, her voice still unsteady. She closed her eyes as if trying to recall the event. "After I talked to Laine, that's Miss Sibley, on the phone, I did what she said and called the police. I've never been so frightened in my life."

The elderly woman looked so shaken, Jeff walked to her side and rested his hand on her shoulder.

She looked at him with a thankful gaze before she continued. "So I hurried to the kitchen door, waiting for the police, but when a car pulled up, I was confused for a minute because it wasn't marked. A man rushed to the door, and like a fool I opened it. I thought it was a detective—you know, like the TV programs."

"You're not a fool, Mrs. Dexter. That made sense." Jeff's empathy rose for the distressed woman.

Her hands still trembled as she nestled them in her lap. "But instead of saying anything, he jerked the door open and pushed me against the wall. Then he demanded to see the kid. That's what he called Becca."

"Oh, I'm so sorry, Mavis," Laine sympathized. "Did he hurt you?"

"No, no, he just knocked me against the wall, like he did you. I told him she was gone. . .kidnapped, but before I could say anything else, you burst in."

The officer turned to Laine. "Could you fill me in on what happened next?"

Laine told him about Mavis's phone call and what happened as she came into the kitchen. As she recalled the event, she slowed and turned to Jeff. "Scott knew Pat? But I don't understand."

"He thought Pat was working for him," Jeff said. "I'll explain later."

She stared at him for a moment, then turned again to the officer. "I guess that was it. When he ran out, you were there. You know the rest," she said to the young man.

The officer ran through the report, verifying the facts, and then walked back outside.

Jeff watched him as he left. "Let's go into the living room where it's more comfortable. You and Mavis can relax and talk. I'll make you a cup of something—tea or coffee. You need to calm yourselves."

Laine didn't argue, so he took her arm, helping her from the chair, then helped Mavis to stand up. When the two women were settled in the living room, he turned on the teakettle and returned to the backyard. The officers were finishing, and when the last car finally pulled away, Jeff returned to the kitchen.

As the kettle whistled, Becca's voice sounded in the yard. Chattering merrily with Pat, she bounded into the kitchen. "Aunt Pat took me for ice cream. And while we were gone, the police came and caught a bad guy. Did you know that?"

"I sure did," he said, tousling her hair. "You'd better go give your aunt Laine and Mrs. Dexter a hug. They were worried about you."

"I know." She hung her head. "Aunt Pat wouldn't let me come in and tell Mrs. Dexter. She said we had to hurry."

As she skipped out of the room, Pat gaped at him. "That kid is a smart one. Even knowing me and with the promise of ice cream, she cried when I made her come along without telling Mrs. Dexter. If I'd been a stranger, she'd have kicked and bitten, I'm sure."

"Good for her," Jeff said, grinning. "And thanks for all your help. I'm glad this thing is over, and I can go back to being me. And get rid of this beard."

"She'll like you either way," Pat grinned, tilting her head toward the living room. "I'm almost jealous."

"Sure you are."

Pat gave him a wink and edged toward the door. "Listen, before she hits me with a frying pan, I'm going to squeak out of here. You can explain everything. I have reports to do."

"I'd say, 'It's been nice,' but. . ."

"No need. So long." She gave him a wave.

When she was gone, he finished the tea and carried a tray into the living room.

Laine looked up, her eyes filled with unspoken questions. Becca nestled in her arm, and Mavis, as white as a new dress shirt, leaned against the chair back as if she were still trying to figure things out.

He handed them each a cup of tea and set the creamer and sugar bowl down between them, then slid onto the sofa beside Laine. "Hope the tea helps. You both look pale—to say the least."

Unexpectedly, Becca turned and faced Jeff. "Do you know where Penny is? She's been gone the whole night and day."

"I think she's at my house, Becca. Sorry I forgot to bring her home." He tweaked her cheek tenderly.

"Can I get her?" She looked at Jeff, then turned to Laine.

"She's right on my porch, and the screen door's unlocked, I think."

Becca eyed Laine for permission.

An uneasy feeling shivered through Laine. "I don't know." She gave Jeff a questioning look.

"It's over, Laine. I'll keep my eye on her. Nothing can happen. . .now."

She studied his face to feel secure with his response, then turned to Becca. "Go ahead, sweetie. But if the screen's locked, hurry back, and Jeff will go with you."

Becca raced out the door, and Jeff stood up to watch the child's progress.

Laine looked up at Jeff. "Since Becca's gone for a second, can you explain some of this mess to me?"

He glanced down at her with an understanding grin. "I noticed you were ready to burst with questions."

Jeff filled them in, speaking as fast as an auctioneer. He offered enough details to explain Darren Scott's plan and Pat's involvement.

Laine glanced at Mavis, seeing confusion linger in the woman's eyes. "I know you're confused, Mavis. I'll explain more later when Becca's not around."

Mavis nodded, apparently understanding enough for the moment.

But Laine had one more question she was hesitant to ask. Taking a deep breath, she plunged ahead. "Jeff, Pat Sorrento—Sabin—wasn't really Kathleen's friend?" The thought brought an ache to her heart.

"That's not true, Laine. Pat told me she originally struck up a friendship with Kathleen so she could get closer to Scott. I think they met in a park one day and chatted. Pat placed herself in places she'd run into Kathleen so they could form a friendship. But in time she became really fond of both Kathleen and Becca. She said she tried to drop hints about Scott without endangering the investigation."

"I wonder if she listened. I suppose that part doesn't matter. I'm glad, Jeff. I'm glad Kathleen had a real friend."

Laine rose and wandered to Jeff's side, then ran her fingers along Jeff's beard. "So are you going to tell me this is part of your masquerade?"

He nodded. "Afraid it is. Something to hide under so I looked a little different. By the way, there's another small surprise."

She waited for the blow, wondering what other pretenses she'd believed.

Jeff turned toward her. "My name isn't Jeff Rice."

"Don't tell me it's Stanley or Aloysius. I'm calling you Jeff, regardless."

"Good. The Jeff part's right. My last name's Reese."

"So you're telling me I have to get to know a beardless man named Jeff Reese?"

"Have to? I hope you want to. He's nearly the same nice guy as that Mr. Rice you're always talking about. The guy who loves you."

Mavis looked at them both with a grin. "Sounds like I should leave and let you two get to know each other. . .alone."

Laine shook her head. "We're rarely alone, Mavis. Have you ever tried to have a moment of privacy with Becca around? It's impossible."

"Now that you mention it. . ." Mavis chuckled.

Thinking of Becca, both Laine and Jeff turned to look out at his yard. When she glanced back at him, she saw the same question in his eyes that she knew was in her own. "Where is she?" Laine asked, concern edging into her voice.

"I was watching. . .until I got distracted," Jeff said. "But she's okay. She has to be."

He darted toward the doorway. "I'll check and be right back," he called over his shoulder as he tore outside.

"I'll come, too," Laine called, bolting after him. Mavis followed, peering through the screen door.

Laine caught up to Jeff as he checked his front porch from the top step. He jerked the door open and called Becca's name, but no answer came. He tested the front door, but it was locked.

Clinging to the doorjamb, Laine's free hand clenched against her chest to calm her pounding heart. "Where could she be?"

"She has to be here somewhere," Jeff answered, striding past Laine to the outside again. She followed him to the edge of the condo, and as they turned the corner of the building, both stopped and then turned to each other in relief. Though their hearts pounded, laughter rose from their throats.

Becca sat on the ground totally lost in her activity, Penny lying neglected on the ground beside her. In Becca's lap, a small, furry calico kitten clambered up her chest, scraping kisses on her hand with its sandpaper tongue as she tried to pet the excited creature. She nuzzled the kitten against her cheek, then caught their gaze. Jumping up, Becca darted toward them with the squirming fur ball in her arms. "Look, Auntie. A kitten."

"Becca, you scared us to death," Laine said, a scowl and grin fighting for a place on her face.

"But look, a kitty." Becca jutted the kitten toward Laine. Her voice piped with excitement. "Can I keep it?"

Jeff chuckled with amusement. "Let's see you get out of this one, Auntie," he whispered.

Laine raised her eyebrow toward him and spoke to Becca. "You didn't listen to me, Becca. You should never scare me like this again. You were supposed to come right back."

"I know, but the kitty ran around the corner, and I forgot." Her eyes lifted to Laine's, pleading. "Auntie, I really love this kitty."

Laine swallowed the emotion rising in her throat. "I'm sure you do." Becca's words struck her heart with more meaning than she could say. Laine knew about love. She loved Jeff, and she loved Becca with her whole heart. She gave Becca a quick hug. "If we find out the kitty doesn't belong to someone else, then we can keep it."

❧

Laine sat alone and recalled the events of the past days. If nothing else, the horrible incidents made one thing very clear: She knew what she had to do. Becca meant more to her than anything in the world. She had to convince Glynnis that the child should remain here with her.

Later that evening when Jeff returned, she described her feelings to him. In a rare moment of privacy, they nestled on the porch while a gentle breeze wafted through the screens. Laine described her mental struggle—the pros, the cons, and the in-betweens of keeping custody of Becca.

"I realize Glynnis hasn't shared the experience of living day in and day out with Becca, so she may not fully understand what it entails. But I have to make her realize that Becca's place is here. When Mavis called me today and I thought Becca might be hurt or I might lose her, I was overwhelmed with desperation. I've never felt such a loss. Not even with Kathleen. Any child is special. And this child is precious to me." She envisioned the small child, nestled in bed with the tiny fur ball at her side. Laine had been relieved when a neighbor whose cat was the mother of the kitten had given permission for Becca to keep the little animal.

Jeff nuzzled his clean-shaven cheek against her face, and she grinned at him, enjoying the new smooth feeling.

But another thought intruded. She turned to face Jeff. "Having you in my life is wonderful. And if Glynnis listens to me, I'll have Becca in my life and Scott Derian—or whatever his name is—out of it, and everything will be complete." She paused and looked at him. "Except for one more thing. If Scott was so certain Kathleen had something hidden, sure enough to kidnap Becca and to break in here, he must have had some kind of evidence, wouldn't you think?"

"Maybe. But maybe it's wishful thinking. People like him get paranoid when they're in trouble. They imagine anything."

"I suppose." A strange sensation rippled through her. Something told her Scott might be closer to the truth than they were. She sighed and rose, crossing to Jeff as he watched out the screen window. "So hopefully, we can breathe again."

"I think we can all breathe again." He stood behind her and wrapped his arms around her waist.

"I'll call Glynnis tomorrow and pray that God gives me the right words." She turned, looking into Jeff's face. "And you know, besides the daily joy of having Becca here, she's given me something I never expected. The Bible says, 'And a little child shall lead them.' Becca did that. She led me—led both of us, really—back to church and back to reading Scripture and—"

"And prayer. A key to everything."

"And to pray." Her eyes welled up with tears. "What had I done all those years without it?"

Jeff chuckled. "You probably prayed without thinking. I did, despite what I said about my faith."

"Me, too, I suppose. I'm sure I did."

"Not wanting to disillusion you, though." He tilted her chin upward.

"What?" Her pulse skipped a beat. *Please, God, not another problem.* "Tell me."

He chuckled. "Don't look so panicky. I just wanted to remind you that when the Bible said, 'And a little child shall lead them,' it was talking about Jesus, not a regular child. Just a point of fact."

"Did you write the Bible?" She elbowed him playfully.

"No."

"Well then. . .it can have two meanings. I know it means Jesus, but remember, we're to have faith like a child. And Becca was our example. Her faith strengthened ours."

"You win." His arm slid firmly around her back, and he drew her closer.

Her upper body molded against his powerful chest where she felt safe and protected. His lips touched hers with a gentle firmness she could never explain, but one that filled her with completeness.

As they drew apart, a chuckle rose to her lips.

"You're laughing at my kiss?"

"No, I'm remembering when you told me months ago about your work—when I said you seemed more like a Superman than a troubleshooter. You said everything so inside out it didn't make much sense."

"That's because I hated to lie to you even though I had to. So I didn't say I was a computer troubleshooter. Remember? I said I was a troubleshooter. Then I said, computers. You put the two together."

"Oh, right! Blame me. Wish I had a tape recording of that conversation."

"Anyway, you have the truth now."

"I'm glad." She squeezed his hand.

He thought a moment. "Except for one thing. And don't panic." He drew his fingers along her cheek. "But it's something that's troubled me for years—something I couldn't talk about. But now I can, and I'm thankful God heard my prayers and took the guilt-ridden feelings away."

"What?" She tried to imagine what had made him serious again.

"I'd spent the past years wanting revenge, wanting to get even with men like Scott. But since I met you and Becca and you've become so important to me, I wanted to see him captured and punished for your safety and no other reason. You and Becca were all I cared about."

Looking into his eyes, she watched his hurt and sorrow melt to a reassuring calm. "I love you, beardless Jeff Reese—or whoever you are."

"But think of how much fun you'll have getting to know the real me. And remember, no matter who I am, I love you with all my heart."

His lips touched hers again, firmer and surer. And this time she definitely believed every word he said.

Chapter 14

After church on Sunday, Jeff suggested that he, Laine, and Becca go for a swim. He grinned to himself, his surprise gathering momentum. He reached Laine's dock before she did, and using the rake, he pulled in a few strands of seaweed. He'd worked hard to clear the shallower water so Becca could play without getting tangled in the drifting weeds.

When he heard a giggle, he looked up to see Becca darting from the house with Laine close behind, carrying the towels and a safety vest. The new kitten, still unnamed, skittered behind them. Once she fitted Becca in a vest, Laine joined Jeff sitting on the edge of the dock, and the two adults watched the little girl splash and play in the water. Their talk was casual, but Jeff knew they still had serious issues to handle before they could close the door on their problems.

But the afternoon was special, no matter what lay ahead, and Jeff's heart kept a wilder pace, waiting for the opportune moment. Finally, while Laine was distracted by Becca's antics, he reached in the small key pocket of his swimsuit and pulled out a tiny box. He slid it on the boards between them.

"Okay, Becca, I've watched enough for a while," Laine said, rolling her eyes at him. "Practice swimming the way I showed you, okay?" She turned her attention to him. "Now," she said, grinning, "we might have one minute."

"One minute, huh?" He slid his hand across her shoulders. "I just found something in my pocket." A secret grin hedged on his lips.

"In your pocket? What?"

He pointed to the tiny box sitting between them.

"What's this?" She stared at the small container. "It could slip through the dock slats if you're not careful." A hint of excitement slipped into her voice.

"Then why don't you pick it up?"

She hesitated and drew the box carefully into her hands. Unmoving, she stared at it.

"So? Open it."

When she lifted the lid, a gasp escaped her. "Jeff, it's a ring. A diamond?" Her eyes widened as she gazed at the stone.

"What else would it be?" He lifted the small ring from the piece of cotton. "I'm asking you to be my—"

The ring slipped from his hand and dropped to the dark cushion of mud beneath the sandy water.

"No!" she wailed. "Becca, don't move, sweetie. Don't stir up the water."

Laine jumped into the gritty lake, and Jeff's heart lifted, remembering the day they'd first met. When she came to the surface, her lovely peacock-hued eyes were wider than he'd ever seen, and his heart pounded.

"Why are you just sitting there?" she asked, her arms flailing.

He grinned without moving.

"This isn't funny. I can't see the ring at all. It's gone."

"You can get one just like that in any Cracker Jack box in town."

Noticeably confused, she peered at him, her face shifting to a scowl. "What are you talking about?"

He gestured. "It's not the real thing like the one in my pocket."

She shook her head with a frown and smacked the water in exasperation. "You! I can't believe you! Why did you do that?"

"I'm just a romantic. Remember how we met? You looked so beautiful and so funny when you bobbed up out of the water. I just had to see you again with that surprised look on your face." He rose and hoisted her to the dock, his arms slipping around her wet, dripping body.

In playful frustration, she pounded his broad chest with her fists. "You're terrible. You scared me."

"I know, but it was worth the look on your face."

"You are an absolute tease."

He spread a towel on the boards, and this time when they sat, he brought out a ring that glinted like blue fire. He slipped it on her finger and kissed her hand. "For better or worse," he asked, "will you marry me?"

"After that dirty trick, I should say no, but I'm no fool. Yes. Yes. Yes."

Becca, watching curiously, paddled to the edge of the dock. "Me, too," Becca said, joining the enthusiasm. "Yes. Yes."

"What, angel? You want to marry me, too?" Jeff asked.

"Uh-huh, me and Penny."

"Okay, then I guess it's a threesome. . .or foursome." He wiggled his eyebrows at her, and she giggled.

"Watch me," she called and paddled along the shoreline for a couple of feet.

Jeff turned to Laine. "You can see how much I impress the girls. I just agreed to marry her, and all she wants to do is swim away."

"But I hope you've noticed I'm not going anywhere," Laine said, offering him her eager, waiting lips.

❧

Laine sat with her hand still clinging to the telephone. She'd waited as long as she could to face Glynnis with her decision, but time had run out. She'd just arranged for the two of them and Jeff to meet that afternoon.

She glanced at her lovely diamond shimmering in the afternoon light. God's hand had guided her life this far even when she had turned her back on Him. The Lord didn't let His children slip too far before His gracious hand lifted them up again and set them on their feet.

So many of her problems had dissipated; her guilt had disappeared when she understood repentance and asked for forgiveness.

Now her loneliness vanished having Becca and Jeff at her side, and her sorrow faded knowing Kathleen's faith had been strong. With Scott Derian—or Darren Scott—out of her life, they were again safe and secure. Her final meeting with Glynnis would finalize it all—except for Kathleen's inheritance. And perhaps she would never know what had happened to those jewels.

Laine uncoiled her fingers from the telephone receiver and walked to the living-room window. Becca sat on the porch, sounding out a storybook to the kitten, who cuddled on her lap.

"You're reading some pretty big words, Becca."

The girl grinned at Laine through the window. "I have to be smart in school. So I'm practicing."

"Good for you." She gazed at her sister's lovely child, who had inherited Alex's Irish coloring, fair skin and dark hair with the bluest eyes. It was time to prepare her, let her know what the day held. . .just in case. Most of all, she needed to know what Becca wanted.

Laine wandered out to the porch and sat on the wicker love seat, watching the child for a few moments before she disquieted her play with questions.

"Becca?"

Becca paused in midsentence, the storybook suspended in front of her.

"Would you come here for a minute so we can talk?" Laine asked.

Her eyes brightened. Without question, she set the book on the side table and the kitten on the floor, then slipped into the seat beside Laine.

Laine kissed her cheek. "I'm going to visit your grandmother this afternoon to talk about you."

"Me?" Becca's curious eyes gazed up at Laine.

"Uh-huh. I'll drop you off at Mrs. Dexter's for a while. Your grandma and I have some important decisions to make. But I'd like to know how you feel, too."

Becca gazed at her without saying a word, listening intently.

"School starts in a few days, and I've waited too long to get you registered. But before that, I have to know which school you'll be going to. Your grandma and I would both like to have you live with us, but you know that's impossible."

She nodded her head matter-of-factly.

"You can visit with both of us. But you have to live in one spot." With her heart thudding in her throat, Laine looked at the child.

"I already live with you, Auntie."

Her answer was simple. "Yes, you do now, but your grandma can give you more things and lots more time than I have. I go to work every day and—"

"And Mrs. Dexter stays with me."

Laine remembered Becca's decisive choices when they shopped for school clothes. The child clearly knew what she wanted. "That's right." She held her breath. "Is that the way you want it to be? Your grandma loves you very much, and she'd like you to live with her, too."

A sudden silence filled the room, a rare silence in Becca's case. For a long time, she looked out toward the water. No emotion—no fear or confusion—etched her dainty face, only serious thought. Slowly, she turned to Laine. "My mommy always said I should love my grandma. But I never saw her. Now, you take me to see her, and I love my grandma."

"I know you do, sweetheart." Laine's chest ached from her halting breath.

"I want to see my grandma for visits. I live with you."

A ragged sigh escaped Laine. "And that's the way you want it? You're sure?"

"Uh-huh. My mommy said if she couldn't watch me, you would take care of me."

"Your mom told you that?" Laine peered at her upturned face. "When did she say that?"

"She always said it. She said you loved me."

Laine nestled the child in her arm, fighting the tears that pushed against her eyes. "Your mommy was right. I love you with all my heart."

"And I take care of Penny like you take care of me."

"You sure do." A new awareness washed over her. She'd worried about Becca's preoccupation with the raggedy doll. Now she understood where it came from. Kathleen must have used the doll as an example.

"Then when I see your grandma today, I'll let her know that this is what you want. I hope she listens to me."

"She will, Auntie. I already told her I wanted to live with you."

Laine closed her eyes, unbelieving. "You did?"

"Uh-huh. Grandma asked me if I could live anyplace in the world, where did I want to live. I said with you."

Laine couldn't speak from the force of the love that pressed against her heart.

❧

Jeff parked the car and glanced at Laine. Though nervous, her eyes were glowing and confident. She'd made her decision about Becca based on every logical piece of evidence she had. Kathleen had willed it, Becca wanted it, and Laine longed and prayed for it. God's will would be done.

He slid from the car, and before he reached Laine's door, she had already stepped to the ground. He took her arm and guided her up the brick steps to the wide, elegant doorway. He'd seen the outside of the huge dwelling before but had never been inside. He and Glynnis had met only a few times while transporting Becca from house to house.

The door opened, and to his surprise, Glynnis greeted them. She, too, appeared confident and collected. They stepped inside, and he gaped at the impressive foyer. Wide solid-oak baseboards and doorframes glistened with varnish and years of polish. Thick plastered walls met a coved ceiling ten to twelve feet above the floor, and a glimmering crystal chandelier glinted in the afternoon light.

Glynnis led them to a wide, deep living room graced by a stone fireplace and heavy brocade furniture. Opulence and wealth spoke out at every turn.

When they were seated, Laine's words lifted from her with grace and ease, and his heart soared to hear her address the elderly woman with her new confidence.

"First, I want to share some wonderful news." Laine extended her hand. "Jeff and I are engaged. We'll be married before Christmas. We've known each other only a few months, but sometimes God's voice rings loud and clear. And I know this is meant to be."

Glynnis took her hand and gazed down at the diamond glinting shards of blue and red fire. "It's lovely. Truly lovely. Congratulations to both of you."

Laine folded her hands in her lap and breathed deeply. "As I said, God's voice sometimes speaks clearly. I've done a lot of Bible reading since Kathleen's death and Becca's arrival. The other day I read a verse that had so much meaning for me I was nearly dumbfounded."

He watched amazed as she pulled the small white Testament from her handbag and opened it to a marked page.

She lifted her eyes to Glynnis. "It's from Philippians, chapter four: 'I know what it is to be in need, and I know what it is to have plenty. I have learned the secret of being content in any and every situation, whether well fed or hungry, whether living in plenty or in want. I can do everything through Him who gives me strength.'"

Jeff studied her when she finished reading. She placed her hands in her lap and sat in silence, the only sound being the even ticking of the grandfather clock beating in rhythm with their hearts.

"I'm not sure if either of you understands what I'm hearing in God's Word, but I'll try to explain. In my early years I struggled for every penny I earned. But worse, most of my life I felt starved for love, hungry for affection, needing someone's accolades. Recently, God's given me those things through Jeff and Becca, but I learned something from these two important people. I learned the secret of being content. It's within me—not something on the outside that I can get from something or someone but inside. It has to do with faith."

She looked at both of them as if searching their eyes for understanding.

"Glynnis, when I first came here, I thought you had so much more to give Becca than I do. You have wealth, status, breeding, so many opportunities that I might not be able to give her. But I've learned that those aren't what makes a person rich. It's knowing God's grace and salvation. It's understanding forgiveness, and it's knowing, no matter how little or how much you have, God loves you.

Becca knows Jesus' love—and I'm thankful that she knows we all love her, too. I believe that—"

"Laine." Glynnis leaned forward, looking earnestly into the younger woman's face. "Thank you for sharing your beliefs with me. But I made up my mind a few weeks ago where Rebecca belongs."

Laine clasped her hand to her chest, tears brimming her eyes.

"She belongs with you. It's where her mother wanted her, and it's where she'll have all the things she needs. I love her, yes, and my money is still hers. I've created a trust fund for her so she can have all the education and travel she'll want someday. But her home is with you."

Laine lifted her hands and covered her eyes, tears rolling from beneath her fingers. "Thank you, Glynnis. Thank you for understanding."

"I asked Rebecca awhile ago where she wanted to live, and she said with you. And one thing Rebecca inherited from her father was decisiveness. She knows what she wants." The elderly woman smiled at them. "It's the best and most appropriate place for her to be."

Through her tears, Laine smiled. "Just to be honest with you, I asked her, too. She said the same thing. But thank you for respecting her wishes."

Jeff drew a ragged breath. If he didn't do something soon, he'd be wiping away his own tears. "All right then, I have an idea. Tomorrow we'll celebrate. Let's have dinner together to show Becca we're all in agreement." He looked at the two women's pleased expressions and accepted their silence as agreement.

Chapter 15

On the way to dinner, Laine silently thanked God for answering her prayers. Her eyes searched the sky, knowing God looked down on her, and she wondered if He was smiling at her, seeing that His love and mercy had formed the plan for Becca's care long before they could ever imagine.

Jeff took them to a lovely restaurant that Glynnis graciously observed was excellent. Laine smiled when Jeff suggested going back to the house for dessert and coffee. She understood. Glynnis had never been inside the house, never seen where Becca lived. It was time.

With their simple dessert eaten, they sat on Laine's screened porch, sipping coffee and watching the setting sun provide a spectacular display for their celebration. Streamers of deep orange, copper, and magenta swept across the horizon with wisps of cerulean blue and deep pink running like dye from the wash of color. Glynnis gave repeated oohs and aahs as she enjoyed the stunning display.

Kitty gravitated to Glynnis's feet until the woman grasped the kitten in her hand and lifted it to her lap. "My, my, little kitten, you do want attention."

"Kitty loves you, Grandma," Becca said, "just like I do."

Glynnis's face flashed with a quick succession of emotions. Becca's words had obviously touched her. "And I love you, too. . .and your kitten." She held the cat up, eye-level. "And what is this tiny creature called?" She lowered her gaze to Becca.

"Just Kitty. It doesn't have a name yet," Becca said with a giggle. "But let's give it one, Grandma."

Despite her exuberance, Becca quieted, looking quizzically at the kitten for a moment. "Is it a boy or girl?"

Glynnis looked at her tenderly and tipped the kitten upside down, then grinned. "I'd say this one is a bonnie lass."

"Bonnie lass," Becca repeated. "That's what we'll call her."

"Well, dear," Glynnis said, "I think Bonnie would be quite enough."

"Sounds like a good name to me," Jeff agreed.

Laine swallowed back the joy that surged through her, watching the child and her grandmother.

Becca slid the kitten from her grandmother's grasp and wrapped Bonnie in her arms.

The conversation turned to other topics, and as the time neared for Glynnis to return home, Becca slid onto her lap with the poor forgotten Penny snagged under her arm. The overloved Bonnie had defensively curled into a ball and slept in the corner of the sofa.

Glynnis wrapped an arm around Becca and eyed the pitiful doll with a sigh. "I guess my efforts were useless." She slipped the doll from Becca's hand and held the toy in front of her. "I don't quite see the charm, I'm afraid. You like this doll best, though, don't you, Rebecca?"

Embarrassed at Becca's disinterest in the lovely doll that Glynnis had given, Laine began to explain the child's preoccupation with Penny, but she'd only begun when Becca took over.

"My mommy told me to take good care of Penny, Grandma. So I do. Mommy said Penny was precious. When she got torn, she sewed her up for me."

Jeff touched Laine's arm. "Your mommy sewed up your doll?" He looked intently at Laine.

Laine's heart skipped a beat. "How did she get torn?" she asked her niece.

Heaving a great sigh, Becca looked at her. "I don't know, but Mommy said she got ripped."

"What do you think?" Jeff asked.

Glynnis flashed a questioning glance at Laine, and Laine looked first at Jeff, then back again to the elderly woman.

"Check it out?" Jeff suggested.

Glynnis lifted the doll's dress. "Yes, she has been stitched." She glanced at Laine. "What do you think?"

Laine felt excitement rising within her.

"I say we check it out," Jeff said. "It can't hurt."

Laine nodded. "I think Jeff's right. If Kathleen told Becca that Penny was precious and she should take good care of her, I think we may have something."

She rose and crossed to Becca, kneeling at her side. "Becca, could we check inside Penny and see if your mom put something inside her? Maybe we're wrong, but no matter what, I promise to sew her back up as good as new."

Though Becca looked bewildered, she nodded her head in agreement. Within minutes, Laine loosened the stitches. She slid her fingers carefully inside the rag doll, and her heart stood still. All eyes were on her.

"What?" Jeff asked. "You found something, didn't you?"

She nodded. "Yes. Here's the answer to our question." She pulled her hand from the stuffing, bringing with it Kathleen's diamond wedding ring, an emerald necklace, and a folded piece of paper.

Glynnis gasped as the gems came into view. "My mother's emerald necklace. I'm so grateful. And the wedding ring."

Becca gazed at the jewels with curiosity. "Are these my diamonds?"

"They sure look like it, don't they, Becca?" Jeff said, standing beside her.

Laine patted her head. "This is where your mom put them for safety. When you grow up, Becca, they'll be yours to wear, but for now, we'll find a safer place for them, okay?"

Becca nodded, studying the pieces of jewelry. But the others focused on the folded paper.

With trembling hands, Laine opened it. A small key dropped to the table. In lengthy silence, she scanned the note, finally looking at the others. "I'll read it," she said.

> This key fits a safety deposit box at the Troy Federal Bank. What I could salvage is there, except these favorite pieces that I kept at home, hoping Scott wouldn't notice the others were missing. A friend suggested I hide these, so I've put them here, praying Laine or someone who loves Becca will find them.

An overwhelming sense of sadness washed over Laine as she struggled to control her emotions. She bit her lip and refocused on Kathleen's note. Then with tears filling her eyes, Laine turned to the child. "But Becca, the best part is a note from your mom to you."

"To me?" Her eyes widened, her voice only a whisper.

Laine furtively wiped away the tears sneaking from her eyes. "Yes, to you. It says:

> Becca, someday you'll be old enough to wear the lovely jewels. I wish I could be there to see you. But most of all, I hope you will listen to these words and hold them in your heart.
> Aunt Laine will help you understand.

Laine swallowed back the lump in her throat, and focusing her misty eyes, she continued to read.

> Do not store up for yourselves treasures on earth, where moth and rust destroy, and where thieves break in and steal. But store up for yourselves treasures in heaven. For where your treasure is, there your heart will be also.
>
> All my love forever,
Mommy

Laine looked from Jeff to Glynnis, then to Becca. Though the child seemed confused, the adults understood. Kathleen's gift to her daughter was far more precious than the diamond ring and emeralds glittering on the table.

❦

While Jeff drove Glynnis home, Laine sat next to Becca and stitched Penny back together. With the raggedy doll back in the child's arms, she tucked Becca into

456

bed and placed the note from Kathleen on the nightstand.

Laine gazed down at Becca with Penny nestled in her arms and Bonnie curled in a ball at her side. Kissing the child good night, Laine bowed her head, praying that she could be the best aunt in the world.

She tiptoed to the doorway, watching until she saw Becca's steady, even breathing, then she closed the door and walked to the kitchen.

So much had happened in these past months. More than she could ever imagine. Today overwhelmed her. God had brought everything to a perfect ending. Every good and wonderful gift she could have asked for had been given to her. And Kathleen's final gift to Becca filled her with awe.

She returned to the porch as Jeff's footsteps sounded outside. He opened the door quietly and paused, looking at her without speaking, then sat beside her on the wicker love seat.

The last vestiges of sunset had melted into the horizon, and the full moon sprinkled the dark water with diamonds of its own, dancing and glinting on the ripples that rolled into the shore. The simple sounds of the quiet night blended into one melody: water lapping on the shore, the chirping of a cricket, and the beating of their hearts.

"You know, Jeff," Laine murmured, "I don't understand why Kathleen didn't tell me about the doll. She never mentioned that poor raggedy thing held what was left of her fortune. What a paradox. One Penny worth a fortune—in so many ways."

"I think you know the answer to that question," Jeff answered. "You said it earlier. Kathleen's treasure wasn't in the doll. Her treasure was her faith in God and Becca. . .and in you, too, Laine. And I imagine she thought she had more time. . .just like you did."

He slid his arm around her, and Laine leaned her head against his shoulder.

Silence hung in the air again, then Laine turned her eyes toward Jeff. In a few months, she'd be his wife. They'd known each other such a short time, but they'd agreed: Their meeting was God's doing, God's gift. They shared the most important things life had to offer: their faith, their values, their trust, and their love.

Jeff studied Laine's pensive face and asked, "What are you thinking?"

"About you. About us, really. I'm thinking how strange things are sometimes. How we met and how much you mean to me."

He lifted Laine's fingers and kissed them. Her diamond sparkled in the moonlight, but not nearly so brightly as the love that glowed in her eyes. She leaned forward, pressing her palm against his cheek, and lowered her lips to his, and he drank in the sweetness of her love, far better than any earthly drink.

He longed to hold her in his arms, to know her as God intended for a man to know the woman he loved, and he knew that time was near. Three months and they would be husband and wife. He smiled, feeling their entwined hands and knowing their hearts were woven together as well.

"Jeff," Laine said, leaning her head on his shoulder, "have we shared all our secrets? You have no other names, identities, worries hiding inside you? Nothing else that I should know?"

He chuckled. "Nope. I laid it all on the table. You know all my secrets. How about you?"

"Not one thing. Everything's in the open. Oh. . .well, except. . ." She paused, gazing at him.

His stomach knotted. "What?"

"I suppose you should know I don't like okra."

"Okra!"

She giggled and pulled away from him, dashing through the outer doorway into the balmy evening air.

He caught the door before it slammed and followed her, catching her by the hand. "Why did you scare me?"

"Oh, I like to see your wide eyes like the first day we met." She chuckled.

"Come here, you." He drew her into his arms and pinned her against him.

"Be kind," she teased. "Don't punish me with your kisses."

"Ah-ha, so that's what you fear."

His lips sought Laine's, and in the rippling moonlight, she clung to his embrace, giving him her lips and her heart. His intake of breath thrilled her, knowing his love was as strong and fervent as her own. Filled with completeness, she raised her eyes to the glowing, star-speckled sky and thanked God for all His precious gifts. On their wedding night, she would share with Jeff her most precious gift. No diamonds or emeralds, not one sapphire, but her pure, untarnished love.

A Letter to Our Readers

Dear Readers:

In order that we might better contribute to your reading enjoyment, we would appreciate your taking a few minutes to respond to the following questions. When completed, please return to the following: Fiction Editor, Barbour Publishing, Inc., P.O. Box 719, Uhrichsville, OH 44683.

1. Did you enjoy reading *Michigan*?
   ❑ Very much—I would like to see more books like this.
   ❑ Moderately—I would have enjoyed it more if _____

   _____

   _____

2. What influenced your decision to purchase this book?
   (Check those that apply.)
   ❑ Cover   ❑ Back cover copy   ❑ Title   ❑ Price
   ❑ Friends   ❑ Publicity   ❑ Other

3. Which story was your favorite?
   ❑ *Out on a Limb*   ❑ *Seasons*
   ❑ *Over Her Head*   ❑ *Secrets Within*

4. Please check your age range:
   ❑ Under 18   ❑ 18–24   ❑ 25–34
   ❑ 35–45   ❑ 46–55   ❑ Over 55

5. How many hours per week do you read? _____

Name _____

Occupation _____

Address _____

City _____ State _____ Zip _____

E-mail _____

If you enjoyed

MICHIGAN

then read:

PRAIRIE HILLS

Treasure in the Hills by Paige Winship Dooly

The Dreams of Hannah Williams by Linda Ford

Letters from the Enemy by Susan May Warren

If you enjoyed

MICHIGAN

then read:

SENECA
Hearts

The past helps set
three romances free

If You Please
Riches of the Heart
Safe in His Arms

TISH DAVIS

If you enjoyed

M ICHIGAN
then read:

DESERT ROSES

Stirring Up Romance by Janet Lee Barton
To Trust an Outlaw by Rhonda Gibson
Sharon Takes a Hand by Rosey Dow